I0747866

THE APEX CYCLE
BOOK 3

WRITTEN BY

M.T. ZIMNY

This is a work of fiction. Names, characters, places, and incidents are either the product of the author's imagination or are used fictitiously. Any resemblance to actual persons, living or dead, events, or locales is entirely coincidental.

Copyright © 2022 by M.T. Zimny

All rights reserved. No part of this book may be reproduced or used in any manner without written permission of the copyright owner except for the use of cited quotations.

Editing by Melissa Ball

Cover Illustration and Special Characters by Maria Mondloch
Back cover photography by Andrew Rossi
Fonts: Cinzel, Marcellus, Roboto, Merriweather

ISBN: 978-1-7356571-5-8 (Paperback)

For Connor.

*You believed that I could write an entire series before I did.
(If you don't like it, please pretend that you do).*

And For Nora.

*I can't wait for you to show me what story you decide to
build.*

Table of Contents

1

Sparring In The Rain

I was way too hungry to care to be sword fighting. Late spring rain slashed at my face, and I tried to blink away the droplets that clung to my eyelashes, searching for the blade I knew would be arcing towards me in the downpour.

I saw the flash of steel moments before it was too late and struck out against the attack. The force of the locking blades sent tremors from the hilt, into my hands, and down my forearms, but I kept my grip. My opponent's toothy grin gleamed in the late-day gloom beneath his single eye.

"Come on, just let me get a hit in," he taunted.

"Doesn't that defeat the whole point?" I kicked him away and tried to flick hair out of my face, but it stuck to my cheek. My ponytail had failed early on in the battle, forcing me to fight to see through both rain and wet locks of hair.

I stumbled back just in time to feel the nick of his sword tip as it grazed me beneath my eye.

"Watch it with the face shots! I don't want anyone losing eyeballs on my watch," Nurse Everly warned. He sat at the foot of the nearby Viking statue, holding an umbrella low over his head to keep it from catching on the sea winds that rolled over the bluff from the ocean. The sky stretched behind him, slate-gray clouds obscuring a sinking sun. Wind-weathered grass carpeted our hill, and the windows of the farmhouse at the foot of the bluff glowed orange in the dying light of day. Even in the rain and wind, the property was peaceful, owed in part to the thick forest that kept us hidden from the rest of McMillan Island.

"I take offense to that, sir!" Sergio scoffed, but his grin remained resolute as he bore down on me with renewed vigor. "There's no shame in losing an eye."

Apparently, once upon a time, I'd been better at sword fighting, but I was starting to think that was a lie. I'd been sparring with Sergio three times a week for as long as I could remember, and I still had yet to win a fight. Granted, "as long as I could remember" was only a few months. Everything that came before, including whatever sword skills I'd allegedly once possessed, had been wiped from my head by an immortal warrior hundreds of miles away.

"The fact that you are down one eye is all the more reason to make sure you don't lose the one you have left," Everly said.

I saw an opening in Sergio's attack and lunged, trying to force him onto defense for a change, but he parried with infuriating ease.

"Look who's finally getting comfortable." His cocky smile twisted. "I think it's time for a *real* test. Everly?"

"That's not fair!" My stomach growled angrily as I deflected another attack from Sergio. Rain mixed with the sweat on his brow, pooling above the black strap of his eye-patch. Save the small slash he'd just carved into my cheek, this was the first time he'd been unable to land a blow in our practices.

"When Sergio's memories spontaneously disappear, we'll test him, too. Don't worry." Everly straightened up where he sat in my periphery. "Avery?"

It was easy to forget about the boy sitting next to Everly. He hardly spoke during these exercises, only participating when forced. Shaggy, blond hair hung around cheekbones that seemed to become more prominent every day.

He cleared his throat, barely audible over the wind, rain, and clashing of swords.

"Samantha," he mumbled, "*remember*."

I narrowly blocked Sergio's blade as it swiped at my legs.

"Louder, Avery!" Sergio called, white teeth flashing in the mist. "I don't think she heard you!"

I scowled. I already knew it didn't matter how loud Avery spoke. It wouldn't work. Whatever Adrestus had done to my head couldn't be reversed, not even by Avery's powers of coercion. I dodged another swing, stepping in a puddle and wincing as cold water splashed up the back of my jeans.

"Remember, *please*."

"I'm trying!" I swung haphazardly at Sergio, and his eye widened in surprise. He deflected it, and again I felt the force of the blow reverberate through my entire body.

"What's your name?" Everly prodded.

"Real or fake?" I danced out of the way of Sergio's blade.

"Both."

"Samantha Havardson and Samantha Fleming."

"And which is which?"

"I don't know!" I struggled to maintain my footing on the slick grass and slid several feet down the hillside. Sergio's eye lit up when he saw his chance, and he leapt at me. I dropped to the wet ground and rolled out of the way. Sergio grunted as he collided with mud and grass.

"Which is which?" Everly repeated. I chanced a glance towards him and Avery in the half-second it took for Sergio to get to his feet. Everly remained at the foot of the statue, dry under his umbrella, but Avery stood, dwarfed by the stone man behind him.

They'd told me the statue was for my dead brother, Avery's father. My dad, too, in a way, since that's what he'd posed as after I'd forgotten my previous life as a medieval viking girl from Iceland. The irony of having lost my memories a *second* time wasn't lost on me.

In one life, the man had been my brother, in another he'd been my father, and in this one he was a bleak reminder of something I couldn't remember. He'd protected my comatose, un-aging body for a thousand years and died protecting me from Adrestus, yet when I looked at the stone effigy, I felt nothing. Maybe it was a side effect of having my memory stripped one too many times or maybe I'd simply always been a callous, unfeeling person. Whatever it was, I at least felt bad about not feeling more.

"Which is which?" Everly said a third time as Sergio charged at me. I struggled to keep up with his footwork while trying to sort through the multiple identities I'd been fed since waking up three months ago.

"Havardson is my real name?" I switched my blade to my left hand to catch Sergio off-guard, but he twisted his wrist and blocked the blow.

A chill sucked at my breath, and ice crystallized where rain struck my face. I adjusted my grip, breaking the ice forming between my fingers. Instead of wet droplets splashing against my forehead, pellets of hail bounced off my head and arms.

"Not fair!" I lunged at Sergio in frustration. "Fleming said no powers!"

"He said I can't fight with my ice blades. He said nothing about freezing other things."

"Brace yourself, Samantha," Everly said from the sidelines. "Avery?"

Avery took a steadying breath that rattled inside his thin throat.

"You need to remember," Avery insisted, more earnest than before.

It was like this every time. It had started with just Avery, sitting with me in the living room, imploring me to remember. When that didn't work, Everly suggested combining my exercises with Avery with my exercises with Sergio, theorizing I might be more susceptible to Avery's powers if I was busy actively trying to not get skewered.

When that didn't work, either, Fleming suggested combining Avery's powers, fighting with Sergio, *and* my background recap tests. Safe to say, I wasn't expecting my former life to come rushing back any time soon.

"And your *third* name?" Everly asked.

"Eydis," I mumbled, more focused on the tip of Sergio's blade, which glittered with newly formed ice. Something about my Viking name made me feel awkward, maybe because it reminded me of the stone man that oversaw the fight. The silver sword locked in the pedestal at his feet looked much more lethal than the dull practice swords Sergio and I used.

My breath rolled from my lungs in cloudy puffs, and icicles formed on each spoke of Everly's umbrella. I made a sloppy lunge for Sergio. He stepped aside and nicked me again, this time on my bicep.

I'd been so sure that today had been my day to finally win. I lunged again with increasing desperation.

My frozen hair crackled in my ears as I struck out for Sergio. I didn't want to fight. I didn't want to study. I didn't want to remember.

"Sammy, please remember. You need to," Avery said.

I tried. I really did. Maybe if Avery's powers worked, everyone would leave me alone. Sergio flicked his wrist, whipping his blade in a tight circle. My sword flew from my hands.

I slipped on the frozen ground and landed hard on my backside. Rain soaked through my jeans. I wiped ice from my face and found the tip of Sergio's blade inches from my nose. I'd lost. Again.

"Come *on*!" Avery cried in frustration.

"What?" I snapped. "I'm trying!"

His pale face turned red, and his eyes narrowed at me.

"Obviously not!" He pointed an accusing finger. "Otherwise you would've remembered *months* ago!"

"Avery." Everly's tone had a warning bite, but the thirteen-year-old ignored him.

"I'm tired of this!" he snarled. "Samantha's broken, and for some reason you all think I'm the one who can fix her, but I can't, and I'm hungry and cold, and it's raining, and I *hate* this stupid statue!"

He spun to kick his father's statue before bounding down the hill in a huff.

"That's enough for one day, anyway." Everly furrowed his dark brow as he watched Avery run back to the house. "Perhaps he'll be in a better mood when his mother returns in a few days."

"I won, right?" Sergio offered me a hand. I took it, but instead of letting him help me up, I pulled him down using a maneuver he'd shown me the week before, and flipped him over me.

"Let's call it a draw." I grinned, getting to my feet. Sergio lay flat on his back in the icy mud, scowling at the clouds.

"That doesn't count. The match was already over, and it wasn't sword fighting."

"Then why'd you teach me that move?"

"Back to the house. Now." Everly's command was jarring and sharp , and I twisted around to see a small fire flash in the upstairs window of the farmhouse. Sergio frowned at the flashing signal.

"Is it another drill? Fleming didn't mention we were due for one."

"It's not a drill." Everly's low and serious voice sent a thrill of fear and excitement down my spine. "Hurry."

I scooped my sword up from the grass where it had landed. Maybe I was finally done waiting. Maybe Adrestus was here to exact his revenge like the others had said he might.

"Okay, but I *did* win, right?" Sergio asked as we ran down the slick hillside, trying to remain upright on the wet grass. "I'd disarmed her and had her at sword point when—"

"That doesn't mean the match was over!"

"It doesn't matter," Everly growled. "Get in the house."

Everly paused in the gravel driveway, looking down the dirt road into the shadows of the trees, and I hurried after Sergio onto the old wooden porch and into the house. The living room was dark and inviting, filled with the smell of lasagna baking in the oven of the adjoining kitchen. Fleming stood at the open door nestled beneath the steps of the wooden staircase that led up to the second floor.

"Downstairs. Keep the swords with you." His glasses perched on top of his head, and his button-up was protected by an apron. I could see the angry burn scars that marred his arms as he held the door open for us.

"Is it him?" I asked, listening to Sergio's footsteps thunder down the stairs into the basement. Fleming's eyes grazed the cut Sergio had left on my cheek.

"A car turned down the drive. Might just be a lost tourist, but better safe than sorry."

An odd mixture of relief and disappointment flurried inside me. Everly deadbolted the front door behind us as I filed into the closet under the stairs. I pushed past heavy coats to find the secret staircase and followed the flickering orange glow that emanated from around the corner at the bottom.

The basement was a cramped room with a low ceiling and concrete walls, adorned by a single bookshelf against the far wall. Amanda provided the only light, the flickering flame in her hand sending shadows dancing through her shaggy pixie cut. Sergio stood near the doorway, his sword blade catching the light of Amanda's fire. I avoided Avery's gaze from where he hunkered in the corner, a hamster cage clutched against his chest, as I adjusted to make room for Fleming and Everly.

"Amanda," Fleming hissed, and Amanda curled her fingers inwards to snuff out her flame. Silent darkness settled over us. Fleming bumped against me, and I hugged myself in an attempt to be smaller.

Car doors slammed shut overhead, and footsteps on the porch drew my heart into my throat. Whoever had come down our drive couldn't be tourists.

Adrestus had found me. The man who'd wiped my memories and killed my brother was finally here after months of us hiding. I tightened my grip on the flimsy sword, hoping the three months of sparring with Sergio would be enough. This is what we'd been working for after all.

"Amanda," Fleming whispered, his hand on my shoulder, "open the passage."

Wood grated against concrete as Amanda pushed the heavy bookcase across the floor. Her tiny flame reignited to reveal a dark tunnel, the dark maw of which sucked at the light from her fire as well as any hope that I might finally be done running and hiding.

Fleming pressed forward against my shoulder.

"Sammy, it's time for you to leave."

2

Speed Dial

Firelight danced on the metal rims of Fleming's glasses as he surveyed me, but I backpedaled away from the hidden passageway.

"I'm not leaving without you all." I scanned their faces, ready to fight them. I wouldn't leave. They couldn't make me.

"Someone needs to close the passage behind you." Fleming kept his voice low, and a distant, underground breeze whistled through the tunnel to ruffle his unkempt hair. "Amanda and Sergio will take you and Avery to the camp. Everly and I will be right behind you."

"I'm staying," Sergio growled. Ice glittered as it coated his blade. Fleming nodded solemnly. I was the only person in the room he had any real authority over seeing as he was my guardian.

"If he stays, so do I!" I said. "I'm not afraid."

"You never are." Fleming bit back a sad smile. "Go for Avery's sake. He'll need you."

"No." I brandished the practice sword. I didn't want to go with my nephew, and I doubted he wanted to go anywhere with me. "Adrestus is here for me, right? I'm not letting anyone get hurt standing between us."

Fleming's face turned red in the light of Amanda's fire, but before he could scold me, a voice called from up the stairs.

"Alex? Are you down there?" Footsteps sounded on the stairs.

My stomach unclenched, and my knees turned to jelly. Fleming closed his eyes in relief. Alison poked her blonde head around the corner, her braid hanging loosely over one shoulder.

"You're all down here!" Her eyebrows shot up her forehead. "You didn't think *we*—"

"You weren't supposed to be back yet!" Fleming leaned back against the wall and pressed his hands over his eyes, forcing his glasses up his forehead. "And we didn't recognize your car."

Alison blushed in the firelight, and she tucked a stray lock of blonde hair behind an ear.

"It's a long story." She scanned the small room and locked eyes with me. As Avery's mother, she'd once pretended to be my mother as well. Sometimes, like right now, the way she looked at me made me think she was still living in that delusion. "We'll explain upstairs."

I followed the others back up to the living room, listening to Amanda push the bookcase back into place in front of the secret passage. The ice on Sergio's blade hissed as it dissipated into steam, and he rolled his head side to side as we climbed the stairs together.

"Thought that was it for a second," he said. "Almost would've been nice to see some action. I'm tired of waiting."

I grunted a noncommittal response. It was more a matter of when than if, and while I didn't want to admit it, I agreed that it might be a relief when the time came for us to finally fight.

We pushed through the curtain of coats and stumbled into the living room.

"Any progress?" A man in a zip-up hoodie stood at the front door. Unkempt scruff clung to his chin, and the low-light of the living room deepened the shadows under his eyes. He took a long sip from an oversized travel mug, looking at me over its rim. While I didn't remember anything beyond three months ago, I knew Trev Baker didn't like me now, and he certainly couldn't have liked me then, either.

"Nothing yet." I shrugged as Alison pulled Avery into a hug he didn't look entirely invested in. He stared at me, unreadable, as his mother pressed his face against the coat fabric of her shoulder.

Mr. Baker scowled.

"Avery was here for a week and no breakthrough?"

Avery turned red in his mother's arms.

"I can't miss what I don't remember, and I'll make new memories," I suggested blithely, trying to alleviate whatever guilt Avery might be feeling.

"If we don't find out what it is Adrestus erased from your head—"

"He erased everything," I snapped. "Mystery solved."

"But we don't know what it is he's trying to hide from us and if it might help—"

"Leave them alone, Trev," Fleming warned from the kitchen. "Are you going to introduce us to your guest?"

I looked to the couch, noticing the girl there for the first time. She hugged her backpack close to her chest and looked to be about Avery's age. Her dark curls were pulled into pigtails that puffed out like clouds on either side of her head.

"This is Joni." Alison sat next to her. "She's the daughter of one of the families we were looking for. Her sister's already at the camp, but their powers make it difficult to be near each other so she'll have to stay here."

Fleming popped back into the living room from the kitchen to survey the girl.

"Joni?" he repeated. "Joni Bradford? Naomi's sister?"

Naomi. I clung to the name, but I didn't know why. Maybe I'd heard them mention her before, though they were usually careful not to mention specifics around me.

"The rest of the Bradfords have, unfortunately, been taken to New Delos," Alison said darkly. Stony silence fell over the room, and Joni's small smile now seemed more brave than nervous. Her family were prisoners, and she was stuck here with strangers. "We found Joni with her aunt. After we picked her up, someone started tailing us. We switched cars and came back early after we were sure we lost them."

"Maybe be a little more careful with those details?" Mr. Baker glared at me from the corner of his eye. "If Adrestus was able to erase the kid's memories, he might be able to pick out information about us from her head as well."

I crossed my arms and sank into the armchair. Three months of not knowing who I was, three months of losing sword fights to Sergio, and three months of being kept in the dark out of fear Adrestus was able to use my head as a direct pipeline of information.

I couldn't blame them, of course. From what they'd said about the guy, Adrestus didn't sound like someone to take lightly. Still, it was annoying being treated like a liability, even if I was one.

Everly dropped his med-kit in my lap and sat down on the lumpy ottoman next to me. I groaned but offered my hand.

"Can't this wait until after dinner?" I grumbled, acutely aware of Mr. Baker watching us. Everly took my hand in his, and his powers rushed across my every nerve as he assessed me for injuries.

"It'll only take a moment. The cut on your cheek isn't deep, so you escaped stitches."

"You're welcome," Sergio sang, taking a spot on the couch across the living room and reaching for the TV remote.

"Next time I'm here, we'll do a finger prick test, too." Everly pulled an antiseptic wipe and a band-aid out of his kit.

"Goodie." I winced at the cool touch of the wipe. I knew the finger prick was important. It would let Everly know if I was still immortal or if the effects of letting a magic stone soak in my neck for an entire millennia had finally worn off. That didn't make it fun, though.

"You said you were followed?" Fleming said, drawing attention away from Everly and me. "Are you sure you lost them? If they find us—"

"Yes, I'm sure." Coffee sloshed out of the top of Mr. Baker's travel mug. "Some of us actually know how to do our jobs."

"We were able to reach a few families before we had to come back," Alison interjected, "so keep a watch out for them at the coffee shop the next few days."

"I'll let Brooke know," Amanda grunted.

"We didn't have time to stop by Esther and Weaver's, so we'll have to make another trip to restock your Serum supply, Jacobi," Alison continued to Everly.

"Careful." Baker eyed me again.

"I already know the Serum comes from Dr. Weaver," I snapped. It had only been a few weeks ago that Sergio had slashed my leg open, requiring Everly to dose me with his miracle Serum. He'd explained it came from an Apex with a healing factor who lived on the mainland, helping us from across the water.

"And we've confirmed that Schrader has Apex tapping into phones." Alison glared Baker into submission.

"Oh, no," I said dryly, eyeing the lasagna Fleming was setting out on the dining table. "What am I gonna do now that I can't call all my many friends?"

Sergio bit back a smile. He was the closest thing I had to a friend, and most our time together was spent with him destroying me in sword fights.

"Even so, it'll make communication with—" Fleming cut himself off, his eyes flickering over to me. "It'll make communication difficult."

The adults ate on the back porch, where Alison and Trev continued their report, a safe distance away from me and anyone who might be listening in through my head, while the rest of us ate in the living room, watching the nightly news.

Sergio shushed us, even though we'd been eating in silence, when New Delos took up the screen. Buildings glittered atop the water, shining in the early summer sunlight, before being replaced by a shot of a dome-roofed governmental building. A bronze statue boasted a caped man in the rotunda in front of the building. Sergio cranked up the volume.

"...forming the parliament of the newly minted nation. Earlier today, the parliament voted John Ratcliffe as their Prime Minister, further cementing the infant nation's sovereign status."

"Ew." Sergio scowled and shoveled lasagna into his mouth. "Hate that guy."

Amanda shushed him, her plate of food getting cold where she ignored it on the coffee table, to better hear the rest of the news story.

"...communication to and from the island is still down, with reports claiming damage from the flood continues to make life in New Delos difficult, causing some to speculate the city was prematurely cleared for habitation."

"What does that mean?" Joni asked.

"Calls aren't going through to New Delos," Sergio explained with a frown. "It's made things difficult for us trying to communicate with—"

He ducked out of the way of Amanda's flying fork. It smacked against the peeling wallpaper behind him, leaving a splatter of pasta sauce.

"Hey, that was my blind side! You could've hit me!"

"I was trying to." Amanda gave me a pointed look. "Careful what you say."

I blew a strand of tawny hair out of my face.

"I'm right here," I mumbled.

"That's the problem." Amanda peeled a noodle off her top layer of lasagna and maneuvered it into her mouth.

"...city engineers have yet to complete the investigation into what caused New Delos to slip into the ocean nearly half a year ago—"

"Now we're done." Amanda hit the remote, and a static pop accompanied the TV going dark.

"They weren't finished." I frowned.

"Too bad. I got tired of seeing John Ratcliffe's face on the screen." Amanda tossed the remote back to the table and leaned back in her seat.

"When do I get to see my sister?" Joni asked, pushing pasta around on her plate. Amanda and Sergio shared a grimace.

"We can talk to Fleming about it in the morning," Amanda promised. "Even with your powers, I'm sure we can try something."

"I can feel that you're just trying to make me feel better." Joni gave a wavering sigh.

"You can sense when someone's lying?" I asked. Joni raised an eyebrow at me.

"No, I feel emotions. But you should already know that. I thought you were my sister's roommate."

Sergio cleared his throat, and Amanda looked at the ceiling.

"I was roommates with an Apex?" I asked.

"It doesn't really matter, does it?" Sergio shrugged. "It's not like you can see her, and if Adrestus—"

"It sort of matters! I have a *friend* on the island, and no one thought to tell me?"

"Yeah! And that friend is me!" Sergio grinned, and I had half a mind to flick lasagna at him.

"But bringing this girl over might help jog my memories and reverse whatever it is Adrestus did to my head!"

"It wouldn't work," Avery muttered darkly from his arm chair. His head bowed over an untouched plate of lasagna while his hamster turned on its wheel in the cage next to him.

"You'll figure it out," Amanda said in a rare show of encouragement. "Apex abilities are tricky, and without knowing exactly what Adrestus did to Samantha's head—"

Avery looked up to glower at the room.

"My powers aren't working because I don't *want* her to remember. When she does, she'll tell you all that I'm the one who made her forget, *not* Adrestus."

"What?" I stood up, and my plate slipped from my lap. Noodles and marinara splashed across the wooden floor, but I hardly noticed through my rising anger. "You're doing this to me on *purpose?*"

"I *am* trying my best to help you, but I'll get in trouble when you remember! It's making some kind of mental block for me."

"Great, now that we all know, that mental block is gone," Sergio spat, standing with me. "So make her remember!"

"I'm sorry. That's the third time I've told you all this." Avery frowned, and I knew what he was going to do a second before the words left his month. I lunged across the room in a bid to stop him, but it was too late. *"Forget I said anything."*

Forget.

"Sammy? What's wrong?" Sergio drew his practice sword. I blinked in confusion, unsure why I was in the middle of the room.

"I don't know." I looked down at my lasagna, splattered across the floorboards.

Avery bent his head over his plate, unbothered by my sudden lunge.

"Is it Adrestus? Is he back in your head?" Amanda asked. "Is he making you do things?"

I shook my head, not sure where the wave of anger that washed over me had come from.

"She's fine," Avery said. "Everyone calm down."

The adrenaline seeped away, and Sergio sat back down as I bent over to clean my lasagna off the floor.

"Right." Sergio nodded. "Nothing to worry about, unless you count the fact Sammy *still* hasn't won a single sword fight."

I brandished my fork at him.

"I'm going easy on you. We both know your ego can't handle losing to me."

He gave me a crooked grin and took a large bite of lasagna.

"Tell yourself whatever lie you need to, Havardson," he said, "but we both know when I'm back here later this week, I'm giving your other cheek a cut to match the one I gave you today."

The adults came back into the house much later looking sullen and uneasy after their discussion. Joni was nodding off on the couch, and Amanda had already disappeared to her bedroom. Alison beckoned for Avery to gather his things, and I pushed myself from the armchair to help.

A funny look passed over his face as I reached for his hamster cage on the end table, and he messed with the cell phone in his hands.

"Can you carry him to the car for me?" he asked without meeting my eyes.

"Happy to!" Night had fallen, and the passing summer rain had left puddles in the gravel driveway that I danced around to get to the car.

The hamster in the cage bustled across his wood shavings, startled by the sudden movement, and Avery followed me out to the front porch.

"He's a cute hamster."

"His name is Knut." Avery shoved his things into the back seat.

"Knut?" I watched Knut's whiskers twitch up at me in the light that poured out from the car. "You named him after my brother?"

"I didn't know you remembered your brothers." Avery glared at me over his shoulder, still leaning into the backseat.

"I have my old journal," I explained. "It's where the last version of me wrote about the first version of me, so Knut is in there along with the rest of the old family."

Knut burrowed into a pile of wood shavings. Avery twisted around to sit on the edge of the seat with his feet on the driveway gravel. His shoulders fell with the force of a sigh.

"They're my aunts and uncle," he finally said. "I wish I could meet them."

"You've got me! I'm your aunt." I lifted the cage to show off the hamster. "And this version of Knut!"

Avery hunched his shoulders and looked past me down the long, dark driveway that disappeared into forest.

Knut poked his furry face out of the wood chips, and I wondered if the Viking Knut had been the kind of guy who'd have a sense of humor about his nephew naming a hamster after him a thousand years in the future.

"Mr. Hendricks got him for me."

I'd heard stories of Amanda's father, Mr. Hendricks.

"The way Amanda talks, he doesn't sound like the kind of guy to go around giving hamsters out to thirteen-year-olds."

Avery let out a dry laugh.

"I used my powers to make him." The mental image of a thirteen-year-old boy manipulating a grown man into buying him a hamster was objectively funny, but Avery's brow furrowed.

"If you were able to do that, then you'll be able to get my memories back no problem."

He glared at me and leaned back into the car.

"When you say things like that, it makes us both look stupid."

For a moment, the only sound in the room was the low rumble of the voices inside the farmhouse and Knut breaking through a sunflower seed.

"Don't be so hard on yourself." I handed the hamster cage to him, and he sat with it in his lap. "It's probably my fault your powers aren't working."

"Samantha, *remember*." He looked at me hopefully, as if catching me off guard might've done the trick. I shook my head.

"Maybe I'm immune to your powers," I suggested. Avery flicked his hair out of his face, and his cheeks turned pink. The corner of his lips tugged upwards.

"Samantha, you should remember everything up to the last week of your lost memories." He raised an eyebrow, looking cautiously hopeful.

"Why not the last week?" I asked.

"Fine, everything but the last day." The flicker of hope fell from his face when I shook my head. "That doesn't make sense! I don't care about the rest of it! It should've worked!"

"What happened the last day that I'm not allowed to remember?" I frowned.

"Never mind, it doesn't matter. Just *remember*."

"It's okay if it doesn't work. I'm fine without my memories." Still, I closed my eyes and tried to let Avery's command compel my lost memories forward.

"You got them back last time you lost them," Avery mused.

"Right." I narrowed my eyes. "Fleming said Adrestus has some guy that basically tortured me into remembering."

"The Inculcator, like me and Mom. He makes illusions, but he was still able to fix you." Avery leaned forward, too young to be looking as serious and foreboding as he was. "Maybe he could fix you this time, too."

I stared at Avery, unsure of what he was getting at.

"It doesn't matter if he can. I'm here, and he's in New Delos."

Avery's hands clenched into fists, and he took a steadying breath before pulling his phone from his pocket.

"What are you doing?" Something like dread gnawed at my chest.

"The news was wrong, you know," Avery said quietly. "There *is* a way to call New Delos. Only one line works. I figured it out the other day but hung up when someone answered."

"No." Blond, thin, and growing up much too fast, Avery should not have been able to make me so gut-wrenchingly nervous. "Stop it. It's not that important."

"It's my fault you lost your memories. And I'm going to make sure you get them back."

"It's your fault—?" I stammered. "Do the others know?"

"No, and they won't find out. I can do this without Mom or Hendricks or Fleming or Everly." He dialed a number on the phone, and his thumb hovered over the "call" button.

I turned and tried to run back to the house but a single word from Avery froze me where I stood.

"*Stop.*"

My heart screamed in my chest. I knew Avery was powerful, and I knew he had an Apex ability that would be very dangerous in the wrong hands, but I'd never been afraid of him. Not until now.

"Avery, you need to tell them," I whispered. "She'll help you. She'll help *us.*"

"Samantha, *stay quiet*, all right?" He jammed the "call" button, and my lips pressed together, unable to cry for help.

Avery set his phone down on Knut's cage and set it to speaker mode.

It rang twice before a raspy-voiced man answered.

"Thank you for calling the Schrader Museum of New Delos. You've reached Miles. How can I direct your call?"

I was choking on my beating heart as Avery looked up at me through a curtain of shaggy, blond hair.

"Hi, Miles." His voice cracked. "I need to speak to the curator, please. I need to speak with Adrestus."

3

The Boy With One Arm

Avery was met with silence that crackled on the other line. I want to grab the phone away. I wanted to yell for help. I was useless.

"I'm sorry, sir, we don't have anyone by that name working here," the man on the phone droned. "Our head curator is Dr. Cunningham, and he's currently—"

"Right!" Avery cut him off. "Dr. Cunningham! That's him! I need his help."

I screamed in my head for Avery to hang up the phone. As much as I hated hiding from Adrestus, this was *not* how I wanted to solve it. Avery avoided my eye and bent over his screen.

"You can set an appointment to come in and meet with him, but our curator is a busy man," Miles rasped. "Do you have a name?"

Avery met my eye and gulped.

"Avery Havardson. I'm Vidar's son."

Maybe his powers worked over the phone. Avery could still change his mind and tell this secretary not to say anything to Adrestus. The silence on the other end seemed to stretch into eternity, and Avery and I stared at each other while I silently begged Fleming to come bursting from the house.

"Let me transfer you," the man finally said, and my stomach dropped at the sound of the call transferring.

"Who is this?"

The voice was deep and sharp and horribly familiar, nagging at me through a fog of lost memories.

"We're on McMillan Island, and she doesn't remember anything. You fixed her once, come fix her again."

He hung up before Adrestus had the chance to respond and flung it over his shoulder into the car.

"What've you done?" I breathed, finally able to speak. He'd doomed us. Not just him and me, but all the others I knew were hiding somewhere on the island.

"It'll be fine," Avery insisted, but I didn't know if he was talking to me or to himself. "I can use my powers on him. He'll be under my control, and once you're fixed, I can send him away again and make him forget."

"No." I shook my head. "We have to leave the island. We have to hide! I won't let you lead him to us!"

He raised his head to look at me.

"Then I'll make you forget, too."

I *couldn't* forget. They'd kept me from the others for their safety because they thought Adrestus was in my head, but it had been *Avery*. Joni had told me I had a friend on the island. I could meet her. I didn't have to be alone anymore.

"If you were going to make me forget, then why bother telling me what you were doing at all?"

He watched Knut amble across his cage.

"I didn't want to do it alone. I was scared to call the man that killed my dad, but you've faced him before. It wasn't so scary with you here."

"Avery, please," I begged. "You can still fix this. You can call him back and tell him not to come and force him to never bother us again!"

"I will! When he's here, I'll make sure he never comes back. I can tell him to stop kidnapping Apex, too. I know it'll be scary, but it'll work out. Trust me."

"You need to tell Alison and Fleming. We need to prepare, we—"

"No." Avery smoothed his forehead, forcing himself to look resolute. "Sorry, Sammy. Adrestus is on his way. But let me worry about that. You, you can *forget this ever happened.*"

I tried to cling to the memory of the phone call and of Avery telling me it was his fault I'd lost my memories three months ago, but it slipped away. No. *No.*

The front door of the farmhouse creaked open.

"Sammy? Avery? Are you out here still?" Fleming called.

There was something I needed to tell him. But what? Avery was buckling Knut's hamster cage into the middle seat of the back of the car, and I frowned.

"Yeah, we're over here." Why couldn't I remember what I wanted to say?

Gravel crunched, and Fleming rushed out into the night with Alison, Mr. Baker, and Everly.

"Joni said she sensed fear," Everly explained in a low rumble. "Is everything okay?"

"I think so." I shrugged, though I couldn't shake the feeling haunting my gut.

Avery popped his head out of the backseat.

"Ready to go." He grinned, unaffected by whatever nerves were shaking me. "Bye, Sammy. See you in a couple days."

He closed the door, and Alison pulled me into a good-bye hug, but I stared at the dark car windows over her shoulder. For whatever reason, I very suddenly did not trust my nephew.

"Hey, loser." A finger tapped against my forehead, and I rolled over in bed, away from Amanda's voice, unsure of why she was in my room. "Fleming says you have to go to work with me today."

I opened my eyes to the darkened wall of my tiny bedroom. The digital clock showed it to be four AM and I growled incoherently.

"C'mon, move it." My comforter whipped away from my shoulders, and I drew my knees to my chest as the cool, morning air dissipated the cozy comfort of my bed. "He has to go to the camp today, and you can't be left alone. Brooke's picking us up in twenty."

My cheek smarted where Sergio had cut it, and I still couldn't shake the heavy sense of unease from the night before, but I powered through, jostling around both Amanda and Joni in the upstairs bathroom as we got ready.

I rubbed make-up into my neck, trying to hide the scar that ran down its length to my collarbone. Fleming said it was too recognizable, and I needed to keep it hidden in public. Joni watched me in the mirror, pulling her hair out of a silk sleep bonnet that matched the periwinkle pajama set she'd worn to bed.

When gravel crunched outside, signaling Brooke's arrival, I grabbed my bag along with the silver necklace I kept on my nightstand. I struggled to clasp it behind my neck as I ran after Joni and Amanda into the cool morning.

The necklace was a simple chain with a dog whistle bent into a V-shape, perfectly mirroring the V-shaped burn scar on my sternum. It wasn't a conventional piece of jewelry, but I'd been wearing it the day I lost my memories. Maybe that was why it felt important to me.

Brooke looked over Joni and me in surprise as we piled into the back of her sedan.

"We're on daycare duty today," Amanda grunted, leaning over to peck her girlfriend's cheek. "Fleming had to leave early this morning, and Samantha needs round the clock protection. I'll tell you about it later."

Her eyes met mine in the rearview, unwilling to reveal more.

Morning haze drifted between trees and settled over the underbrush of McMillan Island. The sun was still working its way over the horizon, and the first tendrils of day pushed through the trees, casting the wooded road in gloom.

"I don't mind the extra company. Sammy is always welcome to stay at the coffee shop." Brooke's warm amber eyes smiled in the mirror. Where Amanda was brash and sullen, Brooke was everything inviting and kind. "Who's your new friend?"

"I'm Joni." Joni leaned forward over the center console. "Do you know my sister?"

Amanda pushed Joni back into the backseat.

"Baker says we can expect a couple families today," she said.

"I'll have my aunt make sure the cars are ready."

Quarry Bay was a cute, oceanside town, and while this time of year brought swarms of tourists to the farm island, it was always quiet early in the morning. We bumped down the main street towards the water, and Brooke parked a block away from her aunt's waterside coffee shop.

The shop sat on the pier, jutting out over the water, so every footstep echoed over the warped floorboards. The windows wrapped around the seating area, their edges green and foggy with sea grime without losing their charm.

"Make yourself useful," Amanda grunted and pointed to the tables with their upturned chairs. "First ferry gets here in about forty minutes."

Joni and I helped pull chairs off tables, setting them up in time for customers while Amanda and Brooke went behind the counter to prepare the vats of coffee and brew themselves espresso to prepare for the work morning. They spoke in hushed voices, waiting to talk until the screaming steam of the espresso machine could mask their conversation.

Whatever had drawn Fleming away from the farmhouse must've been serious judging by Brooke's neat frown.

The wall-mounted phone rang, interrupting their conversation.

"That's going to be him." Amanda rolled her eyes as Brooke answered the phone.

"Orca View Coffee Shop, you've got Brooke." She paused, and I heard the low rumble of a man's voice. "Yes sir, we've got the full menu."

She winked at us and hung up.

"He can just *ask* if we made it to work safely," Amanda grumbled, coming around the corner to unlock the front door and drop off drinks for Joni and me. "There's no need for Fleming to talk in code."

I stared out the window blankly where I sat with Joni, watching the ferry pull into the terminal. Amanda had said something to Brooke about expecting families. I wondered if they would be on board the boat and how we were supposed to help them.

Joni pulled a book out of her bag and disappeared behind the pages, leaving me alone with my sketch pad and pencil. I liked drawing, but it had lost a bit of its appeal ever since Everly had assigned an hour of it a day, hoping that the artistic process might trigger some long-lost memory in me.

The bell over the front door signaled the beginning of the first morning rush and ferry boat travelers trouped in, searching for morning coffee. Amanda and Brooke handled the rush effortlessly, and I sketched them onto a blank page. Amanda didn't have much of an eye for art, but Brooke would appreciate it.

"Sammy, a little help?"

I looked up to see Amanda pointing at a spill on the far end of the counter. She and Brooke were both busy with customers, and I left Joni to grab the rag from behind the counter.

"Does this mean I'm on the payroll now?" I quipped. Amanda raised an eye as I spread the warm mocha around the countertop, somehow creating more of a mess.

"I'm not sure what you're doing constitutes billable work."

The bell over the front door rang out, pulling Amanda's attention away, and two boys walked in.

The one in front scowled under carefully gelled brown hair and bushy eyebrows. His friend lingered behind him, lanky and lean with messy brown hair and thick-framed glasses that perched on the end of his long nose. His cheeks reddened when he saw me, and his eyes grew wide. I looked down at the countertop spill, wondering how bad of a mess I was making to elicit such a reaction.

"Two coffees." The first boy sauntered up to the register with a strained politeness pulling at his face. His friend looked away with his hands in the front pocket of his hoodie. Amanda stood rigid at the register.

"Why are you here?" she hissed.

"Hello to you, too," the boy grunted. He gave me a sideways look while his friend continued to look everywhere except me.

"Tell my father I don't need help. I've got it under control."

"I'm sure you do, but excuse us for not taking the chance to get out of that god-awful camp. Two coffees."

My head snapped up at the mention of a camp, and my eyes locked with those of the second boy. The red of his cheeks deepened.

"You need to be more specific," Amanda said through gritted teeth.

"Aren't they all just coffee?"

"No," his friend muttered, the red in his cheeks extending to his ears.

"Oh, my god," Amanda groaned, watching a line form behind the boys. "Just order hot chocolates and get out of my way. We're busy."

"Yeah, fine," the boy grunted. "Two hot chocolates then."

"Size?"

"You're hurt." The second boy was looking at me again, and I raised a hand to the cut Sergio had left below my eye.

"Leave her alone," Amanda snapped. "Drink size?"

"That cut looks deep, does—"

His friend elbowed him in the side, shutting him up.

"Sixteen ounces. Both of them."

"Great, that'll be—"

"It's on the house," Brooke stepped in, having finished making a round of lattes. Amanda scowled and pulled two cups from a stack and scribbled names onto them.

"That's not how my name is spelled," the boy with the gelled hair snapped. "Andersen is 'E-N', not 'O-N'."

"And you'll be lucky if I don't 'spit-N' your drink," Amanda growled. "Get out of my face, Andersen."

The boys stepped away, and the hair on the back of my neck told me the one was staring again. I could see him in my periphery, his hands still in his hoodie pocket and his thick framed glasses tilted towards me.

"He's doing this just to bug me!" Amanda hissed to Brooke. I finished mopping up the mess and slipped behind the counter to return the rag and bucket.

"Your dad?" I asked, and Brooke pressed her lips together in a silent warning to not egg Amanda on any further.

"He doesn't think I can handle you on my own." She glared at the boys, and in her fury, forgot she was steaming a metal jug of frothy milk. She yelped in surprise and dropped the jug, shaking out her burnt hand.

Hot milk splashed across the floor, and I got to work with the rag and bucket still in hand.

"Did you burn your skin?" Brooke fretted, taking Amanda's hand in hers.

"You have fire powers," I snorted. "I didn't know you could burn."

"Oh, good." Her dry tone made my cheeks warm. "I'll let my hand know that it's actually fine."

She disappeared into the back for the first aid kit, and Brooke took over the drink making.

"Everybody burns, with the exception of her mother. That's her Apex ability. Amanda is only burn-proof when she means to be," Brooke explained. She capped the drinks and handed them over. "You take care of these. I'll clean up this mess."

"If Amanda's dad sent them, does that mean they're Apex?"

Brooke clicked her tongue.

"You know we aren't supposed to talk about that with you."

"So they are?" I looked over at the boys. They'd found a seat in the corner. The one with the gelled hair slumped in his chair while his bespectacled friend sat rigid and alert.

"Take them their drinks, Sammy," Brooke said gently. "And don't press them. If I know Roy Hendricks, and unfortunately I do, I'm sure they're here as a punishment, not a privilege."

I took the drinks from Brooke and came back around the counter. I read the name on the first cup as I approached their table.

"Wesley?"

The boy with the glasses whipped his head around, and his eyebrows shot up.

"You know my name?"

I flashed him the side of his cup where Amanda had scrawled his name in messy handwriting. His face fell.

"Oh. Right." He pulled his hand out from his pocket, and I blinked in surprise when I saw red plastic where there should've been fingers of flesh and bone. A low, mechanical whir issued from the joints, and he gingerly unfurled his prosthetic fingers and clamped them around the cup. His gaze lingered on my neck. "I like your necklace."

My cheeks flushed with sudden defensiveness.

"You're making fun of me."

His ears turned red.

"No, I just— I like your necklace."

"It's old trash on a chain," I frowned. The other boy, Andersen, snickered.

"It's not *trash*," Wesley asserted. "You wouldn't wear it if it was garbage."

"I have terrible taste." I liked that I had been wearing it when I first woke up out of the memory-less fog, and I liked that it matched the upside-down "V" shaped scar on my sternum exactly, but I wasn't about to explain that to a stranger.

"It's nice."

"Mmhmm." I pressed my lips together. He was definitely teasing me. I glanced at the cup in my other hand. "Andersen, spelt E-N, not O-N."

Andersen grimaced instead of saying thank you, but he at least didn't poke fun at my necklace. I tucked the silver whistle under the collar of my shirt as I retreated back to Joni's table.

"You make that boy sad," she murmured without looking up from her book.

"*He* makes *me* sad."

"No, he annoys you. But you make him sad."

I rolled my eyes. Whatever curiosity I'd had over the two Apex boys had completely dissipated.

The door to the backroom swung open, and Amanda stormed out, ignoring Brooke as she strode to the wall-mounted phone. She jammed it to her ear, squinting at the boys. Andersen glared back.

"Roy sent us *babysitters*," she snapped into the phone. I heard Fleming's voice rumble distantly on the other line, and Amanda's face contorted. "I don't care that he's my father, his name is Roy, isn't it?"

She caught me staring and glared, so I made busy with my sketchbook while I continued to eavesdrop.

"He sent *children* to watch us! ...Code? What code? Fine, the menu has a surprise item today, and it tastes like overstepped boundaries."

She slammed the phone back on the receiver.

The bell over the door rang again, and a family of three hurried in, looking around cautiously and shouldering bulging backpacks. A young girl clung to her parents, and the three of them kept their heads down as they approached the counter. Unlike the morning's other customers, these ones looked scared and out of place.

"Amanda," Brooke whispered. Amanda's tense shoulders relaxed.

"The Pomeroys," she hissed back. "Their kid was a sophomore when I was a senior in high school. Where are the keys?"

Brooke beckoned for the family to follow her into the back, and Andersen and Wesley gave each other a meaningful look.

"Who are they?" Joni asked me under her breath.

"One of the families," I said. "But I don't know what that means."

"They don't tell you much, do they?" Joni snorted. I deadpanned at her, and she suppressed a laugh, returning to her book. Brooke returned from the backroom without the family and nodded to Amanda, who redialed the phone.

"The Pomeroys are on their way," she said into the receiver, then glowered. "I don't care about your secret code! No one is listening to us!"

She slammed the phone back onto its mount, angry steam rising from her fingertips.

The morning wore on, each hour bringing a fresh wave of tourists fresh from the ferry boat, excited for their farm-island summer getaway and in desperate need of caffeine to get them started. I tried to focus on my sketchbook, but Wesley continued to watch me from his and Andersen's corner table. After a while, Brooke called me back to the counter and handed me two more cups of hot chocolate.

"Refills for the boys." She nodded at their corner table. Amanda snorted something about Brooke being too nice as I retreated back to Andersen and Wesley.

I made a point to hand Andersen his drink first.

"I'm sorry I made fun of your necklace earlier," Wesley murmured.

"It's fine." I went to hand him his drink, and he revealed his red, robotic hand a second time. The cool plastic brushed up against my fingers as he grabbed the cup.

"Eydis." The voice that sounded in the back of my head was low, authoritative, and familiar. I startled at the sound, and Wesley's prosthetic fingers contracted around the cup with too much force.

The lid shot off the cup, and hot chocolate splattered Wesley's face as well as the front of my shirt. I shouted as hot liquid seeped through to my skin, and Wesley jumped to his feet, choking on an apology.

I dabbed at my shirt, still glancing around the cafe for whoever had said my Icelandic name.

"It's fine," I mumbled, stepping back from Wesley and holding my shirt away from my stomach even though the liquid was already cooling down. He reached out, as if to help. "Really. Don't."

I hurried to the single-occupant bathroom, which was mercifully empty, and I pressed the door shut behind me. The hot chocolate stained the light fabric of my t-shirt, and I grumbled as I got to work with a wet paper towel, scrubbing at the stains over the sink.

"Eydis, dear," a voice purred. "You doing alright? That looks to be a right mess."

I leaped back from the sink at the sound of the man's voice, the same one from before and as clear as if it were in the room with me. In the foggy mirror over the sink, I'd expected to see my own startled reflection gawking back at me, but instead, there stood a dark-haired man with porcelain-pale skin and a gaping, bloody wound where a left eye should have sat opposite his sparkling-blue right eye.

I may not have remembered the man, but Fleming had forced me to study enough to recognize Adrestus when I saw him.

4

Through the Veil

I shrieked and grabbed the broom in the corner of the bathroom, ready to javelin-throw it through the mirror when wood splintered to my left. Bright light poured into the bathroom, and I stumbled back, falling to the floor. Wesley stood in the doorway, having ripped the wooden door from its hinges, still holding it by the doorknob.

"Get out!" I screamed and threw the broom at him instead. He raised an arm in defense, and it clattered to the ground as Amanda, Brooke, Joni, and Andersen rushed in behind him.

"Move!" Amanda shoved past Wesley to grab me by the shoulders where I sat on the tile. "What's wrong? What happened?"

I stared past her into the mirror, but Adrestus was gone. My mind reeled trying to make sense of what I'd seen. Was Adrestus in my head after all?

"I think I saw—" I cut myself off. He had commented on the mess on my shirt. He could see me. I dropped my voice so only Amanda would hear me. "I saw Adrestus."

"What? Where?" Wesley had somehow heard me and glanced around the bathroom, ready for a fight. Adrenaline propelled me to my feet, and I shoved him in the chest, forcing him back out of the restroom.

"Who do you think you are bursting in on girls in the bathroom?" I demanded. "And look what you did to the door!"

He was still holding the door by the doorknob, but it was completely removed from the frame.

"I heard you scream, I—"

"Sammy," Amanda pulled me back. "What do you mean you saw Adrestus? Is he here? Are we safe?"

Brooke cleared her throat, and turned to the rest of the cafe. The other patrons were trying to peer into the bathroom, and my face grew warm with embarrassment.

"Nothing to worry about," she chirped. "Just a spider, is all. We've got it handled."

"A *spider?*" I seethed. "I'm not afraid of *spiders!*"

"It was a *really big* spider!" Brooke insisted.

"Sammy, focus!" Amanda was in my face again. I pointed at the mirror.

"He was there, missing an eye."

Amanda and Wesley both went to inspect the mirror, leaving Andersen and Joni to gawk at me from the doorway.

"It couldn't have been him," Wesley said. "I would've heard him."

"I'm not a liar," I bristled.

"But do you even know what he looks like?" Amanda frowned at me.

"I've been studying!" I insisted. "I've seen his pictures!"

I looked back at the mirror, sharp pain tingling at the back of my skull. His voice had sounded so familiar.

"You should take her to Fleming," Andersen suggested. "He's at the camp so Everly could check her out, too."

"I don't need medical attention," I snapped. "I'm fine."

"No, he's right. Plus, Alison should take a look. She might be able to tell if someone has been in your head," Amanda said, "but we still have at least one more family coming through the shop today, and I'm *not* leaving Brooke if there's any chance Adrestus is anywhere *near* McMillan Island."

"You're supposed to be protecting *her!*" Wesley pointed his plastic hand in my direction.

"I can take care of myself, thanks." I grabbed the broom off the floor. "I need Amanda to *drive* me, not protect me, same way I don't need *you* ripping doors out of the wall."

Color rose in Wesley's face.

"Fine, protect yourself, but if Amanda can't drive you, we can," Andersen said, folding his arms across his chest, and I felt my shoulders relax.

"You'll take me to the camp?" I asked Andersen.

"Yup."

"Fine." My initial shock at the apparition in the mirror was already ebbing. I'd probably imagined it, spurred on by the images of the New Delos curator I'd been forced to study. More than anything, I wanted to see this secret camp they'd hidden from me for the past three months. I pointed at Andersen. "*You* can take me. *He* can tag along if he wants, but he has to leave the bathroom door."

Amanda stepped aside to let me follow the boys to the cafe entrance. A thrill of wonder cut through whatever horror remained. I was going to see the camp where Everly, Sergio, and Avery were always disappearing to and no one could stop me.

"I can come back and fix the door," Wesley said, leading the way to a gray sedan. "I didn't mean to break it."

He held the passenger door open for me, and I glared, instead turning to open the back door.

His shoulders heaved with the effort of a mighty sigh, and he relinquished the front seat to Andersen instead before crossing in front of the car to take the driver's seat.

"Are you old enough to drive?" I asked. He glared at me in the rearview in response.

"He is, but you'll definitely want to buckle up," Andersen sneered.

"I'm a good driver!" Wesley scowled. He glanced back at me in the mirror and grimaced. "Can you cover your eyes?"

"Why?" I recoiled.

"If Adrestus is in your head, he'll see where we're hiding."

I folded my arms at him to let him know I wasn't happy with the instruction but obliged, leaning back in my seat and closing my eyes. The car shuddered as Wesley turned the key, and we bumped through the small town of Quarry Bay until I felt us turn onto the main road.

"If Adrestus wanted to download information from my head, wouldn't he have been able to get whatever he wanted *before* he wiped my memories?" I asked.

The boys were silent, and I grinned, knowing I'd stumped them.

"There's still things he might try to find out," Wesley finally grunted. "You're safer this way."

"What if him downloading information from my head is *why* he erased my memories? What if the damage is already done?"

"It's been three months. He would've made a move by now if that was the case."

Winding through the island's roads with my eyes shut was making my stomach churn.

"Can I open my eyes now?"

"No," Wesley snapped. "It's safer for you with them closed."

"I have no idea where we are. I've only ever been between the farmhouse and Quarry Bay."

"Just let her open them." Andersen grunted, and I blinked my eyes open before Wesley could argue. We barreled past trees and farms, catching glimpses of ocean beyond forests and bluffs.

"What? No!" Wesley looked at me in the mirror. "You're making yourself a target!"

"I'm already a target." It wasn't like they could force me to keep my eyes closed.

Wesley glared back and shook out his right arm. He held it towards Andersen as we passed an orchard full of tourists.

"Little help?"

"Can't it wait?" Andersen recoiled.

"It itches."

"I'm not itching it for you."

"I'm not asking you to! Just take it off."

Andersen's eyes flitted back to me in the back center seat before he begrudgingly raised a hand.

"Remember to unclip the electrodes," Wesley said.

"Yeah, I know." Something metallic clicked inside Wesley's sleeve, and Andersen twisted his wrist in midair. I watched as Wesley's red arm twisted, too, and slipped out of his sleeve, floating towards Andersen's hand. Three white wires dangled out of the back of the arm like detached nerves.

"You're a telekinetic Apex? And *you* break doors?" I asked as Andersen plucked the prosthesis from the air.

"I do more than break doors." Wesley glared at me in the rearview mirror, and I scowled back.

"And you're friends?" I continued.

"No," Wesley and Andersen said in tandem.

"*Best* friends?" I pressed. "Begrudging buddies who go on superhero missions together?"

"We're roommates." Wesley shook out his right sleeve. "The cover's still in there. It itches."

"It's going to be sweaty." Andersen shook his head.

"I can help." I leaned forward over the center console.

"I'd rather stay itchy, thanks." Wesley glared at the road.

"No need to be a jerk about it. What do you need?"

"I'm *not* making you get my prosthesis cover," Wesley said vehemently. "It's all the way up my sleeve!"

"Don't be a baby. You already barged in on me in the bathroom. What's there to be shy about?" I grabbed the hoodie sleeve, and Wesley let me roll it up until I found his arm. Black fabric covered the residual limb, clinging to his skin, and I gingerly prodded at the covering. "This? You want this off?"

"Fair warning, it probably *is* sweaty."

I peeled the cover away from his arm and let the sleeve fall back down around his elbow. Andersen recoiled when I dropped the cover in his lap.

"Do you know Sergio? He lives at the camp, I think. He's missing an eye, and *you're* missing most of your arm." I looked at Andersen with curiosity. "Are you all missing body parts? What're *you* missing?"

The car swerved again, and I fell back in my seat.

"Okay, I lied a little bit." Wesley raised his residual limb towards Andersen, most of the sleeve hanging limp. "I need you to itch it."

"That's where I draw the line." Andersen pushed his arm away.

"No, you drew the line at helping him get the cover off."

Wesley bent over the wheel to itch his arm against his leg. The car swerved and Andersen swore.

"Just let go of the wheel, I've got it!" Andersen snapped. He raised his hand like he did before, and Wesley let go of the wheel to itch his arm. We hurdled around a bend in the road, and I clutched my seat, waiting to careen through the guardrail, but Andersen turned his hand, and the wheel followed suit.

Wesley's eyes met mine in the rearview mirror as he readjusted his hoodie sleeve, and I remembered what Joni had said about me making him sad.

"You okay?" Wesley asked, reclaiming the steering wheel.

"Just carsick." It wasn't a complete lie. "You're roommates, then, but not friends? I thought people were supposed to be friends with their roommates?"

"You're one to talk," Andersen snorted. Wesley shot him a look.

"You mean because of Amanda?" I looked over my shoulder down the empty wooded road. "We're housemates, not roommates. It's different and we get along just fine."

Wesley skirted around a couple of cyclists on the road, and I watched farms appear and disappear between trees and clearings, boasting orchards, petting zoos, and lavender fields.

"How far away is the camp?" I asked, leaning forward again.

"Another half hour," Wesley said. "If you're not feeling good—"

"I'm fine."

Andersen procured a plastic bottle of water from beneath the seats.

"This should help with motion sickness." He passed it to me, and Wesley narrowed his eyes.

"What?" I asked, untwisting the bottle cap. "He's just giving me water."

"It's nothing," he mumbled and hunched over the wheel.

I had more questions about the camp, but Andersen cranked up the radio, and I fell silent, memorizing the twists in the road despite fears of Adrestus using me to learn the way, too. After driving for much longer than I thought possible on the small island, Wesley turned down a dirt road. I sat up, expecting to see cabins between the trees, but the forest thickened around us for another fifteen minutes.

Wesley flicked the headlights on. The late-morning sun barely broke through the dense canopy overhead, and the trees ahead seemed to cast darker shadows still.

"Don't freak out at this next part, okay?" Wesley warned.

"Says the guy who was ripping bathroom doors from walls less than an hour ago," I retorted, but clutched the plastic water bottle in apprehension.

The car rolled to a near-stop, and despite the headlights shining into the dark, the shadows of the forest smothered them just feet ahead. As we crept forward, the dark pressed in until it felt like night.

I could make out the outline of Wesley and Andersen's heads, lit by the failing headlights, but everything else was cast in perfect shadow.

"It's okay," Wesley insisted in the front seat. "It's just the Shadow Veil. It's a security thing."

"I'm *fine*," I lied. The dark was oppressive, and I wondered how we'd ever find our way through, or *back* for that matter. But then, just as the headlights were about to extinguish entirely, the shadows began to lift. The forms of trees reappeared outside the windows, and a grassy field lay before us, dotted with white cabins set against an azure ocean backdrop. Figures ran between buildings, and I saw people sparring beneath a gnarled cherry tree, its red leaves bending and dancing in the sea breeze.

"Welcome home." Wesley grinned in the mirror, then frowned. "Well, not home-home. Not your home, anyway. My home. Our home. For now, at least."

I unbuckled my seatbelt and shifted closer to the window as Wesley pulled up to a grand, three-story colonial-style building with a high porch that boasted white columns supporting the eave.

The front door slammed open, and I shrank away from the window at the sight of a man storming down the porch steps, leaving in his wake fiery footsteps that billowed in the wind before snuffing out. A blue windbreaker billowed behind him, and his round cheeks turned tomato-red under his rimless spectacles. His hair was thinning, and his nose was austere, as if sharpened by decades of looking down it at those around him, but the family resemblance to his daughter Amanda was impossible to miss. Though, that might've been in part to the fire that wicked off his fingertips.

"If you've abandoned your post, I swear I'll have you both swimming laps in the ocean until the orcas adopt you as their own!" He froze in his tracks when he saw me in the backseat. Mr. Hendricks ripped the passenger door open and yanked Andersen out by the wrist. Wesley's prosthesis fell to the gravel from Andersen's lap.

"Wait!" Wesley stumbled out on the driver's side but Mr. Hendricks was already yelling.

"You were supposed to *watch* her!" he bellowed. "Not bring her back like some kind of stray!"

"But she saw—"

"I don't care if she saw God himself descending from the clouds," Mr. Hendricks cut Andersen off. "You've compromised the entire camp bringing her here! This crap might've flown when Alexander Fleming was running the place, but now you've gotta abide by *my* rules."

"Roy!"

Mr. Hendricks stopped his tirade, his fingers still wrapped around Andersen's wrist, and whipped around to face Alison where she stood in the doorway.

"Perfect timing." He let go of Andersen to gesture to where I still sat in the backseat. "We need a memory alteration."

"What?" My heart jumped painfully. I pushed the door open, and Alison's face softened at the sight of me, despite her furrowed brow. "No! It's okay. I'm not a liability!"

"Adrestus has a direct line into your head, and you wanna pretend like your very existence doesn't threaten all of us?" Mr. Hendricks was literally fuming. Puffs of smoke lifted off his arms as he struggled to contain his rage. I'd heard a lot about Amanda's father, and it was becoming very clear why she hated him.

Wesley bent over to pick his plastic arm up out of the dirt, but Mr. Hendricks smacked it back to the ground as he stepped towards Wesley.

"Why is she here?" he demanded.

"I saw Adrestus in a mirror. They thought it best to bring me to Fleming."

Alison's face paled while Mr. Hendricks's turned yet a darker shade of red.

"Alex isn't here! He left half an hour ago!" Embers sparked off the tips of his fingers. "You might've led Adrestus straight to our camp! Today of all days! When we know he's on the move! Endangered every Apex and all the families we've taken in!"

"Adrestus is on the move?" I asked. It now made sense why Fleming had left to come here so early in the morning.

"Enough!" Mr. Hendricks whirled on Wesley. "Go signal for a lock down, and tell Hannah to double the Shadow Veil."

"Her name's Heather," Wesley glowered.

"Do it. And tell Parker what's happened. Make sure every university student that's fit to defend us is uniformed and ready." Mr. Hendricks spoke through clenched teeth. He turned to Andersen. "You, I imagine Everly needs your help in the infirmary."

The boys nodded their understanding and scurried away, leaving me at the mercy of Mr. Hendricks and Alison.

"Are you okay? Tell me exactly what happened." Alison cupped my face in her hands, peering into my eyes as if she might find the apparition of Adrestus still lingering on my retina.

"Take her to Everly." Mr. Hendricks looked out over the camp, as if expecting Adrestus and his warriors to fall upon us at any moment. "See if he's messing with her head again."

Alison put an arm around my shoulders, and I let her lead me up with the porch steps into the building.

"And call Fleming, and tell him to come pick her up!" Mr. Hendricks chased after us. "I will not have Betas putting *my* camp in danger!"

The inside of the house boasted high ceilings and bare, wooden floors. The room immediately to the right upon entering housed an ornate desk, around which several high school students clustered, all trying to look at a computer screen together.

"Sammy?" A girl with dark brown hair looked up from the computer, and a breeze stirred the room despite all the windows being closed.

The other students looked up, too, and I shied away from their curious stares.

"Samantha!" An older boy with dark skin, a bleached buzz-cut, and a sling around his arm raised his eyebrows at me. "Are you here because of the news that Adrestus left New Delos?"

He fell silent as Mr. Hendricks swooped into the house after us. The computer beeped shrilly, and Alison continued to shepherd me down a hall.

"We're on lock down!" Mr. Hendricks barked. "Everyone who can still walk needs to suit up."

The students scattered, casting me furtive glances as they fled the room.

"Why did they all know me?" I asked. "Joni said her sister was my roommate. Is she around, too?"

"You went to school with them," Alison explained. "They were your classmates. Of course they know you."

I should've been scared. Adrestus was on the move and had just appeared to me in a bathroom mirror, but all I felt was the sting of knowing there had been a camp full of people who knew me, who seemed to *like* me, after I'd been hoarded away for three months.

The back room of the house stretched across a long wall. Windows looked out over the fields that dropped off and turned into ocean, and midday-light poured in over the row of white-linen beds that lined the opposite wall, each one occupied with a student. Everly sat at the far end of the room, donning lavender scrubs as he showed Andersen how he was wrapping a girl's ankle.

"Samantha's here!" The girl in the bed nearest to me pushed herself into a sitting position. Her leg was propped up on a pile of pillows, and she winced as she adjusted herself. Limp ringlets fell over her shoulders, and she brushed them back with an arm painted in deep burn scars.

Every face in the infirmary turned to look at me before shrinking back against their pillows at the sight of Mr. Hendricks entering behind us.

"How very much like old times," Everly said wryly, stepping back to let Andersen finish the bandage he was working on. An orange tabby cat sat at the foot of the bed, watching us approach with wide, emerald eyes. "To what do I owe the pleasure?"

"She thinks she saw Adrestus," Alison said in a low voice once we reached Everly's end of the room. The girl with the freshly wrapped ankle yelped.

"She saw Adrestus?!"

The room erupted in gasps and questions, and Everly glared at the girl.

"Yes, thanks, Desirea. That was definitely something we wanted announced to the room."

The girl blushed but leaned forward.

"Is he on the island? Is that why he left New Delos? What happened?" She stared accusingly at Andersen. "Why didn't you say anything when you came in?"

"I didn't *see* him, exactly," I interrupted. "He was in a mirror."

More mumblings and whispers rippled across the beds.

"Can we maybe go somewhere a little more private?" Alison hissed. Everly ushered us into the next room, which was a disorganized cross between an office and a storage closet.

Alison sat me in the office chair and leaned over, gently pressing a hand against my temple. Her brown eyes flitted between mine. She pressed her lips together.

"Someone was in here recently, yes," she murmured. "Seems like they've gone now, but it just as easily could be fingerprints of Avery's powers."

"What exactly did you see?" Everly pressed.

My stomach twisted, and I looked askance at an open box of black and gray body armor. A shoulder pad with a yellow number "12" painted on it stared back at me.

"It looked like the pictures I've seen of him except he was missing an eye and bleeding all over the place."

"I imagine he looked a bit like he did when you gauged his eyeball out?" Everly suggested. I blanched.

"I—what?" I looked at my hands in horror.

"Why would he show her that, of all things?" Alison asked. "Is he putting memories back?"

Everly knelt down to look me even in the eye.

"Maybe. Last time she was regaining memories, they seemed to come back in odd ways, but this feels different. I don't recall her ever mentioning seeing them in mirrors, though she was never my most forthcoming patient."

"I'm right here," I snapped. "You don't have to talk like I'm not. Why did no one tell me I removed a man's eyeball? And to that point, why did no one tell me I have friends here?"

"If it's not a memory, then someone put it there," Alison mumbled. "Adrestus has a man working for him who's an Inculcator like Avery and me."

"The one who forced her old memories to return last time," Everly nodded. "He's likely behind her losing everything else."

"Or I imagined the whole thing?" I suggested.

"That'd be quite the coincidence, you imagining Adrestus in a mirror the very day we get word he's mobilized off New Delos," Everly murmured.

"Speaking of, was no one going to mention that to me?"

Alison and Everly shared a look of guilt but jumped when the door slammed open, revealing Mr. Hendricks in his blue windbreaker.

"He's sending warnings, that's what it is," Roy fumed. "And if he can put images in your head, he might be able to pull images out, too. Now that you've seen the camp, he'll know *exactly* where we are!"

"That's not how an Inculcator's powers work, Roy," Alison reminded him.

"Either way, I want her memory of this place *erased.*"

"It's fine, though!" I stood up, sending my chair reeling backwards into a shelf of first-aid supplies. "No one's in my head except me!"

"Alison, fix this!" Mr. Hendricks growled.

I watched my fake-mother warily, ready to fight if I had to.

"You know I don't know how to do that."

"Then get Avery in here and make *him* try!"

"Avery can't alter memories either! Roy, he can't even get her old memories *back!*"

"I won't have a Beta knowing where we're hiding, especially one vulnerable to Adrestus's mind-attacks!"

Someone cleared their throat and the four of us turned to look at the girl in the doorway behind Mr. Hendricks. Dark hair hung in a curtain of braids down her back, and heavy bags pulled on her eyes, one of which looked purple and bruised against her dark skin. She locked eyes with me, and her lips twitched as she suppressed a flicker of surprise. Her resemblance to Joni was uncanny, and I knew she must be the sister the others had mentioned. I knew I must be looking at the girl who'd once been my roommate.

"What is it, Bradford?" Mr. Hendricks snarled.

"Everly, it's Heather," the girl said. "She's passed out. The Shadow Veil is down."

5

Catching Up

Everly rushed back into the infirmary, and I cautiously followed behind Mr. Hendricks and Alison. The girl in the far bed with the ringlets moved out of the way as Wesley carried in a girl with long, black hair, holding her as effortlessly as he'd pulled the bathroom door from its hinges. A student with big ears that stuck out of shoulder-length brown hair followed close behind, trying to help Wesley but was held back by the angry scowl on Wesley's face.

Wesley set the girl down on the vacated bed, and her head lolled to the side. It was hard to look directly at her, like her outline was blurred and shifted.

"You've overworked her again." Everly took the girl's hand in his. Mr. Hendricks tensed next to me.

"We have to keep the camp hidden!" Mr. Hendricks pointed at a boy in a middle bed. "You! Frankie! Give the camp some fog cover until Hannah is able to go back out."

"It's Freddie, sir," the boy corrected, his pale face turning red, highlighting the purple bruise that spread across his cheek.

"Go!" Mr. Hendricks barked. "They could already be on their way here!"

"No one is looking for the camp!" Everly spun to face Mr. Hendricks. In all the sword fighting sessions he'd monitored, in all the times he'd assessed and tended to my bruises and cuts over the last three months, I'd never heard him raise his voice.

Freddie struggled out of bed and limped into the hall, but the rest of the room fell silent, and the orange tabby cat hurried under a bed.

"Samantha *just* saw Adrestus, and you have the arrogance to assume they aren't looking for us?" Mr. Hendricks seethed. "If we aren't ready—"

"We *aren't!*" Everly gestured around the room. "A fourth of your team is in here! They aren't ready for a brisk walk along the beach let alone Adrestus's army!"

"They're more powerful than they've ever been." Mr. Hendricks beamed at his injured students with pride. "They're in here because they're giving more than they've ever been able to."

"They're children. They don't owe anyone anything, least of all their health." Everly sat down on a stool next to the unconscious girl and pointed to a cabinet under the window. "Andersen, hand me a bag for Heather."

Andersen hurried to comply while Mr. Hendricks's chest swelled.

"That's a waste of our resources, Jacobi," he warned. Everly took the bag of clear liquid that Andersen brought him. "She'll sleep it off and be fine. If we run out of Serum—"

"The Serum is here to heal students. If you didn't push them so hard, this wouldn't be a problem."

"If they were stronger, they wouldn't need pushing!"

"Enough!" Alison stepped between the two men. "I'll contact Weaver about securing more Serum soon. Trev and I can schedule a trip as early as next week. Roy, I'm sure the camp is safe for now. There's no way Adrestus knows we're here. Jacobi, do what you need to do."

Mr. Hendricks breathed heavily through his nose, but Alison stood her ground.

"Where the hell is Alex?" he finally said. "Why hasn't he come to pick her up yet?"

"I imagine it's because no one's called him." Alison raised an eyebrow. Mr. Hendricks unholstered a phone from the clip on his belt and jammed it to his ear.

"I swear, no one at this camp does anything but me. A bunch of lazy, entitled— Alex." His eyebrows began to smoke as soon as Fleming answered on the other end. "Where are you? The coffee shop? Your kid isn't there. Come get her."

Fleming's voice echoed through the speaker.

"Why is she—"

Mr. Hendricks hung up.

"Alison, she'll wait in your apartment. I don't need her snooping."

I flushed under the accusation and the accompanying stares.

"Naomi, would you show Samantha to my apartment?" Alison asked through gritted teeth that she tried to pass off as a smile.

"Everyone else needs to suit up and man the perimeters," Mr. Hendricks barked.

"But my ankle—" Desirae raised her hand at her bed at the end of the room.

"Either walk it off," Mr. Hendricks said, halfway out the door, "or turn in your uniform and go stay with families in the neighboring camp if you insist on being useless."

Desirae looked to Everly for help. He mouthed the words "it's okay" and motioned for her to stay in bed.

"I'll go try to find Val. If anyone can reign him in when he's like this, you'd hope it'd be his wife." Alison sighed. "Let me know if you need anything."

"If you could get Roy to stop pushing these kids past their breaking point, that'd be great." Everly held another hand out to Heather. She stirred feebly, and her eyelids fluttered. Andersen pressed a wet rag to her forehead.

"I'm trying," Alison promised, and with a fatigued attempt at a smile, she exited.

While a few of the students managed to struggle out of bed and follow the adults out of the infirmary, most stayed, casting each other sideways glances, and the unspoken words that passed between them were clear: "If we stay in bed, he can't kick us *all* off the team, can he?"

"Right." Naomi fixed a strained smile on her face, looking me up and down. "Mrs. Havardson's apartment. Upstairs with me, please."

The boy who'd followed Wesley in pressed against the doorframe to make room for us to pass.

"It's good to see you again, Sammy," he mumbled, his eyes on the floor.

"Don't talk to her." Wesley's snarl caught me off guard, and the boy blushed and shrank further against the door frame.

"He was just saying hi." I spun around to face Wesley. He wrinkled his nose.

"Trust me. You don't need *him* saying anything to you."

"Sorry," the boy mumbled.

"No, I'm sorry," I insisted, glaring at Wesley. "Sammy."

I held a hand out to him, and he looked between my palm and Wesley.

"He's not the boss of either of us," I sniffed. "You can shake it."

He took my hand, though his handshake was weak and awkward.

"Anthony. I know you don't remember me, but we were friends," Anthony said, eyes back on the floor.

"Oh, yeah," Wesley snorted. "One hell of a friend."

"Wesley, stop." Naomi's cool voice made Wesley's cheeks turn pink. "It's fine."

Wesley looked like he wanted to say more but cast Anthony a resentful glare and sauntered past us down the hall and out onto the front porch.

"It was great to meet you, Anthony," I said and followed Naomi to the main staircase that ran up the center of the building. I watched her curtain of braids swing between shoulder blades as we climbed to the third floor. "What's that guy's problem? He's terrible."

Naomi smirked over her shoulder at me.

"Wesley's not that bad. He could stand to be nicer to Anthony, sure, but Anthony's no saint, either."

"What did Anthony do?"

The stairs ended at the third floor landing, flanked by two doors which led into two different living quarters. Naomi stopped at the door on the left and scratched at her chin.

"It's a long story. Probably best not to go into it. Either way, here we are!"

She pushed the door open, and I glanced around the cozy living room that connected to a small kitchen. Beyond that, I could see two bedrooms and a bathroom.

Avery slouched on the living room couch, watching the small wall-mounted TV, and startled when we walked in.

"Did it happen?" he asked, pushing himself up straight. "Is Adrestus here?"

"We're fine," Naomi insisted. "Sammy's just visiting."

"Mr. Hendricks is letting you come to the camp now?" He raised a blond eyebrow at me.

"I think this might be my first and last visit," I admitted. He fell back into a slouch and returned to the TV, pumping the volume up. Something bumped up against my foot, and I looked down at a hamster rolling in a ball. I bent over to scoop him up in my arms, grinning at him through the green plastic. "Hello, Knut."

Naomi helped herself to a glass of water in the kitchen, watching me as she did.

"Sorry." Her cheeks darkened with a sudden blush. "It's hard not to stare. It's been a while since I've seen you."

"Rumor has it we were roommates." I followed her into the kitchen and peeked inside the fridge but closed it without grabbing anything. Even if Alison was my Sister-In-Law-Turned-Adoptive-Mother, going through the food in the kitchen felt intrusive.

"The rumors would be true," Naomi admitted. She maneuvered around me to check the fridge for herself and handed me a cup of applesauce. "You're hungry, right? She won't mind. Hendricks is strict about snacks so Alison keeps this well-stocked knowing we all sneak up here for extra food."

"So we were friends?"

Naomi smiled and nodded.

"Of course. I think we annoyed each other sometimes, but we were definitely friends."

Commercials blared on the TV, and I leaned against the counter watching the light of the television dance across Avery's glazed face.

"Hopefully I wasn't too annoying," I mumbled. I didn't know the girl next to me but something about her was relaxing.

"I'm talking to you now, aren't I?" She grinned. "I think I annoyed you with my powers, and in turn, you tried to keep secrets. Standard friend stuff."

I slurped at the applesauce.

"And now everyone keeps secrets from me, so we're even?"

Naomi twirled a braid around a finger, and her smile twisted.

"There was more to it, but..."

"But it's a secret?" I gave her a resigned scowl when she shrugged an apology. "I suppose that's fair. Sorry for whatever it was I did. You seem nice."

"It doesn't matter," Naomi laughed. "You can't remember it."

"But you can," I pointed out. "So where does that leave us?"

She thought for a moment, swishing the water in her cup.

"It leaves us on pause. You'll get your memories back, and we can talk about it then." Her grin widened. "And in the meantime, I'm going to get a kick out of how much you can't stand Wesley. It's *killing* him."

I grimaced.

"It's not that I can't stand him, he just comes off a bit strong. He got mad at Andersen for giving me water and made fun of my necklace." I wrinkled my nose. "And he burst in on me in the bathroom."

"That keeps happening to you for some reason."

"With Wesley?" I recoiled away.

"No." She shook her head and bit back a smile. "And to be fair, you did the bursting in last time."

"On *who?*" I screeched, and Avery shushed me from the couch. I glared at him, and Naomi tittered anxiously.

"Trust me, if you knew, you'd be glad you forgot."

She turned to set her cup in the sink and paused to look out over the green field. Across the grass, there was another collection of cabins and what looked like a large, indoor pavilion. Naomi's smile slipped from her face.

"Is my sister okay?" she whispered.

"Oh. Um, she seems alright, all things considered. Sorry about your family, by the way. I heard..." I trailed off. No wonder we'd had issues as friends. I was an idiot to forget that, as Joni's sister, she would've just found out her family had been taken by Adrestus.

"Don't feel bad," she insisted. "I'm glad she's alright. I know you'll watch over her. As for the rest of my family, they're tough."

"I'm still sorry," I said. Naomi tapped her fingers against her glass.

"I'm glad I get to see you today," she sighed. "Even if you don't remember me and I might not see you for another three months."

She paused and whipped around to look at Avery. He froze under her stare, and for a second I thought he might be scared.

"What?" he asked.

"What're you watching?" Naomi demanded, swooping into the living so fast that she almost kicked Knut as he traversed across the floor in his hamster ball. "You reek of guilt!"

He dove for the remote, but she grabbed it first and held him at arm's length.

"It's nothing!"

"'Drowned City: The New Delos Story'?" Naomi read from the screen. She jammed the power button and tossed the remote across the couch. "What're you doing watching that with Sam right here?"

"It's a documentary!" Avery pushed her away and retreated to pout on the far end of the couch. "It's educational!"

"You were there," Naomi deadpanned. "You know what happened. This is all going to be Schrader Industries propaganda."

"Why can't he watch it?" I'd enjoyed chatting with Naomi but didn't like how quickly things had shifted back into keeping secrets from me. "I already know New Delos sank."

Naomi chewed on the inside of her lip.

"It's nothing," she said too quickly. I plucked the remote from where she'd discarded it and turned the TV back on. The documentary rolled old news footage of what looked like the inside of a middle school gym filled with rows of cots.

Tangled, tawny hair jumped out at me from the screen, and I pointed.

"That's me!" The Samantha onscreen held a small fish tank, barely discernible in the back corner of the gym. "And that's my fish!"

The footage cut, shifting to aerial shots of the flooded city. Naomi wrestled the remote away from me and shut the TV off just as the narrator began intoning about a single casualty, despite the flood's severity.

"We were all there, Sam." Naomi's dark eyes were steely and serious, all signs of her previous mirth evaporated. "We're probably all in the background somewhere."

"So why can't I watch it?"

"You can, but you don't want to." She handed the remote back in a show of good faith. "As your friend, I'm telling you, forget everything to do with New Delos flooding."

I snorted but discarded the remote back on the couch cushions.

"Consider it forgotten."

"You know that's not what I—" She froze and stared into space. The tiniest trickle of blood issued from her nose. "Oh. That's not good."

She stumbled towards the door, tripping on the coffee table. Avery steadied her, but she forged forward.

"What? What is it?" I demanded.

"It's Adrestus!" Avery gasped.

"No." Naomi shook her head, her nose bleeding heavier. "It's Joni. Joni's coming."

She twisted the doorknob, stepped out onto the landing, and collapsed.

6

A Midnight Snack

Avery shot up from the couch and backpedaled away from Naomi where she lay on the floor, as if whatever was afflicting her might come for him next. I hurried to her side as her eyes fluttered open, and she reached out, digging her fingers into the wooden floor to drag herself to the stairs.

"I want to see her," she choked. I looked back at Avery, but he was pressed against the farthest cupboard in the kitchen, shaking his head.

"You mean Joni?" I pulled her to her feet, and she half relied on me, half on the stairway bannister. She was heavier than she looked, and the way her biceps pressed against my back made me self-conscious of my own arms.

Maybe if Everly added weight training to my regimen, I wouldn't lose to Sergio so often...

I shook thoughts of finally defeating Sergio away and refocused on guiding Naomi down the steep steps. Outside, a car door slammed shut.

"What happened?" Fleming's sharp bark echoed in from the driveway.

"Your kid put us all in danger, that's what!" I winced at Mr. Hendricks's accusation.

"Like hell she did! Where is she?"

"Both of you calm down!" Alison demanded.

"I don't hear your sister out there," I murmured to Naomi at the bottom step.

"She's there." She pulled away from me, falling against the front door. Streams of blood ran from both of her nostrils now, pooling above her lip and spilling down her chin.

The door swung open beneath her, and she fell forward onto the porch into Mr. Hendricks's arms. He startled and dropped her, but Fleming was there to catch her before her head hit the wooden planks.

"What've you done to my student?" Mr. Hendricks roared and surged towards me with literal fire on his heels. I staggered backwards, but before Mr. Hendricks could reach me and do whatever he was planning on doing to me, Andersen stepped between us, coming out from the back with Everly.

Everly rushed to tend to Naomi, but Andersen stood firm in front of me. Mr. Hendricks halted and narrowed his eyes.

"Out of the way, Lewis. She's a traitor, and it is not your job to protect her."

"Except it literally is," Andersen snarled. "That's why you sent us to the coffee shop in the first place."

Mr. Hendricks's fire flared, leaving burn marks in the wood at his feet.

"Joni," Naomi whispered, and Fleming whipped his head back to his car.

"Alison, check the car!" Fleming snapped his fingers at the sedan. Alison and a frizzy-haired woman I didn't recognize hurried to Fleming's car. "Open the trunk!"

"It's Joni!" Alison called, reaching into the open trunk to help Joni climb out. Naomi managed to lift her head to her sister, her lips breaking into a weak smile.

Mr. Hendricks rounded on Fleming.

"Who the hell do you think you are driving around the island with a middle schooler in your car trunk?"

Fleming flushed red.

"I didn't know she was in there! She must've slipped in when I stopped to pick her and Sammy up from the shop, just before *you* called!"

"Naomi!" Joni broke free of Alison and stumbled up the steps to her sister, falling when she reached her. Naomi reached out and ran a hand across Joni's cheek, stroking her with her thumb.

"Been a while, weirdo."

"What's wrong?" Joni's brow furrowed, a small trickle of blood working its way out of her nostril.

"Nothing's wrong," Naomi promised, laying her head on her hand. "I missed you. Do you feel alright?"

Joni wiped the blood from her face and nodded.

"Better than you do, I think."

"Your powers are still growing," Naomi murmured.

I looked to Andersen, and he frowned.

"Empaths," he said. "They feel emotions, but when they get too close to each other, they feel what each other is feeling, and it amplifies their powers until it's unbearable."

"Divulging team secrets?" Mr. Hendricks snarled. Andersen sneered back at him, and the frizzy-haired woman tried to pull Mr. Hendricks away.

Naomi ran her thumb across Joni's cheek one last time, and her eyes fluttered closed.

"Naomi?" Joni pushed herself up and shook Naomi's shoulder. The blood over Joni's lip was already drying, and her energy was returning quickly. "What's wrong with her?"

Andersen stepped away to help Everly lift Naomi into his arms. Her arms hung loose at her side, and her head lolled forward onto her chest.

"She lost consciousness," Everly sighed. "She'll be fine once you're out of range."

"Don't worry." Fleming patted Joni's back, and tears sprung into her dark eyes.

"But it's my fault," she gasped. "I didn't mean— I missed her is all. I wanted to see my family again."

Alison helped Joni to her feet and back down the stairs. Fleming brushed dirt from his pants and straightened up to look at me.

"What happened?" he asked.

"I don't know." I shrugged. "We were upstairs, and Naomi fell over all of a sudden—"

"I mean with you. At the shop."

The cool summer breeze did little to help the heat in my cheeks.

"Nothing." I looked askance at Mr. Hendricks. He opened his mouth to argue, but the woman shushed him. "Just imagining things, I think."

Imaginary or not, I didn't want to talk about the Adrestus in the mirror in front of Mr. Hendricks any more than I already had. Fleming must've picked up on that inclination, and he beckoned me down the steps, leading me down with a hand on my shoulder.

"I don't want to see her back at this camp, Alex," Mr. Hendricks warned.

"And if you do? You wouldn't draw attention to yourself by calling the cops."

"Her being here puts us all in danger," Mr. Hendricks glared. "The second she becomes too much of a liability, I hand her over to Adrestus myself."

Fleming paused on the bottom step. His grip on my shoulder tightened.

"Roy!" the frizzy-haired woman snapped. "She's a kid! Stop that."

"Winnie's a kid, too. Their age doesn't make their choices any less consequential," he growled.

"Winnie's our *daughter*." The woman stepped away. Now that I knew she was Mr. Hendricks's wife, the resemblance to Amanda was unmistakable.

"And I suppose you're going to blame me for her, too?" Roy's voice rose, but his wife stood her ground.

"Listen to Val, Roy," Fleming interrupted. "She's always understood both your daughters better than you do."

"Don't you of all people lecture me about family," Mr. Hendricks warned. "Winnie made her choices, and Samantha is making hers when she puts the rest of us in the crosshairs."

"Both of you, stop." Alison closed the sedan door, leaving Joni safely in the backseat.

"My brother made his own choices, too, but you were fine with those." Fleming's words dripped with uncharacteristic bitterness.

Fire erupted in our path, and its warmth washed over my face. Fleming pulled me back before the flames could burn me, and he reeled around, his hands in fists. "You nearly burned Samantha!"

Mr. Hendricks glowered at us from the top step. Val tugged at his arm, but he shrugged her off.

"Only the weak get burned, Alex. Now get off my property."

"Vic bought this property. It's *mine*," Alison warned, but Mr. Hendricks was already stalking back into the house.

"Sure, but the *team* is mine, and if she leads Adrestus here, I'll happily give her up. So if you do care about keeping her safe, I better not see her again." The door slammed closed behind him in Val's face. She turned to give us a look of utter hopelessness, and Alison took the steps two at a time to rush to her side.

"Alex," Alison started, holding Val around the shoulders as they sank onto the top step.

"Save it," Fleming snapped, crossing in front of his car to get in the driver's seat. I slipped in on the passenger side but Fleming hesitated with the door open. He looked at his feet, his glasses balanced on the end of his nose, and then looked up to face Alison and Val. "They're just kids. He forgot that with his own daughters. Make sure he at least remembers now that he's in charge of forty of them."

"We're doing what we can, but you know how he is. Maybe if you asked for the job back—"

"Tell Jacobi and Sergio we're still scheduled for Thursday."

"Alex?"

Fleming froze with his hand on the top of his door.

"We really need to be going, Alison."

Alison chewed on her lip.

"Trev wanted to talk to you."

"I need to get the girls home. I don't have time—"

"He had a dream."

Fleming stood still for a moment, his knuckles turning white where he gripped the door.

"I'll see you around, okay? You take care, Val. We always have room for you at the farmhouse if—"

"It was about you." Alison interrupted. "Trev had a dream, and it was about you."

A slight shudder that I thought I might've imagined ran across Fleming's face.

"Bye, Alison." He fell into the driver's seat and slammed the door shut without looking back. Gravel sprayed from under the tires as he peeled out of the driveway, back towards the tree line.

I sat with my hands in my lap, not daring to speak as Fleming seethed in the driver's seat. He slowed down as we passed a group of four students, all wearing black and gray uniforms with matching helmets that covered the top halves of their faces. They paused as we passed, each with a different number painted on their shoulder armor. Number Seven raised a red plastic hand to wave good-bye.

Our headlights refracted through the fog, and trees took shape in the gloom.

"What does that mean?" I asked. "If Mr. Baker has a dream about you?"

Fleming's cheek dimpled where he chewed on it.

"Joni, how are you feeling?" He looked at the rearview mirror, and I knew that was the end of the discussion about Mr. Baker and his dreams.

"I didn't mean to hurt her." Joni's voice was tiny and muffled in the back seat.

"It wasn't your fault," Fleming assured her. "*I'm* the one who's sorry. I should've noticed you get into the car."

Joni hiccuped.

"I'm never going to see my family again, am I?"

"We don't know that. Naomi's working to find a way to control—"

"So, no. I'm not. You don't have to dance around it."

"I'm not—"

"I can be sad about it now and move on," Joni explained, "or I hold out hope only for it to crush me later. I'll think I'll settle for being sad, thanks."

Fleming glanced sideways at me, maybe hoping I'd have something to say, but I thought Joni made a good point and let it be. I fell back in my seat, and the car forged forward into the dense mist that had fallen over the forest.

"This fog is from an Apex, right?" I mumbled, taking a stab at small talk.

"It's Freddie," Fleming said. "Usually Heather puts up a Shadow Veil, but apparently Roy can't be bothered to not push my students to their breaking point."

"I'm sorry I got you in trouble." I looked at my lap. Fleming gave me a double take in my periphery.

"No. Sammy, no. Roy isn't the boss of either of us, and like Alison said, he doesn't even own the land his camp is on." He drummed his fingers on the steering wheel. "We don't have to talk about what happened at the coffee shop if you don't want, but do you think if you saw Adrestus in the mirror, maybe it was a memory coming back?"

The thought hadn't occurred to me, and dull hope fluttered in my naval before Joni's recent sentiment about hope echoed in the back of my head. Maybe she was right, and it was best not to hope at all.

"Yeah, maybe it was."

We broke through the fog, and Fleming sped up down the dirt road. I found myself trying to memorize every twist on the road. As horrible as Roy Hendricks was, a strange sadness clung to me. I thought it might be something akin to nostalgia, but with memories that only spanned the last ninety days, it was hard to be sure what nostalgia was supposed to feel like.

The faces that lit up when I walked into the infirmary, chatting with Naomi like we were old friends, the way Andersen had gotten between Mr. Hendricks and me... It wasn't that Sergio, Amanda, and Brooke weren't great, but I wanted friends who were my age, not college students.

Speeding past lavender farms and pastures of shetland ponies, I was feeling more horribly alone than I had before seeing Adrestus in the mirror. I'd even take Wesley's company over leaving, as rude as he'd been.

My stomach clenched, and I rolled the bent-metal whistle of my necklace between two fingers.

"When do I get to see friends again?" I turned to the window and scowled, trying to count the lavender fields, immediately embarrassed at having asked the question.

"Did you remember them?"

"No." I dropped my necklace and leaned against the window.

"Samantha, are you not happy at the farmhouse?" Fleming asked. Joni snorted in the backseat, answering his question for him.

"I'm happy." I was safe. I was cared for. I was lonely. "I guess I feel like the world's on pause until Adrestus makes a move or until you're all dead of old age, and I'm still an immortal teenager, all alone."

"No, of course not," he insisted, but I kept my eyes on the passing farms. "I know this isn't a permanent solution. We're still getting our bearings. Once you have your memories back, we'll make our next move."

"Hmm," I grunted.

"I know three months probably feels like a long time when it's all you know, but I promise, we're not stuck here."

I pushed my forehead up against the glass. Three months didn't *feel* like a long time, it *was* a long time.

"And Everly is coming over in a couple days to see if you are still losing your immortality. We aren't going to leave you."

"Right." I tried to smile at him but couldn't get the corners of my mouth to work for some reason. He was doing his best with what Roy was allowing him, I knew that. He probably felt just as stuck as I did, but it still sucked.

He ran a hand through his hair, pulling at the strands and making it stand up awkwardly on one side of his head. He chewed on the inside of his cheek for a moment, and then raised his eyebrows behind his glasses.

"Your birthday is next week," he said. "We could do something for it. A real party. I'll make Roy agree to it. All your old friends, we can invite them to the coffee shop after closing. Mr. Everly will drive them. He'll know who to bring."

"Really?" I straightened up, trying to keep hope at bay. Mr. Hendricks could still say no. "Naomi? And Andersen?"

Fleming frowned.

"You want Andersen there?"

"He was one of my friends, wasn't he?"

Fleming opened his mouth, then closed it, smiling wryly.

"You know what, yes. Yes, he was."

"And we'll eat sushi?"

Fleming's lips pressed together, but he nodded. He hated sushi, but it was my birthday, not his.

"Of course. It's your first birthday in a thousand years, isn't it? You can have a millennium's worth of sushi. I might pack a peanut butter sandwich for myself."

"Fair." With something to look forward to for the first time in my waking memory, the grin I gave Fleming was genuine. "Enjoy your sandwich. I'll eat your sushi for you."

He laughed and shook his head, and I settled into the passenger seat, counting the lavender farms with renewed optimism.

That night, I lay in bed and traced the thin remnants of the cut Sergio had left on my cheek the night before, listening to Joni snoring softly on her cot. A light rain pattered on the roof, and it gurgled down the gutter outside our window.

The light of my digital clock, reading one AM, caught the edges of curling paint, but I couldn't sleep. I was too busy focusing on the darkness of the ceiling, projecting mental images of the road that wound around the perimeter of McMillan Island and trying to recreate the turns and bends between the farmhouse and the Apex Camp.

I had friends on the island. The thought electrified me, and I wondered if they lay awake at night thinking about me, too. I nestled into my pillow, the terror that had come with the mirror apparition that morning forgotten, replaced with daydreams of belonging somewhere other than the salty farmhouse, when I heard my name.

"Eydis."

The husky whisper scraped at the back of my head, and my eyes flew open again. Joni lay with her back to me, her shoulders rising and falling with steady breaths. It couldn't have been her. The voice had been too masculine. Too similar to the voice I'd heard that morning just before running to the bathroom and seeing Adrestus in the mirror.

No. I had to be imagining things. Footsteps sounded from downstairs, though that wasn't uncommon at this hour. Amanda was known to sneak out for the occasional midnight swim in the cove.

I wouldn't have worried if it weren't for the distinct clinking of metal that accompanied every footstep. As far as I knew, Amanda didn't wear metal to go swimming.

I slipped out from under my covers, shivering more from apprehension than the nighttime chill, and pulled the bedroom door open as silently as the old, squeaky hinges would allow.

On the upstairs landing, I strained to listen for more footsteps and instead heard the clinking of mugs in the kitchen. Someone hummed to themselves as I reached the bottom of the stairs and snuck through the living room. I turned the corner into the kitchen, and my heart burst with electric fear.

A man in black armor stood at the stovetop, pouring hot water from a kettle into a mug. The orange glow of the stove light pressed against his silhouette, highlighting the creases and folds of the tattered red cape that hung off his shoulders. A box of teabags sat on the counter next to a black, metal helmet adorned with a magnificent red plume.

Fear rooted my feet to the floor of the kitchen entrance. The man turned, blowing across the top of his steaming mug. Green light from the microwave clock bounced off a metal eye cover while the blue of his right eye seemed to glow in the dark.

"Hello, Eydis," Adrestus crooned. "I've been trying to reach you all day."

7

The Warrior In My Kitchen

It wasn't possible. It couldn't be possible. He couldn't be here. But he was. My sword was clear across the living room in the umbrella stand where Sergio and I kept them, but fear paralyzed my legs and throat, leaving me helpless. Adrestus took a sip of his drink and screwed up his face.

"You know, I've never been a big fan of tea." He set the mug down on the counter. "I know. What kind of immortal warrior doesn't like tea? You'd think it'd grow on me after a couple of centuries, but no. Too bitter."

"Get out," I rasped, barely able to force the words through my throat. "Get out, now."

My eyes darted down the adjoining hall towards Fleming's bedroom door.

"Don't bother waking the others," Adrestus said, reaching for the box of teabags. "I'm not *really* here. I'm an image planted into your head, and I just want to talk."

My chest loosened, but only a little.

"You *are* in my mind." A chill ran through me. I was a liability. Going to the camp had been a mistake. "I-I knew it."

The eyebrow over the metal eyepatch raised.

"This is the first time we've been in your head since your stay at my tower."

"Liar."

"Swear on my life, Eydis, and you and I both know how much weight that holds." He gave his mug a melodramatic swirl, and then held it up as if toasting to me. "Has *someone* been in your head?"

"Don't act like you don't know." My fingernails dug into the palm of my hands as I curled them into fists. "You took everything from me. All of my memories. Now give them back."

Adrestus froze with the mug half-raised to his lips.

"After all that work we did to get them back, your memories are gone? *Again*? Good god, Eydis, it's like trying to carry water in a sieve with you." He set the mug down and raised his hands in a show of innocence. "I've only ever tried to return your memories to you. I'd never take them away."

He was a liar. The others had said so. But a new, different panic rose in my chest.

"Then what happened to my memories?"

He ruffled his dark, silky curls with one hand.

"I'm the wrong person to ask. Perhaps posit that question to your captors if you'd like an answer."

Captors?

"How are you here?" I demanded. "You said you're an image in my head. How does that work?"

"You remember Gregor, of course. Although...no. Sorry. I forgot. Gregor helped with your last bout of amnesia and can project images into the minds of others, so consider this more of a video-call than anything else."

"But I could hear you down here. I can see you drinking the tea you found in *our* kitchen."

"He projects *really good* images. For one, this is tea I had Miles pick up for me. I'm drinking it in my kitchen, and you see me drinking it in yours. I don't know exactly how it works, so you'll have to ask Gregor next time you're around." His lips curled with the last few words. "Speaking of, I wanted to let you know, we're coming to save you."

My hands curled into fists, and I shook my head.

"You're coming to kidnap me, you mean."

"If your memories are gone, how do you know you can trust the people keeping you? Do they keep secrets? Do they control where you go and when?" He picked his mug back up and tried another sip of tea before frowning and giving up on it, setting the mug down on the counter. "I do *wish* I liked tea, even if it was just for aesthetics. No one takes a museum curator who doesn't drink tea seriously."

"I'm serious." My voice wavered. "If you come anywhere near me—"

His face softened, and he stepped forward, then hesitated when he saw me recoil.

"Oh, Eydis," he frowned, "what lies *have* they been feeding you?"

Rain rattled against the kitchen window, and I sized Adrestus up. He wasn't much taller than me, but even though he looked like a young man, maybe in his early thirties, I knew he was much, much older.

"If you hurt my friends—" I warned.

"Friends don't erase friend's memories." His eye widened earnestly, and he reached for my hands, but I drew them back. "They fear you, and they fear what you and I have worked so hard to build. The pieces are taking their final places, and soon we'll have it. A world united. Peace between nations under my singular flag. And after everything you've done to help—"

"But you killed my dad," I stuttered.

"Your *brother* you mean? The man who placed you in a coma for a thousand years until he conveniently woke you up in time to weaponize you against me?"

"But you did kill him?"

He sighed and rustled his curls again. His cape swished around his ankles.

"I'm not happy with how things panned out, I'll admit. I was trying to save you."

"So yes," I snarled, "you did."

"Eydis, why would I lie to you? I'm on the cusp of achieving what I've worked towards for two thousand years. I don't *need* you for that to happen."

"Except that you want revenge."

He laughed, and the sound made me want to trust him. I pushed the feeling away. Good guys didn't show up in kitchens at one in the morning wearing armor and capes.

"I'm two thousand years old, not *twelve*. I'm about to rule the world. What need would I have for revenge?"

"Why would my friends want my memories gone?" I demanded, unable to quell the panic rising my chest. What if they weren't my protectors at all? What if they *were* the bad guys?

"To make you easy to control, I imagine," Adrestus said softly. "And they've done it before. Your memories of middle age Iceland? Gone. All to make you a compliant prisoner."

I chanced taking my eyes off him to glance down the hall towards Fleming's bedroom. He was so *sincere*. He wanted me to be safe.

"You still don't believe me, do you?" Adrestus sighed. "Just like before. I'll take my spot in the first global throne room whether you're by my side or not. I'm here because I *care*."

"No."

"I'm coming to save you, whether you like it or not, Eydis. You may not thank me yet, but you will. On my life, you will." He grabbed his helmet, and the long, red plume swept the mug off the counter. It shattered on the floor, and I stumbled back as Adrestus stepped towards me, his cape billowing up behind him.

"Sammy?"

I yelped at the sound of Fleming's voice and slapped my hands over my mouth as the overhead light flicked on, revealing an empty kitchen.

"It's fine!" Fleming blinked in the light. He'd pulled a checkered bathrobe over checkered pajama pants, and a metal bat rested over his shoulder. He pushed his glasses over his nose and glanced around the kitchen. With his unkempt hair and plaid-on-plaid bed wear, he looked considerably less villainous than Adrestus had in his dark Spartan warrior get-up. "I thought I heard voices."

"And what? You heard them mention a baseball scrimmage match?" I scowled at the bat on his shoulder, and he lowered it, letting it thunk against the wood floor.

"I heard glass breaking."

I scanned the kitchen floor, but the broken mug had disappeared along with Adrestus.

"No glass, and I just got down here," I lied.

"You look pale." He frowned. He raised a hand to my forehead, but I ducked away. "Why are you down here? You should be sleeping."

"I was just thirsty." I knew I should tell him Adrestus had been in the kitchen. So why wasn't I?

My stomach clenched. Fleming had been kind, and he'd cared for me. Had it all been to keep me in line? My birthday party next week, was that to keep me complacent? If I told him Adrestus had been here, that he'd promised to rescue me, would Fleming make me forget?

"Do you feel alright?" Fleming asked.

"I'm allowed to get water, aren't I?" I snapped.

"Sure, but—"

"Great."

I marched across the kitchen and made a show of grabbing a glass from the cupboard. Fleming's baseball bat scraped lightly against the floor as he lifted it back up.

"At least try to sleep, alright?"

He slinked away, back towards his bedroom, and I leaned my forehead against the refrigerator, trying to calm my racing heart. When I heard the bedroom door close, I set the water glass down, still empty.

Adrestus was right about them blocking out my memories once. They'd admitted to writing over them to create Samantha Havardson out of Eydis, and it was true that Adrestus had been the one to bring back my memories last time.

From what the others had said, he couldn't be trusted, but they made it clear they didn't trust me, either. They'd cared for me, sure, but Adrestus was right. It had kept me compliant.

But if it *was* a trick? I needed to tell the others Adrestus was coming.

Except he had no way of knowing where we were, so maybe I'd take my time, watch my captors, and figure out for myself who it was I could trust.

The night passed restless and slow, but whatever plans I'd formulated in my head to avoid Fleming the next day withered away when he told me I was headed back to the coffee shop while he took Joni shopping.

In the rising light of day, away from the uncertainty of night, it was clear that Adrestus had to be lying, but the tiniest possibility that he might be telling the truth kept my mouth shut.

He couldn't know where we were. Despite his promises to rescue me, the threat had to be empty, and I still had time to figure out on my own who I could trust. For the time being, I was safe, even if my stomach now felt like a lump of lead.

"Joni didn't arrive with much," Fleming explained as we bumped down the gravel drive. "I'm going to take her to some of the shops in Quarry Bay. You're free to join us, but I thought you might be happier with Amanda and Brooke."

I pressed my lips together and nodded. He wasn't wrong, but his understanding and thoughtfulness annoyed me in a new way. Adrestus's question lingered in the back of my mind, playing on a loop like a song stuck in my head.

Do they control where you go and when?

Yes. But how was I supposed to know what was thoughtfulness and what was control?

"Did you get any sleep last night?" Fleming asked as we turned onto the main road. I twisted my lips. Was he suspicious? Did he know who I'd spoken with?

"I was fine. Just thirsty."

I peeked at him from the corner of my eye, taking note of the dark circles under his eyes. Fleming didn't *look* like a villain, and he didn't act like one either. Roy Hendricks on the other hand...

He took a different road into Quarry Bay than I was used to, driving towards the water on a side street rather than the main road. I thought it might be a superfluous covert maneuver until I saw the colorful canopies and booths on the parallel road, blocking off the usual route.

"What's that?"

"The Lavender Market," Fleming explained with a frown. "It started today and goes for two weeks. Tourists love it."

He drove the car as close to the coffee shop as the market would allow. I looked out the windshield and scowled when I saw a familiar face waiting on the sidewalk.

Wesley stood apart from the throng of tourists with a nervous smile plastered to his face and his hands hiding in his hoodie pocket.

"I don't need an escort," I growled as I stepped out of the car.

"You'll live," Fleming retorted. "Which is the entire point, actually. We should only be gone a couple hours. I have my phone on me so if you need—"

I closed the door behind me before he could finish and begrudgingly joined Wesley on the sidewalk. A ferryboat harkened its arrival with a long, drawn out horn, and he winced but kept his smile in place.

"Hey, Sammy."

"It's Samantha." I made a point of walking ahead of him.

"You used to let me call you Sammy." He caught up to me with an awkward hop-skip. Suddenly self-conscious, I grabbed at my necklace. My shirt collar was too low to hide the dog whistle under today. Even worse, the V-shaped scar on my sternum was on full display.

"My friends can call me Sammy. You can call me Samantha."

"But we *are* friends."

I stopped at the front door of the cafe to cross my arms at him. He blushed under my stare.

"You're my babysitter," I said. "And yesterday, you broke the bathroom, were rude to Anthony *and* Andersen when they were nice to me, and made fun of my necklace."

"Look, if you just *remembered*—"

"But I don't, do I? Someone took my memories, and I'm left relying on all of *your* rules."

I pushed into the cafe. What should've been a mid-morning coffee rush of tired tourists was an empty coffee shop. Brooke burst in from the backroom, joining Amanda at the register when the bell over the door signaled our arrival, and the customer service smile slipped from her face.

"Oh. It's you. I thought we might finally have customers."

"Slow morning?" I ignored Wesley walking in behind me and took a seat at a table near the counter.

"Why have a standard coffee when you can have a lavender latte? The market always messes with business apparently." Amanda nodded towards Main Street. "If we didn't have Apex families scheduled to come through today, we wouldn't have opened at all."

Wesley hovered awkwardly behind my seat until Brooke came from around the counter to hand him a hot chocolate. He took the drink, glanced at the empty seat next to me, but opted to slink back to the same corner table he'd sat at the day before.

"My aunt is trying to get booth space." Brooke frowned at the street. "With a booth and a little bit of lavender syrup, we'd be in good business. Maybe I'll go see what ingredients I can wrangle up from any of the vendors."

"No customers isn't such a bad thing." Amanda messed with her phone. "I can finish listening to that podcast I was telling you about."

"The depressing one?" Brooke frowned.

"It's the one that talks about the news."

"Yes. Exactly. The depressing one."

"It's this or murder. What will it be?"

"The news is fine." Brooke looked to me and sighed in resolution. "Hot chocolate? Or something stronger?"

"Everly will kill me if I have coffee," I admitted, flipping my sketchbook open to my work from the day before. "Something about it making the immortality wear off slower."

"Then I suppose it won't matter if he kills you." She winked. "I'll whip up something good, and he'll never know."

Amanda cranked up the volume on her phone and set it aside as the podcast host read out his daily story for the empty cafe.

"...next month when the world's leaders meet for a peace summit in the newly minted *country* of New Delos. With Prime Minister John Ratcliffe at the helm..."

"Peace summit?" Brooke raised an eyebrow. "I thought he wanted world domination."

"To him, they're the same thing." Amanda scowled at a tiny flame that danced between her fingers. "It's probably a trap, and it's definitely not our problem as long as we're here."

"...meanwhile," the podcast continued, "Apex continue to flock to the island city from around the world, finding refuge in their new home..."

"Flocked?" Amanda scoffed. "Abducted more like."

"Joining us today is former New Delos resident and international news correspondent Finley Knight. Hello, Finley."

"Hi, Michael. Good to be here. The new parliament of New Delos is working closely with Schrader Industries, who first developed the Epsilon Initiative, to open the country's doors not only to Apex but also to those willing to undergo a procedure and grants super-human abilities. These first generation Apex, also known as Epsilon, are thought to only make up ten percent of New Delos's population, though that number is expected to climb."

"So, superpowers," the host clipped. "There's an obvious draw there that goes without saying, but ten percent doesn't *seem* like all that many. Where's this stall in growth coming from?"

"It remains unclear," his guest explained. "Schrader Industries hasn't been very forthcoming with its research or the procedure's associated complications, and with communications to the island still cut off after the flood, it's been hard to talk to New Delos citizens who've undergone the Epsilon Procedure. So far, it seems safe to assume that something as fantastical as superpowers must come at some sort of cost, we just aren't sure of what that cost is just yet."

Brooke reached across Amanda to turn the podcast off while Amanda stared blankly at the fire in her hands.

"That's enough of that," Brooke murmured. "Like I said, it's depressing."

"Is that legal?" I asked. "Not telling people the risks of becoming an Apex?"

"New Delos is its own country now." Amanda shrugged. "I'd wager whatever Adrestus says is legal must be legal."

I tilted back in my chair.

"Maybe it's not such a bad thing the city sank," I mumbled darkly. "Seems like it would've been better left at the bottom of the ocean."

"Don't let the others hear you of all people say that." Amanda snapped out of her reverie. "That might be a bad look."

"It's about three out of ten." Wesley looked up from his corner. I wrinkled my nose at the nonsensical answer, and Amanda snorted.

"What's that have to do with the city sinking?" I asked.

"Nothing." He nodded at Amanda's phone. "The success rate for the Epsilon Initiative. I heard a couple of their scientists talking back when I was trapped there."

He cut off to clear his throat and looked out the window, itching his right inner elbow through his hoodie where I knew the prosthetic arm connected to his residual limb.

"The procedure only works on thirty percent of people?" Amanda blanched. "No wonder they haven't made that public. That's embarrassing."

"No, only thirty percent of people survive."

"Oh."

My stomach flipped, thinking about the people who would undoubtedly be rushing to New Delos for their own dose of superpowers, unaware that the venture would sooner land them in a morgue than a hero's pedestal.

However, before I could think too hard about what this might mean regarding the trustworthiness of the apparition I'd seen in the kitchen, the bell over the door rang out. A single customer walked in, smiling at the exposed rafters and salt-stained windows.

The kid, hardly older than myself, must've really liked coffee because he had a confident air that bordered on something like triumph as he looked at the menu behind me. He was definitely still in high school with a clean-shaven face and bright cheeks that glowed against alabaster skin.

"Welcome in," Brooke chirped from the register.

The kid beamed around the shop space, still taking in every last detail.

"I've heard this coffee shop has exactly what I'm looking for," he said, "but is there anything you recommend?"

His gaze came to rest on me, and he shook back silky, dark curls that hung in his face, revealing hauntingly familiar ice-blue eyes.

8

Quinn

He turned back towards the menu, but I remained frozen, unable to get his eyes out of my head. They looked just like Adrestus's, though he had twice the number Adrestus had sported the night before. Not to mention, he was decades younger.

"We've got whatever coffee or tea you feel like." Brooke smiled. She seemed at ease and Amanda was uninterested in the boy entirely. They were sooner to recognize Adrestus than I was, and I let my shoulders relax. Fleming's incurable paranoia was rubbing off on me.

The boy laughed and struck an apologetic face.

"I'm not super big into tea, actually. Maybe a white-chocolate latte with extra foam?"

"You don't like tea?" I repeated. Adrestus had said the same thing. He turned back to look at me, and my cheeks burned, but his icy blue stare was kind.

"I mean, it's *fine*," he admitted, pushing silky black curls back out of his face. "But why have tea when you can have something with a whole day's worth of sugar intake in it?"

I let myself laugh. Disliking tea wasn't unique to Adrestus. I didn't like it that much either. That didn't make me in league with the villain any more than it did this kid.

"Name?" Brooke pulled a marker cap off with her mouth.

"Quinn." He looked back at me and flashed a smile that inexplicably made me want to make him think I was cooler than I was.

"Visiting the island, Quinn?" Brooke made small talk as she rang up his order, and Amanda got to work on the latte.

"Fair-weather resident, I'm afraid. My parents live here during summertime."

"Ah." She smiled, handing him his change. "The worst kind of islander."

"Hey, Brooke." Amanda shook a near-empty milk carton at her girlfriend. "We're almost out of milk."

"We're not due another delivery until later tomorrow." Brooke frowned at the dusty wall clock. "We might have time today to pick some up from the general store to hold us over until then."

"Did I cause a problem?" Quinn's blue eyes wrinkled in concern. "I can order something else, it's fine."

"As long as she doesn't mess it up, it should be okay," Brooke assured him over the whistle of steaming milk. She wiped her hands off on her apron and stepped into the back room.

I glanced back at Wesley, who had his eyes trained on the docked ferry outside, his hot chocolate untouched, and the tiniest of frowns fixed to his face, as if he was concentrating on something far away. He seemed distracted so I chased Brooke into the back.

"Everything okay?" Brooke asked when I entered the cluttered backroom. Shelves boasted bags of coffee beans and spare equipment, and she stood at a desk that overflowed with papers and junk in the far corner, pulling cash from a till box.

"Yeah," I said too quickly. "Actually, I'm free to go pick up milk if you like."

She narrowed her eyes at me as she locked the money box.

"Alone?"

"It's only a few blocks away." I tried to look nonchalant so she wouldn't see through my plot to get out from under Wesley's watch. "And you said you wanted lavender syrup to make a special latte with, right? I can explore the market and find what you need."

Brooke fanned herself with the money in her hand.

"You stay between here and the general store." Her face softened. "You can take the back door out to the alley if you want to leave more discreetly."

She passed the money to me and winked. She'd seen through to my ulterior motive after all.

"Thanks," I mumbled.

"Don't be too long, but enjoy the market if you can. It may steal our customers, but it's good fun."

I pushed through the back door in the alley behind the cafe and basked at being out from under watchful eyes for the first time in my living memory. I took a moment to myself, leaning against the wood paneling of the cafe with my eyes closed and my face towards the sun, relishing the early morning warmth against my cheeks.

"Care if I join you?"

I opened my eyes to see Quinn sipping his extra-foamy latte, smiling behind his cup and his blue eyes glittering in the sunlight. Whatever initial apprehension I had about him was gone, and I was surprised to find a weird sense of comfort seeing him there.

"It's Quinn, right?" I nodded at his name on his cup.

"Oh, she's perceptive."

"If by perceptive you mean literate? Then yes."

He laughed, and I pushed off the wall to follow him towards Main Street.

"And you're Samantha." He blushed when I gave him a wary look. "Sorry, I heard one of the others say it. I promise I'm not some kind of stalker."

"Right," I laughed. "I'm not interesting enough to stalk anyway."

We rounded the corner out of the small alley, and I stared up the hill at the double row of booths that stretched along the street all the way to town hall. At first glance, it looked to be mostly soap vendors and fresh-cut lavender-centric flower arrangements, and I wasn't sure where to start regarding Brooke's lavender syrup.

"Oh, nice! They've got lavender ice cream!" Quinn took my hand and pulled me forward into the market.

"Lavender *what?*"

"You've never had lavender ice cream?" He blanched, his blue eyes beaming.

"I always pegged lavender as more of a soap flavor."

"You mean a soap *scent,* not a *flavor.*"

"You don't know me. Maybe I eat soap."

He laughed and shifted his weight to his other foot.

"Then I promise even soap eaters will enjoy this ice cream. I get it every time I visit McMillan Island."

"Which is every summer, sounds like," I teased. "What was it that you called yourself at the shop? A fair-weather resident?"

"My family has a house out here that we stay at through the summers."

"They say the best kind of snob is a rich snob."

He gave me an embarrassed grin.

"It's my parents' money, so I'm not sure if that makes *me* a snob."

"Oh, it does." I nodded sagely as we stepped forward in line.

"We come every June as soon as school is out," Quinn explained. "Mostly for halibut fishing, but the lavender ice cream makes it that much more worth it."

"As long as the ice-cream isn't halibut flavored." I grimaced when he gave me a strange look. "Sorry. That was funnier in my head."

"It was moderately funny out loud, too."

"You're just trying to make me feel better."

He pulled a wallet from his back packet, and I blushed.

"No, don't," I said. "I have money."

"As do my parents. Let them pay." He waggled the wallet, but I was already pulling loose dollar bills and quarters from my pockets. They spilled across the sidewalk, clinking as they bounced. We both crouched down, hurrying to pick them up before the line moved again.

He handed me the last of my coins as the couple in front of us got their ice cream. Quinn caught my eye and flashed a smile as he ordered two cones.

"Make one of those a double-scoop, actually," he said, his blue eyes still locked with mine. Somehow, in the last five minutes, this boy with the haunting eyes had made me forget about New Delos, my lost memories, and the fact that Adrestus had been in my kitchen less than twelve hours ago.

Quinn handed me my ice cream, and my face split into a grin.

"I thought it'd be more purple."

"Why?" he laughed, leading me away towards the other booths.

"Lavender is purple. This looks like vanilla ice cream trying to pull some sort of scam."

"Try it." He stopped walking to watch me and ran his tongue across his own ice cream as he waited. I stared back at him with an intrepid smile before taking a cautious taste. I smacked my lips, surprised at the floral sweetness.

"It's not bad," I conceded. I was more at ease talking to Quinn than I had been talking to anyone in the last three months. Finally someone who didn't know more about me than I did. Someone who wasn't keeping secrets.

"Not bad? It's the best."

After picking up Brooke's lavender syrup, we walked among the booths, standing back as we inspected the foods and crafts to keep our ice cream from dripping over the various wares.

"How long have you lived on the island?" Quinn asked.

"For as long as I can remember." I smiled at my own inside joke.

"Maybe we've passed by each other at some point. What part of the island do you live on?"

"Not too far from here, I—"

"Sammy, don't!"

Someone grabbed my shoulder, and I spun around to see Wesley. Ice cream sloughed off my cone and splattered across the pavement.

"What are you doing?" I snapped. His cheeks burned bright, and he pulled his hand back, watching Quinn. "You better not have been following me!"

"Do you know this guy?" Quinn looked over Wesley, and I saw his eyes falter as they passed over his prosthetic arm. He bit on the inside of his cheek, apparently deep in thought.

"Not really." I'd finally been having a normal moment with a normal person, and Wesley had to barge in. "Shouldn't you be back at the coffee shop?"

"I—" His eyes flickered between Quinn and me. "I needed fresh air. Also, Brooke says she needs the milk sooner than she thought she would."

That was a lie.

"If you have to go, that's okay," Quinn said. "This time ice cream, maybe next time you can go halibut fishing with me and my dad."

"I would really love that." I smiled extra wide, just to annoy Wesley. "Also, I'm having a birthday dinner next Tuesday at the cafe. Maybe you'll stop by?"

"Wouldn't miss it," Quinn promised. He nodded awkwardly at Wesley then flashed me one last grin, and disappeared into the crowd.

"What's your deal?" I spun on my heel to face Wesley.

"What's *my* deal? You're the one running off with strangers!"

"Only stranger I see here is you."

Wesley's face fell, and his arms dropped loosely at his sides. A twinge of guilt threatened to snuff out my anger, so I shoved it down and marched past Wesley towards the Quarry Bay General Store.

"He could be working for Adrestus," Wesley mumbled, walking fast to catch up.

"And you know that for a fact?"

"No, but—"

"I'm not allowed to have fun, then? Is that it?"

"I had a bad feeling about him."

"He bought me ice cream!"

I barged into the general store, and an old woman behind the register raised an eyebrow at us. Wesley flashed her a sheepish smile and lowered his voice.

"Sometimes bad guys can be nice," Wesley hissed. "When we first met Adrestus, we thought he was a sweet, old museum curator who was maybe a little too enthusiastic about his statues, and then he tried to murder you. Technically he *did* murder you—"

"Did Quinn look like Adrestus?" I snapped, grabbing milk from the refrigerator and wishing I could shove Wesley inside.

"Now that you mention it—"

I cut him off with a cold deadpan. He blushed again, and I hoisted the milk jug into my arms and stalked down the aisle towards the register.

"Quinn had one more eyeball than Adrestus and looks about half his age, I think we're in the clear."

"Adrestus has de-aged himself before, and one of those eyes could have been fake or an illusion. He's got this guy who works for him who—" He cleared his throat and smiled awkwardly at the cashier as I slapped my money on the counter.

"You sound ridiculous."

"Okay, fine, *but* I wouldn't be surprised if they were related somehow. Maybe the Halibut fishing dad of his is actually—"

"That's right!" I pressed the heel of my hand to my head in feigned realization. "I forgot Adrestus was super into fishing. How could I be so careless? Good thing you were there to stop me from making any halibut-related decisions."

I beelined for the market, knowing it was the shortest route back to the cafe and wanting to be free of Wesley.

"I'm sorry, okay?" Wesley's tone shifted, but I didn't trust his new gentle edge. "Maybe I panicked, but we need to be careful."

I stopped on the sidewalk, hugging the milk and staring out at the glittering bay.

"For how long?" I asked. Wesley came around to look me in the face. His glasses balanced on the end of his nose, and he pushed them up with a red, plastic finger. "How long do we need to be careful?"

He gulped.

"Until this is all over."

"And if it's never over? You follow me for forever, scaring off any regular person who has the audacity to try to be my friend?"

"I can be your friend!" Wesley's face turned red as he suggested it.

I shoved past him, bumping against his shoulder.

"Fine, we don't have to be friends, but I'm still supposed to be watching you!" he called after me, but I skirted between market-goers, trying to put as many people between us as I could.

"I don't work for Roy Hendricks, so I don't get how that's a *me* issue," I called back, looking over my shoulder to watch him struggle to keep up.

He caught a lucky break when the crowd thinned, and I scowled at the sound of his bounding footsteps catching up.

"At least let me carry the milk for you."

I hugged it tighter, and I kept my eyes forward as I traipsed down the hill.

"Mr. Hendricks didn't send you here to carry milk."

"No, but—"

"He sent you here to watch me. So watch me."

"Is this because of the door I broke yesterday?" he asked. "Because I promise I wasn't trying to be weird, but I heard screaming and—"

"It's not because of the door," I said hurriedly, my cheeks flushing. "It's because you're nosy and overprotective, and I don't even know you."

"But I'm telling you that you do!" The way his glasses magnified his eyes made him look that much more helpless and desperate.

"And because you supposedly know me, you get to decide who I hang out with during my free time?"

Wesley shook his head, unable to hide his frustration any longer.

"God, Sammy, if the real you could hear you right now, she'd have a fit."

The words cut unexpectedly, and Wesley's face told me he immediately regretted them.

"I *am* the real me," I snarled. "It's the version of me that exists in your head that isn't real."

As I approached the cafe, I watched Wesley's reflection in the front windows getting farther away.

"Sammy, wait!"

"What did I say about calling me Sammy?"

I stopped with a hand on the door to look back at him, and I remembered Joni's words the day before.

You make that boy sad.

"I'm sorry. I really am just trying to help. We all are. We're the good guys here."

"I've met Roy Hendricks," I snapped. "So far, *both* him *and* Adrestus seem like assholes, but only one of them has had me followed."

"That you know of."

I scowled at him and ripped the door open.

"Good bye, Wesley."

"Right. Sorry."

I let the door shut behind me without looking back, but I could sense Wesley still standing where I'd left him on the other side of the window.

9

Grim Tidings

Amanda stayed at the cafe until the final ferry came through, but the Apex families she and Brooke were expecting never showed. They trudged home for dinner and gave Fleming mirroring tight-lipped shakes of their heads as he reheated leftover lasagna. He frowned and stepped away to make a phone call, though it didn't last long.

The next morning, when it came time for me to go prepare for my training session with Sergio and Everly, Joni followed me outside, eager to put distance between herself and Fleming's lingering anxiety.

The path down to the hidden cove was slick after another night of early summer rain, but the sky above promised a hint of warmer summer days to come. I made my way down the rough steps to the secret beach, carved from the bluff by centuries of waves breaking the clay cliffs down into sand. The rougher ocean water no longer beat against the shore, as the cliff had eroded enough to form a sort of protective barrier around the small inlet.

"What are we doing down here?" Joni scrambled to keep up.

"Training." The scraps of blue in the sky reminded me of Quinn, but I needed to focus on my upcoming bouts against Sergio. Today *would* be the day I crushed his ego. "The sand doesn't hurt Sergio as much when I throw him to the ground."

"You do the throwing?" I could hear the smirk on Joni's face.

I skipped the last two steps, landing in the sand and feeling the grains slip between my feet and sandals. It was peaceful down here, but I rarely visited. For some unplaceable reason, the cove made me sad.

I slipped my sandals off and walked to the water's edge. Out beyond the cove's protection, Amanda swam laps in the open ocean, her favorite way to spend her days off.

"When do I get to try and see Naomi again?" Joni stuck a bare foot into the water and recoiled. The overhead sun was warm on our skin, but the ocean was still frigid this time of year.

"I'm the last person who would have an answer to that."

The sound of gravel crunching drifted down into the cove, and I looked up the bluff. When Everly's bald head glinted in the sunlight overhead, I sighed in relief to see he'd left Avery at home. However, he hadn't brought Sergio, either.

Instead, Wesley followed in his steps in joggers and a hoodie with his eyes cast downward, missing his glasses.

"Where's Sergio?" I demanded as they descended into the cove. Wesley blushed under a mess of brown hair.

"Sergio was needed for a special trip to the mainland today." Everly's smile wavered, and I knew whatever had dragged Sergio off the island had to do with the missing families. "Regardless, it's high time you sparred with someone new."

I crossed my arms and tried to look passive, but as harmless as Wesley looked with his messy hair and oversized hoodie, I'd seen him rip a bathroom door clean off its hinges. Everly had brought me yet another opponent I could not win against.

"What about the other kids?" I asked. "Like Andersen?"

Wesley blanched, and Everly chuckled, taking a seat on a bleached-white driftwood log.

"You've trained plenty with Wesley in the past, even if you don't remember it." Everly set his bag down and motioned for Joni to join him. I rounded on Wesley, who continued to stare at me with his lips pressed tightly together.

"Trained with Wesley for what?" I frowned. Wesley gulped, but Everly shrugged.

"Just trained."

"Can he even sword fight?"

"No swords today," Everly said. "We're doing hand-to-hand combat. Start with the basics."

Wesley kicked his shoes off in the sand next to my sandals and pulled his hoodie off over his head.

I gulped.

Sure, he was lean, and his hoodie had dwarfed his figure, but the muscles in his shoulders and biceps were taut and toned. My eyes drifted to his scarred right elbow. He'd left the prosthesis at home with his glasses, but I doubted that would affect my chances against him. I was definitely looking at another day of getting my ass kicked.

"Right," Wesley said slowly, shaking out his arms. "The basics."

He looked at me warily, and I wondered if he was as scared of me as I was of him.

No. I wasn't *scared* of him. I clenched my fists. He was annoying. That was all.

"If you had to guess what a good ready position looked like, what would you do?"

I tried to relax my shoulders and shifted my weight to the balls of my feet, raising my hands in fists in front of my face.

"Perfect." He mirrored my stance and waited. A surging swell of water washed over our feet.

"Now what?"

"Hit me." He patted his chest as if showing me where to strike. I looked back at Everly for reassurance. "I can take it. Promise."

I took a steadying breath, and muscle memory guided my fist through the air, aiming an uppercut at Wesley's abdomen.

The cove flipped around me, and I landed on my back in the wet sand, gasping for breath. Wesley's face spun overhead, framed by messy brown hair.

"That wasn't bad." He offered me his hand. I ignored the gesture and staggered to my feet, shaking sand out of my ponytail.

"You didn't warn me!"

"Adrestus won't warn you either."

"The guy's had two thousand years to learn how to fight." I spat sand out of my mouth and into the salty brine that lapped at the beach. "I'm not going to be able to beat him no matter how much I train."

"It's not about beating him, but a matter of lasting long enough for help to come."

I looked him up and down. Sure, he looked intimidating, but I wasn't going to give him the satisfaction of knowing I thought so.

"Help meaning you?" I scoffed.

Wesley blushed.

"Or Amanda, or—"

I lunged, and Wesley staggered backwards, spraying sand as he went. I kept him on the defense, but he danced out of reach of my fists. The movements felt as natural as they had when I'd first picked up a sword against Sergio, though there was something stale and disjointed about them, as if I was learning to walk again. Still, I thought I finally had Wesley when I tripped on a stray bit of driftwood.

Wesley saw his chance to grab me around my wrist and pull me off balance as he spun me around and struck me in the back with his residual limb.

I fell to my knees as the breath and dignity rushed from my lungs.

"Sammy, are you okay?"

I looked over my shoulder at Wesley, his mouth pulled into another concerned frown that he had no right to wear.

This training exercise was useless. I wasn't learning anything. He bent down to check on me, and I pushed him away.

"Do you need a break?" Everly asked, and the question made my temper rise. All I was accomplishing was convincing Wesley I needed his protection.

"I'm not done." I squared up again, but Wesley watched me with apprehension.

"I didn't mean to hurt you," he said.

"We're sparring. You're supposed to try to hurt me."

He swallowed hard and looked to Everly, who gave him a reassuring nod.

"Yeah, fine." He raised his fist back into the ready-position.

"Don't go easy on me." I would prove I didn't need his help. I didn't need anyone's help.

"Promised you I wouldn't, didn't I?"

I cocked my head, confused, and he bolted forward. I dodged his attack and stumbled backwards in the sand, keeping my eye on him as he pivoted and redoubled his efforts.

Dodging was easier than attacking, though self-preservation instincts might've been playing a role. Wesley's attacks were fast and strong and looked liable to do more than knock the breath out of me. His fist whistled past me in a near miss, and I ducked under his arm to deal another uppercut to his abdomen on his unprotected right side.

He grunted, seemingly surprised at the force of my hit.

"Better tell Mr. Hendricks I don't need your help watching me anymore," I sang, kicking up sand as I skirted away from his counter-attack. "I'm sure I can handle boys in coffee shops on my own."

"And thank god I'll be there when that attitude gets you murdered again."

My temper peaked, and I barreled into Wesley, arms around his waist, forcing him backwards into the water. We landed in the surf, and a wave lapped over our heads, pushing us back up the beach in a tangle of limbs.

"Samantha!" Everly ran to the water's edge.

Wesley pushed himself into a sitting position next to me, salt water rolling down his face.

"Good tackle," he mumbled. Salt water burned in my throat as I coughed it up, fighting to breathe.

Everly held out his hand, and as I took it for help up, I felt his Apex powers travel along every nerve from my hand to my feet.

"You don't seem hurt." He frowned. "Wesley?"

He helped Wesley up next, but before he could make a diagnosis or lack thereof, Wesley waved him off.

"I'm fine." He pushed wet hair out of his eyes and tried to smile at me. "That was pretty good! You'd make a good linebacker. That's a football thing."

"I know what football is."

"Oh. Sorry. I wasn't sure with all the..." He trailed off and pointed meekly at his temple. When I continued to glare, he cleared his throat and tried to pass the hand gesture off as another finger-comb through his hair.

"It's just personal memories that are gone." I tried to rub sand off my face, but felt it smear across my cheek, mingling with water.

Wesley's cheeks flushed a deep red.

"That didn't go quite as I'd hoped." Everly rubbed his head. I staggered to the center of the cove, preparing for the next round, but Everly shook his head.

"I think we need a break."

My fists fell to my sides, and I gawked at him.

"We only just started!"

"And now we know where your skill level is to better help me plan the next session."

He was making excuses. He didn't want us hurting each other. Wesley's shoulders drooped in defeat, and he swiped wet hair off of his forehead.

"We came all this way for five minutes of fighting?" he asked.

"That and leftover lasagna for lunch. Plus, Samantha is due for an immortality check." Everly pulled the strap of his bag over his shoulder. I glanced nervously at Wesley.

"Can we *not* mention immortality in front of strangers?" I hissed. To my horror, Wesley looked back at me.

"No, it's okay," he insisted, and I wished he'd stop being so nice. "I already knew."

"Does everyone know?" I demanded.

"Just Naomi and me," Wesley promised. "Oh, and Andersen, I think."

Joni perked up at the mention of her sister and led the way up the steps back out of the cove, berating Wesley with questions. I pretended to be fixing my sandal strap so I could walk up alone.

By the time I caught up with them at the house, Fleming had already shown Wesley to the shower, and Everly finagled with the settings on the microscope he'd set up on the kitchen table. I was half-way up the stairs to my own shower when he called me back.

"Not yet." He shook his bag at me, and I rolled my eyes.

"Do we have to do that now?"

"Do you want to know if you're still immortal?"

"That's a tricky question." I trudged back down the stairs and fell into a chair at the table.

Everly set out his tools and glanced down the hall at the sound of the shower starting.

"You and Wesley were good friends once. That's why I brought him. I thought you'd be more at ease with him around, but that seems to have been a miscalculation." Everly jabbed my thumb with a sharp tool, and I winced. "Though I'd be lying if I said I didn't bring him here for his own benefit as well."

"Right. Because I was such a challenging opponent."

"I brought him here because he needs a friend, not an opponent. There's a decent chance he's about to get some very bad news." Everly fixed serious, dark eyes on me.

Joni watched with interest as Everly dropped a spot of red blood on a glass slide and then pipetted a drop of clear liquid over it.

"What's that?" Joni leaned over the dining table to watch.

"Once a week, I run a test to see if Samantha is still immortal." Everly dropped a second slide over the first and nodded at the microscope. "Plug that in, and I'll show you."

I pushed my chair out from the table. Low voices rumbled down the hall as Wesley and Fleming exchanged words. Even if Everly was right and Wesley did need a friend, it wasn't my job to fill that role. It was another expectation for me to be like the girl they all knew. Another expectation I couldn't live up to.

I fell back onto the living room couch and drew my heels up, half-hiding behind my knees. Besides, if Joni was right and I made Wesley sad, I was probably the last person he needed.

"Can I join you?"

I raised my face from my knees to look up at Wesley in his hoodie and borrowed New Delos University Alumnus sweatpants. His cheeks were pink from showering, and his hair lay flat and wet. I shuffled closer to the armrest, and the couch creaked as it took Wesley's weight. He wrestled with the loose sleeve of his right arm.

If I was his best option for a friend in Everly's eyes, Wesley couldn't have many friends at the camp.

"Here," I sighed, leaning over to help roll his sleeve up.

"Wow!" Joni crooned from the table. She had her knees up on her chair and her hands planted on either side of the microscope with her eye pressed against the eyepiece. "Samantha, your blood is weird."

"Let me see," Everly chuckled, taking a turn at the microscope. He adjusted the dials on the side. "Still immortal, then, but slightly less so compared to last week."

"How can you tell?" Joni continued to crowd around Everly, begging for another turn.

"I mix a drop of Samantha's blood with a drop of concentrated rat poison, and I'm able to watch if the cells react the same way a normal person's blood would or if they're resistant. Look again."

Joni reclaimed the microscope.

"Tell me I'm at least aging," I groaned, leaning my head back over the couch cushion to stare at the ceiling.

"Looking at old samples, I can confirm you are in that sweet spot where you are aging but still unkillable."

"So we won't have to cancel your birthday party," Fleming teased from the kitchen.

I held a hand over my head, looking at the ways the skin wrinkled and stretched over my knuckles.

"About time," I mumbled. "You know how hard it is to look this young for an entire millennia?"

Wesley grimaced, as if unsure if he should laugh or not.

"You did better than Adrestus on that front at least," he quipped. I rolled my head to the side to get a better look at him. "He turned old, but you stayed—"

He cut off and blushed.

"Stayed what?"

"Nice looking."

"Don't try to win points with me. It won't work."

"Samantha, you already eviscerated the poor kid with your linebacking skills," Everly chuckled, removing the slide from the microscope. "No need to come at him with a sharp tongue, too."

He slipped the slide into a black case, tucking it away in the corner. I couldn't see what was inside with his back to me, but Joni leaned over and cooed in fascination.

"What's *that?*"

"A separate project, though not entirely unrelated." Everly tucked the encased slide with my blood droplet into the larger case, and when I moved to try to see inside, he shut it and latched the metal fastenings.

"Someone's coming down the road," Wesley announced, cocking his head to the side. Fleming came out of the kitchen and gave Everly a nervous look.

"Trev shouldn't be back this soon."

"Could be because everything was fine," Everly said.

"Could be the opposite."

True to Wesley's warning, a knock sounded on the door a minute later, and Trev Baker stepped into the entryway. His eyes wavered over Wesley, and his frown tightened. Sergio stood behind him, still on the porch, his usual arrogant smile replaced by a haunted grimace.

"Trev." Fleming stepped into the living room, wiping his hands off on a kitchen towel. "What did you—"

Mr. Baker held up a hand.

"Esther's dead."

Stunned disbelief buzzed through the room, broken by the microwave beeping in the kitchen. I tried to make myself small on the couch. I didn't know who Esther was, but somehow the news of her death still felt like a punch to the gut. Someone was dead.

"She's an Apex," Fleming stuttered. "Adrestus considers them assets, no matter whose side they're on. Why would he—"

"She betrayed him, remember?" Mr. Baker glowered. "I'm sure he wasted no tears killing her. She had a hand shaped bruise on her arm, and her veins had turned dark."

"An Apex, then." Everly lowered his head into his hands.

"And Weaver?" Fleming demanded.

"No sign of her."

"No more Serum then," Fleming sighed.

"One woman is dead, and another is missing," Mr. Baker snapped. "Keep things in perspective."

"Don't with that fake outrage." Fleming fell back into the armchair. "You're just as worried about our resources as I am. Adrestus is getting closer, and there's no point in stationing a replacement on the mainland."

The repercussions of Baker's grisly discovery dawned on me slowly. There would be no more families coming through the coffee shop. There would be no more families rescued. We'd done all we could, and all that was left to do was stay hidden with what we had.

"But what about everyone still left?" Wesley's voice wavered, and Mr. Baker's expression darkened.

"Wesley—" Fleming tried to start.

"Not everyone is here yet!" Wesley clambered to his feet. "My mom and my brother, they're not..."

Mr. Baker's neck bobbed as he swallowed. Wesley's hand hung at his side, and his fingers curled into a fist.

"What?" he demanded. "What is it?"

But the crack in his voice told the room he already knew exactly just *what* it was that Mr. Baker wasn't telling him.

"Mr. Fleming?" Wesley turned to Fleming, his back still to me, and as annoying and horrifying and confusing as I found him to be, my heart broke for his sake. "Where's my family?"

"Daniella and Benson Isaacs were scheduled to arrive at the coffee shop yesterday," Mr. Baker said with a clinical clip, avoiding Wesley's eyes. "When Alison and I go searching for families, we send them to Esther and Dr. Weaver, who send them to McMillan Island's favorite coffee stop. It's dangerous to give them complete directions in case they're...they're captured."

He dropped off and finally looked up to Wesley.

"And?" Wesley pressed.

"Your family and one other group failed to arrive on time so we went to check on Esther and Weaver. The house was ransacked, Esther was dead, and the packs of Daniella and Benson Isaacs were in her living room. From what we could tell, they'd only just arrived when they were ambushed."

I stared at the space between Wesley's shoulder blades.

"I— " he started to say, then finally twisted around to look down at me on the couch. His green eyes widened in a silent plea for help. I shrank in my spot. "I need a break."

Wesley's legs moved mechanically as they carried him out of the living room, past Everly and Joni at the kitchen table, and out the back door onto the porch.

"Thank you for that, Trev." Fleming scowled. "*Very* helpful. *Incredibly* tactful. You couldn't have handled that better."

"Skip the sarcasm." Trev stalked across the living room and into the kitchen to help himself to the lasagna that was still in the microwave. "Better to rip the bandaid off than baby the kid."

The floorboards creaked next to me, and I looked up at Sergio. He had his glass eye in today, and I was struck by how much it looked like the real one. Something about the way it moved when he glanced towards the back porch gave away that it was a prosthesis, though.

"Don't worry about him," he said softly. "He'll pull through."

"I'm not worried," I lied. Joni scoffed, falling into the armchair Fleming had vacated, and I glared at her.

"I am," Fleming said, still looking out at the back porch. He turned his gaze to us, his eyes sweeping over his options before landing on Sergio. "Will you go check on him? Just make sure he's alright."

The couch jostled as Sergio took the seat next to me.

"I'm not the person he wants to see right now." He cast me a sideways glance and crossed his arms. Fleming shook his head.

"That's not fair to Samantha," Fleming said. "We can't expect her to take care of Wesley when she doesn't remember him."

Sergio grumbled under his breath and pushed himself back off the couch.

"Wait." I spoke without thinking, catching Everly's eye. He'd known Wesley was going to be getting this news. *This* was why he'd brought Wesley today. They weren't here to help me train at all.

Maybe the others were telling the truth, and Wesley and I *had* been friends and now some remnant of that was bleeding through or maybe I just felt like I could relate to feeling as if I'd lost everything, but I couldn't shake the guilt and pity that settled in my stomach watching Wesley escape out the back. I pushed myself off the couch and Fleming frowned.

Sergio fell back into his seat without giving it a second thought, but Fleming's brow knit.

"Are you sure?"

"Might as well make myself useful somehow, right?" I squared my shoulders and stalked to the back door, ignoring the stares that followed me.

Outside, salty wind nipped at my nose, but the June sun was warm against my shoulders. I scanned the property, knowing Wesley couldn't have made it far. The pit in my stomach deepened when I saw his silhouette sitting in the dirt in front of the Viking statue with his knees curled to his chest.

I thought maybe he didn't hear me approaching up the hill behind him, but as I reached the top step of the dirt pathway, his shoulders hunched, and his head lowered.

"You didn't need to come up here."

I looked up at the statue that towered over Wesley. Maybe I was hoping to find some inspiration as to what to say there, but his stone face was as stoic as ever.

"I know." I sat in the dirt next to Wesley. "But I'm here, and you aren't the boss of me."

He rested his head against his knees, watching me from behind a shock of wind-ruffled hair with red-rimmed eyes.

"Right." He gave me a weak smile and looked up at my dead brother's statue with a stare that filled me with guilt and jealousy.

"Did you know him?" I nodded at the statue.

"I did." His voice cracked. "Not as well as I would've liked, but he was there when I was hurt and scared. He told me everything would be okay."

"Was it?" I knew the answer already, but I hated seeing the reverence on Wesley's face for the man I should've remembered better than anybody. However, Wesley's mouth twisted into a wry smile.

"I'm not there anymore, so I guess it turned out alright."

"And where's 'there'?"

"Where my mom and brother are now." He wrapped his arm around his legs and tucked his chin into his knees, glaring at the statue's feet. "I couldn't protect them. And I couldn't protect—"

He cast me a sideways glance and squeezed his legs tighter. I searched for the right thing to say.

"At least you know they're alive."

He recoiled.

"I didn't think they *weren't* until just now! Why would you say that?"

My cheeks burned, and I tried to look nonchalant to keep from alarming him further.

"Adrestus killed Esther, didn't he?"

"Yeah, that's not exactly good news, either!"

"But he left her there!" I scrambled. "He doesn't pick up his messes so wherever he took your family and all the other families he's kidnapped, we know they are at least alive."

Wesley chewed on his lip.

"Take it from someone who *has* been his prisoner, being kept alive isn't exactly a mercy." He waved what was left of his right arm at me, and my gut lurched.

"They're your *family*. It's a good thing they're alive."

"I didn't say it wasn't!" he balked. "Why are you up here, anyway?"

"Because everyone keeps saying we used to be friends, but I'm finding that increasingly difficult to believe."

Wesley stood up and glowered down at me.

"We *were* friends. We *are*. But it isn't fair for either of us to send you up here." He cast the statue one last furtive glance and stepped back towards the path down the hill. "I should leave. They'll need me at the camp if Adrestus is getting closer."

I scrambled to my feet, too, but he was already leaving. He was annoying, but a dull, longing ache that I couldn't explain reverberated deep in the pit of my stomach.

"Wait, I'm sorry!"

He hesitated and looked back, sadness and confusion pulling at his eyes.

"Don't be," he murmured. "You're doing your best."

He grabbed onto his elbow, wrapping his fingers around the folds of knot I'd tied the sleeve into earlier, and he trudged back towards the house.

I glared up at the stone face of my brother's statue.

"Thanks for the help," I snorted and rushed to catch up to Wesley.

I caught up where he stood next to the back porch, swaying slightly in the wind. He glanced back at me, looking nervous.

"Don't," he warned under his breath.

"I get it, I suck at being a friend. I—"

He held a finger up to his lips, and voices drifted out from inside the house.

"You aren't pushing her hard enough." Trev Baker's voice was sharp.

"We shouldn't be eavesdropping," Wesley warned, but I stepped around him and sat down on the edge of the porch.

"Then they shouldn't be talking about me," I hissed. "Besides, you're eavesdropping, too."

"This could all hinge on her," Baker warned Fleming inside. "If she never remembers—"

"And if she does?" Fleming cut him off. "She'll run off and try to fix everything on her own! My job isn't to push her, it's to *protect* her."

I leaned my head between my knees and scratched at my ears, trying to drown out Fleming's words. I caught Wesley's eyes and tried to appear more nonchalant.

"Running off doesn't sound like me." I shrugged.

He let out a dry, quiet snort.

"No, it does. Trust me."

"She's not the one who needs protecting, Alex." Mr. Baker's voice carried a dark foreboding.

"I don't want to hear it," Fleming snapped. "I don't care."

"You're too close to the girl. I've been dreaming."

"I know."

"About *you*."

"I *know*."

Wesley's eyes were bright green against a pallid face.

"We really shouldn't be listening," he whispered, but neither of us moved.

"They're just dreams, Trev," Fleming said coolly. "They've been wrong before."

"Rarely."

"When Paul knew he was going to die, he took matters into his own hands and made everything worse for everyone." In my three months at the house, I'd learned not to mention Fleming's dead ex-hero brother. If Fleming was talking about him now, he was serious.

"Paragon was going to die no matter what. You can still avoid it. That's the difference."

The bitter taste of iron wafted over my tongue, and I realized I was biting my cheek.

"No." Fleming's voice turned dark. "The difference is I'm not afraid of death. I won't abandon that girl. I'm all she has."

My fingernails scraped against the wood slats of the porch as I curled my hands into fists, painfully aware of Wesley's eyes trained on me as he listened to the men inside.

"It's every night, you know." Trev heaved a tremendous sigh.

"That's good news for the others if my death is the only one appearing to you. I've made my decision. I'm staying with her."

"Fine. Watch over Samantha. But I can't promise the others won't retaliate after it finally happens. No matter how hard you try to protect her, she won't be safe after she murders you."

10

First Birthday in 1000 Years

I was going to murder Fleming. I tried to swallow the bile in my throat, but the force of my beating heart seemed to keep it in place.

Wesley's face, feet from mine, was pale and scared and somehow miles away, gawking at me from the end of a dark tunnel that closed in overhead.

"I—" I wanted to look for an escape. I wanted to run. I wanted to disappear into the dirt. "I need to go."

My feet moved automatically, propelled forward by the screaming static in my head.

I was a murderer. Maybe not yet, but I would be. Mr. Baker had said it himself. His dreams were rarely wrong.

I was going to kill Fleming. After everything he'd done for me.

Adrestus late-night kitchen warning tugged at the back of my head. Who were the good guys? Who were the bad guys? If I killed Fleming, I was the bad guy. Unless *he* was the bad guy? But Adrestus had killed Esther, whoever Esther was. Didn't that make *him* the bad guy?

"Sammy, wait!"

"Don't call me Sammy."

The cove. I realized that's where I was headed. Back to the waterside, and the sandy beach that made me sad for something I couldn't remember.

Each step down the clay-carved stairway was mechanical, and I kept my eyes trained on the blue of the ocean, wondering what would happen if I simply didn't stop walking.

My feet met sand.

I was going to kill Fleming.

"Samantha!"

Wesley skirted in front of me, throwing his arm out to block me from going any further.

"Leave me alone."

"Just because Trev Baker says—"

"You heard him. His nightmares almost always come true. If I walk into the ocean, this one won't."

He dropped his arm to massage his temples.

"You can't walk into the ocean."

"It's not like I'll drown. You heard Everly. I'm still immortal. Which, apparently, is more than Fleming can say because I'm going to—"

Wesley grimaced and held a finger to his lips as my voice rose.

"No one can hear us down here," I snapped, but lowered my voice all the same. Amanda was still swimming in the water beyond the cove. If she found out what I just had—

I didn't want to think about it.

"Listen, I know Mr. Baker," Wesley insisted. He reached out as if to put his hand on my shoulder, but drew it back and tugged on the collar of his hoodie. "He's never been a fan of you. Don't ask me why because I don't know. But there's a chance he's blowing things out of proportion because he's never liked having you around."

"You're doing a terrible job of making me feel better." I sidestepped Wesley but opted to sit down in the sand instead of walking aimlessly into the ocean.

Wesley kicked up sand as he sat down a respectable distance away.

"Just returning the favor," he said dryly. He put his hand on the sand between us, and I glared at it. "Don't worry about Fleming. As soon as you get your memories back, the future Trev Baker saw will shift, and you'll both be safe."

I narrowed my eyes at his knuckles, still unwilling to look him in the face.

"What difference will getting my memories back make?" I wanted to hope that the future Baker had seen could be avoided, but if it hinged on my abilities to regain my lost memories, those hopes weren't high.

"The Samantha I knew wouldn't kill Fleming."

My fingers contracted, and grains of sand slipped through my knuckles as I made twin fists.

"But I would?" I looked up from his hand into his eyes, unable to hold my anger in.

"No! I didn't mean—it's just—" He struggled to backtrack, tripping over his words, and I got back to my feet. He hastened to do the same.

"You don't trust me?" I snarled. "You really think I'd murder Fleming?"

"Never, but—"

"That's not what you just said." I stepped towards him, and he stepped back. I knew what physique and strength he was hiding beneath his hoodie, but he was more afraid of me than I was of him. "You said the *old* Samantha wouldn't kill Fleming, but I'm not the old Samantha."

"No, I just meant that it would be a big enough shift to change the future." His eyes were still red from crying over his family, but my pity for him was long gone.

"And did you consider that maybe I *am* going to remember, and *that's* what leads to me murdering him?" If Adrestus was right, and Fleming and the others *were* responsible for my lost memories, maybe that was the exact future they'd been trying to avoid when they'd done away with them. The exercises with Avery were just a farce, meant to keep me complacent.

I refused to be complacent.

"No offense, but I think I would know the old Sammy better than you," Wesley said.

"And I know myself better than *you* do." I pointed up towards the house. "I'm done talking to you. Leave."

His face broke.

"But—"

"You said it yourself. They'll need you at the camp." I crossed my arms and sat back in the sand. "So go."

He brushed his hair back and sighed.

"Right. Bye, Samantha."

"And Wesley?" I called. He paused on the bottom steps, frowning. "Don't tell the others what we heard. Please."

He nodded, and I didn't understand the sadness that welled in my chest as I watched him leave.

It was best the others didn't know that I'd overheard Baker and Fleming. If they knew that I knew what was coming, they might decide to be rid of me after all, and while I didn't trust them any more than they trusted me, where else did I have to go?

I would be safe for now, I thought as I watched Wesley disappear over the lip of the bluff. All that mattered was that he kept his mouth shut while I figured things out.

Fleming was better than me at pretending everything was okay. If I hadn't overheard his conversation with Baker about his impending murder, I wouldn't have suspected anything was off. Nothing out of the usual, anyway.

Meanwhile, I did what I could to avoid both him and Amanda over the next few days, unable to look at them without feeling overwhelmed with guilt and panic. I caught Joni staring at me, perplexed, on several occasions and usually took that as my cue to take a walk up to the bluff or down to the cove, even though I wasn't very fond of either location.

It's possible Fleming and Amanda thought I was shaken by the news of the missing families and the dead woman across the water, and I spent the weekend letting them think that to be the case. I stayed out of their way, and they stayed out of mine.

At least, until the smell of burning waffles woke me up early Tuesday morning.

I rolled over in bed, glaring at the morning light that broke through the window curtains and wrinkling my nose at the acrid smell.

"Doesn't smell good, but they've been trying very hard." Joni raised her eyebrows at me from her cot. Her silk sleep bonnet was still fastened over her hair, and her nose was shoved in a book. "They're nervous. Maybe they think you won't like breakfast, but they've been up a while with very loud emotions."

I groaned and pushed myself out of bed.

"I'll go put them out of their misery, then."

"Please do."

I shuffled down the stairs to the sound of a hissing whipped cream canister.

"I'm not letting you feed that to my daughter!" Alison's voice wafted up the staircase. "Let me call Jacobi. He's better at this than both of us. I knew I should've brought him with me."

"It's fine. I'll eat the burnt one," Fleming's voice assured her.

"They're all burnt."

"No, we scraped most of the black off this one! You can't even tell with all the whipped cream on there."

I tiptoed around the corner, still rubbing the sleep from my eyes. Alison and Fleming had their backs to me, all of their focus dedicated to the plates of waffles in front of them.

"Smells great down here," I lied. Alison's long, blonde braid smacked Fleming in the face as they spun to face me.

"You're awake!" Alison beamed, and Fleming held a plate of heavily whipped-creamed waffles aloft.

"Happy birthday!" His apron was splattered with waffle batter, and his fingers were red with strawberry juice. "Take a seat! First birthday in a thousand years!"

They may have been crunchy, but the waffles weren't totally irredeemable. The guilt in my navel tasted worse than the burnt edges, but as soon as I tried to sort out my feelings in my head, they got wrapped up around each other, and I settled with focusing on the fresh strawberries to distract me.

"We should've put birthday candles in them." Fleming frowned at my half-eaten waffle, but Alison shook her head.

"We'll sing at dinner. Penny is making the cake so there's a much lower chance of burning it."

I perked up at the news that Brooke's aunt was in charge of the cake. She made all the pastries in the cafe, and there was a reason they were an island favorite.

"You'll be there?" I asked, and Alison nodded.

"Oh, yes. I was planning on it anyway, but now I'm on driving duty. A certain nurse announced that anyone who'd been friends with you was free to come and turns out, you were more popular than you might think."

"Or they're lying to get away from Mr. Hendricks," I pointed out, and Fleming choked on his waffle. "How'd you get him to agree to this anyway?"

"That would be Everly again." Fleming forced his burnt waffle down but smiled. "He went with a 'ask for forgiveness instead of permission' sort of strategy."

The chair beside me scraped against wood, and Joni fell into the seat.

"Nice." She grinned, loading a bowl with whipped cream and berries. Fleming pushed a plate of blackened waffles her way, and she wrinkled her nose at them.

"You have to have more than cream and berries for breakfast."

"Right, because charcoal is famous for being part of a balanced breakfast," Joni mumbled, grabbing a waffle.

I poked at the remains of my breakfast. The guilt was back. Alison and Everly both had to know about Mr. Baker's dream, yet they were still trying to give me a good birthday.

I didn't understand.

"What is it?" Fleming pushed his glasses up to keep them from fogging up in the steam of his coffee, and he peered at me with concern.

"It's nothing."

"That's a lie," Joni snorted. "She feels guilty and sad and a little bit scared."

"Joni!" Alison snapped. "You can't just announce people's feelings out loud."

"Why not? If I have to feel them, why can't I say them?"

Alison gave me an apologetic glance.

"Okay, you and I are going to go have a chat about using our powers responsibly. Come on. Bring your bowl of whipped-cream. We're taking a walk."

Joni added another handful of strawberries to her bowl and followed Alison out onto the back porch.

Fleming leaned back in his chair and sipped on his coffee.

"Sorry about her," he said. "It's hard to adjust to powers when they manifest, and she hasn't had a lot of guidance. I probably should've been trying to help her more these last few—"

"It's fine." I gulped and looked askance. My cheeks were burning after Joni had laid out all my feelings for everyone to gawk at. "She's just a kid. Thanks for the waffles."

I tried to escape to the kitchen with my dirty plate, but Fleming was quick to follow.

"I know it was rude for Joni to broadcast how you're doing, but now that she has, are you okay?"

Why was he being so nice? I turned to look up at him, and his eyes wrinkled with worry.

"I'm..." I didn't want to admit that every time I looked at him, all I saw were the many ways in which I might murder him. "What if no one has fun tonight?"

Something like relief passed over his face, and his shoulders relaxed.

"We are all going to have a blast. You don't have to worry about that. I've taken care of everything." He set his plate down on the counter, most of his waffle still intact. "Even if you don't remember most of it, you've been through so much. You deserve a celebratory night surrounded by friends.”

I wanted him to stop. It was only making me feel worse. I fixed a smile on my face and nodded.

“Right. It’ll be fun. And if not, at least there will be sushi.”

“Yes, the key to any good night. Raw fish.” He took my dirty dish and flashed a reassured smile. “It’ll be fun for us all. Just wait.”

By the time we drove into Quarry Bay that evening, the lavender market had boarded up shop for the day. Most of the tourists had vacated the town for their vacation rentals, leaving the streets sleepy and peaceful despite the evening sun that continued to beat down onto the oceanside town.

The shimmering water out past the tiny port was broken up by forested islands that seemed to float on the ocean’s surface, and I felt a thrill when I saw the tall, black dorsal fins of an orca pod cut through the water, rising and dipping about a hundred yards out. If it wasn’t so lonely, I might’ve been happy hiding here forever.

Amanda waved from the sidewalk as she made her way from the lavender market, wheeling an espresso machine on a cart in front of her. She looked tired after a day of brewing lavender lattes for the island’s tourists but managed a smile when she saw us coming from the car.

“Late to your own party?” she teased as Fleming led Joni and me to the front of the cafe. I looked at the darkened windows behind her, dubious that anyone could be inside.

“Yeah, sounds like an absolute rager in there.”

Fleming adjusted his tie with a sly grin on his face. He’d chosen his most festive neckwear for the occasion, donning a pattern of pink flamingos in various hats against a blue background.

“I guess we’ll just have to enter and see,” Fleming said.

I pushed through into the shop, doing my best to keep expectations low, but the lights burst overhead, and a cheer of “Happy Birthday!” went up.

I blinked in the sudden light, trying to make sense of the cacophony that greeted me. I'd never seen the cafe so full of people. Everly and Alison stood near the back, beaming at their hard work. Avery stood close to his mother and the only one there without a smile. The tables were full of students, and someone barreled into my side before I could make out any more recognizable faces in the crowd.

"Do you know how furious I was when I regained consciousness last week to find out you'd been at the camp and I'd missed you?" The girl pulled away, and I recognized Heather, who'd been exhausted to the point of collapse when I'd seen her at the camp.

"You're okay!" I beamed, relieved despite not really knowing her.

"Sammy!" Behind Heather, I recognized Anthony and Andersen standing with a girl with the blonde ringlets. The girl blushed when I made eye contact.

"You probably don't remember me." She stuck a hand out. "I'm Remi."

I grinned and took her hand.

"We were friends, then?" I asked, and her blush turned a deeper shade of red.

"Not really, but I like to think destroying the city together might've brought us closer together."

I froze, unsure of what her words meant, but before I could dwell on them for too long, new hands pulled me away.

"We owe you for this." The girl who'd been afflicted by a twisted ankle when I'd seen her in the sickbay wrapped me in a hug. "It's Desirae. And this is my twin, Mike."

They had matching, short-cropped curly hair that made them look very much alike despite not being identical.

"We weren't friends with you, we just heard there would be sushi," Mike joked, and Desirae elbowed him, flinching and holding a hand to her own side as she did.

Sergio waved from a table behind them where he sat with two other boys. One was a dark-skinned boy with bleached, buzzed hair, and the other was sturdily built with freckles that splashed across his nose.

"Nice tie, Mr. F!" the boy with the buzzcut called. He pointed as his own neck as he spoke. "It's got Fleming-o's. Get it? Like flamingo?"

"Yes, very funny, Justin." Fleming adjusted his tie again.

"No Naomi?" I looked up at Fleming, and he fixed a strained smile to his face.

"It's too soon to try putting her and Joni in the same room," he explained, and behind him, Joni pretended to be overly interested in the work of the sushi chef behind the counter.

I glanced around the room again, trying to take in all the faces. Naomi's absence wasn't the only one I noticed. I'd hoped Quinn had enjoyed our time together at the lavender market enough to come, but I couldn't blame him. The way Wesley had treated him, I'd probably steer clear, too.

And then, there in the corner sitting with Everly, I saw Wesley, looking around the cafe meekly, as if embarrassed to be there, and my temper flared.

I thought I had made it clear, especially after our last conversation on the beach, we were *not* friends.

"What are you doing here?" I pushed through the crowd to get in his face, and he shrank back against the window.

"Fleming said to bring all your old friends," Everly answered for Wesley, who gulped. His eyes flickered behind his glasses to my dog whistle necklace, and I shoved it back under the collar of my shirt.

"We aren't friends," I asserted. Not only was Wesley annoying, but seeing him now, my fears over Mr. Baker's warning to Fleming came flooding back.

"Sammy." Everly's voice was low and gentle while somehow remaining reprimanding. "Wesley is here to celebrate you. That's all that matters."

Alison nodded next to him, and I looked back to Wesley, afraid and wondering if he had told anyone what we'd overheard.

"Happy birthday," he mumbled. Maybe it was best I didn't agitate him. I couldn't trust him anymore than he trusted me, and I didn't know if snapping might make him tell the others what we'd heard together.

"Whatever. Thanks." I shrugged, and Brooke appeared at my side to press a plate of sushi rolls into my hands.

"Find a seat!" she sang, on her way to deliver more sushi. "There's more on the way."

I let Heather pull me into a seat next to her at a table with Remi, Andersen, and Anthony. I watched Remi curiously, wondering again what she might've meant about us destroying the city together. It had to be some kind of inside joke. I knew I wasn't capable of much, let alone wrecking New Delos, and she looked harmless with her pink cheeks and blonde curls.

"You'll bring some sushi back to the camp for Naomi, right?" I asked Andersen. He froze with a mouth full of rice and shrugged, but Anthony answered for him.

"Of course we will! She was sad she couldn't make it, but you get it." He pushed his dark brown hair back from his face and smiled. "It's so weird eating dinner with you again, you have no idea."

"I really don't," I laughed and turned to Heather. "And you, you made the Shadow Veil that surrounds the camp? Is that your Apex power?"

She grinned mischievously, and the light leeched from the room.

"Heather, stop!" Desirea called out in the dark, and the light returned. I glanced nervously at the sushi chef behind the counter.

"Is it safe to show off your powers here?" I asked.

"Don't worry about the chef." Heather shrugged. "He's an Apex, too. His kid is on the University team."

I sat back and looked around the room.

"So everyone in here is an Apex?"

"Everyone but you, Fleming, Brooke, and Miss Penny," Remi explained.

My eyes landed on Wesley where he sat with the adults, hunched over his plate.

"And what's Wesley's deal?" I asked. Anthony and Heather fidgeted in their seats.

"What about him?" Andersen grunted.

The other kids in the cafe all ate and laughed together, but Wesley kept his head down, and I wondered if it was my fault.

"He's sort of rude, isn't he?" I prodded. "And a little intense?"

"Wesley's been through it," Heather said carefully.

"We all have," Remi snapped. She pulled back her sleeve to show off an arm marred by ugly burn scars. "Or did I imagine the part where I burnt off half the nerves in my arm? And Wesley *is* rude."

"At least you still *have* both arms," Anthony said. "Don't listen to Remi, she's his ex."

"Don't listen to Anthony, he's a suck-up trying to make us all forget he sold us out last winter," Remi shot back, blushing furiously.

Andersen rubbed a knuckle against his temple.

"Don't listen to either of them," he growled. "Samantha, as glad as I am to hear you finally admit that Wesley is the worst, because he is, Heather is right. He's been through it. He died, lost an arm, his family's been kidnapped, and his best friend hates his guts."

"He died?" I blanched.

"So have you." Andersen raised an eyebrow.

"Right, but Wesley's not immortal. How did he die and come back?"

The others avoided eye contact with each other, and Remi turned an even darker shade of red.

"The details are fuzzy," she mumbled.

"Another fun fact about Wesley," Heather whispered, "is he can probably hear this entire conversation."

I looked towards Wesley in horror, and he turned and locked eyes with me, confirming what Heather had suspected.

For a moment, guilt and panic paralyzed me, but the sound of the bell above the door ringing snapped my attention away from Wesley. A boy stood in the doorway, holding a brightly colored gift bag and smiling assuredly despite every face turning to face him.

"Samantha, happy birthday!" he called, shaking black curls away from his bright, blue eyes. Quinn had remembered my invitation.

11
Advance Guard

If Quinn noticed the hostile stares from the other partygoers, he pretended not to as he circled the room to make his way to my table. He reached my table just as Fleming did, who put a protective hand on my shoulder that kept me in my seat.

"Who's your new friend, Samantha?" he asked through gritted teeth.

"Quinn." Quinn held his hand out to Fleming. "We met last week, and she invited me. You must be Samantha's dad."

"Of sorts." Fleming kept his hands on my shoulders, rejecting Quinn's handshake. "You didn't tell me you made a new friend, Sammy."

His fingers tightened on my shoulders, but I shook him off and stood to take the gift bag Quinn had brought.

"You didn't need to get me anything," I insisted, acutely aware that the entire cafe had gone silent.

"Rich snob, remember? It was nothing." Quinn flashed a crooked smile. "You'll want to get that in the freezer pretty quick, though."

I peered inside the bag at the gallon of lavender ice cream.

"Great, there's a freezer in the back room," Fleming said, his hand back on my shoulder. "Let me help you with that."

He steered me towards the counter, and I tried to give Quinn an apologetic smile before disappearing into the back. I kept my back towards Fleming as I crossed the cramped back room to the freezer and took my time nestling the gallon container there.

"What the hell, Samantha?" When I turned back to Fleming, he had his hand over his face, massaging his temples as he leaned against the door.

"My birthday, my guest list," I mumbled. "Quinn's nice."

"We don't know *who* he is. Where's his family?"

"Probably at their fancy vacation home. They like fishing, I think."

Fleming dropped his hand to smack a shelf, and his cheeks inflated with barely contained anger.

"Adrestus has left New Delos. Esther is dead, and Dr. Weaver is missing. I know Quinn probably is a nice young man, and I know you're lonely but—"

"I don't know Esther or Dr. Weaver. I don't know *anything*," I shot. "I don't know the friends out there that Everly and Alison brought. They're nice, but Quinn makes me feel normal. Why is that so bad?"

"Even if you don't remember them, your friends in that cafe would do anything for you," Fleming insisted. "They'd do the same for any of their teammates."

"Teammates?"

The word hung between us, and the idea of it seemed to expand, pushing me farther from Fleming, farther into my forced isolation.

Fleming's throat bobbed, and his anger dissipated into stricken guilt.

"I mean they care about you as much as they care about each other."

"That's not what you meant," I accused and took a shaking step forward as the pieces fell together. "Why do they all care so much to be here? How do they all know me?"

"Sammy, look—"

"I was on the team, wasn't I?"

Fleming's face was the only confirmation I needed, and discovery and betrayal gnashed inside me.

"When Roy took over, he kicked you off," Fleming finally said. "He has a hard and fast No Non-Apex rule that he lives by."

I breathed heavily through my nose, trying to reassess the last three months through the lens of this discovery.

"I was on the team," I repeated dumbly. "I didn't just have friends, I had teammates."

"It didn't end well."

"That's a terrible reason not to tell me."

"You're right." He shrugged. "I didn't tell you because I didn't want you feeling even more lonely than you already were. I thought I was protecting you, and I wasn't. I'm sorry."

His apology caught me off guard, and I wondered if he offered it solely to try to weasel one out of me.

"Great. Not accepted. Can I go back to my party now?"

"No, you can't, we—"

"First birthday in a millennium, right? That's what you had called it." I cocked my head at him, and he sighed.

"Right." He stepped aside. "If Quinn makes one wrong move, it's over. And tomorrow isn't your birthday anymore, so we'll be revisiting this."

"Great."

I shouldered past him and fixed the most carefully crafted smile to my face. I would have a good night just to spite him.

Quinn had taken up a spot at my table, and Wesley had followed suit.

"Why are you—" I started but was interrupted as Miss Penny came out carrying the cake with lit candles and leading everyone in a birthday song as she paraded the dessert to my table.

I smiled awkwardly as the room sang to me and leaned over to blow out my candles. An odd thrill passed through me as I realized this was the first time I'd ever blown out candles on a birthday cake.

Miss Penny took the cake away for cutting, and Heather turned towards Quinn.

"So, rich snob, huh? How rich are we talking?"

Quinn gave a coy smile and shrugged.

"I don't know my parents' exact worth, but we have three vacation homes."

Wesley scoffed.

"Is it old money?" he asked. Quinn scratched his head, thinking.

"How old does money have to be considered old money?"

"I don't know, couple thousand years maybe."

Quinn smiled politely, still confused, and Anthony laughed.

"He's not *that* old, Wes. Plus, he has both eyes."

Remi groaned and slid her hand over her face in embarrassment.

"Both of you stop. You're being weird."

Brooke came by with plates of cake and gave me an uncertain smile. The table fell silent as we all stared at our cake pieces.

"I wish Naomi could be here," Wesley said, interrupting the silence. "She usually has a pretty good read on strangers."

Quinn shrugged and took a large bite of cake.

"I'm not sure I'm the stranger at this table."

Wesley bristled, and his fingers dug into the table top.

"And what's that supposed to mean?"

"I get the feeling you aren't very close to anyone here."

"They're my friends!"

"Yet none of them will make eye contact with you."

"Stop it," I warned. Quinn blushed and went back to eating his cake. "It's my birthday. If I say you have to tolerate each other, you have to tolerate each other."

"You're right," Quinn said. "Sorry, Sammy."

"Her name is Samantha," Wesley snorted but avoided the glare I sent his way.

"Sure." Quinn flashed a smile in my direction that felt like it was meant for just me somehow, like an inside joke I didn't quite understand but appreciated all the same. "Thought any more about halibut fishing?"

Wesley's face turned bright red, and I took too much joy in answering Quinn.

"Fishing sounds amazing. When are you going out on the water next?"

"Sometime in the next couple days if the weather stays nice. We could pick you up. You said you live near—"

The phone behind the counter rang out, and the silence that fell over the room must've disrupted Quinn's train of thought because he fell silent, too. Brooke hurried to answer the phone.

"Alison, it's Roy." Brooke held the phone out, and Alison frowned in concern as she hurried behind the counter.

"You did get permission to come here, right?" Fleming asked Everly, who nodded. Alison kept her face composed as she nodded along to whatever Mr. Hendricks was saying on the other line, but it was impossible to miss the color draining from her face.

The cafe stayed silent as she waved Fleming and Everly over to whisper to them.

"What's happening?" Quinn asked, and I shrugged.

"Thank you everyone so much for being here to celebrate Sammy," Fleming announced to the cafe. "Take some cake for the road if you like. I hope we get to see you soon."

And just like that, my first birthday in a millennia was over. I didn't have the heart to watch my supposed friends file out of the cafe and kept my eyes on the warped wooden floorboards, trying to stave off the same loneliness that had plagued me after my initial visit to the camp.

It was worse this time. These had been my teammates. I had been one of them. The only reason I wasn't was because I had no powers.

Wesley lingered at the back of the group, and while I hoped he'd leave without saying anything, I knew that was too much to ask.

"Please don't go fishing with him," he begged, quietly enough so that the adults didn't overhear.

"As if Fleming would ever let me."

"I'm—" He screwed up his face. "Happy birthday, Samantha. I'll tell Naomi you said hello."

I watched him follow the others into the darkened streets, wondering what Roy Hendricks could've said to make them all leave so suddenly.

"I should head out too, then, right?"

I jumped at Quinn's voice and made sure Fleming was still across the cafe with his head bent towards Amanda, Brooke, and Miss Penny as he filled them in on whatever had been passed over the phone.

"Right." I nodded, and Quinn smiled apologetically.

"I'm here if you ever need anything." He stepped out into the night. "I know you don't have a phone, but the island is small and I'm around. You hang out with an odd sort of people, but if you need *anything*..."

"Thanks, Quinn."

"I'm serious." He winked. "I'm here for you."

Fleming appeared at my back with Joni in tow.

"Car. Now." His curt tone carried something I couldn't place. Agitation? Excitement?

Joni and I had to jog to keep up with his long strides to the car, and he pulled away from the cafe before we'd had the chance to buckle our seatbelts. I knew his stony, tight-lipped frown well enough to know not to be the first to break his reverie.

"Are we being followed?" We were halfway home when he finally spoke, peering into the rearview mirror.

"There's a car, but it's far away," Joni said from the back. Fleming grunted, then took another moment to himself before speaking again.

"Roy says we've received word from Dr. Weaver. She's alive."

"Oh." The knot in my chest loosened. I'd been expecting bad news. but if the missing woman who supplied us with health serum was okay, that didn't seem so terrible. "That's good, right?"

"Very good. She couldn't say much over the phone, but she's set a rendezvous. Alison and Trev are going to go meet her to find out what happened and possibly relocate her back to the camp."

"Then why do you seem nervous?"

"It's tricky." Fleming frowned, still watching the headlights in the rearview. "It could be a trap. Adrestus might be watching her. Anything could go wrong."

He pulled down our dirt drive and turned off the car lights, waiting for the car that had been behind us to pass. When it did, Fleming turned the car back on and sighed in relief.

"Whatever happens next, we need to be very, very careful," he warned.

However, his warning felt hollow after three months of waiting around. Having been assured that nothing was immediately wrong, I was much more worried about having forgotten my lavender ice cream back at the cafe.

With the Dr. Weaver revelation taking precedence over everything else, I went another day without sword training with Sergio and Everly. I was starting to miss our sessions seeing as there was little else to do at the farmhouse. Miss Penny had Amanda working in a booth at the Lavender Market all day, and Joni was obsessing over a puzzle on the coffee table.

By the time evening rolled around, I'd resorted to scratching idly at a water ring on the dining table and thinking about the gallon of lavender ice cream waiting for me in the cafe freezer. Maybe if I could convince Fleming that Quinn was a normal, trustworthy kid, he'd let him come over. Even if Quinn was, against all odds, secretly an evil despot, at least that'd be more interesting than puzzles.

Brooke was over, waiting for Amanda to get off work, and had just finished setting out extra blankets on the couch for Avery's stay when car doors slammed outside. Fleming poked his head out of the kitchen as Mr. Baker, Alison, and Avery came through the front door. His face fell when he saw the bouquet of flowers in Alison's arms.

"Already?" he asked. Avery looked down, and Alison smiled sadly.

"Not quite, but I imagine I might miss it if we're away too long."

"What?" I looked between the adults, and Alison pressed her lips together.

"It's been six months since Vic died." She rubbed a flower petal between two fingers. "Avery picked these out from a roadside stand on the way over."

Avery blushed and hunched his shoulders towards his ears.

Discomfort weighed heavy in my stomach. What if they expected me to feel a certain way? I didn't remember Vic, or Vidar, or whatever his name had been. If I wasn't sad enough, would they be offended?

"Right." Fleming nodded importantly and slipped into his shoes by the door. "We can go set those out before we leave. Samantha?"

My cheeks burned when they turned to look at me, and I wanted to disappear.

"We'll visit the statue with Amanda later," Brooke said, coming to my aid. "You're picking her up in town when you drop Alison and Mr. Baker off at the ferry, right?"

Fleming nodded again, and I stood rigid as he led Alison and Avery back onto the porch. I tried to quell the flurry of guilt that swirled in my head.

"Thanks," I mumbled to Brooke, and she smiled kindly.

"What for? Amanda would hate to be left out. Would you like a top off, Mr. Baker?" She took Mr. Baker's travel mug from him, and I followed her into the kitchen to avoid being left alone with Mr. Baker before he could accuse me of committing murders I hadn't done yet.

Besides, I wouldn't be able to see the statue from the kitchen windows and didn't want to watch Alison and Avery laying their flowers down at my dead brother's stone feet.

Vidar had supposedly been important to me once, too, and as much as I didn't want to share in the pain of the others, a strange jealousy creeped inside of me. I wanted to remember the man that the others felt so much reverence for. Even if it had all been a clever act, I wanted to remember what it felt like to have a dad.

When they returned, Avery's eyes were rimmed red, and he ducked away from his mother when she tried to hug him goodbye.

"I'll try not to be gone long," she called after him. "Once we've checked in with Dr. Weaver and received supplies, we'll be headed back."

"Brooke is in charge for the next thirty minutes," Fleming said, loading Alison and Trev's bag into the trunk of the car. "I'll be back with Amanda pretty quick, and I have my cell—"

"We'll be fine," Brooke assured him.

"Watch after your brother, Sammy," Alison called, ducking into the passenger seat.

"It's the last ferry of the day, so if we could get a move on, that'd be great." Mr. Baker rapped his knuckles on the roof of the car.

"Couple days, tops," Alison repeated and closed her door.

"Thirty minutes," Fleming warned from the driver's side. "There's leftover lasagna in the fridge. Heat some up for dinner."

He closed the car door, and Brooke snorted.

"Isn't that lasagna from last week?"

"Unfortunately, no," I sighed, watching the brake lights disappear down the wooded drive. "It's one of the few things Fleming makes."

"Then lasagna it is."

Avery was already halfway up the stairs when we walked back in.

"No Knut this time?" I asked, wondering why he hadn't brought his hamster.

"Everly's watching him." He stomped the rest of the way up to the second floor. He'd never struck me as a happy kid, but the last week, his attitude had progressively soured.

Brooke and I ate our lasagna in the living room, helping Joni with the puzzle, but when Brooke left to take our dirty dishes to the kitchen, Joni sat up and gnawed on the inside of her cheek.

"Mrs. Havardson said it's impolite to announce other people's feelings." Joni frowned at her puzzle.

"It is." I mentally braced for whatever one of my innermost feelings she was about to bring up.

"But what if someone is feeling a lot?"

"Is everyone okay?" I squinted at her. She looked around nervously, but Brooke had her back to us in the kitchen.

"I think someone might need help," she whispered, "but I don't know who."

"Avery?" I glanced at the stairs. "He does seem off."

"No. They're not inside."

I looked to the dining window, half-expecting to see someone on the back porch, but all I saw was the sun-dyed orange of the ocean.

"Do they feel dangerous?"

"They feel sad, I think. But it's confusing. Like angry but not."

I gave Brooke one last glance. Joni's powers were new, and I wasn't convinced it wasn't Avery she was sensing. I didn't want to worry Brooke, and what were the odds someone infiltrated the property the moment Fleming left us unprotected?

I tiptoed out to the front porch to peer in the lengthening shadows of the property. Joni came up behind me to point up the hill, and I followed her gaze up to the lone figure standing before the Viking statue. Long skirts billowed in the wind, but otherwise, the mystery woman was as still as the statue she stared at.

"I think it's her," Joni mused. "Do you think Mr. Hendricks sent her?"

"Probably. Go back inside. I'll check."

"What if she's dangerous?"

"You said she needs help. I'll be fine."

It was possible a lost hiker might've found their way to our bluff, but even from here I could tell she wasn't equipped for a walk in the woods in her long skirt. She was more likely a camp student, sent by Mr. Hendricks to undermine and embarrass Fleming.

The sky blazed orange in the light of the dying day, and the statue cast a long shadow over the woman that spilled down the hillside. The woman looked tall, willowy, and harmless with a hood pulled up to protect herself from the wind.

However, as I ventured up the bluff, unease crept inside me. I watched the wind play with the folds of the woman's skirt, and even without Joni's powers, I could sense something about her felt off.

She must've heard me as I came up the hill, but she kept her eyes locked on the face of the stone man.

"It doesn't look much like him," she sighed when I came up beside her. "You'd think if they were going to put up a statue for a guy, they'd at least make an effort to have it resemble him."

She turned her gaze on me, and the sunset glinted off her gray eyes. I staggered backward, taken aback by her unabashed familiarity with which she surveyed me. She was too old to be one of the students, and I was quickly realizing I should've grabbed a practice sword from the umbrella stand by the door.

"You knew him?" I stuttered. I considered myself tall, but this woman was much taller.

"I wasn't there when he died, though I wish I had been." Maybe she was a college student, or one of the adults running the camps. Maybe that was wishful thinking. "It must be something incredible, to watch someone so old snuff out."

"I—" I wasn't expecting that. "I wouldn't know."

"No, you wouldn't, would you?" she sighed. "I remember the first time I saw someone die. A home invader. We did what we needed to protect ourselves. I wonder if Vidar fell as hard as that man had."

As harmless as this woman looked, with her dress and hooded-cardigan hanging off her thin frame, the hair on the back of my neck stood up, and a distantly familiar feeling rose in the pit of my stomach. I hadn't known real danger in my three months of memory, but now, the growing sensation of dreadful peril greeted me like an old friend.

"Are you lost? I-I can help you find the road." I knew she wasn't lost. She'd come to this statue deliberately. She ran her hand along the hilt of the sword that rested in the pedestal.

Hungry gray eyes raked over me, lingering on the ugly scar that crept along my neck. She pulled her hood back, and long, white tresses fell from its confines, billowing backwards in the wind.

"No, I'm not lost." The corners of her mouth twitched. "You're exactly who I was looking for."

12

Firestorm

I'd heard about the woman with white hair. They'd called her Mira. I knew she turned those she touched into puppets, and the hungry way she looked at me reminded me of a cat scheming up how best to play with its food.

"It's absolutely horrid to keep a relic like this out here in the elements. You would've thought *he'd* have taught you proper sword care." Her thumb brushed over the sword hilt as she surveyed the statue's face. "He wasn't as great as they all say. He loved to be a martyr. How stupidly selfish."

It felt too coincidental for Adrestus's right-hand woman to appear the moment Fleming had left me unprotected. She must've been watching the house.

"You knew him," I said. Fleming and Amanda would be back any minute. I just had to keep Mira busy until then. "You work for Adrestus."

Her face softened at the name and somehow the gentler features made her all the more frightening.

"It feels like so long ago that I first tried to rescue you to bring you to him," she said. "*He* would never have abandoned you. Not like this one."

She reached up and rested a hand on the statue's stone chest.

"Vidar didn't abandon me. Adrestus murdered him."

"Adrestus did what he had to in order to protect you. Vidar, meanwhile, abandoned you the day he left you at that school and drove away knowing who and what you were, knowing you could never be safe, wanting to keep his *new* family safe from *you*."

I bristled. I had no memory of the man. For all I knew, she could be telling the truth, but her words felt like sacrilege.

"No." I shook my head. "He thought the school was safe, near the team, with Fleming."

"Alexander Fleming?" she crooned, tearing her eyes away from the statue to look at me. "Then Vidar Havardsson didn't abandon you, he was just a fool, leaving you in the care of a man who eventually would."

"Not Fleming."

"Oh?" She scanned the darkening hillside. "That's funny, I don't see him."

The wind caught her hair and dress, twisting them with the breeze.

"Just because someone has to run an errand does not mean they're leaving you!"

Joni was sure to know something was wrong. She'd feel it, and maybe she and the others could escape while I distracted this woman. I'd fought Sergio plenty of times on this hill. I could fight this strange woman, too.

Granted, I'd never won a single fight against Sergio, but maybe today I'd get lucky.

"Dear Eydis, don't you see I'm here to rescue you? I'll take you to Adrestus. He would never abandon you, as he has never once abandoned me. He took me when I'd been discarded, and he's watched over me ever since. And now, he's building a reality where no one will be left behind, and everyone will have their place. Why can't you see he's not the villain here?"

"I don't need rescuing."

Mira ran her fingers over the stone hands that held the sword in its place in the pedestal.

"I have to admit, I was hoping you'd make this difficult."

Cracks ran along the stone where she touched it, and when she pulled her hand away, rock turned to dust, breaking off the statue in chunks until he was missing his arms up to his elbows. Metal whispered against stone as she drew the sword out of what was supposed to be its final resting place.

The others had not warned me she could use her powers to disintegrate stone, and I shuddered to think what it would do to skin and flesh.

A shrill and panicked shriek echoed across the property, chilling my chest and churning my stomach.

"Oh, and I brought a friend." Mira brandished the sword. "It's about time I had a turn with this thing."

I danced out of reach of the blade. Sergio had disarmed me enough times in practice, and I'd become *very* good at prolonging fights.

Mira's look of a manic joy gave way to frustration, and then fury as she continued to hack the air. She lacked Sergio's finesse and skill with a blade, but she was relentless in her attacks.

"SAMMY!" Avery's scream cut to my core like a spire of ice. I spun towards the house, searching for him in the gathering dark, and there he was in the front doorway where a hulking mass of a man dragged his flailing form back into the house.

Wind whistled over metal behind me, and I turned back almost too late, catching Mira's wrist in my hand.

"Well, see?" she purred. "You were bound to mess up eventually."

Her free hand shot out from the depths of her cardigan, and her fingers wrapped around my bare neck.

Her powers took hold immediately. My body locked up, and I strained against the muscles in my face to watch my fingers, still wrapped around her wrist, relinquish their grasp one by one against my will.

"So, little Viking, just how immortal are you?" Mira whispered, lowering her sword arm.

Unable to so much as flinch, I was forced to watch a serene grin spread across her face as hot agony splintered through my flank.

Pain umbrellaed from my left side, and the taste of metal washed over my tongue. Mira released me, and my knees buckled beneath me. The blade slid from my body as I collapsed to the grass.

I curled in on myself, clutching at the wound. Mira leaned over, and her white hair pooled on the ground inches from my face as she made a show of wiping the blade in the grass.

"Sit tight, alright? I won't be long."

I gasped for air, watching Mira's skirts swish around her ankles as she slinked down the hill towards the house. Towards Brooke and Joni and Avery.

"No." My protest was a soft rattle, inaudible over the wind. My fingers were sticky as I tried to stem the blood. If what the others had told me was true, this was far from the worst I'd suffered, but I could barely even think through the pain. I gritted my teeth, and forced myself to let go of my side and dig my fingertips into the loamy ground.

I pulled myself forward, crying out through clenched teeth. All those training sessions with Sergio…I'd never won a single match, and now here I was, bleeding out on the hillside.

Don't think, I told myself. *Just breathe. Just move.*

I crawled down the hill on all fours, spurred on by my friends' screams. A body hit the living room window and slid to the floor.

Every movement felt like being impaled all over again, and the wound burned as sharply in my back as it did in my abdomen. Mira had ran me all the way through. Immortal or not, I knew I was in no condition to save the others, but I couldn't *not* try.

The hillside evened out as I reached the base, and the gravel of the driveway bit at my hands and knees. My shadow elongated ahead of me. Rocks sprayed, and I turned to see headlights bearing down on me. I braced for impact, but the car braked hard, fishtailing onto the lawn at the last moment.

"Sammy!"

My elbows gave out at the sound of Fleming's voice, and I fell to the gravel.

"She's hurt!" Amanda flipped me over onto my back, and her hands pressed against the wound in my stomach.

"My bag! Grab it!" A canvas bag dropped next to me.

"What happened?" Amanda demanded. "The others, are they—"

"Mira," I said through a clenched jaw. "She stole the sword and..."

Brooke's shriek ripped the night in half, and Amanda abandoned me in the gravel to run into the house, the light of her fire crackling against my eyelids.

"Amanda!" Fleming bellowed, rifling through the backpack. "Don't do anything rash!"

He procured a plastic tube from the bag's depths. It was one of Everly's more clever inventions; a one-time-use shot of Serum for a pinch.

"No," I murmured. How much blood had I lost? The night was getting cold. "I can't die. Don't use it...the others...."

The needle went in just above the entry wound, and I winced.

"It won't heal you completely, but it'll do for now." Fleming helped me to the car, forcing me into the passenger seat. "Stay here!"

I tried to protest, but a spasm of pain rippled across my abdomen. The shot of Serum worked fast, itching and burning as it stitched tissue back together, though there was nothing it could do about the blood loss I'd already suffered. Dark spots danced in my vision as I slumped back in the seat, trying to focus on the open front door of the house.

Screams issued from inside the house, but Amanda and Fleming were here. They'd be okay. They had to be okay.

The front window exploded in an array of glass and flame. Mira landed in the front yard, and despite the force of Amanda's attack, she jumped back on her feet in a swirl of skirts and hair. Amanda leaped from the broken window, the ends of the hair she'd been working so hard to grow back out smoldering.

"If you can walk, go help the others!" she yelled without taking her eyes off Mira. "If Hackjob so much as touches Brooke, I'll kill you!"

A column of flame rushed towards the sedan where I sat, and I stumbled from the front seat before I could be caught in the collateral damage. My side still ached, but Avery was inside.

I ran past Amanda and staggered into the house.

The massive man named Hackjob took up most of the living room. His bulging muscles strained against his coat as he fought Fleming, his scraggly hair nearly brushing against the ceiling of the old farmhouse.

Brooke bent over a crumpled body by the dining table, and my heart jumped into my throat when I recognized Avery's hoodie. I skirted around the fighting men, and Fleming howled at me as he ducked out of the massive man's reach.

"I told you to stay put!"

I collapsed next to Brooke and Avery, my injuries forgotten and my stomach churning at the sight of Avery's blank stare.

"What's wrong with him?"

"Look for a white patch." Brooke pulled at Avery's sleeves to check his skin. "Mira uses them to paralyze her opponents, and Avery is the most dangerous person here. There! I knew it!"

She gently lifted his head to reveal a white sticker behind his shaggy blond hair at the base of his neck. Brooke peeled it away, taking care not to touch the sticky side. Avery's arms twitched, and he gasped, trying to push himself up on his hands and knees.

A mighty crash sounded behind us, and I turned to see Hackjob throw Fleming into the far wall of the living room. Fleming slid down the wall and collapsed on the floor. The hulking man turned towards us, and Brooke pushed herself in front of Avery and me with her arms outstretched to protect us.

"Let's not make this messier than it needs to be." Hackjob's shockingly white teeth seemed to glow as he grinned in the falling dusk. He ripped the TV from its wall mount and brandished it like a weapon.

"You're afraid." Avery's voice was hoarse from the paralytic, yet it seemed to reverberate through the room. Hackjob lowered the TV and blinked stupidly at Avery, as if enraptured. "You aren't safe here. You're *so much more scared than you've ever been before.*"

A shudder passed over Hackjob. His pupils dilated, and his chest fell and lifted as his breathing quickened. Avery smiled smugly, and for a moment, I thought he might've rendered Hackjob immobile.

But then, Hackjob lifted the TV again and shattered it against the nearest wall. Bits of glass and plastic exploded across the room, and Hackjob howled in blind panic. He waved his arms over his head, warding off some unseen attacker.

"Move!" Brooke ushered us towards the back door, but her voice caught Hackjob's attention. He squared up and charged.

Avery pushed Brooke out of the way, and his chest expanded, ready to give another order.

"STO—"

Avery's cry was cut short as Hackjob delivered a fist to his throat. Avery slammed backward over the table, gagging and clawing at his neck, scrambling to get away, and Hackjob screamed in terror as he barreled through the glass of the back door.

"Avery!" I jumped to Avery's side as he slid from the table, his throat rattling for air. His eyes bugged out of his head, and he beat on his chest with one hand. "He can't breathe!"

I looked around for help, but Fleming was still dazed on the floor, and Amanda and Mira were a whirlwind of skirts and fire in the front driveway.

"I've got him!" Brooke put a steadying hand on Avery's shoulder, propping him up in a sitting position. Avery let out a gasping rattle, and tears of pain cascaded down his face. "He's making sound, so he's breathing, but his trachea might be partially crushed."

"Avery, I'm sorry." I pulled him into an embrace, his chest rattling against mine. "Brooke, where's Joni? Is she safe?"

"Already downstairs. Take Fleming down—"

She cut off as the firelight outside extinguished, casting us into darkness.

"Amanda!" Brooke abandoned Avery to run to the front porch, and I chased after her.

"Avery, go downstairs and find Joni!" I chased after Brooke despite the spinning room and my shaking legs. She didn't stand a chance against Mira.

Fleming called out after us, but I slid my practice sword out from the umbrella stand as I ran out the door.

Mira stood triumphant over Amanda's limp body in the driveway. Fleming's sedan was engulfed in flames, and the light of the inferno pressed against Mira's darkened outline.

"NO!" Brooke leapt from the porch, and when she landed, she kept pace, spraying gravel up under her sneakers. She swung a fist, and Mira grunted as her cheek took the brunt of Brooke's knuckles. Mira staggered backwards in shock but grinned through the blood that trickled from between her lips.

"And you must be Brookie!" Delight turned Mira's voice shrill. Brooke raised her fist for another strike, and I strained against the thin, fragile tissue that had fused my abdomen back together, forcing myself to run against the searing pain.

I grabbed Brooke by the back of her shirt and drew her back before Mira could strike her, and I took the brunt of the heavy sword hilt that Mira brought arching downwards.

"Caught a second wind, did you?" The flat of the blade slapped against my side, striking my injury. Dark spots burst in my vision like ink blots against the light of the car fire, but I tried to raise my practice sword against Mira.

She laughed as she batted it away and sent me crashing to the gravel next to Amanda with a swift kick to my abdomen. Brooke stood over us with her hands in fists, ready to go down with a fight, but I knew she was like me.

She had no powers. She could not beat Mira anymore than I could.

"Amanda used to talk about you, you know," Mira crooned, dragging the tip of the sword in the gravel next to her. I tried to get up, but a spasm of pain kept me in the dirt. "Back when she was my perfect little puppet."

"Stop talking," Brooke warned through gritted teeth.

"The pretty little control chip in her neck, it's still there isn't it?" Mira continued. "They're near impossible to remove. I bet I could reboot it. I would so love to have my puppet back."

"You won't ever touch her *again!*" Brooke launched herself at Mira, but Mira was ready this time. She caught Brooke's fist and pulled her in close as every muscle in Brooke's body turned rigid.

Mira turned Brooke around to hold against her body, her long, pale fingers clasped against Brooke's neck and face.

"What do you think, Amanda? Would you like to go back to New Delos with me? Should we bring Brookie this time?"

I struggled to push myself up, noticing for the first time that Amanda didn't look injured. Mira must've paralyzed her the same way she'd paralyzed Avery inside. If I could find the patch and remove it, we stood a chance.

"Let her go." Fleming's voice boomed over the yard

"You're injured, Mr. Alexander." Mira clicked her tongue. "I came to collect the Havardson kids. Let me have them, and I'll let you have Brooke."

"We have help on the way."

"That's a lie. No one is coming, and you're all alone. Now, if you don't mind, on your knees, please," Mira purred. "My powers work by secreting neurotransmitters through skin to skin contact. Imagine what I could do if I learned how to develop neurotoxins instead. It might only take a couple seconds of contact to be lethal."

"You're the one who killed Esther." Fleming's fingers flexed upwards at his side, the tiniest signal to stay where I was. *Play dead*, they said. A sharp bit of gravel dug into my temple, but I obeyed, remaining limp next to Amanda.

"She was a traitor. But this cute thing could still escape tonight unscathed if you cooperate, so why aren't you on your knees yet?" Mira pointed to the ground at Fleming's feet with the sword. "It isn't pretty, what my neurotoxins do to the skin."

Fleming heaved a mighty sigh. He was in no condition to fight anyway, and in the flickering fire, I saw his eyes dart to Amanda and back to Mira as he put his hands up and struggled onto his knees. I wondered how many of his ribs were broken.

"Thing is," Mira mused, "we don't really have any need for little Brookie. I could just let her go, but then she might do something pesky like alert your friends, and I've been *dying* to retry my neurotoxin trick."

"Don't—!" Fleming cut off in a cry of pain as he strained against his injuries.

I dug my fingers into the gravel, ignoring the splitting pain in my flank, but Mira was already running the back of her hand against Brooke's cheek. She lifted her chin with a single fingertip. Brooke's eyes widened, and the skin beneath Mira's finger became mottled and discolored.

Burnt plastic stung my nose, and a white patch on Amanda's arm went up in flames.

"NO!"

A column of fire seared across the driveway, and I shielded my eyes against the blaze. When I opened them, Amanda had Brooke's convulsing body in her arms. I scrambled across the gravel to help Fleming to his feet.

"WHAT'VE YOU DONE TO HER?" Amanda shrieked. More flames broke from the ground, and heat licked at my back.

"Inside! Now!" Fleming screamed. He tried to usher me towards the porch, but Mira appeared out of the inferno, wielding the sword. Metal flashed in the fire, and I pulled Fleming out of her reach just as she swung the sword.

Fleming fell backwards with a grunt. The tip of the blade in Mira's hands was stained red with blood, and fire glinted in her gray eyes as she raised the sword again.

I raised my flimsy practice sword to hers, and the way Sergio had flicked his wrist in the rain the week before replayed in my head as I replicated the movement.

The heavy sword spun from her hands, and Mira was forced to retreat as I struck out with my weapon. Fire erupted between us at the behest of Amanda's howls of grief and desperation. Mira screamed from the other side of the fire, and her dark shadow stalked back and forth, searching for a way past the flame.

Nearby, at the center of a ring of scorched gravel, Amanda cradled Brooke in her arms. Brooke's head lolled back, and her dark hair dragged in the dirt where she lay eerily limp.

Not Brooke. The clenching in my stomach had nothing to do with the barely-healed wound. *Not Brooke.*

"Sammy! She's not dead!" Joni cried, and I spun around to see her helping a bleeding Fleming into the house. She struggled under his weight but pointed a finger at Brooke's body. "I can feel her!"

Amanda lifted her head, and her arms tightened around Brooke.

"She's not dead!" I repeated, yelling over the roar of the fire. Amanda's eyes widened, and shaking hands searched for a pulse against the ugly, purple skin of Brooke's neck.

I hurried to help Joni drag Fleming inside before he crushed her tiny middle-schooler frame.

"I'm fine," Fleming gasped, despite his bloodied shirt. "It's shallow. She barely got me."

Avery scrambled out of the way as Joni and I lowered Fleming onto the couch. The door slammed shut behind us, and Amanda collapsed in the entryway, clutching Brooke's limp body. The fire outside raged on, keeping Mira at bay, and firelight flooded the living room, pouring in through the shattered window.

"She hurt Brooke." Amanda sobbed with her back against the front door. Brooke's head tilted back in her lap, showing off the ugly purple bruise radiating out from where Mira had touched her. "We need Serum."

"Mr. Fleming needs it, too," Joni said, peering at Fleming's shirt.

Guilt nudged at my barely-healed injury. Our only Serum had been wasted on me. If we wanted to save Brooke, we'd have to get her to the camp, and with Mira now pacing blithely on the other side of the fiery barrier, odds of success were slim to none.

"Call Everly." Amanda pointed at Fleming's cell where it had fallen in the rubble of the broken TV. Avery snatched it up and punched Everly's name, and heavy, defeated silence fell over the living room when the tone on the other end indicated no phone service.

"I'll go." Fleming tried to push himself off the couch but fell back against the cushions, unable to move any further.

"Sammy," Amanda choked. "I won't leave Brooke."

My heart twisted when I realized what she was asking. The camp was clear across the island. Even if the hole in my spleen had for the most part stitched itself up, I had lost a lot of blood. I didn't want the weight of Brooke's survival resting on my shoulders.

"I don't know the way."

"He does." Amanda nodded at Avery. He gulped and tried to speak, but could only manage a weak rattle from the back of his throat. "My fire is keeping us safe, and Joni is too young to go in your place."

"Hackjob is still out there." My eyes flickered to the broken porch door. "And there might be others, maybe already at the camp. Maybe Adrestus himself is somewhere on the island."

"We have to try," Amanda begged, stroking Brooke's bruised face. "Even if it takes all night, I'll keep the fire going. I have to."

I looked to Fleming, but his face was grim. We were out of options. Avery opened his mouth to give his input, but only a pitiful rasp came out. He gingerly prodded at his throat and winced.

"I know." Fleming nodded as if he understood what Avery was trying to say. "You'll be okay. Sammy, you can walk, right?"

Cold had settled over my body, and I couldn't feel my legs as well as I would've liked, but I nodded. I could get to the camp. I would make sure of it.

Avery walked with stiff steps across the living room to the closet under the stairs and disappeared into its depths. I glanced back at Joni, scared and shivering in the corner, Amanda, tenderly brushing hair from Brooke's face, and Fleming, staring back at me with a set jaw and pallid face.

"Sammy—" He started, but I gave a half-hearted thumbs up and self-assured grin that felt like it belonged to someone else.

"No need to worry," I assured him. "I've heard that I've faced worse."

"Vic would be proud of both of you." Fleming's face was stony in the light of the fire.

My smile failed, and I held his gaze a moment longer before turning towards the closet and slipping past the coats to the secret staircase.

13
Point of No Return

I started down the passageway ahead of Avery, not looking back as I listened to the bookcase grate back into place as Joni closed the secret tunnel behind us. Avery's footsteps echoed as he hurried to catch up.

Fleming said the tunnel had been carved out and reinforced by several of Sergio's classmates, but something about an underground passageway dug by a couple of university students didn't make me very trusting of its integrity. My side ached, and I was already winded by the walk, but I didn't dare lean against the tunnel walls for support out of fear of bringing the whole thing down.

"We're going to be okay." I tried to instill as much confidence as I could into the words. Shadows pushed against the beam of my flashlight, and the dark quiet was suffocating after the chaos of the fight. Walking down the gentle downward slope of the tunnel felt like falling down the esophagus of a titan, into some new unknown oblivion, but if I stuck to the plan, if we were able to find someone who could help us, we might stand a chance. Brooke might stand a chance.

Avery responded with a raspy whimper.

"We'll get out of the tunnel and make our way towards town," I said. "If we can find someone from the team or Brooke's aunt, anyone with a car, we'll be back here in less than two hours."

The plan was flimsy at best. It might get island police involved, but I could count the number of people I cared about on two hands and still have fingers left over. Most of them were back there, depending on us, so it was a better plan than nothing.

The gentle lapping of waves echoed up the passageway, and a cool breeze stirred my hair. I grabbed Avery by the wrist and hastened us towards the silver moonlight that bounced off the wall at the end of the tunnel.

Salt air greeted us as we came to an entrance that let out into a hidden cove. Lazy waves smacked against the rock, but the tide wasn't so high that we were left without dry passage to the nearby pebbled cove.

Avery pointed upwards, his eyes wide and round, reflecting moonbeams and a soft green glow.

Green streaks painted the night sky, dancing in time to a soft, electric hum. The fingers of emerald light reached towards the water, and its reflection reached back.

"An aurora," I sighed. The lights flooded me with familiarity and longing, but their presence sent a thrill of foreboding through me. Auroras were rare here, especially this time of year. It was too much of a coincidence that they would appear tonight of all nights.

I took Avery's hand and led him around the water's edge, refusing to look at the painted sky. I stepped lightly enough to not disturb the loose, wet rocks underfoot, and they shifted and crunched softly as we went.

There was no easy path from the beach and up the steep incline into the forest. Avery tried to say something, but could only rasp through his throat injury. He pulled on my arm to try to stop me, but I forged onward.

It was easier to crawl up the incline on all fours, and I pulled on sturdy ferns and salal bushes to drag myself forwards. Avery stayed in front of me, and I cheered him on quietly from behind.

When we made it to the top of the cliff, I was slick with sweat and could feel my heartbeat beneath the fragile tissue that had fused my abdomen back together.

I leaned against a tree for support, and Avery rasped another meager attempt at speech. We'd barely made it off the property, and I already wasn't sure how much further I could go.

"S-s-s," Avery hissed. His face swam in front of mine as he tried to force words through his throat. "S-s-s-s…"

"Sammy?" I asked. "Are you trying to say 'Sammy'?"

He shook his head aggressively then fell to his knees. He dragged his hand through the dirt, and I shined the flashlight over the single word he'd written in the dust.

"'Sorry'," I read, looking at the tracts his fingers had left. "It's not your fault Avery."

His shoulders shook, and tears splashed over the R's he'd drawn in the dirt. He nodded and dragged a hand back over his work, underlining his apology.

"Come on." I tapped his shoulder. "If we don't keep moving—"
Avery flung his arms around my waist, shaking with hoarse, painful sobs.

I stared at the top of his blond head in surprise. He'd never seemed fond of me, even if I was his sort-of sister. I had no memories of him as my brother, but as he cried into my blood-stained shirt, a protective instinct washed over me.

I knelt down with him in the dirt and held him by the shoulders, forcing him to look at me.

"Whatever it is, it's okay," I assured him. "I forgive you, alright?"

But he sobbed harder so I pulled him into a hug and let him cry into my shoulder. This was not the time and definitely not the place for a meltdown, but how was I supposed to keep going with him in this state?

"I forgive you," I murmured, brushing his hair with my hand. "Whatever you did, it'll be okay. People make mistakes, but right now, Brooke needs us."

His forehead rolled against my shoulder as he nodded.

"S-s-s-s…"

"I know. You're sorry. Make it up to me by helping me save the others, okay?"

He pulled away and dragged a hand across his face. He gave me a weak smile in the light of the flashlight, but it fell from his face at the distant sound of a branch snapping underfoot.

We froze, listening to the forest sounds and the distant lapping of the ocean against the bluffs.

"Maybe it was just a deer," I breathed after we were met by several drawn out seconds of silence. "We should probably keep—"

The unmistakable sound of a body crashing through underbrush sent a new wave of adrenaline coursing through my body, and I pulled Avery to his feet.

"WHO'S THERE?!" a rough voice bellowed in the dark, far off but unmistakably Hackjob. "I'LL FIND YOU! I'LL FIGHT YOU!"

"Run!" We tore through the underbrush, letting low branches smack our faces and feeling our clothes rip when they snagged.

Pain bloomed in my left side, and the forest warped in a mosaic of shadow, moonlight, and soft, emerald green. A tree root caught my foot, and I fell into the underbrush, sprawled on all fours.

Pain ripped me apart from the inside as my wound burst open. I gagged on my own breath and screamed through gritted teeth.

Avery stopped, and in the light of the flashlight, I saw his mouth form my name.

"Keep going!" I shouted. Tears of pain clouded my vision, but I saw him shake his head and look past me in horror. Branches snapped, and underbrush shook at Hackjob barreled towards us.

I braced for a fight. Even though my side spilled blood to the forest floor, even though I'd seen the damage Hackjob had dealt Fleming, even though I know I didn't stand a chance, I could buy Avery time. He could still make it to the camp.

"Go!" I pushed the flashlight into his hands and took up the best fighting stance I could manage. Instead, Avery pushed me back and shined the light in Hackjob's eyes. He bellowed and swatted around his head, striking out at invisible foes.

Avery's last command was still affecting him.

"STOP IT!" Hackjob screamed. "I know you're there!"

He charged forward blindly, and I snatched the light from Avery, holding a finger to my lips. I flung the flashlight as far as I could into the trees, watching it spin through the forest and disappear. I held back a cry and cradled my abdomen, as if that might keep me held together in one piece.

"You won't escape me that easy!" Hackjob roared and chased after the light, still flailing his arms at the air.

We waited until he was a safe distance away and then ran, tearing through the undergrowth again, this time without the aid of the flashlight. I couldn't breathe deep enough as each lungful of air sent spikes of pain shooting across my side, and the dark of the trees seemed to get denser.

It was a temperate summer night, but the cold was growing heavier.

Fingers snapped inches from my face, and I blinked at them, dully registering the mud that pressed against my cheek. I didn't remember falling.

"S-s-aahh-m..." Avery rasped, shaking my shoulder and snapping his fingers.

"I'm good, I'm good," I wheezed. Hackjob screamed in the distance, and Avery pulled me back to my feet. "Keep going. You'll go faster without me."

He shook his head and tapped his ear. I froze to listen, and the smallest flutter of hope flickered in my chest. In the dark, intermittent cars rumbled down an unseen road.

Hackjob's frustrated roar ripped through the forest, and we jumped when a frightened deer bounded out from a nearby bush. Avery swung an arm over me, and I was grateful for his most recent growth spurt as he helped carry me through the woods. The cold that had settled over me seemed to be dissipating, replaced by a bleak nothingness.

Yellow lights flashed between trees as we got closer to the road. Avery hitched me up, adjusting his grip, and we struggled forward. We broke through the final brambles and stumbled onto the pavement of the dark, windy road.

Avery froze a moment, trying to orient himself, then nodded assuredly and pointed down the road to our left, in the direction of Quarry Bay. We staggered forward, but Avery's arms gave out, and we fell together on the edge of the roadway.

The pavement hummed, and I struggled to my feet, tugging on Avery's jacket. A car was coming, and we were sitting in the perfect spot to become roadkill. He helped me towards the ditch on the side of the road, but the car slowed, and I tensed up. The passenger door flew open.

Quinn gawked at us with a pale face, sitting at the wheel leaning across the front seat with his hand on the passenger door.

"Samantha, what—"

"Quinn!" My relief gave me the strength I needed to stumble forward. "Please! You need to help us!"

Quinn's brow settled, and he nodded, taking my blood-stained clothes in stride.

"Of course. Where do you need to go?"

I leaned against the back window fighting to stay awake as Quinn's car hurtled down the country backroads of McMillan Island. Avery sat in the front seat where he could point Quinn in the direction of the camp. Every few minutes, Quinn would glance back at me, shaking black ringlets from his face and checking that I was still alive.

"I'm fine," I mumbled, my cheek pressed against the window.

"You're bleeding."

Avery tapped Quinn's shoulder and pointed down a side road.

"I'm not *actively* bleeding, I *was* bleeding."

"Oh, good, you're improving," Quinn said wryly. "At least I know you won't stain the upholstery of my dad's car."

I grunted, then forced myself to sit upright and look out the back window.

"What's wrong?"

"Nothing." A car followed at a distance, but it was tourist season. There would be other cars on the road, though it did make me nervous.

"And you aren't going to tell me what happened?"

I twisted back to face forward, eyeing a car coming towards us in the other lane with apprehension. Quinn peered at me with curious concern over his shoulder for as long he could before having to look back at the road.

"Maybe later."

Avery signaled another turn, and Quinn hit the brakes harder than he needed to. I winced as the seatbelt dug into my abdomen.

"Sorry," Quinn mumbled. "My depth perception isn't what it used to be."

He caught my eye again, adjusting the mirror so he had a clear view of me leaning against the window.

"Are you going to get in trouble?" I asked.

"I think I'm in the clear."

"Your parents don't care if you load bleeding strangers into your car?"

"I thought you weren't actively bleeding?"

"Sorry, *bloodied* strangers."

"You aren't a stranger, Sammy."

I checked to see if the car behind us had followed us through the turn, but the road was cast in darkness. Still, I couldn't ease the tension in my gut, and something in the back of my head was screaming that we were still in danger.

I squashed the feeling down, telling myself it was residual adrenaline and the fact that Brooke was still dying back at the house. Avery and I were safe. We'd be fine. Quinn had rescued us, and we'd get to the camp with plenty of time for Brooke.

Roy Hendricks might throw a fit, but that was it. He'd send his team to take care of Hackjob and Mira. We were okay. The danger had passed.

Avery pointed again, and the front of the car dipped as Quinn turned onto the dirt road. The dark of the night forest pressed in around me, and I tried to find comfort in the haze that was settling over my head.

The headlights dampened, and Quinn gave them a test flick, but Avery shook his head and beckoned him onwards.

"What's happening?" Quinn sounded more curious than alarmed. "My lights aren't working."

"Shadow Veil." I didn't have the energy to elaborate. Quinn looked back and tutted.

"No, you're definitely *actively* bleeding."

"Hmm?" I patted at my side, finding it warm and sticky. I pushed wet fingers against my neck, searching for a pulse. If there was one there, it was weak. If I died, would I stay awake? No one had explained how the immortality thing worked.

I blinked slowly, watching Quinn's blue eyes dim in the rearview mirror as the Shadow Veil slipped over us, slowly plunging us into darkness.

Or maybe it was death closing in and pulling me into the shadows of the next life before my immortality could drag me back.

But then the dark lifted and despite the late hour, the camp was alive with light and activity. Cabin windows glowed and rock music that had been imperceivable from the forest blared from the main building. Dark shadows milled along the fields, running and fighting as they trained into the evening.

Good. I hoped they were warmed up.

Our headlights drew the attention of the nearest students, and by the time Quinn pulled up in front of the main building, Mr. Hendricks, Everly, and an entourage of students were flooding down the steps while I continued to bleed in the back.

No, the bleeding had stopped.

Crap. If I wasn't bleeding then I was definitely dead.

The car door disappeared beneath my slumped body, and hands caught me as I fell out into a set of clean, lavender scrubs.

Everly low voice swore overhead.

"Give me space!" he shouted, and his chest reverberated in my ear as he carried me to the grass and laid me down.

"What the *hell* is she doing back here?" Mr. Hendricks's voice demanded. A foggy retort built somewhere in the back of my head, but my lungs felt empty, and I let my words die on my tongue.

"Sammy, are you awake?" Everly's face overhead was outlined by green aurora.

"We were attacked." I struggled to bring air into my lungs to speak. "Brooke needs help."

"And you led them here?" Hot hands grabbed at my shoulders, and sparks of fire drifted into the green of the aurora as Mr. Hendricks tried to shake me.

Everly shoved him back.

"Andersen, I need Serum and a bag of A or O blood. Whichever you can grab first." Everly tapped my face, trying to hold my gaze. "Stick with me, Sammy. You've been through this before."

"What's going on?" A new voice cut through the chaos, and Everly swore again.

"Get Wesley out of here!" he growled as Mr. Hendricks shouted for someone to call the university camp.

"Is she...?" Wesley's voice cracked.

"Oh, I'm totally dead," I wheezed, answering the question I knew he was too afraid to ask.

Andersen appeared at Everly's side, juggling bags of fluid.

"What about the kid?" Andersen nodded behind me. I lolled my head to the other side. Avery leaned against Quinn's car, his hands balled up in front of his mouth.

"Sammy first."

I winced as something sharp pierced my inner arm.

"Make yourself useful if you're going to hover." Everly pushed two bags of fluid into Wesley's arms.

"The phones are dead." I recognized Anthony's voice call from the porch. "We can't call the university team, but Justin is running over there now."

"Tell me what happened." Mr. Hendricks tried to get close again, but Everly held out a hand, keeping him at bay. Val Hendricks was there too, holding her husband by his arm, unaffected by the fluttering flames that rolled off his shoulders.

"Is Amanda alright?" she pressed.

"Brooke is dying. She needs Serum." I looked at the tubes sticking out of my arm as I said it. "Amanda's holding them off, but I don't know how long she can manage."

"And Alex?" Everly asked.

"Injured. Not in danger."

Everly touched my hand and sighed.

"And there's a heartbeat. Welcome back to the land of living."

"Being dead wasn't nearly as restful as you'd think."

"You can relax now." Everly's smile was strained. "We'll take care of things from here. Avery, you next. What's hurt?"

But I couldn't relax. Something was still nagging me, but I couldn't quite remember what. I felt as if there was something important I needed to warn the others about, but *what* was it?

"Sammy!" Naomi came bounding across the field as Wesley helped me sit up, supporting me between my shoulders with his plastic hand. Naomi crouched next to us. Her braids were coiled in a knot at the top of her head, and her cheeks were flushed from running. "My sister, is she—"

She cut off as bright lights broke through the forest behind us.

Three SUVs burst through the tree line, spitting gravel and dirt as they careened towards the house. Wesley tried to pull me to my feet, but Mr. Hendricks yanked me from his arms and threw me against the side of Quinn's car.

"What've you done!?" he bellowed.

"Roy!" Val tried to pull her husband off of me. "She's just a kid! She's here to help Amanda!"

"She's sold us out!" The flames on his shoulder flared, eating into his windbreaker. "Everyone, prepare for a fight! If the camp goes down, we go down, too!"

The high-beams of the SUVS drowned out the light of Roy's fire as they surrounded us. A white-haired head appeared from the passenger seat of the nearest vehicle, and the relief I felt at knowing Mira was no longer at the farmhouse was short-lived. She leaned against the car door, tall and waif-like in her burnt cardigan, her smile looking as poisonous as the toxins she secreted from her fingers, despite the ash smudged across her cheeks.

"We don't want trouble!" Roy pushed me to the ground, and I fell hard in the gravel, still attached to the bags of fluid by tubes. "Take the girl."

"That easy?" Mira asked. Boots shifted in the gravel as more car doors opened, and more of Adrestus's cronies filed out.

"You leave us alone," Mr. Hendricks boomed. "And you leave the families under our protection alone."

"Children are *not* bartering chips, Roy!" Val snarled, and gentle hands pulled me from the ground. She turned me around, and her eyes scoured me for scrapes.

Mira laughed, and I looked back at her to watch her twirl a lock of singed white hair around a finger.

"It's tempting, but I'm not the one in charge," she purred.

"I mean, if they're just offering her up, I don't see why not." Quinn climbed out of his driver's seat.

"What are you—" I demanded, but Quinn waved a hand and cut me off.

"You're on, what, your third version of yourself now?" Quinn asked. "Despite all the identity crises and the thousands of years, you know what never changes? How adorably naive you are. Really, it's my favorite thing about you. Gregor, you can let her see me now."

The blond man next to Mira nodded, and whatever illusion had been draped over Quinn shifted. His cheekbones sharpened, and his eyebrows thickened as he aged an extra fifteen years. His vacation-wear melted from his body, leaving him in tight armor that hugged his frame, and his left eye flickered from view, occluded by a metal patch that glinted in the wavering light of the headlights. He was the same man I'd seen in the bathroom mirror of the cafe and the same man drinking tea in the kitchen at one AM.

Wesley had been right after all, except it wasn't that Quinn was in league with Adrestus— he *was* Adrestus.

Val pushed me out of the way to stand between me and the warrior, but before anyone else could react, most of them probably too stunned by his sudden appearance, Adrestus pulled Val in and embraced her by the head and neck.

A single, spine-splintering crack echoed across the camp.

"This has been fun," Adrestus sighed as Val collapsed at his feet, "but I'll be taking Eydis home now."

14

Negotiations

Val Hendricks was dead. The image of her mangled body at my feet, accompanied by her husband's inhuman wail of anguish, was so horrid and so unthinkable that my mind rebelled against the idea that it could be real.

Because it couldn't be. Because even though I'd been dead myself just minutes ago, something as gruesome and violent as this simply could not exist. Hell erupted around me as fighting and flames broke out. Mr. Hendricks howled in tortured rage that sounded miles away, and Adrestus was drawing closer, stepping over Val's body to reach out for me, but I couldn't move. I wouldn't move.

Moving would make it real. Reacting would somehow solidify this cold reality.

"Sammy, we've got to go!" Arms dragged me away, and I finally raised my eyes from Val's body to Adrestus's scowl inches from my face. His fingers grazed the front of my shirt, and I thought he might have me, but Wesley was faster, pulling me out of the warrior's searching grip.

"Don't make me remove your other arm, boy!" Adrestus lunged after us, but the back door of his car peeled itself from the car frame and bowled into Adrestus's back.

"I've got him, take Samantha!" Andersen cried out as purple flames rose to meet the red fires stoked by Roy Hendricks's screaming cry. The infernos hissed and sizzled where they met in the air, drowning out the sounds of fighting and the mighty beating of leathery wings from an Apex who had taken to the sky.

Wesley tried to put an arm over me, but I pushed him off, searching the tangle of firelight, shadow, and brawling figures.

"I won't leave Avery!" I shrieked.

But I couldn't find him.

What if Adrestus found him first? What if he did to him what he did to Val?

"He'll be fine!" It was Naomi at my other side now, helping Wesley to shield me, but I fought back against their lead.

This was my fault.

Val was dead because I'd led Adrestus here. By the end of the night, she might not be alone. They all should've let Mr. Hendricks hand me over.

My fleeting strength abandoned me, and Wesley and Naomi dragged me up the steps into the house.

"Find my missing Apex!" Adrestus roared outside. "And bring me Eydis!"

Metal groaned and burst, and white light flared through the windows as the car Andersen had been using to fend off Adrestus caught fire. Dark spots burst in my vision as the light faded and was replaced by swirling purple that flickered down the hall.

"Faster!" Andersen burst through the door after us and chased us over the warped hall floorboards to the infirmary. "Watch your heads."

We stumbled into the infirmary, and the row of bed frames shuddered and grated across the floor. Wesley covered my head as the beds shook themselves free of their mattresses and flew to the windows and door to barricade us in.

"We can't stay here!" I cried. Andersen glared at me from where he stood in the center of the room with his arms outstretched, sweating from the telekinetic effort of holding our barricade. "Avery is out there. And Brooke—"

"She needs Serum," Andersen finished for me. "The cabinets under the window. Fill a bag with as much as you can grab. When the building burns, we'll lose whatever's left behind."

Wesley tore through the cabinets, pulling out bags of clear fluid while Naomi disappeared into Everly's office.

"Everly said to get what we need and to meet him at the boathouse," Andersen continued as Wesley and Naomi worked. "He has a plan, and last I saw, he had Avery. Avery's safe as long as he sticks with him."

I nodded blankly, clutching my own two bags of fluid. I was helpless. I was useless. I was better off going with Adrestus and giving the others a chance to get the Serum back to Brooke.

A metal pole nudged my arm, and I flinched away.

"It's an IV stand," Andersen explained. "You need to keep those elevated."

I nodded again and hooked my bags on the pole with shaking hands, trying to forget the image of Val broken in the dirt.

"I need a backpack," Wesley called just before the window behind him shattered. He threw himself over his stockpile of Serum in an attempt to shield it from the barrage of glass as purple firelight flooded the infirmary and sucked the heat from the room.

A body slammed against the bars of the bed frame barricade, and a leathery set of four wings beat against frigid air.

"Andersen!" Wesley yelled, backpedaling away from the window with as many bags as he could carry.

"It's fine, she can't get in."

A woman's face snarled at us from the other side of the mash of bed frames, and she reached through the bars to grasp at air.

"I found a bag!" Naomi called from the office and threw an old, gray backpack into the infirmary. I wheeled my IV pole over, trying to feel useful, trying not to listen to the screams and cries that wafted in through the broken window. I grabbed the bag but hesitated at its unexpected weight.

"There's old clothes in it," I murmured, reaching in to pull out the black fabric.

"Leave it." Naomi's back was to me as she foraged through the drawers of Everly's desk. An orange cat huddled in the corner, leering at us through dilated pupils. "The shirt you've got on has a huge, sword shaped hole in it. You can change later."

I pulled out a single shoulder pad painted with the number "12".

"Will it fit?"

Wesley joined me, piling bags of Serum into the backpack on top of the old team uniform.

"I've got a feeling it will."

"Are we good?" Andersen asked through gritted teeth.

Wesley threw the backpack over his shoulder.

"Ready."

"Not ready!" Naomi cried, ripping open a file cabinet.

"The building's on fire. I can smell it. We need to leave," Wesley insisted.

"I can't yet. You take Sammy and go. We'll catch up."

"We?" Andersen squawked. "What's this about we?"

Naomi looked up from the mess on Everly's desk, pleading with Wesley.

"I need to find something before it's caught in the fire. We'll meet you at the boathouse."

"Naomi—" Wesley tried to argue.

"I'm your captain, Wes. Take Sammy. Get out."

He clenched his jaw but nodded.

"Andersen, let us out."

Andersen tried to blink away the sweat that bled into his eyes.

"Be quick."

That was the only heads up he gave before the bed frame keeping the winged woman out crumpled and bent, folding in on itself to shoot out the window. The woman shrieked as her wings became tangled in a mess of metal.

Wesley grabbed my arm and led us in a full sprint for the window. I screamed in protest, clutching my IV pole like a jousting lance as we vaulted into a freezing mosaic of purple flame and landed hard on the frost-burnt grass.

A ball of orange fur streaked past us as Everly's cat made a break out of the burning building behind us. Smoke filled my lungs, but before I could catch my breath, Wesley had me on my feet again, sprinting past purple and orange flame to darkened bluffs that overlooked the ocean.

Smoke turned to fog as we broke free of the fires and left the sounds of fighting behind us. I pulled my arm away from Wesley's grip and stumbled to a stop on the dew-laden lawn.

"What are you—" Wesley started.

"You go," I panted. I knew what I needed to do. "Get the Serum back to Brooke and Fleming. Adrestus won't bug you anymore. I'll make sure he leaves you alone."

Wesley shook his head, and the disbelieving smile that flashed across his face caught me off guard.

"And here I thought you weren't the same Samantha as you were before."

"What's that supposed to mean?"

"I thought when you lost your memories, you'd changed. But this is the exact crap you've always tried pulling." He took my hands in his, his plastic fingers whirring as they closed over mine. "You're not turning yourself over to Adrestus."

"I can stop this. I can make sure no one else gets hurt."

"Last time you said that, I lost an arm, and Vidar died. Nothing will stop Adrestus. He's like a wildfire. You give him anything, and it'll only fuel him until he's devoured everything."

"I—" I was worse than useless. Stay or go, I was a liability. No matter what I did, people would end up hurt and dead.

Wesley pulled me towards the bluff, and I followed on numb, stiff legs.

"I'm sorry about your arm."

"It wasn't your fault."

"Sounds like it was."

"You aren't the one who hacked it off."

The bluffs were smaller than ones at the farmhouse, and as we dropped down a rickety set of wooden steps towards the beach, the fog cleared, revealing dark water and an old shed built against the cliffside. A shadow moved in the shed window, and I hesitated on the stairs.

"It's Heather," Wesley assured me. "She's inside with Anthony and Remi. I can hear them."

The beach sand turned silver in the moonlight, and green ribbons of light wove between the stars overhead. The black water of the ocean lapped against the shore, slapping against a paved ramp that led to the shed.

The shed door creaked open, and a gesturing hand hastened us forward across the breeze-stirred sand. The door widened as we approached, and a body slammed into mine as soon I was in the safety of the darkened interior.

"You're alright, thank god." Heather squeezed me tight before moving on to Wesley. "You got Everly's instructions, then? I hate running while everyone is still up there fighting."

The shed was cramped, and most of the space was taken up by a thirty-foot boat under a tarp. Moonlight through the bay door window bent around the base of its hull where the tarp didn't quite reach, highlighting the metal frame of the truck trailer it rested upon.

"Take it up with Everly," Remi said, peeking out the window. "Here he comes now."

Anthony watched Wesley with apprehension, but Wesley was determined to ignore him, instead fussing with the bags of fluid I still carried on my IV pole.

"You're almost done with the Serum, but I don't know about the blood transfusion." he murmured.

"Here." Anthony pressed a granola bar into my hand just as my stomach growled.

"How'd you know I was hungry?"

"The Serum will do that. Hendricks is pretty strict when it comes to food, but a few of the university kids sneak us snacks to keep on hand."

The door swung open, and Everly swooped in. His lavender scrubs were dirty with ash and blood, but he ushered an unscathed Avery ahead of him.

I threw myself at my brother, tangling us both in a mess of IV tubing. He leaned his head forward onto my shoulder with his arms hanging loose at his side, quiet and still.

"Are you still hurt?" I asked. "We have Serum. Nurse Everly can—"

"I'll heal Avery when the danger has passed." Everly scanned the dark recesses of the shed and frowned. "Where's Naomi? And Andersen?"

"They'll be here," Wesley grunted, still eyeing Anthony with distrust.

"Right." Everly nodded. "No reason we can't get started. Anthony, Heather, and Remi, into the boat. Wesley, get the boat in the water."

I flinched at the loud rattle of a large metal door lifting, revealing the concrete ramp outside. Anthony and Remi pulled back the tarp and climbed up as Wesley lifted the end of the trailer. He grit his teeth as he pushed against the trailer and wheeled the boat onto the beach with the strength of an All Wheel Drive truck. Everly hoisted Heather up into the boat as it creaked towards the water. Then he held his hand out to Avery.

Avery grabbed my arm, and his fingers dug into the bruises I knew were forming under the IV needle.

"He stays with me," I asserted.

"Adrestus wants both of the Havardson children." Everly held a hand up to stop Wesley from wheeling the boat into the water. "You're safer split up, but you'll see him tomorrow when this is all over. I promise."

Avery let go of me, and I tried to pull him back, but he shook his head. He rasped something, maybe another misplaced apology, but when nothing but painful air escaped his throat, he shrugged and turned away. Everly lifted him into the boat after the others.

"Heather's in charge," he said, signaling for Wesley to continue pushing them into the ocean. "Remi, you should be able to interface with the GPS and the radio. Contact Alison and Mr. Baker. They'll meet you on the mainland. Anthony, you're on defense. Keep the wind strong, and none of Adrestus's Apex will be able to reach you."

Wesley waded until the water reached his waist and unlatched the boat. The boat rocked with the gentle waves as it floated free of the trailer. With a signal from Everly, Remi started the engine, and Avery cast me one last glance before they puttered away from the shore.

"Naomi and Andersen are here." Wesley wrung salt water from the edges of his shirt.

"Get the trailer back in the shed before anyone sees it," Everly instructed. "It's time to go."

Naomi and Andersen were two dark shadows against the cliff face as they descended towards the shed and met us at the bottom. The lip of the bluff glowed orange and purple as the fighting raged on, but with the thick layer of fog that hovered over the camp, no one seemed to have noticed the lonely boat speeding away from McMillan Island.

"Did you get it?" Everly demanded as Naomi and Andersen flew down the last few steps of the stairway and sprinted to the cover of the shed. Naomi nodded breathlessly and procured a thin, black case.

"You had that at the house the other day," I remembered. "What—"

"Later, Samantha," Everly promised. He took my arm and started unwrapping the tape that fastened the IV tubes in place. "We need to move quick. The cars Adrestus's Apex came in, I imagine they'll still have the keys in the ignition. If not, Andersen's powers should do the trick. Stop for no one."

I winced at the sharp tug of a needle pulling out of my arm, and Everly patted my elbow in apology.

"And you?" Naomi asked. Everly's jaw tightened.

"I need to stay with Roy. He's understandably distraught, and if no one is here to pull in the reins, he will burn himself until there is nothing but ash left."

He ushered us towards the stairs, and I rubbed my arm, happy to be free of the needles but still dizzy from blood loss.

"Keep that close," Everly murmured to Naomi ahead of me. Her top knot bobbed as she nodded, and I eyed the case under her arm, wondering what was so important that she had risked staying behind to find.

"Are you feeling okay?" Wesley asked. The backpack of Serum bounced on his back as we climbed the steps back to the bluff. I didn't want to join the fray again. I didn't want to run to the cars and see Val's body, or the bodies of anyone who might've joined her.

"Absolutely peachy." My stomach grumbled, but I'd stashed Anthony's granola bar in my pocket. I could snack later.

"Samantha knows the way to the house. Listen to her, and stick together." Everly crouched on the top step and surveyed us. "I know you haven't all always gotten along, but you are strongest when you are together."

"You sure you can't come with us?" Andersen gulped. "The Serum—"

"You'll do fine." Even though he smiled at Andersen, his words instilled renewed courage in me, too. "Just like we practiced. I'll make a nurse out of you yet."

He turned towards the camp, and the glow of the fires gleamed against his bald head. He set his jaw, nodded, and motioned for the camp.

Naomi was the first to follow Everly into the fog and smoke, back towards the sounds of chaos. Metal clashed against metal somewhere in the mess, and the ground shook with the force of somebody's powers, but it was impossible to make out much of the fighting as we sprinted for the series of bright, white lights that marked the high-beams of the SUVs.

I kept my eyes on Andersen's backpack as we sprinted. Everly disappeared into the smoke to our right, running towards the flaming main building where purple fire raged, flecked with spots of red and orange where Roy Hendricks's fire fought for a foothold.

The cars took shape ahead of us, their doors wide open and their engines idling. Most of the fighting had migrated away from the driveway, giving us a clear shot to safety.

We were going to make it.

And then my collar tightened around my throat, and red heat seared across my front.

"Sammy!" Wesley screamed somewhere on the other side of a wall of flame, but I couldn't make him out through the dark spots that bloomed in my vision. Someone had me in a chokehold, and I scratched at his arms. My fingernails did nothing against the sleeves of his windbreaker.

"I always knew it'd be you who led him here. Everything I've worked for, ruined by a Beta!" Flecks of spittle dotted the side of my cheek as Roy Hendricks screamed in my ear. "And now my wife is dead because of you!"

Beyond the flames, the vague shape of Wesley threw the backpack to Andersen and Naomi.

"I'm trying to help," I choked. "Brooke is—"

"Another Beta," Mr. Hendricks hissed. "Not worth the trouble. Not worth my wife having her neck snapped!"

His hand burned against my neck, and I swung my elbows backwards, trying to make contact, but Mr. Hendricks threw me to the ground.

"Wes!"

I didn't know why I called out for Wesley. I still barely trusted him, but in my state of panic, it was the first name that sprung to my lips.

"I'm coming! Sammy, I'm—"

"You'll stay out of this, boy!" Mr. Hendricks howled. "That's an order!"

"Never."

"You listen to me or you're off the team!"

"Then I'm off the team!"

A long stream of whip-like fire cracked against the air where it issued from Mr. Hendricks's raised fist. A callous grin mangled his face, and his fire reflected against the lenses of his thin-rimmed glasses.

"It all comes down to you, when I think about it." He gave his fire-whip an experimental snap in the air. "Alison was a fool to wake you, and she was a fool to keep you under her protection. Nothing good comes from Betas who think they are bigger than they actually are."

I tried to roll away, but he brought the whip down. Snapping heat broke over my shoulder. Its crackle disguised the sound of my cry, and Mr. Hendricks saw his chance to lurch forward, taking me in his arms again.

"Take her! My deal still stands! Take her and leave us be!" Mr. Hendricks screamed at the air. The skin of my wrist blistered where he grabbed me. Wings beat the air overhead, and I squinted at the smoke-filled sky, trying to make out the outline of a four-winged woman unable to fly any lower thanks to the heat of the fire.

Mira's cheshire grin materialized in the flames. Her flowing skirts had singed up to her knees, showing off bruised and bleeding alabaster legs while her white hair smoked. I tried to twist away as Mr. Hendricks pressed me forward.

"Take her!" he said again. Pleading. Desperate.

She reached forward with toxic, spindly fingers. I struggled against Mr. Hendricks's hold on me. I couldn't let Mira touch me. She might kill me or control me or take me to Adrestus or—

"Roy, you coward!"

Blunt force collided into my side, and the world flipped so that the burnt remains of the lawn were against my face. Mr. Hendricks collapsed in the dirt next to me, and I scrambled away before he could grab me again. New arms wrapped around me, and I screamed in protest, but it was Everly's face that appeared in the smoke.

"I've got you. You're safe," he promised, but the tongue of Roy's fire-whip came down over Everly's shoulders. He dropped me, wincing in pain and turning to stand between me and Mr. Hendricks.

"Leave her, Jacobi!" Mr. Hendricks snarled. "I'm trying to end this!"

"She's a child! This is not what Val would want!"

"You dare speak to me about what Val would want?" The whip cracked again. Everly ducked out of its way and tackled Mr. Hendricks around his middle, slamming him into the ground.

New hands found my shoulders, and I jumped.

"We need to move!" The lines of Wesley's face deepened in the dancing firelight, and I let him help me to my feet.

"Oh, how I do love a reunion. Is that Ares?" Mira cackled. Wesley froze at the name, and I pushed him out of the way as Mira bore down on us with hungry, outstretched hands.

"Move!" I screamed, and Wesley came to his senses a moment too late. Mira's hand was an inch away when Everly yanked her back. His muscles strained against his scrubs where he had Mr. Hendricks's in a head lock while he tried to get a better grip on Mira with his free hand.

Cardigans unfurled as she twisted in his grip and locked her fingers around his neck.

Everly released Mr. Hendricks and straightened up mechanically as Mira's powers took hold. Mr. Hendricks scrambled away, but Mira ignored him, staring at Wesley and me over her shoulder.

"I'm getting very tired of people getting in my way. It really is a shame," she said, hardly audible over the flames, "this one is more of a liability than an asset."

I tried to scream a warning, but her fingers were already tightening around Everly's neck. Black bruises spread along his veins, and his eyes widened. His mouth opened and closed until he was able to gasp a single word:

"Run."

His eyes lolled back, and Mira let go. Everly, strong and sturdy and constant Everly, dropped to the dust where he moved no more.

15

Confessions

I'd seen Mira's hand on his neck. I'd watched his skin darken as the poison claimed his veins. I'd watched him fall. But the dead man on the ground couldn't be Everly.

New arms constricted around me, but it didn't matter because Everly was dead, and it was my fault. Adrestus could have me. Maybe it was better this way.

"Hold on!" It was Wesley's voice, haggard and broken, in my ear, and I hung off his neck, watching Everly's body get farther and farther away. Mira's face contorted in a laugh that was swallowed by the roars of the fire.

"We can't leave him." I tried to let go of Wesley, but he had me in his arms as he ran for the forest.

"Sammy, he's gone."

I tightened my arms around Wesley's neck. I'd led Adrestus to the camp, and now Everly was dead.

"You don't need to carry me," I whispered. "I can run."

"You aren't fast enough," he mumbled into my hair as he adjusted his grip on my legs. I choked on a dry sob, catching my breath and refusing to look away from the fiery camp until we'd turned a corner, and it was lost through the trees. "Naomi and Andersen went ahead. We need to catch up."

The dark of the trees pressed around us, and the only things that existed were Wesley's chest jostling against me and the static in my head. The faint red glow of taillights hastened Wesley forward.

The SUV skidded to a halt, and the back door flung open. Moonlight that filtered through the tree canopy highlighted the braids that had fallen from Naomi's top knot when she leaned into the dirt road. My hand locked with hers, and she pulled me into the backseat as Wesley leaped into the passenger seat up front.

"You're getting slower," Andersen grunted as we slammed our doors shut. I twisted around to look out the back window, half-expecting to still see flames and the silhouette of Everly's body.

"Drive." Wesley wheezed for air.

"I don't have my license! You—"

"I said drive!" Wesley retched, bending over in his seat.

"What's wrong?" Naomi struggled to lean forward between the front seats as Andersen floored the gas pedal. "What's happened?"

Wesley's shoulders shook too hard for him to answer, and I swallowed the bile in my throat.

"Everly's dead."

Andersen hit the brakes so hard that Naomi nearly ended up on the dashboard, and I slammed into the back of Wesley's seat.

"They're following us, you have to keep going," Wesley croaked.

"He's not dead." Andersen looked back at me. "Why would you even say that?"

"Mira killed him," Wesley said.

"Naomi's powers would've felt him die! He's not—"

"Drive, Andersen," Naomi whispered. She extricated herself from the front and fell back against her seat. "We must've been too far for me to feel him."

Her fingers dug into the upholstery as she held the edge of her seat in a death grip.

Everly had been one of my few friends, but I hadn't realized how much the others must've cared for and relied on him. Andersen watched the road with a wide-eyed stare and tight lips. The car fishtailed when he pulled out onto the main road, but still, no one spoke.

The road curved and bent with the island coastline. At one point, I was sure the car was about to flip with the force of taking a corner too fast, but Andersen raised a shaking fist, and the four wheels slammed back to the pavement. Naomi strapped on her seatbelt but no one seemed to want to break the heavy silence.

I knew they were silently mourning Everly, but part of me wondered if maybe they were thinking that staying with me would put them next in line to join Adrestus's growing body count.

"I'm sorry," Wesley choked.

"Don't be," I murmured. "It was my fault."

"The last thing he'd want is you two competing for blame when neither of you are actually at fault." Naomi pulled the rest of her braids from her top-knot and let them fall against her shoulders. "Focus up. We aren't done yet."

But the road was empty and strangely peaceful. The aurora overhead danced stronger than ever now that we were far from the smoke and fog of the battle.

Maybe Roy would fend off Adrestus. Maybe no one would follow us to the farmhouse. Maybe it would all be okay, and in the morning we'd discover that after a close shave with Mira's toxins, Everly was in fact alive.

"Are they still following us?" Andersen asked. The road banked inwards, away from the coast and patches of moonlight flickered overhead as we raced beneath tree coverage.

"They will be," Wesley warned.

"Then should we *not* go to the farmhouse?"

"They already know where it is." I checked the back window, searching for headlights. "We just have to beat them there."

The engine revved as Andersen accelerated.

"Careful," Naomi said as we took another turn too fast.

"I'm fine," Andersen growled, accelerating down a straightaway. I pressed back into my seat and buckled my seatbelt just in case. Andersen scowled at me in the rearview mirror at the sound of it clicking.

"There's an animal or something up ahead," Wesley warned. "I can see the bushes moving. If it's a deer it might—"

"If you wanted to drive then you should've—"

A cloaked figure stepped out of the undergrowth and into the white light of our high-beams, unbothered by the oncoming vehicle.

Tires squealed against pavement, and we shrieked Andersen's name as he veered the SUV off an embankment.

For a moment, I was weightless in my seat, held down only by the seatbelt I'd been smart enough to buckle at the last minute. Then, the front wheels smashed into earth, followed by the back end of the car, each impact sending shockwaves up my spine.

We careened through the undergrowth, ripping up bushes and ferns until the trunk of a cedar tree brought our trip into the forest to a violent halt.

My ears rang, filling my skull with a shrill, high-pitched note. The engine of the SUV hissed through the static, and someone cried out in pain. Naomi's shaking hands fumbled with her seatbelt, and in front of her, Andersen slumped over a deployed airbag.

"Wesley?" I mumbled, fighting against my own seatbelt. My door didn't want to open at first, but with a little prompting from my shoulder, it burst open, and I tumbled out into a patch of ferns.

The front passenger door was in worse shape than mine, but I managed to yank it open, revealing Wesley, bent over his lap and clutching his leg.

"Dislocated again," he moaned through gritted teeth.

"This has happened before?" My tentative hands hovered over his jeans, unsure how to help.

Wesley's face whipped towards mine, and his mouth opened in a warning shout. Hands grabbed me from behind and threw me to the ground.

A hooded face looked down at me, and moonlight highlighted the contours of a macabre theatre mask, its features pulled into a permanent frown.

I tried to scramble away, but was too disoriented to make it far. A gloved hand shot from the robes and yanked me back to my feet to slam me against a tree.

"So you lost your memories. Again." The voice that issued from behind the mask was surprisingly young and feminine. "How convenient that you get to forget all the lies they fed you while I still remember them as clearly as if they'd actually happened?"

She pushed the mask up, revealing a face too young to look as haggard as she did, with heavy, sleep-deprived eyes and the remnants of an old bruise blushing her chin. She may have been shorter than her sister, but even in the dark she looked enough like Amanda for me to guess who she was.

"You're Winnie." I choked against her grip. I was grateful she hadn't inherited her father's Apex genes. She was frightening enough without flame powers. "Amanda's sister."

But if she was Amanda's sister, that meant her mother was dead.

"Amanda's sister. Your pseudo-friend." Strawberry blonde clumps of limp hair hung in her face as she surveyed mine. "Just a bunch of words that don't matter."

"Your mom—" She deserved to know what they'd done, but her grip tightened, and I choked on the words.

"I'm over being defined by my proximity to people I don't give a crap about." She pulled the mask back over her face, and her voice became muffled. "I'm Dion, and I'm the one who's bringing you to Adrestus."

I shook my head. She didn't know. She deserved to know. I tried to loosen her fingers with mine, but her grip was strong, and I was still dazed and dizzy.

"Run!" Wesley launched out of the dark, having finally freed himself from the passenger seat. Winnie danced out of the way in a swirl of cloaks. Wesley was moving much slower than he had at the camp and kept all of his weight on his right leg. He tried to block a kick from Winnie, but it landed against his left hip, and he cried out. "Sammy, go!"

I hesitated when Winnie struck Wesley again, but a hand on my shoulder pulled me back.

"Get this out of here." Naomi shoved the backpack of Serum into my arms. "If the worst happens, destroy the case inside before Adrestus takes it."

She sprinted to Wesley's aid, and I scrambled around the side of the car. Andersen was slumped over the steering wheel with shattered glass sparkling on his shoulders.

"Hey!" I tapped his face through the broken window. His eyelids fluttered, but other than that, he made no effort to acknowledge me.

The door was jammed, folded in on itself like an accordion, forcing me to crawl halfway into the window to unbuckle Andersen and extricate him from the wreckage. He slumped to the ground, and I went down with him.

"Hey, wake up!" I shook his shoulder, and when he didn't move, I swore under my breath. "This is gonna suck for both of us."

Sergio had once shown me how to hoist someone over my shoulder, and I did my best to replicate his instructions. Andersen was heavier than I expected, but with my wound healed thanks to the Serum, I was feeling stronger than I had all night. His head lolled against mine as I leaned forward to hold him in the world's worst piggy-back. I was done with the difficult part. Now it was a simple matter of moving forward.

With the backpack of Serum strapped across my chest and Andersen's feet dragging in the dirt behind me, I staggered deeper into the woods. Naomi and Wesley couldn't take too long. Amanda's sister wasn't an Apex, but I bit my lip in worry as well as strain when I took into account that Wesley was injured, and Naomi didn't have powers that aided her in a physical match up.

My shoes squelched as I stepped into a marsh that had been invisible in the dark, but even as mud found its way between my toes, I moved forward. If I stopped, Andersen's weight might become too much. It was impressive I was able to carry him at all considering I'd been dead just a few hours ago.

When dry ground returned beneath my feet, I was soaked up to my knees. A root caught the toe of my shoe, and I lurched into the dirt with a strangled yelp.

"Dammit, what—" Andersen wriggled free of my arms as I spat dirt from my mouth. "Where are we?

His words slurred, and he gawked up at slivers of aurora visible between the tree canopies.

"You crashed the car."

"Right." He shook his head and pressed a hand against his temple. "And the others?"

I brushed the dirt from my face and stood up, offering a hand to Andersen.

"They're fighting Winnie Hendricks."

Andersen ignored my hand and forced himself to his feet.

"So you took me and ran?"

"It was more of a labored hobble."

"You should've left me." He took the backpack from my arms to sling over his shoulder and turned to lead the way deeper into the woods.

"That's a weird way to say thanks. Instead try, 'thanks for carrying my very dense and very unconscious body into the forest after I crashed us all into a tree'."

"Sure. Thanks."

He held a tree branch out of the way so it wouldn't swing back and smack me.

"What's the plan now?" I asked.

"Everly said to stick together, and that's what we'll do. We need to find somewhere safe to wait for the others, then we'll heal up and continue." He pointed through the dark at a pinprick of orange light. "There's a house up there. It might have a barn we can hide in."

As it turned out, the house had several barns and multiple sheds, including a small, dilapidated building hiding twenty yards into the trees. It had the bearings of a forgotten children's fort, complete with musty couch and a shelf of tattered boardgames that looked like they hadn't been touched in years.

The door broke off its rusted hinges when we tried it, and the floor was littered in forest debris that had blown in through the broken window. I watched the distant home warily, but it was a large property, and the house was far enough away that the occupants wouldn't hear us.

Andersen leaned back on the old couch, rubbing his temple. His eye was swollen shut from the crash, but he was at least conscious.

"Do you need the Serum?" I dropped the backpack next to him, but he shook his head.

"It won't help a concussion. Brain injuries use a different type of Serum and a lumbar puncture."

"Is that hard to do?"

His open eye deadpanned at me.

"You don't know what a lumbar puncture is? You've had at least three."

I tapped my head, crossing the shed to the busted window.

"Right. How could I forget?"

"Whatever. To answer your question, no, they aren't easy, and even if they were, and if we *did* have the supplies, I'd never let you anywhere near my spine with a needle."

I peeked out the window into the trees. A light breeze rustled the leaves, and moonlight percolated through the canopy, painting the forest floor in silver shadow.

"What if Naomi and Wesley can't find us?"

"They will."

"What if they aren't looking? What if Winnie—"

"A Beta doesn't stand a chance against Wesley and Naomi," Andersen snapped. "Don't tell them I said that."

"Beta," I repeated. The ghost of something like resentment and stubborn pride welled in my throat at the word. "That's a non-Apex."

"Right, sorry."

"Why are you sorry?"

"It's not a nice thing to call someone." Andersen blushed in the moonlight.

"Then why'd you say it?"

"I—" His mouth opened and closed as he searched for an answer. "Probably the concussion."

I slid to the dusty floor to lean against the wall beneath the windowsill. Andersen slouched on the couch with his head against the cushions, watching me with his open eye.

He glowered, as if annoyed to be stuck with me, but then the corners of his mouth twitched, pulling into a frown. I tried to shrink into the shadows.

"Sorry," I whispered.

"It's fine." His voice cracked, and he sniffed. I drew my knees to my chest. Andersen was *crying*.

"You were close with Everly, right?"

He blinked up at the ceiling, and tears tracked his cheeks.

"Everyone was. He'd fixed us all at one point or another."

"And you worked in the infirmary with him?" I rubbed the bruises my multiple IVs had left on my arm.

He sniffed again and dragged the heel of his hand across his face.

"Yeah. That was a more recent thing, though."

"Do you want to be a nurse, too?"

"I don't know. I think I'm just trying to make up for things." A shuddering exhale shook his body, and he went back to massaging his temples.

"Don't be too hard on yourself." I scratched at a bit of wood coming up from the floorboards. "You can't have done anything too horrible."

I tried to give him an encouraging smile, but his frown deepened.

"You really don't remember anything."

"I know we knew each other, didn't we? Fleming told me I was on the team back when he was still in charge. You and I would've been in the same grade."

"We weren't exactly friends." Andersen stared back at me, stoic resolve set on his face.

"That's okay," I laughed. "I can't remember why I didn't like you, so it doesn't hurt to be friends now."

He shook his head.

"I wasn't— I don't know. You didn't *belong*. Not in a bad way. You just weren't one of us, and I didn't know how to handle that. And everything came to you so *naturally*. It wasn't fair." Bitterness soaked his words, and he looked back at the ceiling. "I hated you, and you hated me back. If you had your memories, you would still hate me."

I swallowed.

"You're being too hard on yourself. Forget whatever happened. I already have."

He leaned forward on the couch and looked back at me over a broken nose.

"No. I can't. I didn't mean to, but I—" He choked on the words, and fresh tears fell down his face.

"Seriously, it's okay," I insisted.

"Dammit, Samantha! Stop being so nice!"

I shrank back against the wall, but despite his outburst, he couldn't be mad. He was hurt and in pain. I just felt *bad*.

"I was mad that you joined the team, so I pulled a prank on you. It went wrong. I was mean and bitter and proud, and I can admit that but what I did—"

"It was just a prank." The look on his face scared me. "You don't have to say anymore."

"It wasn't just a prank," he said darkly. "Sammy, I—I accidentally killed you that night."

My chest went cold, and I scoured Andersen's face for a hint of a joke. He was abrasive, sure. But a murderer?

"You *what*?"

We jumped at the sudden voice, and I leapt to my feet.

Silver moonlight framed Naomi's silhouette where she half-carried Wesley in the doorway.

"Naomi, I—" Andersen's struggle for words was cut short when Wesley broke free of Naomi's supporting grip and lurched forward. Before he could attack Andersen, however, his leg gave out, and he collapsed to the floor.

"If that's true…" He propped himself up on his arm, and his left leg splayed out at an odd angle. "I'll kill you, Andersen. I swear I will."

Andersen pulled his legs up onto the couch, out of Wesley's reach.

"Sammy, tell me he's lying." Naomi kept her face hidden behind a curtain of braids as she helped Wesley back to his feet, but her words shook with an unspoken threat.

"You know I don't remember," I gulped.

"I'm sorry, I—" Andersen started.

"The night you threw her in the ocean." Wesley leaned against Naomi for balance. "That's the prank you mean, right?"

"You drowned?" Moonlight that poured through the window bounced off Naomi's wide, brown eyes.

"No." Andersen's hands curled into fists, and he tucked his head over his knees. "She froze to death."

"I *defended* you!" Naomi dropped Wesley on the couch, which Andersen hastened to vacate. "Over and over I told Sammy to go *easy* on you and to try to understand. And all that time, you'd—"

Stark realization washed over her, and despair pulled at her features.

"Sammy, why didn't you say anything?"

I looked between her and Andersen, unsure of how to feel.

"I don't know," I whispered. "This is all news to me, too."

Andersen's chin trembled, but he didn't let anymore tears fall.

"I'm sorry," he said again. "You can leave me here, I wouldn't blame you."

"No!" Naomi jammed an accusatory finger against his chest. "You *don't* get to play the martyr!"

"I'm not trying—"

"You're going to help us get to Fleming and the others, and then you're never going to speak to me again."

"Naomi—"

"I felt *bad* for you!" Her voice rose. "Poor Andersen with no friends after his girlfriend told the world he was an Apex. Poor Andersen who can't go home for Christmas because it's too dangerous. Poor Andersen collapsing under the weight of his own insignificance every day, and yes, I felt it."

"There were others," Wesley growled. "You weren't alone the night you threw Sammy in the ocean."

Andersen shook his head.

"They don't know."

"They don't know that they're accessories to *murder*?" Naomi hissed. "Oh, well lucky them. They can still sleep at night!"

"It's not their fault!"

"Whoever they were, as soon as this is over, I'm making sure you're all off the team."

Andersen hung his head, and Wesley reached for Naomi's hand. She pulled it away.

"*What*, Wesley?"

"I hate to say it, but I think we might all be off the team. Even if Roy doesn't kick us off, I'm quitting."

"Fine!" she spat. "We'll make our own team without them and without Andersen."

"Naomi." My voice was quiet. Tiny. I half-expected her not to hear me.

"You!" She rounded on me, braids flying around a face streaked with righteous tears. "Why aren't you angrier?"

"I'm a little angry," I mumbled, "but he seems sorry, and it's hard to be mad about something I can't remember."

"Must be nice." She spun back around. Andersen shied as away as she snatched the backpack from the couch and ripped it open. Her shoulders relaxed a tiny fraction at the sight of the case on top of the bags of Serum, and she pulled out one of the fluid bags to study it.

She unraveled a roll of silicon tubing and a case of needles from the backpack's front pocket, but stalled, squinting at Wesley's jaunty leg.

"Do you need help?" Andersen finally asked. Naomi's nostrils flared.

"Wesley's hurt."

"I'm fine," Wesley said, but a withering glare from Naomi shut him up.

"It's his left leg." She held the bag of Serum close to her chest, frowning and refusing to look at Andersen.

"I think my hip dislocated," Wesley grunted.

"Again?" Andersen blanched.

"You can put it back in, right? Everly taught you how?" Naomi asked. Andersen nodded weakly.

"I watched Everly do it a couple times. It's going to hurt, though."

"Yeah, I know." Wesley gripped the couch cushion. "Just do it fast. And as soon as it's better, I'm gonna kill you."

"That's fair." Andersen took the IV tubing from Naomi, and Wesley scrambled backwards on the couch.

"No. No way. You aren't coming near me with a needle."

"I will if you want to walk after this."

"You're a high school sophomore, not a doctor!"

"Technically we're juniors now."

"That makes zero difference!"

"Do what he says, Wesley. " Naomi frowned.

Wesley screwed his eyes shut and took a steadying breath.

"Yeah, fine. Can you guys wait outside?"

Naomi gave Andersen a withering look.

"If anything happens to Andersen while we're out there," Naomi warned, "I'll make sure it gets ruled an accident."

Andersen's grip tightened around the bag of Serum, and he looked to me for help, but Naomi was already pulling me towards the door.

Branches and rocks crunched underfoot as we made our way to a felled log that overlooked the shadows of the surrounding forest.

"You should cover your ears," Naomi said, taking a seat.

"Why?"

Too late.

A splintering crack accompanied a muffled cry from the shed behind us.

"It's quiet out there." Naomi stared into the dark, eyes wide and hungry for what little light the moon offered.

"That's good. We'll be able to hear if anyone is coming." I tried to sound like I knew what I was talking about as I took a seat next to her. "Plus, your powers should sense anyone who approaches us, right?"

She frowned.

"That's how they work, yes. It's fine. We left Winnie unconscious in the back of the SUV. She's in no shape to follow us."

My stomach growled, and I dug into my pockets for the granola bar Anthony had given me. However, I must've lost it in the forest and came up empty handed.

"We didn't pack any snacks, did we?"

"Sorry. I imagine the Serum left you hungry." She held up the uniform she'd stashed in the bag. "I did grab this out of the bag, though. It's a bit cleaner than what you're wearing."

I ran the spandex fabric through my fingers.

"Mr. Hendricks would be furious if he saw me in uniform."

"All the more reason to put it on."

I stepped away into the privacy of the woods, and after spending longer than should have been necessary to unstick my bloodied shirt from both my stomach and my back, I slipped into the black outfit. The left sleeve was missing, ripped off at the bicep, and I felt silly without the armored layer that I'd seen the others wear, but it was comfier than my ruined shirt and jeans.

I stepped back out of the shadows and waved my bare left arm at Naomi.

"I think it's missing a piece. I feel bad for whoever was wearing this when that happened."

"That would be you."

My stomach flipped.

"Oh."

Wesley cried out again from the shed, and Naomi's smile slipped away.

"Are they okay in there?" I asked.

"How should I know?"

"Your powers?"

She blushed and tried to look busy tying her braids back.

"They're fine. They'll let us know when we can come back in." She looked at her lap and frowned at her hands. "I wish you would've told me about Andersen."

"I know," I whispered back. "I'm not sure why I wouldn't have, but I'm sorry."

"I'm sorry, too." She avoided my eyes as I reclaimed my seat next to her. "I never should have told you to put up with him or made excuses for his behavior."

"You didn't know."

"I still knew he was a jerk to you. Sometimes I think I just tried to broker peace for my own benefit. I got tired of feeling all the anger you had for each other. It was selfish."

"You don't seem like a selfish person," I said softly, and suddenly, her arms were around my shoulders. I froze in shock before relaxing into the embrace and hugging her back.

"This isn't fair," she mumbled into my shoulder. "It's been so long, and I've missed my friend."

Part of me felt weird, like I was playing a lie. Naomi missed her friend, but I didn't remember being that person. At the same time, though, after the night we'd been having, I wanted nothing more than to be the Samantha that she knew.

So I hugged her back and, for just a moment, pretended that I remembered.

16

This Side Of Midnight

The green of the aurora overhead faded as the first signs of dawn seeped into the sky. Dew clung to the underbrush that lined the deer trail we followed through the forest, but my old uniform proved capable of keeping me dry. I'd thought the closer we got to the farmhouse, the more at ease I would be, but my anxiety grew with every step. I didn't know what might be waiting for us upon our return.

Wesley hobbled ahead of me, unfettered by the IV still attached to his arm. He'd led the charge into the woods as soon as he'd been able to put weight on his leg again, aided by the make-shift hip brace Andersen had fastened out of Wesley's shirt.

Now, his bare arms, covered in bruises from Andersen's many attempts at administering the IV, were covered in goosebumps as well while his back remained covered by the backpack. His Serum bag hooked to the top handle and bounced with every step. I counted his strides, taking what comfort I could in the fact that each one brought us closer to Brooke.

"I smell fire." Wesley stopped walking to crouch lower in the bushes. "And we're nearing the road."

"Fire means Amanda still has the barrier up," I said. "Which means Brooke is still alive."

A car rumbled up ahead, and I pushed against the backpack to make Wesley limp faster. We'd move faster along the road. We were almost there. This hell was almost over.

I would never complain about being bored and lonely on this stupid island again.

The tree line broke, and we stumbled out onto the side of the road. To anyone else, it might've looked like any forested roadway, but I knew the drive between the farmhouse and Quarry Bay well.

"The driveway is up ahead!" I took the lead from Wesley, setting the pace.

"Naomi, stay on alert. We'll have to hide if you feel anyone coming."

"You're the ears," Naomi reminded him. "Best to have both of us on alert."

"Best if *all* of us—" Andersen started to say before Naomi interjected.

"We'll let you know if we need you to murder anyone."

We were forced back into the bushes as we went to avoid being seen by passing cars, but this early in the morning, they were few and far between. Finally, I recognized the turn onto the gravel drive and surged forward.

"Here! We're here!" I shouted, and Wesley shushed me. I glared at him and crossed the street to duck down the private drive to the farmhouse. I felt safe back under the tree cover, and the others had to run to keep up with me.

Wesley smelling fire was a good sign, but I was still nervous. Anything could've happened since I'd left.

"Bushes!" Wesley warned behind me, and I ducked into the salal and huckleberry plants that lined the drive as a black SUV shook the gravel. We crouched together in the bushes to watch it pass. I tried to see past its windows, but the tint was too dark.

We waited until it disappeared behind a bend before crawling out of our hiding spot.

"It was a full car," Wesley said grimly. "Naomi, what did you feel?"

She bit her lip and shrugged.

"Hard to tell. Like you said, there were a lot of people inside." Her cheeks darkened with blush.

"Your sister's at the house," Wesley reminded her as we continued down the drive. "Do you think you should hang back? Your powers—"

"I'll be okay."

"Right," Wesley said slowly. "Can you at least feel the others? Are they okay in there?"

She stopped in her tracks as we rounded the corner, and my stomach turned to lead. The light of the protective, fiery dome that encapsulated the house highlighted Naomi's cheekbones, and she gulped.

"Doesn't matter how they're doing if we don't have a way in."

Adrestus had beat us here, his silhouette unmistakable as he paced in front of the dome, either searching for a way in or ensuring there was no way out. Whatever the answer, Amanda had been using her powers for the last ten hours straight and would be running on fumes.

The SUV that had passed us on the road joined two others in front of the house, and another fifty yards away, the sleek body of a helicopter waited against an early dawn backdrop. It was good news for those still back at the camp because Adrestus's entire crew seemed to be here now, instead.

"There's a secret passage," I said from where Wesley had ushered us into the safety of the tree line. "It's down the coast not too far from here, and it leads to the basement."

"Then that's the only option." Naomi signaled for us to fall deeper into the woods. The others slipped back into the brush, but I gave the farmhouse one last glance as the doors of the latest SUV to join the siege opened.

A man in slacks and a button-up stepped out. I hadn't seen him at the attack on the camp, but I recognized him from the television. John Ratcliffe, the new Prime Minister of New Delos, had come to aid Adrestus in his mission.

"Why is—" I started to ask, but then he turned so I could see the limp body he carried in his arms. Heather's long, dark hair hung limp and wet as her head lolled to the side.

Another Apex went to pull a second unconscious body from the car, and Anthony rolled in their arms.

And if they had Anthony and Heather, then they definitely had—

I lunged forward, but arms pulled me back into the bushes. Wesley's hand clamped over my mouth, and I was forced to watch in silence as Remi and Avery filed out of the SUV next, upright and conscious, but with their hands bound behind their backs as Mira shepherded them towards the helicopter.

"We can't fight them," Wesley said in my ear. "The camps will send back up. Our priority is getting help to the others."

"So we go through the passageway like we planned," Andersen said.

"I'm not letting Avery out of my sight," I hissed.

"You're going to get yourself killed!" Wesley shot back.

"What's twice in one night?"

"Fine," Naomi conceded. "Andersen, you find the passageway and help Brooke. Wesley, give him the backpack."

Wesley wiggled out from under the backpack and ripped the IV from his arm.

"Thanks for the biohazard." Andersen flinched away from the free swinging needle as he took the bag. Naomi dug through the backpack to get into the black case, but I was too focused on Avery to pay her too much attention.

"Follow the woods to the coastline," I said to Andersen, my eyes on the farmhouse. "When you come to a cove, find the passageway in the rocks. From there, it's a straight shot."

He grimaced and nodded before slinking deeper into the forest. I refocused on Avery where he stood in front of Adrestus.

"What're they saying?" I asked Wesley.

"Don't know. The fire's too loud."

I scowled and sank lower to the ground.

"But why is Adrestus still here?" I murmured. "Why park his helicopter in my yard instead of leaving the island?"

"Because they know this is where you're headed," Naomi replied grimly. "They'll stick you on that helicopter, and you'll be gone."

John Ratcliffe loaded Heather and Anthony in the helicopter cab, and Remi was forced to file in after them, but Adrestus kept Avery by his side, deep in conversation.

The minutes crept by, painfully slow, and I didn't know if it was the rising sun washing out the light of the fire or Amanda's dwindling energy, but the flaming dome seemed to be dissolving little by little. Hopefully Andersen was moving quickly.

I straightened up when Adrestus pointed towards the helicopter, and Mira pushed Avery towards the open cab.

I stood up. Wesley tried to pull me down, but I pulled my hand away from his plastic grip.

"What are you doing?" he hissed.

"They're taking Avery. It's like Naomi said, they put him in the helicopter and he'll be gone."

"We have to wait."

"They're going to fly away with him!"

"I know he's your brother, but—"

"But he's also a dangerous weapon in the wrong hands. That woman can control anyone she touches, so what happens when Avery's throat is healed, and she has control over his powers?"

"And what are you going to do?" Unable to pull me back to the ground, Wesley stood up to challenge me. "Charge down there and demand they hand Avery over?"

"At least I'd be doing something to help!"

"Or you'll get yourself captured!" Wesley's face reddened to the color of his plastic arm. I wished he hadn't used his shirt to fashion a hip brace. He looked stupid without one on. "And remember what Mr. Baker said. Maybe it's best you avoid battle with Fleming so close."

I thought my ears might burst from the pressure of the blood that roared in my ears, made all the louder by the iron clamp of my jaw.

"What did Mr. Baker say?" Naomi whispered.

"Nothing," I spat. "I'm *helping* Fleming, and you want to stand by and do nothing."

"You don't care about Fleming, you only care about Avery! If you actually thought through a plan for once in your life, you'd see that!"

I stepped back from Wesley, my heart thundering.

"I've thought it through," I assured him. "Worst case scenario, I end up on the helicopter and never have to see *you* again. Plus, Fleming will be safe if I'm in a prison cell."

"Sammy—"

"It's Samantha," I snarled, and before Wesley or common sense could stop me, I charged out of the woods.

Wesley and Naomi called out after me, but I kept my eyes on the figures that rushed to form a line between Adrestus and my dead sprint. Fire glinted against bronze as he drew his sword

A set of four wings spread out, and the winged woman took to the sky. She hurtled towards me, and I raced to meet her, bracing for her attack, but she zipped overhead.

Naomi cried out behind me, but I ignored her. Adrestus was getting closer, and I refused to look away, and I refused to back down. I would do whatever it took to keep Avery out of that helicopter. I hadn't been training with Sergio for nothing. I could fight Adrestus. Even if I lost, Wesley and Naomi might still be able to get Avery to safety.

Adrestus's sword glinted in the firelight as he raised it to Avery's neck.

"I thought you might be joining us," Adrestus called out, and I stumbled to stop in the gravel drive, breathing heavily and locking eyes with Avery's terrified grimace. "I think there's been a bit of a misunderstanding between us, Eydis, and I hate to threaten your nephew, but I'm afraid there is little else that might make you think."

Fire crackled and snapped, filling the static in my head. I was horrifically outnumbered, though most of the Apex flanking Adrestus appeared battle-worn and tired. A strangled cry overhead brought my attention upwards, and Wesley dropped from the sky, landing hard on the ashy remains of the lawn.

Mira stepped forward and crouched next to him, taking a handful of his hair in hand and holding him against the ash. He groaned in pain as she pulled his head back, as if to allow him to better watch the proceedings. The winged woman landed next to them and folded her wings against her back.

"You're confused, Eydis." Adrestus kept his tone even and low. "These people aren't who they say they are. Please, I'm not here to hurt you. I'm here to rescue you."

"He's lying!" Naomi's shoulder bumped mine as she pushed forward to take up the space between Adrestus and me. Thin metal glittered in her hand as she brandished a long needle ahead of herself like a sword.

Adrestus lowered his blade away from Avery's neck, and a blond man stepped forward to pull my brother away.

"Careful, child," Adrestus crooned. Curiosity and amusement mingled on his face as he studied the needle in Naomi's hands. "That could put someone's eyes out, and I haven't many to spare."

"I'd be more worried about losing your immortality than your eye." Naomi's voice shook, but she held the needle steady.

"Oh?" His grin widened. "And what risk might you pose to my immortality? Pray tell, before I get bored and decide to see how well your needle holds up against my blade."

Adrestus gave his sword a gaudy twirl, but Naomi held firm, unintimidated.

"Everly figured it out using samples of blood affected by the Lapis. He reverse engineered the cellular mechanisms he observed to create something to counteract the immortality and then coupled it with a potent poison." From my vantage point on the ground, I could see the corner of Naomi's mouth turn up in a grin. "One prick, and even you will die."

Adrestus, however, threw his head back and laughed. His followers gave each other nervous glances, as if unsure if they should join in, and Adrestus took up pacing in front of Naomi. She turned herself to keep the needle pointed at him as he moved.

"That's impressive if true, though I doubt it. The first Lapis took years to create and perfect. One man couldn't reverse engineer that in a mere matter of months."

"Everly could. He did." Naomi's grin slipped into something more like a grimace. "He made a prototype designed to block the Epsilon Gene rather than immortality, and I can attest to its effectiveness firsthand."

"Naomi?" Wesley's gasp sounded behind me. "You didn't. Say you didn't."

"It's not permanent." Naomi gulped, keeping her eyes on Adrestus.

"You didn't sense Adrestus when he arrived at the camp," Wesley said slowly. "And when Everly...you didn't..."

"Yes, Wesley, I know. We can talk about it later, okay?" Naomi said through gritted teeth.

Adrestus stopped his pacing to survey Naomi carefully. The crease in his brow betrayed the first hint of unease I'd seen grace his face since his appearance at the camp.

"I'll be damned. Perhaps Jacobi Everly was more valuable than I gave him credit for." He flashed Mira a disapproving glare. "Next time, try not to murder anyone who might come in handy. The nurse may have been a genius, but assets are useless to me dead."

"Jacobi what?"

I didn't know how long Fleming had been standing on the porch, hidden by the wall of flame. He leaned against a wooden post that supported the porch eave, clutching at the wound in his abdomen and staring at me through the fire with an expression that begged me to tell him it wasn't true. Everly wasn't dead.

"There he is!" Adrestus clapped. "It's about time you joined us, you've been cooped up inside for so long I thought you might be dead, too."

"You're a liar." Fleming let go of the post and staggered forward on the porch as far as the flames would allow. Andersen came out of the house behind him, his face orange in the light of the fire.

"Look, with everything coming to light, I'm just as cut up as you about it!" Adrestus put up his hands in a show of good faith. "I've tried for centuries to recreate the Lapis, and the one man who might've been capable of it is dead on my watch."

"Everly saved us." My voice was hoarse and barely audible even to myself, but Fleming must've been able to read lips. The color drained from his face.

"Have you not been listening? Dear Eydis, I told you I was here to rescue you, did I? Jacobi Everly was not your friend. He was trying to kill you."

I faltered. He was lying, but why did he seem so sincere?

"That's not true."

"Come with me, and I'll explain everything," Adrestus promised. "Your adoptive mother, she'll help explain. She and Trev Baker should be safe on New Delos by now, I'd think. Gregor, any word on that?"

The blond man holding Avery nodded solemnly, and my heart skipped a beat.

"If you do anything to Alison I'll—" Fleming roared.

"You'll what? Cower on a porch while children fight your battles for you out here?" Adrestus gestured towards Naomi, Wesley, and me.

"Amanda, Andersen, do it now!" Fleming cried. The flames split, and Fleming leapt from the porch. With a flick of Andersen's wrist, the sword in Adrestus's hand zipped into the air, rising to meet Fleming.

Fleming caught the blade midair and brought it back down in a swooping arch that carved a path of red through Adrestus's chest.

The warrior fell to his knees, and as his followers rushed to close in on Fleming where he stood triumphant, Adrestus held up a stalling hand.

"Stay back," he warned, staring up at Fleming with an unnerving ease. The dark of his thin body armor only did so much to hide the seeping of blood beneath the fabric.

I stepped forward, taking the needle from Naomi, and joined Fleming's side.

"Is everyone okay inside?" I asked.

"They will be," Fleming replied through gritted teeth, and I held the needle out, mirroring the way Fleming held the sword to Adrestus's neck.

"Nobody intervene," Adrestus warned his followers in a low voice, still unfettered by the gash in his chest. "Eydis, I'm not against you. We've always been on the same team."

"He's a liar. You know he is." The sword shook in Fleming's hand.

"Who are you going to listen to?" Adrestus asked. "The one who came to rescue you, or the ones who want you dead?"

My hand tightened around the needle.

"You killed Everly."

"Everly *made* the weapon in your hand!" His face softened with pity. "Who do you think they were going to test it on? We're the same, Eydis! As long as they are against me, they are against both of us!"

"She stabbed me!" I pointed the needle at Mira where she still stood over Wesley.

"Sure, Mira got a bit overzealous in her methods, but she knew you couldn't die! In fact, if you actually sat down to talk with her over dinner, you'd be surprised at how well the two of you would get along." Adrestus kept his hand up, signaling for his followers to stand back. "Just because your captors may seem kinder does not mean they are your friends."

"They cared for me," I said through gritted teeth. "They gave me a place to stay and taught me to fight."

"Even lab rats are fed and kept in comfortable cages. A complacent lab rat is a good lab rat, and what were you if not a test subject for their little poison? I'll admit, they've done an excellent job at convincing you that they actually care about your safety."

"Her safety is our number one priority," Fleming snarled, and Adrestus scoffed.

"Which is why Roy Hendricks was so quick to offer her up? Tell me, Eydis, would an adult who cared about you do that?"

"You called me naive," I reminded him.

"Yes, you'd have to be to fall for their tricks *again*! The girl there even admitted it. They created the poison in your hands using blood exposed to the Life Elixir. They used you to create a weapon that would kill you because they don't believe either of us belong in this century."

Goosebumps erupted over my arms, and I looked towards Naomi. She shook her head vehemently.

"We'd never use your blood without your permission!" she insisted.

"Then how did you make this?" I shook the needle, my panic rising. Adrestus was the villain, so why was he making sense?

"From me." Wesley's voice quaked behind me, and my beating heart rose another inch up into my throat. "I had a bit left after—"

"You helped them make a weapon to kill me?"

"No! They said it would help stop Adrestus, I—"

"You can't believe that," Adrestus tutted. "We're the same. They know that. Why else would they have erased your memories?"

He looked up at Fleming accusingly.

"You took her memories," Fleming asserted. "The same way you took Everly and everything else."

"I did not, but don't take my word for it." Adrestus panned his gaze over to Avery and the blond man he'd called Gregor. "Perhaps the young Mr. Havardson can shed some light on the matter."

Avery rasped out a response, and I lowered the needle to stare at him. His brown eyes were round as the full moon that had watched the carnage of the preceding night.

"Convenient of you, asking the boy who can't speak to back you up," Fleming snarled.

But as I shook my head in disbelief at my brother, I remembered the way he'd broken down in the forest, and I remembered the single word he'd written in the dirt.

Sorry.

"Oh, but Eydis knows now, doesn't she?" Adrestus murmured. "You can see it on her face. Avery took her memories, and he called me here to return them to her."

"No," Fleming said. "He—"

"He did," I breathed. The entire world had flipped. We'd spent so many hours trying to restore my memories, but we could've spent a lifetime trying and it never would've worked, because it was *Avery's fault.*

And the others, they must've known. How could they not? Like Adrestus had said, a complacent lab rat was a good lab, and that was all I was.

A test subject, a mechanism by which they could defeat Adrestus.

"You're wondering now if they knew," Adrestus whispered. "If Jacobi Everly was in on it, too. If he'd been the one to ask Avery to erase your memories so you wouldn't fight back. So you'd be easier to manipulate and slaughter."

"Everly would never!" Fleming roared and lifted the blade, arching it towards Adrestus's bare neck.

"No!" I screamed. Nothing made sense anymore, but I knew Adrestus knew the truth. Adrestus was the only one I could trust to make sense of the last three months I'd been kept in the darkness and whatever secrets my consciousness was suppressing from before that.

Because it *had* been Avery all along and Everly *had* built a weapon that could kill me, and regardless of who I could trust, those two things I knew to be true, and that was enough for me to not let Fleming kill Adrestus.

I raised the needle as I tackled Fleming to the ground. He dropped the sword in shock, and I swung down with the only weapon I had on hand.

"Sammy, no!"

A sudden force ripped me away from Fleming moments before the needle could pierce the skin of his neck, and I was met with Wesley's bare torso and his arms around me.

"Fall back!" Adrestus bellowed. "Leave the girl! Eydis knows the truth now, it's up to her to decide what she does next!"

"Get off me!" I beat against Wesley's chest and slipped from his grasp. I tackled him around the middle, the same way I'd tackled him the day on the beach, forcing him to the gravel with a hand on his throat. He went slack under me, giving up the fight. "You've been against me this whole time!"

"No, I—"

"You helped them build a weapon to kill me!"

SUVs peeled out of the driveway, but crunching metal told me Andersen's powers hadn't let them escape far. Screams and orders echoed into the early morning.

"Into the woods!" one of them cried, and the overbearing roar of helicopter rotors revved to life.

"Sammy. Sorry, Samantha." Wesley shook his head against the gravel. "We're on your side! Adrestus is lying to you."

"Adrestus didn't erase my memories!"

"Neither did I!"

"You helped them build a weapon to kill me!"

"I swear I didn't know what they were working on! But I'm not going to let you murder Fleming. I won't let Trev Baker be right."

He could fight me if he wanted. He would win if he did. I may have had him pinned against the dirt, but we both knew it was because he was letting me hold him there.

But why? Why wouldn't he fight back?

The flickering light of the fire played against the edges and valleys of a V-shaped scar on Wesley's sternum.

I froze, every muscle still tensed as I gingerly traced the scar with a single finger.

"Sammy?" His fingers wrapped around my wrist, and he pulled my hand back.

"Where did you get that?"

"It's a burn mark," he gasped. "From your necklace."

"How?" I demanded.

"You have one, too," he said. My heart hammered in my chest just behind where my own scar burned into my skin. Why did Wesley and I have matching scars?

"You can trust me. You *need* to trust me."

But I couldn't trust anyone.

"They're taking Avery!" Andersen's cry snapped my attention to the helicopter. Andersen fell to his knees with his shaking arms outstretched, tethering the machine to the earth with his kinetic powers, but his grip was slipping, and I watched in horror as Avery wrestled against the blond man in the open cab. His mouth formed my name.

I abandoned Wesley in the dirt and sprinted for the helicopter struggling to lift off against Andersen's hold. Avery clawed at the air in the open cab, trying to escape from Adrestus's grip on his shirt collar.

"Avery!" I fought against the helicopter's wind and through the tangle of hair in my face. "Give him back!"

I pushed off the ground with every last bit of energy I had left, and my elbow hooked around the helicopter's landing ski while my legs dangled beneath me. Someone yelled behind me, but the blades overhead were too loud for me to make out their words.

And even as the ground got farther away below me as Andersen's kinetic grip weakened, I knew I was so *close*. Avery was *right* there.

Avery reached out for me through the open cabin, trying to call my name. Frustrated tears spilled down his face.

It had been Avery. It had been Avery all along, but I realized I didn't care. He was still my brother, and I wouldn't let anyone take him. I reached towards him even though I didn't have the strength to climb. I'd lost too much this night to lose him, too.

His eyes cleared, and his brows furrowed in concentration. He mouthed a single word.

Remember.

Remember.

Warmth sprang behind my eyes, and my heart threatened to choke me where it beat in my throat. My grip broke. I slipped from the landing ski, falling back into open air.

A lifetime burst in my mind, and I was everywhere at once.

I felt cold nights under an aurora, warmed by the laughter of my sisters. The touch of moss beneath bare feet as waterfalls roared. A pale boy with black hair and blue eyes on a gray beach insisting he could help. My sword in his gut after he'd slain my family.

And I was on a ferryboat, watching a colossal man of bronze materialize in the fog, and then I was puking on someone's shoes. I hid under a table. A car trunk closed overhead. I was on a cold floor as a knife dug behind my collarbone. A broken fencing foil pierced my abdomen. Fire melted a Paragon statue while a man stood in front of me in a wet peacoat with his arms outstretched. I was falling in a lightning storm. A blade pushed through my father's chest.

I stood on a windy bluff as night swallowed the bay. Three words rang out.

Just forget it.

Arms smacked against my back, and a body buckled beneath me, absorbing the force of my fall.

"Samantha." They set me down in the gravel as gently as they could. "I'm sorry. I'm so sorry, I—"

I'd failed. Overhead, the helicopter shrank into the sky, and numb shock buzzed in my head as I took in the green eyes glittering with tears above me.

"Wes?" I struggled to my knees, keeping my eyes transfixed on him.

Wes.

How could I have forgotten Wes? His face broke, and his hand shook as he reached slowly and gently for my cheek.

"Sammy?"

I nodded weakly into his palm. His lips twitched, and I thought he might smile, but then stabbing, unbearable pain shot through my head. Whatever was keeping me grounded to the earth snapped. I slumped against Wesley's chest, feeling his arms wrap around me as darkness rushed in.

17

Aftermath

The dull ache of my back dragged me into the world of the waking. I shifted in bed, trying to shake the stiffness that had settled over what felt like every muscle. My head throbbed like it had been filled with sand, and my brain was heavy and muddled.

Voices whispered down the hall, but I couldn't make out what they were saying. I pried my eyes open, and the dark room took shape around me. It had to be the middle of the night, but I didn't feel tired.

I groaned as I pushed myself up to swing my feet over the bedside. Whatever I had been dreaming about had left a bad taste in my mouth, though the details were fuzzy at best and already slipping away.

My stomach growled, and I smacked my lips, trying to wet my sandpaper-dry tongue. When I stood up to venture to the kitchen for a late night snack, however, my knees buckled as if surprised by my weight. I caught myself on the bedside table, but my head spun with the room. I closed my eyes until it stopped and then pushed myself back to my feet.

The barren white walls of the hallway outside my room were lit only by the living room light down the corridor. The carpet felt freshly cleaned and soft beneath my feet, and I kept a hand on the wall in case my legs gave out again.

"What if it doesn't work?" The voice was gruff and deep, and reassurance blossomed in my chest like a late winter flower. *Dad.*

"It will," a more feminine voice assured him.

"And everything is all set?" Dad asked.

"Val and Roy finished moving the house in yesterday, and we have our ferry reservation booked. We'll be fine."

"And you're sure this is the safest place?"

"Vic, I'd stake our lives on it. There hasn't been a legitimate threat to the city since before Paul died."

Dad snorted.

"And his brother—"

"Alex will watch over her. I promise. He's never failed me."

"You haven't seen the man in nearly fifteen years."

"It's Alex. He was always—"

"Yes, I know, he was always the best of you. But is he the best for her?"

"You'll get a few days with her before we leave. It'll be okay."

The couch was the only piece of furniture left in the living room. Everything else had already been packed and taken to the new house on New Delos. Dad and Mom sat on it with their backs to me, their heads bowed towards each other.

"Dad?" My voice came out raspy, as if I hadn't used it a long time, though I couldn't have been asleep for more than a few hours.

Dad twisted around on the couch, his face going slack behind his tawny beard.

"Eyd— Sammy!" He stood up cautiously. "You're awake."

"Sorry." I hugged my shoulders and glanced to the kitchen. I was starving, but the thought of food made my stomach roll. "I think I might be sick."

"Right." He nodded. "Come here. Let's get you some water."

He led me into the kitchen. Despite the late hour, he was still in his jeans and button-up. He pulled a bottled water from the fridge.

"Thanks." I twisted the top off, and he watched me in a way that made me think he'd never seen someone open a bottle of water before. "What?"

"Nothing. You said you didn't feel well?" He pressed the back of his hand against my forehead, and his storm gray eyes narrowed in concern. "Alison, she's warm. Why is she warm?"

Mom lingered in the kitchen entryway, her blonde hair braided over one shoulder and her hands wringing.

"Symptoms are to be expected, all things considered." She gave me a warm smile as I took a swig of water.

"I'm fine, and you're both being weird," I said. "Stop it."

Mom laughed, but Dad continued to look worried.

"You're sure?" he asked. I nodded, drinking more water, but then my head buzzed, and the kitchen spun.

A moment later I was staring at the ceiling from Dad's arms. He'd caught me just before I'd hit the ground, and water gurgled as it emptied from the fallen bottle.

"Alison, help!" he cried. "Something's wrong!"

"She's fine." Mom hurried to my side, and together, she and Dad set me back on my feet. "See? Just a stomach bug. Let's go back to bed, alright? We've got a big week ahead of us."

We shuffled back down the hall, and Dad hovered close behind me, ready for another dizzy spell. The door opened to my right, and a messy blond head stuck out from inside.

"Sammy?" Avery said sleepily. Mom and Dad froze, and I waved weakly at him. "Why's everyone awake?"

"It's alright, Avery, go back to sleep," Mom said gently.

"But Sammy's up. It's not fair that Sammy gets to be up but not me."

"I'm older than you," I teased.

"Sammy's going back to bed," Mom explained.

"But—"

"Goodnight, Avery."

Dad followed me to my bed with a fresh bottle of water.

"Sorry," I mumbled, crawling back under my sheets. "I didn't mean to scare you."

His beard scratched my forehead as he bent to kiss it.

"It's okay, kid. Everything's good now."

He snuck back to the hall and hesitated in the doorway. It was too dark for me to read his face.

"What?"

"Nothing," he said. "I just missed you, and this is weird."

I laughed into my pillow.

"You're the weird one," I said, already feeling sleep pulling me back into its clutches.

"Yeah," he chuckled. "I suppose I am."

He closed the door, and I fell back into darkness.

"Dad!"

I sat upright in bed, pushing quilts off of me. Midday light streamed in through the window. My chest heaved with labored breaths, and I looked around my bedroom. The events leading up to my black-out flooded back.

I leaned over the bedside and retched, but there was nothing in my stomach to vomit. Everything hurt. My head was splitting, and sharp pains radiated from my abdomen. Val, Avery, Mom, Everly. I pressed a hand over my mouth, willing the scream I felt building in my chest to stay down.

Something crashed outside, and I peeked behind the window curtain. Andersen stood in the driveway with a white bandage wrapped around his head. Three cars in varying degrees of destruction lay around him. One grated against the ground and creaked as it righted itself. Andersen bent over with his hands on his knees to catch his breath.

Andersen who'd hated me for puking on his girlfriend's shoes and stealing his favorite seat in class. Andersen who'd murdered me. Andersen who'd saved my life several times.

I raised a shaky hand to my mouth.

I remembered Andersen.

They were there. My memories. All of them. Or, the real ones at least. Not just from my time on New Delos, either. Iceland was there, too. Eydis and Samantha had both been crammed back inside my head.

I was both of them, again. I was *me.*

Fresh bile forced its way up my throat.

The door slammed open and hands grabbed my hair, pulling it up out of my face as I heaved onto the floor.

"Sammy?" Naomi asked, wrapping a tie around my hair. "It's you, right?"

I wiped my mouth on the back of my hand and straightened up to look at my friend. She'd changed into a set of Amanda's jeans and flannel, but her face was still streaked with dirt. Her hungry eyes searched my face for traces of her friend.

I fell into her arms, and she held me. I'd been without my friends for so long.

"Avery," I cried. "He—"

"I know." She patted the back of my head, and hot tears fell onto my shoulder.

"And Everly's—"

"Yeah." She squeezed me tighter.

"Is everyone else—"

"They're fine." She pulled away and wiped her face. "Everyone here at least. We haven't been to the camps yet."

I struggled to my feet.

"Take it easy, okay?" she insisted. "We gave you more Serum, but you haven't eaten in a while."

I grimaced at the bruises that had been added to the insides of my elbows. Andersen either had a long way to go before he reached Everly's caliber of IV administration or he needed to avoid poking people with needles while concussed.

"You built a weapon that could kill me." I looked out the window. Dad's statue sat on the top of the bluff, and seeing it there was like a fresh sword blow to my spleen. I was waking up from a bad dream into a nightmare. Dad was dead, and the months I'd lost mourning him pressed in on me.

"I did," Naomi admitted. "Or I at least helped. But your memories are back now. You know we'd never—"

"It's fine." I gave her a weary smile. "I would've helped, too, if Everly had let me in on it."

Everly. My hands shook at the memory of how his body had collapsed amid dust and ash. I wondered if he was still there.

"Sammy, how do you do it?" Naomi croaked. She sat back on my bed, tugging on a braid.

"Do what?"

"It's so quiet," she whispered. "I thought I hated how loud everyone's feelings were, but now, I can finally hear mine clearly, and they're so much louder. I can't bear it."

She bent over her lap and pressed her hands over her ears. I pulled her into another hug.

"You'll get used to it," I promised. "And it isn't always like this. Somedays, the good emotions are the loud ones."

"But it's so lonely," she gasped between heavy breaths.

"That's normal," I mumbled into her hair.

"And Everly..."

I held her tighter. Without Everly, I wasn't sure we'd ever feel whole again.

"I'm sorry," she cried. "You just got back, and I'm immediately a mess."

"What's neat is that now I can remember all the times you comforted me when I was the mess," I said. The door creaked open, and I looked over Naomi's shoulder.

Wesley looked small in the t-shirt Fleming had loaned him, and the bags under his eyes were heavy. His left hand gripped his right arm where red plastic met skin, and he gulped.

"Hey, Samantha."

My stomach clenched, and I put a hand over the healed remains of my stab wound.

"Oh my god, stop lurking, you ghoul." Naomi leaned over to pull Wesley into our embrace. I sank into their arms, finally feeling like maybe things could be okay despite all that still went unsaid between us. I was with my friends again. I remembered all the times they'd helped me and been there for me, and my cheeks burned with shame at the thought of having doubted them.

Naomi broke free first, pretending to push braids away from her face as she wiped her eyes.

"I need to check on Joni." She forced a grin and pointed to the wood floor on her way out the door. "You might want to clean that up."

I grimaced at the pool of stomach bile.

"I've got it." Wesley reached for a box of tissues on my dresser. I tried to stop him, but he ignored my attempts. I drew my feet up onto my bed, still in the black underclothes of the team uniform.

My team uniform.

"Thanks," I said. "Are you okay without your glasses?"

He looked up from the trash bin to finally look at me. There were new creases in Wesley's face I hadn't noticed before. His eyes and mouth had harder lines, and his jaw was clenched in a way that signaled something more than the usual migraine brought on by forgoing his glasses for too long.

"Yeah. I mean, no, but it's okay. Andersen's checking to see if any of the cars are drivable. I'll get my glasses back once we return to camp."

He was avoiding my eye again, instead scanning my bedroom walls that I'd papered with old sketches. For the first time in months, I was close to him in a way that counted for something, but he seemed miles away, walled off by some invisible barrier that was still keeping us apart.

I stood up from the bed and stepped forward mechanically. If I didn't knock down whatever wall stood between us now, I wasn't sure I'd ever find my way back to what Wesley and I once had.

"Sammy, what—?"

I buried my face in his chest and balled his shirt in fists against his back. He kept his arms out to the side for a startled moment, but then he was squeezing me, holding me under his chin. He'd gotten so tall.

"Thank you." My voice was muffled against his shirt.

"For what?"

"For not letting me murder Fleming."

He cleared his throat and looked out at Andersen in the driveway.

"Nah, don't mention it. It was less about you and more about not wanting to listen to Trev Baker gloat about being right."

I sighed, but the borrowed shirt pressed against my face didn't smell like him and didn't quite fill the space in my chest like I wanted it to.

"I missed you," I admitted.

"You didn't remember me." He tried to laugh, but the sound caught in his throat.

"I still missed you. I just didn't know it."

His hand pressed against the back of my head.

"I missed you, too. And I'm glad you're back."

"It was Avery," I said into his collar. "He was able to get my memories back at the end."

Wesley tensed in my arms.

"But why would he erase them in the first place?"

"Doesn't matter."

"And Andersen. If he actually murdered you—"

"Definitely doesn't matter."

Wesley pried me away, holding me by the shoulder with his prosthesis while his other hand pushed hair behind my ear.

"It *definitely* matters."

"I walked in on him in the bathroom that one time, so I think he and I are even now." I pulled Wesley back towards me to hide against his chest. "Oh my god, I *walked in* on Andersen in the *bathroom*. I could've done without that one coming back."

Another car slammed outside.

"I'm serious, Sammy. Why didn't you say anything?"

I craned my head back to look up at Wesley's red-rimmed eyes.

"Can we table Andersen murdering me for now?"

There was too much to process. Avery and Mom were captured. Everly was—

"Yeah. We'll talk about it later. Sammy, I'm...I missed you, too, but you should go see Fleming."

I scowled, wanting to disappear back into Wesley's shirt.

"He's gonna be weird."

"He's not okay."

"Right." For all the times Fleming had been there for me, I wasn't sure I knew how to be there for him. "Fine."

We tiptoed down the stairs together, and Wesley gave my hand a final squeeze before slipping outside to help Andersen. Amanda and Brooke held each other on the couch.

Brooke was pallid, and her neck still bruised, but she appeared better off than Amanda, whose face was swollen and blotchy from crying. Her mom was dead, I remembered. She would've heard the news by now.

I gave them their privacy and shuffled into the kitchen at the sound of a teapot whistling. Fleming stood over the stovetop and looked over his shoulder with heavy, dead eyes.

"You're awake. In more ways than one, I hear."

"Yeah." I hugged myself and looked sideways at the box of tea.

The first day of class. A guardianship form with his signature. A screaming match in the empty street of a sinking city.

"Good. Good." He nodded, and his mug quaked. He stayed the shaking by holding it with both hands. "I, uh— Well. Welcome back."

Christmas stockings. His voice calling for me on a crowded boardwalk. Crying in his arms next to Vidar's lifeless body.

Amanda and Brooke's low murmurs drifted into the kitchen, and Fleming's throat bobbed as he threw back tea that I knew was still too hot.

"Pack a bag." He forced a casual air into his tone. "Once Brooke is feeling up to it, we're headed to the camp. Depending on what we find there, we might not be coming back."

He set his mug down, still mostly full, and made to exit the kitchen with his head down, as if that might hide the tears on his cheeks.

"I'm sorry." I could only whisper. If I talked any louder, my voice might've betrayed my grief, too. I looked up at him, and his lips pressed together in an attempt to keep his chin from trembling.

I didn't know the first thing about comforting people, especially not the man who'd been forced into the role of quasi-guardian of an immortal Viking child hellbent on messing up everything she touched, but Fleming's shoulders relaxed.

"You don't have to comfort me, Sammy. I'll be alright."

"You shouldn't be sad alone."

He rested a hand on my shoulder.

"He would be very proud of you," he murmured.

"I almost killed you last night."

"And he would've been so impressed." His hand dropped away, and he stalked down the hall to his room with his head low, trying to hide the shaking of his shoulders.

As crowded as the SUV was, it was quiet. Insufficient seating forced Naomi, Joni, and me into the open trunk. I clutched a backpack of my few belongings, trying to keep my pet fish Floundersen's travel tank still as the car wound down the road.

We stopped at the scene of our crash from the night before, but Winnie was no longer in the wreckage where Naomi and Wesley had left her. Amanda's face was unreadable as she climbed the bank back to the road.

As we continued down the road, my stomach became unsettled, but I wasn't sure if it was unease at what we were headed towards or motion sickness. I turned to face forward in the trunk, holding onto Wesley's seat back as we turned down the forested road that led to the camp.

Dense fog and hazy smoke drifted through the trees, making the forest seem thicker. When we cleared the tree line, the haze lingered, lying over the grounds. Angry, black burn scars cut through the lawn in a mosaic of mottled patterns, and the main house loomed out of the mist, still standing, though half of it had been burnt out.

"Nobody's here," Wesley whispered. "They must all be at the neighboring camp."

The car shuddered to a halt, and we filed out in silence. The heavy fog suppressed all sound except that of the waves against the beach, though the ocean was invisible through the clouds. Fleming stood at the front of the car, facing the half-burnt building with his arms limp at his side. As we walked to join him, we saw the form lying on the ground, still in his lavender scrubs, right where Mira had left him.

Fleming staggered forward. Joni shook her head, and Naomi drew her closer. Wesley grabbed my fingers, and I searched for whatever comfort our shoulders brushing together might bring me.

Fleming dropped to his knees on the burnt grass, and a faint, angry hiss issued from Everly's body. An orange head reared up from the crook of Everly's arm and batted his little paw at Fleming. Everly may have been abandoned, but Tonka had watched over him through the night.

"Please," Fleming said softly to the cat, "it's okay. I'm his friend."

He bowed his head, and Tonka curled up on Everly's chest, no longer hissing, but his tail swished apprehensively.

"Someone's coming," Wesley warned. We looked to our left, and figures took shape in the smoke and haze.

"Friends?" Amanda growled.

"Not the word I'd use, but yes."

Flecks of flame gave shape to the wisps of fog and illuminated the shape of a man striding towards us.

"You aren't welcome here, Alex!" a voice boomed.

Embers danced off Amanda's fingertips. The firelight in the fog flared in response, and Roy Hendricks stepped out of the mist.

18

Housekeeping

Embers on either side of the driveway sparked into the fog like fireflies, and Amanda marched to meet her father.

"You left him in the dirt?" she demanded. "Is Mom out here in the cold, too? Did you leave her behind?"

"Your mother has been cremated." A new voice said, and two more figures emerged from the fog next to Roy. The woman who'd spoken was taller than Roy, and her hair hung over one shoulder in box braids similar to Naomi's. It had been a while since I'd seen the head of the University team, but Professor Parker hadn't changed much.

"Cremated?" Amanda's fires snuffed out, and Brooke stumbled forward to take her hand. "Without me? But she can't burn."

"Everybody burns." Roy sniffed. "Even your mother in the end. And you weren't here. Maybe if you'd never quit the team—"

"This isn't the time, Roy," Fleming said, still kneeling in the dirt, staring at his friend.

"We heard the car and came to make sure it wasn't Adrestus." The third figure crossed the drive to join Fleming. Her short, gray hair lacked its usual luster, and with her neck bruised and her arm in a sling, Coach Reiner was in the roughest shape of the three adults who'd joined us.

"Were you just going to leave him here?" Fleming asked.

"We hadn't had the chance to retrieve him yet," Parker said softly. "We'll take him back now. Your students will be relieved to see you."

Mr. Hendricks balked, but Parker ignored him, joining Fleming and Reiner.

"My wife is dead because of them," Mr. Hendricks fumed. "And you want to take them in?"

"Where else can they go?" Parker snapped.

"That's not our problem. Let Alison figure that out when she and Trev return!" He faltered at the looks on our faces.

"Adrestus has them," I said. "And Avery, too."

Mr. Hendricks stared at me, unflinching.

"You did this," he murmured. "All of it."

"Roy, if you'd like to continue to be welcome at *my* camp, you'll stop," Parker warned. "Otherwise, feel free to stay here."

"The door, Andersen," Fleming said. Naomi stroked the top of Tonka's head until the tabby let her scoop him into her arms. Andersen opened the car as instructed, then hurried to help Fleming and Reiner lift Everly in their arms. I turned away, unable to watch. With both Eydis's and Samantha's memories back in my head, I didn't think I could take anymore bodies.

Roy walked back to the university camp alone while I followed the brake lights of the SUV across a foggy field spotted with birch trees. It was difficult to make out the neighboring camp through the mist, and as far as I could tell, it looked a lot like the high school camp, but with more buildings that were closer together.

Wesley walked beside me, and six months worth of unspoken words bubbled in my throat, but our somber march didn't seem fit for conversation. Instead, I tried to focus on Naomi and Joni walking hand in hand ahead of us as we slipped through the mist-woven trees like ghosts.

Reiner and Fleming beat us to the camp and parked in front of a mess hall built of logs. A tarp whipped in the wind on the building's side where it covered a gaping hole, though the camp seemed to have otherwise escaped greater damage in the night's attack.

The people who gathered around the SUV didn't look so lucky. Injuries ranged from black eyes to splinted legs, and unless the university team had a large cache of Serum hiding somewhere, our backpack of remaining fluid would never stretch enough for everyone.

"Holy crap, Sammy, you're okay." Sergio broke from the group to pull me into a hug. The sudden familiarity of his embrace had little to do with my returned memories of him and everything to do with remembering what it felt like to have older brothers a thousand years ago.

"I'm at least doing better than you'll be next time we spar." I gave a broken laugh. "You don't stand a chance now that I remember all my old tricks."

Sergio pushed me away to gawk at me. His glass eye always caught me off guard with how life-like it looked.

"You're kidding." He looked to Wesley for confirmation, who nodded. Sergio's tired face broke in a grin. "It's gonna be so embarrassing for you when you still lose."

A wail issuing from the center of the crowd cut our reunion short, and Sergio's face fell. Cries rippled out from the SUV.

"I didn't want to believe it," Sergio murmured. "But he's really..."

The crowd cleared a path, making way for Fleming and Reiner. Soft gasps followed in their wake as the students crowded to get a better look and confirm for themselves that the man who'd put us all back on our feet at some point or another was indeed gone.

We followed the crowd into the pavilion mess hall, but Fleming and Reiner disappeared with Everly's body into a back room. Families huddled together along the long tables while Roy and Professor Parker conversed on a raised dais at the front of the hall.

"Might as well sit," Naomi suggested and sank onto a table bench. Joni sat next to her and reached to take Floundersen's tank from my hands.

"Fish have simple feelings," she murmured, setting the tank on the table in front of her. "It's quieter when I focus on him."

Andersen took a seat at our table, too, though he was careful to leave several open spots between him and us.

"I'm going to kill him," Amanda was saying as she and Brooke joined us. Her eyes were red with tears and rage. "I will. I'll do it."

"I know," Brooke assured her.

"Dead less than a day," Amanda spat. "I bet he cremated her just to see if he could make her burn. She was the one person he couldn't hurt, and he hated that about her."

She glared at her father where he stood on the dais, and I absolutely believed that Amanda had what it took to murder him. However, patricide would have to wait because Fleming and Reiner returned from the backroom. Reiner joined Parker, and their heads bobbed as they spoke.

Fleming fell into the seat at the far end of our table, and Wesley leaned towards him.

"What happens now?" he asked. Fleming raised steely eyes to Dr. Parker and pressed his lips together as he watched the University team leader step forward.

"Since you're all here, now's as good a time as any to take care of some housekeeping." Dr. Parker's voice carried through the room, and the whispers fell silent. "Unfortunately, I'm sorry to officially announce that Nurse Jacobi Everly died in last night's attack. In keeping with his Jewish tradition, we will bury him tonight before twenty-four hours have passed since his departure. All are welcome to attend."

Everly's passing was no longer news, but the announcement still drove stakes of ice through my chest. Joni hunkered lower, narrowing her eyes at Floundersen, as soft cries wafted through the pavilion. Naomi put a protective arm over her shoulders.

"In the meantime," Dr. Parker continued, "we cannot stay here. The McDougall family has graciously invited us to their family ranch, but the trip will be long, and we'll have to leave the camp in waves to avoid detection. The first group will depart early tomorrow morning."

Dismayed shouts rose from the crowd. The families who'd taken refuge here had already uprooted their lives once. Now that Adrestus knew where they were, they'd be forced to leave again.

"That's not all," Roy prompted behind her.

"No, it isn't," Parker admitted through a strained smile. "Not everyone will be going to the ranch. Those of us in fighting condition will be returning to New Delos—"

Roars erupted from angered parents as well as from students hungry for blood.

"*If* they are legally of age or are able to secure parent permission!" Dr. Parker tried to shout over the crowd.

"And if our parents are prisoners?" Isabelle stood up, her long hair flurrying in a burst of wind.

"We'll discuss it. We need all hands helping to break camp. Report to your Team Captains if you'd like to be on the team headed to New Delos. Otherwise, assignments will be posted later tonight."

I whipped my head around to look at Fleming. Parker's directive didn't include us. We weren't with the team anymore, but I wasn't about to become a refugee, not when my mom, brother, and friends were Adrestus's prisoners. If anyone was going back to New Delos, I would be sure I was among them.

Fleming avoided my gaze, though his furrowed brow told me he knew I was looking at him.

"High school team, stay." Roy held a hand up for attention, and the high school team members slowly sank back into their seats, casting each other nervous glances.

"What about us?" Andersen whispered. Fleming shushed him, and we followed his lead and remained seated as the families and college students climbed out from the benched tables and exited.

"Countless injuries. Four abductions. Two dead, including my wife," Roy thundered. "This is why we follow orders!"

He yelled the last two words. Joni put her hands over her ears.

"Had your teammates followed orders, they, along with Avery Havardson, might still be here." Roy's eyes found mine. "Nurse Everly would still be alive."

My stomach clenched. He had the *gall* to blame *us*?

"Moving forward, anyone who so much as breathes without permission will be off the team."

"Roy, don't be—" Dr. Parker tried to interject.

"It's my team."

"They're kids."

"I need the three captains up here to discuss assignments moving forward. The rest of you—"

"You mean the four captains," Justin interrupted. He'd been at my birthday, but with my memories intact, I felt like I was seeing him for the first time in months.

Roy grinned hungrily and squared his shoulders.

"No, I mean *three*." He gave Naomi a vindictive smile. "Apex who disobeyed orders to fall back and protect this camp last night are no longer on the team."

"*Roy*," Professor Parker hissed.

"It's *my* team, Diane. I get to kick out anyone I deem a liability."

Naomi and Wesley gave each other resigned glances, but Andersen clenched his fists and looked to Fleming for help.

"But where will we go?" he asked under his breath.

"New Delos," I said. It was the only answer, even if Fleming didn't want to admit it.

Roy beamed over his students.

"This means when we recover Remi, Anthony, and Hannah, they will *also* be off the team."

"Her name is Heather." Olivia's voice rang out over the crowd as she stood up.

"Sure." He nodded. "Heather. Whatever her name is, she's off the team."

Roy stepped off the dais to stalk down tables to the exit, leaving his students in a hushed silence.

"Then I am, too."

Roy froze and slowly turned back from where he stood at the pavilion doors. Olivia's chin stuck out in defiance.

"You won't be missed," Roy boomed. "Anyone else coward enough to walk away?"

"Me." Freddie's puff of hay-colored hair rose from the table. "I mean, I'm not a coward, but, you know."

Everest, whose black hair was now long enough to keep in a low half-ponytail, stood up next to him.

And the floodgates opened. Isabelle, Justin, Desirae and Mike, Marcus and Jen, then all of the rest, abandoned their seats, though I made note that Skyler, who had always hated me, was the last and scowled at the ceiling as he did.

Roy shook with poorly contained rage as he surveyed the students that had been his until a moment ago.

"You make me ashamed to be an Apex," he spat. "You would rather hide on a resort ranch than defend the world?"

"We'll go wherever Mr. Fleming decides we should go." Justin crossed his arms and stood resolute. Smoke curled off Roy's fingertips as he drew them into fists.

"You think you'll be safe with a Beta?" he snarled.

"Yes." Justin didn't waver.

"No." Fleming stood, his shoulders sagging but unmistakable pride written across his face. "You are all so strong and brave and deserve the world, but I don't have the resources necessary to lead you. I'm honored that you all think so highly of me, but I have nothing. With the team, you can still—"

"There is no team without you," Isabelle said.

"Perhaps we should discuss this outside?" Professor Parker, still on the dais, raised an eyebrow at Roy and Fleming. Behind her, Reiner watched with careful interest.

"I won't step down," Roy seethed. "And you can't make me without the other two thirds of the Apex Council. If Alex hadn't sent that screw-up of a child to our camp, both my wife and the medic would still be alive."

"You're going to call me the screw-up?" My words rang clear before I could contain them, and now that they were spilling out, I let the dam come crashing down. "Both your kids hate you. So does the team. You can blame me all you like for Everly's death, but I saw what happened, and you might as well have killed him."

Devastating silence fell over the hall, and Roy's shoulders heaved with angry breaths.

"Sammy, what do you mean?" Fleming asked.

"I mean Everly died because he was trying to stop Mr. Hendricks from handing me over to Adrestus."

Fleming's chair scraped against the wooden floor as he stood and strode across the room towards Roy. I braced, waiting for Fleming to hit him, but he stopped when his face was inches from Roy's.

"Tell me she's lying."

"I warned you if she became a liability, I'd hand her over. My wife died because of her. I was doing what I could to save the rest of us."

"Jacobi is dead because of you!" Fleming shoved Roy in the chest, and he stumbled back.

"Don't make me burn the rest of you, Alex. You don't have anyone left to put you back together."

Fleming's fist swung and a cocky half-smile tugged at Roy's face. A cry went up from the students, and I leaped to my feet, but Amanda was faster. Searing white flames erupted around Roy's outline, but before he could torch Fleming, Amanda pulled him back from her father's fire.

She grabbed Roy by the face, forcing her way through his flames, and threw him to the ground. He gasped for air, and his fire snuffed out as Amanda stood over him.

"You call them cowards, but the only coward here is you," she said. "Don't hide behind Mom's death when we both know you've resented her for years for only giving you one Apex child."

"And what a disappointment you turned out to be, throwing everything away for the sake of a Beta." Roy pushed himself to his knees to glare at Brooke. "If she hadn't needed Serum last night, Samantha never would've led that pack of murderers here."

"You don't get to talk about murderers," Fleming spat. "Not while your hands are painted in the blood of everyone I've ever cared about."

"Your failures are yours." Roy staggered back to his feet. "You hid in the shadow of your brother, letting him elevate you into something you never were and never will be. Eydis may have brought Adrestus here, but you're the one who allowed her on the team in the first place."

My heart stopped. Roy's eyes met mine, and a sinister curl tugged on his lips. He knew what he was doing. He knew what he'd done, and it didn't go unnoticed by the others.

"Eydis?" someone snorted. "Like the Scourge Queen?"

"Does he mean Samantha?"

"Okay, but not like *literally*, though, right?"

Wesley's hand found my knee under the table. I felt the stares of the room locked on me, but I couldn't look away from Fleming, whose face reflected my own panic back at me. I wasn't ready for everyone to know.

Fleming set his jaw and took a steady breath.

"I made my own way onto the team," he said, "and I became coach on nobody's merit but my own. If anyone used my brother Paragon to elevate themself, it was you."

The mutterings about Eydis ceased, sucked into a vacuum as the room instead tried to process Fleming's words. He'd kept his brother's identity so close to his chest for more than a decade, and now he was letting it go in a last-ditch effort to keep mine hidden.

"Wait." Mike stood next to his twin sister, and every face except Fleming's and Roy's turned to look at him, daring him to ask what everyone was thinking. "Your brother was Paragon?"

The room held its breath, and Fleming slowly turned away from Roy to face his former student.

"My brother's name was Paul Fleming," he said, "and yes, he was the hero known to New Delos as Paragon."

19

In The Ruins

Fleming braced himself for the thousands of questions the room was sure to have for him. Instead, a quiet reverence filled the space that only seemed to weigh on Fleming more.

"You think you can usurp me by throwing his name around when we both know I was more his prodigy than anyone?" Roy sneered.

"I'm not usurping you," Fleming frowned.

"What do you call this?" Roy gestured towards his students, a ball of flame rolling off his hand as he did. The students ducked as it bounced through the air before dissipating into smoke. "And now you invoke Paragon's name to solidify their misplaced allegiance!"

"My brother is not someone to revere." Fleming turned to address the room. "Anyone who follows me because they think my relationship to him gives me extra rank should know that is not the case. Paragon may have been a symbol of justice and safety, but Paul was as flawed as any man."

Justin raised a hand.

"All due respect to your brother, Mr. F," he said, "but we never knew Paragon. We know *you*, and if you aren't in charge of Apex Team, then we don't want to be on it."

I nodded along with Justin's words, as did most of the room. Fleming looked over us in stunned silence and pushed two fingers up behind his glasses lens to rub his eye. Roy lurched forward as if to try fighting Fleming again, but Amanda stepped between the men.

"I knew I had my work cut out for me when I took over a team that had been operating under Alex all this time, but never could I have imagined such staunch cowardice and blind, misguided loyalty." Roy turned back to Professor Parker, his visage warped by the waves of heat that rolled off of him. "That's it then. I quit."

He gave the team one last withering look, as if daring them to cheer for his departure, and when no one did, his last ounce of fight fled, apparent in his falling shoulders.

When the pavilion door slammed shut behind him, Dr. Parker cleared her throat.

"Looks like your old position has opened back up, Alex."

Mike clapped, but Fleming shook his head, and Mike's applause died.

"Students were hurt under my leadership. I quit because I believed myself unfit to lead. I stand by that." Angry cries interrupted him, and he was forced to wait for them to subside before continuing. "I knew no matter who replaced me, you all still had Nurse Everly. I don't know how to do this without him, but the last thing he would've wanted was for you all to be left with no one."

"Is that a yes?" Professor Parker asked tentatively. "Lord knows I have my hands full enough with the college kids."

Fleming's eyes flickered over me, carrying a trace of fleeting concern that he was quick to suppress.

"I'm honored to accept my old position."

"Now can I clap?" Mike hollered, and nervous laughter broke across the hall. Fleming ran his fingers through his hair.

"If you must, Mike."

Applause exploded through the room, and Fleming shook his head as he walked down the table length to shake Dr. Parker's hand. The team fell from their seats in their rush to surround him, jumping and whooping in hard-won celebration.

I glanced at the door where Roy had made his exit. He may have been gone, but there was still a hollow pit in my stomach.

"Everything okay, Sammy?" Naomi asked when I stood.

"I just need to go check something."

It was easy to slip outside unnoticed, and I squinted into the fog. The flames that rolled off Mr. Hendricks's shoulder made him easy to spot, but he'd already made it halfway back to the burnt-out husk of the high school camp headquarters. I jogged to catch up, and he turned around when he heard me coming.

"Here to gloat?" he snarled. "The little Viking got her way. Congrats."

"Where are you going?"

"You heard me. I quit."

"You could still stay with the Apex families."

"And watch Alexander Fleming screw up from the front row? No thanks." He turned back towards the high school camp. "I've been waiting nine months for Winnie to come home, and now I'm free to go fetch her myself."

"I'm not sure Winnie is going to let you do that."

Mr. Hendricks narrowed his eyes, and embers floated off his back.

"She's just a kid. She doesn't know what she's doing."

"Lots of kids don't know what they're doing, but they don't run off and join the first villain in bad cosplay they find."

"I'm not about to take parenting advice from a child who's spent the last millennia in a coma. I love Winnie. I trained her the same way I trained Amanda until it was obvious she didn't get our gift."

"And then you cast her aside."

"Don't mischaracterize it. I adjusted our expectations. I was a good father."

"Obviously."

"Vic was no saint, either."

"But that's just it." There it was. The reason I'd followed him out. The question that had plagued me since I first discovered my true identity. "If you hate me so much, why corrupt your own daughter's memories for my sake? Why offer to help my parents at all if I'm nothing but a worthless Beta? Because you're right. I'm not special, but you still dragged Winnie into this mess."

Contempt curled Roy's lip.

"This is about closure? You don't care about my family. You care about yourself and your own clarity of conscience," he sneered. "You and my kid had one thing in common: neither of you had any friends. So Alison went into both your heads and fixed both your problems. Then you woke up and got too big for yourself."

"Right, because us Betas exist to serve your superhero egos. The only reason I got mixed up in any of this was because Winnie tried to sell me to Adrestus, just like you did last night."

"I'm not responsible for Winnie's transgressions," Roy deadpanned.

"No, both your daughters hate you for reasons completely unrelated to how you've treated them."

Grass wilted and died under Roy's feet as he closed the distance between us. I held my ground, sticking my chin out as he approached.

"Because you know so much about fathers and daughters? How many fathers have you gotten killed now?"

My stomach fluttered, and I reigned in the urge to smack him across his stupid face. Instead, I smiled coyly and crossed my arms, refusing to be intimidated by someone as weak as Roy Hendricks.

"You mock their deaths because you don't know what it means to be willing to die for someone you love."

"Those who are strong enough don't need to lay down their life." He pivoted around to continue stalking across the field. "As much as I dislike him, I hope Alex knows what he's getting into with you. It's only a matter of time before he joins the pile of bodies you've accumulated."

His words were like electricity, and I stood shaking, unable to move as Roy faded into the mist.

He was wrong. Trev Baker had been wrong. Wesley had stopped me from killing Fleming, and now that I had my memory back, Adrestus couldn't trick me into murdering anyone.

Fleming would be fine.

He had to be.

Breaking camp turned out to be much more of an undertaking than I'd anticipated. I wanted nothing more than a moment alone with Naomi or Wesley, but they were kept at the camp's perimeter, watching for unwelcome guests, while I was stuck packing kitchen provisions.

I kept my eye out for Fleming. I needed confirmation that I was indeed back on the team, and I needed to know that I would be among those headed to New Delos. However, he was busy making preparations for Everly and presumably avoiding me in an effort to dodge the very questions I needed answered.

When night fell, however, my questions would have to wait as Wesley, Naomi, and I finally reunited after a long day of work to join Everly's funeral procession. With bowed heads, we joined the silent crowd walking down the forested pathway lit by lanterns Brooke and Amanda had lovingly set out in the hours before.

An owl hooted a mournful canticle overhead, welcoming us to the clearing that would be Everly's final resting place. I'd watched him die less than twenty four hours ago. Maybe it was a side-effect of my memories returning, but the world seemed to be moving so much faster now.

A college student at the clearing's center raised his hands over the dirt in front of him, and the earth rolled beneath his fingertips, leaving a gouged-out hole, six feet deep. Naomi exhaled next to me, and I reached for her hand.

"Sorry," she whispered. "My powers are waking up again."

In the clearing full of mourners, it was difficult to fathom what that might feel like to Naomi as her empath abilities returned. I squeezed her hand, and she squeezed back.

The crowd shifted, and we stepped to the side to make room for the pallbearers and the wicker basket coffin. My last day as Samantha, we'd laid Vidar to rest. How was it we were doing the same for Everly my first day back? I stared at the moss at my feet, knowing if I let myself look at the others, I'd get lost wondering who we'd be burying next.

Andersen and Sergio were among the six pallbearers, joined by a college student I didn't know, Coach Reiner, and Angie, the battle scarred nurse that served the University team. Fleming took the final spot, leading the way at coffin's head with an ashen face.

They lowered the wicker casket into the grave and stepped back to join the crowd along the perimeter of the clearing. I flashed back to Vidar's funeral and the way Fleming had stepped up to stand with Mom, not because he'd been particularly close to her dead husband, but because he'd known she'd needed him there.

I gave Naomi's hand a final squeeze, and she understood, dropping her hand so I could slip around the perimeter of the clearing. My heart rose to my throat as I stepped to Fleming's side. At first, I thought he didn't notice me.

But then, he raised a hand and rested it on my shoulder. His fingers shook, but being there for him let me selfishly focus outside of my own pain. Everly had fixed so many of us. It was cruel that none of us were able to return the favor.

The earth-moving student rolled the dirt back into place over Everly and his casket. As he disappeared, I wondered if Roy had been right. If it had been my fault Everly was killed. If the team was better off without me.

Moss rippled across the clearing, spiraling out from a college student named Boonsri. She bowed her head in concentration, focusing on covering the upturned dirt in clovers. Ivy wound up the trees, adorning Everly's final resting place in moonlit green.

Desirae and Mike took turns reading a prayer, but a soft buzz had fallen over my brain, dragging me into a numb, hazy grief. I stared at the clovers that now dotted Everly's grave, and I memorized their arrangement like it was a constellation.

Maybe I would see the same pattern in the night sky and know that Everly was still somehow watching over us, keeping us safe, keeping us whole from wherever he was now.

We didn't have the resources for a proper reception. Most of the food had been packed up, but a few college students snuck into Quarry Bay for hot chocolate mix and marshmallows. Amanda and Sergio heated vats of water down on the campfire-spotted shore, and though summer had reached McMillan Island, the night was cool.

I clutched my styrofoam cup, and the heat of the watery hot chocolate inside kept me rooted to the beach. Wesley pressed a shoulder against mine where we sat on a driftwood log around one of the campfires that flickered in the sand. Naomi and Andersen sat opposite us, a cold distance apart, the flames casting long, flickering shadows up their expressionless faces.

"Fleming and Parker are letting students with missing parents go to New Delos," Naomi finally said. "I think it's because they know I can't go to the ranch if Joni goes, but it opens the door for you, Wesley."

I looked up from my hot chocolate.

"If you guys go, then I do, too."

Naomi and Wesley gave each other looks, and I scowled, kicking sand into the campfire just to watch it sizzle.

"You need Fleming's permission," Naomi reminded me.

"I'll do what I want, and he knows that. I'm not leaving you guys again," I asserted. Naomi's lips tightened, and my chest constricted. "What aren't you telling me?"

"Nothing." She shook her head too aggressively, but Andersen interrupted before I could press the matter.

"I got permission from my mom," he grunted.

"Why are you sitting here?" Naomi snapped. "We don't like you."

"Neither does anyone else."

"It's fine." I gave Naomi a warning glare. She wrinkled her nose, but left Andersen alone. "Tell me what you know about the New Delos assignments."

She swirled her hot chocolate and looked off into the distance, choosing her next words carefully.

"Adrestus hates you, Sam. If you go to New Delos, he'll target you. I know you want Avery and Alison back, but—"

"Of course I do," I nodded, "and even if I go back to New Delos, I might not save them. I'm not naive enough to believe that anymore."

Naive. That's what Adrestus had called me. The word made my skin itch.

"Sure, but we need talent at the ranch, too. We still don't know how Adrestus found us here—"

"It was Anthony," Wesley asserted. "Who else would've sold us out?"

I was thankful that the dark of the beach hid the blush that rose to my cheeks. It had been Avery, not Anthony. I trusted Wes, but I needed to know he would do everything it took to save my brother.

"He has spies." I shrugged. "It could've been anything that tipped him off. We won't know for sure if Anthony is innocent until we save everyone."

"We being those assigned to return to New Delos," Naomi reminded me.

"Which will include me."

"Have you spoken to Fleming about it?" Naomi braced herself.

"No, but you have, Captain. What did he say?"

Naomi looked off to the side.

"I think you should talk to him about it."

"He's sending me to the ranch?" I was standing, but I didn't remember getting up. Naomi looked down at her feet, and I threw the rest of my hot chocolate into the fire.

I stumbled over sand, ignoring Naomi calling me back as well as the grains of sand that slipped inside my shoes and scratched against my feet. Isabelle raised a hand to me in greeting from where she sat with the other high school juniors around their fire, but I pretended not to see her.

Six months separated from my friends, half of which, I didn't even know who they were, and Fleming was sending me away the moment I reunited with them? Fury propelled me forward. He should know better by now than to tell me where I could and couldn't go.

The charred ruins of the high school camp sat atop the bluff to my left, and as I climbed the steep steps up the cliff face, I focused on the blackened walls of the main building. The night air, so cool a moment ago, felt balmy against my neck.

"Sammy!" Wesley called out as I started the march across the camp borders. "Sammy, wait."

My shadow elongated ahead of me in the beam of a flashlight.

"You're definitely back, then," Wesley sighed, catching up. "Always running off."

"I'm not running off." The back of his knuckles brushed against mine, and I pulled my hand away. "You're going to New Delos, aren't you? With or without me."

"He has my mom and brother, Sammy. I have to."

"And what about *my* mom and brother?" I continued my march to the burnt-out building ahead. I couldn't blame him for opting to go. I would've chosen the same.

"I know, but it's dangerous, especially to go together. Adrestus tried to make me kill you," he said, keeping pace with me. "He almost succeeded. And then I lost my arm and—"

"Do you blame me for losing your arm?" I whispered. He looked at me in horror.

"Of course not! But I'd sooner lose my other one than be forced to fight you again."

"So you agree with Fleming. I'm better off at the ranch."

"That's not what I'm saying."

I took the flashlight from Wesley to shine it up at the house. We stood in front of the ruined porch, and while the right side of the house had been reduced to charcoal and brittle beams, the left side was still largely intact.

"Why are we here?" Wesley asked. "It'll be dangerous inside."

"As dangerous as going back to New Delos?" I tested the bottom step of the porch, and when it held my weight, I continued to the front door. "Avery and Mom have things upstairs. If we're packing up, I want them, no matter where I go."

Wesley continued to nervously hiss my name as I ventured into the house. The stairwell had been saved from the brunt of the fire by a closed door, but I exercised caution as I wound my way up to Mom and Avery's apartment on the third floor. Bits of wall were missing from the stairwell, and I shone the flashlight in the holes left behind by the fire.

The door to Mom and Avery's apartment was charred and fell inward off its hinges when I tried to open it, but the living room behind it was untouched by the fire.

Avery's school books were still stacked on the coffee table, and his bedroom door in the back hall had been left ajar. I poked my head inside and felt my heart break all over again.

His wall was covered in drawings, not unlike the ones I'd taken to drawing before losing my memories. He was talented for being so young, and Dad's graphite face stared passively back at me from many of the leaflets.

I frowned at Avery's dresser. Knut dug beneath his cage shavings as I got closer, and I wondered if he knew how close he'd been to becoming barbecued hamster.

"What's that?"

I jumped at Wesley's voice.

"Avery's hamster. He named him after my brother."

"Avery named his hamster Avery?"

I found an old backpack in Avery's closet and began loading it with Knut's food bags and hamster ball.

"No. He's named Knut."

"A Viking."

"Yes."

And I remembered him better than I ever had. Stronger and bigger than Vidar. Kinder than our father, Havard. About to marry a pretty girl from our village when he died. To me, it didn't feel as if a thousand years had passed since I'd seen him last, but just a few months.

"How would Knut feel about being a hamster's namesake?" Wesley joined me at the dresser.

"He would've said something stupid, like there's never been a stronger, tougher hamster than this one." I threw the bag over my shoulder, and Wesley took the cage between his arm and prosthesis. He flashed a jaunty grin, but I knew it was forced. If we were about to be separated again, there were still things I needed to say. If the worst happened, and I never got the chance...

I refused to think about that possibility.

"Wes," I said, and the tone of my voice wiped the smile from his face. "I'm sorry for the things I said to you this week. I was confused about what was happening, but what I said was hurtful."

"It's okay. It wasn't really you."

My heart sank at his words, and I shook my head.

"It was, though. Just because I didn't remember anything doesn't mean I wasn't still Sammy."

"That's ridiculous," Wesley laughed. I knew he was trying to make me feel better, but he was doing the opposite. "Of course you weren't *Sammy*. I mean, you were, but you weren't, you know?"

"I *don't* know," I asserted, wishing we could be having this conversation anywhere other than Avery's bedroom. "The whole point is that it's been Eydis or Samantha Havardson or Samantha Fleming. I'm all of them because they're all just me."

"But that doesn't mean you meant the things you said."

I shoved past him to the hallway, my frustration returning.

"But I *did* mean it!" I marched into Mom's room. "Just because I have more context now doesn't mean I didn't mean those things when I said them. So, I'm sorry."

I looked back at him from where I stood at the foot of Mom's twin bed. Her room was simpler than Avery's without the wall decorations and hamster supplies.

"Right." Wesley nodded. "I'm sorry, too. I don't want you to feel like I only care about one aspect of you. I'm excited to get to know all of you."

The knot in my chest loosened.

"Thanks, Wes."

"I'd give you a hug, but my arms are full thanks to Canoe."

I snorted, feeling my face break in a smile.

"It's Knut. Kuh-newt. Not Canoe." I turned to Mom's bedside table. I wasn't in any of the pictures in the family photo album that rested there, but I couldn't bear to leave them behind.

"Ok. Knut. Were your other brothers' names harder or easier than that to say?"

"Vidar was my only other brother." I moved to Mom's closet and rifled for anything she might want to save. "I had three sisters, though."

"That's a lot of sisters," Wesley choked.

"Gunhild, Hjordis, and Erika."

"I can spell one of those."

I laughed, pulling out a dark gray hoodie that was nicer than the one I had on. It smelled like Mom.

"Hjordis, right?"

"Oh, easy. That starts with a Y."

"Nope."

"Did you even use a normal alphabet back then?" Wesley asked, following me back to the living room. "Isn't spelling all made up anyway?"

I scanned the living room and kitchen. If it weren't for the charcoal door laying across the entry, the space would've looked as if Mom and Avery had just stepped out for a walk.

"We'll—"

Wesley cut himself off before he could say the words I'd heard so many times now.

We'll get them back. How many people had Adrestus taken from me at some point? My eyes flickered over Wesley's red arm. Even if we did rescue Mom and Avery, what condition would they be in?

"Knut was the oldest." My voice cracked. I went through the kitchen cupboards, wandering aimlessly through the space Alison and Avery had lived in without me. I was stalling. I didn't want to leave the apartment. It was my family's last home. "Then there was my sister Gunhild."

"Gunhild is a girl's name?"

"It's not as bad as Eydis," I snorted.

"Eydis is a great name!"

"There's a reason little girls still get named Erika and not Eydis." I turned to watch Wesley set Knut and his things down on the coffee table. "You got that?"

"I'm good. Knut and I are bonding." His right fingers whirred as he relaxed his grip, and he stepped away, rubbing at his elbow. "Tell me about Erika."

"The youngest," I sighed. "She was still so little when Adrestus…"

"Right. Sorry. You don't have to—"

"It's the first time I've been able to tell anyone about my family." I moved to the living room closet, shining the light between the three coats that hung there to inspect the boxes in the farthest corner. "Erika was a handful but the sweetest handful you'd ever meet."

"Being difficult ran in the family, then?"

The large duffle bag in the back corner of the closet looked familiar. The zipper was undone, and the contents spilled out across the dusty wood floor. The flashlight caught the glossy sheen of printed photographs.

"Someone's been in here," I said sharply, half-crawling into the closet to drag the duffle bag out.

"Someone like Alison?"

"No." I shifted through the pictures. When I'd first found Paul Fleming's belongings in his brother's apartment over Winter Break, there'd been more of them, cataloging Paragon's time as a high schooler and college student. Now, the only pictures left were the ones with Fleming in them. "Someone like Roy Hendricks."

I shined the flashlight into the duffle bag. When Fleming had gifted Paul's things to Alison, I knew he'd handed over Paragon's signature cape. Unless she kept it somewhere else, Roy had taken that, too.

"He took your mom's things?" Wesley asked. "Why?"

I shrugged and shoved the things into the bag before Wesley realized they'd been Paragon's. I didn't want to talk about Fleming's dead brother. Knut's wheel creaked, and I sat on the floor in the mouth of the closet. There was nothing left in the apartment important enough to grab, but I still didn't want to leave.

"We should head back," Wesley whispered.

Every time Adrestus has taken someone from me, I'd felt so alone afterwards. This time, Alison and Avery were gone along with three of my friends. But now, I had Wesley, even if only for a fleeting moment.

"Wes." I lowered the flashlight to cast our faces in shadow. "What was it you were going to say to me?"

His silhouette stilled, and while I wished I could see his face, I kept the light low.

"I don't know what you mean."

"Yes." I reached for his hand where it rested on the floorboards, and I ran my fingers over his knuckles. His hand shivered under mine. The memory of him standing in the surf rushed back as forcefully as the tide that had washed him away. I could see him lifting me to safety. I could see his mouth move, inaudible over the roar of the wave that broke over him. "I think you do."

"I barely remember that day, Sammy. Especially considering I almost died."

"You *did* die," I reminded him, trying to keep my tone light in spite of everything. "And you *do* remember because you were going to tell me right before Avery—"

I broke off. My dumb, *stupid* brother. The thought of him in Adrestus's clutches made me heartsick.

Wesley's fingers wrapped around the palm of my hand.

"You really want to know?"

Moonlight filtered in through the window and glinted off his eyes. Had he moved closer? Had *I*? After so many months apart, I wanted to be as near him as possible. I wanted to get lost in the folds of his sweatshirt where they wrinkled across his chest.

"I really want to know."

We were close enough now that I could see his eyes waver as they oscillated between mine.

"I thought that might've been it for me, and that I wasn't ever going to see you again, so—" He gulped, and I wondered if I raised a hand to his cheek if I'd be able to feel him blushing. He looked away and then looked back with sudden steel in his eyes. "Sammy, I—"

"Hello, Eydis."

I jumped away from Wesley and spun to face the kitchen at the sound of the voice.

There by the sink, unnaturally bright in the gloom of the apartment, Adrestus stood in a linen suit, eating a lemon bar. He licked powdered sugar off his thumb and grinned.

"Hope I didn't catch you at a bad time."

20

According To Plan

This visage of Adrestus was only in my head, but that didn't make him any more welcome.

"What is it?" Wesley stood up, too, unaware of Adrestus brushing powdered sugar from his suit jacket in the kitchen.

"Nothing," I said.

"Oh, you're with friends?" Adrestus said in mock-apology. "That's it, then? You've decided to trust them? I know we left in a hurry, but you were being difficult and then, well, who would've thought Paragon's brother had *that* in him?"

He drew a hand across his chest, mimicking the path the sword had taken in Fleming's hands.

Wesley peered into the kitchen, squinting to see what I was looking at.

"Sammy, come on," he said. "You're freaking me out."

I gritted my teeth and refused to look directly at Adrestus.

"Just be quiet a moment." If I ignored him, maybe he'd go away.

"Not telling them I'm here," Adrestus tutted. "You've decided not to trust them after all. I was wondering if you would, especially after seeing the way you went after poor Alexander Fleming."

He didn't know my memories were back. Not only that, but he couldn't see Wesley. I had more power here than I thought.

"The silent treatment, I see," Adrestus said. "Fine. I was just popping in to let you know your nephew and Alison are safe, if you care."

"I care," I said.

"Great," Wesley said slowly. "I care, too."

"Not you." I dug my fingers into the palms of my hands.

"What's happening?"

"It's complicated." I still hadn't told anyone how Adrestus had appeared to me last week. Maybe if I had, things wouldn't have turned out the way they did.

"I asked Avery if he had any messages for you," Adrestus continued, finishing off his lemon bar. "I know you're busy right now, but don't worry. He made it quick, and so will I. All he wrote was 'Knut'. That's your dead brother, isn't it? Though, I suppose Vidar is also your dead brother now."

I looked at the hamster, still running on his wheel. Avery was worried about him. The priorities of a thirteen-year-old.

"Is it Adrestus?" Wesley whispered.

"Yeah, that's right." I nodded, talking to both Adrestus and Wesley. I held a finger to my lips to stay the panic in Wesley's face.

"How? Where?" He looked around the room again, ready for a fight.

"Not here."

"I know you're busy," Adrestus said, "but if you *do* manage to get away, we're here for you. Waiting. The same way I've been waiting a thousand years. Remember, I'm not your enemy, Eydis."

He fizzled from view, and I exhaled, dropping back to the floor. I tried to pull at my hair, but Wesley's fingers wrapped around mine.

"It's okay," he said. "Is he gone, then?"

I nodded, still breathless.

"It was just an image, like a video call," I finally managed. The ember of an idea whispered at the back of my head, the tiniest flicker of both hope and dread. "And he doesn't know my memories are back."

He didn't know I was back to my normal self. He didn't know I knew what he was trying to do. He didn't know how vulnerable that made him. How much easier it would be to get close to him now.

For the first time since plunging my sword in his gut all those centuries ago, I had the upper hand, and I wasn't going to waste it by hiding.

"Are you—"

"He doesn't know I got my memories back." I squeezed Wesley's fingers.

"Avery didn't tell him?"

"Avery wouldn't know. He tried to give them back to me in a last ditch effort."

I pushed myself to my feet, leaving Wesley bewildered on the floor.

"But what did Adrestus want?" he said.

I struggled to take Knut's cage into my arms. My head spun with thoughts that raced to outrun the dread that crept inside me.

"He wanted to tell me he's still waiting in case I decide not to trust you all."

"Good thing he's immortal, then, because he's going to be waiting a while." Wesley took the hamster cage from me.

I blinked back the film of tears that sprang unexpectedly to my eyes and turned my back to Wesley, pretending to gather my scavenged finds from the apartment into my arms.

"Sammy?" His voice was careful and afraid. He must've come to the same conclusion as I had. The path forward was obvious and horrible. "Sammy, no. You can't. I know what you're thinking, and I won't—"

"Won't what?" I spun to face him. "You won't *let* me? Haven't we had this conversation before?"

"This is different!" he cried. "You know it is! I only just got you back! Sammy, *please!*"

"You don't even know what it is I'm thinking." I wanted to hear him say it. Maybe if I heard the words come from somebody else, I'd realized how ridiculous of an idea it was.

"You're going to join him."

It *was* a ridiculous idea, but it was one that would work.

Wesley turned on his heel and yelled down the charred staircase, Knut still in his arms.

"It's just us!" he called, then looked at me over his shoulder. "Fleming's here. They saw our flashlight in the window."

I leaned against the kitchen table and pinched the bridge of my nose. Adrestus's visage was still plastered on the inside of my eyelids, and I tried to will it away as I listened to Fleming come up the staircase.

"What are you doing here? Do you know how dangerous this building is right now?" Fleming grabbed my shoulders, and I opened my eyes to an angry, worried frown that softened at the look on my face. "What is it? What happened?"

Dr. Parker lurked in the doorway, scanning the living room for invisible enemies.

"She saw Adrestus." Wesley locked eyes with me over Knut's cage. "She's going to go join him."

Fleming's fingers tightened on my shoulders.

"What? Why?"

"He doesn't know my memories are back," I explained. "How many times has he had someone on the inside sabotaging us? This could be our only chance at getting the upper hand and stopping him."

"Absolutely not." Fleming shook his head. "You've had bad ideas before, but this?"

"I'm the only person who will be in any danger this time."

Moonlight from the window glared against Fleming's glasses, making his expression impossible to read.

"Samantha," he said slowly, and I backed away. "I can't let you do that. New Delos isn't safe for you."

"Nowhere is safe for me!" My voice rose. "Not here, not the ranch, and not New Delos, but this is my fight! And you want to bench me!"

"What I want is to keep you alive."

"But not everyone gets to stay alive, and you don't get to decide who does and who doesn't."

Fleming's shoulders swelled with indignation, but I stood my ground.

"You dare—" he sputtered. "Not two hours after burying Jacobi—"

Dr. Parker reached forward to rest a hand on Fleming's shoulder, and he spun, looking like he might fight her there in the darkened living room of my kidnapped family.

"She's right, Alex." Dr. Parker's face was heavy.

"I'm not going to offer her up on a platter!"

"Nor should you send her to the ranch. You know her better than I do, but you're kidding yourself if you think that's where she belongs."

My interactions with Dr. Parker had been few and far between, marked by distant reverence amplified by my lack of familiarity with the woman. Yet for some reason, here she was, going to bat for me against Fleming, and I clung to the hope that fluttered in my chest.

"She's just a kid." Fleming flung his hand out towards me, and I straightened up, as if to appear older and taller.

"So are the forty students you and I will be leading into New Delos tomorrow night," Dr. Parker said darkly. "But Adrestus has just added two powerful inculcators in the shape of the Havardsons to his toolbox, something that bodes all the more sinister with his so-called Peace Summit next month. Samantha is in a unique position to ensure we all get on the island safely."

"To put her in danger like that—"

"Is out of the question," Dr. Parker nodded in agreement.

"What?" I demanded. "But you just said—"

Dr. Parker held up a hand and stalked into the kitchen to look out the window towards the distant camp. She surveyed the moonlit property for a moment, and I could feel Fleming's eyes boring into the side of my head.

"I said you'll help us get onto the island safely. We'll send you to the island with an advance guard. You'll keep Adrestus's attention, giving the rest of us the chance to sneak in unnoticed."

"Absolutely not," Fleming fumed.

"With the right people in place, he won't be able to get close to her." Dr. Parker turned away from the window and leaned against the sink. "It's the distraction we need."

"I'll do it," I said, finally looking at Fleming. "It'll be easy."

"We don't need Sammy on the island to use her as bait," he argued. "Adrestus only needs to think she's nearby."

"If anything makes him suspicious, he'll know we are up to something. Our chances are better with Samantha." Moonlight caught her teeth as she grinned at me. "And like she said, it's her fight, too."

Fleming stood defeated in the living room, and the harrowed look on Wesley's face told me he wasn't sold on the idea, either.

"Please," I whispered. "I don't want to be alone at the ranch."

"You'll have Joni," Fleming promised, but his helpless frown told me he knew I'd be miserable.

"I'll run away. I'll find a way to New Delos alone or with the team."

Fleming looked between Dr. Parker and me. A final flicker of desperation pulled at his face, but then his resolve fled, and his shoulders fell. I'd kept good on my promises to run off in the past. He could not control me.

"I'll gather the captains." He held me in a gaze that carried the fear and weight of a half-year's careful protection. With Everly dead, Alison captive, and his New Delos home abandoned, I was all that he had left to lose. "Better go get some sleep, Samantha. We leave early in the morning."

The smallest kernel of guilt pierced my soaring heart as Fleming retreated back into the stairwell, but nothing could spoil the victory of the moment for me.

I would not be left behind. I would see to it firsthand that my family and friends were safe. I would make sure Adrestus failed at whatever he had planned for the Peace Summit.

However, the chill of the night air as I followed Fleming outside reminded me of just what I was walking into and the dark repercussions of what I knew needed to be done.

Wesley carried Knut in his cage next to me, and I tried to refocus my thoughts on him rather than the impending mission.

"You're nervous," I murmured.

"It's a good plan," Wesley assured me, stopping to stare up at the stars. He pulled his glasses off, and I wondered what the night sky might look like with his super-vision. "You'll be with us, and you won't have to hand yourself over to Adrestus. Everyone wins."

"Right." I nodded. The moon illuminated the shape of his nose against the dark backdrop, and somehow with everything that was happening, I found myself wondering once again what it was he had said to me just before the waves claimed him.

I couldn't bring myself to ask. Whatever it was, it would only make me feel worse about the fact that this time tomorrow, if everything went according to plan, I'll have horribly betrayed Wesley.

I'd let them think I'd agreed to be their bait, but my plan was better. I needed to join Adrestus.

Sleep was hard-won that night, taking a backseat to make time to anticipate who Fleming would team me up with the next day. Whoever it was, I would have to be able to outfight, outrun, or slip away from undetected.

By the time I was sitting on a truck bumper the next morning, waiting for Fleming, I'd compiled a solid list of contingencies in my head, but a few teammates remained who I knew I didn't stand a chance against. I mentally listed them, hugging my backpack closer to my chest.

I'd handed off both Floundersen and Knut to Joni earlier that morning for safekeeping at the ranch, knowing the animals would be a small comfort to her.

"So you got them to let you go?"

I jumped at Amanda's voice. She'd slunk up to the truck silently. Her shaggy pixie cut caught the ocean wind, and the dancing strands of hair helped to hide the fatigue on her grief-laden face.

"Sad you won't be seeing me at the ranch?" I teased. I wanted to ask how she was doing after losing her mother, but she'd never forgive me for prying.

"Annoyed I'll be seeing you on New Delos," she snorted. "I can't get away from you."

I pushed my backpack aside and straightened up.

"But you aren't on the team," I stammered. "Unless you rejoined? But then Brooke—"

"Parker knows she needs me, and she knows better than to assume Brooke is useless just because she's a non-Apex." She gave me a wry smile and readjusted the duffle bag she carried on her shoulder.

"You're going back for Winnie?" I'd never pinned Amanda as the sisterly type, so her scowl was unsurprising.

"I don't give a damn about Winnie," she grunted. "But last winter, I was trapped in my own body, lighting myself on fire to try to escape, and Remi seared the nerve endings out of her own arm to free me. And now, they have Remi."

She pursed her lips and looked to the side, watching Brooke help a family load into a van. Amanda may have been moody and proud, but she was nothing if not loyal.

"Right." I nodded. "In that case, I'll see you there."

Somehow, I didn't feel as guilty lying to Amanda. When she figured out what I'd done, she'd understand. She would do the same.

Behind her, Fleming approached the truck with Naomi, Wesley, Andersen, and Sergio in tow, and I swore under my breath. Of the list of teammates I knew I'd struggle to escape from, Naomi and Wesley had been numbers one and two.

Amanda turned to see who I was looking at and gave a low laugh.

"Good luck. See you soon, alright?" She clapped me on the shoulder and went to help Brooke load families into the available cars.

Sergio winked at me as he threw a tarp into the truck bed.

"This is the team?" I faked an enthusiastic smile.

"In a sense." Fleming frowned. "You'll be with Andersen and Naomi running distractions while Wesley and Sergio make sure the bases are habitable."

"More accurately, you're the distraction while Andersen and I are there make sure you don't do anything stupid." The dried blood on Naomi's lip indicated her powers were back, and her red-rimmed eyes told the story of a goodbye to Joni that had been both physically and emotionally painful. "Granted, I'm perfectly capable of doing that myself so I'm not sure why Andersen's here."

Fleming held the truck door open and signaled for us to file in.

"It's Andersen's rocky friendship with Sammy that makes him the *least* likely to enable her."

"Friendship?" Andersen and I said in unison.

"Exactly," Fleming deadpanned. "Now, load."

I shuffled into the cramped backseat next to Naomi, jamming my knees up against the front seats, and Wesley crammed in next. Naomi rested her head against the window with her eyes closed. As horrible as it was that her powers backfired like this after seeing Joni, hopefully she was too exhausted to sense my brewing conspiracy.

Andersen and Sergio joined Fleming in the front of the truck, and as abruptly as we'd arrived the day before, we were leaving the camp. My stomach twisted when I thought of all the friends I hadn't had a chance to say goodbye to. They thought they'd see me later that night. I'd make sure they didn't.

"You good?" Naomi murmured with her eyes still closed. Heat rose in my cheeks, and I shrugged against her and Wesley's shoulders.

"As good as anyone else. Why?"

"You're hard to read."

Trees, ocean, and farm passed outside the truck windows in a blur, and I played with the thin metal of my whistle necklace in an attempt to keep my nerves steady. By the time we pulled into Quarry Bay, I was already sore in my seat, but Fleming refused to let us out even after we'd boarded the ferry.

"Too dangerous," he clipped, undoing his seatbelt. "Besides, we need to go over the plan. We aren't sure we'll be able to communicate once you're on the island since Adrestus seems to be blocking cell tower and radio signals."

I relaxed against Wesley's leg, figuring I might as well get comfortable if I was going to be trapped in the back of the truck for the entirety of the ferry ride and subsequent five hour drive to the boat terminal for New Delos. Robotic fingers whirred as they unfurled to rest on my knee. I grabbed them, knowing the gesture would give me more comfort than it would Wesley.

"Once it's dark, the rest of the team will make our way to New Delos. Your job is to distract Adrestus," Fleming continued. "That does not mean fight Adrestus. It does not mean try to rescue your lost friends and family. *Nor* does it mean infiltrate enemy lines."

Fleming looked at me over the rims of his glasses, and I gave a placating thumbs-up.

The ferry shifted beneath us as we pulled away from the dock, and I tried to look through the rows of cars to get a last glimpse of Quarry Bay. Under other circumstances, I might've liked living here. The darkened windows of Orca View Cafe stared at me from the rickety boardwalk, and I turned away.

If this all went okay, if we came out unscathed, maybe I'd come back.

The day's travels passed in a sleep-deprived blur, interrupted by moments of waking up with my cheek pressed against Wesley's shoulder after not realizing I'd drifted off and several stretch breaks, where we were allowed to run into gas stations in pairs for the restroom and snacks.

As we followed the coast, I watched the horizon for the first glimpse of New Delos. When it first appeared, glinting orange in the light of the steadily sinking sun, my stomach flipped.

Fleming pulled off the main highway, found an empty park that overlooked the ocean, and shut off the car. He twisted in his seat to look at us all and sighed.

"This is where Sergio will take over. Customs into New Delos will be lax. Adrestus wants people on the island, after all, but we're still going to hide the four of you in the truck bed while Sergio drives onto the ferry."

We tumbled from the car on stiff legs and convened with Fleming at the bumper. The ocean wind was stronger here than it had been on McMillan Island, rolling over the coast unencumbered by straits and islands. I nestled into the collar of my hoodie. It was the same one I'd stolen from Mom's closet.

"Check in as soon as you're on the ferry, ten minutes before exiting the ferry, and again as soon as you're safely able to once off the ferry," Fleming instructed. His eyes raked over us one last time, counting our heads, making sure we were all accounted for.

"We'll be fine," I promised.

"I've heard that before."

"And I'm bound to be right when I say it one of these days. We'll all be back under Schrader Hall before you know it," I assured him. "At the latest, in time for breakfast tomorrow."

The orange of the setting sun cast his face in gold, and he hugged himself to brace against the wind.

"Sammy..."

I knew why he was hesitating because I was thinking about it, too. The last time he'd put me in a boat and sent me to New Delos without him, I'd been captured, Wesley had lost his arm, and Vidar had died.

"It's different this time," I lied. "You'll be right behind us."

Andersen pulled himself into the truck bed first and offered a hand to Wesley. Wesley ignored him and jumped up on his own.

"Right," Fleming grimaced. He patted my shoulder awkwardly. "Remember, check in—"

"Twice on the ferry and once we're off," Naomi parroted. She helped me into the truck, and I gave Fleming one last self-assured smile before lying back between Wesley and Andersen. Wesley shifted as Naomi settled in on his other side.

A tarp rustled, and Fleming, his expression unreadable, pulled it over the truck bed, obscuring the twilight sky.

"Quick question." Sergio sounded muffled outside of our hiding spot. "I'm technically in charge, right?"

"You can try, but I don't think anyone's in charge of those four." Fleming's voice hid an exasperated laugh. I swallowed the bile in my throat. He was going to be so disappointed in me.

The cool metal of the truck bed, already sapping the heat from my body, rumbled beneath us. I clutched my backpack against my chest, unsure of the next time I'd see the man who'd become the closest thing I had left to a father.

21

Together

The cool glass of the ferry window helped calm my nerves as I watched the horizon swallow the last mark of daylight. The sun broke through the oncoming night to highlight the ocean ahead in hues of red and orange. As Fleming had predicted, getting onto the New Delos ferry had been easy, and without him there to make us stay in the truck, we'd ventured up to the passenger deck to stretch our legs.

The vinyl of my bench dipped as it took Wesley's weight next to me.

"Anything feel off?" he asked in a low voice.

"We're fine. No one's suspicious." Naomi faced me on the opposite bench. "Where's Sergio and Andersen?"

"In the galley," Wesley said before he and Naomi fell silent. I raised my eyes to see them staring at me expectantly.

"Can I help you?" I gave them a nervous laugh and lifted my forehead from the window glass.

"You've been quiet," Naomi shrugged.

"I was tired." My scowl inched into a reluctant smile. I'd missed them, even if their powers gave me no privacy. "It's weird to be going back to New Delos. I was just here with my family, thinking I was about to have a completely normal school year. I had no idea about anything. I'd only just woken up from my coma."

Naomi studied me, biting her lip.

"How much do you remember now?" she pried. "You don't have to say if you don't want to, of course, but I'm curious."

I picked at the plastic booth seat.

"All ten months of Samantha are there, and I think all of Eydis is there, too, but it's like forgetting a funny story until someone reminds you of it. When my earlier memories started coming back, I had to fight them off or else they'd completely take over, like they were happening in real time."

"Erika," Naomi said softly, and I jerked my head up. She blushed. "The night Hephestae attacked the New Year's Festival, you kept saying someone had taken Erika. Were you in a memory then?"

I chewed on the inside of my cheek. I'd always felt the most guilty about tiny, innocent Erika.

"Erika was my youngest sister. Raiders invaded our settlement and tried to carry her off. That's what I was remembering."

"Was she okay?" Naomi's brow creased, and I curled my hands in on themselves. She and Wesley were sitting so still, but there was something that felt good about telling someone at long last what I'd gone through as Eydis.

"My father saved her." In my mind, I saw the head of Havard's arrow embed itself in the raider's neck as he ran away with my sister over his shoulder. "He killed the man who grabbed her, but I—"

My voice caught, and I tried to swallow again, but my mouth was dry. How much should I tell them?

"Sorry," Naomi whispered, and Wesley shifted closer to me. "I shouldn't have pried."

"It's not you. I killed a man." I cringed as the words left my mouth. Wesley tensed next to me, and Naomi's eyes went wide as her jaw tightened.

"Oh."

"To be fair, he was threatening us."

"No one's blaming you for killing a medieval raider, Sammy," Wesley said through a quivering laugh.

"I'm glad Erika was okay." Naomi tried to pivot the conversation, but Wesley gave her a warning glare.

"Adrestus killed her eventually. He killed everyone." I cleared my throat and tried to lighten the mood. "It wasn't all bad. Iceland has geothermal springs. There was one near my settlement, and in the winter, we'd swim under the northern lights and play games in the water."

I grinned at the memory of pushing Gunhild into the pool. Mother had yelled at me for getting Gunhild's coat wet, but it had been worth it.

"That sounds amazing." Naomi nodded.

"That sounds cold," Wesley corrected her.

"It wasn't if you stayed in the water. I swam in the ocean a couple of times. *That* was cold." I grinned. "Remember when I passed out in the pool?"

"That was another memory?" Naomi asked.

"Sure was. Same with when I fell off the cliff in The Apex Games against Sergio."

"What were you remembering that made you fall off a cliff?" Wesley laughed, but I winced.

"I don't remember," I lied, shoving away the memory of a teenage-version of Adrestus pressing his lips against mine. Naomi frowned, and I wondered if she'd felt the wave of disgust and unease that came with the memory.

"Who wants hot chocolate?" Sergio and Andersen appeared, bearing cups of hot chocolate. Naomi and Wesley both made a point to take their cups from Sergio.

"Thanks," I mumbled, taking Andersen's spare drink. He screwed his face up, as if he wasn't completely comfortable doing me any favors but knew better than to fuss with Naomi and Wesley there.

The deck filled with gasps of admiration, and passengers crowded around the window.

A man of bronze pushed his way through the drizzle of rain that had started to fall outside. Paragon, immortalized in massive statue form, looked just as he had on my first voyage to New Delos. His wide, pupil-less grin caught the footlights illuminating him from his pedestal, and his cape of metal furled out behind him, frozen in an invisible wind.

Naomi, Wesley, and Sergio looked at it with new reverence.

"I still can't believe *that's* Fleming's brother." Naomi shook her head in awe.

"Sammy knew," Wesley said. "Right? You and Adrestus talked about it last winter."

I'd almost forgotten Adrestus had tried to talk to us about Paul Fleming when he'd captured Wesley and me.

"You both knew?" Naomi snapped. "And didn't say anything?"

Wesley shrugged.

"It seemed like a secret. Although," he looked at me, "how did you know before Adrestus told us?"

"I figured it out just after you beat me in the Final Trial, actually," I admitted.

"But why keep it a secret at all?" Wesley asked. "I get Fleming wants to be his own hero and all that, but it's *cool*."

I watched the behemoth statue pass, thinking of how he'd lit a building on fire to die a hero rather than succumb to an incurable illness.

"Paragon wasn't the hero everyone thinks he was," I said simply. Andersen grunted in agreement and Naomi frowned.

"He was a fraud." Andersen shrugged.

"Watch out, everyone," Naomi sneered. "Andersen is passing judgment. If anyone's a fraud—"

"He's right," I interjected. I tried to catch Andersen's eye, but he looked away.

"How? Was he a non-Apex, too?" Sergio asked.

"No," I scowled. "He committed arson, with Roy Hendricks's help no less. It was the same fire that killed him."

Andersen stared at the floor, but Naomi, Wesley, and Sergio gawked at me. I hoped Fleming didn't mind me airing his brother's dirty laundry, but I couldn't stand the thought of Paul getting the legacy he'd tried so hard to secure for himself.

I ignored their looks and instead watched the city emerge from the gathering marine layer. Lights of yellow, orange, and blue lit the windows of the city against the darkening ocean. New Delos was fast approaching, and Wesley's prosthesis whirred behind me as he flexed his robotic fingers in anticipation.

And then, in one fluid wave, the lights of the city extinguished, leaving behind a dark shadow on the ocean where it had been a moment before.

I leaped to my feet and pressed against the window, trying to better see the island.

"What was that?" Naomi hissed, pressing next to me. "The city— it's gone."

"No, it's there," Wesley said gravely. "Look."

A single line of lit windows hung suspended eighty-some stories over the city.

"It's like the power's gone out except for that one floor." Sergio vied for a spot at the window for a better look.

I set my jaw and exhaled heavily through my nose. I knew who lived in the top floors of the tallest building in New Delos.

"That's Adrestus's home." I fell back into my seat. The others followed suit, watching the window with new apprehension. We hadn't anticipated sailing into a blackout.

"We're okay," Naomi assured us, though she gripped the windowsill forcibly enough to make her hands quake. "He won't even be able to get near us."

I nodded and watched the lightless mass of New Delos get larger and larger ahead of us, until it stretched up into the marine layer like an open set of jaws ready to clamp down.

When we returned to the truck on the car deck, we piled back into the backseat, not bothering with hiding in the truck bed in case someone spotted us crawling under the tarp.

A thrill of panic tightened my chest as the boat bumped up against the dock, and Naomi reached for my hand, though I wasn't sure if it was more for my comfort or hers. I focused on the bumper ahead of us as traffic unloaded from the car deck and rolled into the city.

The streets were lit by the headlights of cars and the feeble beams of cellphone lights from the straggling pedestrians. New Delos had once been as alive at night as during the day, dancing with lights and full of people. Something about this dark, new city felt oppressive.

"Naomi," Sergio asked in the driver's seat, turning left at the first defunct traffic light, "check communications. My phone says no service."

She pulled a small box from her bag and shook her head.

"Nothing," she confirmed. "Just like Fleming thought."

"So we'll have no way to stay in contact?" Wesley fretted.

Sergio pulled into a car lot that overlooked a park and boat dock. The headlights illuminated a rusted play-set, and what little ambient light rose from a nearby neighborhood pushed against the silhouettes of trees. Most of the letters had fallen off the park sign, but I still recognized Northshore Park. Hackjob had beaten Wesley to a pulp here once.

"We have to trust the plan, and we have to trust everyone is able to rendezvous at the campuses by the end of the night." Sergio flicked the headlights off, and heavy darkness rushed over us.

I fought the grim satisfaction that rose in my chest, lest Naomi feel it and get suspicious. When I made my move, Naomi wouldn't be able to call for back-up. All I needed was to get Andersen on my side somehow. Otherwise, I wasn't sure I could get away.

We snuck into the park bathroom, holding our uniforms close. Sergio and Wesley would suit up completely while Naomi, Andersen, and I only put on the torso parts of our uniforms. We'd be hiding in plain sight and could only wear what was easily concealable under our jackets.

In the dark of my bathroom stall, I struggled to fit the tight layers on. My uniform was still missing its left sleeve, and I tried to rub away the goosebumps that covered me from bicep to wrist.

I felt along the stall door and pushed it open. The glowing helmet visor that Wesley held under his arm lit the sinks in a dull, green light, and I searched for his face in the gloom.

"Sorry." Wesley patted the helmet. "The others are already outside, but I thought you might need the light."

"You can't tell I'm wearing armor under this, can you?" I tried to see my reflection in the darkened mirror.

"You look fine," Wesley assured me. He set his helmet down on the sink and surveyed where the edges of my armor pressed against my hoodie. "I hate that I won't be out there with you."

"We'll be okay. Adrestus can't get close with Naomi's powers keeping a lookout." I hated lying to him and couldn't stand to look him in the eyes. I nodded at his helmet. "You should put that on. If someone sees you—"

"It's just us here. We're fine."

I stepped closer to Wesley in spite of myself, and my hand bumped against his chest plate. His forehead met mine, and I closed my eyes, pretending I could see him on the other side of my eyelids. His gloved hand snaked through locks of hair at the back of my head, and his fingertips gently pressed against my scalp, holding me close.

"What's wrong?" he whispered.

"Every time we get close like this, something tears us apart." Something like me.

"Not this time." He held me closer, and I burrowed my face into his chest, wishing he was still wearing his hoodie so I could disappear into its folds and hide from the crushing guilt. Instead, his armor felt hard and uncomfortable, but I pressed into him all the same. "For now on, whatever happens to us, happens to us together."

I tried to swallow the bile that rose to my mouth, but it caught on the lump in my throat.

"Together." By the end of the night, the word would be a knife in his back.

Someone hit against the metal door.

"Hurry it up, would you?" Sergio barked.

Wesley's arm tightened around me a moment longer and then released. I fought the urge to pull him back but instead let him grab his helmet from the sink.

"See you soon, okay?" he said, hoisting his helmet up to pull over his head. I reached up and held it there, taking in his features one last time. His long nose, messy hair, and nervous smile. The muscle in his jaw tightened when I placed my hand over his cheek, basking in its warmth.

"See you soon."

I withdrew my hand, and he secured the helmet over his face. The light in the visor dimmed, and we were cast in total darkness.

22

Traitor

I couldn't bring myself to watch Wesley and Sergio disappear into the shadows of the park. I'd said my goodbye, whether Wesley knew it or not, and I wanted my last image of him to be that of his face holding me in his gaze.

Andersen clapped his hands together, and I tried to refocus.

"How does this work?" Andersen asked. Like mine, his jacket hid the bulk of his torso armor. "Do you dial Adrestus in your head?"

"I don't think it's a two-way channel." I tried to untangle a knot the breeze had worked into my hair. Before the flood, the docks we now stood next to had been full of yachts that helped to dull the ocean wind. Now, the moorage sat empty, giving the wind an unfettered path through the park. "We need a phone."

"I have mine." He pulled his cell phone from the front pocket, and I snapped it from his hands.

"Perfect."

"There's no service," Naomi reminded me, but I was already dialing the number I'd made sure to memorize before coming here.

"Not if you call the right place." I held the phone out so Andersen and Naomi could hear it ring. Naomi furrowed her brow in the dull light of the screen.

"But how—"

"Thank you for calling the Schrader Museum of New Delos. You've reached Miles," a familiar voice drawled over the speaker. "Unfortunately, we are about to close for the evening, but if you'd like to call back—"

"I need your boss," I cut him off, holding Naomi's eyes with mine. My fingers shook with fear and excitement.

"Adrian Schrader will be available tomorrow."

"Your actual boss. Adrestus. I need to talk. He'll know how to find me."

Miles was quiet a moment. Then—

"Eydis?"

I hung up and, mustering as much strength as I could, threw Andersen's phone into the ocean.

"What are you doing?" Andersen seethed. "That's my phone!"

"You're telekinetic." I shrugged. "Pull it back if you like. Just know that it puts us at risk of being tracked."

Naomi nodded, tying back her braids.

"She's right, and we should probably get away from here in case he is able to trace the signal." She beckoned for us to follow her out of the park and into the surrounding neighborhoods, though Andersen took a moment to gawk into the dark after his phone.

Adrenaline propelled me after Naomi. Low buildings rose around us, interspersed with fleeting headlights and the occasional window candle. Light rain fell as we put as much distance behind us before the light tugging in the back of my head signaled Adrestus's arrival.

I stopped between two pubs lit by candles and phone lights. Naomi and Andersen followed suit, and Naomi took me by my shoulders.

"Is it him?" she asked. I pushed her away as a cheshire grin melted into view, and there he was, in his favorite striped apron, stirring a bowl of chocolate batter.

"Eydis, my dear! My associate thinks you called the museum, but surely that can't be right." The vision looked out of place in the alley, wearing his apron and slippers. He dragged a finger through the batter and licked it. "Maybe too much cocoa?"

"I'm in New Delos, actually."

The bowl dropped from his arms, disappearing before it hit the ground. Flecks of chocolate splashed up to dot his apron.

"Oh?" He dropped his voice, and though his eye stared ravenously, I knew he couldn't really see me.

"You said I was still welcome." I leaned against the alleyway brick, ignoring Naomi and Andersen's wide-eyed nods as they tried to follow my half of the conversation.

"You ran away?" Adrestus crooned. "Where are you now?"

I turned to look back at the top of Schrader Tower, a sole beacon of light on the darkened island.

"I'll be at the boardwalk in an hour," I said. "Come find me there."

He sucked batter off his thumb and furrowed his brow.

"And this isn't a trick? How do I know you're actually here?"

"Trace the call. I made it from the island."

His mustache twitched as he smirked.

"Were you followed?"

"No."

"How can you be sure? I can increase security around the island if it makes you feel better."

I hesitated. That was the opposite of what we were trying to get him to do.

"It wouldn't," I said carefully, "but do what you want."

"Very well. Boardwalk. One hour."

The shadows reclaimed his visage, and I exhaled, rubbing the heels of my hands over my eyes.

"You good?" Naomi asked, and I nodded.

"Never better." I pushed off the wall and forced a smile. "But we need to move. The whole neighborhood will be crawling with his people if he traces the phone call."

We wove between shops and townhouses, bowing our heads against the rain and trying to avoid attention. My chat with Adrestus had left my lungs empty and my hands shaking, but my resolve was intact. There was no better way to uncover the reason for his Peace Summit than from behind his frontlines.

It was impossible to tell how much time had passed when the tugging in the back of my head returned.

"Eydis, my dear."

My stomach squirmed as Adrestus appeared before me donning a black suit and polished shoes, standing in the misting rain. I grabbed Naomi's wrist to silently warn her, but I couldn't help the smirk that pulled at my lips. Adrestus glowered behind a carefully constructed smile, the strain of which was apparent in the way his one eye wrinkled. He was annoyed.

"Yes?"

"It's been an hour. Where are you?"

"I'm still by the ferry terminal."

He chewed on the inside of his mouth, making his cheek dimple.

"You said you'd be at the boardwalk."

"I got lost in the dark," I lied. "You didn't forget to pay your energy bill, did you? Because—"

"I get it." A muscle in his jaw jumped. "We're on our way. Stay there."

He faded from view, and I flashed a triumphant smile up at his tower. Seeing him the second time was less intimidating. I was the one in power. I held the cards.

"He's annoyed," I said. "I think I can lead him on for a little bit longer before we give it up."

Just a little bit longer before I had to give Naomi the slip. Just a little bit longer before I faced Adrestus on my terms.

"Don't get too cocky," Naomi warned. "We're playing it safe, okay?"

"Right. Safe." I nodded. "And the safest place is now the boardwalk since he's certain we aren't there."

"That's a bit close to Schrader Tower," Andersen interjected. "If Naomi gets too close, and her mom is up there—"

Naomi took Andersen's words as a direct challenge and marched forward.

"Don't tell me what I can and can't handle," she spat. "Sammy's right. It's the safest place."

I followed her into the rain, and Andersen's footsteps splashed after us.

"But what's our endgame? I don't want to be out in this weather all night."

"Right, wouldn't want to catch hypothermia." Naomi's braids hit me as she spun around to face Andersen. He took a step back and put his hands up in surrender.

"That's not—"

"Not what you meant? Same way you didn't mean to kill Samantha?"

I put a hand on her shoulder, and she let me draw her away.

"Later," I warned under my breath. I looked back at Andersen. "I'll eventually tell Adrestus I chickened out and went back to the mainland. With any luck, he'll chase me there while we swing around the south end of the city and up towards the campus."

Andersen nodded, knowing better than to voice whatever reservations he had left, and followed behind us with his head down.

The handful of times I'd been to the island's western boardwalk, it had been alive with people enjoying the shops, no matter the time of day. Now, large parts of the boardwalk were missing, presumably destroyed in the flood, and the only shops to have survived were the mobile kiosks that now lined the edge of the pavement where it met wooden plank.

The usual crowds had been replaced with quiet, scattered pedestrians, huddling between propane lamps that offered dull heat and a meager, orange glow that caught the bronze edges of a new statue installation.

A Paragon statue had once stood among the shops of the boardwalk. Now, Prime Minister John Ratcliffe's likeness watched over the dilapidated waterfront. A wave of metal water crashed up against his back and fanned out, freezing him in a moment of feigned heroism.

"Wavemaker." Naomi murmured Ratcliffe's superhero name with distaste.

"It's just a statue." Andersen forged onward to get a better look at the food options.

"Just a statue?" Naomi repeated. "He paved Adrestus's way to take over the island! His daughter *ruined* your life when she told everyone you were an Apex."

"I'm not scared of a statue."

He sauntered over to a cart advertising kebobs of meat and fruit, his dewy hair glowing in the orange light of a nearby lamp.

"He's trying." I shrugged at Naomi.

"Why do you keep defending him? You spent months hating him, and now that I know what he did to you, you want me to be cool with it?"

Andersen held up a few fingers as he ordered food. Naomi was right. I had hated him. But somewhere between being forced into Fleming's custody together and then working as a team to destroy New Delos, I'd forgotten how to keep doing so.

"He murdered me," I said slowly, "but he's also saved my life. He got lucky I didn't stay dead, and I think he and I are both doing what we can to make the most of that second chance."

"Even if you're over it, I'm not. I reserve the right to hate him for your sake."

Andersen returned with several skewers of meat and fruit. Naomi scowled and scanned the surrounding sidewalks.

"You sit. I'll take a lap and make sure the area is as safe as it looks." Her eyes flickered over Andersen, and I suspected she was looking for an excuse to escape him. She slipped away as Andersen fell onto a rusted metal bench that looked out over the vast blackness of the open ocean.

I sat down next to him, letting the hum of the food vendors' generators fill the space between us. Andersen tore into his food, but I held my kebab in one hand while I pulled my dog whistle necklace from under my hoodie with the other. I rolled the thin metal between two fingers, thinking if anything went wrong, I could use the whistle to signal to Wesley.

"Eydis."

I dropped the necklace in surprise. Adrestus stood on the sidewalk in front of me. For a horrible moment, I thought he'd caught up with us, but a couple of pedestrians passed around him, and I knew he was still in my head. He wore a careful scowl that matched his black-on-black suit and undershirt in mood and tone.

"I'm starting to feel a little jilted." He folded his hands carefully in front of his chest, and his blue eye bore into mine. I reached over to smack Andersen's shoulder.

"What?" He craned his neck around. "Is it him again?"

"Sorry, sir." I smiled sheepishly. "I got hungry and used some change to come to the boardwalk."

"We *are* at the boardwalk, you idiot!" Andersen leaped to his feet. "You're supposed to send him away, not towards us!"

"Oh, good. You found the boardwalk." Adrestus's thinning patience was apparent on his face. "Because I've been all over the island. In the rain. In a cashmere suit."

"Right, very sorry. I promise I'm at the boardwalk this time."

"*Samantha!*" Andersen hissed. "He'll come here! Before I've finished my kebab!"

Adrestus's eye flashed angrily.

"I don't like playing games," he snarled, "and I don't like playing the role of the fool."

"Understandable. You know, I can see the top of Schrader Tower from here," I offered. "It's a walkable distance, right? I'll come to you. No need to keep chasing me around the city."

He grinded his jaw, and his lip twitched.

"If you aren't there by midnight, I swear I'll return to that backwater island and—"

"Do it. I'm not there, and I don't care what you do to the people who are."

The muscles in his shoulders relaxed ever so slightly.

"Midnight," he repeated.

"Midnight."

He dissipated into nothingness, and I collapsed back in my seat, no longer hungry.

"What the hell?" Andersen took Adrestus's place in front of me. "You told him where we are! And when you don't show by midnight—"

"I need your help."

He blinked once, then twice, and deflated. He fell back on the bench, staring blankly at the dark water.

"You're joining him."

"This could be our only shot at playing him at his own game. I'll find the kidnapped Apex. I'll figure out what this Peace Summit is about. We'll stop him faster this way, before he hurts us."

The others cared too much to let me walk into the lion's den. But Andersen? He was practical and wouldn't be blinded by friendship.

But his stony facade seemed to be an attempt at covering the out-of-character worry that now creased his brow.

"Naomi would never allow it, and you can't outrun her."

"I don't need to make it the whole way," I said darkly. "If we're right and Adrestus is holding the families in Schrader Tower, Naomi won't be able to get close. Not while her mom is nearby."

"That's... That's underhanded."

My cheeks warmed with shame.

"It might not come to that," I said. "Not if you do your part and hold her off long enough for me to get all the way to Adrestus."

"I can't beat her!" he blanched. "You've seen her fight. There's a reason she made captain as a sophomore."

"So wrap her in a lamppost! It'll be easy for you."

Andersen blushed and tried to hide behind his kebab.

"Sure, technically, I could, but—" He cleared his throat and refused to meet my eye. "I won't. Not against my friends. Not since—"

He gulped and took too big a bite of meat.

"Since you threw me in the ocean?"

His lips tightened, and he swallowed his food.

"Everyone will think I let you go because I hate you."

"That's not entirely untrue, though."

"But I don't," he scowled.

"Don't what?"

His eye twitched.

"I don't—" He glanced around and struck a face, looking like his next words caused him great physical pain. "I don't hate you."

I recoiled.

"Ew, don't get all gushy on me all of the sudden."

"I'm not!" he said, too loudly, and then hunched his shoulders over his food. "But you're tolerable, okay?"

"I was kind of counting on you hating me for my plan to work, actually," I admitted.

"The more you talk, the better your chances."

"Fine, don't help me because you hate me. Help me because it's a good plan."

"And who's going to keep Wesley from murdering me when he finds out what I let you do?"

I crossed a leg over my knee, trying to look at ease.

"I'm doing this with or without your help." I shrugged. I could see Naomi's bowed head coming towards us, stepping around the small groups of people that dotted the boardwalk. "Once Naomi figures out where I'm leading you, she *will* try to stop me. Don't think about it too much. You'll give us away."

"But—!" He cut off as Naomi fell into the empty chair.

"No sign of Adrestus. Have you heard anymore from him?"

"Not yet." I stood up and finished off my kebab. "But we should keep moving. I'll send him to the mainland next so we can make our way to campus."

I tried to shove down my festering guilt until it was hiding somewhere neither I nor Naomi would feel it.

The rain picked up as we wove deeper into the city, and puddle water seeped into my tennis-shoes, making me wish I had my uniform boots to go along with the torso armor hiding under my hoodie. I kept a hand on my necklace and my eyes on the glowing windows of Adrestus's penthouse.

The closer we got, the better my chances of escaping Naomi became and the harder my heart drummed against my sternum. My luck couldn't hold. I knew that. It was only a matter of time.

And then time ran out.

"We need to go further south." Naomi stopped, nearly invisible in the dark of the alley we were passing through. "If we go much farther, I'll be in range of my mom, and we should try to avoid getting too close to Adrestus's home."

"I thought we could make it to the central park first so we'd have tree cover."

"The park doesn't go south," Naomi pointed out. "And it's way too close to the tower. If my mom is up there, I won't be able to get under the tree cover at all."

"Oh." We'd been making such good progress. "I don't know why I thought it led south."

It was a weak lie, and my focus wavered for a half-moment as I forged onward.

It was all Naomi needed.

"Wait." She grabbed my bicep, and I tried to will my beating heart to calm itself. Naomi squinted at me in the dark. I knew she was trying to make sense of the blend of guilt, fear, and panic that gnashed inside of me. "You've been on guard all night but not just for Adrestus, I think."

She craned around to look at Andersen. He took a step back, and her fingers tightened around my arm.

"And *you*," she hissed. "You've reeked of deceit since we left the boardwalk."

Andersen and I locked eyes, and I saw him gulp.

"Naomi," I said slowly, "I can save your family."

Damp braids swung as she spun back to me. I grabbed her wrist where she still had my bicep in her grip and tried to loosen her fingers.

"That's why we're here," she said. "To save the people Adrestus has kidnapped and stop whatever he has planned. And we're doing that as a team. Together."

That was the word Wesley had said, too. Another spike of guilt grabbed at my chest. How many times had I broken her trust now? I'd lied about my identity. I'd run off without telling her more times than I could count. What was once more?

"I'm sorry," I gulped. Whether Andersen had made his decision to help me or not, the time had come for me to make my move.

I twisted my arm free of her grip, feeling her nails dig into my skin through my several layers of hoodie and uniform. I sprinted as fast as I could, but didn't even make it to the end of the next alley when the collar of my hoodie tightened around my neck. Naomi threw me against the wall, knocking over a metal trashcan that rattled down the alley.

"You can't be *serious*?" She pressed her elbow against my throat, pinning me against brick slick with rain water. "After *everything*, after *Everly*—"

"Let me go!" I kicked her off me and tried to run again, but she grabbed me from behind before I made it more than two steps.

"We *just* got you back, Sammy! *I* just got you back! He already has my family. I won't let him take you, too!"

Her arms locked around my chest and her cheek, pressed against mine, was wet. Maybe it was just rain on her face.

"Naomi..." I whispered. A burning tightness rose up my throat and into my nose. My eyes itched. "I'm sorry. I—"

Her arms disappeared, and her fingernails scrabbled at the back of my neck. Thin metal pressed into my throat and snapped as my necklace broke in her hands.

"Go!" Andersen shouted, struggling to hold Naomi back. Tears tracked her face, and she let out a feral scream.

"Don't you *dare*, Samantha! Don't you *dare* leave me!"

I hesitated.

"Samantha, *go!*" Andersen repeated, his face contorting with the effort of containing Naomi.

I turned away before the sight of Naomi struggling in Andersen's arms could destroy my resolve. Her screams of protest tore at the back of my brain, echoing in my head as I sprinted towards Schrader Tower.

At least I wouldn't be there when she had to tell Fleming what I'd done. Or when Wesley found out. Rain cut at my face, and I scowled at the sky as I ran.

I fought back a sob. I missed Naomi and Wesley so badly that it made me ill, and I wished for nothing more than to return to when they'd been training me in the fall. When we could end the day over frozen yogurt and worry about class projects. Adrestus had just been an apparition back then. A mystery to crack.

I burst free of the buildings and welcomed the shadowy embrace of the park trees. The branches left on the trunks drooped and sagged, and in the dull light of Schrader Tower, the leaves looked more orange than green despite the season. Water pooled over the cobbled walkway, and pale, sickly trunks rose on either side of me like skeletons.

"Sammy, you coward!"

I spun around to meet Naomi's fist as it collided with the side of my head. The park flipped, and I landed in a puddle, the falling rain swirling overhead in a dizzying array. I waited for Naomi to attack again, but she coughed next to me, her braids floating up around her face in the puddle water.

"That's...that's a dirty trick." Blood streamed from her nose, and her eyes shifted in and out of focus. "Using my own mother against me... maybe you belong with Adrestus after all."

Sudden convulsions shook her body.

"Naomi!" I pulled her into my lap, and she blinked up at the sky.

"I haven't felt her in two years." Tears pooled in her hairline, and I wiped them away.

"I'm going to get her out," I promised.

"And then what? I go back to never seeing her again? I already used up the only dose of power blocker Everly made."

"You will. I promise." I located a bench nearby and staggered to my feet, straining under her weight.

"You promised you wouldn't lie to me anymore," she choked. "You promised me the Lapis before Vidar destroyed it. What good are your promises, Sammy? I won't let you go. I won't—"

Sudden, searing pain exploded in my head, and I cried out, dropping Naomi as agony washed over me. It was like a thousand nails screeching against a chalkboard in my mind. It was unbearable. It was distinctly Naomi.

It felt like she was tearing me apart from the inside, and I fell to my knees, grabbing at my hair. Metallic heat warmed my sinuses and blood dripped from my nose and into my mouth.

"Stop," I gasped. "Naomi, please."

Naomi stood over me, her strength having returned as quickly as mine had evacuated. It was as if the affliction of her powers had been turned on me instead. Was this what it felt like for her to be near her mother and sister?

"I don't—" she stammered. "Sammy, what—"

And then the pain disappeared as suddenly as it had come, and Naomi collapsed in the grass, unconscious.

I sat catching my breath, too stunned by this new power of hers to move until I remembered the promise I'd made to Adrestus. I wiped the blood from my face and staggered forward, taking my friend in my arms to lay her down on the bench.

By the time she woke up, it would be too late. I'd be with Adrestus. I'd been a bad friend, but maybe I'd be able to at least give her back her family.

Naomi's final attack left me shaken, and I made slower progress through the rolling knolls of the park than I had wanted. Bleached branches cast zig-zagging shadows across the path. Schrader Tower loomed overhead, its top floors disappearing into a halo of hazy, white light, but I kept my eyes on the path ahead.

The Schrader Museum took up the bottom four floors of Schrader Tower, and its white face and decorative columns reflected the dim solar garden lights of the park back at me through the last of the trees. My breath turned shallow and my palms clammy. Every instinct screamed at me to run from the building where I'd been hunted, where Wesley had lost his arm, where Adrestus had murdered Vidar.

But I would find Mom, Avery, and my missing friends. I would beat Adrestus. I would see Naomi and Wesley again.

The trees parted, and I stood across the street from the grand, white steps that led to the museum entrance. Adrestus stood on the top step in a halo of light emitted by lamps above the doors. Mira lingered just behind him, impossible to read from this far.

"Cutting it a bit close to midnight, my dear," Adrestus called as I strutted across the street to meet him. Something akin to distrust laced his words, and I couldn't blame him. He'd spent the last few hours chasing me across his own island.

"So?" I forced a laugh in an effort to hide the quake in my voice. "What do I care if you go back to McMillan Island? They wanted to use and discard me like a lab rat. If you can promise me better than that, then I don't care what you do to them."

I stopped on the bottom step. Adrestus's face was lost to shadow thanks to the light directly above him, but I thought I saw his mouth twist into a smirk.

"I can promise you *much* better."

"But you left me behind," I accused, getting the jump on him before he could claim I'd stayed behind of my own volition. "You said you were there to rescue me, but you lied. You just wanted my nephew."

"No, he was just my consolation prize. He belongs here, just as you do." He stepped aside and beckoned to the door behind him. "It's been a thousand years since you were stolen from me."

"Glad to be back." My stomach lurched. I wanted to vomit.

I inhaled, savoring my last taste of freedom, and took the first step up to the doors.

"Wait!"

The cry calling out from the dying trees behind me was desperate and begging and resolved. It hung in the air, echoing off the face of Schrader Tower as if to knock the breath from me twice.

No.

This was not the plan. This was not *my* plan.

My brain slowed, and the museum steps seemed to freeze around me. I looked back at the figure running out of the protection of the mottled shadows. He stumbled to a stop in the middle of the street and bent over, leaning against his knee with his one arm, wheezing for air.

The lamplight glinted off the thin silver chain that hung from his hand. My dog whistle necklace.

He raised his green eyes to meet mine, and his jaw tensed in anger and terror and stubborn loyalty.

"If she joins you," Wesley panted, "then I do, too."

23

Underwater, Underfoot

Wesley's cold, determined gaze held me as he addressed Adrestus. Sweat slicked his brow, and his shoulders heaved with the effort of having sprinted across the island to reach me in time. He was mad. Really mad. He may be willing to follow me into hell, but I wasn't sure if he was willing to forgive me.

"They're tricking us," Mira hissed, and my stomach dropped.

"No!" I ripped my eyes away from Wesley to look up at Adrestus. I couldn't abandon the plan now. It would put Wesley in danger, and as furious as I was with him, I couldn't have that. "I swear, I had no idea he was here."

While Mira looked ready for murder, Adrestus smiled.

"If it's a trick, it's a poor one," he mused.

"He must've followed me, I—" I stopped. I couldn't raise suspicion. I couldn't give Adrestus a reason to search the island for more of my teammates.

"Yeah," Wesley panted. "I followed her. Alone."

He locked eyes with me again, limping to the bottom step, my necklace swinging in hand. Naomi had ripped it from around my neck. She must've used it to call him.

I tried to shake my head, hoping the tiny movement would be imperceptible to Adrestus, silently begging Wesley to notice and take heed. He stared back at me with a hard brow and set jaw. He stepped up to meet me, and my chin tilted up towards him in defiance. His hair was messed up and his cheeks pink from running, but his eyes narrowed at me.

"*Leave,*" I hissed.

His jaw clenched. He was furious. He was terrified. He wasn't going to back down.

"Roy Hendricks kicked me off the team." Wesley made the lie look effortless, maybe because it was technically true. "I don't have the team anymore, and you have my family. There's nowhere else for me to go. Ares was the name you gave me, right? Congrats. You got Eydis back along with your god of war."

"I don't trust them," Mira asserted. "It's too easy."

"It doesn't matter if they're trustworthy or not," Adrestus grinned. "We have their friends. We have their families. Even if they didn't want to, now that they're here, they'll have to obey."

I suppressed a shudder as the many holes in my plan came to light. It had been stupid of me to come here. It had been even stupider of Wesley to follow.

"You cut off his arm," Mira reminded Adrestus. "Why would he want to come here if not to return the favor?"

"Apex Team used me to develop a weapon that could kill Sammy," Wesley asserted. "My choices are slim, but my allegiance is to her. If Sammy decides she belongs at your side, then that's where I belong, too."

Adrestus's smile strained, but he nodded and stepped to the side, gesturing to the museum entrance with a sweeping motion.

"Then who am I to deny you a front seat to the bright new future we'll build together?"

Wesley's shoulder bumped against mine, and we climbed to the top step together. Mira stood aside with Adrestus, and I felt her eyes on my back as I passed through the main doors.

My final remaining shred of sense searched for a last-second exit, feeling very much like I was walking into the open mouth of a hungry crocodile as I stepped into the dark, empty museum atrium.

My sneakers squeaked with puddle water, and the sound echoed off the marble floor and high ceiling, accompanying the sound of the water fountain that splashed and gurgled at the center of the space.

"Apologies," Adrestus murmured. The door clicked shut behind him. "But there's something still nagging me."

Wesley stepped back, but I stood my ground.

"And?"

Adrestus brushed invisible dust off his shoulder and leaned against the locked door.

"Mira killed you the other day," he continued, and I placed a hand over my abdomen where the sword had pierced my spleen. "Yet here you are, still reaping the blessings that the Lapis bestowed upon you."

"Everly said I'll run out." It felt sacrilegious to speak Everly's name in front of his murderers. "That's bugging you?"

He laughed softly, and it was hard to ignore the tension in Mira's shoulders, like the raised hackles of a cat.

"No, not at all. But it *is* important, I promise you." He swaggered forward. "I need you to prove your loyalty."

"We're here, aren't we?" I fought the instinct to take up a defensive stance.

"Yes, but are you here because you wish to be or because there is nowhere left for you? And will you be loyal to me or..." His gaze rolled from me to Wesley, "... to each other?"

"I don't even know him!" I stepped away from Wesley, hoping it might sell the lie.

"Mr. Isaacs, you said you're loyal to *Sammy*, and are therefore loyal to *me*. But those who follow me are loyal to me and me alone. I'm happy to have you, but if I have to break whatever allegiance you have for the person you thought Eydis was, then so be it." He pulled a long knife from his belt, and I recognized the thin blade as the one he'd used to dig the Lapis out of my neck back in October. He tossed the knife, and it skittered across the tiles before coming to stop at Wesley's feet. "Last time you were here, you both declined to obey. If you want to prove that you're on my side, kill Eydis."

"But—"

Adrestus held up a hand to cut off my protest.

"You'll come back. You always do. But it's important that I know Ares is willing to kill for me." His mouth twisted, and panic rose in my chest. It had been so stupid to think I held all the cards. "As for you, even if you don't remember your past transgressions, it's important that I know you're willing to die when I tell you to."

"So you're making us fight?" Wesley's voice cracked. Why had he followed me? Why had I come in the first place?

"Fight?" Adrestus's eyebrows hitched upwards. "Oh, no, dear thing. Not fight. Simply kill. And die. Obey. No need to spar over it. You can use that knife if you wish, though I'd prefer if you kept her bleeding to a minimum."

Wesley stooped to pick up the knife. His hair hung in his face as he stared at the blade, hiding his expression.

"Of course, whether you do or don't, you're here now, and we'll still be able to make ample use of you," Adrestus crooned. "You can kill her *or* you can refuse, in which case, Mira will force you to kill her anyway."

Wesley turned to look at me, his green eyes wide with terror.

"It's okay," I rasped, though my hands had turned numb. My calves bumped up against the fountain as I stepped back. "I'll be alright."

His shoulders trembled, and I tried to look calm for his sake. If we wanted to beat Adrestus, if we wanted to have any chance at all, if we wanted to avoid becoming his prisoners, we knew what we needed to do.

"You shouldn't have followed me," I breathed, barely audible to myself, though I knew Wesley, and Wesley alone, would hear my words. "Because now you have to do it, Wes."

"Sammy." He mouthed my name, anguish written in the shadows of his face.

"Do it."

The knife slipped from his grip, and it clattered to the floor. Mira tensed, ready to intervene.

"Wesley—" I started to beg, but then he closed the space between us, and my hoodie collar was balled in his fist. His eyes wavered between mine. He didn't have it in him to do what he needed to do next.

I lifted my hands to his wrist and held him there. It wouldn't be worse than the deaths I'd already suffered.

I fell backwards into the fountain, pulling Wesley after me. The water closed over my head, and with the first lungful of liquid, my resolve deserted me, and survival instincts took over.

My mind went blank, overcome by the screaming demand for air, and I struggled to return upright as the world blurred and darkened overhead. I kicked against something sturdy, and Wesley's hand tightened around my jacket collar.

Relief and disappointment swirled around me in the dirty water of the fountain. Wesley, who made me feel safe. Wesley, who now needed to kill me to keep us both alive.

Bright lights popped in my vision, and just as the world was starting to feel heavier, a muffled cry echoed overhead, and water rushed around my ears as someone pulled me from the fountain.

I fell to the tiles. Grimy water burned and grated at my throat as I coughed it up onto the floor, my elbows shaking with the effort of supporting my weight.

Why had Wesley stopped? They'd hook him back up to Mira's control device again. They'd force him to wreak havoc and do their bidding. They'd make him do far worse than killing an immortal girl.

"Wesley, you need to kill me!" I gagged. A hand caressed under my chin and lifted my gaze. I tried to recoil away from Adrestus's face so close to mine, but his fingers tightened, digging into my cheeks.

"Ares isn't the one who showed you mercy," he growled. "I am. *I'm* the reason you are spared another death tonight. *I* did that for you."

He released my face, and I craned my neck to look back at Wesley. He stepped away, his face lost in shadow.

"You both did well," Adrestus said, rising to his feet. "How lucky for you both. Mira, take Eydis to your quarters. I'll handle Ares."

Mira's hand clamped around my wrist, and I tensed, waiting for her control to sweep across my nerves. However, it never came, and I staggered to my feet myself.

"Wesley, are you okay?" I asked as Mira led me to a side hall. He bowed his head and ignored me, but I kept my eyes on him as long as I could before he disappeared around the corner.

No, he could never forgive me for this.

With no power in the city, I was afraid we might be forced to climb eighty flights of stairs, something I was sure my quaking legs couldn't do. However, after Mira led me through the back offices of the museum, she stopped at an elevator. A gentle chime sounded its arrival, and Mira shoved me into the lift. I pressed myself into the corner, ready for Mira to try and hurt me somehow, but she stayed on her side of the elevator, leaning against the windowed wall as we rose up and over the darkened city.

"He may have opted to trust you," she finally murmured as she watched city streets spotted with flecks of random light disappear in a cloud of fog beneath us, "but I know you better than he does."

"You don't know me." I worked to keep the snarl out of my voice. She'd murdered Everly for no reason other than she could, but I'd avenge him better if I kept my cool for now.

Her lips pulled into a cold smile, and she pushed her long tresses behind an ear.

"Perhaps not."

The elevator came to a halt high above the streets of New Delos. We were in the upper floors, back where I'd been half a year ago. This time, I wasn't a prisoner.

At least, I didn't think I was. Mira hadn't used her powers on me yet, even if she did look ready to throw me out of the window.

The doors slid open, and she led the way to the right down a gray walled corridor. Less than half of the rounded lights that rested atop the sconces were lit, casting their glow across the tiled floor. The high ceiling was topped with ornate crown molding, and the doors were farther apart than those in a hotel or dorm, suggesting generously sized suites behind them.

Mira stopped at a plain, gray door.

"You touch anything I don't give you express permission to touch, and you die." She pushed into the apartment.

It wasn't fair that a murderer was allowed to live in as luxurious of an apartment as this one. Candlelight from the marble kitchen island reflected off the massive window that stretched from floor to two-story high ceiling. Orange light flickered off the second-floor walkway's metal railing as well as the banister of the floating stone staircase that wrapped up the side of the living room.

Mira walked to the open-concept kitchen and pulled a bottle of pink wine from the stainless-steel fridge. She gestured towards the low, black couch that ran along the far windowed wall of the sunken living room.

"That's the best I can offer you for now." She took a long draw of the wine straight from the bottleneck, and I looked between her and the sofa.

"Can I have a change of clothes?" I raised my arms in front of me, showing off my soaked hoodie. She smiled through narrowed eyes and lilted into the living room, making a show of climbing the stairs while drinking.

I backed into the living room, tracking Mira up to the second floor. She opened a door in the middle of the hall to reveal stacked laundry machines, and rifled through the dryer until she found a suitable change of clothes for me.

She dropped them over the railing, and I stepped back, letting them fall to the ground rather than try to pluck them from the air.

"Bathroom's around the corner." The pink wine swished in its bottle as she gestured to my right. I gathered the clothes from the floor and gave Mira one last wary glance. She leaned against the second floor railing, her long white hair cascading over the banister.

In the candlelit bathroom, I made quick work of peeling my wet clothes from my body and tried to keep my breathing under control.

Wesley was still downstairs with Adrestus. He could be in mortal peril, and I was eighty stories away from him.

Why had he followed me? Why had Naomi called him with my whistle? And was Naomi okay? Maybe I should've carried her farther from the tower before leaving her.

I tugged on the collar of my borrowed t-shirt as I exited the bathroom. I hated wearing the clothes of a murderer, but the shirt and leggings were at least dry. Mira had left a pillow and blanket on the couch for me, and I stepped down into the living room, looking out the darkened window.

Any moment Fleming would be hearing about how I went rogue again and how Wesley had followed me.

I hoped he knew I was sorry.

I sat back on the couch and startled when I saw Mira still leaning against the railing overhead. Her cascading hair stirred with the rise and fall of her shoulders, looking ethereal and terrifying from her perch on the second floor.

I lay back and closed my eyes, trying to block her out, but after another few minutes, I opened them again to glare at her.

"You don't need to stand there all night."

"So many years at his side, and I've never doubted Adrestus," she murmured. She stared down at me like I was a zoo animal in an enclosure. "Until tonight. We attacked you. I killed your nurse friend. I killed you. Yet here you are, wanting to join the team."

I sat up on the couch.

"He trusts me."

"He trusts no one," Mira laughed, "and he has no practical use for you whether he trusts you or not. You're a trophy. A trophy that even after everything you've done, he continues to underestimate. But that's why I'm here. To stop you when his judgment ultimately fails."

"He invited me here." I leaned back, trying to look self-assured. "I'm not going to fight you or anyone else."

"Fighting is who you are," Mira hissed. "He told me how you first stole the Lapis from him. How you tried to murder him after you killed your family—"

"I didn't kill anyone!" My borrowed blanket fell in a crumpled heap on the floor as I rose to my feet.

"What would you know, little amnesiac? We all know what you did, even if you don't remember it, how the Scourge Queen killed those who loved her most."

I scowled and fell back onto the couch, pulling the blanket back up over my legs. She was trying to goad me into a fight. I wouldn't let her.

"Be assured, when you screw up, and I know you will, I'll make what I did to that nurse look like a mercy after I'm through with your precious Wesley."

I waited for her to slink away, but she remained overhead. I refused to let her intimidate me and fluffed my pillow before turning towards the low back of the couch.

When sleep finally came, it only held onto me for a feeble, few hours before I awoke to a sore jaw, courtesy of Naomi's final sucker punch. For a split second, I thought I was back in my bed at the farmhouse, and then I opened my eyes to Mira's vaulted ceiling, lit by first rays of dawn streaming over the glittering city. My eyes flickered to where Mira had stood watch as I fell asleep, but she must've tired, too. The second floor hall was empty.

My stomach lurched when I sat up, upset by lack of sleep as well as worry over Wesley. I looked at the front door, wondering if it was locked and if I would be free to go find him, but I knew that doing so would land us both in more trouble than we were already in.

The candles on the kitchen island had burnt out overnight, and I ran my hand over the impeccably-clean white marble countertop. As nice as the massive island and stainless-steel appliances were, it wasn't the fanciest kitchen I'd ever been in. That title still belonged to Adrestus's living quarters.

I hoped Wesley was somewhere nice, too, and not locked up in some lab.

I opened the fridge, though I was too nervous to eat, and shifted through a row of Greek Yogurt containers, investigating the various flavors. A row of pitchers filled with juices crowded the middle shelf, but when I bent down to get a better look, sudden blinding pain erupted in my head as something collided with my temple and pushed me to the floor.

Strawberry blonde hair blurred overhead, and I tried to blink my eyes back into focus.

"Mira!" my attacker shouted. "We've been infiltrated!"

She placed a foot on my chest, though I was too stunned to try to get up, and leaned down, her strawberry blonde hair swinging forward to frame her jaw.

"How the hell did you get in here?" Winnie snarled. "And why the hell are you wearing my clothes?"

24

Just Like Old Times

I pushed Winnie's foot off my chest and tried to scramble away, but she grabbed a handful of my hair and dragged me to the living room.

"Winnie, stop!"

She threw me to the floor, and Mira's plush living room rug pressed against my face.

"Mira!" Winnie howled again. With both my scalp and my dignity smarting, I grabbed her leg and flipped her to the floor. Her hand pressed my head into the carpet while I trapped her in a leg lock. "Let go of me!"

"You first!" The rug muffled my words, and Winnie pressed down harder.

"Why are you wearing my clothes?" Winnie demanded again. "Is this supposed to be some sort of disguise?"

"Yes, you saw right through my plan! I was going to infiltrate Adrestus's ranks using your musty old yoga pants!"

"They are *not* musty *or* old, you *hag*!"

"HAG?" I found Winnie's face with my hand and pushed her away. She released my head, but grabbed me around the torso and flipped me so I was looking up at the ceiling.

Mira stared down at us from the second floor, boredom pulling her mouth into a neat frown.

"Stop her!" I squawked at Mira. The morning light that poured in through the window highlighted the bags under her eyes that the dark of the night had hidden the night before. Her skin was ashen, and her usually silky hair seemed to hang limp.

"Why?" She drew her lips into a coy smile, though it looked heavy on her face. "What do I care about how you and Winifred resolve your issues?"

"Resolve our—?" Winnie repeated, her voice muffled. "Mira, she's *intruding*! She stole my clothes! Her friends are probably nearby, ready to attack!"

"Yeah, that's what I said, too." Mira floated down the stairs, her floor-length cardigan billowing out behind her. "Take it up with Adrestus. He's the one who let her in."

"Exactly!" I wheezed, my head at a weird angle. Mira stepped over us, unbothered by our wrestling match. "So let me go!"

"You can't be serious!" Winnie cried. "We can't trust her! She—"

"She's here, and she's not going anywhere, even if she wants to." Mira pulled a milk carton from the fridge.

Winnie finally let go, and I rolled away, rubbing my scalp.

"We're just conveniently forgetting that she escaped once?" Winnie balked.

"Only prisoners escape," Mira crooned from the kitchen. "Eydis isn't a prisoner."

Winnie scowled at me and rose to her feet.

"Fine, but my clothes are *my* clothes."

"We'll get her new clothes, but until then—"

"And I'm not sharing my room with her."

"She's not staying on my couch. It's velvet."

"Then make Lana take her!"

"Adrestus sent her to stay with us." Mira's voice wrapped around a poorly concealed warning. "Besides, it's nice to be back living under the same roof, is it not?"

"No," Winnie asserted, "it's *not*. What are we going to do if she turns on us? It's not like you can help."

Mira's eyes hardened over the bowl of cereal she was pouring, but Winnie was too busy fixing her hair in the far wall mirror to notice.

"Your powers don't work?" I watched Mira curiously.

"They work fine," Mira growled. "And unless you'd like proof, I'd shut your pretty little mouth before I melt it off."

"Oh?" Winnie chirped. "Didn't you accidentally poison yourself the other day? Samantha's on our team, now, isn't she? Shouldn't she know about her own teammate's limitations?"

Mira's haggard face twisted.

"You poisoned yourself?" I asked, a sick sense of retribution rising in my gut.

"She's got this cute new trick," Winnie sang. "Neurotoxins. But when she uses them, she poisons herself, too."

"Winifred," Mira warned.

"She has to develop an antidote for herself while she poisons her target, but if she's running low on fuel, that becomes tricky."

I looked back at her gray skin and heavy eyes. She was paying the price for what she did to Everly, but it still wasn't enough. I would make sure she paid in full.

"If you're finished divulging our secrets," Mira hissed, "Adrestus needs you with the interns today."

With her bowl of cereal in hand, she whisked towards the door.

"But I hate the interns," Winnie groaned. "What about you? Where are you going?"

Mira's eyes glided over me, and I gulped.

"I need to discuss plans for our newest team additions with Adrestus." She sneered at me through a mouthful of cereal.

"Additions?" Winnie straightened up. "As in more than Samantha?"

"Another classmate of yours," Mira said sweetly, halfway out the door. "Mr. Wesley Isaacs."

"Wesley's here?" Winnie blanched.

The door slammed shut, and Winnie turned to me with her mouth hanging open.

"He followed me." I shrugged. Winnie blinked several times in rapid succession and shook her head.

"You're idiots. Both of you." She stalked into the kitchen to make her own bowl of cereal and flicked on the overhead lights.

"The power's back?"

"For now." She may have been shorter and blonder, but Winnie's resemblance to Amanda threw me off guard.

An invisible knot wound its way across my chest, and I tried to swallow the lump in my throat. Despite everything, maybe I needed to be nicer to Winnie. Her mom had only died a couple days ago.

"I'm sorry, by the way." I sat back on the black couch and wrung my hands.

"About what?" She glared at me suspiciously.

"The other night."

Her glare dissolved into an eye roll.

"Oh. That. I wasn't close with Everly."

I faltered. She didn't know. She didn't know about her own mother. They hadn't told her.

"What?" She took a bite of dry cereal, staring at me from the opposite site of the kitchen island. "Look, I'm sorry he's dead, but he got in the way."

I looked away, scratching at the fabric of Mira's sofa. I couldn't bring myself to tell Winnie about her mother. She was unlikely to believe me, anyway.

Winnie's bowl clinking in the sink brought my attention back to her as she made to follow Mira's path out the door.

"Wait." I stood up. "What am I supposed to do?"

Winnie glanced around the living room and shrugged.

"Maybe take a shower? You smell like crap."

"I'm just supposed to stay here?"

"Mira said you're not a prisoner." She spread her arms wide. "Go wherever you like. Just stay out of my room."

She disappeared into the corridor, and the door slammed shut.

By the time the city power shut off again sometime after the sun dipped back below the horizon, I'd eaten seven packs of greek yogurt and taken three showers. No matter how many minutes I spent throughout the day under the rainfall shower head of Mira's bathroom, I couldn't seem to get the smell of the fountain water out of my hair.

I needed to see Wesley but didn't dare leave the apartment. This had to be a test. Adrestus had to be watching, waiting to see if I would seek out my friend. I refused to fall for it.

I explored the apartment instead, poking my head into both Mira's and Winnie's bedrooms and figuring out how to wash my jeans and hoodie in the upstairs laundry closet. And then I paced, counting the number of steps between the walls of Mira's living room. If I kept moving, I wouldn't be tempted to seek out Wesley. I wouldn't fail whatever test Adrestus was putting me through.

The next morning, back in my freshly washed jeans and hoodie, I waited for Winnie or Mira to give me new instructions, but again, they left me behind in the apartment.

I at least saw some company this time. Several men came through to assemble a new twin bed in Winnie's bedroom, and I figured I might as well officially move myself in, arranging the new bedsheets and neatly folding my borrowed yoga pants and t-shirt on the foot of my new bed.

"Mira!" Winnie's angry shriek signaled her arrival back home sometime after I'd finished a dinner of cherry yogurt. "She's in my room!"

She stood in the doorway to our bedroom with disheveled hair and black cloaks that hung off her shoulders. Her theatre mask dropped to the floor as she spun around to scream for Mira again.

"She can't keep sleeping on the couch," Mira called back. "She'll ruin the upholstery."

Winnie opened her mouth to snarl some new insult my way just as the power cut yet again, and instead she cursed at the ceiling.

"Is this a nightly thing, then?" I watched the surrounding buildings go dark out the window that took up the far wall of the room, lounging on my bed, forcing myself to look at ease just to frustrate Winnie. "The blackouts, I mean."

Winnie slammed the door closed in response.

I couldn't do a third day alone in the apartment, and the next morning, I tiptoed into the kitchen, hoping to catch Winnie or Mira before they left for the day.

"Good, you're up." I jumped at the sound of Winnie's voice, and she peeked out at me from behind the open refrigerator door. "You have orientation for your new internship."

"Oh." An internship hadn't been what I was expecting. I was, after all, Adrestus's Scourge Queen, scourge of the Apex, killer of the Apex Father. I looked down at my borrowed shirt and yoga pants. However, maybe an internship was exactly the best way to snoop. "Great. I'll go change."

"Into what? I've seen your jeans. There's giant holes in the knees."

"So let me borrow something." I blushed.

She frowned at my yoga pants.

"Nah. You're good."

She led the way to the front door and out into the main corridor, forcing me to keep pace while throwing on my sneakers. I watched the space between Winnie's shoulders as I ran my fingers through my tangled hair. Hopefully this wasn't too professional of an internship

She stopped in front of another door and knocked.

"Who lives here?" I asked. She rolled her eyes and sighed.

"The secretary. And Wesley."

I inhaled sharply, hoping she didn't notice, and forced my face to stay passive. It was a relief to know Wesley was safe, but suddenly I didn't feel ready to face him.

The door swung open, revealing my least favorite of Adrestus's followers. Miles wore all black, and his gray-flecked brown hair was already fighting the hair gel he'd used in an attempt to tame it. An earpiece hung from his ear, and he held a steaming mug of coffee. His lip curled into a sneer, and as much as I wanted to scowl back, I needed him to believe I didn't remember who he was or the countless times I'd ran face first into the force fields he could create.

"I'm here for Wesley." Winnie crossed her arms at Miles. "It's orientation day."

"I think you mean *Ares*," Miles chided. "Don't let the bossman hear you using names that he didn't choose, *Dion*."

"Like you aren't bitter you got passed up by another kid for a spot in the New Parthenon."

Miles's smile fell, and he straightened up, though he wasn't much taller than us.

"I'm needed for more important work—"

"Managing Adrestus's calendar? Answering his phone? Sure, Miles. You're the real backbone of our operation."

"I don't just answer—" His face twisted, and the earpiece blipped blue. He spoke into an unseen mic. "Schrader Museum. You've reached Miles."

He stepped aside, and I peered around Winnie to get a better look into an identical apartment to Mira's but with larger, leather furniture. Wesley stepped out from behind Miles to join us in the hall, dressed in a black henley and dark jeans. I held my breath, taking in his every detail, searching for injuries, trying to read the glower that cast a shadow across his face.

He adjusted his glasses, avoiding my eye and nodding half-heartedly at Winnie. He looked as bone-weary and stretched thin as Mira had. I didn't know who I was angrier at: him for following me or me for not somehow preventing him from doing so.

"Great." Winnie faked a smile. "Bye, Miles. Try not to break a sweat answering phones."

She marched down the hall, not bothering to check if we were following. Wesley strode ahead, and I reached for his elbow, trying to get his attention, but he pulled his arm away and sped up.

"Idiots. I let Andersen punch me in the face." Winnie hit the elevator call button. She turned to cross her arms at us as we waited. "I had a black eye for a week because I helped you escape last time you were here."

"I lost my arm, Winnie." Wesley frowned, and we stepped after her into the elevator. "I don't care about your black eye."

"Exactly. You lost an arm. Did you come back to make the other one match?"

"Your dad kicked me off the team." Wesley still refused to look at me, instead staring out over the glittering city through the windowed walls. "I didn't have anywhere else to go."

"So you followed Sammy," Winnie finished for him. "But she doesn't remember you. How *tragic.*"

The elevator doors opened to a corridor busy with workers in business suits and pencil skirts that made me feel even more self-conscious in my yoga pants and sneakers.

I hesitated in the elevator, and Wesley tilted his face towards me without meeting my eye.

"You look fine," he murmured, "and you passed your chance to turn back a while ago. No use getting cold feet now."

He trudged forward, rolling his loose sleeve up with his left hand, and I ignored the lump nerves had brought to my throat, hurrying to follow him, Winnie, and the distant sound of forks clinking against plates.

Winnie stopped at the entryway to a cafeteria.

"This is the employee cafeteria." Winnie crossed her arms and nodded behind her. "The Student Internship ambassador will come find you for orientation. Until then, try not to run off. Or do. I don't actually care."

She made her exit, bumping against my shoulder harder than she needed to. I stared at Wesley, but he kept his eyes trained on the omelet bar on the far wall.

"Wesley—"

"He's watching us," he said.

"Of course he is. Are you okay? Did he hurt you?"

He pushed his way through the breakfast rush, surveying the spread of oatmeal, omelets, sausages, and waffles. After being cooped up in Mira's spacious apartment for two days, the employee cafeteria felt claustrophobic with its kitschy low-rise carpet and sensible one-story ceiling.

I wanted to be mad at Wesley. For following me. For acting distant. For looking stupidly good in his henley while I looked like a doof in my borrowed yoga pants. Anger turned to guilt, which made me angry again, and if he wanted to refuse to look at me, then fine. I wouldn't look at him, either.

I shoved through the crowd to the cereal bar, ignoring the sound of Wesley following after me.

"Slow down, alright?" he said under his breath, joining me at a stack of bowls. "We need to keep together."

"Oh, do we?" I hissed. "You don't get to invite yourself, act all moody, and then snap at me for not being the ideal teammate."

"First of all, you've never been an ideal teammate." Wesley kept his voice low as he poured his cereal.

"I take offense to that."

"Good."

"You can still leave, you know," I dumped milk into our bowls too aggressively. It slopped over the sides and pooled on the counter, but I moved on towards a cup of spoons.

"Are you going to leave that mess there?"

"Why wouldn't I? It's Adrestus's milk."

"Technically, I think it's Adrian Schrader's milk."

"If you care so much about Schrader's milk, you clean it." I whisked away, stepping around tables in search of somewhere to sit and somewhere Wesley *wasn't.*

"Sammy, wait!"

I fell into a seat at a small table by a window and angrily stirred my cereal. Wesley caught up with a new wet spot on his shirt.

"What is—"

"I spilt Adrian Schrader's milk trying to keep up with you." He took the seat opposite mine, and I begrudgingly slid my napkins across the table. He accepted them and dabbed at his shirt. "I'm sorry I'm acting moody."

"And?"

"I'm not sorry for following you." He narrowed his eyes at me. "I wasn't going to let you come in here alone. This was stupid, even by your standards. And after what happened that first night—"

His throat bobbed as he swallowed hard, and I softened just slightly.

"He won't do that again," I said, though I didn't believe it myself. "We passed his test, and he doesn't want to risk me running out of Life Elixir."

"He knows we're friends. He might even know I—" His cut off, but his green eyes finally found mine. "He's unpredictable, and we're safer if we distance ourselves from each other."

"You chased me into the most dangerous place in the world for either of us and *then* decided we should keep our distance?" I bristled. "Were the two days in solitary not enough distance for you?"

"I knew you were okay." He frowned. "I could hear you down the hall, not well enough to make out what you were saying, but you talk to yourself."

"I'm glad you had peace of mind while I didn't know if you were even still alive," I snarled. "I was fine until you followed me here. If distance is what you want, then *fine*."

I made to get up, but he reached across the table, and I froze when his hand rested on mine.

"I mean emotional distance. If he finds out we care for each other, he'll take it out on both of us. I promise, if I seem moody, it's not because of you."

"Oh, ew," a voice overhead said, and Wesley jerked his hand back. "When they told me we had new interns I didn't realize it was you two."

A mini-blazer and chic pencil skirt loomed over our table, and I slowly turned my head to look up. I recognized her voice, but the less rational part of me was still hoping maybe I was wrong.

Nope.

Jamie Ratcliffe, our ex-classmate, Andersen's ex-girlfriend, daughter of New Delos's first Prime Minister, stared down her nose at us.

25

Island Royalty

Jamie dragged a chair over from a neighboring table and sat down with her hands tucked into her lap, as if she were afraid she might touch us if she wasn't careful.

"You're the student rep for the intern program?" I laughed. After Adrestus nearly had me drowned two nights prior and spending every minute since in the home of the woman I'd watched kill Everly, Jamie's presence was a strange relief. She was horrible, but she was just Jamie. Harmless, safe, horrible Jamie. "Nice to hear that nepotism is still alive and well."

Jamie's face flushed, and she shook out her platinum curls.

"The summer internship program is through Schrader Enterprises, not our governing system. I'm here on merit alone."

I snorted, and Wesley kicked my foot in warning.

"Great, so we're interns. What does that mean?" Wesley asked, and Jamie struck a face.

"You didn't read the program description before applying? The internship is run through the museum, but we're helping with Peace Summit preparations." She rolled her eyes and crossed her arms. "I need to have a chat with whoever is in charge of hiring. I can't believe they let in a couple of ill-prepared Apex sympathizers."

Wesley and I exchanged a look. Jamie didn't seem to know how we'd come to be at Schrader Tower, nor did she seem privy to the fact that Wesley was an Apex and I was an undead Viking. To her, we were still a couple of nobodies in her first period history class. She knew nothing of Adrestus and the larger powers at play on New Delos.

"The museum?" Wesley pried. "You work with Cunningham?"

"It's *Dr.* Cunningham," she sniffed. "I'm his most trusted student worker, which is why he made me intern ambassador. Unfortunately, that means I have to deal with you two. That said, I'd like to make quick work of this so let's get a move on."

"Worried I might throw up on you again if you spend too much time with us?" I nettled, and she turned redder still.

"Sammy," Wesley warned under his breath, "no one is puking on anyone."

He gathered our cereal bowls and carried them to a bussing cart while Jamie blinked after him.

"This might be a dumb question," she admitted, "but has he always been missing an arm? Or is that new?"

"You were classmates for two years," I reminded her. "And you can't honestly say how many arms he had during that time?"

"Excuse me for having better things to worry about than Wesley Isaacs." She forced a smile as Wesley rejoined us and then took off towards the elevators at a brisk walk. "Orientation will take a few hours, and then we'll meet with the other interns to go over preparations for the Peace Summit."

She spun to face us so suddenly that I nearly ran into her in my haste to keep up.

"I get to be on the main stage," she beamed. "Sitting in front of the world's greatest leaders, and I swear if you somehow ruin that for me, I'll make sure you are never eligible for the Epsilon Initiative when we're older."

"Oh, no," Wesley muttered under his breath as we followed her onto the elevator. "Whatever will I do if I'm not gifted superpowers?"

I bit back the smile that tried to sneak onto my face in spite of our dire position.

"Did you say something?" Jamie raised an eyebrow at us as she selected the floor for the museum office. "I *really* wish they'd run the applicants by me. What were they thinking letting you two into a program as prestigious as this one?"

The doors slid open to the familiar white walls of the museum office. Exhibits adorned in tapestries peeked at us from beyond the glass double doors, and Miles's raspy voice spoke from behind a dual computer screen.

"Any nation wanting to establish an embassy in New Delos will have to adhere to the guidelines set out in Addendum B of the New Delos Peace Summit bylaws," he was saying. "Yes, ma'am, you need only elect one for the initiative. *Then* we can talk embassies."

"This is the museum office, but you probably know that." Jamie gestured around the office and then pointed to the computers. "And that's Mr. Miles. He's the receptionist."

Miles peeked at us from behind his desk set-up.

"I'm *not* a receptionist. I'm Schrader Industries top managerial coordinator and—"

"And that's a nice mouthful of words to say that you're embarrassed to be in a position typically occupied by women," Jamie sang. "If you're gonna be sexist, don't be such a coward about it."

"I'm not sexist," Miles scowled. "I *am* tired of teenage girls thinking they're clever."

"But not teenage boys? Sexist," Jamie sniffed. "Careful, I'm island royalty. My father is—"

"Prime Ministers aren't royalty," Miles shrugged, "and neither are you. I see the new interns are with you."

He dug into his desk drawers and threw a couple of key cards onto the counter.

"White?" Jamie blanched, holding up a white keycard. "Why do they get white clearance? Not even *I* have white clearance!"

She waved her silver keycard, and Miles smiled smugly.

"I'm just doing what I'm told."

"But White Clearance has access all the way up to Schrader's Penthouse!" Jamie squawked. "I'm the Prime Minister's daughter! I'm the head Intern! If anyone—"

"I suppose we're *both* outranked by someone who thinks these two brats should have access to the top of the building. Hurry up with the tour. Schrader is catering a luncheon for the intern team in Conference room 42-C at noon and expects you all there."

"Great." Jamie marched to the glass doors of the office. "Schrader better be there. I need to ask him why these losers have better clearance than me."

Jamie dragged us through the museum, keeping a brisk pace, as if getting us through the tour faster would bring her face to face with Schrader sooner. Only my first visit to the Schrader Museum had been relatively uneventful. Since then, the exhibits had been marred by memories of being hunted and bleeding out on the cold marble tile.

"Adrian Schrader's great grandfather, Grier Schrader, was the man who built New Delos." Jamie's designer shoes echoed in time with her pace. "It was his solution to the Apex problem, creating a place to section them off and to protect the rest of the world."

"I thought he built it as a place for them to be safe from discrimination." Wesley frowned.

"It was a mutually beneficial arrangement." Jamie shrugged, walking us past pictures of the island mid-construction. "In time, they became too unruly even for New Delos, but now with the Epsilon Initiative, *anyone* can opt into Apex powers and even the playing field."

"What incredibly sound logic that is." I rolled my eyes.

"If you have an issue with it, why are you here? I can get your clearance revoked," Jamie snapped.

"How? I have more clearance than you." I looked at Wesley in mock surprise. "Hey, you don't suppose we can get *her* clearance revoked?"

Jamie's face reddened, and she forged onward into the next exhibit.

After our tour, she brought us to a new elevator and up to the middle of the building. Spacious halls wound between cubicles, and late morning sun spilled in from the windows.

"This is headquarters for Peace Summit planning," Jamie explained. "You'll spend a lot of time here performing administrative tasks like transferring calls, sending emails, and scheduling appointments for the incoming ambassadors and leaders."

"Appointments?" I remembered Wesley in the cafe, reporting the Epsilon Procedure's thirty percent survival rate, and my stomach flipped.

"For the Epsilon Initiative. Superpowers are New Delos's top export. We are a small country, but everyone wants what we have. What better way to secure our place in the world?"

"But what's to stop them from using their new powers against us?" I asked. "And is it safe?"

"It's not our problem," Wesley warned.

"And where *do* we give them superpowers?" I pressed, trying to milk Jamie for information. "There has to be some sort of clinic or lab or…"

"Floors fifty-two through sixty-four are dedicated to Epsilon Development," Jamie said smugly. "Not even White Badges have access there, so don't feel too special."

"What about silver badges?" I pointed at her silver key card, and she flushed again.

"Don't get cute, Samantha. I still outrank you. You probably only got access to the top floors because they want you to clean Schrader's toilet."

"At least I get to *see* Schrader's toilet. That's more than you can say."

Jamie looked ready to burst with indignation, and I could see a fresh lecture swelling in her chest, but I was saved when a suited man poked his head out from a cubicle.

"Miss Ratcliffe!" he beamed. "Just who I needed! Spain called today with a question about the seating arrangement at the opening ceremony. Do you have a moment?"

Jamie grinned importantly and smoothed the creases in her blouse.

"Of course." She turned her gaze on us as the man disappeared back into the cubicle. "Don't go too far."

She whisked out of sight, and I snorted.

"How much you wanna bet that guy is only pretending to need her because he wants her daddy to give him a City Hall job?"

Wesley grabbed my arm to pull me around the corner, then checked back down the hall to ensure it was clear and pushed his glasses up the bridge of his nose.

"Cool it. We're supposed to be on their side now, remember?"

"Oh, come on." I rolled my eyes. "It's *Jamie*. She makes it so easy. If we're going to be in here, might as well have some fun."

"You're making our job more dangerous," Wesley hissed.

"She has information, and she's happy to share it if it means showing off her rank," I pointed out. "Now we know where the labs are, and I bet they don't take up all twelve floors between fifty-two and sixty-four, which means we might know where the kidnapped Apex are as well. *And* we know Adrestus intends to turn his Peace Summit guests into Apex."

Wesley leaned against a wall. The office space beyond our hall was festive as people hurried between cubicles and called out to each other. Everyone was in good spirits as they put together the minutiae of the upcoming summit.

"Jamie would've told us all that without you antagonizing her."

"Our existence antagonizes her. Excuse me for giving her something to actually be mad about."

"Don't push me, Sammy," he warned in a low growl.

"Or what? You'll give me the cold shoulder? Oh, no."

"Excuse me for keeping us safe while Adrestus is watching us."

"Don't use Adrestus as an excuse. Just admit you're mad at me."

"I'm beyond mad. I'm furious."

"Mad and furious mean the same thing, dingus."

Wesley pushed his glasses up to pinch the bridge of his nose and drew in a long, shuddering breath.

"The moment we're in too much danger here, I'm making a break for it and taking you with me," Wesley said. "Push me, and I'll make that call earlier than you would like."

"I didn't ask you to come here!"

"And I'm not going to ask you when it's time to leave."

"So you get to make all the calls? Wesley Isaacs, you are the most—"

"I'll follow your lead, Sammy." His anger with me was fading in a calm frustration, but I realized I preferred his ire to whatever this was. I could push back against anger, but this adjusted attitude of his only made me feel guilty. "I followed you here, and I'll keep following you. Despite the better judgment of *everyone*, I trust you to know what you're doing. But the one thing you don't know how to do is quit, so I reserve the right to have that *one* responsibility as long as we're here. Okay?"

No. No, it wasn't *okay*. It was infuriating.

"I know how to quit."

"Says the thousand-year-old who's died how many times now?"

"I thought I told you not to go too far?" Jamie came around the corner, and I glared at Wesley for not being more careful with my secret. "We aren't paying you to run off on the clock."

"We're getting paid?" I asked.

"Only if you count this catered lunch, which I do *not* want to be late for."

She took off at her usual fast pace, and I stomped after her, still fuming over Wesley and his boundless supply of audacity. We passed a row of conference rooms until Jamie stopped in front of one labeled "42-C". She peeked through the thin window above the door handle and whipped back to face us, her cheeks flushed.

"Okay, Mr. Schrader *is* in there. I swear, if you embarrass me—"

"—then I'll consider it a lunch well spent." I smiled sweetly and let myself into the room before I could let her enter first.

Dazzling, mid-day light poured in from the expansive window opposite the door, brightening up a mouthwatering spread of Thai cuisine. Schrader stood at the end of the room and beamed when he saw us burst in, but I ignored him, instead staring at the dozen student interns seated at the long table.

Winnie was there, lurking in the corner with a scowl, and I recognized most of the other students from school, but I didn't have the wherewithal to remember their names. Not when I was too busy gawking at two faces near the head of the table that I was both relieved and terrified to see.

The steam rising from the troughs of food bowed in a wave, and the hair around my face stirred in a sudden breeze.

"*You!*" Wesley hissed, pushing forward.

"Hey, guys," Anthony grimaced, trying for an awkward wave that Heather, sitting next to him, grabbed and pushed back into his lap. "What're you doing here?"

26

Measuring Up

Wesley stood rigid in the doorway, and Jamie pushed her way through.

"It's a door," she snapped. "You're supposed to walk through it."

She strode across the conference room with her chin up. She stopped in front of Schrader to shake his hand before dropping into the seat next to the one that bore his suit jacket.

"Wesley, we have to sit." I bumped against his shoulder in an attempt to prompt him forward, but he stood firm.

"I knew it," Wesley hissed under his breath, still focused on Anthony's reddening face. "I told you it was him."

"It wasn't Anthony," I said through gritted teeth, offering the room of staring faces a terrible attempt at a casual, toothy grin. When Wesley still refused to move, I side-stepped him, shuffling around the room's perimeter to sit in the empty seats next to Heather and Anthony.

I tried not to give them any attention. Winnie was lurking just behind us and most likely studying how I reacted to their presence. Still, I tried to assess them for signs of injury in my periphery as Schrader addressed the room.

"That should be everyone!" He clapped his hands, and Jamie straightened up in her seat. "Excellent! Mr. Isaacs, the door, please."

Wesley stepped in on rigid legs, and the door creaked shut. Schrader gave him a tight-lipped smile and gestured to the empty seat beside me.

"Please. Sit." The light streaming in through the panels of window behind him cast Schrader in diffused shadows. "It's a genuine honor watching this internship program grow, and I can say with confidence, New Delos's future looks bright with such capable young students helping to helm our ship into the bright, new world of tomorrow."

Jamie interrupted him to clap, and Schrader's narrowing eyes betrayed the slightest hint of irritation. The wheels of the chair beside me squeaked as Wesley pulled it out, drawing further attention away from Schrader's speech. On my other side, Heather tapped against her bouncing knee, and Anthony stared into a steaming vat of phad thai with a clenched jaw.

"All that said," Schrader began again, his eyes meeting mine, "eat up! You'll need all the energy you can get with these busy weeks ahead of us."

He lowered himself next to Jamie, and she pulled him into immediate conversation. I hated how good the food smelled. Pride would have me forgo the meal, but after two days of little more than Greek yogurt, I conceded and loaded my plate with spring rolls.

"You should eat," I whispered to Wesley.

"Anthony sold us out. Why else would he be sitting here?"

I looked back at Anthony, and he tried to smile again.

"Heather's here, too," I said.

"It was Anthony." Wesley kept less care to be quiet. "It's just like last time."

An arm brushed against my shoulder, and Winnie shoved me out of the way to lean over my plate and fill hers with food.

"It wasn't Anthony who told us where your dumb team was hiding," she hissed. "And maybe keep your voice down in a room full of interns."

She flicked Wesley's head as she leaned back, and he rubbed his hair ruefully.

"But he—"

I elbowed him, and he finally shut up. Heather cleared her throat and pressed her hand against my knee under the table with trembling fingers.

"So, you guys signed up for the internship program, too?" She tried to look casual, but a light sheen of sweat had broken out across her forehead.

"It's not what you think." I dunked a spring roll in the sauce platter between us. "I came here because I wanted to. Wesley followed."

He ignored my pointed glare, instead scanning the faces of the dozen other interns.

"Samantha, you didn't." Heather groaned.

"It's still not what you think." I wanted to tell her it was a ruse. I wanted to let her in on my plan. But I couldn't, not with Winnie right there.

"Whatever it is you've done," Heather shook her head, "you're both idiots."

"I may be an idiot," Wesley started, "but at least I'm not a traitor."

He glared at Anthony, who shrank back in his seat.

"It's not what it looks like," Heather assured us. "It's not like last time."

"It's exactly like last time."

The nearest interns cast us nervous glances, and Schrader seemed to have noticed the building argument as well, watching us instead of pretending to care about whatever it was Jamie was saying to him.

"You need to calm down." I tried to warn Wesley out of the side of my mouth.

"You're telling me to calm down? After you've been picking fights all morning?"

"I wasn't picking fights, I was just having a bit of fun!" The rest of the room had gone quiet, and I tried to lower my voice, but it was too late. The attention was on us.

"I'm not going to eat lunch with someone who sold us out twice!"

"You're going to eat lunch with him because we're all on the same side now."

"Did you not hear me? He sold us out! Everly is dead because of him!"

"It wasn't Anthony who sold out the team, you moron, it was Avery!"

I didn't know when either of us had stood up, but Wesley and I were face-to-face, standing over our lunch. His chair had toppled backwards, and I waited for him to yell, but he stood silent, his green eyes wide with shock and malice behind his glasses.

Every eye was on us, and even Schrader held his tongue, waiting to see what might happen next.

A faint wind stirred my hair.

"Everly's dead?" Anthony's voice came out tiny and broken.

The room felt ten times smaller than it had a moment ago.

"Samantha?" Heather prodded. "He can't be...he's *Everly*."

"He's dead," I whispered, finally tearing my eyes away from Wesley.

"Who are you talking about?" Jamie demanded. "Everly? Like the school nurse Everly?"

"It was Avery?" Wesley's eyes glazed over in a thin film of tears, but he blinked them away, leaving only anger.

"Not now, Wes." The food didn't smell good anymore.

"And you *knew? And* you knew I thought it was *him*!" Wesley pointed at Anthony. "You let me hate him, and you didn't say anything?"

"You would've hated him anyways!" I snarled.

Schrader made a show of standing up and reclaiming the room's attention. I sat back down in my chair, determined to let the room's gaze shift off of me.

"Jamie, I think it's time the team got a tour of your father's Schrader Tower offices, don't you?" Schrader suggested, watching me as he spoke.

Jamie perked up, all thoughts of the dead school nurse forgotten.

"Right now?" She scrambled to her feet. "I'd be more than happy to show them the way. It's not nearly as nice as his City Hall office, but—"

"Yes, what a lovely plan. Everyone, follow Jamie." Schrader crossed around the table, and Jamie rushed to pull the door open for him. Schrader turned his strained smile on our corner of the table and circled us with his finger in the air. "Except you five."

As soon as the last intern had filed out after Jamie, carrying a plate piled high with Thai food, Schrader marched across the room to face us.

"I'm glad to see the obvious enthusiasm and passion, but maybe we should keep personal disputes personal, hmm?" He pushed back his sandy hair and adjusted the smile on his face. "We don't want to alarm the other interns, do we?"

"No, sir," I said through gritted teeth.

"Good. I'm glad you agree." He took another steadying breath. "Unfortunately, I've had to inform Dr. Cunningham of this dispute. Dion, if you could look after Eydis, Mr. Schultz, and Miss Hisakawa."

"What about me?" Wesley stammered.

"I have something *else* for you up on floor sixty-four. I'll show you the way."

The slightest hint of fear chased the anger from Wesley's eyes, and for a fleeting moment, they begged me to hold him here. Winnie gripped my arm in a silent warning, and Wesley's face turned dour again. He turned away to follow Schrader to the door.

A man in a button-up in the outside hall raised a mug of black coffee to us in a salute through the open door as Schrader and Wesley took their leave.

"You interns never seem to take a break!" His jovial smile faltered at the looks on our faces. "No need to be so serious! I swear Schrader is working you kids too hard."

Winnie pushed me aside to cross to the door and slam it in the man's face.

"Idiots," Winnie muttered to herself, falling into the nearest chair. "They're all idiots."

"You work for Schrader, too," I reminded her.

"No one works for Schrader."

"What's he going to do with him?" I demanded. "What's on floor sixty-four?"

"Oh, now you care about repercussions." Winnie's shoulders relaxed, and she sighed, wheeling her chair to the window and spinning blithely. "Some labs. Some prison cells. Don't worry. Adrestus likes him too much to hurt him."

"Sammy, what you said about Everly, what happened?" Heather pried. "He was there when we got on that boat. That can't— that can't be the last time we saw him."

I buried my face in my hands, suddenly missing my two days of isolation.

"Mira killed him." I watched the back of Winnie's head as I said the next part, gaging her reaction. "As you know, there were a few casualties that night."

If Winnie knew her mom was dead, she made no indication that my words bothered her. Heather fell back into her seat, and Anthony's shoulder-length dark hair flurried about his head, wrapping itself into windswept knots.

"And you and Wesley, were you captured, too?" Heather said, holding back tears.

Winnie became still in her chair. I fixed a cold visage to my face and straightened up in my seat.

"I'm here because I decided to join Adrestus."

Heather scoffed and pushed away from the table.

"Yeah, right. Why are you actually here?"

I took a big bite of spring roll.

"I'm serious. Avery is the one who erased my memories, Fleming and Roy were keeping me prisoner, and Everly was developing a weapon designed to kill me. The only person to tell me any sort of truth in the last half year was Adrestus."

"And you listened to him? You're a bigger idiot than I thought. You actually joined him? Willingly?"

I turned away. Guilt made it difficult to look at her and Anthony. They were only here because they'd been trying to get Avery to safety.

"And Wesley?" Anthony's voice cracked.

"Roy kicked him off the team. He had nowhere else to go." I shrugged. "He kicked you guys off, too, by the way, so you might as well get comfortable."

A soft knock sounded at the door, but I didn't bother looking up as it creaked open. Winnie's chair wheeled backwards several feet with the force of her standing up so abruptly, and a silky voice set my nerves on end.

"What's this about my newest interns causing a disturbance?"

I jerked my head up to see Adrestus in a navy linen suit. He smiled, his neat beard turning upwards at his mouth corners. He at least seemed more "Doctor Cunningham, Museum Curator" than he did "Adrestus the Unkillable" at the moment and walked with a casual step. He draped his suit jacket over the back of the nearest chair and surveyed the room.

Behind him, a woman with a pixie cut carried a small, leather kit. A wool shawl that appeared much too heavy for the oncoming summer was buttoned at her shoulder, and her angular face had a kind smile fixed under a button nose.

"Eydis, I'd ask if you remembered Lana, but I'm thinking the answer might be no." Adrestus stood aside to let Lana pass, and he reached over to close the door behind her.

"She was at the camp." It was hard to recognize her in her shawl, but I knew the heavy fabrics hid the four leathery wings that protruded from her back.

"Oh-ho! You're right! She *was* there that night. Excellent memory. Well, perhaps not *excellent*, all things considered, but I digress."

Lana turned her smile towards me, looking much kinder than she had when swooping overhead, illuminated in flame.

Adrestus sat in the chair at the head of the table and helped himself to some poor intern's abandoned plate of food.

"I'd hoped Schrader capable of reigning in high schoolers. If the other interns were to learn about Apex Team, well, it'd be more of a distraction than anything." He beckoned Lana forward to set her kit on the table, and she pulled out a ribbon of measuring tape. "No matter. I needed to see you all today anyway so it works out. Miss Hisakawa, you first."

Heather took a step back, but Lana held up the measuring tape as if to show her she meant no harm.

"Just taking measurements," she sang. "It's time you all got your costumes."

"Thanks to Lana's unconventional physiology, she's adept at creating her own clothes," Adrestus explained. "She's fallen into the role of Team Seamstress."

"What costumes?" I asked.

"Your Pantheon costumes! You should see the sketches," Adrestus grinned. "I think you'll like it, and who knows, Eydis, it might just jog some old memories."

"You keep calling her Eydis," Heather said slowly. She let Lana approach her with the measuring tape and held her arms out so Lana could collect the measurements she needed. "Her name is Samantha."

My hands clenched at my sides, and I briefly considered making a break for the window and hoping for the best when I hit the pavement.

"Of course!" Adrestus boomed. "I forgot you didn't know! Eydis, I'll let you do the honors."

I looked at Heather and Anthony, their tired eyes wide and scared, and maybe I should've been upfront all along. Maybe all of this could have been avoided somehow if I'd only been more open.

"The Scourge Queen Eydis. I'm her."

Heather dropped her arms to deadpan at me with a hitched eyebrow. Lana tapped her shoulders, and she begrudgingly raised her arms again but shook her head.

"You're kidding. *That's* what they're telling you? And you believe it?"

My face flushed.

"It's the truth," I tried to explain. "Fleming—"

"You want us to believe that you're a thousand years old? And that the giant statue down in the museum is supposed to be you?" Heather's face reddened. "This isn't some make-believe fantasy game, Samantha! My parents are in a cell! Remi could be dead! And you're here because Adrestus made you feel special by telling you were some kind of ancient queen?"

Lana tapped Heather's shoulders, and she dropped her arms again.

"But she's come back from the dead before," Anthony mumbled behind me. "Wesley saw her get her neck snapped."

"Yes! By *him!*" Heather pointed at Adrestus.

"Hold still, please," Lana chided, her smile still fixed upon her face.

"Just because she had a magic rock keeping her alive doesn't mean she's a Viking. They're lying to her, Anthony. Don't play into it."

I could tell her that Fleming and Everly knew. I could tell her that Wesley and Naomi knew. Something, maybe guilt, maybe embarrassment, kept me quiet. Anthony's face screwed up in thought.

"I guess it is a little far-fetched," he finally conceded.

"More far-fetched than being gifted wind-channeling powers? More far-fetched than my existence?" Adrestus inquired. "Samantha Havardson and Eydis the Scourge Queen are one and the same, whether you choose to believe it or not."

Heather snorted in contempt.

"Sure, and I'm the Easter Bunny." She retreated to the chair farthest from Adrestus as Lana finished up her measurements and moved on to Anthony.

"The Easter Bunny would be a fine addition to my Pantheon," Adrestus chuckled, "but you'll make a fair enough goddess of the underworld and shadows should you prove yourself."

"I don't understand," Heather said, crossing her arms in front of her chest.

"In a few, short weeks, the Peace Summit will see a new era ushered in," Adrestus explained. "A new age marked by new gods. Only the most powerful will reign at my side, including you if you prove yourself."

"And by most powerful, you mean the easiest to control," Heather retorted. Adrestus laughed.

"Don't undersell yourself, Miss Hisakawa. You are one of the strongest Apex to come through New Delos." Adrestus gestured towards Lana where she worked on taking Anthony's measurements. "Lana here recently qualified for my Pantheon, though we're still workshopping her new name."

Lana blushed, and her pink lips pressed into a pleased smile. She looked kind, and I wondered if she knew the horrors Adrestus had committed, and, if she did, what horrors she'd experienced in her own life to not care.

"Are you an Epsilon?" Anthony blurted. Lana's eyes widened in surprise at the question, but then she laughed.

"No, I was born Apex, though my wings didn't come in until later. Just in time for middle school."

She unbuttoned her shawl, letting it fall to the floor. Her shirt boasted an open back, and her four wings shuddered as she stretched them. Light permeated the skin-like membrane that stretched over bone. She beat them once for show, and my hair flew back with the force of the wind.

"Many Apex have the luxury of choosing to live in privacy," Adrestus said. "Lana never had that choice. Luckily, she's just as capable of flying with four wings as she was with six."

She kept her back to me as she continued Anthony's measurements, and I frowned at the two scarred stumps of bone hiding beneath the folds of her bottom set of wings.

"I was seventeen." She scooped her shawl up from the floor and refastened it around her shoulders. "I went to see a movie with friends when a group of boys stopped us. They'd heard about the girl with wings."

My stomach churned, and Adrestus nodded for her to continue when Lana faltered.

"They were younger than us, but we were outnumbered. They ripped my coat off to see my wings for themselves, and they called me a witch. One had a pocketknife. They only got through one wing before the police came. I'd never be able to fly with five wings, but with four, I'd at least be balanced, and there was still a chance."

"You cut off your own wing?" I blanched.

"The only hope I had left was the thought of flying out of that place. I begged my father until he found a doctor he could pay under the table to do it for us."

"*This* is what we're fighting for," Adrestus asserted. "A world where Apex can live free."

Winnie kept her gaze fixated out the window, stony and passive, impossible to read. She hated Apex and had told me once that she saw them as little more than tools to be wielded. It seemed strange Adrestus could unify people with such diametric world-views.

"If you wanted Apex to live free, you wouldn't murder them." Heather's tone had a bite to it, and I watched Adrestus, waiting to see how he responded.

"You must've heard about Jacobi Everly's passing. I was sorry to hear of it, too."

"People die." Winnie shrugged. "That's what happens when they get in the way. Vic died because he got in the way. Everly died for the same reason."

"Oh, yeah?" I snarled, unable to help myself at the mention of Vidar. "It's the same, then, for your—"

Adrestus stood up and clapped.

"Excellent. That takes care of measurements for those two. Dion, would you escort them back to the museum? Show them the training gym on your way. I expect them there tomorrow after work hours so I may assess their abilities for the Pantheon."

"What about me?" I frowned.

"Oh, no," he laughed, and I hated the heat that rose to my cheeks. "No, no, no. Eydis, you will stay right here with me for a moment."

"See you, Sammy," Anthony mumbled as he and Heather followed Winnie back out through the dining room. Adrestus leaned back in his seat, throwing his feet up onto the table to better recline. A plate of food fell to the floor, but he paid it no attention.

"Does Winnie not know about her mom?" I demanded as soon as the door shut.

Adrestus furrowed his brow at me and clasped his hands across his chest.

"What's wrong with Winnie's mother?"

"She's dead." I hated the bluntness of my words.

"How terrible," Adrestus murmured. "And how did she pass?"

I stared at him blankly.

"You killed her."

"Did I?"

"At the camp."

"Ah." He nodded and pushed off the window, walking back towards the kitchen. "She should've stayed out of my way. If you don't mind, I'd appreciate you not telling Dion about her dead mother. Not until after the Peace Summit, at least. It'll only upset her, and there's nothing we can do about it now."

"The summit is four weeks away." Lana approached with her measuring tape, and I held my arms out for her. "How am I supposed to live with her and not say anything?"

"Oh, I think you'll find the strength to keep it to yourself. It would be a shame if I had to, ah, terminate her employment before then."

A cold chill rolled over me, and I tried to suppress it so Lana wouldn't notice.

"You mean kill her?"

"Only if she made it necessary. She's a good little pet and tends to do what she's told, though I still question whether it's out of loyalty to me or resentment of her father. So, if she *must* learn what came of her mother, I'd like to at least get another few weeks of good work out of her. Besides, after the Peace Summit, it won't make much of a difference, now will it?"

He lifted his chin to grin at me from behind locks of silky, black hair.

"Why not?" I tried to hide the catch in my voice.

Adrestus's grin widened, and he bit his lip, appearing to savor some private thought.

"We dreamed of this once upon a time. I wish the Eydis back then could see us now."

"I wish I remembered her," I lied. I remembered her all too clearly. I used to hate her for falling for Adrestus's tricks, but I'd come to realize it wasn't her fault. It wasn't *my* fault.

"She'd only get in our way." Adrestus shrugged. "Your temperament has improved bounds now that she's gone."

Quiet rage rolled inside me, but I kept the storm contained.

"So I get to join the Pantheon, too?" I asked as Lana bent down to measure the length of my leg.

"The Pantheon is no place for my Scourge Queen," Adrestus laughed. "You will be by my side, the way we once dreamed. *If* you can prove yourself."

I gulped.

"What does that look like?"

"To rule over the Pantheon, you must be greater than them. I won't make you fight them all, but take your pick of one. If you can defeat them in combat, you'll stand at my side at the Peace Summit, and we'll watch the world bow to us."

"You could fight me!" Lana suggested. "I would be honored."

I blushed and ran through my options in my head. I knew Adrestus wanted to parade me as a trophy rather than actually rule together, but I could use a spot on the Peace Summit stage to my advantage.

"Winnie," I said. "I'll fight Winnie."

Adrestus roared in laughter, and Lana hissed between her teeth as if she wasn't sure that was the right choice.

"Winnie has trained in combat her whole life," Adrestus reminded me. "First under Roy Hendricks, and then me. Are you sure?"

"Positive." Even if she was a skilled and brutal fighter, she didn't have powers. She was the only one I was sure I had a chance against.

"That settles it." Adrestus kicked his feet off the table and stood up. "If you win, you'll have earned back the title of Scourge Queen, and you'll take Winnie's spot on the stage."

I faltered.

"No, I don't want her spot. Why can't we both be up there?"

"If I don't give her something to lose, it wouldn't be much of a test for you, would it?" He leaned against the table. "Thank you for your help, Lana. I look forward to seeing the costumes."

Lana nodded and repacked her kit, leaving me alone in the conference room with Adrestus. His single blue eye studied me, and I avoided his gaze, instead looking at his "Head Curator Badge".

"By the way, I've been wanting to ask you, does this mean anything to you?" He dug into his pocket and revealed a silver chain dangling from his fingers. A crooked dog whistle glittered on the end, forming a lopsided

"V". My necklace. Adrestus rolled the whistle between two fingers. "Ares had it on him the night you two arrived."

"It's just an old necklace I used to wear." I wanted to grab it. I wanted to hide it. I wanted to hurt Adrestus for daring to touch it.

"Suppose I'll throw it out, then." He shoved it back into his pocket, and I resisted the urge to trace the burn scar on my sternum that matched the "V" of the necklace.

The door reopened, and Winnie stomped back inside. Adrestus raised a single finger to his lips in a silent warning to keep quiet about Winnie's mother.

I nodded wordlessly, wishing he wouldn't stand so close.

"Do you want her to go back to the interns now?" she asked.

"Take her to your apartment. I think that was enough for today. Training tomorrow after work. Dion, you know the place." He looked up as I passed him, making my way to the door. "And Dion, I could've sworn we sent clothes to Eydis the other day. Why is she still in leggings?"

My face burned, and Winnie's cheeks flushed. Her wide eyes met mine.

"I was washing them," I lied. "Sorry. I'll make sure to wear something nicer tomorrow."

Adrestus nodded approvingly, and Winnie narrowed her eyes at me. If she had purposefully hidden my new clothes, I wasn't sure what Adrestus would do in retaliation. However, hidden clothing was nothing when compared to a hidden dead mother, and the least I could do was take some heat off her back.

Winnie stood aside to let me into the hall, and I saw a glint of silver as Adrestus pulled the dog whistle necklace back out of his pocket to study.

27

Six Seconds

As much as I wanted to, I knew better than to search out Wesley. I would have to trust that he was okay and that I would see him in the breakfast line the next morning.

However, he didn't show and after a full day of mindless interning with Jamie, there was still no sign of him. Whatever had happened on floor sixty-four with him and Schrader must have ended in disaster. By the time Winnie was leading me to the training gym on the floor beneath our apartment that evening, it was taking every bit of self-control to not throw all my plans out the window in a blind panic searching for Wes.

Winnie, meanwhile, refused to look at me. She'd been furious since discovering I would be vying for her position on the Peace Summit stage. I struggled to keep up with her in my new pencil skirt and a blouse that didn't fit my shoulders quite right as she took us down a corridor. At the far end of the hall, I could make out a glass wall that overlooked a spacious training gym.

A stairway on the other side of a glass door led down to the matted floor. Wooden bleachers pressed against the wall directly beneath us, offering a place to comfortably view the training proceedings as well as the two-story window that made up the far wall.

"Locker rooms are there." Winnie jerked her thumb behind us. "Put your stuff wherever and don't take too long. Mira will be furious if you aren't down there when she arrives."

She pushed through the glass door to march down the stairway to the gym floor where Heather was stretching.

The locker room was much nicer than the locker rooms of the Apex Team training facility and sported polished wood lockers, black marble floors, and mahogany benches. I pulled my new sneakers and gym clothes from my bag and stored my business attire in an empty locker.

Anthony exited the guys' locker room just as I came out of the women's, and he blushed when he saw me.

"Just like old times, right?" he mumbled. "Not that you remember. But you, me, Heather, and Wesley. All training together again. Makes me miss Naomi, though."

"Have you seen Wesley?" I blurted, unable to contain myself.

"Sure, he's in there." He pointed at the locker room and furrowed his brow as relief choked the air from my lungs. "Are you okay—?"

I shoved past Anthony into the guys' locker room, but before I could get around the corner of the winding entryway, Wesley's voice called out.

"Go away, Samantha."

I froze, staring at the tiled walls of the entryway and chewing on my lip. Those were not the words I wanted to hear.

"I know you're still there," he sighed.

"I just wanted—"

"Leave."

I crossed my arms over my chest and squared my shoulders. It wasn't fair that he could hear me from a distance and know I was okay while I was forced to wonder if he was still alive anytime he wasn't in my direct line of vision.

"I'm coming in," I asserted. "So, I don't know, make sure you're dressed."

I marched around the corner before he could protest. He looked up from a wooden bench, wearing joggers and an athletic t-shirt made of thin fabric.

"You're okay," I said simply. He frowned at me.

"I spent the day stapling together 'Welcome To New Delos' pamphlets in a cubicle, so I don't know about okay, but sure."

The tension that had been building in my chest all day finally loosened.

"Are you mad at me?"

"Am I—" His eyes widened, and his mouth dropped open. "Sammy, how could I not be?"

"Because of Avery?" I asked. He stood up from the bench to pull me farther inside.

"Because of you!" He paced in front of a row of sinks. My heart skipped a beat when I noticed the dark carbon-fiber fingers of his right hand.

"What's that?" I pointed at the prosthesis, and he stopped to look at his palm.

"It's new."

"Is that why they wanted you in the labs?"

"Yeah." He gave his fingers a test wriggle, each one moving independently of the others, something I'd never seen his 3D-printed plastic fingers do.

"I thought they were going to hurt you."

He looked up from his carbon-fiber hand, glaring at me through the locks of hair that hung in his face.

"Nothing to worry about. Just replacing the arm they cut off last winter."

"Right. Sorry."

Wesley extricated his residual limb from the confines of the prosthesis and shuddered. For a moment, something akin to relief crossed over his face, but then the knot in his brow returned, and he set the arm on the bench.

"You hate it," I murmured.

"You can't make arms overnight," Wesley said. "It takes time, and you need proper measurements, but they had this ready for me. They knew I'd come back."

A chill shook my spine, but I shook my head.

"Adrestus was just hedging his bets. Plus, kidnapping is kind of his thing. Once he decides something belongs to him, he won't stop until he has it. He decided you were the Ares of his new pantheon, and he made plans for when you came back."

"That confirms we're playing into his hand."

"We can leave," I whispered. Wesley froze, rubbing the scarred skin of his right elbow. "You get to decide when we leave. If that's what you want to do, then—"

"No." His eyes flashed, and he jammed the arm back on. "Not yet. I saw them, Sammy. My mom and brother. Yesterday. They walked me right past their prison cell."

"Prison cell?" I repeated. When Vidar had been a prisoner under Adrestus, he'd been kept in a small, luxury apartment.

"Everyone they've kidnapped the last few months is there," Wesley said.

"My mom?" I pressed. "Avery?"

Wesley scowled.

"You should've told me about Avery."

"I was going to."

"When?"

"Eventually."

"Did you think I wouldn't save him if I knew it was all his fault?"

I gulped. I knew Wesley was better than that, but when he said the words out loud, I realized there was some truth to the accusation.

"I want to get everyone out safe, and I didn't ask you to help me, Wes."

Wesley squeezed his eyes shut and massaged the space between his eyebrows with a knuckle.

"You shouldn't be here. We need to keep our distance. I'll see you in the gym."

He dropped his hand, and I caught a flash of purple bruising under the collar of his shirt.

"What was that?" I lunged forward, defensive ire rising in my gut as I reached for his collar to further investigate the familiar discoloration. Wesley wrapped his fingers around my wrist.

"It's nothing," he said, his face so close to mine now that his breath broke over my cheeks in a sweet heat.

"What did they do to you?" My head tilted back to look him in the eyes.

"Nothing."

"Liar. That's a bruise from one of Mira's patches. They paralyzed you. Why?"

He exhaled through his nose, his breath washing over me a second time. They didn't need to paralyze him to give him a new arm.

He held my gaze, locking me in a stand-off until he finally relinquished my wrist to pull back his collar. A faint purple bruise discolored the skin underneath.

"I'm fine," he murmured, reaching around me to close his locker. I held my breath as he leaned in close, refusing to let his familiar smell quell my fury. "The patches don't work well on me, anyway. Something to do with my powers probably."

"Wesley, show me the back of your neck."

He placed his hands, flesh and carbon fiber, on the lockers on either side of me and slumped forward so his forehead rested against mine. I welcomed the pressure of his skin against mine, but didn't dare move, afraid if I tried to embrace him, he might scare.

"I told you to leave."

"Not until you show me your neck."

With a final sigh, warm against my cheeks, he pulled away, turning to reveal the purple bruise that painted his skin below his hairline

A lump of fear and rage rose in my throat.

"Did they put in a new chip?" I whispered.

"Everly never took out the old one. It's too close to my spinal cord." He turned back to me, rubbing his neck. "They did a manual reboot and refilled it with Mira's neurotransmitters as a precaution."

All it would take was a flick of a switch, and Wesley was their puppet again. I shouldn't have come to check on him. If they knew I still cared about him, if *Adrestus* knew...

"I should leave," I said quietly, retreating to the exit.

"Sammy," Wesley croaked.

"I'm sorry, Wes. You're right. We can't talk anymore. Not until we're out of here."

I whipped around the corner, out of the locker room.

"The ladies' room is across the hall," a voice purred. Mira stood at the far end of the corridor. Her form, typically obscured by flowy fabrics, showed off muscles that rippled beneath her athletic wear.

"Right." I nodded. "I got turned around, I guess."

I pushed through the glass door and descended the stairs to the main gym floor. Heather looked up as I hurried down the steps, and I went to join her in stretching by the bleachers.

"Still no Remi?" I asked. I looked around the training space, but it was only Heather, Anthony, Winnie, and myself. Up above, Wesley joined us ahead of Mira, who followed at a more leisurely pace.

"Mind your business," Winnie grunted from where she stretched. "If Remi's whereabouts were something you needed to know about, you'd know about it."

Heather pressed her lips together.

"And here you thought you joined Adrestus because of how liberal he is with the truth," she snorted, keeping Winnie out of earshot. "For what it's worth, Remi is here somewhere. We didn't make it far after we'd escaped the island, thanks to Jamie's dad and his hydrokinesis. They knocked me out first, probably so I couldn't escape, but Anthony says he saw them grab her before knocking him out, too."

"Unless they dropped her in the ocean somewhere," I muttered darkly. Heather frowned.

"Don't say that. They can't have."

"Sorry. You're right." But I'd seen Adrestus cast aside those he deemed worthless before, and Remi's computer interfacing abilities had caused him more trouble than she was probably worth in his mind.

"Excellent, everyone's here!" Adrestus's silky voice crooned out over the gym, and my stomach dropped. He stood on the top step of the stairway, looking out of place in a cashmere suit and black polished shoes. "Don't mind me. I'm merely here to observe the creation of my

Pantheon's final pieces. Let's start with a sparring assessment. Would the gentlemen mind getting us started?"

I felt Wesley's eyes on me, but when I glanced his direction, he'd already looked away. Heather tugged on my shirt to get me to move, and I begrudgingly took a seat with her and Winnie on the wooden bleachers. Wesley gave his new arm a test punch, swinging it through the air. Anthony gulped.

"It's not a very fair match up," I mumbled. Wesley and Anthony squared up, and Adrestus paced in front of us, carefully assessing their stances. "Wesley could crush Anthony if he wanted."

"Who said he doesn't?" Winnie snorted.

"Focus," Mira hissed, sitting down a healthy distance away, watching Anthony and Wesley size each other up. "You're next."

Wesley moved first, lunging across the space, and Anthony propelled himself backwards with a burst of wind to avoid the attack.

"Excellent!" Adrestus's voice boomed as Wesley forced Anthony onto the defensive. "Both of you, *good*."

Wesley hounded Anthony across the room, and I gripped the wood of the bleacher beneath me. Anthony's defensive maneuvers turned the gym into a wind tunnel, and while they were effective in keeping Wesley away, it was making it hard to stay in my seat.

Anthony faltered near the window and dove out of the way as Wesley came at him with renewed fervor. His fist collided with the glass, and white fissures spiraled out from the point of impact. Anthony stood wide-eyed, looking at the cracked window where he had been standing just a moment before.

"That could've killed me! What are you doing?"

"He's fighting like a god worthy of my Pantheon." Adrestus shrugged.

Wesley lunged again, using the same move, and Anthony released a hurricane force gale that blew the glass out of the splintered window. Wesley blew onto his back and landed dangerously close to the room's edge, his chest heaving. Anthony stood a few yards away, his shoulder-length hair stirring in the wind that rushed in from outside.

"There he is! Excellent!" Adrestus steadied himself in the gale. "I was beginning to wonder what it might take to get something like that out of you. Your grandmother was New Delos's first major hero."

"Zephyress." Anthony wiped the sweat from his brow.

Adrestus smirked and paced around Anthony, sizing him up. When he got close to the broken window, I fantasized about pushing him out and watching him drop.

"I remember her well. She could fly, yes?"

Anthony gulped and nodded.

"She's the only one in the family who could get her wind strong enough."

"She's the only one in your family *so far*."

Anthony's hands balled into fists at his side.

"My cousin got close once," he admitted. "Then she almost broke her neck. Or maybe she did break her neck? I don't remember exactly."

Adrestus stopped his pacing when he was face to face with Anthony and smiled.

"But you aren't your cousin, are you? I bet you could figure it out. You've come so far in the measly few months you've had these powers."

"Well, I—"

"In fact, I'd be willing to bet that once you really put your best effort in, it takes you less than, say, six seconds to learn."

"Six seconds?" Anthony repeated.

"Sure." Adrestus shrugged. "It's simple math and physics. Calculate the velocity of gravity with this height and it comes out to roughly six seconds before hitting the museum steps down on the street."

Anthony backpedaled from Adrestus, and Heather wrapped a warning hand around my bicep.

"No!" Anthony cried. "You can't. I'll die!"

"Nonsense!" Adrestus beamed. "I have complete faith you'll figure it out with seconds to spare. Sometimes all we need to reach new heights is a little push."

"You're going to push me?" Anthony blanched, his knees shaking.

"Not quite." Adrestus grinned wider still.

He spun back, his foot tracing the arc of a round kick that Wesley didn't see coming.

"NO!" I screamed, and Heather's hold on me tightened, pulling me back as Wesley's eyes widened, and he toppled backwards out of the shattered window.

28

Stolen Skies

A hand clamped over my mouth, trying to stem my feral scream. Winnie's arms joined Heather, both of them fighting to hold me back while I stared at the empty window, horrified and furious.

Whatever plans I'd had to infiltrate Adrestus's ranks had been kicked out the window with Wesley, and now I would make sure New Delos and whatever else Adrestus had built was razed into the seabed of the ocean, where he and his dreams of a new world could rot.

"Six seconds!" Adrestus yelled. Anthony crumpled to his knees, tears streaming down his face.

"Please!" Anthony tore at his hair and bowed with the force of the sobs that racked his body.

"Tick, tock!" Adrestus yelled. "If one friend's broken body isn't enough, I've got plenty others I can throw! It may be too late for Ares, but what about Miss Hisakawa? Or Eydis? I can throw her all day, and she'll come back every time until you figure out how to save her!"

I tore away from Heather and Winnie, feeling fingernails scrape against my arms in a last ditch effort to hold me back. I leaped across the gym and lunged for the ledge, but Adrestus stopped me with an elbow to my ribcage. I fell to the matted floor, gagging on air and tears.

Anthony's six seconds were up.

Wesley would be dead.

I saw Adrestus's foot just in time to raise an arm to my face and save myself from a broken nose, but the force of the kick still dazed me. I tried to struggle back to my feet, but Heather returned to my side, holding me back.

If I hadn't come here, Wesley wouldn't have followed me. If he hadn't followed me, he wouldn't be...

The steady thump of beating air pulled my attention back to the window. A set of wings blocked out the setting sun, turning red as light permeated the leathery membrane of skin that stretched between bone. Lana lighted into the room, and as the sunlight shifted around her, turning dark silhouette into shades and detail, I saw Wesley in her arms, eyes wide and hair windswept, but otherwise unharmed.

"Wes!"

I rushed to tear Wes away from Lana, squeezing him tight to try to stop his and my quaking.

"I'm okay." His shaky breath stirred the hair by my ear. "Sammy, I'm alright."

Pain exploded in the side of my head, and the room flipped around me as an unseen force ripped me away and threw me on my back. Adrestus's face shifted in and out of focus overhead.

"If I didn't know any better," he seethed, "I'd say you're having loyalty issues. If I want Ares to fall eighty stories to his death, then that's what he's going to do."

I nodded breathlessly. My head smarted, and my chest hurt, but Wesley was alive.

"I've given you both room, board, and power at my side." Adrestus bent low next to my ear. "I can take that all away, and I'd hate for Lana to not be there to catch your friend next time."

He brushed my forehead with the back of his hand, and I rolled onto my side to escape his touch.

"Lana, take Ares to the infirmary." Adrestus straightened up to survey the room. "I want him in peak condition for the next time I throw him off the building. Mira, continue the lesson. Eydis, with me."

I clawed my way to my feet, my ears ringing. Anthony was still on the floor, wiping the tears from his face while Heather comforted him. Wesley kept his back to me, but Winnie met my eyes and shook her head. I couldn't tell if it was a reprimand or a warning, and I followed Adrestus into the hall, apprehension knotting my stomach.

His polished shoes tapped against the tile as we passed the locker rooms and the elevator. He didn't once check to make sure I was following until he'd reached a communal lounge with low furniture, a kitchenette, and a rain-marred view that turned the city gray.

Adrestus stopped at the window, looking out over his manufactured kingdom, and his shoulders rose and fell with a sigh.

"I thought you didn't remember the boy." Adrestus raised a finger to the window and traced the course of a raindrop that clung to the glass.

"I don't."

"I hope for your sake there are no remnants of old allegiances lingering in that leak-riddled head of yours."

I was too reactive. I knew Wesley was too valuable of a puppet for Adrestus to discard so easily. I would have to be more careful.

"I'm sorry," I said. "I hadn't ever seen someone thrown from a building before. That's all."

He held my gaze for a moment, then turned back to the rain-stained window.

"I'm worried about you."

"Don't do that. I'd hate to be the cause of even more wrinkles."

He looked at me over his shoulder. I braced for another hit, but the corner of his mouth twitched.

"You haven't teased me in over a thousand years. Most people are too afraid to do that." He stepped closer, and the tips of his fingers found my chin. "I want to warn you, Eydis. I've only ever made the mistake of allowing misplaced loyalty once. It was a long time ago, and it nearly cost me everything."

"Me?" I asked. He let me go and pursed his lips.

"No, if you exclude the bit where you tried to kill me and steal my immortality, you were perfectly loyal." He looked back out the window at some unseen memory. "Their names were Tiberius and Ignatia. They taught me it is better to have followers than it is to have friends."

"Tiberius and Ignatia?" I repeated. The names felt old, much older than me.

"Tiberius, Ignatia, and Quintus. We could've had everything, but their loss is your gain. It won't be them by my side, but my Scourge Queen. If you don't make their mistake, that is."

"Quintus." I flashed back to the boy in the coffee shop. "Or Quinn for short."

He gave me a wry smile.

"It's not a story I've told anyone. Not even you. But you don't need the full story to learn its moral. I am your leader, your savior, your everything. Any loyalty to anyone or anything who is not Adrestus the Unkillable will be culled." He stalked past me to the lounge exit. "Go rest. I imagine Miss Ratcliffe will have plenty for you to do in the morning."

And he disappeared into the hall, leaving me to wonder just what Tiberius and Ignatia had done and what hell Adrestus had loosed on them in retaliation.

Jamie did indeed have plenty for me to do over the next few days. I kept my distance from Wesley, knowing if I so much as looked at him too long, Adrestus might be inspired to throw him from the upper floors again. We caught up with each other in the fleeting moments we shared in the breakfast line, though neither of us were making headway in discovering Adrestus's plans for the Peace Summit.

The summer rain lasted the entire week, letting up on Friday as if to celebrate with me that I wouldn't have to listen to Jamie squawk about her father until after the weekend. After work, I sat on Mira's low-back couch, rubbing the feeling back into my feet after another day of business attire and watching the setting sun cast long shadows across the living room.

The slamming of the front door brought my attention to the entryway.

"Going dark early tonight," Mira announced. Her arms were laden with grocery bags, and she threw them up onto the counter.

"What time?" Winnie asked. She leaned over the second floor banister, trying to better see Mira.

An electric pop sizzled overhead, and the room was left in deep, orange shadow cast through the window. Mira spread her arms wide.

"Now, it would seem."

I turned back to the city to watch the lights blink off in a wave, like a black shadow spreading out over the buildings. The hum of the emergency generator buzzed through the room, powering little more than than the kitchen fridge.

"Don't get too comfy," Mira continued. "Adrestus wants you both patrolling. There are reports of a middle-aged man in glasses lingering near Schrader Tower. Apparently he's been asking about a girl."

I clenched my jaw to keep my face from betraying the flipping of my stomach. I'd hoped Fleming wouldn't come search for me. After a week, I'd thought I was in the clear. Obviously, that had been stupid to think.

"He wants us to go now?" Winnie's distaste for the idea was evident in her tone.

"No, he was thinking at your earliest convenience." Mira's words dripped with sarcasm and poison, but Winnie didn't seem bothered. "Find Eydis something to wear. Her costume isn't ready."

I looked up at Winnie in time to see her strike a sour face and stomp towards her room.

"Are you coming or not?" she snarled from out of sight, and I hurried up the staircase.

She threw open our closet door and pushed hanging clothes to one side, revealing black cloaks that trailed to the floor. I'd seen her in the Dion get-up before, and I wasn't eager to share in the honor of wearing the creepy uniform.

"I don't have to wear the mask, do I?" I asked.

"I only have one." She ripped a cloak from the closet and threw it at me.

"I could wear my old uniform." I glanced around the room in search of my torso armor.

"Lana took it." Winnie pulled a kevlar-padded chest plate over her shirt and buckled it in place. "Don't worry, this'll pair well with the yoga pants you stole."

She flashed me a fake smile and disappeared into the folds of her cloak. I frowned at the black fabric in my hands, certain I was going to look ridiculous creeping around back alleys in a glorified Halloween costume.

Not that it was any less ridiculous than the armor and helmet of the team uniform, I realized, and pulled it over my shoulders with a heavy sigh. The fabric was heavier than I'd expected it to be, and it had a strange, synthetic feel when I rubbed a fold between two fingers.

"It's fire-proof," Winnie explained, catching me studying the fabric as she fastened the ghoulish white mask over her face.

Of course it was fire-proof. With a father and sister with fire powers as her sworn enemies, it made sense Winnie would want to be as immune to their attacks as possible.

Once changed, I walked through the darkened corridor towards the elevator with my head down. It was embarrassing enough that Winnie could see me in my sneakers, yoga pants, and borrowed cloak. I didn't need any of Adrestus's other cronies seeing me in this ridiculous get-up, though I knew they'd be watching.

Adrestus would have eyes on me all night, seeing how I might respond to coming face-to-face with Fleming if we found him. I would have to fight him. I hoped he understood.

Downstairs, Winnie led me through the empty museum by the light of emergency LEDs and out a side door in the alley beside Schrader Tower. I craned my head to look up at the glowing top floor where Adrestus still had full power to his apartment and gasped.

Shifting hues of green danced across the night sky, painting the stars with streaks of white and emerald. For a moment, the city disappeared, and I remembered shivering in a field of snow and ice, ignoring the biting cold to stare up at a technicolor sky while my mother called my name, begging me to come in before I froze.

"The aurora borealis?" I breathed. How did a piece of home end up trapped in the sky over New Delos?

Winnie followed my gaze and sniffed.

"It's an electromagnetic field made by one of our Epsilons. No calls in or out of the island. Miles's phone line is the only exception. Disrupts radio signals within its field, too. We used it when we went to find you on that backwater island you were hiding on."

I'd seen the same aurora on McMillan Island, but my memories of day-long nights spent under its light had still been locked away by Avery at that point.

"Is there a place we could see it better?"

Winnie sighed, and, to my surprise, beckoned me after her.

"Yeah, whatever. You can see it best by the water."

I kept my head craned backwards as we walked, unable to look away from the dancing lights. The darkened island was silent around us, but a faint hum buzzed in my ears.

"That's the electromagnetic field you hear," Winnie murmured, as if reading my mind. "It's always there, but you can't see it during the day or if it's cloudy like it's been all week."

It looked so much like the real thing. A thousand years may have worn on since I'd seen a natural aurora, but thanks to the coma, it felt like no time at all had passed since I'd snuck out with my younger sisters to watch them dance. Erika in particular had been enthralled by the lights.

I wondered if Vidar's spirit had found its way to the rest of the family. I wondered if he and Erika watched the lights together from a new angle.

"We're on patrol, remember?" Winnie hissed. "Unless you think we might be attacked from above, keep your eyes on the streets."

I tore my eyes from the sky, peering into the shadows that enveloped us.

"Winnie, why aren't you an Epsilon?" I wasn't sure what brought the question to mind, and I was asking it before I could think better of it.

"You asked me that before, you know."

"I don't remember before," I lied. Back then, she'd told me Epsilons and Apex were nothing but tools to her.

"It's not a pleasant procedure." Her cape rippled as she shrugged. "The risk isn't worth it, not when I don't need superpowers to be Adrestus's right hand woman."

"I thought Mira was his right hand woman."

Winnie laughed and pushed her mask up so I could look her in the eye by the light of the aurora.

"For now. She's been at his side longer than most of us, but she'll disappoint him eventually. Every Apex ability has its limits, and he's about to find hers. But me? Powers aren't what make me special. *I* make me special, and I am boundless."

She flicked the mask down over her face, and her cloaks fanned out as she turned on her heel to continue down the shadowy street towards the water.

"Is it because of your dad?"

Her steps faltered, but she forged forward. For a silent moment, I thought she'd opted to ignore me. When she finally spoke, her voice was callous and hard.

"I spent the first ten years of my life being told I was special. From the moment I could walk, I spent every day learning to be faster, stronger, all around better than everyone else. When Amanda's powers manifested, he was so proud and told me soon I'd be special, too."

"But it never happened," I said slowly.

"When my powers didn't manifest, Dad had my genes tested. The idea that one of his children might not be an Apex had never crossed his mind so he'd never thought to test me before. When my results came back as negative for the Epsilon gene, the way he screamed, you would've thought it was the worst day of his life." Winnie held her head high and defiant, spitting on her words as she spoke them. "I'd given up my childhood to push myself to become some great hero, and when I turned out to be a dud, I was cast aside. No more training with Amanda. No more speeches about how I was going to change the world. No more dreams about becoming stronger than Paragon himself. All I was good for was to be brainwashed into remembering a fake past, all so you could have a friend."

"So you won't become an Epsilon because you don't want to give your dad what he wanted?"

"I won't become an Epsilon because I won't be used ever again, not by my father, not by Adrestus. *No one.* I will become stronger than Dad and stronger than Amanda, and I'll make Roy Hendricks eat the words he said to me when I became his greatest disappointment." She squared up and tilted her head back to look at the shifting lights in the sky, pushing her mask out of the way. "He said I'd be nothing without his powers, but when I'm helping Adrestus run this world, I'll have my father and sister on their knees, begging for mercy, and they will know which of us is stronger."

"What's Amanda have to do with Roy's bad parenting?" My heart ached for Winnie in a way I hadn't thought it still capable of, but a strange defensiveness reared its head inside me at Amanda's mention. "Adrestus already enslaved her once, and she was a disappointment, too."

"Oh, yes," Winnie said with a gleeful twill. "She quit his precious Apex Team. Plus, she was an excellent swimmer and quit that, too. To top it all off, she brought home a Beta."

"But Brooke is great—"

"Tell that to my father. He was furious!" Winnie laughed. "If it weren't for my mom calming him down, he might've burned down the whole island there and then."

Mrs. Hendricks... I bit my lip and tucked my chin so that my hood fell further over my face.

"Your mom, Winnie, she—"

"Dion." Winnie cut me off. A gust of ocean wind cut through the alleyways, and her cloaks billowed out around her. She turned back towards me, her mask back on her face and glinting green in the reflection of the aurora. "My name is Dion. Adrestus's goddess of madness and destruction. There is no Winnie."

"You aren't a goddess, though," I said carefully. "Look, I know your family hurt you but—"

"I *am* a goddess because after the Peace Summit, I will be worshiped as one of the New Pantheon. People like my father believe the world should be run on birthright and that you stay in the position you are born into.

But *I* decide who I am and who I will be." She gestured to the ocean behind her, which bled with hues of green. "There's your pretty lights, Eydis. They're beautiful, sure, but remember who put them in the sky for you."

I gulped. The electromagnetic field had its function, turning New Delos into an island in a whole new way, cut off from the rest of the world for the most part, but I didn't like the insinuation that Adrestus had put the aurora in the sky as some sort of gift to me.

"I'm sorry your family sucked, Dion," I sighed, "but don't think that means I'm going to roll over and let you have the spot on the stage at the Peace Summit."

"Oh, no. I'd never expect that of you. I will win and deserve every honor I receive because while I may be a goddess, I am a goddess of my own making."

I walked up to the railing that looked over the water. Besides the short bursts of ocean gales, it was a relatively calm night, and the glass ocean surface danced in tandem with the sky. Standing on the edge of the darkened city looking out over water, I felt like I was standing at the edge of the universe, and I might float out into dark nothingness.

"We didn't come out here to sight-see," Winnie reminded me. "We'll get back faster if we split up. I trust you can make it back to the Schrader Tower without my help?"

I turned back to look at the single dash of yellow light eighty-seven stories above the street.

"It shouldn't be all that difficult," I muttered.

"Great. Take this and radio me if you see anything."

"But I thought the aurora disrupts radios?" I took the small communicator in my hand and turned it over to inspect it.

"Special frequency. Don't ask me how because I don't know." She adjusted her cloaks and straightened up. "You go round the north side of the tower. There's some abandoned buildings there that were damaged in the flood and haven't been repaired yet. It would be the perfect place for someone to hide."

I had a sneaking suspicion that this was some sort of test Winnie was putting me through, and if that were the case, I was determined to give her a flawless performance, even if Fleming *was* hiding in the buildings.

Winnie made a show of heading south as I turned towards the north, my eyes back on the sky. I didn't like this new pity I had for her. It was easier to work against her when she was just the overzealous sister, envious of her superhero family. Even if her hatred for Amanda was misplaced, it was easy to see where her bitterness had come from. The only person Winnie didn't seem to harbor resentment for was her mother, and when she eventually found out that Val was dead and I had known all along?

I shuddered. There was nothing I could do about it now. I'd have to wait until I came to that bridge to burn it.

The magnetic humming of the sky permeated my skull as I walked through the shadows of skyscrapers. In this part of the city, slabs of concrete were criss-crossed by haphazard cracks. I stepped over a larger crack, ignoring the burning of blisters in my new sneakers. My cloaks billowed out around me as I whisked around a street corner before a lone car could catch sight of me in its headlights.

The buildings Winnie had wanted me to check were easy enough to pick out. The windows that weren't boarded up were cracked and shattered, making entry into the first building easy. It was hard to tell what sort of establishment it had been before the flood, as most of its contents had been gutted.

"I'm in the first building," I whispered into the comm device.

"Please don't whisper and sound all creepy about it," Winnie snapped back. "See anything?"

"Sure," I said, clearing my throat, "let me find the lights real quick."

Winnie's heavy sigh came through the comm as static.

"There's a flashlight on the comm device, genius."

I found the button on the side of the communicator, and a beam of white light extended ahead of me. Dried kelp and old litter spread across a rotted tile floor. A row of cash registers sat abandoned under boarded windows, and grimy water dripped from the ceiling, adding to the puddle of rot in the room's center. A set of escalators rusted to my right, leading to a second floor.

"It smells horrible." I pressed a hand over my mouth and nose, trying to stem the stench of decay.

"Water damage does that. Don't fall through any floors."

I froze, inspecting the tiles ahead of me. They were discolored and displaced by the swollen wood beneath them, but otherwise looked sturdy.

The building creaked overhead, but it sounded more like floor settling than it did footsteps. My heart jumped all the same, and I tightened my grip on the communicator.

Tile and wood bowed beneath my boot, and I stepped back as part of the floor dissolved, revealing the black void hiding beneath the rotting tiles. A distant splash sounded from the abyss, and I gulped.

"Keep me updated," Winnie sighed. "It's dead down here. Total waste of time."

Winnie fell silent, and the only sounds were my careful breathing and the squelching footsteps of my shoes as I tried to cross to the busted escalator. The floor creaked underfoot, and I froze, testing my weight little by little until I was confident the floor could hold me. I shifted forward, sweeping the area with the light, catching nothing but rot and dust particles in the beam.

I looked back at my feet, watching each step with care, until a new smell lingered with that of blight, itching at the back of my throat.

Smoke.

The green light of the sky leaked in through the second floor windows, illuminating the outline of a man standing at the top of escalators.

"Wi—!" I stumbled backwards, but the floor cracked and shuddered underfoot. My boot punched a hole in the tile, and I fell onto my back.

For a moment, I lay with one leg dangling into the black abyss hidden beneath me, marveling at how lucky it was I hadn't fallen all the way through. But then a terrible, squelching splinter rang out, shattering the floor, and I shrieked as the darkness below swallowed me whole.

29

Fire and Brine

For the brief moment where I hung suspended in dark nothingness, I thought I might fall forever. The illusion broke with stale water slapping across my back. I dropped a short few feet through the brine, smacking my head against the rubble hiding beneath the surface, but I hardly noticed it through the blinding agony that seared through my left leg.

Piercing, excruciating, and all-encompassing, the pain was the only thing that existed, and I howled through gritted teeth, my screams bubbling through the water and twisting through my hair, until my face broke the surface, and I choked on pungent air. I'd fallen into absolute darkness, but I didn't need to see to feel the white-hot pain of metal rebar impaled through the meat of my thigh.

I tried to swallow my cries, but they fought their way through my throat as guttural, feral growls. Shaking, tentative fingers found the metal rod protruding from the back of my thigh, straight through to the front.

Panic welled in my chest, and I bit back a renewed, carnal need to scream. My quaking hands searched the floor beneath me, finding the base of the rod where it stuck out from the rubble. The fact that I managed to dislodge it from the broken concrete was a small victory. I was blind and in excruciating pain, but with the rod loose, I could move. I struggled to my feet and inhaled sharply as raw muscle constricted around the metal goring my leg.

The stench of the flooded basement hit me as violently as the rusted rod had skewered me, and I raised my hands to my mouth to keep from gagging. Knee-deep ocean water that had likely been here since I'd flooded the city clung to my cloak and clothes, thick with grime and fetid foam.

Debris rained into the water around me, and I raised my arms to protect against falling pieces of tile and wood. When the destruction settled, I was left with the sounds of disrupted water lapping against the distant edges of the basement and my own haggard breaths.

I stumbled forward blindly and collapsed to my knees. Overwhelming pain threatened to drag me into unconsciousness, and as much as I wanted to let it, I knew I'd drown in the rotting water if I did.

Something sloshed far to my right, and I froze, biting down on my slime-soaked hand to keep quiet. Rattling breaths, rapid and heavy, echoed off the high ceilings of the rotting chamber.

I was not alone.

The thick, muscular body of some unseen sea creature bumped up against my thigh. I recoiled from the touch, landing on my backside in the water and jostling the foot-and-a-half length of metal that still protruded from my leg.

I bit back a scream of pain and strained my ears against the deafening silence, but all I could hear over my heartbeat roaring against my ear drums was the distant sloshing of water.

I took a slow, careful step forward when an arm shot from the darkness behind me, wrapping around my torso, and a hand slapped across my mouth. Flames leapt from the arms like vambraces, illuminating a nearby row of toppled shelves that lay like fallen dominos in the murk and turning the water and slime the color of coagulating blood.

"I'm here for Winnie Hendricks," a low voice growled in my ear. "Take me to her, or you'll have barnacles growing on you by the time your comrades find your body, if you haven't been picked apart by the crabs first."

Roy Hendricks had come to collect his daughter.

Maybe I should've been relieved it wasn't Fleming after all, but trapped in Roy's grip with rebar stuck through me like I was a chunk of meat on a spit, Fleming was who I needed the most. Bitter disappointment dulled the pain in my leg.

"Screw you," I choked. Winnie's borrowed cloak kept Roy's fire from burning me as I swung an elbow into his ribcage. His fire flickered out, and I surged forward on uneven strides, but my shadow jumped ahead of me as the flames reignited.

Fire erupted around us in a ring, illuminating the piles of debris, floating chunks of flotsam, and the distant gleam of defunct escalators from which the fire had cut me off.

I spun back to face Roy, pulling the hood of Winnie's cloak low over my face.

"You know where my Winnie is." Soot painted the top half of Roy's face in a crude recreation of Paragon's mask, and he wore all black. Thin streams of whip-like flame issued from both his hands, trailing behind him as he stalked forward. "That was her voice on your radio."

His fire whip cracked as he brought it down, and I raised an arm to deflect it away from my face, but cried out as the tongue of flame snapped and wrapped around my unprotected forearm.

"You think I won't kill you?" he seethed. "I know who you work for, and I know he's done far worse. I'm not afraid to do what I have to do to save my daughter."

He yanked on his end of whip, and I fell forwards next to a rusted, overturned shopping cart. The fiery constraint dissolved with a hiss when it hit water, but the second whip was already snapping overhead.

I let my shoulder take the brunt of its lick, and while my cloak saved me any burns, the sharp tongue of the flame was as cutting as any other lash. Roy lumbered forward, and flames rose off his shoulders in premature triumph.

I struck out at the water, scooping it with my hand and sending a big enough spray upwards to obscure his vision. I reached for the shopping cart, grabbing it with both hands, and with a mighty heave, I swung it, pivoting on my good leg to smack Roy upside the head. He staggered sideways, and I pounced, giving him no time to gather his bearings.

He was larger than me, but I had the upper hand and pinned him under the water, plunging us both back into darkness as his fires extinguished. I held him there, feeling him thrash beneath me, thinking darkly of how I had been in his position so recently, knowing the panic that was screaming in his head.

I wouldn't drown him. Not all the way. I just needed to weaken him.

But the water around my hands turned warm, then hot, and then it was blistering, hissing as it turned to steam around me. I cried out and stumbled back, clutching my hands close and gritting my teeth in pain.

As Roy rose from the water, his flames rose with him, rolling off his back in a cape-like sheet.

"That's how you're going to play it, then?" he growled. I squared up, holding my blistered hands in front of me in painful fists. "You would *murder* me, would you?"

"You were going to murder me first," I snarled. He raised his hands and brought them down in an X-shaped motion. The whips reignited in his fists.

"I can tell you're young. I've worked with kids your age," he said darkly. "There's so many rules about discipline these days. You can't properly raise a hero or a kid anymore because you aren't allowed to discipline them."

He cracked a whip for show and splashed forward. When I tried to step back on my injured leg, a whip snapped and snagged my cheek, burning my skin and drawing blood.

My leg collapsed under me, and I fell back in the water as the second whip broke overhead, snapping down at me hungrily. I kicked at the water like I had before, and again, the whip dissolved with a hiss, but he was ready this time.

A third tongue of fire wrapped around my raised calf, and I screamed in pain as the flame seared through Winnie's yoga pants and into my unprotected skin.

I lowered my chin, trying to hide my face under the hood, but Roy sloshed forward to get a better look. I winced as yet another flame whip tore at my shoulders, pinning my arms to my side. Roy transferred his end of the line to his other hand, holding both my leg and shoulders in position as he bent over me and flicked my hood back.

His face contorted in the flickering firelight. The fire constraints dissolved, but a new ring of flame erupted around us, dancing on the surface of the water.

"You," he growled. "I *warned* them about you!"

"I guess you were right all along." The salt water was like knives in my burns, and the pain in my left thigh was threatening to drag me into unconsciousness, but I bit back the tears to flash an insincere smile. "Whoops."

A twisted smile tugged on the corner of his lips.

"How that must've simply destroyed Alex's poor, Beta heart," he sang. "But let's put thoughts of Alexander Fleming's innumerable failures aside for a moment because I'm a humble man. I'm not here to gloat, I'm here to take my daughter home. So, Eydis, Samantha, whoever the hell you are, where is she?"

I backpedaled in the water until the heat of Roy's flames pressed against the back of my head.

"I'm not telling you." I struggled to my feet and lunged. His boot rose from the water to meet me in my stomach, and I fell back to the water, gagging on bile and salt.

"Do you think she'll come looking for you?" he mused. "Maybe she will when she hears the sounds of your screams?"

The whips reappeared, this time with extra tails. There was no escape. I held myself up on shaking arms and glared up at Roy through grime-soaked locks of hair.

"Really, dear," he grinned, "I take no pleasure in this."

He raised the whips, and I screwed my eyes shut and tucked my face into my shoulder.

The crash of debris overhead mingled with the crack of Roy's whip. Rotting wood and tiles cascaded into the water, and Roy bellowed in anger.

"You!?"

A red cape trailed in the water next to me, and firelight glinted off a raised carbon-fiber arm. Thin streams of flame wrapped around the sleek black wrist.

"Don't you *dare* touch her," Wesley growled.

"I had it under control," I groaned.

"Yeah?" A new voice called from the furthest corner. "It definitely looks like it."

Roy spun around, his fire expanding, traveling along the ceiling, so that he could see Winnie better where she stood at the top of the escalator with her mask pushed up to the top of her head.

"Winnie!" He stumbled towards her, splashing haphazardly through the water, Wesley and me forgotten. "Winnie, it's me!"

She flicked the tragedy mask down over her face, the curves catching the red of her father's fire.

"Ares, take him alive."

Wesley tackled Roy from behind, a column of flame sent him stumbling backwards.

"Wes!" I ripped my cloak from around my shoulders.

I staggered through the water, propelled by adrenaline, gathering the cloak in my arms. Wesley took it, unfurling its folds as he launched himself at Roy a second time.

He covered Roy in the cloak, and the water around them steamed and bubbled as they thrashed. Winnie stalked down the steps of the escalator, stopping two steps above the water.

"Hey, Dad!" she called. Roy stopped struggling under the cloak, and Wesley pulled it back from his face so he could look at his daughter. "If you want to talk, we can do it with my boss, yeah?"

"Winnie, come home," Roy begged. "You have no idea how badly we've missed you. And your mother—"

He bowed his head, unable to talk any further.

"We can talk about it up there." Winnie nodded upwards in the direction of Schrader Tower. "Otherwise, I'll have Wesley leave you down here for whatever bottom feeders are hiding in the dark."

I gave Wesley a nervous glance. Our entire story we'd fed to Adrestus hinged on him believing Roy was still in charge of Apex Team and my memories were gone. If we gave him the chance to talk to Adrestus, our story would fall apart, and the chip in Wesley's neck would be activated.

Wesley stared back, equally panicked.

"Wes—"

But he was already taking care of it. Wesley arced his fist upwards into Mr. Hendricks's chin. The man's head rocked backwards as he slumped forward, and the fire he had cast around the basement extinguished with a hiss.

"What did you do?" I demanded.

"It'll be a concussion at least," Wesley murmured, taking the unconscious man into his arms. "It'll be difficult for Adrestus to get anything out of him for a few weeks, and by then, hopefully we'll be gone."

"You idiot, now you've got to carry him!" Winnie shouted from the escalator. The white light of her communicator hit us square in the face.

"Sammy, you're hurt!" Wesley gasped.

"It's nothing," I said through gritted teeth, limping towards Winnie's communicator light.

"You have a metal rod sticking out of your leg!"

"Hadn't noticed."

"Holy crap, Sam." Winnie whistled as I limped closer. "I'm definitely not getting those pants back."

Pain spasmed through my leg as I reached the escalator, and a splash sounded behind me as Wesley unloaded Roy into the water to help keep me standing.

"Wesley, he's unconscious!" Winnie squawked. "You can't just drop my dad in the water!"

"Then you get him!" Wesley scowled, trying to put an arm around me. I almost let him until I remembered the device in his neck, and shoved him off.

"You're already wet! I'm not getting in there," Winnie said.

Wesley begrudgingly pulled Roy's limp body from the brine and flung him over his shoulder before trying to help me.

"I'm fine," I hissed. "Winnie, get us out of here."

My various burns, cuts, and impalements made it hard to stay upright, especially as my rush of adrenaline fled my body, leaving me unsteady. Another spasm of pain rocked my leg, and I fell against Wesley's shoulder. My last remaining bit of adrenaline stoked my frustration, and I grabbed onto the rod where it jutted out of my thigh.

Without thinking, without feeling, and without hesitating, I ripped the rebar clean through and cast it aside into the dark waters.

"Oh, my god." Winnie's saucer-like eyes reflected the white of the communicator light. "You did *not*."

"Like I said. Perfectly fine." I stood back up. For a half-moment, I really thought I'd shown them and that I had salvaged a hard-won victory for myself. Then, nauseating pain rolled over me, and the last thing I was aware of was the sound of Roy Hendricks's body splashing back into the water and Wesley's arms cradling me as the ground rushed upwards.

30

Busywork

Low voices murmured overhead, pulling me out of a fever-induced dream featuring a school trip to my family's Medieval longhouse in which I had to juggle keeping my cover as a normal, modern teenager without being recognized by my Viking neighbors. It was a task made infinitely more difficult by the bits of metal I kept finding wiggling their way out from under my skin.

The whispers and low lights were a relief after such a dream, but the pain in my leg made me wish I was unconscious again.

"No, she's fully vaccinated," an achingly familiar voice said. "Including tetanus."

I turned towards the voice and cringed when my hair, dried and caked in basement ocean grime, crackled in my ear.

"You vaccinated an immortal Viking?" Adrestus's voice hid a laugh.

"She could still get sick. Vic said they both had the plague in the fourteenth century."

"Fair point. Been there myself. Not fun."

"I have tetanus?" I rubbed my eyes, and the corners and shadows of Mira's living room took shape around me, lit by the dim light of her never-ending candle collection. The familiar press of the black sofa cushions pushed against my back, and I found Mira, watching me from behind the second-floor railing with a bandage around her elbow.

"Despite your best efforts, no." Adrestus knelt at the side of the couch in a white button-up, his hair unkempt so that loose curls hung in his face. His metal eyepatch glittered in the candlelight. "You didn't die either, which I'm told is quite the feat for you. You did need a transfusion, but luckily you and Mira have the same blood type."

I willed myself not to think about Mira's blood coursing through my veins, and fought against my aches and burns to sit up. A woman sat on a kitchen barstool, her blonde hair braided over one shoulder and her brow knotted with worry.

"Mom!"

I lurched forward, reaching for her, but Adrestus put a hand on my shoulder to hold me back.

"I'm afraid I can't allow that." He pressed me back against my pillows, and my injuries forced me to obey. "Her powers work by touch, and I can't risk her downloading any secret messages into your head."

Mom watched with careful composure, her hands in her lap and her brow creased as she studied me from afar.

"You ripped a metal bar out of your leg," she said, "and somehow it's not the stupidest thing you've done recently."

"Where's Avery?" I asked.

"He's fine," Mom promised.

"Alison, we have everything we needed from you, unless there was more in Samantha's medical history."

I silently begged her to stay. I wanted to run to her, to tell her I'd come to rescue her and Avery, that I hadn't actually joined Adrestus.

"No," she murmured, "but Roy is allergic to penicillin."

"I'll pass that along to our medics."

"Sammy, I—" Mom stepped off her stool, but Adrestus held up a hand.

"That's all we needed from you Ms. Taylor. Mira, if you would assist her."

"It's Havardson," she sniffed as Mira came down the stairs to meet her. "Stay strong, Sammy. I assume you know what you're doing."

I watched her exit, wanting to go after her, knowing I couldn't. She hesitated in the door to flash an assured smile before Mira prodded her into the hallway.

"My *gods*, Eydis!" Adrestus fell back in an armchair and ran a hand through his curls. "It's a miracle your history teacher doesn't have more grays. Are you always like this?"

"Can't remember."

He laughed and shook his head.

"Our team sutured your leg, and we medicated and bandaged your burns, though they didn't appear too extensive. They also gave you a round of antibiotics, but I think a shower might be what you need more than anything."

I stared at the far door, wondering how far Mom's room was and if she was staying with Avery or if they were keeping them separated.

"You could've asked her my medical history in her room."

"This felt more efficient, somehow." Adrestus scratched his beard, and I avoided his eye by staring at the lump my feet formed under my blanket. "You did well against Roy Hendricks."

"I fell through a floor and immediately impaled myself."

"Either way, you beat him."

"Wesley beat him." I rolled my eyes. "I got burned and skewered."

"I'm sure you had it under control. Unfortunately, with these injuries, I doubt you'll be able to face off against Dion for a seat at the Peace Summit."

"What?" I threw the blanket off to further inspect my injury. Winnie's yoga pants were in tatters, cut away from my left leg at the upper thigh. Beneath the bandages, my heartbeat pressed against gauze, which probably wasn't a good sign.

"The blanket was keeping the smell in." Adrestus turned up his nose and leaned away.

"I can still fight!" I insisted. "It doesn't even hurt!"

"That's a lie, and I know it because I've been stabbed before. Several times, most of them courtesy of you." He tapped a fingernail against his metal eye patch.

"I'll beat her anyway."

"No offense, Eydis, but you couldn't even beat her father. Your grit is something to be admired, but sheer willpower alone won't win you a spot on my stage."

"Roy has fire abilities. Winnie doesn't."

"Who do you think trained Winnie for most of her life, until he found out she was a Beta and a waste of his time?" Adrestus shrugged. "He did a good job of it, too. She's a talented fighter, and she'll use your injury to her advantage. She's not afraid to fight dirty."

I glared at my leg, willing it to fuse the puncture wound back together. Everly would've been able to fix it, Serum or not. White linens balled in my fists.

I needed to be on that stage at the Peace Summit. I needed to be able to stop whatever it was Adrestus was going to try. I needed to beat Winnie.

"Then train me."

"Pardon?" A disbelieving laugh escaped his lips.

"I have three weeks, don't I? Train me."

His blue eye wavered, oscillating between mine as I silently dared him to take the bait.

Train me. Let me get close. Tell me the plan. Put me center stage so I could ruin everything.

"That's how it used to be with us, right?" I asked. "You said we were friends when we first met. Did we never spar?"

He sighed and stood up.

"Heal first."

"I only have a few weeks!"

"We may not have the healing Serum the Apex Team kept in supply, but our medicine is advanced. Give it a week. You'll still be shaky on your feet, but one week from today, I'll train you."

He stared down at me with his lips parted in a crooked smile. He wanted Eydis back so badly that he had forgotten that she'd had been the one who walked into his tent with a concealed blade and smiled sweetly at him just before running him through.

And I was happy to do it again.

For the second time since arriving at Schrader Tower, I was trapped and useless in the confines of Mira's apartment, waiting for my injuries to heal while Winnie left daily to train. She'd been sullen since we'd taken her father prisoner, though he had yet to wake up thanks to Wesley's final hit.

As far as Wesley was concerned, the only indications he was surviving our stay were the spreading bruises and grumbling complaints about having to fight him that Winnie brought home each night. I was scrounging up food in the kitchen one evening, leaning against a crutch, when she came in and shoved me out of the way for an icepack.

"What the hell are you doing?" She gawked at the glass of juice I'd just poured myself. "That's Mira's!"

"So?" I shrugged. "It's been in the back of the fridge for more than a week. She's obviously not drinking it."

She slapped my cup into the sink.

"It's laced with scorpion venom, moron," she snarled. "It's how Mira learns new toxins and their antidotes."

I watched the juice wash down the drain.

"Winnie, are you going soft?" I wrestled with a yogurt lid, struggling to use my hands through the layers of bandages that covered my burns. "A week ago, you would've let me drink that."

She scowled as she pressed her icepack to her shoulder.

"It wasn't a mercy. Adrestus wants you to go to City Hall with Jamie tomorrow."

She was right. I would've rather drank scorpion venom.

"Why can't any of the other interns be Jamie's personal assistant?"

"Because you impaled yourself and aren't cleared to train, so you have to do this instead."

"But I'm cleared to run after Jamie all day? On crutches? Have you seen her walk? I'm not convinced she *isn't* an Apex with the speeds she reaches."

Winnie hitched the icepack up higher on her shoulder.

"If I can go toe-to-toe with Wesley for two hours, I think you'll survive chasing after Jamie."

With that, the lights snapped and darkened overhead, just as they had every night since my return to New Delos, and Winnie slinked out of the kitchen.

Squirming into my internship attire the next morning proved difficult given my number of bandages and the fact that my left leg was screaming in pain. I was running late by the time I stumbled downstairs, caught myself on the bottom step with my crutch, and pivoted into the kitchen.

Mira, with her white tresses pulled back into an elaborate bun, leaned against the island to watch me struggle to throw together a sandwich and fill a water bottle.

"You could help if you like," I mumbled, straining against my injuries to reach for the peanut butter.

"I gave you two pints of blood the other night. That's help enough." She grabbed her things from the counter as she waltzed to the front door. "Try not to fall through any more floors today."

I scrambled after her with my lunch in a paper bag, unable to catch my breath until I was in the elevator dropping eighty-five stories to the museum office where Jamie waited with an impatiently tapping foot.

"Good god, Samantha, what happened to you?" Jamie's eyes flickered from my disheveled hair to the bandages that peeked out from under the hem of my pencil skirt.

"I fell."

"If this impedes your work, I might have to have a chat with Mr. Schrader." She wrinkled her nose at me and led the way to the office exit.

"You should probably check with your lawyer father before trying to use my injuries as an excuse to get rid of me."

"He's prime minister now, not a lawyer."

"Then ask your lawyer mom."

She whirled on me, platinum curls flying.

"Is that supposed to be funny?"

"She's a lawyer, too, isn't she? I've seen her ads."

Jamie's nostrils flared under narrowed eyes.

"She left us because of Dad's new powers."

Jamie twisted back and marched even faster down the corridor to the main atrium of the museum. I half-hopped, half-skipped to keep up.

"I'm sorry," I mumbled. "I didn't know."

"She was weak and not cut out to be a part of our new nation."

I laughed in spite of myself, and Jamie glared at me from the corner of her eye.

"What's so funny?"

"In a weird way, you remind me of Winnie. It's a wonder you two never got along."

"Ew." Jamie shuddered. "Never say that again."

A sleek town car idled on the outside curb, and the driver opened the back door for us. I slid in after Jamie, maneuvering my crutch across my lap.

"A pleasure, Miss Havardson," a husky voice murmured, and I craned to see around to Jamie's other side. John Ratcliffe, with his gelled back graying blond hair and broad shoulders, looked cramped in the town car. His usual smirk had been replaced with a wary glare, and he regarded me with something like suspicion.

"This is the staging plans for the Crystal Amphitheater, right?" Jamie took her father's clipboard from his hands.

"The what?" I asked as the car pulled forward.

"The Crystal Amphitheater? At Schrader Hotel?" Jamie glared at me over the clipboard. "Where we're hosting the summit?"

"The summit isn't going to be at the tower?"

Jamie looked at me like I'd just kicked a puppy.

"Where, Samantha? Where would we have the summit in Schrader Tower? Tell me."

"That's enough, Jamie." Mr. Ratcliffe put an arm around his daughter and pulled her closer, keeping his eyes forward.

"Who are all these people?" Jamie frowned at the clipboard. "Adrestus? Siedon? Mira? Why are they sitting up front with me, and where are you?"

"They're code names," Ratcliffe said, plucking the clipboard back.

"Why don't I have a codename?"

"Because you aren't an Epsilon."

I tried to focus out the window. It was the first time I'd been out on the streets of New Delos during the day since my arrival. From the top floors of Schrader Tower, it was difficult to see the damage the city had incurred in the flood, but cracked sidewalks, boarded up windows, and dying trees were all too visible up close. Each sign of destruction weighed on my conscience, building in my heart like a monument of the pain I'd inflicted on the city and its people.

It was a relief when we turned the corner to City Hall. The opulent, white building with its domed roof and corinthian columns had been restored, and the bronze Paragon statue that stood in the center of a plaza glittered in the summer morning sunshine. Jamie squared her shoulders and smoothed out the wrinkles of her skirt. When security guards in suits opened the car door for us, she stepped out like she owned the place.

Ratcliffe gave me one last dubious look, then followed Jamie up the sweeping, stone steps to the polished-wood doors. I jammed my crutch under my arm and tried to follow, but a hand on my shoulder held me back.

"You have a special assignment today, Miss Havardson." A cool voice accompanied the hand that grabbed my shoulder. A lean man in a suit pushed sunglasses up to reveal eyes so pale blue, they almost looked white against his dark skin. He would've cut an intimidating figure if he wasn't wearing the same careful trepidation that John Ratcliffe had borne towards me. "Follow me."

I obliged, keeping my eyes on the short, twisted locks of hair he had pulled back into a low ponytail as he led the way into City Hall.

"And who are you exactly?" I asked. Without looking back, the man held up a hand, and a tiny, purple flame danced on his fingertip.

"Felix Grimaldi. We met on McMillan Island."

The stone parquet floor cut an elaborate pattern across the expansive City Hall foyer. Marble columns stretched upwards, supporting several floors of exposed halls and a massive, domed roof. While Jamie and her father continued across the main level, Felix pointed to a sweeping staircase.

"That way."

I'd only been inside City Hall once, just after sinking New Delos using the control booth that had been suspended somewhere beneath the floor. That day, City Hall had been alive with terror as the scramble to evacuate began. Today, it was empty.

"Where is everyone?" I asked.

"We try to keep them out of the offices. They don't like listening to the screaming."

I faltered on the steps and looked back at the foyer.

"Screaming?"

"Don't worry. She's been docile lately."

He continued to the third floor, and I hobbled after him, burning with questions to which I knew he wouldn't give the answers. The click of my crutch on tile echoed throughout the building, and I looked over the white railing to see if Jamie and her father were still downstairs, but they'd disappeared down some unseen offshoot.

"Here." Felix unlocked a polished wooden door that creaked forward into a dark, high-ceilinged room with rows of filing cabinets and shelves of boxes. "You'll be in the back."

He led the way through a maze of cabinets to a dusty desk hiding in the back corner. A boxy monitor rested atop the desk, and Felix bent down to flick on a chunky tower. The screen lit up blue.

"Have a seat." Felix gestured to a rickety chair as I threw my lunch and water onto the desk. "You'll be combing through Project Heracles video today. Once upon a time, a man named Paul Fleming was in our employ, though you might know him better as Paragon."

"Yeah, I know who he is." Rows of electronic files populated the screen as a knot worked its way into my stomach.

"During his tenure, we compiled hours of security and training footage of his efforts with us." Felix opened the first file, and a video of a college-aged Paul took over the screen, shot from an overhead security camera. "He was a loyal employee and an enthusiastic hero, eager to work with

Adrestus. We need you to go through everything and determine if the video in question might prove useful in supporting that narrative."

The Paul on screen looked like his brother, though a bit broader and with an infectious grin. He stood at the museum office desk, drumming his hands against the desktop.

"I have a meeting with Dr. Cunningham," he told the secretary.

"I'm making propaganda?" I asked. Felix shook his head.

"You're simply compiling evidence that Paul was on our side." He made a show of dragging the file into a folder labeled "Project Hephestae".

"You want these for Amanda Hendricks?" It had been over half a year since Adrestus forced her into the role of Hephestae, and I couldn't quite figure out the connection between her and Paul Fleming.

"The Hendricks girl is a lost cause," Felix said. "She won't be our Hephestae. Her father will."

I froze in my seat, looking at Paul's digitized face. The man Roy Hendricks revered above all others. The hero he idolized. If there was a way to use Paul to convince Roy to join Adrestus, it would surely work.

And Roy would be a thousand times more volatile as Hephestae than Amanda ever had been.

31

Light Training

Most of the Paul Fleming footage was useless, but the few videos that showed him enthusiastically following Adrestus were enough to make me realize it wasn't propaganda that I was gathering. It couldn't be propaganda if it were true. Fleming's brother had been on Adrestus's side all along.

It was hard to be disappointed with the man. None of the footage proved that Paragon had known Adrestus's true nature. Rather, Paul was young and easily swayed with promises of a utopia that he could help bring about.

Several hours in, I dragged yet another video into "Project Hephestae" and flicked open my water bottle. It was bold of Adrestus to try to win over Roy at all. He'd taken both his daughters and killed Val. Imprisoning Roy was a safer bet, but Adrestus must've determined him to be worth the risk.

I took a swig of water, and a sharp, metallic taste broke across my tongue. I sputtered clear liquid over the computer keyboard, coughing and gagging at the unexpected taste.

This was not water.

I stared at the bottle in horror, replaying my morning hurry in my head. Mira's bottle had been on the counter, too, before she'd taken it. Mira, who drank scorpion venom for fun.

I braced for sharp pangs of poison that never came. Maybe I'd gotten lucky. Maybe it was one of her drinks that she hadn't laced with toxins.

I smacked my lips, feeling braver. The metallic taste lingered. The distant memory of a glass of cider set against a lavish dinner spread of ham and disembodied arm nudged at the back of my head. Something other than poison churned my stomach.

Mira wasn't just poisoning herself. She was also dosing Life Elixir. I stared at the bottle with renewed horror. Like Adrestus and like me, Mira was immortal, and she would be furious when she discovered I'd taken her Elixir.

I glanced at the exit, then at the incriminating bottle. She'd kill me. Then she'd wait for me to come back and kill me again. I could not return to the tower with a bottle of stolen Life Elixir, whether I'd taken it on purpose or not.

I limped into the aisles of towering file cabinets to find the bottle a new home behind a row of manila folders in a random drawer. I stashed it away and slammed the drawer shut, hoping this would be enough to cover my accidental crime.

"This is a stupid waste of time," a voice, familiar though younger than I was used to, cut through the rows of cabinets, and my heart soared.

"Fleming?" I hissed.

"It's not a waste of time!" Paul's voice replied, and disappointment weighed in my stomach. It was just another video.

"I don't want to work for Schrader." The Fleming on the screen was barely older than me. In his t-shirt, his bare arms were unmarred by the burn scars they now bore, and he waited with Paul at a desk.

"You're studying history. You'll be lucky to work for anyone." Paul was shorter than his brother, though not by much, and his chest pressed against the confines of his "Schrader Industries" hoodie.

"I could always teach," Fleming shrugged.

"Or," Paul grinned, identical to his many statues, "you could let Schrader make you a hero. It took some convincing, but he's willing to give you a shot."

"Your recommendation was wasted," Fleming said. I sank into the office seat, watching him run his fingers through his hair, guilt gnawing my insides. "You should've brought Roy instead."

"Roy's nothing more than hot air. Schrader told me about a project they're working on, and if you join, Roy will have nothing on you. They've got this guy working for them, and he's incredible. He'll take care of you. Just wait and see."

"What project?" Fleming adjusted his glasses, looking at his brother suspiciously.

"Let's just say, you might not be a Beta for that much longer."

Fleming stood up and shook his head.

"No. That's ludicrous. And maybe I like being a Beta? Maybe Roy has nothing on me whether I have powers or not?"

"Oh, come on!" Paul groaned. "Don't get all prideful! We could be heroes together!"

"Suppose pride runs in the family." Fleming slammed the door as he exited, and Paul sank his head into his hands.

I dragged the file into the reject folder. Nothing in this video would convince Roy to join Adrestus.

Fleming didn't feature in any more of the clips, though Paul talked about him often. Their spat in the office footage didn't seem to have permanently marred their relationship as Paul only ever spoke positive things. Those clips went straight into the reject folder, and while I enjoyed hearing about Fleming, to save time, I started dumping any video in which Paul mentioned him.

By the time Felix returned, my eyes were sore from staring at the computer all day, and I was thirsty, having had no water. It was a relief to finally be leaving the cramped records room. I kept my eyes forward as I followed him to the hall, hyper-aware of the cabinet I'd stashed Mira's Life Elixir inside. Hopefully, it would rust there, and Mira never found out I'd stolen her bottle of the most precious liquid on Earth.

Jamie waited by the City Hall entrance, her foot tapping impatiently just as it had that morning when waiting for me by the elevator. The click of her toe filled the wide, empty space of the foyer, but as I followed her and Felix into the setting summer sun of the front plaza, I thought I heard something else.

A single, drawn out scream, high pitched, panicked, and distant, rooted me to the top step of City Hall. I spun around, every nerve on end, but the heavy, wooden door slammed shut in my face, and the scream was silenced.

Mira was furious when I returned to the tower. She wouldn't admit why, but I knew it had to do with her missing Life Elixir. Luckily, stashing away the evidence seemed to have been my saving grace. She tore apart the kitchen in search of her bottle, and I was able to slip upstairs without notice.

Her sour mood continued into the next few days, but I was able to stay out of her way by busying myself with intern work in the offices. I caught glimpses of Wesley between tasks, but we were both careful to keep our distance. Instead, I clung to Heather, even if she made her fury with me and my apparent betrayal very well known. Still, she was my friend, and I felt safe near her. In a few weeks, I'd be able to tell her it was all an act, and she would understand.

At the end of the week, I was no closer to learning anything about Adrestus's plans, but I had least graduated from my crutch. My leg still ached, but I was able to get around by limping, which meant it was finally time to start my training sessions with Adrestus. As much as I knew I needed the practice if I wanted to stand a chance against Winnie, I wasn't eager to spend more time with the warrior.

I'd fought him before, and not just in the handful of times we'd clashed over the last few months, but a thousand years ago, sharing our cultures' sparring techniques with each other. As I made the solo journey back to the training gym after work on Friday, a seventeen-year-old version of Adrestus lurked in my memories, grinning from across a mossy clearing. That Adrestus had been a ruse. A cruel trick so I would give him information on my people and the surrounding settlements.

But as I approached the gym, I thought my reveries of Adrestus must be messing with me. On the other side of the glass wall that overlooked the training mat, down by the open edge of the broken window, Adrestus looked just as he had all those years ago.

"Eydis! Welcome!" He rushed up the stairs to grab the door, and I choked on the air in my lungs.

I'd been expecting Adrestus, the apparent thirty-something year old in an eyepatch. Instead I was greeted by Quinn, no older than seventeen with both blue eyes intact and glittering.

"Is this Gregor again?" I gestured at his renewed youth. "Is he in my head making you look this way?"

Quinn— No, *Adrestus* beamed back.

"Darling Eydis, Gregor is always in our heads. But, yes. This is how I looked when we first sparred."

"You looked like this on McMillan Island." I strode past him down the stairs to the mat, suppressing a chill from the salty wind that poured in from the gaping window.

"That was more out of necessity than sentimentality. I would've been recognized, and the rescue would've failed." He flashed a smile, and I rubbed a knuckle against my temple, as if that might negate the visage of teenage Quinn that Gregor was projecting into my head.

"Gregor's powers," I asked, setting my bag and water down next to his at the bottom step of the stairs, "how do they work if he's not here? Can he see us? Is he projecting an image over you?"

"He puts the expectation to see what he wants you to see in your head, and your brain does the rest, making for a flawless mirage."

"If I poked your eye, would I feel an eye patch or an eyeball?"

Amusement tugged at Adrestus's lips.

"Here," he murmured. I tensed up when he grabbed my hand and lifted it to his face. I thought he might jab my finger into his mirage eyeball, but instead he pressed my palm against his smooth, porcelain cheek. He held it there, his hand warm and balmy on top of mine. "What do you feel?"

"Skin."

"Exactly." He released my hand, and I resisted the urge to wipe my palm off on my leggings. "Yet, I still have a full beard. Gregor's powers are incredible, yes?"

I shook out my shoulders and turned away, pretending to take a moment to stretch. Adrestus had once said Gregor's powers of inculcation were second only to Mom's, but I was starting to wonder if he'd been underselling his favorite henchman.

"Where are the swords?" I asked, glancing around.

"You'll be unarmed against Dion, so you'll train unarmed as well."

A sudden blow to my back made stars dance in my vision, and I collapsed to my knees, gasping at the pain from the attack as well as the sharp ache in my injured leg.

"Lesson one." Adrestus's face swam behind a film of tears, blue eyes grinning behind loose locks of hair. "Never turn your back."

"We weren't fighting yet!" I struggled to my feet.

"Never turn your back on *anyone*, friend or foe," he growled. "Though, in my experience, true friends will stab you in the front."

I pivoted, keeping him in my line of sight as he paced in front of the window. The afternoon light cast deep shadows across his tight-fitting undershirt.

"Like I did." Stab a guy one time, and he's sure to complain about it for the next millennia. Hopefully he wasn't about to use our training sessions to exact little bits of revenge on me.

"Yes," he mused, "but it's less cowardly, watching the realization and disbelief dawn on their face just before the light leaves their eyes. Sticks with you longer, though."

He lunged, and I tried to dance away, but my bad leg was like a stilt underneath me. Adrestus knocked me off balance, and the room flipped.

The matted floor greeted me with a slap, and I lay still for a moment, waiting for the pain in my leg to subside before pushing myself back up.

"If true friends stab from the front, and I shouldn't turn my back, what option does that leave me?" I grunted.

Adrestus smirked, and the face took me back a thousand years. He'd looked at me like that often. He kept his right eye towards me as it was the only one that actually worked.

"If you turn your back to me, you can't see incoming attacks. If you keep your front squared up, you are making yourself a larger target. So what should you do?"

I scowled and stepped one foot back, turning my shoulder towards him.

"Good." He pushed hair away from his face and attacked a third time. When I fell this time, something tugged in my thigh, and I clenched my jaw to keep from crying out. "You're making this too easy! You're a smaller target, sure, but you're an immobile one!"

His foot arced in a downward kick. I rolled away, compartmentalizing the pain in my leg, telling myself I'd handle it later.

"Better!" Adrestus called out, and I dodged yet another attack. "But can you keep this up? You can avoid me until we are both another thousand years old, but you dodging only delays the inevitable!"

I scrambled back to my feet and narrowly avoided Adrestus's fist to my face.

"You're on your feet! Now what, Eydis? We can't dance forever!"

I kept my shoulder to him and bobbed and weaved, though I could tell by the jaunty smile on his face that this was nowhere near his maximum level.

"Come on!" he goaded. He kept his right eye towards me, but if I could get on his left side, he'd be blind. I could attack. I—

Knuckles smashed into my ribs, and the mat disappeared from under my feet as Adrestus threw me to the ground.

The air deserted my lungs, and I was left choking on pain. I rolled onto my hands and knees, pressing my forehead into the mat.

Adrestus kneeled down beside me, blurry behind tears of pain and frustration.

"May the pain be a reminder," he murmured. "It doesn't matter if I do or don't trust you because you are powerless."

"I don't care if you trust me or not," I growled through gritted teeth and shoved him away. "I'm not here to get on your good side, I'm here because I'm sick of getting trashed every time I fight anyone!"

I fought my way to my feet, clutching my side where Adrestus had struck my ribs.

"Now, that's not being fair to yourself." Adrestus crossed his arms, triceps straining against synthetic fabric. I wondered how much of their form was real muscle and sinew, and how much was aided by Gregor's illusion. "You don't get trashed *every* fight! You pulled my eye straight out of my head! That's very impressive!"

"Roy Hendricks threw me around that basement like an old dog toy," I snorted. "His daughter is going to do the same in two weeks."

"You want to be by my side that badly?" His eyebrows softened.

"What I want is to not be a human punching bag!"

"With the number of times you've been stabbed, I'd say you are more of a pin cushion."

I scowled and lunged, hoping to catch him off guard. He clasped his hands behind his back and side-stepped out of my reach.

"Being angry is no use," he said, dodging another swing. "It makes you more vulnerable than strong."

"I'm not angry, and you aren't teaching me anything!"

"You're keeping my target small, and you've kept moving." He danced out of reach of another attack. "The anger could be better managed, but baby steps!"

I faked him out with a swing towards the left side of his face before gritting my teeth and pivoting on my injured leg to come at him with a round kick.

It seemed like forever ago that Wesley had gone over the mechanics of a good round kick with me, and the laced top of my sneaker collided with Adrestus's blind side.

He remained upright, but raised a hand to his cheek in surprise. I put all my weight on my right leg, hoping I didn't set back my injury too much.

"That was..." Adrestus swallowed. "Who taught you that?"

I leaned away.

"Don't know," I lied. He grunted, his smug grin nowhere to be seen.

A beeping drew his attention to his bag by the stairs, and he crossed to check his phone, still rubbing his face.

"That'll have to do for today," he murmured, frowning at his screen.

"You're already done?" I'd finally gotten a good hit, and he was quitting?

He dropped his hand and stalked back to me. I had been the same height as him a thousand years ago. Gregor had done him the liberty of adding a few inches to his stature.

"Oh, Eydis, I'll never be done with you." He reached forward to brush his thumb against my chin. "But we've been summoned. Roy Hendricks is waking up soon."

32

The Trade

Hopefully Wesley had hit Roy real good, otherwise, my tenure at Schrader Tower was about to end. Roy would tell him my memories were back and that he had been the one kicked off the team, not Wesley.

Somewhere between the gym and a familiar plush carpeted corridor, Adrestus had transformed from Quinn the seventeen-year-old to Dr. Cunningham, the thirty-something-year-old museum curator.

Gregor stood in front of a nondescript door that looked like all the others, but something about it made my stomach clench, and a haunting sense of deja vu swept over me.

"Is he inside?" Adrestus asked, and Gregor nodded solemnly. "Excellent. Lead the way, Eydis."

Gregor stood aside, and the door handle buckled at my touch. Ambient light filtered in through windows, though the sun had already traveled to the other side of the building, casting dull, dusty shadows across the room.

Rhythmic beeping accompanied the sound of low voices murmuring around the corner, and a uniformed medic lowered her eyes as she hurried to clean up an abandoned game of cards that sat on the TV tray. The couch that sat against the window was adorned with an old pillow and a wrinkled blanket. I wandered further in, ignoring the medic and following the window around a corner and into a small kitchen, where dishes sat on a drying rack. Two plates. Two mugs. A frying pan that had been used to cook a long since eaten frittata.

Beyond the kitchen, a door was left ajar, and I could make out a bed in the shadows. The man lying in the blankets wasn't my dead brother, but I wondered if the pillows still held traces of Vidar.

This was, after all, the apartment Adrestus had held him in until the day he'd broken free to save me. The day Adrestus had put a sword through his chest.

"Forgive the mess." Adrestus came up behind me, watching the medics in the bedroom tend to Roy. "We never had the chance to clean out the last tenant's things before moving Roy in. This was the apartment of Vic Havardson, also known as Vidar."

"Hasn't he been dead a while?" I asked. He was testing me. He had to be. A medical assistant gathered up the game of abandoned solitaire. I turned away to stare out the living room window where ugly cracks in the window marred the cityscape view, radiating out from a point just above the couch back.

My last day with Vidar, I had drawn our stick figure family in the fog of our breath as it clung to the window. Our mother and father, Solveig and Havard, our brother Knut, our sisters, Gunhild, Hjordis, and Erika. Each reduced to circles and lines dragged through condensation. The figures were long gone, but the cracks converged in the glass where I thought I had left them.

"Believe it or not, I was fond of the man. I think we'd come to an understanding by the time he died. We were almost friends. I couldn't bring myself to pack up his apartment." Adrestus frowned at the apartment as another assistant brought him what appeared to be his dry-cleaning.

In my mind, I saw the length of a silver blade protruding from Vidar's chest, glistening with blood and rain, put there by Adrestus, who was audacious enough to claim they'd been friends.

I forced the muscles in my face to relax.

"I'm sorry for your loss."

The corners of his mustache turned up in a satisfied grin.

"That means a lot, Eydis. Thank you." He threw his dry-cleaning over his shoulder. "Go take a seat. I'll be there in a moment. I can't have my newest Pantheon member meeting me in my gym clothes."

He left to change in the bathroom, and I shuffled forward into what had once been Vidar's bedroom. Roy lay unconscious against the pillows, hooked up to machines that beeped slow and rhythmic. Slits of light cut across the bed, leaking in between window blinds.

"Wesley must've hit him good."

I jumped at the voice and twisted to look at the woman sitting at Roy's bedside. She glared at me from behind locks of blonde hair that had fallen loose of her braid, but her frown was tight with worry.

"Alison." I wanted to fall in her arms and cry, but that wasn't an option, not with Adrestus in the next room over. Her eyes darted to the door, as if to ensure the medics were out of earshot.

"What've you done?" Her tone had the sharp bite exclusive to angry parents, and I tried not to shrink from her admonishment.

"I've joined—"

"Don't give me the crap you're feeding Adrestus. He's already told me. I don't believe it. Why are you here?"

I narrowed my eyes at her, not willing to give up my charade just yet, in case it put her in danger somehow.

"You called me Mom the other night." Her eyes glistened in the shadows, and my stomach dropped. "You haven't called me that since losing your memories."

A weird relief filled my chest. She knew. She'd known for a week, and I somehow felt less alone. I wanted to hug her and search for comfort in her embrace.

"He doesn't know. You can't—"

"I won't, but when we get out of here, you're grounded."

"Fleming's in charge of me."

"He's grounded, too. Does Roy know your memories are back?"

"Why do you think Wesley hit him so hard? As soon as he wakes up and tells Adrestus—"

"I'll make sure he doesn't."

Mom slipped Roy's glasses from his bedside table. She lifted them to his face to slide them over his nose. Her pinky finger grazed his cheek, and his eyes twitched beneath his eyelids, then fell still.

"You better not be touching him, Alison," Adrestus's voice chided from the kitchen. He stepped into the room, now wearing a cashmere suit. "Who knows what I'll have to do to poor Avery if you use your powers."

Mom settled back in her chair, and I tried not to look at Roy. Had she altered his memory of my memories returning? It was almost too much to hope for.

"I was only helping my friend," Mom said flatly, her arms crossed.

A medic hurried in from the kitchen and to Roy's bedside.

"Sir, he's waking up," he said and stepped back as Roy's eyebrows knit and unknit.

"Play the video," Adrestus commanded. "Alison, you'll be interested in this, too, I think."

The TV on the wall opposite Roy lit up, and a familiar bit of footage took up the screen. A young Paragon grinned at a desk.

"I have a meeting with Dr. Cunningham," he chirped. "Should be under 'Paul Fleming'?"

"Paul?" Roy raised a hand to his head but froze when he noticed the IV line hanging from his wrist.

"Good morning, Mr. Hendricks," Adrestus sang, reaching up to pause the TV. "That was quite the nap you just had."

Realization broke over Roy's face, and he jolted into a sitting position and pressed against the headboard in an attempt to find an escape. He extended a hand and paled when no fire sprung to his fingertips.

"What've you done to me?" he demanded. "Where's my fire?"

"That's a precaution." Adrestus shrugged. "Mira's busy today and couldn't be here to keep you under control, but we had a spare control chip lying around. Cooperate and we won't have to use it more than we already are."

Roy rubbed the back of his neck, feeling the bruise that overlaid the control chip injection site.

"You're fine, Roy," Alison murmured. He gawked at her, noticing her for the first time. "We're prisoners, but we're fine."

"Prisoners?" Adrestus frowned. "Hopefully not for much longer after you've seen what I have to show you."

"I don't understand." Roy shook his head. "I was at the camp and then I..." His eyes drifted upwards, finding me in the corner by the window. He lurched forward before collapsing back against the headboard. Unable to get up, he pointed an accusatory finger in my direction. "You! You tried to drown me!"

"So? I still have burns from *you!*" I held up my hands to show him.

"I want my daughter." Roy leaned back, gathering what dignity he could scrape together.

"That was Ares," Adrestus said. "I'm glad he's cooperating with us, but perhaps he was a little overzealous when he knocked you out."

"Ares?"

"Mr. Wesley Isaacs. He claims you kicked him off the team so he came to me for a new home."

I held my breath, hoping Alison's tiny pinky graze had been enough to overhaul Roy's memories.

"I was right to if the first thing he did was run to join *you.*"

I let out a shaky breath. Wesley and I were safe.

"Mr. Hendricks!" Adrestus placed a hand over his heart in feigned offense. "That hurts. What might Paul think if he saw you speaking so callously of me?"

"Paul?" Roy's face softened, and he gripped his blankets. "Paul was *good, and* you're—"

"Evil?" Adrestus grinned. "Pray tell, why do you think I'm so bad?"

"You took my Winnie—"

"Miss Winifred joined me willingly. I've given her purpose."

"You were going to burn down the city—"

"According to whom? Her? I recall *Eydis* being the one who destroyed the city." Adrestus pointed at me and laughed. "You've been playing Alexander Fleming's game. But Paul? He believed in me and my vision."

Roy shook his head, and the video on the screen resumed, skipping ahead to show Paul and Adrestus standing in the training gym.

"This doesn't look like office space," Paul laughed nervously, glancing around the gym.

"I know what the job listing entailed, but we think we might have something better for you," the Adrestus on the screen said. He appeared older, like he had when I'd first met him as Dr. Cunningham, innocent museum curator. "I know who you are. I know about your Apex abilities."

Paul staggered backwards and shook his head.

"No, you must be mistaken. I—"

"You are the strongest Apex New Delos has seen in generations." Adrestus circled Paul, carefully surveying him. "And Adrian Schrader wants to make you our newest hero. Our *greatest* hero."

"You invented Paragon?" Alison stared at the screen, blank-faced. Adrestus paused the video again.

"We created Paragon together. Paul was a dedicated follower. It's a shame what happened to him. Perfectly preventable, too. I was devastated when he fell ill. I can recognize superior power when I see it, and Paul was the greatest of all my children."

"Stop talking," Roy growled, but Adrestus forged onward.

"This was years after this video was taken, of course, and by the time he became sick, we'd been working together for nearly half a decade. Luckily, I had a solution. I may not be able to cure cancer, but I *did* have the means for immortality, as thin as my resources were." Adrestus shook his head, and I might've believed he was actually remorseful if it weren't for the grin on his face. "I offered him a simple trade. He could have enough of my Life Elixir stores to overcome his disease, but he would have to bring me something in return."

Roy sat transfixed, breathing heavily through his nose.

"Paul would've given anything to get better."

"There was one thing he was unwilling to give up. Like I said my resources were running out, and I didn't have my Lapis to renew my stores. We were trying to recreate a new Lapis, but we needed more— ah, materials, if you will."

My stomach clenched, thinking about the jagged scar that marred Anthony's flank, the one that had given him his powers. I knew the type of "materials" Adrestus liked to deal in.

"The non-Apex children of Apex typically carry one of the two Epsilon genes. Livers, and their regenerative properties, were of interest to us in our quest to make a new Lapis. So I asked Paul for something very, very simple. I would cure his cancer in exchange for his brother's liver."

The room swooped around me. Adrestus didn't seem to notice, still focused on Roy.

"It's Alex's fault?" Roy croaked.

Adrestus nodded solemnly, but Alison scoffed and looked away.

"How things might be different if we'd had another fifteen years of Paragon. Alexander Fleming's life would've been a small price to pay, and we would've made strides with his sacrifice."

Roy's shoulders heaved with labored breathing as he tried to make sense of what Adrestus was saying.

"If keeping Paragon around was so important, why not give him the Elixir anyways?" Mom whispered. She shook with anger, and her nostrils flared, but she remained seated, silently quaking.

"I was running out," Adrestus growled. "My Lapis was missing, hiding in a comatose child's neck."

"But why Alex?" she demanded. "And why put that on Paul?"

"Paul was the best of us," Roy said, staring at his hands. "Those genes were wasted on a Beta like Alex, but if their secrets were waiting in his liver, ready for the taking—"

"No one's organs are 'ready for the taking'," Alison snarled. "You can't be buying this? After everything Adrestus has done?"

"Alex could've saved Paul!" Roy's fingers curled into fists, and smoke escaped between his fingers.

"No, *he* could've!" Alison pointed at Adrestus. "And he didn't because he felt entitled to someone else's *organs*!"

"I created the Apex and their families." Adrestus frowned. "They exist because of me."

"Is that why you've taken so many of them prisoner? To do tests on their livers and try to make a new Lapis?"

Adrestus surveyed Alison with deadly ire, but even he knew better than to touch her and risk succumbing to her powers.

"It's a shame," he murmured. "I thought if anyone could be swayed by Paul, it would be his old fiancee."

"After what you did to my husband? To my family?" Alison hissed.

"Then I'm afraid you're a lost cause. Gregor!" Adrestus beckoned Gregor into the bedroom from the kitchen. "Take Mrs. Havardson back to her cell. And you, Mr. Roy Hendricks, enjoy the show. I have hours of footage that corroborates Paul's past with us. I hope you find it enlightening."

I tried to meet Mom's eyes as Gregor led her from the room, but she kept her gaze forward.

"Eydis!" Adrestus barked, and I jumped. "With me!"

He whipped out of the bedroom, and I scrambled to follow him. Poorly contained anger forced heavy exhales through his nostrils he marched from the suite and into the hall. My stomach was churning at the revelation that Paul Fleming had only died because he wouldn't turn his brother over to Adrestus. Fleming hated his brother, but if he knew...

"Was she right?" I dared to ask, breaking Adrestus's furious silence as we neared the elevators. "Are you building a new Lapis with the prisoners?"

"I have a supply of Life Elixir to last me another two millennia! I have plenty of time to figure out how to make a new stone. What I *don't* have is Roy Hendricks's trust, and for some reason, your fake mother is determined to undermine my efforts!" He punched the elevator button.

"What do you mean 'figure out how to make a new stone'?" I repeated.

Adrestus turned pale and then did something I'd never seen him do before: he retreated, abandoning the elevator to continue down the hall. I chased after him.

"You didn't make the first Lapis, did you?" I accused. "All this time I assumed you were making a new one, but you don't know how!"

"That's enough!"

"Where'd the first one come from?" I demanded. "How'd a boy in Ancient Greece come across a magic rock?"

He spun back around, having made it to the stairwell.

"Rome. It was Ancient Rome. I'm not *that* old."

"Rome? But your whole theme—"

"It's not a theme, it's an aesthetic!"

"I always thought you were Greek."

"I've traveled so long, I don't think I'm anything anymore. I was never Greek, but I'd hardly call myself a Roman either."

"Ignatia is a latin name." Maybe I should've let it go, or maybe it would offer clues into what Adrestus was planning.

He head jerked around towards me, and I couldn't tell if he looked more angry or surprised.

"Yes. Ignatia was Roman, too."

"Was she the first person you killed?"

"No." His lips curled.

"Tiberius, then?" I asked, remembering the names he'd told me in warning after he'd thrown Wesley from the training room window. "What about dinner?"

I clasped my hands behind my back. Dinner with Adrestus was the last thing I wanted, but I was desperate for information.

"You want to have dinner? With me?" He raised a dubious eyebrow.

"I want to hear what it was like back then. Why rely on history books when I have you?"

The simpering words made me want to vomit, but they served me well. Adrestus stepped aside to let me walk ahead of him into the stairwell.

"I suppose the company might be nice after that disaster," he murmured. "Then come. It's high time I told someone about who I was before I became Adrestus."

33

The First Epsilon

When Adrestus led the way into the dining room of his apartment, I half-expected to see the bloody mess I'd left behind the last time I'd been here. The dying daylight pouring in from the long, windowed wall turned the white tablecloth orange. In my head, I saw the flash of a silver sword followed by the splash of red and Wesley's disembodied right arm lying limp on the table, his fingers curling in towards his palm.

The wall opposite the window sat empty, and I felt a flicker of triumph when I saw the barren hooks that had once held my sword captive. I took comfort knowing it was safe with Fleming, somewhere Adrestus couldn't parade it as a trophy.

I sat at Adrestus's kitchen island as he cooked dinner. The smell of seared duck accompanied the crackle and pop of heated oil, and I glanced to the white furniture of the sitting room to my left, then down the windowed hall to my right. Now that I was alone with him in his home, I was having second thoughts about my plan to extract information.

"I'm not too much of a cook, I'm afraid," he chuckled as he tended the stainless-steel stovetop. "Baking is more my forte, though I appreciate the opportunity to prepare you a meal, again. You hardly tasted the food last time I tried."

I responded with a wan smile. The ham dinner he was referencing had been cut short by a severed arm and a gouged-out eyeball.

"It smells great."

He carefully lifted porcelain plates of meat and vegetables.

"I know duck can be an acquired taste." He set the plates on the marble island and took the stool next to mine, still wearing his blue and white striped apron over his button-up.

"So," I said, "Ignatia?"

I took a large bite of duck, hoping to hurry dinner along. I never thought the day would come where I was eager to get back to Winnie, but her sullen silence and occasional melodramatic outbursts were preferable to Adrestus's company.

Adrestus swallowed his first bite of duck and set his fork down. He propped his elbow on the countertop to rest his head in his hand.

"Quintus Dio," he said. "That was my name. Ironic, isn't it, that my surname meant 'divine-like'? However, 'Quintus' never quite seemed big enough for me. Adrestus is the name of a warrior. I took it from the stories my friend used to tell me. He said it was the name of a king who couldn't be conquered."

"Your friend?"

"Tiberius. He was the Greek apprentice of an alchemist. I was merely the son of a Roman governor ruling over what had once been Sparta. Tiberius may have been the one with the fantastical stories and aspirations, but I was the one with the means to make them reality."

"Okay, then, Quintus Dio," I said, pushing bits of seared duck across my plate. "You and Tiberius were buds in a colonized Sparta. You were a rich boy, and he was the apprentice of a what?"

"An alchemist." His mustache twitched at the sound of his original name. "Like a chemist, but a little more fantastical. For centuries, alchemists around the world had a singular goal, and they called it the Magnum Opus."

"The Lapis. Your magic immortality rock." I rubbed the scar on my neck. It was strange to think something so coveted had spent a millennia hiding behind my collar bone.

"No man knows when or how he'll die. Is it not a worthy goal to answer the question by making sure it never comes to pass?"

"No man except Trev Baker," I snorted. Adrestus set his fork down and furrowed his brow against his metal eye patch.

"Trev Baker knows when and how he'll die?"

"I thought you knew." I gulped. I didn't care much for Trev, but he was a prisoner somewhere in this building. Hopefully I hadn't landed him in any trouble. "That's his power. He sees deaths."

"Trev never disclosed his abilities to us, only that he was indeed an Apex," Adrestus murmured. "How is it that he knows?"

"He dreams it, I think." Heat rose in my cheeks. I'd been trying to make a joke and now was being interrogated. "It's why he's always guzzling caffeine. To avoid seeing his friends die when he sleeps."

Adrestus stroked his beard.

"Trev Baker excluded, no one knows when death may come, and the Magnum Opus may have been the divine goal of many an alchemist, but only one person succeeded in creating not just one, but two."

He'd told me a long time ago that there had been two stones until he'd accidentally destroyed one.

"One for you and one for Tiberius?" I asked.

"One for me, one for Ignatia, and I killed Tiberius before he could create a third."

"Oh. So who was—"

"Just listen to the story!" He abandoned his dinner and beckoned me to follow him down the windowed hall. I slipped from my stool, uneasy about following Adrestus deeper into his home, but I had little choice in the matter. "Tiberius's master was old and increasingly desperate to succeed in his creation of the Lapis. He was just on the cusp of discovery, too, when age beat him to the punchline, leaving Tiberius floundering for direction and purpose."

"Which is where you stepped—"

"Which is where I stepped in, exactly!" He stopped in front of a wooden door and pulled it open to let me into a sort of office.

Mahogany shelves lined the walls, giving off a thick, cozy scent in the light of a glass desk lamp. Old trinkets in glass cases lined the shelves, and alcoves showed off oil paintings in gold frames. I stopped at the first one, staring at the face of a man I didn't recognize. His skin was a shade darker than Adrestus's and his brown hair slightly lighter. His brow was serious, accented by a long, handsome nose.

Adrestus poured himself a glass of red wine he'd procured from a nearby shelf.

"And there he is. Painted him myself, the best my memory would allow, anyway. Tiberius and I met as children when his mother worked in my home. I grew up listening to his stories of gods and titans. I came to adopt them as my own, not as religion mind you. Rather, as a model. After his mother died, the alchemist took him in. Six years later, he showed up in my family's garden. He needed help. Resources. In return, he could stop us both from aging."

"And you believed him?" I looked at the next painting over. Adrestus's self-portrait of his teenaged self spoke to his skill with a brush and canvas. He looked just as I remembered him.

"No. He'd told me many stories, but this was the most farfetched of them all. I helped him anyways. I was bored, and I had what he needed."

"Which was…?"

"People." He took a sip of wine. I tried to keep my face passive but must've done a poor job of it. "Don't look at me like that. People are and always have been a resource. Some are more expendable than others."

"Why—" My voice caught as I thought of Fleming and the trade Adrestus had offered Paul. "Why did you need people?"

"*Tiberius* needed people because we couldn't very well test an immortality rock on ourselves. We'd have, at most, two tries to get it right."

"You tested the Lapis by killing people?"

"To see if they stayed dead, yes. I don't get what's got you all nervous. Tiberius's master had a way of luring in travelers that hadn't raised suspicion. Dying on long journeys wasn't exactly a rare occurrence at the time, but Tiberius found he wasn't as capable at bringing in lodgers so he turned to me."

"And where did *you* get the people?"

"As the governor's son, I had access to our jails, and no one so much as blinked when I showed up to take handfuls of prisoners at a time."

"How many?" No wonder he felt no remorse for how he treated people. We must've looked like nothing to him after killing so many.

"Somewhere upwards of fifty, I'd wager, before the first prisoner survived death. I thought we'd failed again, but as we were carrying his body into the woods, he stirred in my arms.

"But the effects weren't permanent. That first prisoner to survive came back a few more times, but after a week, the stone's power had worn off. We needed a more permanent solution. If only we'd had *your* innovation and thought to stick the stone into our own necks. Alas, we weren't so creative, and several more prisoners had to die for it."

He stood in front of the portrait of a girl with bright green eyes and curly, blonde hair. Freckles spotted her nose, and her smile was kind and innocent.

"And then, we came to a prisoner, no older than fifteen. She was a thief, but I rescued her from the prison and gave her great purpose." Adrestus stared at the portrait with the same possessive hunger he'd regarded me with so many times, and a strange protectiveness rose in my chest on the girl's behalf. "She would help us test a modified form of the Life Elixir, introduced directly to the nervous system. Perhaps that was the key to immortality. It was a key, to be sure, but to a very different door than the one we were trying to open."

He turned to me to grin in the low light of the office, sipping at his wine.

"The nervous system?" I balked. "Like her brain?"

"Spinal cord, actually. It was messy. We didn't have tools that allowed for finesse, but after lots of screaming on her part, we'd done what we'd set out to do and waited for her to wake so we could give her the hemlock and test our latest theory.

"But when she woke, she woke with literal fire pouring from her hands. She refused to drink the poison, and with the new powers we'd given her, we were powerless to force her to do anything."

"It's a wonder she didn't kill you." I wrapped my arms around myself, wishing that the poor prisoner *had* killed Adrestus and Tiberius.

"Oh, she tried. We'd never bothered learning any of the prisoner's names. They were naught but lab rats, so we referred to each one as a letter, rotating through the Greek alphabet as needed. But Tiberius calmed her down and asked her for her name."

"Ignatia." I looked back at the demure smile of the portrait.

"To save us, Tiberius offered Ignatia what he'd offered me. Eternal life. He wanted her to join us. She would no longer be an experiment. She'd get to live forever. It was an easy choice for her to make."

"She was the first Apex?" The red cloak Adrestus had painted on her looked similar to the old cord of maroon fabric, carefully folded under a sealed glass case on the next shelf over.

"Oh, yes. And in her honor, we named all first-generation Apex after her assigned Greek letter she'd kept as a prisoner."

"Epsilon," I sighed. Adrestus winked at me and backed out of the room, tapping something out on his phone, as he led the way back to the kitchen.

"Immortality was put on the proverbial back burner. We had the Lapis and were in the process of creating two more. As long as we drank the Life Elixir that the stones created, we wouldn't die, so we focused instead on creating more Epsilons. Prisoners who swore allegiance to us would undergo the Epsilon procedure. The mortality rate wasn't great. Roughly nine in ten prisoners perished in the process."

"But you had Life Elixir." My duck was cold, but it was no matter. I'd lost my appetite. "Why didn't you give them a sip and ensure their survival that way?"

"We tried," he shrugged. "But it didn't work. Even today, the mortality rate for the Epsilon procedure isn't splendid. If some people are destined for greatness, it then follows that some are destined for mediocrity. The elixir rejects them and punishes them for trying to be something greater than they are."

I slipped onto my stool to poke at my dinner with my fork.

"So what went wrong?" I asked. "You had immortality, a growing army, and friends. Why'd you kill them?"

Adrestus stared at the bowl of fruit he kept on the kitchen island, but his blue eye seemed focused on something much farther away.

"Ignatia was wonderful. The way she practiced with her new Apex abilities, the skill with which she talked our experiments into letting us cut open their spines in the hopes they too might develop powers. We spent evenings in my family's courtyard watching the constellations. She told me the stories behind each pattern of stars. I've always liked girls who watched the sky."

I shivered at those words, and though the vegetables on my plate were quickly growing colder, I shoveled them into my mouth to avoid looking at Adrestus. How many frostbitten nights had we spent looking at the sky together? How many auroras had we sat beneath as we planned our future?

"I freed her from the jail. I gave her powers. I offered my family's home and food. And then, just after the completion of the second Lapis, I found her and Tiberius. *Together.*"

Adrestus pressed the head of his fork with his thumb, bending it towards the handle.

"So you murdered her."

"I murdered *him*. I was certain with Tiberius gone, Ignatia would have no choice but to love me back. We had two stones. We didn't need the third. Tiberius's role had become redundant anyway. But how do you murder someone who's immortal?"

"I'll let you know when I figure that one out," I snorted.

"It was actually quite easy. He was jealous of the Epsilons we'd created. All it took was carefully stoking the fires of his envy, until he was fool enough to risk the operation himself and bare his neck for me."

"Was the gamble worth it?" I asked. "He had a ten percent chance of surviving and becoming even more powerful than before. He would've been that much more difficult to get rid of after that."

Adrestus laughed, and I blushed, feeling like he was somehow laughing at my expense.

"Dear Scourge Queen, I would *never* take that risk. The only people I allow to become Epsilons are those I know I can control. No, I took the knife to his spinal cord and made sure he never moved again. As you are painfully aware, the Life Elixir keeps death from being permanent, but does little in the realm of healing."

"So you paralyzed him and left him for dead?"

"I may have been young, but I was no fool. Could you imagine if I didn't wait around and ensure his passing? If he showed up now, against all odds, centuries later? No, one ancient friend waltzing back into the picture has been enough for me this last year." He finished his duck and dabbed at his mouth with a cloth napkin. "I had to wait for his last dose of Life Elixir to wear off. Ninety-three days I waited until, finally, his fleeting immortality lost its hold. Poor Ignatia had no idea. She'd been running an errand in Rome and returned just after his passing."

"What did she do?"

"She stopped looking at constellations in the night sky with me." He took his plate to the sink, dropped it into the basin, and porcelain shattered. "I told her his body had rejected the Epsilon Procedure. She didn't believe me. Tiberius was dead! What more did she have? What did she have that she didn't get from *me!?* So I switched her Lapis out with a failed experiment from years before. It changed colors, similar to the real deal. Tiberius would've known the difference but precious Ignatia...well. She was too wrapped up in her own grief to notice me anymore. She certainly wasn't going to notice her waning immortality."

"Her only crime was not loving you?" It was horrible. It was disgusting. It was unnervingly familiar.

"I gave her a chance, Eydis! I promised her the world. I promised her *everything!* And she denied me! *Me!* I mean—" He paced through the kitchen, pulling at his hair. "Why does this keep happening? I've accomplished godhood, and somehow that still wasn't good enough for either of you!"

He pulled a dirty knife from the sink and whirled around, flinging it towards my face. I fell backwards off the stool to avoid the flying blade, crashing to the kitchen tile.

"I didn't get you, did I?" Adrestus crouched next to me, concern etched into every line on his face. I pressed against the kitchen island, trying to get away. "I'll admit I got heated. It's been so long since I've thought about Ignatia. I didn't know she still had that sort of hold over me."

He pushed the hair out of my face, and I flinched at his touch.

"I'm fine," I insisted, ignoring the shaking of my hands.

"You remind me of her. You always have."

"And you killed her."

"She had to pay for her greed." He nodded sagely. "Same way you did. Your debt is paid, and now there is nowhere safer for you than at my side. For forever. The way it was always supposed to be."

He wrapped my fingers in his palms.

"Right." The single word was all I could manage to gasp. Anything else, and I was sure my voice would give away the fear that held me in its chokehold.

He helped me to my feet and brushed off his apron.

"Mind grabbing that knife for me? It's high time we made dessert. I hope the duck wasn't too filling."

I found the knife by the window and dropped it off in the sink as Adrestus pulled out his baking supplies.

"The Apex and their families that you have as prisoners in the building," I said slowly, "are they your new experiments?"

"I haven't killed anyone, if that's what you're asking," he said, prying open a jar of flour. "They'll serve a separate purpose. One that remains to be revealed."

"And when Paul Fleming worked here and you offered him a cure to his cancer in exchange for his brother, would Mr. Fleming have become another experiment?"

Adrestus turned away from the flour, his apron dusted with fresh powder. He walked back to the kitchen island to pluck an apple out of the fruit bowl he kept there.

"This is a honey-crisp apple."

"I know what an apple is," I mumbled.

"They're sweet," Adrestus bit into the skin, sending up a spray of juice, "but they bruise easily, rendering many of them unfit for sale. Does that make them any less delicious?"

"People aren't apples."

"The answer is no, the bruised apples taste just as good, and to keep them from going to waste, they're squeezed into juice." Adrestus tightened his grip, and the apple broke into large, sticky chunks that fell to the floor. "I know how best to use my harvest. There is a certain greatness found in being ground up as spare parts."

"Is that the future you're building?" I couldn't speak any louder than a whisper. My voice was shaking too much. "Your bright new dominion, built on the spare parts of your victims?"

He took my chin in his sticky, apple-stained fingers.

"Careful. You're starting to sound like you did just before you tried to murder me in Iceland."

"I thought you didn't care if you couldn't trust me," I shot back. "You said I can't beat you even if I tried."

He smirked and let go.

"Doesn't mean you can't be a downright pain in the ass, and you stabbing me is a nuisance I'd like to avoid." He pointed a silicon spatula at the counter. "Cut this chocolate into chunks for me, would you?"

He pulled out two bars of baking chocolate and a cutting board as I tried to settle my racing heart.

"Sure thing, Quintus Dio."

He threw his head back and laughed.

"If anyone else called me that, I'd have them killed."

Music played as we baked giant chocolate chip cookies that reminded me of the ones Wesley's mom had made me once. Adrestus used fancier ingredients, sure, but something about Mrs. Isaacs's baking was still better.

Adrestus bit into one, chocolate goo running into his beard. He closed his eyes and nodded.

"Here's the thing with being the best baker I know. I've sampled so many desserts for the Peace Summit, and none of them come close to what I can do. I'd cater it myself if I wasn't going to be booked all next week."

"So, the Peace Summit." I fought to control my voice. This was it. This was why I was here. "It can't really be about making peace with the rest of the world."

Adrestus marched to the window and pressed his hands against the glass, staring out over the city like a kid might stare into a candy shop. We still had electricity in the comfort of Adrestus's apartment, but the rest of the city had gone dark.

"People are simple, Eydis, and I've had two thousand years to unravel how they work. There is one thing everyone wants above all else." His fingers curled, and I winced at the sound of fingernails against glass. "Power. And while power can make one strong, desire for more power is where man becomes weak. You offer them superpowers, and they roll over. But there's only one place they can get superpowers."

I knew this part already. Jamie had told me all about how New Delos was offering the Epsilon Procedure to incoming emissaries.

"But what's to stop them from using those powers on you once you've handed them over?"

"That's the best part. I own their powers, and their choice is a simple one. Join me or watch their world burn at their own hands."

I pressed against the kitchen counter. It wasn't a Peace Summit. It was a gathering of the troops. The troops just didn't know it.

"Mira's control chips," I said slowly. "You aren't—"

A knock sounded from the dining room. Adrestus twisted away from the window with a familiar, hungry grin plastered to his face.

"I invited a guest to join us," he said. "I hope you don't mind."

Adrestus walked to the sitting room, but I lingered in the kitchen entryway, hovering at the periphery as Mira marched her latest quarry in through the dining room.

Trev Baker stood rigid with Mira's hand on his bicep. One eye was swollen shut, but the other strained against Mira's control to take in the sitting room with its big windows, white plush rug, and matching couches. His bruised face paled, and a glassy film glazed his eye over, but he blinked it away.

Mira let him go, and he stumbled forward to catch himself on the nearest couch.

"Damn," Trev murmured. "I've seen this room before."

34

In These Arms

I'd told Adrestus Trev Baker's Apex ability, and not an hour later, he was in Adrestus's sitting room. I couldn't bring myself to join them, instead staying back in the kitchen, hoping the others couldn't hear my rapidly beating heart.

"Mr. Trev Baker." Adrestus took his seat in a white, leather chair. "It's a pleasure to have you in my home."

"Dr. Cunningham." Trev's eye flitted to where I lurked in the kitchen entryway. "And you. You got us captured."

"Eydis is not the one who told us where you were hiding," Adrestus said. "And don't talk to her about double-crossing when you were a loyal employee of Schrader Enterprises not too long ago. One of Adrian Schrader's favorites, in fact. That's why he chose you to represent the company on The Apex Council, isn't it?"

"And then I got kicked off because everyone but me figured out Schrader is trash." Trev fell back against the cushions of a sofa.

"How embarrassing for you, given your little gift of foresight." A sympathetic smile played on Adrestus's lips.

Trev scowled through his mask of bruises.

"She told you."

My face warmed, and I fought the urge to place my hands over my ears. What if Adrestus forced Trev to list out how each of my friends would die?

"She thought we knew. You were once on the payroll, after all." Adrestus held his hands wide in mock-apology. "But what good are secrets, eh? Surely your powers have burdened you with unbearable truths so allow me to relieve you of them. How exactly do your powers work? Do you view the inevitable? Or do the deaths you dream manifest *because* you saw them?"

"I'm not sure." Trev's mouth dropped open. " I hadn't—"

"You see deaths every time you fall asleep, and you never thought to ask yourself if they only come to pass because your powers make it so?"

"They don't always happen the way I see them." Trev's voice shook. "If I was the one determining how everyone dies, then they would play out exactly as they do in my dreams."

"I can't imagine you have good control over your powers. I hear you have quite the passion for coffee. Trying to stay awake forever and keep the dreams at bay?"

Trev looked at me, his hate apparent on his mottled face, then swiveled his head back towards Adrestus.

"I've seen you die," he murmured, and Adrestus turned deadly still. "It was back when I thought you were just a curator. When Samantha came running and told us all that you were secretly an immortal warrior, I figured she must be lying. I'd seen proof of your mortality. You can't outrun the dark forever."

"Suppose you *do* manifest each death you witness. What do you think would happen if you died before they came to pass?"

"You can't scare me," Trev said. "I already know how this conversation ends. I told you. I've seen this room before."

"My death?" Adrestus raised the eyebrow over his eyepatch.

"No."

Adrestus grinned.

"Then you understand I must take every precaution to ensure your dreams stay dreams. I *am* immortal, and I *can* outrun the dark. It's been a pleasure talking to you. And now, you may finally sleep a dreamless sleep."

"You don't have to kill him." The words spilled from my mouth, and I stepped back, hoping the dark of the kitchen might protect me.

"Why shouldn't I?" Adrestus growled. "I've killed half his precious Apex Council. Weaver, Mickey, Allen. All dead."

"Dead?" Trev croaked, and Adrestus cackled. Dr. Weaver, Mickey, and Officer Allen had only ever been kind to me. They couldn't be dead.

"Dead," Adrestus confirmed. "I would've thought you knew given your gift. Don't worry, Mr. Baker, you'll soon be reunited with your friends. You saw me die, and I'll do everything in my power to make sure that doesn't happen."

"He can be wrong. I was supposed to kill Fleming, but I didn't."

"You dumb kid." Trev's chuckle morphed into a belabored cough. "You didn't stop anything. I still see you murder him every time I close my eyes. Alexander Fleming will die at your hand."

I was trying to save him. He needed to shut up. Why was he saying I was still going to murder Fleming?

"Eydis?" Adrestus whispered.

"Yes?"

"The knife you used to cut up the chocolate, it should still be on the counter."

My eyes flitted over the serrated blade.

"It is."

"So grab it, little Scourge Queen."

I walked with stiff, shaking steps, and the knife sang against the chocolate-stained cutting board as I lifted it. I felt numb and mechanical walking the knife back to the sitting room, and I winced when I stepped into the harsh, white, overhead light.

Adrestus nodded towards Trev, but Trev's expression was haughty and defiant. He saw a future where I murdered Fleming. If Adrestus was right, that could be stopped.

"Kill him."

I lifted the knife ahead of me. Trev exhaled heavily through his nose. He was shaking. I was shaking, too. I knew how this ended, and I knew how this couldn't end.

Even though he'd always been horrible to me, and even if it meant stopping a future where I murdered Fleming, I couldn't kill Trev Baker.

"You aren't the one who kills me, Samantha."

The plush rug dampened the sound of my knife dropping to the floor.

"Mira," Adrestus growled behind me.

Mira stepped up behind Trev Baker and cupped his cheek in her hand. The bruises that were already there seemed to deepen, and his eye found mine one last time before rolling back in his head. His head lolled to the side, and he moved no more.

"Goodnight, Mr. Baker," Adrestus murmured. "May it be a restful slumber."

He rose from his chair to meet me where I stood in the middle of the room. His hand brushed my cheek.

"Next time I tell you to do my bidding, you will do it." His fingers tightened against my skin. "Look at Mira. She obeys even when it causes her pain."

Faint, purple bruises seeming to leak out of the veins in Mira's neck. Her powers were stretched too thin, and she was hardly able to keep herself standing.

The thought wasn't as comforting as I wanted it to be. Not when I knew she was immortal too, and not while Trev Baker's body lay on the couch.

"More training tomorrow." He let go of my face to march into the kitchen. "Rest up, and don't disappoint me like you have today."

As soon as the door slammed shut behind me, leaving me in the dark hallway outside of Adrestus's apartment, I ran. Ignatia's story reverberated through my skull, and I couldn't shake the mental image of Trev Baker's body on the couch.

I couldn't be here anymore. I couldn't watch anyone else die. Next time, Adrestus *would* make me do it. I was sure of it.

I wasn't sure I would remember the way. The doors and walls all looked the same, but I traced the path Winnie had taken me weeks ago until I was standing in front of a gray door, wondering if I dared to knock.

It swung open before I could retreat, and Wesley stood in the doorway, his hair ruffled and his eyes lined red.

"Sammy, what—"

"How did you know I was here?"

He drew the back of his hand across his cheeks, trying to look casual. He'd been crying.

"I heard you coming from down the hall. Why are you here?"

I wanted to fall into him, to hide against his chest, but then I remembered Tiberius's slow, painful death, all because Ignatia had preferred him.

"Trev Baker is dead," I whispered. Wesley closed the space between us, wrapping an arm around me and pulling me inside.

"How do you know?" His voice was soft and low in my ear.

"I saw it happen. He wanted *me* to do it, but—" I swallowed hard, maintaining my composure the best I could.

His arm tightened.

"We can run," Wesley whispered. "We can beat him from the outside."

I'd come down here to do just that, but now that I was here, now that I had Wesley with me, I could already feel my panic ebbing.

"We have to hold out until the Peace Summit. That's when he's making his move."

Wesley took my hand and led me deeper in Miles's apartment. It had the same blueprint as Mira's, and I faltered in the living room to look outside at the aurora before Wesley pulled me towards the stairs with a warning finger raised to his lips.

"Miles is asleep," he said.

I tiptoed after him to his bedroom. A twin bed pressed against the wall opposite a large window, and green, shifting light from the aurora outside spilled across the bare wooden floor.

How did this keep happening? How many people would end up dead because of me? If I hadn't told Adrestus Trev Baker's powers, he'd still be alive. If I hadn't come here, he'd still be alive.

"How," I choked, "how do I screw up so badly over and over again?"

"Your ideas are usually good!" Wesley placed his hand on my cheek and lifted my face to his. "I wouldn't keep following you if they weren't. And in a couple weeks, we'll beat him at the Peace Summit like you say we will, and we'll never worry about it again."

I retreated to the window and shook my head.

"I shouldn't have come here. It's my fault Trev Baker is dead, and if Adrestus realizes that you and I are— he'll kill you. I know he will." Like he did Tiberius. Like he did Ignatia.

"It's not your fault—"

"It *is*, Wesley! It is!" My whisper was strained with hysteria. "I'm the idiot who spilled about Trev's abilities, and Adrestus killed him for it! And apparently I'm still going to murder Fleming!"

"Adrestus killed Baker, not you."

"And who's next? Alison is here. So is Avery. So are you! And aren't you worried about your mother and brother?"

"Sammy, there's too much on the line to lose your nerve this late in the game." He touched my shoulder. "We've got this. You've got this."

"And when something terrible happens, it'll be my fault. It's always my fault, since Iceland."

I knew we couldn't leave. Not yet. Not when we were so close. But something else, a new anxiety, blossomed in my stomach.

"He killed your family. That wasn't your fault." Green light flooded Wesley's green eyes, and my worst secret, the one I avoided admitting to even myself, bubbled up inside me. "What is it?"

The sudden concern in his voice made me wonder how much my face betrayed. My throat constricted. I couldn't breathe.

"It *was* my fault. Back then," I whispered, "he didn't look the way he does now."

Wesley's fingers tightened on my shoulder, and his eyes turned to steel, but he kept quiet.

"He looked like us," I said. "Young, I mean. He was almost a thousand years old, but he looked seventeen."

"Okay." Wesley's voice shook. "So he's grown a few grays since then."

"When he showed up, I was the one who found him, and I was the one who befriended him." I shrugged away from Wesley's hold on my shoulder. "I trusted him, like an idiot, and then, like a bigger idiot, I told everyone else they could trust him, too."

"He tricked you. You don't have to feel guilty over that. Anyone in your position would have—"

"Kissed him?"

Wesley froze, his hand extended towards me as if he were going to draw me away from the window until my words had stopped him.

"What?" His voice cracked, and I wished the swirling, green sky would reach in through the window and swallow me.

"I kissed him." I spat each word. "And he kissed me back, and I—"

The next words festered on the tip of my tongue, refusing to leave until they'd drawn burning tears of shame into my eyes.

"—Loved. Loved him."

Wesley was still frozen, wide-eyed, hand outstretched, and even though neither of us moved, I could sense him getting farther away, drawing back into an unreachable place.

I stared back, my arms wrapped tightly around myself, feeling like I might vomit.

"Sammy..." Wesley finally whispered, and I noticed the tears in his eyes, too. I was broken. I was ruined and had been for centuries. I was just as repulsive as Adrestus because I'd let him make me so.

"Are you mad?" I barely contained the sob that fought its way up my throat. Wesley dropped his hand, and his nose wrinkled.

"Mad doesn't even begin—Sammy. I'm—I'm—" His voice cracked again, and he took a steadying breath. "Holy *crap*, Sammy. I knew you were friends with him, but this—"

"It's okay," I sniffed, drawing my hand across my cheek. I'd expected this. I'd dreaded it, sure, but I'd been bracing for this moment since recovering my memories in full. "I would be angry too. You can leave. I won't blame you, and I won't raise an alarm."

His look of disgust was replaced by one of confusion.

"Leave you? Now?" His jaw hung open and tears glittered green in the lights of the window as the dam broke, and they spilled over his cheeks. "Sammy, no."

And then his arms were around me, his fingers pressed against the back of my head, hard and reassuring as he held me against his chest. I didn't know why he was hugging me, but sobs of relief shook my shoulders, and he pressed me into his shirt harder still.

"You don't hate me?" My voice was muffled by his shirt and distorted with emotion.

"I could never hate you." Hot, wet tears fell through my hair, and I finally hugged him back. "I'm not mad at you. Never at you. But Adrestus, he was an old man, and you were— *are* a kid. He knew what—"

He cut off, jerking away and grabbing at his right elbow, exhaling through his teeth in pain.

"What is it?" I asked, wiping away my tears and letting concern for Wesley's wellbeing push everything else aside.

"It's nothing," he said, teeth gritted. "We're talking about you, not me."

"Is your arm okay?"

He forced a smile, still gripping his elbow stump with convulsing, panicked fingers.

"Yeah. No. Sorry. It's fine," he insisted and then screwed his eyes shut and stumbled back to sit on his bed.

"Wesley..."

"I'm sorry," he breathed.

"Let me help."

A quaking laugh escaped his lips, but he unfurled his fingers to show me the scarred skin at the end of his right arm. His foot tapped restlessly, and I frowned at the sweaty sheen that had erupted across his forehead.

"Sorry," he said again. "I didn't mean to interrupt you. Sometimes it feels like it's still there."

"Does it hurt?"

He exhaled heavily through his nose.

"Kind of. It gets worse when I'm not wearing my arm. Sometimes it just itches, and I can't scratch it. Other times, it hurts. And then there's times—"

He cut off, and his throat constricted as he swallowed.

"There's times it what?" I whispered.

"I can feel my hand as if it's still there. I can feel each finger, and on bad days, I can feel them moving as if Mira is still controlling them."

I wrapped my hands around his elbow.

"And is that what you feel right now?"

He nodded, and his cheeks turned red.

"It's not so bad when I have my fake arm because then I can see my hand isn't moving, and I can move the fake fingers myself and see she's not in control."

"Where's the arm Adrestus built you?"

"I don't want *anything* that monster has touched."

I faltered, my hands hovering over his, and the unexpected sting of his words threatened to reopen every old wound and insecurity.

"No, Sammy. Not like that, I—" His face paled in horror and embarrassment.

"You didn't mean it," I insisted, and while I knew that was true, I couldn't help but to feel like my worst fears had been confirmed. My chin trembled, and I clamped my mouth shut to stop it, but the pressure made the blood in my ears scream.

"I meant the arm. It's—" He screwed his eyes shut. "I can feel her controlling the arm I don't have anymore. It's just a phantom limb thing, but that doesn't make it any better."

"Move."

"Sorry?"

"Scoot back. Against the wall."

He obeyed, though he looked confused, and I pulled the blanket from the foot of his bed. He froze as I crawled across the bed and fell back into his lap.

"Sammy—" he mumbled into my hair.

"Shh." I whirled the blanket over us, wrapping it around his shoulders and bringing it over my arm. I pressed my right arm against his and wiggled my fingers out from under the blanket. "Look. There's your hand."

He was silent for a moment, and I felt his chest rise and fall against my back. My face burned. Maybe this was a stupid idea. Maybe I'd offended him somehow. Maybe he really *didn't* want to touch anything that had once belonged to Adrestus.

"Can you wiggle your fingers?" His breath was warm against my ear, and he leaned his chin to rest on my shoulder. I obliged, wiggling my fingers for him. "Now just hold it still."

I let my hand go limp with the palm facing up, and on my other side, Wesley's left hand mirrored mine. I settled back into his chest, letting him concentrate. I felt his breathing calm, and he relaxed, leaning over me and letting his cheek press against mine.

"Better?" I finally asked. He nodded against my shoulder, still watching the hands in our laps.

"It is actually," he mumbled. "Sammy, what I said before, I'm sorry."

"Stop saying that."

"I *am* sorry, though."

I watched green light shift across our laps, focusing on the rise and fall of Wesley's chest against my back.

"Sammy." His cheek was still pressed against mine. "Nothing Adrestus did changes who you are. You're still Sammy, and you're just as wonderful as the day I met you."

I snorted.

"I'm pretty sure you had to carry my useless self out of a riot the day we met."

"I was stuck under that table until you showed up," Wesley laughed. "You were more help to me that day than I was to you. "

"I'm like a rescue dog you found at the animal shelter. 'Who saved who' and all that."

He lifted his left arm to wrap it around my waist, holding me close, though I could tell by the angle of his cheek against mine that he was still watching my upturned palm.

"I'm being serious."

"So am I."

"You're making jokes about rescue dogs, and I think it's because you can't stand to hear people say nice things about you."

"You've never been more wrong. I love hearing nice things about me. It gives me the fuel I need to be greater than my enemies."

"You're still making jokes. It's okay. I do it, too."

He was annoying, but he was right. I pressed into his chest, wanting to disappear.

"You're just trying to make me feel better," I whispered. "I used to despise Eydis because of what she did, but now I know better. I *am* Eydis, and her memories are as clear as Sammy's, and I've made mistakes as both. I remember my time with Adrestus back then as if it just happened last summer. Because, to me, it did. My family's been dead in the ground for over a millennium, but Vidar and I buried them less than a year ago. And they're dead because I fell in love with the worst person to ever exist."

Wes shook his head against mine, and I leaned into it, pushing my temple against his. I wished I knew what he was thinking. If he was just being nice to make me feel better. If he was scared of me, or grossed out by who I'd been and who I was now.

"Do you remember the day the city sank?" he asked.

"Sure, now that we've recapped Eydis's biggest screw up, let's go over Samantha's."

Green light danced across my open palm.

"Do you still want to know what it was I said to you?"

His heart beat against my back.

"I already know what you said," I mumbled. "You said to tell your mom that you're a hero."

"After that."

He'd come close to telling me twice before. Something had gone wrong both times. Maybe it was better if we left it a mystery. A permanent barrier that could exist between us to keep Wesley safe.

"I said..." The arm around my waist tightened as he held me against him. "I said, tell my mom I was a hero, but between you and me, there's no point in trying to save a world that didn't have you in it."

I stared out the window, processing his words. The last words he'd said before dying. Drowning because he'd used the last of his energy lifting me to safety. He tensed behind me after another long, silent moment.

"I'm sorry," he mumbled. He let go of me, but I found his hand under the blanket and held him there, squeezing his fingers. He took my cue and held me tighter, even as words continued to evade me. "I can't force you to forgive yourself, and you won't be able to find lasting self-worth in the nice things I think about you. But until then, I'm here. I'm right here, Sammy. And I'm never going anywhere."

I twisted around in his lap until I was facing him with my hands cupping his face. I studied him in the dark, making note of the defiant set of his brow and the flush of his cheeks that was nearly undetectable in the shadow. I brushed the tip of my thumb along his bottom lip, the words he'd just recalled still echoing in my head.

He thought the world wasn't worth saving without me in it, but he had it backwards. I may have been asleep for most of it, but the world hadn't even made sense until *he* had come along. He knew my every transgression, and I was still somehow good enough for him.

Maybe he simply had bad taste in friends and girls, but maybe it meant that eventually, I could be good enough for me, too.

I pushed his ever-longer hair back from his forehead, as if to see him better, and his hand pressed against the small of my back.

"I'm not kidding. I'll follow you anywhere and whatever you want, I'll make sure it's yours."

"I want..." I traced the cut of his jawline from his cheek bone to his chin. "Wesley, I want you."

We both sat perfectly still. Adrestus's story of Tiberius and Ignatia nudged at the back of my mind, but here in the dull, green light of the aurora, on Wesley's borrowed bunk, he and I were the only things that existed. So why shouldn't we have what we wanted?

My lips found his, and he froze beneath my touch, then pressed back, holding me tighter still, and it felt like home.

Maybe it was selfish, but I couldn't bring myself to leave. We fell asleep holding each other, Wesley still in his t-shirt and jeans and me in my athletic wear. When the rising sun filtered red through my eyelids, I searched for darkness in the folds of Wesley's shirt. His breath stirred my hair, preceding the gentle touch of his lips against my forehead.

"You need to go. While it's still early."

"No." I rubbed my face against his shirt. It was the first good night of sleep I'd had in a long time.

"What're you going to tell Winnie?"

"That I was up all night training so I can kick her ass next week."

His fingers ran through the knots in my hair. I opened my eyes to see him looking at me, and I wondered if he was thinking about our late night kiss, too.

And then his hand tightened on the back of my head, and panic struck the stillness from his face.

"Wes—"

The bedroom door slammed open, and a new hand grabbed at the back of my head, taking a handful of hair and dragging me away from Wesley.

"Well, well," Miles rasped, holding me by my scalp and wrapping an arm around my torso. "This certainly looks like trouble."

35

Test Flight

My brain whirred, working overtime for an escape, an excuse, anything, but Miles was already marching me down the hall as Wesley called after us, trapped in his room by Miles's forcefield.

"It's okay!" I called back. Don't act guilty. Only guilty people act guilty. Adrestus never said I couldn't see Wesley. If I could wrangle up a good excuse, I could save us both.

Miles spoke into a communicator as he led me down the stairs to his living room.

"Found her," he sneered, and Mira's voice came through the static.

"Excellent. We're waiting."

Miles's grip on my bicep tightened, and I tried to pull away.

"You can let go. I'm coming with you."

"We have a betting pool going, by the way. How long before you slipped up. The boss has blind spots when it comes to you. But now? I don't see how he'll forgive this."

I tried to catch a final glimpse of Wesley upstairs, but Miles pulled me into the hallway to march me down the corridor. My brain buzzed, filling with excuses and cover stories too quickly to cling to any of them. Miles shoved me into Mira's apartment, and I braced for Mira's anger. She waited in the kitchen, and I opened my mouth, ready to stutter out my story, but was cut off before I could speak.

"Dion raised the alarm when she woke up this morning and realized you'd never come back after dinner." Adrestus's voice was low and calm where he sat on Mira's couch, his back to the expansive window.

Miles released my arm, and I tried to rub the feeling back into it.

"I meant to come back." I needed to take the blame off Wesley. "It's not what it looks like."

"Oh? I hope not. Because it looks like your allegiance is still to that boy when I expect nothing less than a hundred percent from all my followers." He rose to his feet, his face cast in the shadow with light from the window pouring in behind him. "Do you know your mistake? The one you made a thousand years ago? I wanted you to come with me. To *follow* me! But who was your allegiance to?"

"My family?" I flinched, then remembered I wasn't supposed to remember all those years ago. "I mean, that's what I've been told."

Mira scoffed behind me.

"Your *family*," she repeated. "Spare us."

"Your allegiance was to your own ambitions," Adrestus crooned, stepping closer to me. "Your family and I be damned."

That wasn't true, but I nodded.

"That's why I went to Wesley last night," I lied. "To learn more about myself. After everything that happened upstairs, when I couldn't do what you wanted me to, I wondered if I had it in me at all. To kill."

I knew I did. I *had*. Not a defenseless man on a couch, of course, but still. I'd taken a life before. But I needed an excuse and preferably one that would appeal to Adrestus's ego.

"So you went to the boy?"

"He knows me, doesn't he?" I shrugged. "I thought he might have some insight."

"And?"

"He said I was a fighter." I nodded. "And he said I threw a knife through your eye so maybe I do have what it takes."

"And then you just...stayed there? All night?"

"I got lost in the hall. All the doors look the same, so I retraced my steps back to his apartment."

"*My* apartment," Miles corrected.

Adrestus closed the space between us, his features finally taking shape in the shadows. He frowned at me, studying my face, as if scanning for traces of Wesley.

"I think..." he said slowly, then straightened up and looked towards Mira. "I think it's time we tested the Whitlock Protocol. Mira, fetch the subjects. Dion."

He looked up at the second floor, and I craned my head around to see Winnie leaning against the banister. Anger stirred in my stomach. She'd sold me out. If she hadn't said anything, Adrestus would have no idea I hadn't returned to the apartment last night.

"Get Eydis something to eat and then bring her to the training room."

"And me, Master?" Miles asked eagerly.

"The museum opens soon, doesn't it?" Adrestus spat, stalking to the front doors. "Go watch my phone."

Miles cast me one last withering sneer before following Adrestus into the hall. Mira, meanwhile, waited for the men to leave before grabbing me by the chin.

My body locked up, trapped under her control, and for a moment, I thought she might murder me the same way she'd murdered Everly and Mr. Baker. She stooped down, bringing her six foot frame to my eye level.

"You're lucky," she whispered. "Anyone else would already be dead. Screw up again, and I'll make the call he's too soft to make himself."

She let go, and I flinched as my faculties returned.

"You pretend to be scary," I jeered, "but I think you're just afraid I might replace you."

"Oh, Eydis," she purred, opening the door and pausing to look back at me, "who do you think *I* replaced?"

The door slammed shut behind her, and I looked up at Winnie where she leaned lazily against the banister.

"You're the dumbest person I know," she said. "You know that, right?"

"Like Mira said, I'm not dead yet." I shrugged.

"Give it time. You usually end up that way anyway."

I crossed my arms and tried to scrape up whatever dignity I had left.

"I'm surprised, Winnie. You never struck me as a snitch."

She raised an eyebrow at me.

"You brought my father here." She pushed off the banister to stalk down the stairs one deliberate step at a time, keeping her icy gaze on me the whole way down. "I came here to get away from him, and now word is you helped Adrestus recruit him."

She stopped when she was face-to-face with me, and even though I was taller by several inches, she stood defiant and proud. A demure smile passed over her face, and she clapped me on the shoulder.

"Don't underestimate my hatred for my father or for you, Sammy. If you do, you *will* end up dead."

I didn't know what the Whitlock Protocol was, nor did Winnie feel like cluing me in as we walked down long, gray corridors back to the training gym. I at least knew Wesley was, for the moment, okay. Adrestus wouldn't hurt him without me there to watch. It was a tiny comfort, but a comfort all the same.

A small crowd gathered at the glass wall that overlooked the training gym, and I walked forward on stiff legs, flashing back to a forced death-match against Wesley. I couldn't do it. Not again. And not with everyone here watching.

Adrestus stood at the center of the crowd with Mira and Gregor flanking him on either side. Heather and Anthony stood near the back, pressed against the corridor wall between the locker room entryways. They gave me a worried glance, but neither dared say anything.

"Perfect timing." Adrestus motioned for Mira to make room for Winnie and me. "The subjects just got into place."

I cut through the crowd to the Adrestus's side, passing scientists in lab coats and members of Adrestus's inner circle, including Felix and Lana. I didn't have a clear view of the training gym until I reached Adrestus's side, and I held in the gasp that fought to escape my lips.

The yellow caution tape that stretched across the gaping wall where the window had once been fluttered in the wind, offering meager protection from the eighty story drop. Wesley stood on one side of the room, pressed against the wall with his eyes screwed shut, as if he were in pain or concentrating or both. His prosthetic arm hung at his side while his left hand massaged his temple.

On the other side of the room, a hulking man strained against metal constraints that had been bolted into the wall. He howled, sounding like a hunted animal wailing in a forest. I grimaced. Hackjob had proven adept at fighting Wesley in the past, and their quarrels usually ended in a broken leg on Wesley's part.

"He'll kill him!" I balked.

"Without the Whitlock Protocol, perhaps he would. Luckily for Ares, today is the day we put the neurotransmitter chips to the test. We need a more sweeping reach than the current one-to-one control, so we installed a supercomputer at the heart of the city that controls the city functions. Today we discover how well it controls people."

My stomach lurched.

"Hackjob will only kill Wesley faster if Wesley can't fend for himself."

Adrestus chuckled, his eyes trained on Wesley.

"If Ares was our intended subject, I don't doubt that. However, for our first test, we'll see if the city's heart has what it takes to quell Hackjob's fury." Adrestus tapped the glass, maybe trying to get Wesley to open his eyes, but they stayed shut. "We aren't exactly sure what your adoptive brother did to Hackjob on McMillan Island, but he hasn't been the same since, trapped in a constant state of terror. It'll be down to the Heart of the City to ensure Ares makes it to the end of the fight."

When Mira had controlled Wesley six months ago, she'd used a tablet computer and motion-sensitive gloves. Today, her hands were empty, and she watched Wesley and Hackjob with poorly contained glee.

"So it's like an artificial mind controlling Hackjob instead of a person?"

Adrestus grinned, resting his hand against the glass.

"Mira's control chips are limited only by the finite amount of neurotransmitter each one holds and the one-to-one operating process. One subject, one controller. But what if we found a way to control two subjects at once? Ten? A hundred? A single person could never do that, but the supercomputer living at the heart of the city? All that remains is to try it."

A chill ran down my spine, and my horror at what Adrestus was implying momentarily stayed my worry for Wesley.

"The new Epsilons and the Peace Summit," I whispered. "You're going to—"

"If things go according to plan, it won't be necessary. Good to be prepared with a back-up plan, though." He set a hand on my shoulder, holding me at his side. "Keep in mind, if you interfere here, Hackjob will be the least of Ares's worries."

Wes hadn't moved, but he would know I was there, listening to my voice and heartbeat from my vantage point on the other side of the glass wall.

"Is the Heart ready?" Adrestus asked.

"She is," Mira purred.

"Do it."

The restraints on Hackjob's wrists and ankles fell away. With a roar, he surged forward.

"Get away!" he screamed. Wesley's eyes snapped open, and he jumped to the side as Hackjob slammed into the wall.

"He doesn't appear under control," Adrestus observed.

"The Heart is still waking up," Mira chided. "She isn't used to asserting her will over another."

Wesley was ready with his knees bent and his arms up, bracing for Hackjob's next charge. Hackjob batted at unseen foes floating around his head before noticing Wesley in the center of the room.

He launched at Wesley, and Wesley hit him with an uppercut to the diaphragm. Hackjob fell to his knees, wheezing. I held my breath, not daring to hope Wesley could come out unscathed so easily.

"Mira," Adrestus growled. "I have a lot of assets in that room. If this doesn't work—"

"It will."

My stomach was just beginning to loosen, thinking Wesley might be okay, when Hackjob's hand swept forward, catching Wesley by the ankle.

Wesley slammed onto his back, and tried to scramble away, but Hackjob swung him around as if he weighed no more than a rag doll.

He let go, and Wesley skidded towards the gaping open edge of the room. His eyes found mine through the glass, wide and terrified, just before he slipped over the room's horizon for the second time in the last few weeks.

Adrestus's fingers dug deeper into my shoulder, but I held back my scream. Wesley's hand was still visible, clinging to the lip of the floor.

"Mira, if you need to override—"

"It'll work," Mira cut off Adrestus.

Hackjob lumbered towards the edge, standing over where Wesley's fingers gripped the floor for dear life and lifted a heavy boot, preparing to bring it down on his hand.

"Don't," Winnie hissed in my ear, as if sensing the shout building in my chest. "You'll get him killed."

Hackjob still stood, teetering on the edge of the room with one foot raised, ready to strike. The lights flickered, once, then twice, and finally a series of electric pops cut the electricity entirely.

Hackjob fell backwards and backpedaled from the edge, a strangled scream rattling in his throat.

"It's too high," he sobbed. "Help me, somebody! Why hasn't anyone come to help me?"

He rolled onto his stomach and held his hands over his head, shivering and crying into the matted floor. Wesley's fingers strained, and he reappeared, windswept but otherwise okay.

He kept an eye on Hackjob's sobbing form and circled to the middle of the room, his shoulders heaving with heavy breaths.

"Is that it, then?" Adrestus asked, pressing his free hand against the glass. "She did it? That was her, right? The Heart?"

A few in the crowd clapped tentatively, but then Hackjob's head snapped upwards, glaring at us through the window with terror and murder etched into his face.

He roared and charged the wooden bleachers, racing up the seats, until he reached the glass that separated us, hitting it with both fists. Cracks spread across the surface, and the crowd fell silent.

"GET OUT OF MY HEAD!" he shrieked, and another fist shattered the viewing window. The crowd screamed and fought against each other to flee down the hall. Adrestus pulled me back a few strides but lost his grip on my shoulder as bodies pushed passed, looking for an escape.

Hackjob jerked backwards, stopped by Wesley, who threw him back down the bleachers.

"Run!" he shouted at the few of us who remained. "Sammy, get—"

He cut off, a sudden rigidity freezing his shoulders, and his quaking hand rose to the back of his neck. I watched him in horror as Winnie hooked her elbow around mine and tried to drag me away. I shoved her off, and she stumbled into Heather, who didn't seem to notice.

"Something's wrong with Heather!" Anthony was one of the few remaining in the hall, and tried to shake Heather free of the same rigid posture that Wesley now possessed.

"Someone's in my head," she murmured. "I—"

"Samantha!" Three voices entwined together. Wesley, Hackjob, and Heather all called out my name at once. "Samantha, help me!"

"That's enough," Adrestus commanded. Someone had knocked him onto his backside, and he sat against the wall. "Mira, end this!"

"Why has no one come to rescue me?" Wesley, Hackjob, and Heather cried in tandem. "It's too high, we're too high."

I backed away until I bumped against Winnie, who held me steady.

"Mira!" Adrestus barked, and Mira poked furiously at a tablet she'd procured from her leather bag.

"I'm trying!"

"Samantha, please." Only Wesley spoke this time, the words pulled from his throat against his will. "It's so high up, and I'm all alone—"

The Heart of the City, the supercomputer at the center of New Delos, had a grip on Wesley, Heather, and Hackjob and somehow knew my name.

"She's overridden the entire system!" Mira cried. "Contact Siedon, and order a manual reset!"

Heather staggered forward.

"Samantha, please," she begged, but her words were not her own. "Everyone is going to die. Help—"

Hackjob's roar split the dark.

"I SAID," he howled, fighting for control against the Heart, "STAY OUT OF MY HEAD!"

"No!" Heather grabbed me with stiff, shaking fingers. "It's too high! Don't! It's—"

Heather collapsed, and I caught her in my arms. Down below in the gym, Hackjob hung in midair just beyond the edge of the floor, frozen in the wind, free from control and free from whatever influence Avery had placed over his mind for the last month. He plummeted from view, and I counted back from six.

"Did you see that?" Adrestus crept towards Wesley where he lay unconscious on the top bleacher and nudged him with his shoe. "The Whitlock Protocol works! She controlled all three of them at once! If she can do that—"

"One of them launched himself out the window, in case you didn't notice," Mira snarled. "She'll never be ready in time, and if Plan A falls through—"

"Gregor will give her some well-needed focus."

I wanted to run to Wesley. I wanted to make sure he was still breathing, but knew better than to do so. Winnie leaned over him, checking his vitals, and I lowered Heather to the floor.

The pieces had fallen into place in my head, and I didn't like the picture they made. The new supercomputer, the nightly blackouts, Hackjob's sudden fear of heights and how his brief flight had been the only thing to cut the control...

And, of course, there was the fact that if I had given more attention to Remi and her computer interfacing powers, I might have sooner remembered her last name was Whitlock.

36

Hand-to-Hand, Heart-to-Heart

The moment Hackjob had launched himself out the eighty-fourth story window of Schrader Tower, Remi, from wherever it was that Adrestus had her hooked up to the city's mainframe, fried the electricity across New Delos. The surge ruined even the generators that had kept the elevators and fridges running during the nightly blackouts.

Hackjob's fate was confirmed soon after the incident in the training gym, but I didn't know where Wesley and Heather had been taken. I knew better than to ask and reminded myself that Adrestus wouldn't hurt Wesley if I wasn't there to serve as audience.

I sat on the couch with my knees drawn to my chest as Winnie lit candles in the kitchen to stave off the oncoming night.

"So," I said, picking at the frayed fabric of my old, ripped jeans. "Remi Whitlock. You knew, I take it?"

"We all have a part to play," Winnie grunted, her back to me.

"Are people going to die?"

Winnie fell silent, and her lighter clinked against the marble countertop.

"Adrestus is intense, but he doesn't kill anyone if he can help it." The first hints of green seeped into the room as the aurora lit up the sky outside.

"You really think that?" I whispered. "Everly—"

"Mira did that, *not* Adrestus." Winnie whipped around to face me. "He could've slaughtered that whole camp, but there was one casualty. *One.*"

My stomach churned as I thought of Winnie's mother and the way Roy Hendricks had screamed.

"Speaking of Mira," I said into my knees, thinking of the bottle of Elixir I'd hidden in City Hall, "how old is she?"

"Younger than you." Candlelight caught the cascading tresses of Mira's white hair as she pushed through the front door. "You should know better than anyone to not inquire after a woman's age, Eydis."

I gave her a wan smile and pushed myself off the couch to retreat to my room. Alone in the dark and hiding under my covers, trying to erase the day's events from my mind, I counted the hours that stood between me and the Peace Summit. The pieces of the plan were finally starting to make themselves apparent, but there was a disconcerting comfort in knowing that, come hell or high water, in less than a week Wesley and I would escape this self-imposed hell.

The elevators were still dead the next day, but Mira sent me to the museum for intern duties anyway. She insisted we needed all hands on deck with emissaries starting to arrive to New Delos, but I had my suspicions that she only wanted to make me climb down eight-five stories and then back up again at the end of the day.

Near midday, a group of foreign delegates came to the museum office. Their grins and nervous laughter mingled in a mixture of accents, and they were in good spirits despite the blackout.

"Sorry about the climb," Miles was saying as he led them in. "It'll be about sixty floors."

"What's sixty floors of stairs once we're Apex?" a man with an enamel french flag pinned to his lapel laughed. "After this, we'll be able to fly down if we're lucky!"

Miles met my eyes as he held the stairwell door open for them.

"If you're lucky, yes," he murmured. My stomach churned, and I wondered how many of them would survive the Epsilon Procedure. I wondered if they knew the risk.

Despite the eighty-plus floor climb with a thigh wound, I still managed to drag myself back to the training gym for another sparring session with Adrestus. Mira watched from the back bleacher, and while I knew she didn't trust me, I was glad to not be alone with Adrestus.

He took the opportunity to express whatever resentment he was still harboring over finding me in Wesley's room. I knew he'd been going easy on me the other day, and now he was more than happy to flex his prowess and strength. By the time I limped back to the showers, covered in bruises, I wasn't sure if training with Adrestus would help or hurt my chances against Winnie.

The next few days passed in a blur of sparring against Adrestus, countless stairs climbs, and smiling emissaries who went up Schrader Tower but never came back down. Intern duties became busier as the Summit approached, and three days out, I passed Wesley in the stairwell on my way to the museum.

I tried to ignore him, but my heartbeat soared. The last time we'd been properly alone had been in his bedroom. I kept my eyes down as we passed, but he grabbed my bicep and squeezed.

"Your fight with Winnie," he murmured. "It's tonight."

"How do you—"

"You have to win, Sammy." He raised his eyes to look at me through messy locks of hair. "If you aren't on that stage—"

He cut off, swallowing hard.

"You know his plan?" I asked. He bit his lip and glanced up the stairs.

"The Heart of the City," he whispered. "It's Remi."

"I know."

"I saw the plan when she was in my head. You're the only one who will be able to stop him."

"That's bad news because I've been training with Adrestus all week. I can't get a single hit in." A metal door slamming shut signaled we were no longer alone.

"I'm not talking about Adrestus." He hurried up the stairs before we could be found.

"Wesley!"

"See you tonight, Eydis," Wesley called back as Felix Grimaldi came around the corner, forcing me to continue my trek to the museum, wondering what Wesley could've meant.

With three days to go until the Summit, I knew my face-off against Winnie had to be soon. Still, Wesley's warning threw me off guard. I'd thought I'd have more of a heads up, but maybe Adrestus wanted me to feel unprepared.

When Mira told me after dinner that Adrestus was waiting for me in the museum, I knew to wear something I could fight comfortably in. With Wesley's warning still echoing in my head, I limped to the museum for the second time that day. Adrestus, in full Spartan regalia, waited by the fountain. The water sat still in its basin, and purple light danced across the marble floor at Adrestus's feet.

"Eydis, dear." He spread his arms wide, and the black metal of his armor glinted purple. Through the windowed entrance, purple flames lined the far side of the street. "The time has come for you to win back your title of Scourge Queen. I wish I could say you've improved over the course of our sparring sessions, but alas. Maybe you'll surprise me."

Metal boots clanged against tile as he led me forward, and I hastened to tie my hair back. A line of silhouettes stood against the purple fire, and I hesitated on the top step of the grand entrance.

"What are we doing out here?" I asked.

"We wanted to provide you and Dion plenty of space to spar. Whichever one of you brings the other to me will be on the stage at the Peace Summit."

"When you say 'brings the other'—"

"Good god, Eydis!" Adrestus stopped halfway down the stone steps to balk at me. Green mixed with purple as the overhead aurora brightened with the darkening night. "It's not a fight to the death! You need only incapacitate her."

I followed him across the street to the figures that stood before the flames. The purple fire sucked the heat from the air, and I shivered under the gaze of the gathered Pantheon. Wesley stood on the end with Anthony and Heather. Wes gave me a subtle jerk of his chin, and I quickly looked away.

"Felix, give her passage," Adrestus commanded, and the flames parted to allow me into the park. "What do you think, Hephestae? Does Eydis stand a chance against your daughter?"

I gulped when the man next to Adrestus raised his gaze to mine. Purple light caught his rimless glasses.

"Winnie may not be an Apex," Roy Hendricks said, "but she is my child. She comes from a line of powerful fighters."

My hopes for Roy had been low, but dismay and disgust broiled within my stomach. Wesley may have hit him hard, but Roy couldn't have forgotten that Adrestus killed his wife in cold blood. The man had idolized Paul Fleming. It had been too easy to sway him to Adrestus's Pantheon.

"On your way, Eydis." Adrestus gave me a nod, beckoning me forward. "Show me that you belong at my side."

I steeled myself and walked forward. A rush of cold accompanied the flames as they resealed the park perimeter. I took a steadying breath and forged forward into the night.

The purple light of the fire didn't reach far into the park, occluded by knolls and dying trees. Green aurora light criss-crossed over long-dry stream beds of concrete, its glow shattered and cut by bleached, leafless branches. My arms erupted in goosebumps, though I didn't know if it was from the nighttime sea breeze or apprehension at the approaching fight.

Through the trees, I caught glimpses of purple fire spreading between the trunks, forming the boundaries of our battlefield. I strained my eyes, looking for Winnie's silhouette standing against the flames.

A whistle sounded somewhere overhead, and I froze, trying to pinpoint where it had come from.

"Come on, Winnie," I called at the sky, my apprehension mounting. I wanted to draw her out before she noticed my nerves. "Come out and face me."

I couldn't outrun her, not with my leg in its current condition. I wasn't sure I could out-fight her, either. Maybe if I dodged enough I could tire her out. In my sessions with Adrestus, I'd become *very* good at dodging.

But she was smaller than he was and probably faster.

Either way, I wouldn't let her continue to hunt me from some unseen vantage point.

"Your dad said you'd do this," I sighed loudly. "He told me to make quick work of you. It's probably less embarrassing for him if I don't draw this out too long.

"You won't beat me, Samantha." She took my bait, but remained hidden. Her voice wafted through the dying trees, echoing off the concrete stream beds. "If you give in, I'll tell them you put up a good fight."

"Is that how you handle your problems?" I goaded. "You wait for someone to give you what you want?"

"Everything I am, I *made*," Winnie asserted from the shadows. "You were handed everything you have. Your second life as Samantha, your spot on the Apex Team, even your friends."

"I made my friends myself."

"What about me? Handed to you with my memories scrambled to make room for a girl that didn't exist?"

A rustling of cloaks pulled my attention upwards, and I leaped backwards, narrowly avoiding Winnie's aerial assault.

She dropped from the trees, her theater mask shining green and purple. Her cloaks whirled as she struck out with a round kick, but it seemed like more of a test than an actual attempt to hit me.

"I'm not going to let you of all people invalidate everything I've done to get here," I snarled as her boot passed within inches of my face.

Winnie lunged again, but my practices with Adrestus were paying off, and I danced out of reach. He'd told me in our first session that anger is a weakness. Lucky for me, Winnie was always angry.

"You grew up being told power was your birthright, and when it didn't fall into your lap, you attached yourself to the greatest source of power you could find," I sneered. "Your daddy let you think you were something special, and when you turned out *normal*, you couldn't bear it and went looking for someone bigger than yourself. All to spite Roy and your sister."

"You don't know *anything*!" Winnie shrieked. She feinted left, and I dodged the wrong way. Her boot collided with my injured leg, and I grunted in pain. She'd always fought by exploiting her enemies' weakness.

Unfortunately for her, she had her weaknesses, too, and I was already under her skin, pulling up on her emotional scabs.

"You call yourself a goddess so that you can hide from your own crippling insecurities." I pivoted, keeping her in front of me, trying to act as if my leg wasn't searing with white-hot pain. "You pretend to be stronger and more important than you are, hoping you might trick those around you into thinking you are powerful."

"You think you know me! You've always thought you know me. But you never have!"

I laughed, working to keep the screaming pain out of my voice.

"Winnie, my nickname was *Scourge Queen*. I know you because I *am* you. All I've known, as Eydis and as Samantha, is the pain of being underestimated. And like you, Adrestus was the first person to take me seriously. But he never valued my strength, only my bitterness. You think you're the first daughter to be disregarded by her father? I was fighting paternal disappointment a millennia before you were even born!"

Her fist smashed into my face, and stars danced in my vision. I stumbled back, avoiding an uppercut that would've left me breathless had I allowed it to hit.

"The difference between you and me is simple," she jeered. I tried to avoid her next kick, but two Winnies shifted in and out of focus in front of me. Her boot hit me square in the chest, and I fell back against a tree. Flakes of bark fell around us, and her gloved hand shot from her cloaks to pin me by my neck. She pushed her mask up, and tracts of tears on her face glistened green. "You were only ever just a name, whether that name was Eydis, Scourge Queen, or Samantha. You killed your family because you knew you'd never amount to more than their opinion of you while I strove to be *better. Stronger!*"

Blood roared in my ears. I could see their faces in my mind's eye. My mother and father. My brothers and sisters. All dead. I'd blamed myself for their deaths, sure, but to suggest that I murdered them?

"I would never kill my family."

Winnie leaned in, her face a simpering snarl.

"Has he not told you?"

"How he murdered everyone I love?"

"Oh, you precious thing." She dealt an uppercut to my diaphragm that would've doubled me over had her grip on my throat not tightened. She leaned in as I choked on air. "I know your family wouldn't let you leave Iceland and how you killed them in your rage. How he denied you after discovering what you'd done, and how you exacted your revenge by trying to add him to your ledger."

"Not true." Fury choked the air in my lungs as much as Winnie's hand against my windpipe.

I tried to kick her, but her knee rose, slamming into my injured leg, and this time, I did cry out.

"What would you know?" she laughed. "You can't even remember the idiot boy who put his life on the line to chase you to Adrestus's side."

My vision ran black from lack of oxygen, but the rage Adrestus had called a weakness gave me the energy to slam my forearm into the inside of her elbow, breaking her hold.

"He's the murderer!" I cried, coming at her again. "Not me!"

I tackled her around her middle, pulling us both to the leaf-littered ground. We rolled into an empty stream bed, where I pinned Winnie. The murky remnant of stream water seeped into the folds of her cloak.

"I would *never* kill my family." I repeated. They'd died so long ago, but to me, it had been less than a year since I'd buried them. Since I'd held Erika's tiny, broken body in my arms and vowed revenge.

"What makes you so sure?" Winnie spat. "Your superior sense of integrity?"

"You of all people want to talk to me about integrity?" Rage boiled over before I could contain it. "You tried to get me kidnapped! *Twice!*"

Flames crackled and popped in the distance, filling the silence that fell over us.

"You aren't supposed to remember that," she finally whispered.

I leaned in, furious tears dripping off the end of my nose to splash against her cheeks.

"And you were supposed to be my friend. Not because our parents decided you would be, but because I *was* your friend. Because as horrible and as manipulative as you were, I *defended* you!" My fist was cocked, ready to fly, and it shook with the effort of holding back. "I spent the next *month* fighting tooth and nail to find you. I had my neck snapped like a twig. And I *still* never stopped looking! Just so you could stand by and watch as your *master* flayed me like a fish on his museum floor!"

Winnie's chest heaved underneath me, but she otherwise lay still.

"You've been playing us." Realization broke across her face. "You've remembered this whole time. You aren't here to join him, you're here to *stop* him!"

My gut twisted as I realized what I'd done, but I couldn't take it back now. The same way Winnie couldn't take back ruining my second chance at a normal life last September.

She bucked beneath me, and her leg came out of nowhere, sweeping me to the side. My head smacked into the concrete of the stream basin.

"I don't need to beat you!" Triumph laced her words. "It's over for you *and* Wesley. He's in on it, isn't he? He's got to be."

"Not too long ago, you helped us escape. Why give us up now?" I scrambled after her out of the stream bed.

"I was being merciful, and you repay me by showing up months later with my dad and trying to ruin *everything!*" She flicked her mask back over her face and stepped towards the pathway. "Not this time. This time, I make sure you don't *ever* get in my way again."

She spun on her heel and sprinted for the park perimeter. I struggled after her, ignoring the way the ground swayed beneath my feet.

Winnie put ground between us at a rate my spinning head and aching leg couldn't keep up with, but I had one last card left.

After all, she had her own weak points, too.

"What about your mother, Winnie?" I yelled. "Does her life mean nothing to you?"

At first, I thought she hadn't heard me, but then she staggered to a stop.

"What's she got to do with any of this?" She pushed her mask up again. "If you're messing with me, I swear—"

I was already regretting what I was about to say, but regardless of this fight and whatever happened next, she deserved to know.

"I'm sorry," I said, and even after all the hateful things we'd hurled at each other, the words tasted like lead in my mouth. Winnie deserved better than this. Val had deserved better. "Adrestus killed her the night he attacked the camp. She's dead."

37

Coronation

Winnie's face was unreadable in the shadows cast by the sky's green glow. The aurora's electric hum hung over the silence, mixing with the distant crackle of freezing flames.

"You're lying." It wasn't an accusation, but a statement, as if her belief in her words might alter reality. "Adrestus would've told me. You've always lied, and you're doing it again!"

"He was waiting until after the Peace Summit." Watching her with her arms hanging limp at her side, I felt as if I was looking in on something private and resisted the urge to look away. "He was afraid you wouldn't react well."

"React well?" Winnie repeated, the hysteria rising in her voice. "But he wouldn't, he'd—"

"He killed her just for standing in his way."

"My mom is dead?" Winnie's voice broke, and she wavered as if buffeted by a non-existent wind. She looked ready to collapse, but then she charged forward, and her fist collided with my face. I fell to the ground, my ears ringing and my head feeling like it had been cleaved open.

Winnie stood over me, angry and distraught, and I didn't blame her for whatever she was about to do.

But then she fell into a crouch, holding her head between her hands. "I never said goodbye. I never got to explain why—"

And Winnie was no longer a self-proclaimed goddess but a scared girl, crying for her mother in the dark. I crawled to her side and placed a hand on her back. I knew what it felt like to lose a mother.

"She's been dead for weeks!" Her voice was quiet. Defeated. "And you didn't say anything!"

"He'll kill you," I said. "I was trying to keep you alive."

"But you tell me now," she spat. "When it benefits you."

"Stopping Adrestus benefits us both," I insisted. "If you give away that I've been playing him, I'm dead. And he'll kill you too when he doesn't need you anymore."

"My mom is gone." Winnie shook beneath my hand. "She never got to see me again. She died thinking I hated her! She probably hated *me, and* I never got to—"

"No. She loved you."

But my heart ached for Winnie. I often wondered if my own parents, my *real* parents, had died hating me, too.

"And my father didn't protect her?" She looked up with sudden ferocity, staring at the distant purple flames.

"He tried." The words were ash in my mouth.

She stared at her hands and curled her fingers into fists.

"You have to hit me."

"What?"

She sprung to her feet and pushed me over with the heel of her boot.

"You have to make it believable that you beat me by force."

"Are you sure?"

"You win, okay?" she spat. "But you have to hit me. I can't escape with Felix's fire blocking us in. I have no other choice. Just don't make me hit myself. Not tonight. Please."

I stood up and brushed the dust from my shirt.

"Where?"

"It'll be better if it's a surprise," she grunted, wiping the tears from her face, and then closed her eyes. "Whenever you're ready. Don't be queasy about it."

"I'm sorry. For everything."

"Now I'm the one getting queasy. Do it before I change my mind. And give him hell at his damned Peace Summit."

I clenched my fingers, remembering the way Wesley had knocked Roy Hendricks out after our basement brawl, and let my fist fly.

I limped towards the line of silhouettes that stood against the purple blaze. Winnie, dazed but conscious, hung limp over my shoulder. The bruise spreading along her jaw told the story we needed it to tell. Whatever came next, I felt strangely assured. For the first time, I had Winnie in my corner.

Adrestus at the center of his pantheon with his hands clutched behind his back, watched us approach with an unreadable expression. Winnie's breath caught in my ear, but she remained limp on my shoulder, defeated and gutted.

"My gods, Eydis," Adrestus boomed. I slid Winnie off my back and laid her at Adrestus's feet. "I'm pleasantly surprised."

Wesley, Heather, Anthony, Mira, Gregor, Lana, Felix, Roy, and John Ratcliffe fanned out on either side of Adrestus. Their expressions ranged from stoic reservation to anxious apprehension. A tenth figure, standing directly next to Adrestus, shrouded in a cloak, averted their gaze.

"I had more to prove than she did." I glanced at Roy, who stared at his daughter with furious disappointment.

"And prove yourself you have," Adrestus laughed. He nudged Winnie with the toe of his boot, and she groaned in pain.

"She probably needs a doctor," I noted. I put a hand up to my temple, and my fingers came away sticky with blood. "And I'm bleeding—"

"Later! Roy, get your kid out of my way." Adrestus clapped his hands, and Roy hurried to drag Winnie back. Gregor stepped forward, carrying a pillow upon which dark metal glinted. Adrestus drew me closer, pushing hair matted with blood away from my face. "The next era is within our grasp, and our Pantheon needs a queen."

I shivered and tried to pull away, but Adrestus's hands tightened around mine.

"Winnie needs—" I tried to say.

"Nearly ten months ago," Adrestus cut me off, "when I heard that the talented inculcator Alison Taylor had a daughter, I wanted to see her for myself. Mira tried to collect you for me on the ferry, and while she was thwarted, she came back with impossible news about the girl and her father. "

Beside my better judgment, I glanced down the line at Wesley where he stood at the end. He kept his eyes forward, into the dark of the park, but the heavy sigh that rolled his shoulders told me he knew I was looking.

"I told Mira she must be mistaken, but then you came to my museum, and while it couldn't be possible, you looked just like my Eydis."

Wesley's jaw clenched. He wouldn't look at me, but I was reassured by his presence all the same.

"Your Eydis?" I dared to ask, turning back to Adrestus.

"But of course. Was it not I who named you Scourge Queen? Was it not my stolen immortality that brought you back to me? In the museum, you had no knowledge of our legend yet the resemblance was uncanny. I redoubled my efforts to bring you to my side.

"Nearly two thousand years ago, I swore to usher in an age of peace the world had never seen before. A thousand futile years later, an Icelandic girl spurred new vitality into my vision. Now that we are poised to take what I swore would be mine in just a few, short days, we should step into this new dominion together." He lifted a circlet of black metal from Gregor's velvet pillow. "It's time I crowned my Scourge Queen."

I stood stiff as he rested it atop my blood-matted hair. The metal felt cool against my forehead, though it stung where it grazed the wound in my temple. Adrestus lifted a sword from the pillow. Its slick blade and simple hilt were made of the same, black metal, and it reflected the freezing, purple fire that raged behind the Pantheon.

"Your last blade was lost to the enemy. May this one prove a worthy replacement." He handed me the sword. Its weight was well-balanced in my grip, designed to emulate the make of the viking sword that was still in the care of Fleming.

"All hail the Scourge Queen," Mira snarled. "She only had to murder and betray to get what she wanted."

"Enough, Mira," Adrestus warned. "Jealousy doesn't suit you."

Mira's mouth clamped shut, but after Winnie's accusations of murder, the words carried an unexpected sting.

"I'm also pleased to announce that, thanks to Gregor's ingenuity, the Whitlock Protocol is perfectly reliable now," Adrestus beamed. "The City's Heart has been tamed. Should Aetos fail, our plans will still succeed."

"Aetos?" I repeated.

"It means eagle in Greek. Eagles were the symbol of Zeus, the most powerful god of the Greek pantheon." He patted the shoulder of the cloaked figure next to him, who continued to keep their head down. "A fitting name for the Apex who will lead us into victory, for when Zeus speaks, all of humanity should take heed and obey."

Obey...

The word set me on edge, and I looked over Aetos's slight frame, my breath catching and my mind reeling.

"Every nation in attendance *will* align themselves with me. With *us*." Adrestus spread his arms wide. "Their resources, their land, and their people will be ours to command. All we have to do is ask nicely. Isn't it so much cleaner than disposing of their leaders and taking what they have by force?"

"Disposing?" I balked.

Adrestus laughed, amused and condescending.

"Should Aetos fail in his duties to make the nations bow, the Whitlock Protocol only works on those we've implanted with Mira's control chips when they undergo the Epsilon Procedure. Because of the procedure's mortality rate, most countries elect lower ranking officials to undergo the surgery. Otherwise, their leaders run a high risk of dying. Should we meet resistance, then we'll dispose of the leaders and use the Whitlock Protocol to take over each country with our new Epsilons."

"But that's..." Evil? Barbaric? I struggled to find the words. "It's not practical! They have entire government systems backing them, not to mention militaries!"

"What's a military compared to my pantheon?" Adrestus simpered. "I admit, if it *does* come to the implementation of the Whitlock Protocol, my hopes aren't high, and I'm afraid we'll have to resort to more drastic measures. But don't worry your pretty, crowned head. We won't have to kill anyone because we have Aetos, and Aetos is very good at what he does."

He crossed behind the hooded figure and leaned over him, grabbing the hood with both hands and drawing it back.

Shaggy, blond hair sprung free, in desperate need of a haircut, and brown, terrified eyes rose to meet mine. It felt like a lifetime had passed since I'd last seen Avery, struggling to reach me from the cab of a helicopter.

"After all," Adrestus continued, "he's used his powers on you enough times. You know better than anyone how effective they can be."

38

One Step At A Time

Adrestus's ceremony finished, and the purple fires extinguished, leaving the Pantheon to cross the street to the museum in darkness. I didn't remember how it ended. Maybe I was concussed from my fight with Winnie or maybe I was too stunned by the revelation that my little brother was the key to Adrestus's plan to subjugate the world. Wesley's warning in the stairwell suddenly made so much more sense.

I was the only one who could stop Avery.

Adrestus was saying something to me, but his words echoed against the back of my skull as I watched the Pantheon climb the stairs to the museum. Avery's blond head bowed as Roy Hendricks led him through the doors, held open by Wesley.

"Eydis, are you listening?" Adrestus scowled. Mira and Gregor waited behind him, stoic in the night wind.

"Sorry," I mumbled. I pressed my fingers against my temple, and they came away sticky with blood. "I might have a concussion. Can I go see the medics?"

He frowned.

"I was asking if you'd like a celebratory dinner upstairs? I know it's a bit late—"

"Can it wait?"

He froze, and I knew I'd made a mistake cutting him off. His brow worked as he tried to force it to relax.

"Do you know how many of my followers would kill to be invited to a private dinner with me?" he asked through a strained smile. "And I quite literally do mean kill."

"I'm covered in blood and dirt." Avery was getting away. I needed to catch up.

"That's always how I liked you best."

I ignored my squirming stomach.

"It won't be much of a dinner if I pass out."

He sighed and looked up at the aurora, as if its lights might calm his irritation.

"Tomorrow, then. Perhaps that's better, dining together the night before our victory." He cupped my filthy cheek in a cold, clammy hand.

I nodded, and the motion made my head spin. Maybe I did have a concussion.

"Looking forward to it," I lied. He turned to Gregor, I escaped to the street before he could insist on accompanying me.

Inside, I caught up with the others at the stairwell. I knew I should stop by the medics who were tending to Winnie in the museum office, but there were more pressing matters at hand. Wesley, lingering at the back of the group, held the stairwell door open for me.

"Your head—"

"Where is he?"

Wesley gulped.

"Up ahead, but you shouldn't—"

I pushed into the fire-lit stairwell and took the steps two at a time, shoving my way through Adrestus's Pantheon. Lana tried to stop me, saying something about my new Scourge Queen uniform being ready, but I ignored her, chasing after Roy, who had one hand on Avery's shoulder while the other held a ball of fire aloft to guide the way.

"Avery!"

Avery's head craned around, and the color drained from his face. Roy whispered something in his ear before turning towards me as Avery continued up the stairs into darkness.

"What do you want with him?" Roy demanded.

"I'm sorry, what do you want with *this*?" I flung my arms out, nearly smacking Felix in the face as he passed us, holding his own purple fire to keep the stairwell lit.

"What do you mean 'this'?" Roy growled.

"All Adrestus had to do was drop Paul Fleming's name, and you came running to his side?"

"You're here, too, aren't you?"

"Adrestus didn't murder my wife."

Roy's face reddened, and the rest of Pantheon glanced back at us as they continued forward. Wesley hesitated before following the others.

"Valerie would understand. If she'd known Adrestus's vision for the world and what side Paul had been on—"

"Then she'd be okay with being a murder victim?"

"Then she never would've gotten in the way." Roy spun around and continued climbing up the steps. "I don't have time for this."

"You've got about eighty floors worth of time, actually!" I called after him, though I was already struggling to keep up. I was exhausted after my fight, and my head pounded in my right temple, but I forged forward and upward while the stairwell got darker as the others and their firelight got farther.

"Sammy!"

I yelped at the sound of my name whispered in the dark.

"Wesley?"

A door creaked open to my left and dim, green light spilled from the windowed hall into the stairwell, illuminating Wesley and Avery's silhouettes.

"You wanted to talk to him, right?" Wesley asked, holding Avery at his side.

I stepped into the green-lit hall, and Wesley guarded the door.

"Don't—" Avery started, but I clapped a hand over his mouth.

"Not another word."

"Let him talk, Sammy," Wesley mumbled.

"He said 'don't'. 'Don't' is a command. He was going to use his powers."

Avery shook his head beneath my hand.

"Come on," Wesley urged.

"Just keep watch." I tightened my grip on Avery's face. "Try to command me, and I'll make sure you don't talk ever again."

He nodded, and I let him free.

"I just wanted to ask you to not be mad," he sniffed.

"Why would I be mad?"

"Because of what I'm going to do at the Summit."

I crossed my arms, trying to ignore the tears in his eyes and the quake in his voice.

"You're not seriously thinking about helping him?" I hissed. "Avery, it's world domination! You're just a kid! You shouldn't be helping anyone take over the world!"

"If I don't, people will die!" he wailed. "You heard him! He'll kill all the world leaders, and he's not going to stop there if that's not enough!"

I paced in the space the hallway allowed, kneading at my aching head with my knuckles.

"Why haven't you used your powers on Adrestus?" I demanded. "Tell him to not take over the world."

"I tried." He at least looked well. He'd been well-fed in the weeks since I'd last seen him and had no apparent injuries. "I really did, as soon as they fixed my throat and I got my voice back. I told him to stop what he was doing and leave everyone alone, but—"

He shook his head. I took him by the shoulders, trying to be gentle but firm.

"But what?"

"It didn't work. Gregor, that blond guy. It was like a brick wall was inside of Adrestus's head, and it felt like Gregor."

"He's an Inculcator, like you and Mom," I said through gritted teeth. Of course Adrestus had defenses in place.

"He knew what I'd done," Avery said. "He knew I'd tried to use my powers on him. So he took me away from Mom, and I haven't seen her since. I don't even know if she's alive."

"She is," I said. "She's fine, I—"

Something in Avery's face finally broke me, and I pulled him in, marveling at how much taller he seemed as I hugged him.

"I'm sorry, Sammy," he sniffed. "I don't want to help him, but if I don't, people will die, and it'll be my fault."

"No one is going to die, and if they do, it'll definitely not be your fault."

He pushed away and picked up my pacing.

"It *will* be! It always is! It's my fault Wesley got hurt last winter! It's my fault he was captured, which was the only reason you came back here, and then Dad died! So that's my fault, too!"

"No, Avery."

"What do you know? You can't remember because of me!"

"Oh." I froze, my heart constricting. "Avery, no."

He'd spent the last several weeks thinking my memories were still lost. I stuck my hand out to stop his pacing.

"Potato chips," I said. His brow furrowed, and he looked at me with concern, as if worried I'd finally lost it.

"What about them?"

"The fake memories Mom and Dad made up for me never really came back. They're like fuzzy shadows, just memories of memories. But the very first time you and I got to be brother and sister, away from Mom and Dad, was on the ferry," I said. Avery's eyes grew wide. "You wanted potato chips for breakfast, and I let you have them."

"How did you know that?"

"Because," I grinned, "I remember. But you can't tell Adrestus."

"Never." He hesitated, then flung his arms around me. "But only if you stay out of the way and let me do what he told me to do."

My heart fell and the sweetness of our reunion soured.

"You can't."

"People will die if I don't." He let go and crossed the hall to join Wesley at the stairwell door. "Not even Dad could beat him. What makes you think we can? The best we can do is try to save as many people as possible, even if that means doing something bad. That's why you sank the city last winter, right? That's all I'm doing now."

He pushed into the stairwell and left Wesley and me alone in the hall. I stared at the door, reeling, wanting to run after Avery, to force him to listen, but I knew it was futile.

"We're stopping him," I finally said. "Both him and Adrestus."

Wesley nodded and shifted his weight from one foot to the other.

"Right, but if we get caught alone again—"

"I get it." I shouldered past him into the stairwell and listened to the distant sound of Avery's quickly receding footsteps. "What floor is this?"

My legs were already numb with exhaustion.

"Eight."

"So only seventy-something to go?" The door slammed shut, and the meager sliver of moonlight that had lit the stairwell a moment before snuffed out, leaving us in total darkness. I stepped forward, ready to make quick, if difficult, progress, but my legs shook, and I gripped the railing for support and guidance in the dark.

"I can still see," Wesley murmured in my ear. "Let me."

I marched up the next few steps, ignoring his offer. If someone saw us...

"I could hear you and Winnie, Sammy. I know you've had a hard night. Let me help you. It's too dark for anyone to see us."

My injured leg buckled, but Wesley was there to catch me. I succumbed to his chronic need to help. He scooped me into his arms, and I clung to his shirt as he carried me effortlessly up to the top of the skyscraper.

I was sure he noticed my shoulders shake as I silently cried into his chest, but he kept it to himself.

Skipping out on medical attention might've been a mistake, as evidenced by my blood-stained pillow in the morning. Everything hurt, and I held in a groan as I forced myself into a sitting position. Winnie had come in some time after me and now lay with her back to the room.

"There's bandages in the bathroom," she grunted.

I gripped my covers, watching her stoic shoulders. Her Dion mask sat on the floor with a large crack running down the middle. Our fight had been fierce, but I didn't remember the mask breaking.

"Any extra pillowcases?" I forced a hollow laugh, glancing at the bloodstain.

"You can have mine." She pushed herself up to face me. Dark circles clung to red, angry eyes, and black streaks ran down her face—remnants of unwashed make-up.

"I'm leaving. Tonight. Don't try to stop me." Winnie shook, though I didn't know if from anger, grief, or exhaustion. Her hair stuck out to the side, bits of twigs, and dirt still tangled in her collapsing ponytail.

"How?" I demanded. Winnie had nothing to lose. If selling me out helped get her out the front door and away from this place, she'd do so without hesitation.

"If I tell Mira I'm going patrolling, she'll believe me." She pulled her hair out of its ponytail and attempted to run her fingers through the tangles. "When I'm not back by morning, it'll be too late."

I sat frozen on the edge of my bed. Her plan was simple. Painless. She'd get away for sure on her own.

"Take Avery with you."

"And force Adrestus to kill people? No, thanks. Plus, I have a better chance of escaping on my own."

"We're going to stop Adrestus at the Peace Summit," I insisted. "But he's more powerful with Avery."

"If you want him out, figure out how to do it yourself."

She pulled her clothes from the closet and marched out the door. I sat in silence until I heard the shower running down the hall.

Winnie *would* be leaving with Avery, whether she wanted to or not. I'd make sure of it.

39
Stage Setting

I wasn't ashamed to admit that I had a bit of a disastrous streak when it came to making plans, but the one rapidly forming in my head was uncharacteristically perfect. Painless, even.

First, I needed to block off Winnie's means of escaping, which meant removing her exit route. What better way than to place Adrestus himself in the museum?

The power grid was still dark, so I took the stairs to Adrestus's penthouse while my plan played out in my head. Maybe I was feeling overenthusiastic because the Peace Summit was the next day, and I would finally be free. There were still places my plan could go wrong, but odds were slim. For once, I was the one in control.

I burst out of the stairwell into the red-carpeted lobby of Adrestus's penthouse with maybe too much zeal, eliciting a glare from Miles where he sat at the circular desk.

"Do you have an appointment?"

I ignored him and strutted down the hall to the plain white door of Adrestus's dining room. I hesitated, unsure if I should knock or walk in. It was a sprawling apartment inside. He might not hear a knock at the door, but at the same time, he might be offended I let myself into his home, and I needed him in a good mood.

A throat cleared behind me.

"You're up early." Adrian Schrader's white teeth flashed in the dark of the hall. He loomed overhead in a tan suit that matched his sandy hair. "Mind grabbing the door?"

I choked on a response and pushed into the dining room before stumbling out of Mr. Schrader's way. The morning sunlight that flooded the room bounced off the white walls and carpet in a dazzling array, made all the more overwhelming by the crooning of Adrestus's orchestral music blasting in the sitting room.

"I heard you did well last night!" Schrader chortled over the music. "I'll bet Miss Hendricks is less than happy, but it'll push her to be better."

"Adrian? I was expecting Gregor." Adrestus's head peeked out from around the corner. "And Eydis, too!"

"Gregor has no more flights of stairs left in him after last night," Schrader laughed. "So I drew the short straw. Though, I'm happy to report that six of the eleven representatives survived yesterday's batch of Epsilon Procedures. They're currently resting in their hotel rooms and should be fit in time for the Summit tomorrow."

My stomach churned.

"Six?" Adrestus turned his music down. "Did we do something different?"

"It was probably just a good batch of subjects," Schrader shrugged. "I have more to report, but Miss Havardson was here first."

Adrestus's face brightened.

"My Scourge, you're just in time for strudel!" He gestured to his dough-stained apron.

"I wasn't planning on staying," I mumbled, then couldn't help but to ask, "How are you baking without electricity?"

He beckoned me into the kitchen. I ignored the way my stomach tightened at the memory of Trev Baker lifeless on the couch as I passed through the white-rugged sitting room.

I wondered what Adrestus did with all the bodies. They had to be piling up with the Epsilon Initiative in full swing, especially if five dead in one day was a low number.

"No electricity required!" Adrestus stood in front of a new oven and propane tank. "I had it installed as soon as the blackout hit. Thank goodness for Ares. I'm not sure who else would have been able to carry it up eighty-seven floors."

Wesley was strong, but the oven looked heavy. Suddenly, spending my days helping Jamie didn't seem so bad.

"Right. It's very nice," I gulped. "Look, about tonight—"

Adrestus's expression turned dark.

"You can't possibly be thinking of putting it off again," he warned. "Last night I can forgive, though your insolence and lack of gratitude won't be forgotten. But to deny me a second night, and on the eve of the Summit—"

"Never!" I gushed. "I just had a request."

"I've already settled on a menu." Adrestus raised a dubious eyebrow.

"That's fine!" I hoped I wasn't coming off as overeager. "But I thought it might be more poetic if we had our victory dinner downstairs."

Adrestus paused, surveying me closely.

"In the museum," I continued when he said nothing. "Close the whole place down, and maybe we can eat in front of our statues."

Schrader burst into laughter, and I recoiled when he ruffled my hair.

"I see why you like her, sir," he quipped. "She's just as melodramatic as you are!"

Adrestus smirked then looked away when his kitchen timer demanded he tend to the strudel puffs in the oven. Hot, pastry-scented air wafted across the kitchen, and the smell of hot food was too tantalizing after several days of eating nothing but cold soup and peanut butter sandwiches.

"It's a long walk down to the museum and a longer walk up," Adrestus said.

Exactly. He'd be out of the way.

"I'll talk to Lana about giving us a lift back up," I smiled. "I'm sure she won't mind."

Adrestus pulled at a bit of pastry, watching the layers flake apart.

"I'll have Miles close off the museum to ensure we aren't bothered," he finally said. "I'll meet you down there at eight."

The museum was completely shut down and closed off. Interns were sent to the hotel instead, and those of us living in Schrader Tower's upper floors were told to keep out as Adrestus made preparations for our dinner. With Winnie's easiest route for escape blocked, I needed to establish her new way out.

I found Lana in the training gym with Anthony. The window had finally been replaced, though Anthony still looked skittish to be near the edge. He narrowed his eyes at me over Lana's winged shoulder when I came down the stairs to make my request.

"I'd be happy to fly you up after dinner," Lana smiled. "The exercise is good for me."

"Actually," I tried to force an embarrassed blush into my cheeks, "if that's the case, would you mind giving me a ride down as well? I hit my head yesterday, and my leg is still killing me."

Lana laughed and nodded.

"Of course!" She ran a hand through her short hair and ruffled it. "That's enough training for this morning, Anthony. You're free to go grab breakfast. There's more jam in the lounge, and if Roy's around, maybe he'll toast some bread for you. See you tonight, Eydis!"

She spread her wings and skipped the stairs, soaring to the top step to make her exit. I tried to make a quick escape after her, but Anthony grabbed my shoulder.

"You're up to something," he accused. "What's Adrestus got you working on?"

"Nothing. Why?"

"You're scheming."

"*You're* being paranoid."

"You may have lost your memories, but you're still the same Sammy, and you'd never ask for help."

I crossed my arms. Anthony had seen through my ruses before.

"The Samantha you knew is dead." Part of me wanted nothing more than to admit the truth to Anthony, but I hesitated. He had betrayed me before.

"You can't trust him," he said, and a soft breeze stirred my hair. "I know his promises sound good, but they're not, and if you don't come to grips with who he is, we might lose the entire world."

"You want to talk to *me* about who I can trust?" I snapped. "Don't think I didn't notice the other day that Remi only took control over Heather and Wesley. You don't have a control chip, which means you don't need one."

Anthony's face reddened.

"He thinks he can control me without one," he spat. "Same way he thinks he can control you. Probably because he's been able to before. It isn't like he sees either of us as a threat. But whatever. Do what you want. No one's ever been able to stop you before. I know I can't, whatever it is you're working on."

He tried to walk past me to the stairs, but I held out a hand to stop him.

"Anthony," I whispered, grabbing his arm. "He doesn't see us as threats, but what if we proved him wrong?"

His bicep tensed under my grip.

"You aren't planning something for him at all," he realized out loud. "Sammy—"

"Do you know where Avery is?"

"He's staying with Gregor down the hall from me."

"Make sure he's on the roof tonight when I meet Lana. Make something up if you have to. Just make sure he's there, okay?"

A heavy pause settled between us, and I stared out the window over the glittering city, holding my breath as I waited for a response.

"I—" His voice quaked over the single syllable, and he cut himself off with a gulp.

"Fear made you break my trust once," I reminded him in a low tone. "Don't do it again. I trust you. You were my first friend on New Delos, after all."

"Sammy," Anthony gasped. "Your memories—"

"They've been back since the attack on the camp." I turned him around to look at me. "If you tell Adrestus, he'll reward you. He might take your powers away like you want."

"I won't tell."

"If you do—"

"I won't." He dropped his hand to mine and squeezed my fingers. "Never again."

I nodded. I'd have to trust him. I hadn't given myself any other choice.

"It goes without saying," I said, moving towards the stairs, "but *don't* tell Wesley."

"I don't even know what it is we're doing. But, Sammy, this Eydis stuff...I know it can't be real, but with how crazy things have been...It's all made up, right? Because there's no way you're an immortal Viking queen."

Sunlight outlined him in gold, casting a halo through his shaggy hair and turning his ears red. It was hard to read his face, but there was a sort of calm apprehension about him. I still might tell him the truth someday. Maybe.

"Don't let Lana see you and Avery before I get there."

I spun on my heel, leaving Anthony alone in the gym. I thought I'd feel calmer as more pieces came together, but nerves mounted in my navel.

However, the plan was already in motion, and I was only missing one, vital piece.

The lounge Lana had mentioned happened to be the same one Adrestus had brought me to the day he kicked Wesley out the training gym window. A kitchenette went unused along one wall, while the other sported the same large windows as every other outside-facing room in Schrader Tower. A center table held the aforementioned spread of jams, and I helped myself to a lunch of crackers and jelly.

I carried a cracker-laden napkin to the windows to look out over the city, towards the eastern boundaries of the island, where I knew the schools were hiding behind skyscrapers. The teams should still be there.

Adrestus would've said something if they'd found them. And tonight, if everything played out how it should—

"Dammit, Sammy!"

Winnie's screech made me drop my crackers, and I spun around just in time to see her charging across the empty lounge at me.

"It's fine! Don't be mad!" I put my hands up to stave off her attack. She halted a few paces away, red in the face.

"It's fine?" she seethed. "Adrestus blocked off the entire museum. He isn't letting anyone through, and word is it's because *you* asked him to!"

"I've got it under control," I assured her. "I thought if the exits were closed, you might be more agreeable—"

"To taking your dumb brother?" She crunched my crackers underfoot and threw a fist at the window over my shoulder. It hit the glass with a thunk, and she held it there, leaning in. "Good plan, genius. How is blocking off the only exit going to make me take Avery when I can't even leave?"

"Winnie, you're smarter than that," I smirked. "There are exits on every floor. I would've thought Hackjob made that clear."

"The same Hackjob we had to peel off the sidewalk?" Winnie gritted her teeth, and her eyes bulged in anger "You idiot, you ruin *everything*. First my mom, now—"

"I'm not the one who killed your mother."

"No, you just told me she was dead and then trapped me here!"

It wasn't fair for her to blame me for her position. After all, she was the one who made the decision to run off with an immortal despot knowing full well he wanted world domination. Still, I couldn't help but feel bad.

"Look, I need you. I don't trust Avery with anyone else, and I can't leave until after the Summit."

"No one will leave after the Summit." The first hints of a summer storm pattered on the window behind me, and I hoped the dark clouds rolling over the city weren't a bad omen. "With or without Avery, Adrestus is going to get what he wants."

I shook my head.

"When you leave tonight, go to the school. Fleming, Amanda, and all the others are hiding in a secret facility under the main hall. Tell them where the prisoners are, and tell them that tomorrow during the Summit is their best chance to save them."

Winnie looked at me with something akin to pity. She retreated to the table of jams and scoured her options.

"It won't matter."

"We have to try. Please, Winnie. At least tell them. Let them make the call. The entire Pantheon will be at the hotel, leaving the tower unguarded."

She settled on a raspberry jelly and fell into one of the seats.

"But why?"

"Because it's what your mom would want."

Winnie glared up at me, and I swallowed the guilt I felt at weaponizing her dead mother. We stared at each other until, finally, Winnie sighed and rolled her eyes.

"You haven't even told me your escape plan yet."

"Easy. Lana's going to fly you and Avery from the roof."

"Lana?" Winnie blanched, dropping the jam jar. "Lana loves Adrestus! She'd never help."

"I know someone who can be very persuasive."

"Avery won't—"

"Not Avery." I grinned. "If you want to escape, then you have to help me break out my mother."

40

Break Out

It was too late to worry if Anthony would uphold his part of the plan. Summer rain splattered against the large windows of Mira's apartment as I paced in front of the couch, waiting for Winnie to come downstairs. She was mad, but she was at least willing to go forward with the plan I'd set in motion.

A door slammed upstairs, and Winnie descended the staircase, brooding under the black hood of a fireproof cloak.

"Twenty-one floors down to your mother's cell, then twenty-three back up to the roof," she recited. "Hope your leg isn't bothering you. I will leave you if you fall behind."

"I'll be fine." I zipped my black jacket up to my neck, vaguely reminded of last September when Winnie and I had gone on our first misadventure together. The night had ended with Wesley springing me from the boot of Mira's car after Winnie had tricked me. It felt nice to be the one in control this time.

I beat Winnie to the door, and she hesitated in the living room, watching the rain batter the darkening city.

"You coming?" I prompted.

"Yeah. Whatever." She turned her back on the window. "You're sure Adrestus is downstairs?"

"Positive," I assured her, stepping into the hall. "He won't get in our way."

We passed Miles's apartment on our way to the stairwell. I hoped Wesley wasn't inside listening. He needed to stay away. If Adrestus did somehow catch wind of our plot, I didn't want him activating the control chip in Wesley's neck.

The stairwell was dark, but Winnie had come prepared with a flashlight and led the way down the twisting steps. I kept track of the floors, watching the numbers in the stairwell decrease in the light of the sweeping flashlight beam.

We stopped when the floor number read sixty-four, and I steeled myself for what might wait in the corridor. I'd been in control until now, but it was Winnie's turn to lead the way.

"You remembered your keycard, right?" I asked. Winnie smirked and leaned into the door handle, eliciting a satisfying, metallic click.

"Clearance level doesn't matter in a blackout."

"That's terrible for security."

"Security doesn't matter either when no one is dumb enough to infiltrate a skyscraper full of super-powered villains."

"I know a couple of people who are dumb enough."

Winnie rolled her eyes, her whites flashing just as she clicked off the flashlight.

"Two rules," she hissed. "One, you will stay close to me."

"I'm not—"

"And two," she snarled, cutting me off, "we're here for Alison and Alison only."

"Right." I frowned. "I'm not about to sabotage my own plan."

"I know how you are," Winnie continued. "You're a bleeding heart *and* stubborn. I don't want you getting ideas about a massive prison break."

I gulped. I hadn't considered who all I might face on the other side of the door.

"They'll get help tomorrow. Avery is the priority right now."

"*I'm* the priority." Winnie pushed into the darkened hallway.

The hall beyond the door was dark and empty, a straight shot to the rain-battered window at the far end of the corridor. Winnie stalked down the hall with purpose while I followed in a crouch.

"What are you doing?" She whipped around to look at me. "If you act suspicious, you'll look suspicious. Walk like you're supposed to be here, and no one will ask questions."

I scowled back but straightened up and tried to instill confidence into my stride. I faltered when I saw a dull silhouette standing against the diffused gray light of night filtering in through the windows ahead.

"Who's there?" a gruff voice demanded.

"It's just us, Kory," Winnie sniffed. "I'm missing your aurora tonight. Can't see a thing without it."

She clicked on the flashlight, and the man named Kory flinched away from the beam. He was tall with hair buzzed short in an attempt to hide a receding hairline.

"It's up there, even if you can't see it. Who's with you?"

"The Scourge." Winnie's voice dripped with disdain, and I blinked in the sudden light as she flashed the light my way. "We're on official business. Wish I could elaborate."

"The Scourge didn't have clearance for this floor."

"She was crowned last night. She can go wherever she wants now." Winnie swung the light back in his direction. "So stand out of the way, we're on a time crunch."

"Which prisoner are you here for?"

My chest constricted, but lying came easy to Winnie.

"Bradford." She lowered the light out of Kory's face. "Something about needing her for an interrogation, but again, I can't say much because you're the one lacking clearance."

I flushed at Naomi's last name. Her mother was a good pick for a cover story. Their family powers were strong, but posed little physical threat.

Kory must've thought so, too, because he stepped aside, holding out a ring of keys. Winnie snapped them from his hands and led the way.

The hall curved with the building, and we walked with the windows to our right. On our left, doors and windows alternated. The first window glowed with light, and the door boasted a plaque that made my heart sink.

Melody Hisakawa
Apex

Hinata Hisakawa
Apex

I looked in against my better judgment. The room on the other side was lit by a ceiling lamp that illuminated a sparsely furnished room. The hum of a hidden generator gave away the source of the electricity, and the names on the door explained why these prisoners had power before even Adrestus's living space.

At least one of Heather's parents would be capable of the same shadow-fueled powers as her daughter. Without light, they weren't prisoners at all, but a liability.

A woman with bright, red curls that fell over her shoulders sat with her dark-haired husband. They leaned into each other with their eyes closed, and I wondered if they knew their daughter was in the building.

I hurried after Winnie and tried to ignore the names on the doors, but the surnames of my friends jumped out at me: Silva, Pomeroy, Chase, Archer.

There had been so many families at the camp. I hadn't realized how many went un-rescued. I stopped again when I saw the name "Trevor Baker". The room on the other side of the window was empty.

"Would you keep up?" Winnie hissed. I tried to hasten my pace, but another name stopped me yet again.

"Winnie, wait."

Winnie spun around.

"I told you, we aren't here to give out charity."

The family on the other side of the glass looked cramped, keeping their heads low as they passed a box of cereal between them in the dark. The matriarch glanced up, sensing me on the other side of the glass, and in the dull light, I recognized Naomi's features on her face.

"What is it?" Mr. Bradford's nervous voice carried through the door. "Who's out there?"

"A friend."

"Winnie, please." I beckoned for the keys.

"We're running out of time."

"So hurry."

Winnie shouldered me out of the way, jamming a key into the doorknob.

"You have thirty seconds before I leave you behind."

The door retracted into the wall, and I stumbled in.

"Where are my daughters?" Mrs. Bradford was on me within seconds, holding me close. I'd only ever met her over Naomi's many video calls, but something about her embrace felt familiar. "I felt Naomi nearby, several weeks ago."

"They're safe. Joni is far away, hiding. Naomi is on the island, waiting."

"Is that Samantha?" A small boy peeked out from behind the cereal box.

"Are we leaving?" Mr. Bradford asked, standing up from his cot. "If you're here—"

"Not yet." My voice broke. "Soon. Tomorrow. I promise."

"Samantha," Winnie warned from the doorway.

"Then why are you here?" Mr. Bradford had been kind and soft-spoken when I'd met him before. I couldn't blame him for the ice in his voice now.

"I wanted to tell you Naomi and Joni are safe and to hold on." I pushed away from Mrs. Bradford, and she patted my head in a motherly gesture.

"You are doing wonderfully," she insisted. "You've been so stressed for so many weeks."

"You've been able to feel me?"

"I had my suspicions it was you I felt worrying up and down the tower. You arrived just after I felt Naomi's presence."

"Sammy," Winnie said again, and I stepped back to join her, guilt settling in my gut, remembering the way I'd tricked Naomi.

"It's fine," Mrs. Bradford said. "Whatever it is, it's fine."

"Tomorrow," I repeated. "Be ready."

Mrs. Bradford stepped back, put her arm around her husband, and the door slid closed.

Winnie jogged down the hall.

"That was stupid," she said. "We've lost time."

She skidded to a stop and stood in front of a window, waving me past her.

"What?"

"I'm not letting you stop again."

I gulped when I read the names "Daniella Isaacs" and "Benson Isaacs". Wesley's mother and brother.

"But—"

"This is taking too long." Winnie reached for my wrist and pulled me down the hall, and I tried to catch a glimpse of Wesley's family through the window. "Think about Avery and Alison."

I pulled my wrist out of her grasp but followed her down the curving hall, ignoring the rest of the doors until Winnie came to stop outside a door that read:

Alison Havardson

Apex

Winnie fumbled with the keys until she found the one that fit in the lock, and the door slid open. A figure pushed herself up into a sitting position on her cot, holding a hand over her eyes to stave off the harsh light of our flashlight.

"Mom?" I gasped.

"Sammy?" Her blonde hair was neatly braided over one shoulder, sporting the few tangles her fingers were unable to work out. "Why—"

"You're leaving," Winnie snapped. "But we need to hurry."

"But Avery—"

"Is on the roof," I gushed. "Come on, before—"

"Before someone catches you?" a voice drawled behind us. A strange static crept into the corners of my brain, buzzing through my skull. I turned to face Kory where he stood down the hall, green light radiating around him.

"Kory, it isn't what it looks like," Winnie said.

"Drop it," Kory sneered, and the static in my head got louder. Winnie winced, and I knew she could feel it, too. The buzzing crescendoed, and I fell to the ground clutching my head. A thud sounded next me, and I forced my eyes open to see Winnie on the tiled floor, her hand pressed against her ears.

"Stop!" she cried. "Kory, don't—"

"You don't like my magnetic field? I thought you told Adrestus it wasn't Pantheon-worthy! That was you, wasn't it, who got Lana promoted over me?"

Tears streamed down my face, and I tried to claw my way to my elbows. I was not about to be thwarted by a man bitter over a missed promotion, but the electricity in my brain scrambled, making it hard to think.

And then, as suddenly as the pain had started, it cut, and Kory fell backwards against the tiled floor. A metal bowl rolled to a halt next to him, having been thrown against his head, and Mom's hand was around my arm, pulling me to my feet.

"Run," she hissed. "I'm right behind you."

Winnie didn't need convincing and bolted back the way we came while Mom bent over Kory's feebly struggling form.

"Samantha, come *on*," Winnie yelled, but I was frozen in place. Kory had seen me helping them escape. He knew I was a traitor.

"It's fine." Alison's voice was warm in my ear, and she propelled me down the hall after Winnie. "I fixed it. He won't remember you were here."

My legs moved mechanically underneath me, chasing the curve of the hall, following the bouncing beam of Winnie's flashlight as she turned down the corridor towards the stairwell. By the time Mom and I were on the stairs, Winnie was already a floor ahead.

"Is he unconscious?" Winnie called down.

"Not for long," Mom called back. "But he can't call for help if communications are still down."

I took the stairs two at a time, straining my thigh, threatening to rip a new hole through the muscle fibers.

"I hope you know what you're doing, Sammy," Mom murmured through labored breaths.

"I've got a general idea," I wheezed back.

We caught up to Winnie, sprinting up the stairs, ignoring the burning in our legs and chests. The flashlight passed over a large "Seventy-Seven" but the thought of ten more floors to climb made my legs heavy.

A nudging pull tugged the back of my head, and I thought Kory had returned, attacking us with a fresh electro-magnetic wave, but then a humanoid shape took form in front us. Winnie stopped, too, seeing it where I saw it, but Mom was oblivious to the apparition dressed in a blue and white striped apron stained with flour and gravy. I should've been used to images of Adrestus appearing before me by this point, but my body turned cold with dread.

"I've just been informed," the apparition started, "we have a prison break on floor sixty-four. Alison Havardson has left her cell and is considered dangerous. My loyal followers, she must be stopped."

41

A Mother's Gambit

The image of Adrestus in his gravy-stained apron remained imprinted on my retina as the apparition fizzled from view. The beam of Winnie's flashlight wavered as she tried to steady her shaking hands.

"Dammit, Sammy!" she snarled. "If you hadn't stopped—"

"What's wrong?" Mom demanded, staring down at us from the same landing where Adrestus's shape had just been standing.

"They know." I doubled my pace up the stairs. Lana would've seen the same apparition. Maybe Avery and Anthony, too. If they were already waiting on the roof, it would be down to Anthony to keep both Avery and Lana in place.

The heavy clanging of metal echoed through the stairwell as doors slammed open floors above us. We froze, staring upwards, and Winnie suffocated the flashlight against her shirt.

"In here!" she whispered, leading the way through the nearest door.

Every worst case scenario flooded my brain at once, none more harrowing than the thought of a chip-controlled Wesley hunting us down. We pressed against the stairwell door, listening to feet thunder down the stairs.

"There's another stairwell for custodial staff," Winnie said. "We still might run into someone, but it's less likely."

"Or," Alison stopped her, "we go up a route no one will be using."

She stood in front of the defunct elevator, and her gaze fell on a glass case housing a fire extinguisher. She broke it open, cast the extinguisher to the floor, and reached in to pull out a metal ax.

Winnie's jaw fell as Alison wedged the head of the ax between the elevator doors.

"No way. It's another ten floors! How are we going to open the elevator from inside the shaft if you can barely do it standing in the hall?"

"They're designed to be easier to open from the inside," Mom grunted.

Metal creaked, and the elevator opened to a dark maw. Stale, cold air wafted over us as Mom took Winnie's light to lean into the shaft, shining the light up and then down.

"The carriage is down another five or so floors, so if we fall, it won't be all the way down."

"Still far enough to kill us!" Winnie hissed. "How are we supposed to climb?"

"There's a ladder." Something about Mom's smile was strained, like she was forcing optimism. She knew Adrestus catching us would be much worse than falling to our deaths. She took Winnie's hand. "You can do this, Winnie. You're brave enough and strong enough."

Winnie's shoulders fell, then tensed, and she nodded with new resolve.

"Right. I know."

Mom winked at me and reached around the elevator side.

"You good, Sammy?"

I tucked my hands into my pockets and narrowed my eyes at her.

"Yeah, I'm good."

I was familiar with her powers, but I'd never seen her use them like that. She'd been so casual in the way she'd grabbed Winnie's hand to instill borrowed courage. She was using her powers for good, sure, but it was still manipulative in a way that I wasn't quite comfortable with.

Worry and fear pushed away discomfort as Mom swung into the elevator shaft with the ax in hand and the flashlight secured between her teeth. Winnie followed, grabbing the ladder and pulling herself into the chasm.

I wiped sweaty hands on my pants. The darkness of the elevator shaft was a mercy. At least I wouldn't be able to see how high we were climbing.

I creeped towards the edge, listening to the clanging of the ax against the ladder rungs and watching the flashlight climb into the endless shadows above. I suppressed a final shiver and reached for the ladder.

Winnie's silhouette climbed ahead of me as I fumbled for the rungs in the dark. The fear of falling numbed the pain in my leg, but my arms ached as I clung as close to the ladder as possible. It was impossible to tell how far we had left to go and how far we'd already climbed.

"S-sammmy..."

The voice that rasped in the dark froze me to the ladder, filling me with a dread heavy enough to make my arms shake with the effort of staying upright.

"What the hell was that?" Winnie yelped, and the voice replied from the oppressive dark.

"*Sammy, run...*"

Fingers wrapped around my ankle.

I shrieked, kicking out at the assailant, and my foot made contact. There was a grunt, and dark wind gushed past me, and I clung closer to the ladder, hooking my elbows around the metal for a better hold.

Winnie screamed overhead, and a shadow swooped over her, pulling at her shoulders and hair, trying to dislodge her. In the light of the flashlight, I caught a glimpse of long, dark hair and a vacant expression.

"What's happening?" Mom yelled through a mouthful of flashlight.

"It's Heather!" I called, helplessly watching Winnie fend off Heather's assault.

Winnie smacked Heather's nose, and she dissolved back into the darkness. Mechanical whirring hummed to life, reverberating throughout the entire elevator shaft.

"Is the power back?" I cried.

"Only if Remi is awake!" Winnie called back. "And I'm guessing they've woken her up if Heather's here."

"And Wesley?" I asked.

"Better not to think about it."

Heather materialized out of the shadows to slam into my side. The light of Mom's flashlight grew dimmer as Heather peeled me from the ladder.

Metal groaned overhead as Mom went at the elevator doors with her ax, and I hung onto the ladder with the tips of my fingers.

"I'm s-sorry," Heather gasped. "I can't fight her."

My fingers slipped from the rung, and I toppled backwards off the ladder.

I held tight to Heather's waist as we fell, and for a moment, we hung suspended as she struggled against my hold. Then, she dissolved into shadow once again, and I tumbled through the air.

Hard metal met my body much sooner than I thought it would, and the elevator carriage shuddered and swayed beneath me. The mechanical whirring was louder here, and I groaned as I pushed myself up, dimly aware that I was rising with the elevator.

"Sammy!" Mom's shriek reverberated through the space, and I blinked away the daze that threatened to overwhelm my brain to find her silhouette leaning into the elevator shaft, light pouring from the hall behind her.

"I'm okay!" I called back. "Keep going!"

The light snuffed out, and for a moment I thought the city's power had flickered out again. However, the elevator carriage beneath me continued to rise, slower than usual, but creeping upwards all the same, and I braced myself.

I leapt into the darkened lobby once I was level with the open doors, and while Heather must've sucked all the light from the room, the rustlings of fighting bodies echoed in the dark.

I was crap at fighting blind, but prepared to jump into the fray just as the elevator carriage doors slid open behind me. Flickering, orange light cast my shadow forward on the crimson carpet and bounced off the round desk of the penthouse lobby.

We'd made it to the top floor, but so had Roy Hendricks.

Fire billowed from the carriage, singeing Adrestus's carpet, and I stumbled backwards into Winnie and Heather where they fought. We fell in a tangle of limbs, and Heather slipped away, disappearing in the shifting folds of our dancing shadows.

The fire behind us strengthened, its heat licking at our backs as Roy descended, his entire being engulfed in flame.

"*No, Roy!*" Mom's scream accompanied her ax spiraling through the air. Our backs cooled as Roy ducked out of the way, and metal rang against metal as the ax buried itself in the far elevator wall.

"Alison, this is what Paul wanted! What're you doing?" Roy screamed. Winnie and I scrambled after Mom, hurrying down a portrait-lined hall to the spiral staircase that led to the roof.

If anything, the light from Roy's flames seemed to be keeping Heather at bay, but Roy yelled after us.

"That better not be my daughter throwing away everything she's built these last months?" he jeered. "And Eydis— I should've known! Loyal to no one but yourself!"

Our feet clanged against the metal stairs, and I hoped and prayed that Anthony was in place with Avery and Lana.

Bitter wind and rain greeted us as we reached what had once been a glass-domed penthouse. Now, heavy construction scaffolding created a frame around us, offering little to stem the summer rainstorm that battered the city. The city spread out beneath us in a mosaic of orange and blue lights, electricity once again restored as long as the Whitlock Protocol was in use.

"Sammy!" Anthony's voice cried over the wind. He had Avery in a headlock with one hand clamped over his mouth.

"Keep going!" Mom propelled us forward across the slick tiles. "He's right behind us."

"Where's Lana?" I demanded as we got closer, and Anthony shook his head.

"She took off after Adrestus sent that message." Anthony's eyes grew wide as Roy emerged from the spiral staircase. Rain hissed and sizzled as it met his fire, and he stalked forward, no longer in a hurry now that we were trapped between him and an eighty-seven story drop.

Winnie took up a defensive pose between us and her father, her strawberry-blonde hair whipping in the wind.

"Don't come any closer!" she yelled. Roy's fire towered into the air overhead, making the metal scaffolding groan. He stopped, his glasses glinting from within his suit of flames.

"Be a good girl, Winnie, and stand aside. You might still redeem yourself."

"Don't talk to me about redemption when you joined the man who murdered my mother!"

"This is bigger than our family!" Roy howled back. "I don't want to hurt you, now move."

"At least now that Mom is dead, she doesn't have to be married to *you* anymore!" Winnie screamed in defiance and sprinted at her father. His fires flickered out in surprise and apparent caution, as if afraid he might burn his daughter.

I tried to run after her, but Mom stopped me.

"Leave them. Avery." Mom reached for Avery, and he struggled harder against Anthony's hold. "Let him go, Anthony."

Anthony released my brother, and Avery wailed.

"People are going to die, and it's going to be my fault! Don't make me leave!"

Alison pulled Avery into a rushed embrace, and her fingertips disappeared into his blond, rain-drenched hair. Her chin wavered, but then her jaw tightened.

"You are so brave, my little Viking," she murmured, "but you need to trust us. I won't let anyone die. I promise."

"But—"

"Anthony." Mom reached out to take Anthony's hand. "Your grandmother was Zephyress, yes?"

"Yes, but—"

"And she could fly?"

Anthony tried to pull away, but Mom's grip tightened.

"I can't," he insisted. "I've tried but—"

"You can," Mom promised, and Anthony's arm stiffened. "You know you can fly."

"Mom, don't." I saw what she was doing. It was risky. Avery and Anthony could die.

Flames crackled and popped behind us, and we spun around to see Winnie jumping out of the way of a column of fire, headed directly at us. Anthony pushed me behind him, and a powerful gale hailed from the sky and forced Roy's flames upwards, igniting several construction tarps in spite of the downpour.

The wind raged, and I fell to my knees, holding onto a pillar of metal scaffolding. Roy went reeling backwards, sliding on the slick, rain-soaked roof, unable to anchor himself in Anthony's gale while Mom had Avery in her arms again. Either rain or tears tracked her cheeks. It was impossible to tell which.

Her mouth formed the words "*I love you*", and then she was pushing her son towards Anthony.

Anthony took Avery in his arms, and wind pulled at their hair. Avery glanced back at Mom over Anthony's shoulders, and I reached out, screaming for Anthony to stop as he leapt from the roof and disappeared over the lip.

Time froze, and I no longer felt the storm battering my face or the heat of Roy's growing flames at my back as I waited, choking on a silent scream of terror.

Mom had sent Anthony and Avery to their deaths.

"What did you do?" I sobbed, watching the edge of the roof. Six seconds. Adrestus had said it takes six seconds to fall to the cement.

"I gave Anthony what he needed to get them both out of here."

I shook my head. She'd been wrong. Just because his grandmother could fly, did not mean—

A silhouette rose on the wind, outlined by the orange city lights, hair flying in the gale. I could just barely make out Avery's face, and his outstretched arm reaching for his mother as Anthony carried them both on the wind, away from this hell.

Winnie cried out in pain behind me, and I spun around to see her on the wet tiles, her triumphant father standing over her with a cape of flames licking off his back.

"For as much as you and your sister fought," Roy growled, "it's a wonder neither of you ever realized how similar you are."

Winnie kicked out at Roy, but his boot collided with her ribs, and she slid across the tiles. Again, I tried to rush to her aid, and, again, Mom held me back.

"A couple of quitters, too cowardly and weak to rise up and meet their destinies!" Roy continued. "You made a name for yourself despite being a Beta! You did that here! With Adrestus! And I was *proud* when I'd seen what you'd accomplished! And then you run away on the eve of your victory? I raised you better than this!"

"You didn't raise me at all!" Winnie struggled to her feet and charged again. Her fist made contact with Roy's face, and his fires flickered.

"Who trained you every day of your childhood?" Roy snarled. "Who gave up his own career as a hero to make you strong?"

"Pitting me against Amanda isn't the same as raising me!" Winnie lunged, disappearing behind metal scaffolding. Roy adjusted, prepared for her attack, but she double-backed the other way, swinging back around to clock Roy under his chin.

He fell back in the rain, landing on his back on the tiles.

"You could've been great, Winnie," he hissed. "Instead, you chose Eydis."

Winnie laughed at the storm, her father at her feet.

"I *am* great. That's the whole point. You thought I was a waste of time and space, but here I am. A goddess!" But for all her talk, when she turned to Mom with wide, scared eyes, Winnie looked more than anything like a child begging for an adult's guidance. "Where's Lana? How am I going to escape if—"

"Eydis, watch out!" Lana shrieked overhead, and I looked up to see her dive through the maze of scaffolding straight for Mom. Mom braced herself, and Lana slammed into her. They slid across the roof in a tangle of limb and wing, and Lana came out on top, pinning Mom beneath her. "Are you girls okay? You did great cornering her—"

She froze, her hands still pining Mom's wrists against the tiles.

"I'm on your side," Mom insisted. "You're on *our* side, and Winnie needs your help."

"No, you escaped, you—" Lana shook her head and fell off of Mom.

Mom kept her grip on Lana as she pulled herself to her knees.

"Adrestus is evil. You're escaping. Take Winnie. Get her somewhere safe."

"Evil?" Her voice quivered.

"You deserve so much better, Lana."

"Don't listen to her," Roy groaned. Winnie turned back to us as Roy called after her. "If you don't stop, they'll force me to hurt you, Winnie! They put one of those damn chips in my neck. They won't let me go easy on you forever."

Winnie ignored her dad and continued her sprint across the rooftop, her cloak billowing out behind her.

"Winnie, no!" Roy twitched, coming to his feet, fighting some unseen force. The city lights blipped, blinking off and on in a single wave of light that rippled across the island, and Roy's fire ignited brighter than ever.

Remi was in control.

A ball of fire that melted metal scaffolding seared across the rooftop. Winnie looked back and watched it bear down, stopping when she saw she couldn't outrun it.

I shrieked a warning that wouldn't help her.

But a dark shape impeded the flame, lifting Winnie up and out of the fire's trajectory. Lana held Winnie in her arms as she flew through the scaffolding, high over Schrader Tower, until she disappeared into the lowest hanging rain clouds.

Roy screamed in fury and scaffolding fell around him, landing with heavy clangs that rang out over the city.

"You don't know what you've done, Alison!" Roy roared. He pointed a flaming hand in my direction. "And *you! You've* been playing all of us! This entire time! When he hears you've shown your true colors, he will turn your bones into the foundation of his dawning empire!"

I staggered away, feeling the wind tug at my back as I neared the building's edge. The charade was over. Mom, Wesley, and I would all suffer for it. Mom took up a stance between Roy and me.

"Roy," she begged, "this isn't you."

"Alex turned you soft," Roy hissed. "You lost sight of what we fought for."

"And what were we fighting for?"

"A better world! One where we would bring peace and be praised for doing so! A world where Paul could've lived!"

"Is that what Adrestus promised you after he killed Val?"

"It's what Adrestus promised *Paul!*" Roy roared, flames building. "Paul believed in him so why shouldn't I? Because if I don't— Alison, I have nothing left!"

Mom dropped her fists and scoffed.

"Winnie was right. Thank god Val isn't alive to see this. I'd say she wouldn't recognize the man you've become, but honestly, Roy, I don't think she'd recognized you in a long time."

Scaffolding bent and fell in Roy's wake, morphed by the heat of his fire. I grabbed Mom's wrist and stepped closer to her.

"Mom," I whispered. There was no escape. Not unless Anthony or Lana came back, and even then, I couldn't leave without Wesley.

"It'll be alright, Sammy." She held me close as we faced Roy together.

"If you won't stand with me, Alison, then I will watch you and your pseudo-daughter both burn on the funeral pyre of the old world."

"Mom, I'm sorry," I choked. At least Avery was safe. At least Fleming would be warned by Winnie.

"It's okay, Sammy. I won't let him tell Adrestus that you helped us." Mom took my face in her hands, and her eyes filled with tears that reflected the city lights. "You've been the perfect daughter."

She leaned forward to kiss my forehead.

Every holiday, every family dinner, every vacation, every lazy Saturday spent doing puzzles on the kitchen linoleum of a house I'd never actually lived in. Denting Dad's car with my bike. Christmas in a power outage. Scraping all the skin off my knees and elbows when I crashed my new skates, and crying as Mom cleaned the dirt and grit from the gashes.

Every fake memory, every day that had never happened, every bit of Samantha Havardson's wonderful, ordinary, invented life rushed back.

"Mom?" I whispered. She pulled away.

"The perfect daughter," she repeated, and then threw herself at Roy while the memories flooded my brain.

"Alison, don't—" Roy screamed, and his light burned brighter, swallowing Mom.

"NO!" I ran after her until the heat was unbearable, and I was forced to my knees. The city lights flickered and died, powering down once again, and the fire snuffed out, leaving two smoldering figures. Despite the rain thundering against the tiles and the soft crackling fires of the ignited tarps that flapped in the wind, the rooftop felt silent. "Mom?"

I crawled forward, watching the rain bounce off charred skin, and horror rose in my throat at the sight of my adoptive mother's burned body. I pulled her into my arms, clinging to wild hope that I might be able to save her.

"Mom, please, wake up. Please." I couldn't be left alone on another roof. I couldn't lose another parent.

Roy groaned and sat up, looking at Mom in my arms. He removed his glasses to wipe the tears from his eyes.

"What a waste. I'm sorry, Eydis," he murmured. "You fought so well. And she wasn't really your mother, after all. And think of how proud Adrestus will be when he hears what you've done."

I choked on a sob at Roy's words. He had no memory of my hand in the escape. Mom had altered Roy's mind, rewriting the events of the night, saving me and Wesley from a grisly fate.

Her final gambit had been that of a hero and that of a mother who loved her daughter.

42

Descent

I didn't know if Anthony, Avery, and Winnie had made it to safety. I didn't know if Heather was okay. I didn't know where they'd taken Mom's body.

I stared at the wall of Mira's apartment in a numb daze with dried blood and rain tangling my hair. The room was a revolving door of Adrestus's soldiers reporting on the failing manhunt for my friends, but the buzz in my head made it impossible to keep track of who had come through.

Adrestus was there, that much I did know. He paced through the room, barking orders as Mira lurked in the kitchen. Roy stood nearby, sporting a blackening eye, put there by Adrestus when he'd first relayed the night's events to the warrior.

However, Adrestus's fury at having lost nearly half of his Pantheon gave way to horrible mirth when Roy told him how Mom had fallen. It was amazing how many details she'd been able to download into his head before succumbing to the flames. The numb buzz in my head dulled as I listened to Roy describe how I'd captured Mom, how she'd begged me to spare her, and how I'd denounced her motherhood before pushing her into Roy's fire.

The sound of Adrestus's cold laughter pried my calloused heart open.

"Incredible," he murmured, stopping his pacing to take my chin in hand and lift my gaze to his. I couldn't let him see my rage, but I refused to act proud of my invented accomplishments. I stared back, blank and cold. "My Scourge Queen has certainly returned, then. Ruthless. Like you were when I first found you."

I swatted his hand away, and he recoiled in surprise.

"I don't like being touched." My voice was hoarse and my jaw sore from clenching it.

"Four members of my Pantheon are gone. You may have proved your loyalty to be true, but if it weren't for the fact that I need you on stage in front of the world's leaders in seven hours, I would have you beaten for your failures."

"I did what I could."

He reached for my face again, and I tried to lean away but wasn't fast enough. His fingers clamped around my cheek, digging into my skin.

"And it wasn't enough." He pushed my face away, but the sting of his fingers was hardly noticeable through the roar in my ear pounding a war drum's tattoo. "Go sleep. I need you alert at the Peace Summit. Without Aetos, my plans are changing, and you've proven yourself ruthless enough to bring them to fruition."

Adrestus and the followers he had yet to send into the city marched from the room. Roy rushed to make sure he was next to Adrestus, following him into the hall with the others until the door slammed, and I was left alone in the apartment with Mira.

As contentious as things could be with Winnie, the apartment felt more dangerous without her.

"So you killed your mother?" Mira lilted out of the kitchen. The dark hid the dark circles of fatigue that weighed on her face, but she walked like gravity pulled heavier on her.

"It was Roy."

"His name is Hephestae now." She stopped with one foot on the bottom step of the staircase, and for a moment, the only sound was the rain battering the massive window behind me. "Though I suppose, if I've learned anything from you, it's that names do nothing to change the person. You're just the same as you were."

"What's that supposed to mean?" Suppressed rage threatened to boil over.

"It means I shouldn't be surprised you killed your mother after what you did to the first one."

"The story about me killing my family in Iceland is a lie," I scowled. "And you don't know me."

Mira's laugh was bitter in the dark.

"I know you better than you know yourself, amnesiac."

Something tickled at the back of my head, something I couldn't quite grasp but concerned me all the same.

"If names don't matter," I asked, pushing the strange feeling away, "what was yours before you became Mira?"

"I've always been Mira," she snarled, suddenly defensive. "And tomorrow I become the right hand of the leader of the New Dominion."

She stalked upstairs, her long white hair swishing with every step.

"Will you, though?" I asked, and I savored the way she turned around slowly, deliberately, furiously. "*I'm* the Scourge Queen, not you."

"You," Mira's voice mingled with the pounding rain, "you are nothing more than a pretty trophy in a crown."

And she whisked into her bedroom, leaving me alone in the dark, which felt all the more oppressive with the light of Roy's murderous fire still burning on the inside of my eyelids.

I watched the sunrise from Mira's couch, cradling the hoodie I'd stolen from Mom's closet. It was the same one I'd worn onto the island, and despite nearly being drowned in the museum fountain while wearing it, it still smelled like her. I breathed in her scent and let a calm fury move into the place of numb disbelief. Adrestus was done taking everything from me. This would end today.

Lana may have been gone, but the ghastly updates she'd made to my costume remained, and I avoided my reflection in Winnie's bedroom mirror as I got dressed. She'd built my Scourge Queen costume on top of the tattered remains of my team uniform, leaving the black undershirt and its missing sleeve as well as the dark torso armor.

I rubbed the shoulder pads where she'd painted over the number "12". Even with the addition of leather armguards, a cloak of black fur, and my dark steel circlet, it felt poetic knowing that underneath it all, I'd be in my uniform when I struck down Adrestus's plans.

Mira had to help me with my make-up and hair, and I sat in stoic silence as she braided tawny tangles back into a wild ponytail and painted heavy liner over my eyes that made the gray of my irises appear cold.

She left the apartment in her own ethereal get-up, dressed in a floor-length red satin dress with a slit up to her waist and her long, white hair braided up in an elaborate twist.

I waited until the door slammed shut before lifting my new sword from where I'd laid it out on Winnie's bed. The dark metal glinted in the morning light that seeped in through the window, reflecting a sense of foreboding off the flat of the blade. Even if he was immortal, if I saw my shot to take out Adrestus, I wouldn't hesitate to make him taste the steel he'd armed me with.

Downstairs, I slid the sword into my uniform's new leather scabbard as I gave the apartment space one last glance.

I did not intend on coming back.

The hall was empty, though sounds of rustling whispered on the other side of the doors that lined the corridor. The whole city would be waking up and preparing for the Peace Summit, ready to watch New Delos step into the sun as a newly minted, fully fledged country.

"Sammy!"

Wesley's call squeezed my chest, but I ignored him, pushing my way into the stairwell, steeling myself for the long walk down to the ground floor. Wesley caught the door before it could close behind me.

"Sammy, what happened—"

I raised my gaze to his, grimacing at his Ares get-up, designed to look like Paragon's old costume, though in shades of black instead of white.

One of Paul's old capes trailed off Wesley's shoulders, and he wore his glasses over the black domino mask secured to his face.

"Are you going to be okay?" I asked. He rubbed the back of his neck, making his red cape ripple. "The chip—"

"I'm not worried. You shouldn't be, either." He came down the steps to meet me and held me by my shoulders. I raised a hand to his, feeling smooth carbon-fiber beneath my fingertips. "You look—"

He stopped himself, blushing beneath his mask.

"Ridiculous?" I whispered.

"Last night," he tried again. "Miles told me. I'm—"

I pressed into him, no longer caring if someone caught us. The game was just about over anyway.

"I'm okay." I searched for the reassuring sound of his heartbeat beneath the dark Paragon uniform. "And I'm going to kill him."

"I know," he murmured, and fingers ran through my ponytail. "But without Everly's Immortality Cure—"

"I can kill him over and over." My fingers clenched, balling Paragon's cape into fists against Wesley's back. There it was. His heartbeat. Thumping in my ear. Grounding me.

"I know, but—"

"But nothing!" I stomped down the stairs, my heavy boots echoing against the concrete steps. Wesley hurried after me, jumping down the last three steps to stand on the landing below.

"We don't want to mess this up," he said carefully.

"I mess things up?" I shouldered past him to continue down the next flight of stairs.

"No, but you're passionate—"

"I don't know what's going to happen," I admitted. "All I know is I want this to be over."

"You and me both."

Wesley and I both jumped as Heather came around the turn in the stairs ahead of us in a skin-tight white suit and gold chest plate under a hooded cape of ivory. Her dark hair stood out against the fabric, and her cheeks were pink and blotchy with burns.

"Dammit, Heather," Wesley seethed, "don't jump out at us like that."

"I thought you had super hearing." She raised an eyebrow at him, and it disappeared under the hem of her hood. She took the stairs two at a time, falling into my arms and squeezing me.

"I'm so sorry, Sammy. Last night, I— How long have you been faking it?"

Heat rose in my cheeks.

"A while."

"And you kept it a secret?"

"I needed to be convincing. And it's not like you would've had a choice anyway when you attacked last night."

She lifted a hand to prod at the burns on her face.

"I'm not going to have a choice if this summit goes sideways, either." She frowned. "Same with Wesley."

A door slammed some number of stories overhead, and Wesley raised a finger to his lips and ushered us down the steps.

"I have a plan for that," he whispered, pulling a white paper sheet from under his dark sleeve.

He passed the sheet to Heather. She stopped in shock, but Wesley beckoned for her to keep moving. I looked closer and realized it was a sticker roll, sporting three white patches that clung to the paper.

"Mira's paralytic?" I hissed.

"If you feel Remi taking over, you'll have a few seconds before she's in total control. Hide those somewhere you can reach them, and when you feel her—"

"Slap it on," Heather finished for him, tucking the patches under her sleeve.

"But you said the patches don't work well on you." I looked at Wes.

"Neither does the implant chip," he murmured.

"But if the paralytic wears off—"

"I'll be fine, Sammy."

"And what exactly is the plan?" Heather asked.

"The moment Adrestus tries to kill someone, we step in." I shrugged.

"And if Wesley and I are on the floor paralyzed, you'll be on your own?"

"By now, Winnie should be with Fleming and others, telling them where to be today. I won't be alone," I said, or rather hoped. I wrung my hands, trying not to imagine a scenario in which the team didn't show.

"Fleming will be there," Wesley assured me, sensing my unease. "He hasn't failed us yet."

"If he's there, it'll be to kill me himself." Even if everything went according to plan, even if we were victorious over Adrestus at long last, I had a lecture waiting for me. Not to mention, Fleming's ire would be nothing compared to Naomi's.

We finished the descent in uneasy silence. Somewhere around the fiftieth floor, Wesley's hand found mine, and he didn't let go until we were outside the museum office.

"With any luck, we won't be climbing back up," Wesley tried to joke. Heather grimaced and pushed through the heavy metal door.

The office was a mess of activity. Interns bustled back and forth, carrying summit programs and tiny flags. Jamie conducted the scene from atop Miles's desk, paying no attention to Miles seated beneath. He had his hands full powering a hand-cranked phone battery that connected to his earpiece by a thin wire.

"What the *hell* are you wearing?" Jamie's indignant screech brought the chaos to a halt, and the only sound was Miles talking into his earpiece.

"Spain sits between France and Portugal. Why— ? Check a map, that's where it *is*...I have never once heard of the country Andorra. Where—"

"Did you hear me?" Jamie stepped off the desk, sticking the landing despite the stiletto heels that stuck out from under the hems of her pantsuit. "I said—"

"We heard you." I couldn't look Jamie in her face. The other interns were all in formal businesswear, and I was wearing a whole bottle of eyeliner. "This is what we were told to wear."

"Not by me, you weren't!"

"No, Miss Ratcliffe. I'm afraid I made that call."

Adrestus's voice, echoing softly in the confines of his metal helmet, sent a chill down my spine, and Wesley, Heather, and I stumbled to make way as he stepped out of the stairwell.

The lamplight of the office glinted off his black armor, throwing the ridges in the metal that curved around every muscle into relief. His red helmet plume and matching cape fell into shadow, taking on the color of thick, rich blood, and his face was lost under the dark cover of his helmet. His right hand played with the bronze hilt that stuck out from his scabbard, but Jamie crossed her arms and set her jaw.

"And why is the local manager of Party Halloween telling my interns what to wear on my big day?" Manicured nails wrinkled the fabric of her blazer sleeves.

Adrestus removed his helmet, and soft, black curls fell in his face. Jamie's composure finally cracked, and she blinked in surprise, though she kept her arms crossed.

"Your big day?" Adrestus grinned, and I recognized the face he made anytime he was about to take pleasure in someone else's pain. "Dear, you've done a stellar job helping me prepare, but this is my great dawn, not yours."

"Dr. Cunningham?" Jamie stuttered. "Look, you're a respectable employee of Schrader Industries and obviously have a flair for costume design, but my father is the Prime Minister and—"

"John Ratcliffe is a puppet who only survived up till now because he got lucky." Adrestus, with his helmet under one arm, unsheathed his sword. Jamie took a stumbling step backwards, but not before Adrestus managed to hook the string of her necklace on the tip of the blade. "You've been a good girl so far, Miss Ratcliffe. I'd hate for you to mess that up today of all days and end up as useless as your mother."

Jamie's eyes widened, and I flinched when a gloved hand pressed against the small of my back. I was very suddenly grateful for the heavy, fur cloak and the extra barrier it offered between me and Adrestus's touch. He guided me forward, and I glanced back at Wesley, who followed with Heather.

Jamie finally found her voice as we reached the far door of the office.

"At least make Havardson take off the crown. It's insulting."

Adrestus stopped, but instead of looking at Jamie, he trained his hungry gaze on me. His blue eye lingered on my crown then dropped to my face.

"Oh, Miss Ratcliffe," he grinned. "What's the point of having pets if I don't get to put them in whatever I like?"

The streets between Schrader Tower and the hotel were eerily still. We drove through empty roads, and I peered into abandoned windows and storefronts from the back of a town car. Adrestus sat with his sword and helmet in his lap, his red plume spilling over on Mira's knees. She had managed to wiggle into the backseat before me, eager to take the middle seat in her long, red dress. I was more than happy to let her be the barrier between Adrestus and me, and I sat with my own sword balanced between my legs, its tip digging into the floor of the car.

"It'll be fine," Mira said in a low purr, and Adrestus grunted, craning his neck to see the road. "The Whitlock Protocol works. We have at least sixty—"

"It would've been easier with Aetos," he growled.

"It would've been messier." Mira shrugged, her satin covered shoulders sliding against my shoulder armor. "You updated your speech, I assume?"

Adrestus grunted again, and the car turned a corner.

The streets lit up. Banners hung off every building side. New Delos citizens lined the sidewalks waving flags and cheering, and up ahead, the hotel glittered in the morning light.

The pavement here was cleaner. Windows glowed with life and electricity, and flags of every country decorated the street lamps.

"How do they look?" Adrestus murmured.

"Positively jubilant," Mira replied, and Adrestus nodded in satisfaction.

"Good. Gregor's done well."

"Gregor's doing this?" I craned around Mira to look at Adrestus.

"Some of it," Adrestus admitted. He grinned out the window. "Do you know how difficult it is to reverse salt-water damage? To make a recently drowned city look new and clean? And don't get me started on the people."

I looked back at the cheering crowds who pressed up against barriers as they shouted and smiled. Avery had mentioned that inculcator tricks like the ones he and Gregor were capable of wouldn't work on Adrestus.

"And what do the crowds look like to you?" I dared to ask.

He paused, as if savoring the question, and his grin glinted white.

"Terrified." And he continued to wave.

43

World Domination, Plain and Simple

The train of town cars carrying Adrestus's Pantheon pulled up to the back entrance of the Schrader Hotel. The building's white-stone face was broken by a massive window glittering across the top floors in the morning sun and reflecting the blue of the ocean. I craned my neck to look up at it, and a black-gloved hand found my shoulder.

"The Crystal Amphitheater," Adrestus sighed in my ear. "That's where you and I will ascend our thrones, one way or another."

Peace Summit staff intermixed with the Pantheon, giving those of us in gaudy costumes a wide berth as they bustled about in preparation for the oncoming event. I tried to find Wesley and Heather in the crowd, but Adrestus steered me forward into the back halls of the hotel.

The back halls of Schrader Hotel were just as opulent as the front lobby, sporting plush carpet and gold-leaf crown molding. Gold-plated chandeliers lit the way, and I wondered if the electricity was real or another trick of Gregor's.

However, we came to a stop at a row of elevators, and Adrestus held me at his side as we waited for the gilded doors to slide open. I caught a glimpse of red cape to my right just before Mira steered Wesley into the adjacent lift.

Adrestus pushed me into ours, and the doors shut before anyone could join us. The elevator shifted, and Adrestus, his hand still on my shoulder, leaned over so I could feel his humid breath against my neck when he spoke.

"I may have one tiny task for you," he growled. "If you don't want to see Ares become redundant in the next phase, you'll do exactly as I ask. You did well against Alison last night, but you aren't finished yet."

The elevator doors slid open to a new corridor. This one was louder, and voices buzzed out of sight. Adrestus stepped around me to exit the elevator, but paused to look back at me.

"If I couldn't have Ignatia, I'm glad it could be you."

I stumbled after him, gripping the hilt of my sword and ignoring the stares of a nearby group of interns. The voices down the hall were too loud. Mira had said there were sixty Epsilons, all presumably with chips. When they were activated, when Adrestus put his plan into action, Wesley and Heather would paralyze themselves, and I'd be left to somehow fend off an amphitheater of Epsilons as I went after Adrestus.

I searched for hints of the team, some sign that Naomi and Fleming were nearby and that I wouldn't be fighting Adrestus and his legion alone. My chest armor was too tight, and I couldn't breathe against its confines.

"What's wrong?" Wesley appeared in front of me, his hands hovering over my shoulders, not daring to touch me with Adrestus nearby.

"Nothing." Everything. We were in over our heads. "It's just— I have a really bad feeling."

His green eyes wavered.

"I know," he said. "Me, too."

His honesty was more reassuring than placations, and I nodded. Wesley— strong, powerful, perfect Wesley— was scared, too.

A woman in a tight bun and pencil skirt yelled at us to line up outside a heavy door of polished wood. I joined Adrestus in the line-up when the woman called my name, just ahead of John Ratcliffe. He was the only Pantheon member in normal attire, opting for a suit more appropriate for a Prime Minister.

Jamie stood with him, tapping her stiletto heel against the marble floor. Adrestus was deep in hushed conversation with Adrian Schrader, so he paid me no attention, leaving me vulnerable to Jamie's attacks.

"You think you can come in here and upstage me today of all days?" she hissed.

"Jamie," her father warned. He gave me a nervous side-eye that dropped to the hilt of my sword.

"I don't know what's going on with you and the curator, but you aren't special, Samantha," she snarled. "You never were, and I don't know who the hell you think you are—"

"An undead Viking warrior."

Jamie blinked in surprise, but quickly covered the look with a scowl.

"What the hell—"

"You want to know who I am." I shrugged, and played with my sword hilt. "My real name is Eydis, and I'm the Scourge Queen who killed Adrestus a thousand years ago."

"That's the stupidest—"

"Jamie." Mr. Ratcliffe gave her the tiniest shake of his head. A strange, new feeling blossomed in my chest. John Ratcliffe was scared of me.

Jamie opened her mouth to spit a fresh retort, but rich, brass tones crescendoed in the amphitheater in the next room, signaling the start of New Delos's national anthem. Adrian Schrader straightened his tie and pushed forward into the dazzling light that spilled from the massive windows of the Crystal Amphitheater.

"If your old self could see you now," Adrestus crooned, pulling his helmet over his face, "Eydis, I think she'd simply *die*."

He followed Adrian Schrader, and I twisted to give Wesley a final look where he stood near the end of the line. Jamie pushed me from behind, and I staggered into the blinding light of the amphitheater.

We entered through a side door that let us out directly onto a stage that stood at the bottom of tiered rows of long, thin tables adorned by national flags. Morning light flooded the amphitheater from the three story window that stretched behind the stage up into a dome of crystal that spat flecks of iridescent light around the seats.

The polite applause of the gathered leaders and ambassadors hitched at the sight of Adrestus in his armor, but then John Ratcliffe and Jamie filed out behind us, and the applause renewed in honor of the Prime Minister, drowning out the sounds of the fountains that gurgled on either end of the stage.

The clapping staggered again as the rest of the Pantheon followed, each in their own themed get-up. Roy was in a black armored suit and face mask, similar to the outfit they'd forced Amanda into when she'd donned the mantle of Hephestae. Mira looked more ready for a movie premier than a war with her backless dress and long red sleeves that clung to every contour of her biceps and triceps.

Next to her, Wesley kept his face forward, scanning the crowds, assessing the situation as the National Anthem continued. I probably should've been doing the same, but somehow, looking at him and Heather bracing for the coming fight felt more important in the moment.

Mr. Ratcliffe and Jamie approached a podium, their hands placed solemnly over their hearts as they beamed up at the green and white flag that hung from the crystal ceiling. I tried to take in the crowd, but the sea of faces and flags blurred in the bright light.

The anthem ended on a sustained note, and the applause swelled. Mr. Ratcliffe waved at the amphitheater, signaling for everyone to take a seat. Cushioned chairs lined the window, and I followed Adrestus's lead when he sat, but had to wrestle with the scabbard of my sword to make my way into my own seat.

The applause died, punctuated by the resounding slam of the heavy entrance doors locking us all in the amphitheater at the top of the sloping steps. I took a steadying breath. This was it.

"It is the greatest honor of my short career as the first Prime Minister of New Delos to welcome each and every one of you to our small and humble nation." Ratcliffe ran his hands along the top of the podium. "To set the mood for the rest of the Peace Summit, I would like to take this moment to honor and assure you all that I will uphold the standards with which you have governed. Your people and your lands will be in the best of hands."

A nervous titter rippled across the amphitheater. Ratcliffe bowed his head in an insincere laugh and raised his hands in apology.

"I know, I know. It's hard to take me seriously. After all, what experience do I have in global domination, right?"

The laughs were more forthcoming this time, but Jamie took a step back from her father.

"That said," Ratcliffe wiped an invisible tear of mirth from his cheek, "I am sorry to announce that the week of negotiations and treaty drafting we'd advertised won't be happening. Instead, we'll be discussing the terms of your surrender."

No one laughed this time, instead casting each other nervous glances behind their desks.

"What's wrong?" Metal clinked as Adrestus rose from his seat. The energy in the room had been cold before, but as Adrestus took center stage, something about the faces lining the rows and rows of seats turned downright hostile. "What don't you understand about fair trade?"

"Fair trade?" An older woman in a navy pantsuit stood up in the front row. "You hijack American territory, sell us back our own product, and expect us to hand over our sovereign lands? Is that your 'fair trade'? "

"Your product?" Adrestus jeered.

"The Epsilon Initiative was developed on American soil."

"My dear, there is no American soil here. Just the titanium that this city was built on."

"By drilling into *our* continental shelf!" The woman's nostrils flared. "And that's enough with the 'my dear'. You will refer to me as Madam President or not at all."

"I thought this might happen," Adrestus crooned, and I recognized the silky quality to his voice that always preceded his outbursts. "I figured you all might be reluctant to hand over what is rightfully mine, so let me lay out your options."

"Rightfully yours?" A new voice spoke up near the back of the room. "And who the hell are you? We came to do business with Ratcliffe, not some freak in a costume."

Adrestus removed his helmet and shook out his black curls.

"I'm the god who is laying claim to this earth. I've walked its soil since before your nations were even the smallest iota of a concept. I've watched mankind misuse this land and each other for two millennia and finally, I'm putting an end to it and claiming headship over your nations."

Yelling broke out through the amphitheater, many of the emissaries now on their feet, though some of them stood unnaturally rigid with wide, terrified eyes. I looked to Adrestus, but all I could make out at this angle was the upturned edge of a cheshire grin.

Movement in my periphery caught my attention, and I glanced over to see Wesley standing at the ready next to Mira while Heather slumped over the cushioned arm of her seat.

The Whitlock Protocol had been activated, and Wesley hadn't been fast enough.

I was alone.

"If you do not concede," Adrestus boomed over the fray, "every dissenter will die."

The angry shouts cut, and I felt hundreds of eyes sweep over the stage, taking in the costumed Pantheon. They thought we were the weapons, still unaware of their frozen comrades.

"If we die, you die, too," the so-called Madam President asserted, squaring her padded shoulders. "Our governments will retaliate with everything—"

"Now that *would* be frightening," Adrestus teased, "if it weren't for the fact that you have no way to communicate with your countries as long as you're here."

"But the livestreams—"

"I have an army of super-powered individuals, and you think I don't have anyone who can trick a camera? I assure you, the livestreams are playing out across the globe right now, showing a very peaceful, very jubilant Peace Summit opening ceremony."

Gregor watched the proceedings with mild interest. Back in October, when Winnie had hunted me through the museum, Adrian Schrader's voice had taunted me as I ran. No one believed me because Adrian

Schrader had been at a televised event on the mainland that very night. Perhaps that had been Gregor's powers at work, too.

"Prime Minister Ratcliffe!" The president pressed her hands against her desk. "What is this? This is *your* country!"

"His country?" Adrestus snarled. "Have you not yet realized who I am? You come here, begging for powers, not so much as blinking when the Epsilon Procedure kills so many of those who undergo it, and you didn't bother learning our stories? Here on New Delos, we all know the legend of the Apex and how they came to be. The tale of Adrestus, the Father of All Apex, and his fall at the hand of the Scourge."

His sweeping gesture towards me brought with it the many stares of the world's greatest leaders, and I shrank in my seat.

"It's just a story, you say," Adrestus growled. "Maybe if you weren't all so damn shortsighted you might've seen that I've been here all along."

"You expect us to believe—" Madam President started.

"It doesn't matter what you believe!" Adrestus laughed. "What do gods do to insolent nations? Look at any creation story. Zeus became angry with humanity and flooded the earth. The man Deucalion and his ark only survived thanks to a warning from Prometheus. Then there's the Epic of Gilgamesh, and Manu, and Noah. Over and over, it's always the same. Men turn their back on their god, so he wipes them out with a flood. Will you dare turn your back on me?"

Stunned silence buzzed through the amphitheater.

"You can't flood the earth," someone shouted from the middle rows. "That's not—"

"Every other creation myth starts with a flood. Why shouldn't mine? New Delos is Deucalion's Ark, preserving my loyal few for the voyage into our new world." Adrestus pointed at the president, and then beckoned her onstage. "If you wish to spare the earth my wrath, then you will be the first to kneel."

Two of her security detail, their movements rigid, yanked her towards the stage. She struggled and screamed, eliciting more panic through the amphitheater. The delegates closest to the doors tried to make a run for it, but orange flames erupted around the room's perimeter.

Epsilons wrestled ambassadors back into their seats, and Adrestus kicked the podium over to make room for the president center stage. Adrestus couldn't kill the president of one of the most powerful countries. He—

He could. And he would. And I was helpless to watch.

"It's time I introduce you all to one of my oldest associates." He forced the woman to her knees and beckoned me forward. "Eydis the Scourge Queen. The only person to ever come close to killing me."

The president looked over her shoulder at me, her eyes wide and horrified, reflecting the red of the flames that continued rage at the room's perimeter. I stared back, unable to move on legs of lead.

"Get up." Adrian Schrader's hand clamped down on my shoulder, and he pushed me from my seat and propelled me forward.

Adrestus stepped aside to make room for me behind the kneeling president.

"She may have nearly killed me, but she's become the perfect pet. May she serve as a warning to you all. You can try to go against me, but I will tame you one way or another." Adrestus's bright blue iris glinted. "Eydis, your sword."

My shaking hand withdrew the dark sword from its scabbard.

"Madam President," Adrestus crooned, "do you forsake your office and relinquish the United States of America into my hands?"

The woman's body quaked, but she kept her head high.

"I do not."

"Then perish. Eydis?"

I looked back at Adrestus blankly, my sword in my hand.

"I—" I croaked. My mouth was too dry. I couldn't talk. Adrian Schrader loomed next to me in a silent threat.

"Remember Tiberius, Eydis," Adrestus snarled.

I glanced back at Wesley, still frozen and staring forward. He'd told me not to worry about him. Mira rubbed her fingers together, as if preparing the toxins brewing beneath her skin.

Wesley had told me he had the situation with his neck chip handled.

He'd been wrong.

Blood crescendoed in my ears. I'd killed before. In Iceland. To protect my family.

I could kill again.

I swung the blade, deaf to the screams erupting throughout the amphitheater, and I braced for the familiar weight of meat and bone on the other end of my weapon.

My blade stopped when it met Adrian Schrader's spine, and I ripped it from his abdomen, the metal slick with blood. He looked down at his cloven torso, then back up at me with his trademark grin in place, and the sound of his familiar, booming laugh echoed through the Crystal Amphitheater.

But Adrian Schrader wasn't laughing. The sound came from behind me, and I turned to see Gregor doubled over as he guffawed.

"That settles that, then," he called out, and I was suddenly struck by the fact that I had never once heard Gregor speak. And his voice was exactly that of Adrian Schrader's.

The president scrambled across the stage, as if afraid I might change my mind about sparing her, and Adrian Schrader's grisly visage shimmered out of existence. It all made sense. Why Naomi couldn't feel his emotions. How he seemed to be in two places at once sometimes.

Adrian Schrader had never existed. He'd been one of Gregor's illusions this entire time.

"EYDIS—" Adrestus howled in fury, but I brandished the sword.

"It's Samantha Havardson," I said, "and you never should've trusted me."

44

Reunions

Adrestus's roar of fury ripped through the screams of delegates as the crowd boiled over with panic and chaos. The Epsilon battalion worked to subdue their leaders, and those that broke free were stopped by the fire that crackled at the room's edges.

It was me against the literal world, and my chance to save the delegates rested on my ability to bring Adrestus to his knees before his Pantheon stepped in.

"So Samantha Havardson is back." Bronze whistled against bronze as Adrestus drew his weapon.

I brandished my sword, moving before he could have the first swing.

He batted my attack away, and the force of our meeting blades reverberated through my arms. I stumbled back and hadn't yet regained my bearings when the flat of his blade slapped against the side of my head, and I crumpled to the floor.

"How long have you been deceiving me?" Adrestus murmured, bending over me to wrap his fingers around my face. "You let me believe the Eydis I knew had returned, but perhaps she really is dead."

"I don't stay dead. And *you*," I pried his fingers back, "will never touch me again!"

I sliced my sword upwards, and Adrestus reeled away, stumbling on his cloaks. I rolled back to my feet, but he was already striking, and I prepared to block or dodge or do whatever I needed to survive just a moment longer.

The first blow forced my sword from my hands, leaving my palms stinging and me vulnerable. I froze as I watched the arc of the second swing, helpless to do anything but hope that when I woke up from this next death, I would still have time to save the world from Adrestus's oncoming flood.

I closed my eyes and braced for the sharp sting of bronze, but instead felt the floor drop out from under my feet. My stomach flipped as the room rushed around me, ending in a sudden, jerking halt that brought me to my hands and knees.

The floor rolled, and a deep, threatening rumble echoed outside like thunder. The blue sky outside the window was broken by plumes of dust as several nearby buildings trembled and collapsed. The short quake may have saved me from Adrestus's sword, but New Delos was crumbling.

Adrestus howled at his captive legion from where he'd fallen to the ground.

"Kill her! Kill her, and bring me her body so I can wake her up and kill her again!"

Hands pulled me to my feet, bringing me face-to-face with the wide, scared eyes of an Epsilon wearing a Canadian flag pin on the lapel of her blazer. I couldn't bring myself to fight back, but my hesitation cost me as her fingers sparked, and a jolt of electricity sent me back to the floor. A new Epsilon jumped in to lift me by my collar and fling me off the stage.

My ribs collided with the edge of the bottom step of the amphitheater, and the vaulted crystalline window swirled overhead. I couldn't fight. I was outnumbered. Fleming was supposed to come help. Maybe he'd finally decided I was too much and had abandoned me.

A dark figure blotted out the sky, jumping off the stage to stand over my body. A red cape fluttered at his ankles, and I curled in on myself, bracing for the worst.

Adrestus was going to force Wesley to kill me.

"It's not your fault." I knew Wesley could still hear me despite being under Remi's control. "We tried. It's okay."

But Wesley looked out at the crowd of Epsilons that rushed to surround us.

"No one touches her!" His furious brow and threatening snarl did not look like the horrifyingly passive faces of those under Adrestus's control.

"Wes—"

"I told you not to worry about it." The hint of a smirk tugged at his lips.

I pulled myself to my feet using Wesley's cape, ignoring the aching in my ribs. Adrestus's heavy boots clanked with each footfall as he approached us from the stage, his Pantheon at his back and Jamie cowering at the foot of the window.

"I'd hoped we could be happy in the next era together," Adrestus mused.

"There is no next era." I spat blood at his feet. "I'm going to stop you."

"My dear, I've already won!" Adrestus called out in triumph. "My Epsilons are in control, and within the hour, every major world leader, your *boyfriend*, and you will be dead while Siedon floods the world, wiping out every trace of the old regime. Didn't you feel us drop? New Delos has disengaged from its physical supports. We're sailing to the center of the Pacific ocean, where no one will be able to stop me, and where my people can live in safety until the world is ready to be reclaimed."

So that was why the floor continued to sway underfoot. Good. I'd thought I might be concussed.

"There's still time," I said, not because I believed it, but because I had to make it true. I couldn't let Adrestus kill everyone.

"To what? Take me out here while I'm surrounded by all my strongest and most loyal followers?" But as he said the words, his brow furrowed, and his jaw went slack behind his beard, as if just realizing the flaw in his plan. "Mira, the tower. Who's—"

The doors at the top of the stairs splintered on the other side of Roy's fire. A figure in red and white stepped through the flames, unaffected by their heat, wearing armor designed to look like the Apex team uniform but in Paragon's colors. I'd only seen him in the get-up once before, but even if I hadn't, I would've recognized the tight frown under the helmet visor anywhere.

Fleming had not abandoned me after all.

Now that he stood at the top of the amphitheater, ready to fight a room full of Apex, Epsilon, and one immortal warrior that he didn't stand a chance against, I realized how stupid it had been to think he would ever leave me, no matter how many times I ran away.

Practical, reliable, protective Fleming. We'd probably die here together.

"You've lost, Cunningham!" Fleming roared, and even though I couldn't see his eyes past his helmet, I thought I felt his gaze sweep over me. The flames sizzled and died, and a dozen helmeted Apex rushed in behind Fleming, one of them wielding familiar twin blades of ice. Sergio was here, too. "Your prisoners are free, and the nearest authorities have been made aware of the situation."

"I am the only authority!" Adrestus growled. "And as long as my aurora is up, the only communication on and off the island is—"

Fleming held up an earpiece. Miles's earpiece.

"Your secretary handed this over as soon as we took your tower. Didn't even put up a fight. Something about it not being worth it? It only took one phone call. The world knows what you're doing here."

But Adrestus grinned wider.

"What are they going to do? Nuke us with their leaders still on board the island?" Adrestus teased. "Even if they wanted to, they can't find us, not with the Heart of the City cloaking us from every radar and every satellite. We're invisible. They can't touch us."

Heavy hands wrapped around my shoulders and yanked me onto the stage. I fought against Adrestus's hold as he pulled me against his metal chest plate.

Wesley cried out after me, but didn't dare move as Adrestus already had me in a headlock that felt all too familiar, with one hand wrapped around my forehead and the other grasping my chin.

He was going to snap my neck.

"Drop her!" Fleming shouted.

I pulled at Adrestus's fingers, trying to free my mouth so I could tell the others to fight. Forget about me. They needed to save everyone else.

"Another move, and she dies," Adrestus warned. "I can't guarantee she'll come back. It's been so long since she touched the Lapis. Surely her immortality has almost waned completely. Will you risk it?"

Fleming and his Apex froze, and Wesley stared up at me in horror. I shouted into Adrestus's hand, refusing to give up the fight.

His muscles tensed around my face, and he leaned in to whisper in my ear.

"If this *is* your final death and there is a plane after this one, send my love to Ignatia. Goodnight, my little Scourge—"

I reached back and found the hilt of his sword resting in its scabbard at his hip. It was heavier and broader than either sword I was used to, but I leaned into its weight, dropping the tip of the blade into Adrestus's foot.

He roared in pain as I slit through boot leather, skin, and fragile bone, and his grip on my face broke. I spun away, whirling the heavy blade, and felt the resistance of thigh muscle meeting the bite of bronze.

And then everyone was moving again.

Fleming led the charge towards the stage, and Roy ran to meet him, though his fire did little to impede Fleming's armor. Meanwhile, Wesley leaped at Adrestus while he was distracted by the open gash in his leg. Mira rushed to defend her master, meeting Wesley with outstretched hands.

"Samantha!" Fleming's hoarse bellow echoed over the sounds of fire, electricity, and brawling. "Get Jamie out of here!"

Jamie pressed against the window, hiding behind her hands, as I charged at her. She shook in my arms but was in too much shock to resist as I pulled her after me to the side door where we'd entered.

Heather's limp form twitched where she remained slumped in her chair. I hoped the paralytic wasn't already wearing off.

"But my dad—" Jamie cried, finally digging her heels in as we reached the door. I looked over her shoulder at my friends fighting for their lives. I didn't want to leave them, but if I could save a single person, even if that person was Jamie Ratcliffe, I would have at least done *something*.

"He's fine!" I tugged harder on Jamie's arm, and she fell in step beside me, prioritizing her immediate survival over her father's wellbeing.

"Samantha, what the *hell* is going on? I wasn't— no one told me—"

"Just run!"

She pulled away to rush the elevators and punched the call button.

"Not there!" I dragged her towards the stairwell, wishing I still had my sword. "We'll be sitting ducks in an elevator if the power cuts."

She slipped from her high heels and followed me into the stairwell.

"You're one of them, aren't you?" she accused between heavy, gasping breaths. "An Apex, right?"

"I'm not."

"But you—"

"I told you. I'm an immortal Viking."

"But that's—"

"Stupid?"

"A little. And Dr. Cunningham—"

"Adrestus."

"R-right." Jamie slid to a stop at a landing between two floors. "Also immortal?"

"Keep moving."

She glanced up the stairwell. We'd managed to put several floors between us and the Crystal Amphitheater, but it was far from enough.

"But my dad—"

"He'll be fine. Fleming won't kill your father."

"Fleming?" Jamie blanched. "That wasn't Mr. Fleming!"

"Right. My bad. But we *really* need to keep—"

"And Adrestus said he created the Apex. And Adrestus is the bad guy. So I was right all along!" She put her hands on her hips. "The Apex *are* evil!"

"Apex are just *people*, Jamie!" I grabbed her wrist and pulled her down another flight of stairs. "Being one doesn't make someone evil, the same way *not* being one doesn't make someone good!"

"Wait!" She stopped again, and I whirled on her, weighing the pros and cons of knocking her out and carrying her down the stairs myself.

"We can't—"

"Adrestus said the Epsilon Procedure kills people."

"Yes. As discussed, he is evil. Hence, why we need to *go*."

Jamie stood her ground, wrapping her arms around her blazer, looking at me for the first time with something other than disdain.

"My mom never said goodbye."

"What?"

"My mom," she repeated. "She left after Dad became an Epsilon. She never said goodbye. But what if she wanted to be an Epsilon, too. And then what if—"

She clamped her mouth shut, and her cheek dimpled where I knew she must be biting herself in an attempt to stave off the tears.

"No." I shook my head, though I wasn't sure. "First we get out of here, okay? And then we find her. I promise."

"What do you know?" Hysteria rose in her voice. "You haven't seen your mother in centuries!"

"I had a mother back then," I admitted. "And I had another until last night when the people upstairs killed her, and they will kill us if we don't leave."

"Or I can go back," she murmured. "Dad's up there. If Mom is— Dad will know where she really is."

She took a step back up the stairs.

"No, Jamie!"

"You're one of them!" she hissed. "Sure you're not an Apex, but you're connected. How can I trust you? At least I *know* my dad won't hurt me."

She sprinted back up the stairs, flashing the dirty soles of her bare feet with every step.

"Jamie!" I hollered after her and started to give chase, but then, the lights in the stairwell blinked off.

"I'm so *sick* of the janky electricity on this *janky* island!" Jamie wailed somewhere in the darkness.

I held my breath, straining my ears. My heart stopped when I could still hear the faint buzz of the fluorescent lights.

"The electricity isn't out," I hissed.

"No?" Jamie screeched. "Nothing about this makes you think that maybe you're wrong?"

Jamie's feet slapped against the stairs as she continued her sprint.

"Jamie, get back!"

A shriek ripped through the dark, and Jamie slammed into me from above, sending us both careening down to the next landing. A hand-like tendril wrapped around my ankle and yanked me away, bouncing me down another flight of steps.

"Samantha, make it stop!" Jamie screamed.

"It's Heather!" I slammed into a wall and swiped at the air, making contact with a woven hood. My knuckles collided with a face, but Heather didn't flinch.

"Sorry," I grunted, and wrestled her to the ground, feeling along her sleeves where she'd stashed the paralytic patches.

I might as well have been wrestling water and sand. She melted beneath me before I could find the patches.

"No escaping," Heather rasped, and the sound echoed in the dark as she dematerialized completely, joining with the shadows.

A dreadful cold crept up my fingers, then to my wrists. I shook my hands, trying to regain feeling in them, but it was as if they were no longer there.

She was traveling, jumping through shadows, and she was dragging me with her.

"Jamie," I gushed, "she's taking me. Get out of here. Outside, there will be others. They'll help you."

"You are *not* leaving me surrounded by these freaks!" Jamie found me in the dark and pulled on my hair. "You're staying here!"

Boot-steps hammered up the stairs towards us. Adrestus's people had gotten ahead of us, and now Jamie had no way out.

"Close your eyes!" A feminine voice barked at us in the dark. Jamie let go of my hair, but I didn't heed the warning.

Blinding light brought tears to my eyes and feeling back to my hands. Heather materialized with her hands on my wrists and blinked in the sudden brightness.

A floor below us, a woman with wild, red curls and clothes that hung off her emaciated frame barreled around the corner. I recognized her from the prison floor. Heather's mom was free, and she was here to save her daughter. A second figure joined her, donning the Apex Team uniform. The number "15" was painted on her shoulders, and long, dark box braids trailed out from under her helmet.

Relief, guilt, and nerves left me unable to do anything but stare back blankly.

Naomi probably hated me. She wasn't here for my sake, but to save the world. Nevertheless, she was here.

"I can only take Heather," Mrs. Hisakawa said.

"Do it." Naomi's voice was sharp, and the lights cut from the stairwell once again.

A rushing sound whistled up the stairs, and I instinctively covered Jamie.

"I've got you, darling," Mrs. Hisakawa's voice whispered in the dark. "It'll be okay."

The lights snapped back on. Mrs. Hisakawa and Heather were gone, and where Heather had stood, a small metal chip fell to the stairs.

I leaned over it, inspecting its tiny, spike-like tendrils. Heather's powers were strong, but her mother had finesse that came with decades of practice. She'd shadow-jumped Heather to safety while leaving behind the control chip that has been in her neck.

"Don't touch it," Naomi barked.

"I wasn't going to." I shied away from the chip as Naomi came up the stairs. She looked down at the chip through her visor then crushed it under her boot. I pressed my lips together, ready for her to yell at me for tricking her and leaving her unconscious in the park.

"Nice make-up," she drawled. I lifted a hand to the thick eyeliner that was running down my cheeks with sweat.

"I didn't pick it."

"I can tell." She offered a hand to Jamie.

"How did you find us?" Jamie wrinkled her nose.

"I felt you," Naomi shrugged, her hand still extended. "I've spent enough time with you both to feel you from a distance. I just had to point Mrs. Hisakawa the right direction, and she transported us here, a few floors off, but pretty close."

Jamie looked up at Naomi through narrowed eyes.

"Naomi?" she finally dared to ask.

Naomi dropped her hand and pulled her helmet off.

"Surprised?" Naomi intoned.

"Not really, actually," Jamie sniffed. "You did stop living with me right after Leif Erickson here showed up."

She pushed herself to her feet, and I followed suit.

"Naomi—" I started, but she held up a hand.

"Did you see the others?" She led the way down the stairs, taking them two at a time, and Jamie hurried to keep up with us, no longer interested in returning to the fight upstairs.

"They showed up just in time. Fleming's probably fighting Adrestus." He was probably fighting Adrestus *if* Adrestus hadn't already killed him.

"Don't worry about Fleming," Naomi shrugged. "He's got one of these on hand."

She reached into the side pocket of her pants and pulled out a syringe. My breath caught at the sight of Everly's immortality cure.

"Mr. Fleming. An Apex," Jamie snorted. "God, I knew they were all jokes!"

"He's not an Apex," Naomi and I said in unison. I cracked a timid smile and glanced sideways at her, but she didn't return the look. I didn't care if she hated me, I decided. I was happy to see her even if she never wanted to see me again after this.

We took the final twist of the stairwell, and Naomi charged at the door, forcing her way into the lobby. Furniture was turned over, and lights had fallen from the ceiling when the city had dropped. One chandelier hung from a single wire over the dining area.

Naomi skidded to a halt, and I slammed into her back.

"Why'd you—"

My chest turned cold, and the glittering lobby of gold and white lost its glamor as dread and fear washed over me.

Adrestus stood triumphant in front of the main exit with Wesley on his knees. Wesley's cape had ripped, and his mask was missing, revealing the black eye that painted half of his face. Unruly brown hair framed wide eyes, but despite the apparent fear on his face, he kept silent, staring at me wildly as Adrestus's fingers dug into the back of his neck.

"Give me the Cure," I growled and held my hand out to Naomi. She pressed the syringe into my grip, and I wrapped my fingers around its contours, imagining it was a sword hilt.

"Careful," Adrestus warned. "I'd hate for that to end up in the wrong person."

He pulled on a handful of Wesley's hair as he spoke, bearing his neck at me. Why wasn't Wesley fighting back? Even if injured, he was stronger than Adrestus. He could escape if he wanted.

"Where's Fleming?" I demanded.

"He put up a fight, but your pesky history teacher won't be bothering either of us anymore."

Naomi gasped, but I shook my head.

"He's lying," I snarled. Fleming couldn't be dead because I was supposed to kill Fleming.

"Mr. Fleming is dead?" Jamie's voice cracked.

"I killed him myself!" Adrestus boasted. "Drove my sword straight through his chest and watched the blood—"

Adrestus's sneer slipped into an uncertain expression, and his eye widened, as if some new horror was slowly dawning over him.

"What—" he gasped, and a bit of blood trickled from his nose. "What are you doing—"

Naomi shook with fury and power, and I remembered how her abilities had overcome me in our fight in the park.

"Is this you?" I whispered.

"Kill him," she gasped through clenched teeth, and I tightened my grip on the vial.

I sprinted across the opulent floor, ignoring a warning shout from Wesley. I didn't care if it was a trap. I only cared to see Adrestus on the floor with his immortality stripped away.

I pushed Wesley aside, and Adrestus made no attempt to fight me off as the needle broke the skin of his neck, and I hit the plunger, emptying the Immortality Cure into his veins.

The skin turned purple, and he grabbed me by the throat, holding me close and forcing me to look into his single eye as the poison spread, discoloring his skin. But I'd won. He would die.

"God," he growled, "that tastes disgusting."

The bright blue of his eye faded to gray, and I thought I was watching him die, but his mouth twitched into a smile, and the purple in his veins receded.

"Sammy!" Wesley grunted, flinging himself at Adrestus, but the warrior stopped him with his free hand. "Don't let her—"

He broke off in a cry of pain.

Her?

"You know," Adrestus said, and his voice morphed, becoming higher. His black hair turned white, and the red of his cloaks shimmered into the red of a silk dress. "It's a shame so many died before you hoping you might *do* something with yourself."

Adrestus's face was gone, replaced by Mira's. Another trick of Gregor's. Adrestus was still upstairs, hopefully bleeding out.

"I'm not dead yet." I raked my boot down her shin, and she growled in pain but kept her hold. Her paralytic neurotoxins flooded my system, and I was trapped in her embrace. Wesley continued to fight feebly next to me, straining against the control.

"Put them down!" Naomi screamed, and her hands tore at my back, trying to pry me away. Wesley collapsed, and Mira let him fall so she could grab Naomi by the throat.

"How lucky that silly mixture was toxin based," she crooned. "It burned a bit, but it was easy to absorb, and in just a moment, I'll be able to recreate it. You were both so eager to see it in action. Which of you would like to taste it first?"

Sweat beaded along her hairline, and I knew she was nearing the limits of her power. Her knees buckled, and she pulled us down with her, refusing to let go.

The revolving door behind her turned, and I thought more help had arrived, but then I saw Jamie sprinting away from the hotel entrance, running to safety in the rubble that littered the street.

"Vidar would be so embarrassed to see you here," Mira murmured. "Imagine taking a sword through the chest for someone so quick to throw that sacrifice away."

Her eyes lit up, and she licked her lips. Burning pain radiated from her fingers where they gripped my throat, but I was trapped, unable to even scream.

"There it is. Burns, doesn't it?"

"No..." Wesley stirred on the floor, unable to rise, but reached out to grab Mira's bare ankle. Her eyes darted to him, and the burning let up just a little as she redirected her energy towards keeping him at bay. "You don't have the energy to kill all three of us."

The pain flared in response, and Naomi cried out next to me, then went limp. Mira let her drop to her floor, and I strained against her hold, searching for signs of life in my friend where she lay.

Wesley collapsed next, sprawled out on the tiles. Mira lurched forward, pushing me to the marble floor. Her gray eyes swam inches from mine. The poison continued to seep into my skin, but it seemed to take all her energy and focus, releasing me from the paralysis. I struggled against her grip, too weak to fight as the world closed in.

"And this is where you die. It's just like last time, when *he* died. How many times had he looked me in the face only to never realize?" Mira's words slurred with exhaustion, and the whites of her eyes burned red as her own powers ate away at her. "I wish I had been there when he died. The hero-brother, who gave everything for Eydis. You always were his favorite."

Her hand seared against my skin, and I struggled against her hold, but the world was spinning with her white-framed face at its vortex.

"He *was* a hero," I managed to gasp. The bright chandelier lights of the lobby dimmed overhead. Was I dying for real this time? Were Wesley and Naomi already dead?

"Even Adrestus loved to talk about how *good* a man Vidar was." Mira shook her head, and her chest heaved with labored breaths as she leaned in closer. "If anyone had stolen his life-giving stone, at least it had gone to someone as *worthy* as Vidar."

The edges of my vision blurred and darkened.

"Vidar *was* worthy..."

"You'd think a worthy man would've recognized his own sister at some point."

I stared up at her, fighting the toxin with every ounce of my being. She wasn't making sense.

"He did," I insisted. "He knew me, he..."

"*You*, the only one of his sisters he ever gave a damn about, and I'm left wondering if he ever even cared about me. He died not knowing his own sister even when he stared her dead in the eyes." Hot tears rolled from her face and splattered across my cheek. "You're the one dying this time, and I'll be damned if I let the same thing happen again."

"I—"

"Come on, *Eydis*." She wavered somewhere between taunting and begging. Sweat and tears dripped off her cheeks, and her pale skin turned ever paler as she reached the limit of her powers. "Don't let me kill you before you figure it out. I told you, didn't I? In front of his statue on that island? The first time I saw someone die was when my sister killed a home invader. You remember when you did that, don't you?"

My stomach flipped.

No.

No.

She was lying. It was a cruel, dirty trick, and it made me strain against her toxin that much harder.

But how could she know about the day I protected my sisters and mother from the enemy raiders who'd broken into our longhouse?

It felt like the ground had disappeared beneath me. I wanted to scream but had no energy left and was forced to stare back at her in silent horror, searching for the faces of my long-dead sisters.

And when I finally saw her there, I was amazed and horrified I hadn't seen her there before.

But how could I have? She'd been so tiny. She'd been *dead.* But Mira had the same gray eyes as our father. The same gray eyes as Vidar. The same gray eyes as me.

"Erika?"

Her lips trembled, betraying the smallest hint of relief.

"Hello, Eydis."

And her eyes rolled back, and she slumped forward just as the darkness took me, too.

45

En Route

Fire surged through my veins, licking at my every cell. I tensed against the pain, waiting for it to pass, but when it did, it came back worse than before, as if each beat of my heart sent the toxin surging through every blood vessel all over again.

Screams issued overhead, but the chaos made little sense as I drifted in and out of consciousness, vaguely aware of the arms that passed beneath me. The minutes bled together, and suddenly someone had my legs while someone else held me under my arms.

Familiar voices shouted, but it was hard to find comfort in them when they were distressed, still fighting, still running. All scared. I clung to them anyway.

Darkness lifted, though only a little, like a stage curtain drawing back, giving only an inch of a glimpse. Naomi's braids hung in her face, barely stirring in the air of her labored breath where she lay on a cot.

I tried to rasp her name, but something sharp broke the skin of my arm, and the darkness returned.

The ground vibrated, accompanied by a low rumble that was vaguely reminiscent of the ferry boats with their massive engines that shook the entire vessel.

Dull pain nagged at my muscles, and I forced my eyes open to the muted, orange glow of lamplight.

"Sammy?" A blurry figure rushed to my side. "Holy crap, you're awake!"

He shifted in and out of focus, but I recognized the bushy eyebrows and the brow, though I was more accustomed to seeing it furrowed in anger than worry like it did now.

"Andersen." I tried to sit up, but my stomach clenched, and I fell back against my pillow. "Is everyone— where—"

"It's fine," he insisted. "I mean, it's not fine. But we're fine. Mostly."

The buzzing lamp that stood tall in the middle of the room did its best to throw its light into the corners of the room. Cots lined the either side of the space, some occupied but most empty with neatly folded sheets set at their feet.

I blinked a few more times, trying to shake the sense of familiarity that the space brought me, before realizing we were in the Sickbay of the Apex Team facility under the school. Naomi lay in the cot next to me with her eyes closed.

"Naomi," I croaked. "Is she—?"

"She's fine. Same as you." Andersen looked up as the door creaked open.

"And Wesley?"

"He's good. I'll go find him for you." He stepped away, making room for whoever had just run in.

"My god, Sammy." Fleming stared down at me with his glasses pushed up on top of his head. His button-up was wrinkled, looking like he'd slept in it more than one night in a row. He twisted to look towards Everly's old office. "Angie?"

The university medic with long, brown hair pulled into a french braid and arms painted in long-healed battle scars hurried from the back office. The pain subsided as she approached my cot, and my heart rate calmed.

"Welcome back, Samantha." She adjusted the stethoscope at her neck and wrapped a blood pressure cuff around my bicep.

"Back?" I repeated. "Did I die again?"

Fleming gave me a sad smile and shook his head.

"No, not this time." The cot creaked and bowed as he took a seat on its edge. So, I was fine. Why did they all look so harrowed?

"Is everyone—" I said quickly.

"All fine. We were able to evacuate many of the summit attendees, but not everyone—" He cut off to clear his throat, and his eyes glazed over for a moment, and I wondered what horrors from the fight he was remembering. "Your friends were very brave. They were able to escape with you but—"

My hand shot to my neck when I remembered how Mira had grabbed me.

Mira.

Erika?

No. I didn't want to believe it.

"I should be dead," I said. "Like, dead-dead."

Angie unstrapped the blood pressure cuff and shuffled to Naomi's bed.

"The Immortality Cure worked to an extent," Fleming sighed. "You aren't immortal anymore."

I was vulnerable. I was breakable. I was free. A weight that I didn't realize had been pushing on me lifted. I could be normal.

"That's not the worst news I've ever heard."

"You only survived because Mira's powers found their limit. Wesley explained what happened. As far as we can tell, she tried to kill him and Naomi, too, but with her energy divided, she wasn't successful in killing any of you."

Fleming seemed to be saying that we were okay. If Mira hadn't been so exhausted filling the Epsilon chips in the weeks prior, we'd probably all three be dead, but the standing lamp made the tight lines in Fleming's frown look deeper than ever.

"What's wrong?" Apprehension knotted my stomach.

"When we took Schrader Tower, we found the morgue."

His voice distorted with pain and emotion, and I could only nod, wordlessly confirming what and who I knew he must've found.

"Was it Roy?" Fleming whispered. Only one person could've been responsible for such extensive burns. I nodded again, and Fleming closed his eyes and bowed his head.

"She died protecting me." A lump rose in my throat. "The same way Everly died. Your friends are dead because of—"

"Because of evil people. And because Alison and Nurse Everly loved you, but that is no more your fault than it is theirs." He opened his eyes to look at me with a fierce seriousness. "I'm a poor replacement for Alison, but you and Avery have me. I promise, Sammy. I won't let anymore harm come to either of you."

Fresh guilt weighed on my stomach, not for Mom or Everly, but because Trev Baker spent his final moments reminding me I was going to kill Fleming.

"Good luck," I sniffed. "I'm not a weird zombie Viking anymore. I'm normal."

Fleming smiled, and to my horror, his eyes filled with tears.

"Completely normal, yes."

"What?" I asked, my apprehension flooding back. He cleared his throat, and I gripped the railing of the cot, feeling the skin of my hands stretch over my knuckles. "We won, right? You said everyone's okay. We got away."

"In a sense of the phrase, yes. I suppose we did."

And Adrestus's threats came rushing back, as did his words after the city had dropped. New Delos was an ark, and he was sailing us to the middle of the ocean.

I stumbled out of bed, ignoring Fleming's protests. I needed to see it for myself. I needed to make sure.

"You need to stay in bed," Fleming chided. "There's still poison in your system."

"Not enough to kill me." My stomach heaved, but I steeled myself and pushed out of the Sickbay.

"Well, no—"

"Then I'm fine."

The atrium was dark and quiet. I'd thought there'd at least be a couple people at the call desk, but all I saw were sandbags piled against the walls. A camping lantern burned at the desk, casting flickering shadows through the empty space. Fleming tried to grab my shoulder, but I shrugged him off and continued into the basement hall of the main school building.

"You need rest!" Fleming called after me.

"I'll rest when I'm dead," I said through a wry smile.

"Samantha, I'm serious!"

"So am I!"

The school was dark, and I relied on slivers of light that trickled down the distant staircase to make my way to the first floor and out the rusted back door.

My heart beat so fast that it hurt, but I wasn't sure if it was from residual poison or anticipation at what I was going to find. I forced stiff legs to jog, then run, then sprint across the empty school grounds, past the cafeteria and the dorms, all the way to the island's edge.

I should've been able to see the mainland from here, especially on a day as clear as today. Instead, blue ocean stretched until it mingled with the blue of the sky. Water churned, and unseen engines roared, propelling us towards the middle of the ocean. Just like Adrestus had promised.

I dropped to my knees. We hadn't won at all. We'd only survived.

"It was a good plan," I insisted quietly, and traitorous tears welled in my eyes as Fleming came up behind me. "I was going to stop him. I thought...I did okay. I did— I didn't want him to hurt any of—"

Tears choked the rest of my words, and I stared at open ocean. The weight of Fleming's hand found my shoulder.

"You did more than okay," he murmured. "You were magnificent."

"Did he flood it yet?"

"No." Fleming climbed down to the lawn to sit beside me in the grass. "We think he's waiting until we're in the middle of the ocean. We estimate another week of sailing at least."

So there was still time. We could still stop Adrestus.

"Then we'll stop him," I asserted. "We still have Immortality Cure, right?"

Fleming blushed and rubbed his neck.

"Afraid not. I tried to use it, but he managed to break the syringe. And we found Naomi's empty syringe with you. It was all Everly ever made, so we're fresh out of ways to kill immortal warriors."

A series of painful coughs that tasted like metal shook my ribs, and when they subsided, my hand came away flecked with blood.

"You're still ill," Fleming said, grimacing at my bloodied hand. "You escaped death, but it might take a week or two for the poison to leave your system."

"How long was I out?"

"The Peace Summit was a few days ago," Fleming admitted. He frowned at the water and itched at his arms. "The poison was potent, but the good news is that Adrestus thinks you're dead."

"What?" I gawked at him. "Why? How?"

"We all thought so for a moment, when we found you in the lobby. I thought I'd lost all three of you." His voice hitched, but he covered with a fake cough. "When we fled, Adrestus gave chase. All of us saw you lying in the lobby with Mira and figured... Anyway, we weren't about to leave you there, but we didn't realize you were all alive until we were halfway back to the hideout. Mira's unhappy about her current living situation and has been less than forthcoming, but we have her downstairs."

"Why'd you take her if you thought she was dead?"

A heavy moment passed.

"After seeing the morgue, I didn't think Adrestus deserved to keep any more dead bodies."

I dug my fingers into the unkempt lawn and clenched my jaw as a flurry of tangled feelings washed over me. Anger, regret, despair, and relief ran together to paint a picture of Erika's face in my head.

"She's my sister."

"Your what?" Fleming croaked, and I told him what she'd said to me. "And you believe her?"

Tiny Erika, who fit so snug in my arms when I'd carried her around our village. I didn't want it to be true that this entire time, the woman who'd been terrorizing me, my friends, my family had been my tiny baby sister.

"I think I do."

Fleming swore softly and buried his head in his hands.

"I'm sorry, Sammy."

"Doesn't matter," I whispered. "It doesn't change anything."

"Of course it matters. She's your family."

"Forgive me for not taking anything you say regarding sibling affection too seriously."

"I said it matters, not that you should be in any rush to reconcile with her."

My laugh was cold and bitter. Even if Mira was created out of the tiny thing that had once been my sister, a thousand years of Adrestus's lies had changed her into someone I didn't know.

I climbed to my feet and trudged back towards the school hall.

"And what's the plan now?" I asked. "How are we stopping him?"

"*We* aren't doing anything. Those of us still in one piece have a plan, but your priority is to rest."

"No time, remember?" I pushed back into the school too quickly, and my head spun. Fleming steadied me with a hand on my arm.

"Angie said it looked like you had a hole punched through your thigh."

"It's better now."

"You're limping, and she said there's a lot of scarring," he said as I forged onward. "And I imagine there's more than just physical scars."

I'd spent the last month pretending to play to the tune of a monster as he threatened my friends, the world, and me, blatantly murdering those who stood in his way and more than once asking me to do his dirty work.

But whatever scars Fleming was worried about weren't going to be healed by sitting back in the med bay. They'd only be fixed by retribution and bringing Adrestus to his knees for the hell he'd forced on me.

After the fresh salt air of the ocean outside, the atrium of the facility felt stuffier than before. I hadn't noticed how thick the air was down here and faltered in the dark.

"So." Naomi's voice echoed through the space, and I froze in the atrium doorway. "You're awake, too, then?"

She'd blended into the shadows cast by the camping lantern so well in the black underclothes of the team uniform, and it was difficult to make her out where she leaned against the old call desk.

"Hey." I grimaced, suddenly self-conscious. Naomi pushed off the desk and crossed the atrium with a limping gait, her face stoic and hard, until she was right in front of me with her nostrils flaring in anger. I gulped, ready to receive whatever punishment she deemed worthy of my bad friendship.

I flinched as she raised her arms, but then they were around me, and her face was buried in my shoulder, pushing her braids against my cheek.

"I hate you so much," she murmured, and only then did I decide her embrace was safe to return. I held her along with all my relief and shame at finally being reunited in my arms, refusing to be the first to let go.

"I think that's fair," I mumbled back.

She pulled away, and the steel in her eyes made me worry she hadn't completely ruled out punching me yet.

"Was it horrible?" she whispered, her hands still on my shoulders. The question caught me off guard, and I tried to stutter an answer, but she frowned and cut me off. "Of course it was. You idiot."

And she hugged me again.

"I'm so sorry." I didn't deserve to get off this easy. I didn't deserve to have her back. I'd left her unconscious in a park. I'd abandoned her, and now Adrestus was going to end the world before I had a chance to make it up to her.

"My family." She stepped away to look at Fleming. "Are they...?"

"Safe and with the others," he assured her. "If you don't feel up to—"

She shook her head vehemently.

"It can't wait. I have to know if it works up close."

"Then lead the way." Fleming nodded.

Naomi looped her hand around my elbow and pulled me toward the corridor that led to the underground parking garage. She paused to cough when we pushed through the door, and I held her steady even as the same poison made me feel heavy with an unfamiliar weight.

"You're going to see your family?" I asked carefully. "Is that possible?"

Naomi nodded, and I watched our shadows elongate down the hall ahead of us as Fleming lifted the camping lantern higher.

"It's a new trick I learned the night you ditched me. I think you felt it."

I swallowed hard and nodded. It was hard to forget the brain-splitting mental attack Naomi had unleashed on me.

"I remember, but how does that help your situation?"

She grinned as we passed into an underground parking garage, veering towards a new corridor that would take us to the tunnels under the university campus.

"I can push any emotion onto anyone," Naomi explained, "but if I'm using my powers like that, I can't feel anyone around me. That's why I didn't sense Wesley and Mira at the hotel. I was too busy making Jamie agreeable to escaping. But this all means—"

"You can get close to your mom." I stopped walking to better look at her. She bit her lip, scared but excited. "Your family can be together again."

"If it works," she murmured. "I got cold feet when we went to free them, and before I could get too close, I escaped with Mrs. Hisakawa. Then Mira happened, and I haven't been able to test if it works as well as I hope."

"It will," Fleming assured her behind us, and we continued forward into the university tunnels. "You've been practicing the technique nonstop the last month."

The tunnels twisted through corridors of rusted doors and peeling sports murals painted over concrete brick. The walk was wearing on me, and I was beginning to wonder how much farther ahead the team could be hiding.

"We've been staying under the university arena," Naomi explained. "We've kept the Sickbay far away though, in case of an attack, to keep the injured safe."

"And Adrestus never came looking here?" I asked. Naomi laughed, then coughed, and wiped a bit of blood from her chin.

"He checked once, but we're good at hiding. I would've thought you knew, considering you were in his inner circle."

I grunted.

"He never really trusted me, not as much as he wanted to."

"We kept busy," Naomi continued. "Remember how easy it was to sneak onto the island? It's been almost impossible to get off. Adrestus doesn't want people leaving, so for four weeks, that's what we did. We smuggled people trying to leave back to the mainland. Then, the other night, Winnie of all people shows up."

I laughed, imagining what sort of welcome she must've received.

"And you didn't chase her off?"

"We thought about it," Naomi said with a wry grin, "but then Anthony and Avery showed up, too, and they told us the plan for the Summit."

I watched her talk, reveling in the sound of her voice and the comforting grip of her hand around my elbow. I'd missed her, and I'd missed the comfort of being with people who didn't want to push me off a building.

The world might be ending, but I was with my friends.

She detailed the month we'd been apart, explaining the missions they'd run, the close shaves they'd had, and she never once asked me what I'd been doing in the meantime. She never once mentioned the limp affecting the leg I'd gored in my fight against Roy. She never once pried into the horrors of Schrader Tower and instead let me lean into the comfort of stories about my friends.

Maybe that was why Naomi kept talking, so that I wouldn't have to.

But then, she cut off as light stretched around the next corner to meet us, and Fleming clicked off our lantern. Hushed voices whispered ahead, and Naomi trembled.

"What if it doesn't work?" Naomi's voice quaked.

"It will," Fleming assured her.

"Gabriella, wait!" a man said, out of view around the corner. "Let's go back to the kids. I don't want to get lost down here."

"No, it's her," a woman said. "I can feel it."

A woman stepped out at the end of the corridor, followed by a man. They froze at the sight of us, and the lamplight of the next hall glittered off the wide grin of the man. The woman raised a shaking hand to her mouth.

"Naomi?" she cried, as if afraid her daughter was some sort of cruel prank and not the child she hadn't seen in several long years.

"I—I can't feel her!" Naomi cried. "Mom!"

Naomi let go of my elbow, and I resisted the selfish urge to pull her back as she ran into the arms of her parents, a screaming sob of relief echoing off the narrow walls of the corridor.

They collapsed in on each other in a tangle of arms, and watching Naomi's parents shower her in kisses and tears, I thought that even if Adrestus did end up flooding the world, my month at the tower would have still been worth it if just for this moment.

"Come on," Fleming sighed. "Let them be. You have people waiting for you, too."

He led me past Naomi and her parents, but a hand reached out from their embrace to take mine. Mrs. Bradford, with her cheek pressed against her daughter's, gave me a watery smile and a gentle squeeze of her fingers.

Their excited cries faded behind us as we turned down a hall lined with lamps. I'd been here before, when I competed in The Apex Games against Sergio before Winter Break. We paused at a set of double doors. The arena and all my teammates were on the other side. A strip of light leaked out from beneath the doors, interrupted by shifting shadows.

"I should warn you," Fleming said, his hand on the door. "There's been a lot of rumors, but by now everyone has heard about the Scourge Queen."

I rubbed the scar on my neck. I'd been accused of worse, but this time the rumor was true.

"How's my make-up?"

"Still there, unfortunately. More or less." Fleming grimaced.

"At least I ditched the crown and fur somewhere."

"It was a bit much, I'll admit."

I squared my shoulders and braced for whatever waited on the opposite side of the door, and Fleming pushed them open.

I stood at the top of a row of stands that looked over a small colosseum-style arena. The last time I'd been here, it had been filled with rocky crags and inclines, providing a dynamic competition space. Now, the terrain was flat and covered by rubber mats.

Cots dotted the floor haphazardly, most of them being used as benches. A table in the corner sported several vats from which steam rose into the air and curled. The area was lit by ambient light that filled the space like sunshine, though the massive overhead fluorescents appeared to be off.

Groups of families and students sat in clumps around the stands as well as the main floor, and I scanned the familiar faces, searching for messy brown hair and a pair of glasses. However, before I could find Wesley, a voice cried out from below.

"Samantha's back!"

I stared in horror at Mike, standing next to his twin Desirea, pointing up at my hiding spot against the wall.

The entire arena stopped to stare up at me. It had been so long since I'd seen most of them, and while many looked excited at my return, I couldn't ignore the few faces of apprehension and outright distrust.

"While the enthusiasm is welcomed—" Fleming started as a crowd gathered below but was cut off by a shout.

"Is it true?" Skyler looked up at me through the railing that separated the stands from the floor. His blond hair, normally gelled into spikes, hung limp in his face, and he leaned on a crutch.

"I'm not entertaining any rumors," Fleming snapped.

"Then just say it isn't true!" Skyler retorted.

"It's not—"

I pushed past Fleming to walk down the steps to the railing, looking down at the gathered teammates and their rescued families. A few of them stepped away as I got closer, and all of them turned silent.

"Is what true, Skyler?" I asked. I felt a flicker of dark satisfaction when fleeting fear passed over his face.

"That you're the Scourge Queen."

"Sammy," Fleming said softly behind me, but I took a steadying breath.

We were probably all going to die anyway.

"My name is Samantha Havardson," I said, "but a thousand years ago, my name was Eydis Solveigsdotter, and yes. I'm Adrestus's Scourge Queen."

46

Breath of Air

The stunned silence that rang out across the arena lasted a few, fragile moments before the barrage of questions broke out. I couldn't answer them all, but one echoed out louder and more horrible than the rest.

"You've been lying to us this whole time?" It was, of course, Skyler who asked it, and the others quieted at his raised voice. "You tricked us into thinking you were some useless Beta—"

"You're the one who thought she was a useless Beta," Andersen spoke up, leaning against a far wall.

"But she *was*—"

"She wasn't useless." Andersen stalked away from his spot to come face-to-face with his former friend. "We just wanted her to be."

"She lied to all of us!"

"I'm not a liar," I asserted. "And I *am* a useless Beta."

"When you left to join Adrestus," Skyler shouted, "was that really a ploy to double-cross him or did you want your immortality back?"

I gripped the railing, biting my tongue. It was hard to make sense of the faces below, and the arena light was too bright.

"You know, Skyler," a new voice joined the discourse from the stands, "I used to think you were too stupid to be an Apex. How refreshing to discover that Apex can be just as dense as us normal people."

Winnie stood with her hands on her hips. Lana shrank next to her, shying away from the stares that Winnie had brought their direction.

"You of all people—" Skyler started.

"Yes, *me* of all people," Winnie snarled. "You pretend the reason you hate Samantha is because she's weak, but you and I both know it's because you'll never *be* her."

"Figures that Adrestus's lapdogs would come to the defense of each other," Skyler sneered just before a snowball smacked him in the back of the head.

He spun to face Sergio, who sat on a cot with one knee up towards his chest as he procured another snowball from the moisture in the air. His hair hung long and haggard, obscuring his eyepatch.

I took my chance to escape, retreating back up the stands as a million more questions flew at my back.

"She doesn't owe any of you any more than she's already given!" Fleming yelled behind me, attempting to quell the crowd. I scanned the floor, searching for somewhere safe, somewhere I could hide.

Then, a flash of red plastic and a shock of messy brown hair appeared from one of the arena passageways on the floor below. I stumbled down the stands to a set of stairs, unable to reach him fast enough, not slowing down until I slammed into his chest and wrapped my arms around him.

"You're okay," Wesley mumbled into my hair. "I wasn't sure, with the poison—"

"I'm fine." I looked over his shoulder where Fleming continued to conduct the attention of the crowd. Wesley drew me back beneath the stands into a lamplit corridor filled with the smell of roasting potatoes and carrots. "Where are we going?"

"My mom and Benson are on lunch duty in the kitchen today," he said, taking my hand. "It's a little more private back here."

"And they're okay?" I stopped, taking hold of Wesley's hands. I'd missed the plastic of his red prosthesis.

"As good as they can be," he rasped through a rapidly fading smile. "That was the worst month of my life. They were there even *longer* than us and were trapped in a prison cell, but I can't stop thinking about how terrible it was."

His voice caught, and he leaned forward. I stepped closer, letting my forehead catch his.

"You were thrown out a window," I pointed out. "You can't compare the two experiences. Neither was more or less terrible than the other."

"Then how are they serving food and helping people, and I feel so—" He broke off to swallow hard, and his hand squeezed mine.

"Scared?" I finished for him in a whisper. He nodded.

"I wasn't scared when I was with you," he whispered. "Even when I knew Adrestus might force me to do something horrible, it was like, if Sammy was there, things couldn't be that bad, you know?"

"That's funny," I laughed softly. "You made me feel the same way."

"I know the world might be ending," he said, "but it's weird. I feel okay. We're all together again."

His lips pressed against my forehead.

I tilted my head back to look at him. The fight against Adrestus felt far from over, but we were still here. We were still surviving and fighting. Together.

"Is everyone doing okay?" I asked. He tried to give me a brave smile, but it wavered.

"Come see." He pulled me towards the kitchen. "The ambassadors and leaders we saved are staying in the university training gym. Dr. Parker spends most of her time there, and that's where Jamie's been, too, though she won't talk to anyone. I guess they found her mom in the morgue."

So Jamie's hunch about her mother succumbing to the Epsilon Procedure had been right.

"And Remi?" I continued, not wanting to linger on thoughts of Jamie's family.

"Still missing." Wesley frowned. "I feel like it's my fault. If she had never rejoined the team—"

"Don't do that to yourself," I snapped. "Remi rejoined the team because she wanted to."

Wesley blushed and turned the corner into the brightly lit kitchen. A cannonball of blond launched at me, ripping me from Wesley to wrap me in a new embrace.

"You're not dead?" Avery choked, squeezing me around my middle.

"Never," I laughed and held my brother close. "Look, Avery, I'm so sorry. Mom—"

"I know." He choked on the words. "It's not your fault. It was *them*."

His hug tightened just to the point of being painful, and he released me. I looked around the kitchen, taking in the faces of my friends.

Wesley's mother and brother helped Mr. and Mrs. Hisakawa chop potatoes and carrots at a steel countertop while Heather stirred a giant vat of soup on a kitchen island from where she sat in a wheelchair. Anthony helped Brooke stack cups and bowls onto a trolley in the corner.

"Samantha." Mrs. Isaacs left her potatoes to pull me into a motherly embrace. She looked like both her sons, with unruly graying brown hair and a long nose. "I swear, if you ever let my son follow you into danger like that again—"

"I won't let him," I promised through a laugh. I looked at Brooke over Mrs. Isaacs's shoulder. "Where's Amanda?"

"Guard duty." She grinned, moving a vat of soup onto her trolley. "I've got to get this to the ambassadors, but it's good to see you, Sammy."

She hugged me as she left.

"If it isn't the Scourge Queen herself," Heather beamed from her wheelchair. She'd found a bow somewhere, just like she used to wear, and had it in her hair. "Sorry about tackling you in the stairs."

"Are you okay?" I looked over her wheelchair, and her smile faltered.

"That was my fault." Her mother frowned beneath the hairnet that kept her red curls away from the carrots she was peeling. "I tried to teleport her without the chip in her neck, and now she's partially paralyzed."

Heather shrugged.

"I can move perfectly fine in the dark," she said, but her optimism looked forced. "And I'd rather be free of that chip than anything."

Her mom kissed the top of her head while Wesley rubbed the back of his neck where his own control chip still sat.

"There you are!" Naomi poked her head through the door, and Wesley left his neck alone to launch at her, holding her tight as her parents and two younger siblings filed into the kitchen after her.

"You're okay!" Wesley beamed.

"Anything that doesn't kill Sammy definitely isn't going to kill me," she scoffed. "Also, leave me with Andersen ever again, and I'll kill *both* of you."

She glared at me over Wesley's shoulder, but then pulled me in and held me there with them.

"You whistled for me to come help when Samantha went rogue!" Wesley shrugged against our shoulders.

Naomi pushed away to frown at him, though her look was one of concern rather than a reprimand.

"I wanted you to stop her, not join her." She looked at her parents, and her face softened. "But I guess it worked out."

"Until the world floods," Anthony said miserably from his corner.

Wesley opened his mouth to retort, but Naomi put up a hand and whispered a gentle, "Don't."

"He wouldn't flood the world if you had left me there," Avery pointed out.

"I wasn't going to let that happen." I frowned.

A pang of guilt shot through me as I looked at my friends and their parents. The Hisakawas, the Bradfords, and Mrs. Issacs were all still here, but Avery had no one left. I couldn't help but to feel at fault.

All he had left were a couple of thousand-year-old aunts, neither of which were equipped to step up and take care of a middle schooler.

"Wesley," I said as the others returned to their soup-making, "where's Mira?"

Naomi frowned at me, and Wesley glanced into the hall.

"She won't talk," Wesley warned me. "No one can get any information out of her, and she's dangerous."

"Take me to her," I said. "It's okay if she doesn't talk. I just need to see her. Please."

Wesley nodded, though his brow knit, and stepped back into the corridor. He led the way through the back halls of the arena that sprawled beneath the stands, walking us past locker rooms towards a flickering firelight. A small flame rested in the palm of a lone figure's hand, its light playing against the fringe of her pixie cut. Amanda looked up from her fire as we approached and held it aloft to better see us.

"Thanks, Wes." I gave his hand a squeeze. "I've got it from here."

"You shouldn't face her alone."

"I lived with her for a month. I'll be fine. I just—" I swallowed, trying to figure out what it was I was trying to say. "I need privacy. Go back to the others. I know Naomi missed you."

He nodded and squeezed my hand back.

"Right. Got it. I'll be down the hall, then." He gave me an assuring smile and backed off, leaving the way we'd come. As much as I wanted him by my side, I wasn't ready for Wesley to know Mira's real identity.

"You woke up," Amanda drawled. She pressed her lips together in disapproval as I got closer, but her eyes raked over me ravenously, and I knew she was assessing my well-being. "Wasn't sure I'd ever see you again."

"You didn't think I'd let Adrestus kill me, did you?"

"I was more worried about what Fleming might do when you returned. He was livid the night you left."

I shrugged away my feelings of guilt and looked around Amanda at the door she was guarding. How fitting that Amanda would be guarding Mira after Mira had used her as a puppet for so many months last winter.

"I need to talk to her," I said, cutting to the chase. Amanda laughed in response.

"Too bad. No one is allowed in. Not even you, Scourge."

I glowered at the nickname but wasn't going to give up that easily.

"She knows where Remi is," I told her. "Saving Remi was your whole reason for coming to New Delos, right? If we find Remi, we can stop the Epsilons and end all of this."

"Oh, gee, thank god you're awake." Amanda rolled her eyes. "We never would've thought to ask her about Remi! What do you think we've been doing the last three days? She won't talk. Even Avery can't crack her."

"She'll talk to me," I insisted.

Amanda lobbed her ball of fire between her hands, tracking its arc with her eyes.

"Oh, yeah? Because of your expertise in tactical interrogation?"

"Because she's my little sister."

Amanda dropped her fire in surprise, plunging us into darkness before she could procure a new flame.

"Your—"

"I just found out," I said.

"That's…" She sighed and ruffled her hair. "That's a lot. Family sucks, dude."

"Sorry my sister enslaved you for three months." I pressed my lips together.

"It was four," she said dryly, "and my dad killed your mom, so, you know, crappy people do crappy things."

She procured a key from her pocket and stepped away from the door.

"I owe you," I breathed, taking the key.

"Nah," she murmured, watching me mess with the lock. "You saved Winnie. That's more than I could've ever asked for."

The doorknob clicked, but I hesitated.

"I thought you didn't care about Winnie."

She shrugged and looked aside.

"Sisters are weird, but I guess you know that now."

I smiled in spite of myself and pressed into Mira's makeshift jail cell.

The room had once been a sports medicine office. Laminated anatomical posters papered the concrete walls, and a row of rusting ice baths lined a sidewall. A haggard figure lay on a cot bolted to the tiled floor, and white hair glowed in the lamplight.

"That better be my dinner," she growled. Metal handcuffs clinked against the bar of her cot as she pushed herself up.

Mira swung her legs over the side of her bed, and the dirty, red satin of her dress rippled. Gray eyes, identical to mine, glinted from behind white hair hanging in clumps from her days-old updo.

"I'm here to talk."

Mira threw her head back and laughed. The sound was coarse, and she broke into a fit of coughing.

"So you survived," she crooned.

"So did you," I crossed my arms, "Erika."

Her lips curled into a cruel smile, and she tried to flip her loose hair over her shoulder to regain whatever dignity she could.

"Erika died the day you abandoned me in your quest for immortality."

"She died the day you let Adrestus in your head."

She sneered at me and tried to straighten up.

"You killed our whole family. Are you here to finish the job?"

I recoiled.

"I don't kill like you do," I spat.

"You struck a man dead when we were children."

"To save you!" Everything about this was *wrong*. How could this vile thing be my sister?

"Why are you here, Eydis?"

I pulled a metal stool over from a desk and sat down directly in front of her.

"Tell me where Remi is," I demanded.

Her handcuff chain clinked against the metal of her bar as she reached out for me.

"You sure you want to sit so close? Are you that eager to taste my toxins again, sister?"

"You can't hurt me," I said, though I leaned away from her fingertips. "I've seen you erode stone. You're still recovering from the other day, otherwise you wouldn't be here."

This time, I was the one to break into a coughing fit, and Mira laughed again.

"It appears I'm not the only one recovering," she tittered. "You and I are both on our last lives, but Adrestus will live on, and he will have what's his. As soon as my powers return, I'll escape and stand at his side once more."

"He murdered you," I reminded her. "And I still don't know how you survived because I buried you."

"Not deep enough, I suppose."

I exhaled heavily. I was letting her under my skin.

"Where's Remi?"

"Right where Adrestus needs her."

"She's not going to talk, Sam," Amanda said from the door. "Just leave her."

"Yeah, *Sam*, just leave me," Mira goaded. "It's what you're best at."

I stood up, and my stool toppled over behind me.

"I never abandoned you!" My voice rose, and Amanda tried to shush me. "I'm sorry for what happened. I never should've brought Adrestus into our home, but I *never* murdered my family. That was Adrestus, and I killed him for it."

"Liar." Mira drew her feet onto her cot and glared at me over her knees, somehow looking more like Erika than ever. "Adrestus saved me."

"You're my sister, Erika," I croaked. "I loved you."

"My name is Mira," she snarled. "Erika is—"

"Don't say 'dead'," I warned. "If Erika was dead, you wouldn't care, but you do."

I gave her one last look of contempt and turned away when I saw tears of anger leaving trails in the dirt on her cheeks. Amanda stepped aside to let me out and locked the door behind me as I wiped furious tears from my face.

"That was probably the worst interrogation I've ever seen," she said, and then did something completely unexpected.

She hugged me.

I tried to compose myself in her arms, but her embrace only drew more tears, so I pushed her away.

"Thanks," I mumbled.

"Like I said, sisters are weird." She shrugged.

I nodded and retreated, unable to get Erika's face out of my head.

Eager to forget about my undead sister, I volunteered to help with dinner and was happy to find myself next to Naomi behind the vats of soup in the arena corner. She grinned as we ladled soup into bowls, and I ignored the curious looks of teammates and their families when they stopped in front of me to receive their dinner.

I tried to catch snippets of conversations, hungry to know the plan to stop Adrestus, but those still brave enough to speak to me weren't interested in divulging attack strategies.

Isabelle, with her bowl extended forward for soup, gushed her gratitude in me for helping Anthony escape. When I tried to pry into team plans, she switched gears, instead filling me in on how Justin and Marcus were finally officially an item, and how if the world was ending, at least she could be happy they finally got together.

Mike and Desirae were less helpful and held up the soup line with demands to know if Vikings actually wore horned helmets or not. Mike's face fell when I informed him that we had no horned headwear.

"But that doesn't mean no Vikings had them," he protested. "Maybe you lived with the boring Vikings. Where were you? Norway? Sweden?"

"Iceland."

"So now we know!" Mike declared. "Iceland Vikings were the kind of Vikings without fun hats!"

"Don't listen to him," Desirae scowled. "I'm sure your Vikings were plenty fun."

"If you have your soup, keep moving." Wesley pushed his way between Naomi and me, his messy hair contained in a hairnet. He pointed a plastic finger away from the table, and Desirae dragged her twin out of the way of the next people in line.

"Thanks," I laughed as Wesley took up a ladle to help dish soup, but Freddie and Everest were next in line. I tried to smile at my fellow sophomores.

"I heard you split Adrian Schrader in half," Freddie blurted, and Everest elbowed him in the ribs.

"He wasn't real. It was fine." I dropped soup into Freddie's bowl.

"Yeah, but you didn't know that. You really swung for the fences. Literally."

I suppressed a laugh. It wasn't funny. It was, in all honesty, absolutely horrific.

"He had it coming." Winnie pushed forward to hold her bowl out to Naomi. She gave me a steely look. "And Adrestus is next."

When our soup vats were about to run dry, Naomi, Wesley, and I scooped the dregs into bowls for ourselves and let our hair free of our hairnets. We sat in the corner, sipping our broth and potatoes, and I watched Avery eating with Mrs. Isaacs and Wesley's brother across the arena.

I'd turned him into an orphan in the same indirect way I'd turned Erika into an orphan.

"You're keeping secrets again," Naomi whispered matter-of-factly.

"You're using your powers?" I asked. "With your mom so close?"

"It doesn't take superpowers to know when you're being secretive," Wesley snorted into his soup.

I sighed and stirred my bowl, leaning against the arena wall.

"I know I've kept secrets before," I said, "and I know those secrets hurt you, but it's different this time. It's personal."

"As personal as being an undead Viking?" Naomi asked.

"Sort of." I gave her an apologetic grimace. I would tell them about Erika eventually, but the wound was too raw. "I'm sorry. I'm not ready to talk about it."

Her face softened, and she reached for my knee.

"I'm sorry I make you feel like you need to keep secrets. I know I've been bad about holding it against you when you don't tell me everything."

"I weaponized your powers and your mother against you to go rogue." I deadpanned. "You aren't the one who should be apologizing."

"That you're *not* off the hook for," Naomi chided. "But I was a little harsh on you about the Viking thing last winter. I can feel when people are keeping secrets, but that doesn't mean I'm entitled to them."

"Whatever it is," Wesley said, "we're here when you're ready."

The horrors of the last month continued to weigh on my chest, but seeing Wesley and Naomi smiling at me over their soup made that weight seem that much more manageable.

"Sammy, a word, please."

I jumped at the sound of Fleming's voice as he approached us. He'd traded out his wrinkled button-up for the red and white base layer of his field uniform, and there was a scruff to his chin I hadn't noticed before.

I nodded and climbed to my feet. The poison still in my system made my head spin, but I followed him under the stands, down a corridor to a lamplit alcove.

"I'm in trouble, right?" I'd been bracing for this for a month. I knew I'd gotten off too easily for going rogue.

"Immense trouble." He frowned at the cot in front of us. "Unfortunately, reprimands will have to wait."

Two swords lay on the cot, shining silver next to black metal. My old sword next to the new one.

"I don't know how to duel wield," I said, and Fleming choked on a disbelieving laugh.

"You get to keep one to have on you just in case." He held out the leather scabbard Lana had built for my costume. I fastened it around my waist and reached for my silver Viking sword. It was an easy choice to make. It slid into the scabbard, and I patted the hilt.

"You're suited up," I noted. "If you're going to stop Adrestus, I—"

"You will stay underground until we're finished," Fleming warned. "University students and adults *only* from here on out. You aren't immortal anymore, and you're still sick."

I frowned at him.

"I just want to know what's happening. If you don't come back, I want to know what it was you were trying to do."

"I'm not sure I owe you that considering all the times *you've* left without telling me your plans," Fleming sniffed, then put a serious hand on my shoulder. "And Samantha, I promise, I will always come back. I'm not going to let anyone, least of all Adrestus, leave you with no one to watch over you and Avery."

I scowled so that he wouldn't see how much those words meant to me. Embarrassed gratitude made the blood in my ears louder, but then Fleming looked around.

"Do you hear that?" he murmured, and I realized the sound wasn't in my ears at all. I stepped back, my boot splashing in a puddle of water.

"Water," I said dumbly, and the distant rushing turned to a roar, accompanied by screams in the arena. "Are we sinking?"

Fleming swore and grabbed the black metal sword before running back to the arena floor. I staggered at the end of the corridor, taking in the sight of water rushing down the stands and cascading into the colosseum. Cots swirled in the angry torrent as my friends and teammates fought against the current to climb to steps to the exit

"Adrestus?" I asked Fleming as water rose to our ankles.

"Maybe," he said through gritted teeth. "That or the Prime Minister wants his daughter back."

47

Fighting the Current

The swirling water that pulled on my legs brought me back to the day I flooded New Delos, and I froze in the corridor beneath the stands. I caught sight of Wesley helping Avery, Mrs. Isaacs, and Benson up the far stairs, and I snapped back into the moment.

Everyone fled towards the exit, fighting the falling water, helping each other where they could, with the exception of one person. Brooke's long hair fanned out behind her as she rushed for a darkened corridor across the arena. As selfless as I knew Brooke to be, there was only person she'd run into a flooding labyrinth for, and if Amanda was still down here, that meant Mira was, too.

Someone yelled my name in warning as I sprinted against the gushing water. My leg wound was stiff, but I wouldn't let Erika drown, and after everything she'd done to Brooke and Amanda, I couldn't imagine Brooke risking the time to save her.

Brooke's lantern cast a dull, yellow glow across the peaks of shin-high rapids, and I followed her silhouette to the old sports medicine room. She called Amanda's name ahead of me.

"Brooke!" Amanda screamed back, and I hastened my stride.

Fire glowed at the end of the hall, and Amanda was on her hands and knees in the water.

"We need to leave! The whole place is filling up!" Brooke cried, but Amanda shook her head.

"I dropped the key. I can't find it in the water." She looked up at me. as I approached. "Sammy, I'm sorry, it's gone."

"Get Brooke out." I joined her in the water, pressing my hands against the tiled floor. "I'll find it."

I had to find it.

"Amanda, burn the door." Brooke commanded.

"It's metal!"

"It's a *school*. Our funding isn't good enough for the nice steel. The hinges will be the weakest."

I stood back and shook my head in disbelief.

"You want to help Mira?" I croaked. "After everything she's done?"

"Of course. We're better than she is," Brooke said darkly. "Amanda?"

Amanda nodded and pressed one hand against a curled fist, creating a makeshift blowtorch. The water surged, and I steadied myself by driving the tip of my sword into the tiles below while Brooke held Amanda, keeping her upright.

The door groaned as the hinges melted away. With a mighty shove of her shoulder, Brooke barreled into Mira's cell.

Mira was on her knees atop the cot, pulling at the chain that linked her handcuffs to the metal railing. Her eyes widened at the sight of us, and her lips drew into a snarl.

"Get out!" she shrieked. "I don't need you!"

"Amanda, get the chain," Brooke said and clapped Amanda on the back. "We aren't letting you drown, Mira."

I held Mira by her arm as Amanda blowtorched the chain. The metal broke apart with a clink, and Mira tried to make a break for it, but I kept a hold on her.

"I didn't need you to help me!" she spat as I pushed her back into the hall.

"I told you," I said through gritted teeth, fighting against the rising current, "I would never abandon you."

Amanda created a trail of flame that clung to the concrete wall, leading the way back to the arena. She and Brooke struggled arm in arm. They could've been out of here by now if they hadn't helped Mira.

"Thanks," I gasped, using my sword to keep me steady while my other hand kept a firm grip on Mira's shackles. "You didn't need—"

"You saved my sister," Amanda grunted. "I saved yours."

"We'll all die because you're weak," Mira snarled, and I gave her chain a warning tug. "You won't be able to fight the current in the arena and once the water gets too high, we'll be sucked back down this hallway to drown."

Amanda's fire trail ran out, and it took me a moment to register that we'd come to the arena. The bright, ambient light that had lit it before had gone out. Amanda lit up the space with a flying ball of fire that revealed the frothing waterfalls that worked to fill the colosseum. The fireball hung suspended in the air, turning the water red.

Mira had been right. We would die here.

"You dumbasses!" A voice screamed at us, and a new sound joined that of the rushing flood. Ice crackled and groaned, stretching across the arena. Sergio stood at the exit overhead, straining to build a wall of ice faster than the surge of water could destroy it. The water cascading down the steps slowed enough for us to wade to the arena's edge and start the climb.

"No!" Mira resisted and tried to pull us both back into the water. "I'll make sure we both die here, Eydis! I won't let you save me! I won't let you win!"

"Leave her!" Sergio shouted as Amanda and Brooke clambered up the stands. I pulled on Mira's chain, and water dripped off the clumps of hair that hung in her face.

"I won't let her drown!" I screamed back at Sergio. Amanda's fireball overhead broke apart as she and Brooke made it to the exit, raining bits of flame over the center of the darkening arena.

A splash sounded as Sergio landed next to me. He dripped with sweat and salt water as he strained to hold the water back. He pressed his helmet into my chest, and in the light of the falling fire, he flashed me a cocky smile.

"Put that on. Wavemaker's got to be near, and we want him to think you're dead."

He lifted Mira over his shoulder, and as much as she struggled against his heroics, she couldn't break free.

"It smells in here," I said as I secured the helmet over my head.

"That's the smell of raw strength and prowess," Sergio grunted. "Now *move*."

I struggled up the steps, ignoring Mira's shrieks of anger and indignation. Sergio's ice dam began to splinter, letting free spurts of water that further widened the cracks in the frozen surface.

"Is that everyone?" I gave one last glance to the arena, sheathing my sword.

"You're the last one," Sergio said. "Turn right."

I skirted into the corridor, but couldn't have turned left if I wanted to. Ice plugged the exit that led to the high school campus, and the water on the other side strained against it, groaning and popping ominously.

Amanda had left a rapidly fading trail of fire, and I limped after it, hoping Sergio was right about us being the last out. I couldn't have come all this way and survived so much just for my friends to be drowned by John Ratcliffe.

Pipes burst overhead, and water sizzled where it met flame, dimming what little light we had left.

"Faster," Sergio said through clenched teeth. He adjusted Mira on his shoulder as he ran, but she'd stopped struggling.

"I don't know if you heard, but I skewered my leg clean through recently," I panted. "I don't go much faster than this."

"And I don't know if you noticed, but my ice won't hold forever. And when it breaks—"

A splintering snap exploded behind us, and water thundered. It caught up to us within seconds, slamming into my back and forcing me forward. Dark water threw me down the corridor, and I was at the mercy of the crushing weight of the torrent.

I curled into a ball, waiting for the current to spit me out, and my head slammed into the floor. Sergio's helmet spared me extensive injury, but I gasped at the force of the hit, inhaling a lungful of burning salt water.

A hand found my collar and pulled me to my feet, and I was back at Sergio's side, gagging and reeling.

"You aren't supposed to drink it."

"Tastes better than your helmet smells," I choked. Water sucked at our waists, and dim, white light glowed from a stairway up ahead. Sergio flipped wet hair out of his face, and my heart stopped when I saw his empty shoulder. "Where's Erika?"

"Who?"

"Mira! Where's Mira?" I shoved him hard in the chest, and he grabbed my arm to propel me forward towards the stairs.

"Lost her when the dam broke. We did our best to save her. Sometimes that's all we can do."

"Find her." My chest and throat burned with salt water, but I forged forward with new strength. I wouldn't let her get away.

But the corridor was still filling with water, and by the time we reached the stairs, it had risen to my chest. Two figures stood on the lowest steps, clinging to the hand rails, and for a brief moment, I thought we'd caught up with Brooke and Amanda before realizing it was Jamie and Andersen.

"I won't go! He's up there! I don't want to see him!" Jamie had her elbow hooked around the bannister while Andersen tried to pull her up the steps. Moonlight poured down the stairs from windows up above. We were so close, but Andersen looked at me helplessly.

"She won't budge," he croaked. "She's afraid of her dad."

"I'm not afraid of him!" Jamie shrieked. "I hate him!"

I pointed up the steps to the exit, rounding on Sergio.

"Mira. Find her. I've got these two."

He shook his head but clambered out of the water to give chase to my sister.

"I don't need your help, Sammy," Andersen growled. "Jamie, we don't know he's up there. There's a dozen different exits, and he could be waiting at any of them. If he's at this one, I won't let him near you."

"He's doing this to get me back!" she wailed. "He won't kill me if I stay down here. It's one big game of chicken to him, and I refuse to let him win!"

Not only was the water rising, but it had started to roll down the steps of our escape, adding to the flood.

"Your dad won't know you're drowning until it's too late," I said. "You'll be dead by the time he realizes."

She whipped her head around to look at me, and I stumbled up a few steps, fighting against the pull of the current. Limp curls clung to her cheeks, and she pursed her lips in stubborn anger.

"He won't kill me," she said again.

"You have to trust us," Andersen begged.

"Trust *you?*" She barked a humorless laugh. "I broke up with you because you're a liar! I can't trust you anymore than I can trust my father!"

Andersen held out an arm, beckoning me farther up the stairs. I slipped in the cascading water, but caught myself and crawled up the steps on my hands. Metal creaked behind me, and I turned to see the bolts holding the bannister in place pop out of the concrete.

Andersen was telekinetically pulling Jamie up the stairs, reeling her in on the railing she refused to let go of.

"Stop!" Jamie wailed. "What do you care if I drown?

"Because he cares about you!" I yelled back.

"Then why'd he lie about being an Apex when we were together? Why didn't he tell me the truth?"

"Because you based your entire personality on hating Apex!"

"Stop," Andersen mumbled. "I've got this."

"No, I won't stop," I snarled. The water frothed at Jamie's neck. "She's being stubborn and prideful, even if it might get her killed. Which, funnily enough, isn't the first time she's done this. So go ahead, Jamie. Drown yourself. I'd say see if we care, but obviously we do, and obviously we can't stop you."

I turned away, but Jamie called out.

"Wait!" Jamie shouted. Something I said must've resonated because she reached for Andersen's hand.

But then, her eyes widened, and her mouth opened in a shriek as she slipped.

"Jamie!" Andersen screamed, and more metal bolts flew from the wall as the banister peeled itself away from the concrete and curled in on her.

She clung to the metal, but the water sucked at her chest.

"Don't let me go," she begged.

"Never," Andersen breathed. "Just stay calm."

Metal creaked as he bent it forward, carrying Jamie towards us, but the water was slick. She slid through the bar, clinging to the wet metal with one hand, her face barely visible at the frothing surface of the water.

"Save me, dammit!" she cried. "Please! Andersen, don't let me go!"

"I won't!" Andersen promised. "Jamie, I've got—"

She slipped under the water.

I grabbed Andersen around the shoulders as he lunged after her, tackling him to the steps before he could do something stupid.

"NO!" he wailed. "Stop, I can still help! I can—"

He broke off in a scream and collapsed in my arms. I dragged him up a few more steps, away from the unforgiving undertow.

"You know," he choked, and his hands curled into fists. "I never did feel like I made up for what I did to you."

"This isn't your fault," I panted, heaving him up another step. For all the dumb things I'd done in the past, even I knew going after Jamie meant certain death. "Please. We need to get out of here."

Voices called out overhead, and Andersen, defeated and broken, struggled to his feet before helping me to mine.

"I hope you know," he murmured, "I really am sorry for everything."

"Andersen, don't—"

But it was too late. He was already in the water, diving after Jamie, disappearing into the dark foam of the flood.

48

Vapor and Ice

Staring at the swirling water where Andersen had disappeared, I knew that I never should have told him that he'd murdered me. I'd done the same thing to him that I'd done to Wesley, giving them both the sick compulsion to be heroes when they didn't need to be.

"Sam!" Sergio's voice sounded distant, but maybe that was because of the relentless roar of the water. He tugged on my arm, and I followed him up the stairs.

I'd seen so much death in the last few weeks, but this—

Sergio caught me as I fell forward and retched. The salt water burned just as much on the way out as it had on the way in.

"We should keep moving." Sergio's voice, which had been sharp and commanding moments ago, was now gentle. "We're out, but it still isn't safe."

Puffs of steam wicked the water out of my uniform, but Sergio shouldn't have been wasting his energy on drying me. I pushed him away and staggered forward through the windowed hall. Moonlight mingled with green aurora, illuminating the main rotunda of the college outside.

A Paragon statue stood in a dried-out fountain basin, identical to the one that stood in front of the high school. Teammates, Apex families, and rescued delegates milled around the rotunda in a daze, checking in on each other, but it was far from everyone who had been hiding underground.

"We've been scattered," Sergio said as we splashed across water-logged tiles. "There's a lot of different exits from the tunnels, so it'll take a moment to regroup with everyone."

Red satin glimmered in the moonlight, but it was hard to feel relief at the sight of Mira held captive on a bench after watching Andersen and Jamie succumb to the flood.

"You found her," I said numbly.

"She didn't make it far." Sergio's arm was around me. I hadn't realized I'd been leaning against him for support. "Hard to get away when handcuffed and sick with poison."

We stumbled out of the college building together. Water bubbled up from underneath the foundation and through storm drains, but it was unable to accumulate into a threat here.

I scanned the faces of those who had made it out from the underground, noting Brooke and Amanda had made it to safety. Anthony stumbled forward to meet me.

"I don't know where the others are," he gushed. "We think some of the team went towards the high school but—"

He broke off as I pulled him into a relieved hug.

"Andersen's gone," I said.

Anthony pushed me away, looking to Sergio for confirmation. After a solemn nod, Anthony's mouth dropped open.

"Not gone-gone. He can't be gone-gone."

"He was trying to save Jamie. He went down a hero."

Over Anthony's shoulder, I caught a glimpse of Mira glaring at me from between the two college students who stood watch over her.

"Not Mira," I reminded myself under my breath, looking at the woman who'd somehow grown out of what had once been my sister. "Erika."

"What?" Anthony asked, and I ignored him, marching over to Mira's bench. The green aurora overhead no longer felt like a piece of home, but a gross reproduction of something that had once been mine, the same way Erika had been.

"Where is he?" I demanded. Mira tilted her chin at me and tried to look proud, though she reminded me more of a drowned cat.

"Who?"

"Siedon. Wavemaker. John Ratcliffe. Whatever his name is. This was him."

"Here I thought you saved me to prove a point about the kind of sister you are. But no, you just want information."

I clenched my fists.

"He's nearby, right?" I ignored her words, despite the way they cut. "Do his powers work long distance?"

Erika sneered, and the look of petulance made me wonder all over again how I never realized her true identity. She used to make the same face at our mother.

Then, the look dropped from her face as the ground beneath us trembled. The Paragon statue in the empty fountain creaked and groaned, then blew to the side, uncorking a column of water that shot upwards out of the pipes.

A voice howled into the night.

"Where is she? Bring me my daughter!"

John Ratcliffe sauntered down the main drive towards the university. His suit was soaked and limp, damp hair hung in his face. Water ran from the geysers he'd formed out of the fountain and drains, rolling across cobblestone to add to the mass of water that was building behind him. The wave rolled and crested but never broke, growing taller and stronger behind the Prime Minister.

"I said, where's my daughter!?" he roared.

The strongest of us were still missing. I didn't know where Fleming, or Wesley, or Naomi, or any of the captains were or if they were even alive. I didn't know if it made a difference.

John Ratcliffe's powers may have been relatively new to him, but they were devastatingly strong.

I stepped forward, but a hand on my shoulder pulled me back.

"Keep that helmet on," Sergio hissed as he squared his shoulders and formed an ice-blade in either hand.

He stalked forward to meet the Prime Minister, standing tall, though I could tell he was nervous by the way he tested his grip on his blades.

"Your daughter is gone," he called. The wave behind Ratcliffe gnashed and frothed, still not breaking, trapped in an eternal crest.

"Liar!" Ratcliffe yelled. "Bring her to me or you'll all be swept into the ocean and left to drown!"

"If you think you can—" Sergio started, but a burst of water shot forth from Ratcliffe's wave. Sergio held his ice-blades in a cross, and the attack dissolved into steam.

Two more water cannons issued forth. One shattered into ice shards, but the second hit Sergio square in the chest. He barreled backwards, landing in the fountain basin. Water rained over him, spurting from the broken pipes, and his ice-blades elongated into javelins. He whirled, building momentum, and let them fly one after the other.

Ratcliffe side-stepped the attacks, though one of the javelins nicked his shoulder, ripping his suit. He roared in pain and fury, but before he could retaliate, the top of his wave froze and dropped sharpened icicles down over his head.

He rolled out of the way and lifted his arms to conduct the water pooled at Sergio's feet. Sergio tried to boil the water off, but it gathered too quickly, sucking him into a floating vortex. Several students charged at Ratcliffe from the side, including Amanda, but the rest of his wave rushed forward, bowling them over and smashing them into the side of the college building.

"You have three seconds to bring me my daughter." Ratcliffe lowered his voice, no longer yelling, but somehow more threatening.

"We don't have her!" Isabelle screamed.

"One!" Ratcliffe held up a single finger. "Two!"

Ratcliffe formed a fist and raised it over his head. The water in the fountain lifted, forming a murky, levitating globe with Sergio at its core. He slashed at the water with newly formed blades, struggling to find the surface. His face strained with the effort of holding his breath as Ratcliffe lifted him higher still.

"Jamie's not here!" someone cried.

"Thr—"

"Stop!" It was Brooke, yelling from where she helped Amanda climb to her feet. "We'll get her for you, but you have to give us a moment!"

"Hurry," Ratcliffe warned. A new wave built behind him, rapidly growing as he continued to absorb water. "I'm going to hold your friend here until my daughter is in front of me. I doubt he can hold his breath much longer."

Brooke cast a nervous glance around, searching for any sign of Jamie, but I knew she wasn't here.

"Or perhaps I should drop your friend?" Ratcliffe called. Sergio's thrashing was getting weaker at the water's center, and there was less steam rolling off the globe. "If he breaks his neck in the fall, it may be quicker and less gruesome. Drowning is a horrible way to—"

"You want your daughter?"

The voice— hoarse, scratchy, and impossible— boomed over the rotunda. I spun around, my heart rising in my chest before immediately plummeting again.

Andersen stood in the main doors of the college hall. Water leaked out of the corridor behind him, rushing past his ankles. Damp hair plastered his forehead, and his shoulders heaved with deep breaths of loathing. Quaking arms clutched Jamie's lifeless body, and he carried her forward. Salt water dripped off of Jamie's hair and clothes, but the girl did not stir. Skin that had once flushed pink with a never-ending supply of indignation and misplaced passion was now dull and pallid.

Jamie had been hateful, vindictive, and cruel, and she had not deserved to die this way.

The wave building behind Ratcliffe collapsed. Despite its size, it didn't crash or roll or surge, but rather deflated in a defeated outpouring of water. At the same time, the watery sphere that held Sergio at its center burst, and Sergio plummeted back to earth.

Anthony and Isabelle cushioned his fall with a gust of wind, and he landed, unmoving, in the fountain. I vaulted over the fountain rim and rushed to his side. I tapped on his face, wondering if it was too late, but then he rolled over, coughing up water.

All the while, Andersen continued his procession until he stood directly in front of John Ratcliffe.

The Prime Minister of New Delos stared blankly at what had once been his daughter.

"What did you do to her?" he rasped as Andersen laid the girl at her father's feet.

"I did my best," Andersen replied. "She died insisting you would never hurt her."

Ratcliffe shook his head, and Andersen stepped back to give him space as he fell to his knees. He pulled wet locks of hair out of Jamie's face and caressed her cheek.

For a second, I was naive enough to think the danger had passed, and I welcomed the quiet of the moment, despite the tragedy it carried. Andersen was okay. Sergio was recovering. John Ratcliffe had lost whatever fight had been raging inside him.

But then, Ratcliffe released a scream of feral anguish, and the ground shook. The gathered students and family shouted in shock as the shaking became more violent. A dull roar grew, and I thought it might be more water adhering to some summons by Ratcliffe, but then the silhouettes of several buildings along the city skyline shifted and crumbled.

Ratcliffe, in his grief, was shaking the entire city.

Behind us, bricks moaned and clattered against each other as the foundations of the college hall gave out. I threw an arm around Sergio to pull him out of the fountain and away from the cloud of dust that washed over us.

Water surged from the wreckage, thick with mortar and debris, and John Ratcliffe continued to howl.

The fallen Paragon statue shifted, grating against pavement, and Andersen grunted in effort as he telekinetically lifted it and hurled it towards Ratcliffe.

A wall of water shot upwards, knocking the statue off course, and as the dust from the fallen building began to settle, silhouettes appeared atop a distant pile of rubble, their outlines glowing green against the aurora-stained sky.

"Is that—" Sergio started to say, but the hope on his face faded as the figures charged.

"Not friends." I gritted my teeth and drew my sword, preparing for the oncoming fight. "Adrestus's Epsilons."

I could see them clearly now, and I recognized the haunted, passive faces they wore as they charged at us over the rubble.

"Don't kill them!" Isabelle shouted, taking up a fighting stance next to Anthony. "They aren't fighting us of their own free will!"

Boonsri, the college student who controlled plants, rushed to join the front line. Vines and roots ripped from the ground at her behest, white and gnarled from salt water damage, but looking all the more lethal for it. I brandished my sword, reminding myself to use the flat of the blade.

"Move!" Sergio shoved me to the ground, freezing a wave of water that rose behind us. The water burst through the ice, sending frozen projectiles across the rotunda. I tried to push myself to my hands and knees, and my fingers brushed against an abandoned set of handcuffs.

"YOU KILLED HER!" John Ratcliffe roared, still clutching Jamie's body against his chest, and the ground shook once again. "You've murdered my only child!"

I lifted the handcuffs to better inspect them in the moonlight. The metal was gnarled and eroded, as if dissolved in acid.

Mira's powers were back, and she was escaping.

A glimpse of red and white disappeared over a pile of rubble, and I leaped to my feet, casting the handcuffs aside to sprint over quaking ground.

"Wait!" Boot-steps thundered after me. "Sammy, stop!"

I ignored Sergio's cries, forging deeper into the city after Erika. I wouldn't let her escape. I wouldn't let her return to Adrestus. I wouldn't let him take my sister back.

"Samantha, I swear on whatever pagan pantheon you hold dear, if you don't stop running, I'll—"

"Lose to me in another sword fight?" I goaded. I jammed my finger up to the microphone button on Sergio's helmet. "Is anyone out there? Can you hear me?"

"First, I've *never* lost to you in a sword fight, and second, that helmet hasn't had batteries or a radio signal in weeks."

I scowled.

"First day of sword training," I panted, watching Mira's red dress turn down an alley up ahead. "I beat you fair and square."

"And I was going easy on you."

"That's your mistake, not mine." I stopped to point where I'd seen Erika disappear. "We follow her, we find Remi. We rescue Remi, Adrestus doesn't control his army anymore, get it?"

The clamor of battle faded behind me. If I could free Remi, then I could free the island. I could free the Epsilons. Adrestus's forces would be hobbled.

Maybe I could face Adrestus himself one last time. I wasn't afraid of him anymore, after all.

I doubled my pace, ignoring the ache in my lungs and the metallic taste of blood on my tongue. Residual poison weighed heavy in my veins, but I fought to keep going.

"Is that why you turned back to save her from being drowned? Because you knew she'd lead us to Remi?"

The suggestion stung, maybe because Mira had also accused me of saving her for my own use.

"You've known me long enough to know that I never think that far ahead."

Sergio grunted something that sounded like "fair enough" as we took a turn. We'd lost sight of Mira, but through the rubble of the city, I could see the glowing domed rooftop of City Hall.

I frowned. I had figured Remi had to be in Schrader Tower, or somewhere near there. When she first took control over Hackjob weeks ago, she'd cried about it being "too high". It could have been because we were high up, but what if it was because Adrestus was keeping her at a height? City Hall was barely five stories tall. Sure Remi was scared of heights, but five stories?

But then I remembered the massive whirlpool that lived under City Hall and Remi shaking in fear as we'd climbed up to a control booth hanging over the vortex's maw before sinking the city.

And I remembered the day I'd spent in the records room and the sound of screaming as the City Hall doors closed behind me.

"I know where she is," I gasped. It was stupidly obvious.

We'd wrecked the old control booth that commanded the city functions. Remi had replaced it.

"Great, so let's go back and help the others!" Sergio panted, but up ahead, Mira darted into a parking structure that sat beneath an apartment building, and despite what I told Sergio and myself, this chase wasn't about Remi.

I sprinted after her into the parking garage. This part of the city had long since been abandoned, evidenced by the broken shop windows and empty parking spots. I looked up at the concrete supports that held the building over us, then pulled my eyes away from the ceiling to focus on the path ahead. I skidded to a stop.

Mira had stopped running and now stood just ahead between two concrete supports.

In the dim light afforded by distant, glowing City Hall, I saw her lips split into a grin, and my body turned cold.

"Get out!" I screamed to Sergio and charged at Mira, hoping to tackle her before she could raise her hand to the concrete.

It took the smallest brush of her fingertips, and the concrete cracked and crumbled, just as Vidar's statue had on McMillan Island.

The building overhead groaned, and Sergio screamed my name as heavy concrete slabs fell around me, plunging me into suffocating darkness.

49

Fates Fall

The building seemed to fall forever, raining dust and rubble. Its collapse brought an odd clarity, like the Universe and I had come to a mutual understanding that this was the end, and why shouldn't it be?

But then uneasy silence settled over the destruction, and the Universe went back on its word. Everything was uncertain again. Relief at being alive mixed with the fear of still having something to lose.

A single beam of dusty, distant light broke through the slabs of concrete where I curled up, protected only by Sergio's helmet.

"Sergio?" I called. A cough racked my chest, and the taste of blood became stronger.

Alone.

I was alone. Sergio could be injured or dead, and Mira was getting away after trying to bury me. I'd been close to the edge of the building when the collapse happened, and loose rocks gave way as I tried to dig myself out, letting more of the dim light in to break across my visored face.

I pushed against concrete, but it didn't budge. I needed Wesley or Andersen or Heather or even Naomi. Anyone.

Because no matter what, no matter how strong I'd become, my strength, my skills, my strategic prowess still paled in comparison to those of my friends.

I was, and I would die, the weak link.

Not every Beta could be as amazing as Fleming, rising to surpass his brother in everything but legacy, or as determined as Winnie, driven by sheer will to prove the world wrong about her.

I knocked away another rock and dragged myself forward, freezing when I heard the rubble shift overhead.

But even if my friends didn't have their incredible powers that let them do the things they could do, none of them would leave me under a pile of broken concrete. None of them would stop fighting. And I wasn't about to, either.

Not while Adrestus was still alive.

But the dust was thick, and my head was turning heavy. I pulled myself another foot, getting ever closer to the light. Blood pooled in my mouth. Part of me had felt lucky to survive the collapsing building, but that would've been a more merciful death than suffocation.

Every lungful of air brought more dirt into my mouth. I was at the opening and reached my hand forward, scraping at loose rubble, but it was too much. I laid my head down and closed my eyes to the dull light, letting it filter across my eyelids.

Then, the glow turned dark, occluded by an unknown something standing at the opening. Fingers wrapped around mine and pulled on my hand, dragging me out of the rubble.

"Sergio?" I murmured. Sharp, concrete edges tore at my sides, and I sucked in my stomach, trying to help worm my way out.

Cool wind met my cheeks, and I coughed up blood and dust. Debris clattered as my savior staggered away, giving me space to push up onto my hands and knees on the rubble pile. Fresh oxygen filled my lungs and cleared my head. I cleared dirt off my visor to better see the brick-laid plaza that sprawled out ahead. Another Paragon statue glinted at its center, grinning in the green aurora, which bled with the orange lights of City Hall, still another mile or so into the city.

My rescuer stood at the feet of the statue. Black metal glittered in the night lights, and red capes fluttered in the ocean wind. I should've known Adrestus would be nearby.

"You." The single word reverberated from inside his helmet, full of loathing and heartbreak. I stumbled away from the rubble, marching into Paragon's shadow as I drew my Viking sword.

Adrestus sauntered forward but stopped several yards away.

"You...you should be dead."

"Surprise." My mouth twisted with the word. I'd told myself I wasn't afraid of Adrestus anymore. It took every ounce of resolve I had left to keep that promise. He'd spent every minute of our training sessions together demolishing me in combat, but something seemed off about him now. His stance was less assured than usual, and the way his shoulders rose and fell betrayed his rapid breathing.

He was off his game. Maybe I stood a chance.

"I won't believe it until I see your face." His voice echoed inside his helmet.

I hesitated. I was safer with the helmet on.

"I said," Adrestus roared with sudden agitation, "show me!"

I removed the helmet, and wind grabbed at my hair. Adrestus drank me in before following suit and letting his metal helmet clang against the ground. His blue eye screwed up in loathing while light bounced off the curve of his metal eyepatch.

"It doesn't make sense," he murmured, wagering another step forward. "I saw your body, and the others—"

"It can't seriously surprise you at this point in the game." I forced myself to laugh, hoping it might keep fear at bay.

"No, I suppose not." His gaze flickered down at my uniform. "You've updated your look."

"The last costume didn't really feel like me," I snorted, thinking of Lana's ridiculous updates.

Adrestus's good eye twitched, and he sneered.

"Whatever it takes to feel like one of *them*."

"They're my family," I snarled. "Which is more than you ever were."

His face contorted, and he drew his sword, swinging it haphazardly. I deflected the blow, though the force of it made me stumble back.

"*I* was your family!" he bellowed. "And *you!* After all this time, you've been *lying* to me! Me! Of all people!"

He swung the sword again, but he was sloppy in his rage, and I danced out of his reach. I'd been right to assume he was off his game.

"You *killed* my family," I countered.

His eye bulged, and he placed an indignant hand over his chest.

"Me? *Me?* You want to call me the murderer after everything you've done?" The next swing caught me off guard, and while I raised my sword in time, the force of Adrestus's blow knocked me to the ground. I coughed into a hand that came away red with blood as I struggled to catch my breath. Adrestus's eye grew wide. "You may not be dead, but you're still sick."

He stood over me, his sword limp at his side, as I tried to catch my breath. I glared up at him, and my stomach turned when I saw tears streaming down his face.

"No," I growled, pointing my sword up towards his face. "No, you *don't* get to cry over me!"

"Why shouldn't I?" he murmured. "All of this, and they can't even heal you?"

I slashed at his ankles, but he stepped out of my range.

"You're weaker, too," he mused. "Much weaker. Here I thought you were back from the dead but this? This is a shadow of your former self."

I shook my head and struggled to my feet.

"You and I," he continued, "we were going to save the world together, and then *you*—"

"Don't act like you viewed us as equals. Don't you dare pretend to have ever valued me—"

"Valued you?" Adrestus's face broke into a snarl. "I admired you more than anyone. I spent years thinking you were better than me and then—"

"I *am* better than you," I said, but my head spun. Adrestus didn't admire me. He was toying with me. He was being cruel.

He lunged with new fervor, and again I struggled to parry but managed to stay standing.

"You were *everything* to me!" he bellowed, and our swords sang as they met midair. "But you threw it away when you *ruined* everything!"

I dodged another sloppy lunge and managed to nick his thigh between plates of armor. He roared in pain and anger and limped out of my range.

"I never did *anything* to you!" I screamed. "You're the one who ruined *my* life! You're the one who used *me*!"

He shook his head, hate pulling at his otherwise handsome features.

"You were everything," he repeated, "and you discarded me like I was nothing. You've been lying this whole time, after taking the only girl I ever loved—"

Rage boiled inside me, and my hands quaked against my sword hilt.

"Loved?" I cackled, cold, mirthless, and furious. "I took nothing because she was never yours to begin with! *I* was never yours!"

I lunged, propelled by sloppy rage. He sidestepped the attack easily and brought his heavy hilt down between my shoulders as my momentum carried me past him.

The air left my lungs, my knees buckled, and I collapsed in the dust. Adrestus rolled me onto my back with the toe of his boot, and he had the audacity to continue to cry as he held his sword point to my throat.

"Save the world," he croaked, tears falling from his chin. "That's what we said we were going to do."

The blade shook in his hands, rattling against the skin of my neck, stinging me, and I braced for the attack.

He licked his lips, still staring down at me. The statue of Paragon loomed behind him.

"Do it," I goaded. "It should be you, after all."

His nostrils flared, and he drew his arm back. I stared at him, resilient and stubborn to the end, but then he cast the sword aside and let it clatter against the brick plaza.

"I won't," Adrestus said. "I won't kill someone I love. I'm not like you."

He gave me one last look of utter contempt and heartbreak, and turned away.

"I didn't kill anyone!" I screeched.

I would make sure his mercy was his last mistake.

I leapt to my feet, and he spun around just as I bore down and shoved the blade between two ribs, the same way I had a thousand years ago.

The same look of awestruck betrayal crossed his face, and he fell back. I leaned into the hilt, watching his chest deflate and his eye widen in the light of the aurora.

I'd thought I'd feel triumph in this moment, when I'd finally put the man who'd ruined my and my family's lives to rest. He couldn't hurt us anymore. He couldn't hurt *me* anymore.

But more than anything, I just felt tired.

"I'll make sure you die this time." I nodded, speaking to myself more than him. "Even if it takes months. Same way you did Tiberius."

He shook his head.

"I don't know...what you're talking about."

"Yes, you do," I growled. "Tiberius! Your friend! The one you murdered!"

"I don't understand." His lips struggled to form words. "Why, Paul?"

My hand slipped. *Paul?* A thousand years of animosity, and as he lay dying on the end of my blade, he had the gall to spend his last moments talking about *Paragon?*

"What's Paul Fleming got to do with anything?" I hissed. "I'm the one who killed you a thousand years ago, and I'm the one who killed you today."

His breath rattled, and his brow furrowed weakly as confusion clouded his pallid face.

"Are you not Paul?" he rasped, the tiniest bit of hope clinging to his words. "Are you not my brother?"

I stumbled off the sword, leaving it embedded in Adrestus's flesh. His chest heaved with the effort of lifting his head to watch me scramble backwards.

Something was wrong. Something was *very, very* wrong, but I couldn't figure out what. White noise screamed in my head, and underneath it, Adrestus's words repeated themselves.

Are you not my brother?

"That was a cruel trick," he murmured. "Making yourself look like Paul when you killed me."

He coughed, then grunted in pain as my silver sword shifted in his chest.

"I didn't—"

"You can't win." His lips ran red with his own blood, and they twisted into a cruel smile. "She's better than you in every way."

I shook my head. He wasn't making sense, and something was very, horribly, devastatingly wrong.

"Oh, dear, looks like you've certainly made a mess, haven't you?" A new voice cut through the static in my head, and I twisted to see Adrian Schrader sitting at the foot of the Paragon statue. "You didn't *actually* think that was Adrestus, did you?"

My knees gave out, and I collapsed in the dust, looking back at Adrestus bleeding out. But then, the illusion flickered. Dark chest armor turned red and white. Black hair turned brown. The metal eye patch flickered from view.

This whole time, I thought I'd been fighting Adrestus, but it wasn't Adrestus gasping for air around the hilt of my blade.

It was Fleming.

50

Spell Break

Trev Baker's prophecy was coming to fruition right in front of me. I crawled to Fleming's side on all fours, begging this to be another illusion. A falsehood. Fleming couldn't die.

His eyes widened, and his lips formed my name.

"No," I whispered. "It isn't you. You were..."

I kneeled at his side, and the world reeled around us.

"Imagine," Adrian Schrader crooned, "your last two fathers died *because* of you, but this one? You put the blade in him yourself."

I found Fleming's hand, gloved in Paragon's colors.

"I'm sorry," I choked, and his dying face blurred behind a wall of tears. "I didn't know, I—"

I glanced around, looking for anything that might stem the bleeding. Anything that might save Fleming.

"You figured it out there at the end, I saw it in your eyes," Schrader said. "But it was too late. You'd already run him through."

Schrader stood over Fleming and me. His light gray suit was spotless, despite the demolition that surrounded us.

"Help me!" I choked, pressing my hands over Fleming's stomach, trying to stem the blood. But even if Adrian wasn't an illusion projected into my head by Gregor, he wouldn't have helped me.

"Sammy, it's okay—" Fleming tried to gasp, but he was cut off by more blood pooling at his lips, and I forced him onto his side so he wouldn't choke. The sword still stuck out of his trunk, red and glistening. My sword. It hadn't been that long ago that the same blade had stuck out from Vidar's chest.

"Now you're just prolonging things," Adrian tutted.

"Get out!" I screamed and slashed my black steel sword at the apparition. He put his hands up in defeat and dissolved into nothing, and I howled at the sky. "Help! Somebody! Please!"

"It's okay." Fleming's rasp was barely audible. His eyelids fluttered closed, and I shook his shoulders, maybe too violently. He couldn't die. He couldn't leave me. "I'm fine."

"No, you're not." Tears fell off the tip of my nose, splashing onto the paved stones of the plaza next to Fleming's face. "It's my fault. Trev Baker said—"

"Trev is dead," Fleming coughed. "Just like all my friends. I never should've outlived any of them."

"What about me?" I cried. "I'm alive still."

He gave a shuddering breath, and I stopped, a hand over my mouth, wondering if it had been his last, but then his shoulders heaved again, and he opened a single eye to look up at me.

"You are the best thing and the best daughter to ever happen to me." He smiled, but his teeth ran red with blood. "Can I call you that? Daughter?"

I nodded, unable to speak, and Fleming closed his eye again, a new serenity passing over his face.

"Good. Now go help the others."

"No." I shook my head. "I've run off enough times, okay? And I'm going to make you proud. I promise. I'll—"

"Sammy." His fingers tightened around my hand. "You already have."

His fingers went limp.

"Please," I whispered, but his breathing was shallow, and he didn't respond when I shook his shoulders. "You can't. Stop it. *Please.*"

I bowed my head over him, crying openly.

"Holy hell, Sammy. What happened?"

I jerked around at the hoarse voice and the sound of shifting rubble. Sergio stumbled down the side of the debris pile.

"You're alive?"

"Of course I am. Is *he?*" Sergio held his left arm against his body as he joined me at Fleming's side.

"Barely." I wiped my tears away, though there was no chance Sergio hadn't seen them already.

"That's your sword in his chest."

"I know." My voice cracked. "It was Gregor. He made me think I was fighting Adrestus. Neither of us knew who we were fighting."

Sergio swore under his breath and winced as he let go of his arm to grab the sword by the blade.

"You have to leave it in!" I tried to bat his hand away. "He'll bleed out faster if you take it out!"

"Not if I do this correctly. Sorry in advance about the smell."

He pulled the blade out little by little until the point that protruded from Fleming's back retracted back into his body. Sergio held it there and took a deep breath.

The metal under Sergio's hand glowed orange. Sweat beaded along his forehead and pooled atop the black strap of his eyepatch.

And then the smell hit me. The acrid scent of cauterizing flesh.

Sergio slowly and carefully lifted the blade from Fleming's body until the blade tip appeared. Bloodied skin puckered and sealed, burning the ripped fabric of Fleming's uniform.

Sergio wiped the sweat from his forehead and handed me the sword, dirty with burnt blood.

"I cauterized what I could, but he's not out of the woods yet. Far from it." He shifted around to Fleming's side and hoisted him up as best he could with one arm. "You go. I've got him."

"But—"

"You'll be faster than me. They need you."

"Your shoulder looks dislocated. You can't—"

"Can't?" Sergio shifted Fleming up over his shoulder in a fireman's carry. "You know me better than that. I *can*. You can. Now go."

"But I can help."

"Gregor made you think you were fighting an enemy. What are all our friends doing *right now* back at the campuses?"

"They're—"

Fighting. They were fighting enemies.

Sergio readjusted his grip on Fleming and nodded back the way we'd come.

"Go."

Maybe Sergio was wrong. Maybe our friends were okay. Maybe the fighting had already stopped. But if Gregor had used that trick on Fleming and me, what was stopping him from using it back at the schools? I knew he had the skills and the power, and what better way to keep us occupied as Adrestus launched his final plan?

I raced the purple dawn that rose on the horizon and chased away the green of the aurora. More buildings had fallen, and I stumbled through debris, ignoring the exhaustion that weighed on every footstep.

Shouts and screams rose as night faded and horror mounted when I realized I could put a name and face to every shriek.

There were no Epsilons here tonight. The only ones screaming were my friends.

I passed the rubble that once had been our favorite frozen yogurt shop, passing into the high school campus and stopped to cover my face from falling glass when a whole floor of school hall windows blew out.

"Stop!" I screamed and sprinted around the building.

The school yard and athletic fields had been reduced to a battlefield, and my friends stood on either front. The rising sun cast long shadows that criss-crossed across the overgrown grass. Another explosion rocked the school hall, and I stumbled back, watching silhouettes pass on the other side of shattered windows.

"Please!" I screamed, charging to the center of the field. A gust of wind knocked me off my feet, and I fell hard on my side. The ground tilted beneath me until I managed to gather my bearings and spin around just as Anthony launched at me, his face almost unrecognizable behind a mask of rage.

I rolled out of the way as he sent another torrent of wind burrowing into the grass where I'd been a moment ago.

"Anthony, it's me!" I put my hands up, begging him to see me past Gregor's illusions.

"You hurt Isabelle! I'll kill you!"

Anthony sent another blast of air, pushing me towards the island's edge.

"It's me, Anthony!" I drew my sword to dig into the lawn, using it as an anchor in his gale. "I'm Samantha! Your friend!"

Anthony shook his head.

"You can't trick me!"

"Adrestus already has! He's in your head, making you see something that isn't real."

Anthony's shoulders heaved with exhaustion and confusion. Behind him, fire erupted near the school hall.

"You don't look like Samantha."

"It's me."

"Prove it!"

I struggled to my feet, leaving my sword upright in the grass.

"You don't *hate* frozen yogurt," I said slowly, thinking of the ruined shop I'd passed. "You just hate that it's pretending to be something it's not."

Anthony's face screwed up, and he shook his head.

"Look through the illusion," I begged. "I'm Sammy."

His face broke in relief and pain.

"It's not real," he murmured. "But everyone— Move!"

Anthony buffeted me with a new gust of wind, and I landed spread-eagle on the lawn. I twisted around to see a new assailant with his hair standing up at odd angles, slicked with sweat and salt water.

"Wesley?" I asked.

Wesley charged, unable to see beyond the illusion, and I curled up, bracing for his hit.

Anthony leapt between us, his arms outstretched.

"Wesley, it's us! Anthony and Samantha!"

Wesley paused next to my sword where it still stood in the grass. He pulled it up by the hilt, and his eyes went wide at the sight of the bloodied blade.

"This is Sammy's." His words were laced with a poisonous warning, and he held the blade up for us to see. "What've you done to her?"

"Nothing! She's—" Anthony tried to say, but Wesley closed the distance between them and backhanded his former roommate out of the way. The sound of a cracking bone split the lawn, and Anthony screamed in agony.

"Stop!" I reached out for Anthony where he collapsed in the grass.

"If you've hurt Sammy—"

"I *am* Sammy!"

He stood over me now. He'd lost his prosthetic somewhere and held my sword over me.

"How did you end up with her sword?"

"Wesley, please." Anthony crawled over to us, holding his broken arm against his body. "You don't know what you're doing."

"I'm saving my friends," Wesley spat. "And if you've hurt them in any way—"

"Yes." Anthony was nearly on top of me in his efforts to stave off Wesley. "I have. I betrayed their trust. I got them hurt. I thought I was doing what was best and that everything would be okay, but it's my fault we're here now."

Wesley's brow furrowed in confusion.

"Where are they?"

"Right here." Anthony patted his chest armor. "But if you can't see us, that's okay. If you have to hurt us, hurt me. I deserve it. But don't hurt her, okay? I know you'll never forgive yourself if you do. Because unlike me, you're a good friend. You're loyal. Too loyal. And you always try to be good. So please—"

Wesley's face broke with horror, and he fell to his knees, turning pale.

"Anthony?"

Anthony half-laughed and half-sobbed in relief.

"Yeah, yeah it's me."

Wesley dropped the sword and wrapped his arm around Anthony, who yelped in pain.

"Your arm." Wesley pulled away to inspect Anthony's arm better. "I did that?"

"It's okay," Anthony insisted. "I almost jettisoned Sammy into the ocean before I realized—"

Wesley seemed to notice me for the first time, and he scrambled over Anthony to pull me into a hug.

"What's wrong?" he said. "What's happened?"

"We need to stop the fighting. It's us. Both sides. Gregor is in all our heads."

Wesley stiffened.

"No." He shook his head. "Not everyone. It can't—"

"Everyone, except Ratcliffe. They're all us."

"Sammy." The way he whispered my name sent a chill down my spine. "Whose blood is on your sword?"

My fingernails dug into his shoulders, and I crumbled into him, shaking but somehow holding back all the tears I wanted to cry.

"Everyone, stop!" Anthony screamed. Wind pulled at my hair. "Listen to me!"

"Sammy?" Wesley whispered as Anthony continued to beg for a ceasefire.

"I thought he was Adrestus. He looked and sounded like Adrestus. He's with Sergio now, but I don't think he's going to—"

I broke off, unable to complete the thought.

"Who?"

"Fleming." I met his green eyes and watched what little color was left in his face drain. His chin quivered, and he clamped his jaw shut, but nodded and helped me to my feet.

Anthony's message spread slowly at first, but Gregor's spell broke one teammate at a time, until there were only cries for ceasefire left in the wake of the fighting.

Naomi limped out from the school hall, followed by Amanda and several others. Justin untangled Freddie from one of Boonsri's roots. A stunned and horrified silence fell over the campus.

And then, the first crying scream split the morning air.

"Somebody help! Please!"

More voices joined in the wailing, calling for aid as they discovered their injured teammates across the two campuses. I sank into Wesley's chest, absently rolling up his empty sleeve, as the cries of my friends rose with the sun.

"You could've all had paradise!" Water seeped up out of the dirt and rolled across the lawn to a new figure. John Ratcliffe held his dead daughter, and his suit was in tatters. A stream of blood issued from his head and down his face. "You could've had everything we were building, but instead you chose pain and death and destruction!"

"The only ones who brought that are you and the so-called master you serve," I spat. Wesley kept his arm around me, and I felt I was supporting him just as much as he was supporting me.

"ENOUGH!" he bellowed and raised a fist in the air. I waited for the ground to tremble or for water to surge, but nothing happened. Ratcliffe appeared to have reached his limit, but then a startled shout rang out.

"The water!"

The ocean glowed orange in the light of the rising sun, but the colors distorted as water rose to obscure the horizon. Ratcliffe roared with the effort of building a tidal wave that towered high over the abandoned dorms of the high school, reaching into the sun-dyed sky.

"No!" I surged towards Ratcliffe, but the lawn had filled with murk, and I fell forward as mud sucked at my boots.

I twisted back to look at the colossal wave, big enough to wipe out not just the schools, but all of New Delos. And then, just as I'd resigned myself to defeat, the wave shrank, receding back into the ocean.

"It's getting smaller," I gasped.

"Not smaller," Wesley croaked, joining me on the ground to hold me by my shoulders. "Farther."

Adrestus's great flood had begun.

Ratcliffe retreated, but we were in no shape to fight him anyway. Jamie may have been the only fatality, but when Sergio limped into our new makeshift camp on the high school soccer field, it was apparent that Fleming may soon join her.

I rushed to his side, watching the haggard and shallow rise and fall of his chest as Angie went to work assessing the cauterized sword wound. I tried to follow her into her medical tent where she treated the worst injuries with Andersen's help, but Wesley held me back.

Most of us had sustained some kind of injury, and we had no food or water for the globe's worth of traumatized diplomats huddled in the bleachers of the field. I hid from them at the back of the bleachers with Wesley and Avery, hoping I wouldn't be recognized outside of my Scourge Queen get-up.

A subdued silence rang out, all the more profound in the absence of the rumbling city engines. A new wave was building on the horizon, but we were helpless to stop it while we waited for Dr. Parker to finish meeting with the team captains.

When the bleachers shook with footsteps as Naomi climbed to join us, Wesley was first to interrogate her.

"What's the plan?" he demanded, but she shook her head and sat down, clenching her fists in her lap.

"What's wrong?" I asked. "Is Fleming—"

"Still alive," she murmured, then leaned forward to hide her head in her hands.

I wanted to ask more, but Dr. Parker limped to the front of the bleachers, leaning against Coach Reiner. She glanced nervously at the delegates, but in the days she'd watched over them, she seemed to have earned their respect and they fell quiet as she cleared her throat.

"We've experienced a harrowing few days and an even more harrowing night," she started. "The plan is survival. We'll send teams to find food, water, and supplies. We'll hold on as long as Adrestus allows us to and re-evaluate after whatever happens next."

"So we're giving up?" a college student stood up at the front of the bleachers.

"Eli, the flood has begun." Dr. Parker shook her head. "Those of us who can still stand are in no condition to fight, and even if we could, we can't stop the tidal waves Ratcliffe is already sending towards the coastline. We've lost. Adrestus has won."

51

Final Team

Nothing could change Dr. Parker's mind, not even when I begged her to send a team to City Hall to save Remi. I understood why, of course. The few of us left standing were exhausted to the brink of collapse and, for the most part, we were *just* kids. We had no way to fight Adrestus's army. No way to stop him.

It would be a suicide mission that flew in the face of Dr. Parker's one and only directive: survive.

As for the rest of the world, there were other Apex out there, living normal lives. Maybe they could fight off Adrestus's great flood.

Fleming still hadn't woken up, but his breathing seemed steady. I sat beside his cot in the medical tent reserved for those with the most extensive wounds. Isabelle lay on his other side, still unconscious after the battle.

"Can you feel him?" I asked. Naomi looked up from where she sat on the floor between Fleming and Isabelle.

"He's okay," she promised. "I've been making sure."

I could see her in my periphery, watching me, but I kept my eyes trained on the steady rise and fall of Fleming's bandaged chest. According to Nurse Angie, he had an infection that she couldn't treat without the proper supplies.

Sergio, with his arm in a sling, narrowed his eyes at me from the cot across from Fleming's. He was sporting a new undercut over one ear where his skin was gnarled with ugly sutures.

"What're you thinking, Sammy?"

"Nothing." I held my breath when Fleming's chest stopped moving, but then the rhythm of his breathing resumed, and I exhaled.

"That's a lie," Naomi snorted and pulled her braids over one shoulder.

"No running off." I shrugged. I could hear Fleming saying the words in my head. "We both know he wouldn't want me doing anything stupid."

I nodded at Fleming, and Naomi settled her chin against her knees.

"We also both know he would expect it."

"You would have to stop me if I tried," I said wryly. "Might lose your captaincy if you didn't."

"The world is about to end. Team Captain doesn't mean anything anymore."

I glanced back at Sergio, but he had fallen into conversation with Marcus, who occupied the cot next to his.

"I'd say it matters more than ever," I laughed softly. "It's not like we have much left to hold onto."

"You're not running away, then? For once, the world's flightiest non-Apex superhero is staying put?"

"Superhero?" I suppressed a dry smile.

"Sure. What would you say instead?"

Mistake? Disaster? A train wreck masquerading as a high schooler?

"I don't know."

The canvas flap at the tent entrance shifted, and Wesley looked in. He tried to smile but looked down the rows of injured and gulped.

"Sammy, you free to talk?" he asked.

I jumped to my feet, worried he bore bad news, but he managed a more successful attempt at a grin and reached for my hand.

"It's nothing bad," he promised, leading me out of the tent. He'd lost his prosthesis in the flood, and I reached over to help roll up the empty sleeve of his uniform as we walked.

"Are you going out tonight?" I asked, nodding at the kevlar armor that covered his legs.

"A group of us are searching for supplies. I don't really want to leave Anthony but..." He shrugged.

"Is he okay?"

"Isabelle hasn't woken up yet, and his arm is broken because of me." His face flushed, and his smile slipped.

We walked towards the dorms where a wooden bench sat at the edge of the lawn, looking out over the ocean. We'd sat there together before, though there had been a boardwalk back then, helping create a barrier between the seat and the water.

"Don't blame yourself for his arm," I sighed, sliding onto the bench. The toes of our boots tapped at the island's edge.

"Then you can't blame yourself for Fleming." He leaned his shoulder against mine, and as terribly as I wanted to return the gesture, I didn't have it in me.

"You had something you wanted to talk about?" I tried to sound casual, but it was hard when we were watching Ratcliffe's newest wave continue to grow on the horizon.

"I know the world might be ending." Wesley's voice wavered. "And maybe it's too early to talk about, but my mom, she wanted me to tell you. You and Avery have a home with us. It's just me, Mom, and Benson, but, you know. It's better than nothing."

My chest constricted.

"You mean because of Fleming."

"I don't want it to be something you're worrying about. When I told you about my dad, you said that your dad could be my dad, too. Then, a few days later, I woke up undead in Adrestus's tower, and your dad was there. He told me everything was going to be okay. Maybe he was trying to make me feel better, but it was the first time I felt like I'd had a dad in a decade."

His hand found mine. "So if you need a family, mine would be honored to have both you and Avery."

I wrapped my arms around him. The spandex of his black uniform smelled musty after the flood, but I pressed my face into his shoulder anyway.

"Thank you, Wesley."

He held me back, and for a brief moment, the world was okay. We would be fine.

"You know I've got you." His laughter was soft in the tangles of my hair. "Always and no matter what."

I pulled away to look at the dying light of day turn his face a cozy orange. He pushed his hair away from his glasses and grinned. Only Wesley could find something to smile about at the end of the world.

"Samantha?" A strained voice came up behind us, and I blushed at Andersen having found Wesley and me embracing. His cheeks tinged pink, too, but his forehead creased with more pressing matters. "It's Fleming. He's not good. I thought you'd like to know."

Maybe it was best if Fleming didn't survive to see our defeat.

I'd rushed back to his bedside after Andersen's warning, and while Fleming's breaths were growing more shallow, he was hanging on. Angie said he was unlikely to last the night. Naomi sat with me, nodding off on the floor of the tent. Dark had fallen hours ago, but I refused to sleep.

He would do the same if the roles were reversed. He'd been there time and time again since I'd started at New Delos Prep. He'd been overbearing, uptight, and rigid, but he'd taken me in without hesitation, without question.

I clenched my fists. There was no way to save him. We had no Serum. I was officially mortal and devoid of Life Elixir and what Life Elixir *did* exist, Adrestus would have under lock and key for his and Erika's personal use.

But then I remembered the acrid taste of my water just a few short weeks ago and a dusty room in City Hall.

What were the odds Mira's bottle was still there? Was it at all possible no one had touched the old file cabinet in the records room?

Don't run off.

That's what he would say. Don't run off, and don't do anything stupid.

I'd ignored that order countless times. It had caused Fleming more trouble than I was probably worth, but why, *why* would I make the *one* time I listen to the rules the one time his life was the one on the line?

I stood, sudden urgency sending waves of adrenaline through my system.

"Naomi." I shook her shoulder. "Help me."

She jolted awake, looking over Fleming in the light of a bedside lantern.

"Did he—"

"Not yet. And he won't. But I need your help." I crossed to the opposite side of his cot, assessing how best to carry him.

"I knew it." She scowled. "You *are* going to do something dumb."

"I can save him," I whispered. "Him and Remi both."

Naomi shook her head and put a hand on Fleming's shoulder.

"Remi's at City Hall," she said. "By the time we get there and come back, it'll be too late."

"Then we take him with us. There's Life Elixir in City Hall. Or there was last time I was there."

"Sammy—"

"I know where it is. " I bit my lip. It would be a miracle if Fleming was still alive in the time it took to run to City Hall, let alone survive long enough to await the return trip. "I can't carry him by myself."

Naomi gawked at me, but her slack jaw worked into a disbelieving grin.

"It's a better plan than nothing," she said darkly, and together, we maneuvered Fleming into our arms.

"Lift with your legs, not your back," Sergio mumbled from his cot. "Is that Samantha?"

"Go to sleep," I hissed. "You're dreaming."

"Yeah, right. If I was dreaming, I'd still have a full head of hair." He raised a sleepy hand to run it over the buzzed hair above his ear. "Tragic."

He rolled over, settling back into his cot, and I exhaled, nodding at Naomi to keep moving.

The makeshift camp outside was asleep. A few college students stood at the far end of the field, but they didn't see us slip towards the school hall, carrying Fleming between us.

My sword, safe in its scabbard, bumped against my leg as we made progress by the light of the aurora. My lungs burned, and I tried not to think about how far City Hall was from New Delos Prep. Fleming was already starting to feel heavier.

When we were a safe distance from the soccer field, Naomi scoffed and shook her head.

"I can't believe you," she said. "This is insane. I hope you know that."

"Of course I know that," I laughed nervously, still watching Fleming for signs of decline. "Just promise me that you'll take care of him after we get the Elixir. You have to let me go save Remi alone."

Naomi nearly dropped Fleming, and I buckled under the added weight.

"Don't talk like that," she hissed. "And if you don't come back, Wes will—"

"He'll move on," I insisted.

"Of all the stupid things you've ever said, that's probably the stupidest."

I scowled at her and adjusted my grip on Fleming.

"No, please. Keep arguing with me. This is exactly the time and place for this, over the unconscious body of our history teacher!"

Naomi blushed in the moonlight.

"If not now, when?"

"Wesley will be fine. And he'll watch over Avery. It'll be okay."

"Wesley will crumble without you. Sam, I—" She tried to hold in a shuddering breath but was unsuccessful. "*I'll* crumble. I *did*. This last month, without you? I won't let you walk in there alone."

"And I won't let you die to save someone who should've died a thousand years ago. It's too dangerous, so help me save Fleming and then let me handle the rest. "

"But that's not fair!" Naomi's voice rose. "Adrestus will kill you. How can you be okay with that?"

"I'm not." I lowered Fleming to the grass to better look at Naomi in the dark. "I want to keep being your roommate. I want to go to college with you and stand next to you when you get married and babysit your kids and do all that other stuff friends who are friends forever do. And maybe I do come out the other side of this, but if I don't, I want you to at least have the chance to do all those things, whether I go down with Adrestus or not."

Angry tears streamed down Naomi's face, and she continued to glare, but her quivering chin gave away her grief.

"I don't want to get married," she said, as if that made all the difference.

"Then I want you to stand by *me* when I get married. Or go on expensive vacations with me if neither of us gets married. We'll buy first class plane seats because we're worth it. And you know what? Even if I *did* get married, you and I would still go on vacations together and eat good food and see the world. And I'm going to fight to make sure that future can exist, but as long as Adrestus is alive, it *can't*."

Naomi stared at Fleming and blinked back whatever tears remained.

"Where would we go on our friend-cation?" She lifted her eyes from Fleming to me.

"I hear Iceland is nice." I grinned. "But maybe somewhere warmer."

"Peru." She nodded sagely.

"Is Peru warm?"

She thought for a moment before breaking into a tearful smile.

"I'm not sure, but it has alpacas."

"Naomi," I said seriously. "I swear, if by some miracle this works out, you and I will go pet all the alpacas that Peru has to offer. But promise me, you'll get Fleming out and leave Adrestus to me."

She nodded and stooped to help lift Fleming again.

"That's not fair," a voice said in the dark. "You guys are going to run off to Peru without me?"

Wesley stepped out of the shadows, bringing with him conflicting feelings of relief and worry. I raised my eyes to his neat frown.

"I thought you weren't going to be back until morning."

"I came back early to be with Fleming. I thought I was too late when I came back to his empty cot, then I heard you two." He looked at Fleming in our arms, and his frown deepened. "Do you need help with whatever this is?"

"It's okay," I insisted. "Go to bed. Please."

"Right. After everything we've been through, I'm going to just go to bed after catching you dragging Fleming down the street."

"Wesley—"

"I'm not leaving. What's going on?"

A sudden fire crackled and popped, casting us in red and orange flickering shadow.

"You haven't figured it out yet?" Amanda held her hand higher, expanding the halo of light that exuded from the fire dancing in her palm. Brooke stood with her arm wrapped around Amanda's and her long, dark hair pulled back.

Winnie and Andersen stood a little farther back, giving each other a wide buffer.

"Why are you all here?" I snarled.

"Sergio woke me, saying something about you kidnapping Fleming to take him to City Hall," Andersen grunted. "I thought the infection in his head wound was making him delirious, and then I thought about it for a half second longer and figured the story probably checked out."

"So you woke up half the camp to come stop me?" I snapped.

"We're not here to stop you, idiot," Winnie snorted. "We're here to help. I'm assuming there's some semblance of a plan here."

"Congrats, Samantha," Amanda snorted. "You've done the impossible and put me and Winnie on the same side."

"For now." Winnie shrugged.

"And Mom and Dad would kill me if I let you go alone," a new voice chimed, and Avery stuck his blond head out from behind Brooke.

"No," I asserted. The others? Fine. But Avery? "Absolutely not. Avery, go back. Mom and Dad would kill *me* for letting you come!"

"Too bad Adrestus killed them because now they can't tell either of us what to do." Avery crossed his arms. "If the world is ending, I should get to at least try to help make him pay."

"He's hurt all of us, Sammy." Wesley stepped in between Naomi and me, taking Fleming effortlessly into his arms. "And Fleming's *helped* all of us. It's not fair to not let us help."

"And I wouldn't say no to a fight against my father," Winnie added. "If Adrestus is at City Hall, he won't be alone."

Amanda flexed her fingers of her free hand, cracking the knuckles as if to agree with her sister.

"And he still has Remi," Andersen reminded me. "You can take care of Fleming and Adrestus, but how are you going to do all that *and* rescue Remi?"

I looked at Avery, but he kept his mouth shut. He could've convinced me to take them all, no questions asked, with a single sentence, and I would've been helpless to deny him. Instead, he waited.

How many times had I run off alone to try to solve things by myself? How many times had I convinced myself that I and I alone had to face Adrestus? And how many times had my friends come to my rescue anyways, no matter what stupid, bull-headed scheme of mine had landed me in trouble in the first place?

Tightness crept in my throat, and I blinked back tears of sudden gratitude.

"Right." I drew my sword. Rays of green aurora bounced off its sheen. "Then I guess we're doing this together."

52

Facing Eydis

Winnie knew the island the best and wasn't keen on keeping close, so she scouted ahead in her fire-proof cloak, ensuring a clear path to City Hall. The rest of us followed by the light of the fire in Amanda's palm. Andersen helped Wesley carry Fleming and carefully monitored his breathing as we went. The farther we got, the more his brow furrowed. We were running out of time.

Naomi winced as we ducked down an alley at Winnie's behest.

"There's a lot of very scared people here." She shuddered. We paused in the shadows of the alleyway while we waited for Winnie to check the next street, and Brooke placed her fingers under Amanda's to gently close her hand, extinguishing her fire.

"You should conserve your energy in case we run into your father," she said.

"I'll always have fire left for him," Amanda said darkly.

"But he's fireproof," Avery pointed out.

"Everyone burns, even Dad."

I caught Wesley's eye. His silent sigh was discernible only by the heavy rise and fall of his shoulders. I'd been prepared to face Adrestus tonight, even if it meant death, and I hadn't even bothered to say goodbye.

Andersen drew away Wesley's attention as he pulled off his glove to press the back of his hand against Fleming's forehead.

"What's wrong?" I demanded. Shallow, labored breaths strained against the bandages around Fleming's chest, and his forehead glimmered with sweat.

"We need to go faster." Andersen pulled his glove back on.

"We're more likely to be seen if we do," Winnie said, reappearing from around the corner.

"If we're seen, we'll deal with it," Naomi asserted. "It's not like we have that much to lose."

"Oh, sure." Winnie turned away, but I could hear the eye roll in her voice. "Nothing to lose except our lives."

Avery bumped up against my shoulder as we followed Winnie, going faster than before. He looked at me with wide, brown eyes that looked just like Mom's.

"Does walking into danger always feel like this?" he asked. "You don't even have powers to protect you."

"Neither do Winnie or Brooke."

Despite having less experience in a fight than even Avery, Brooke looked the most at ease of the group. I was confused at first as to why Amanda had let her join us, but when I looked at Wesley, I thought I might understand.

Despite my fears for my friends, it *was* better this way.

City Hall was directly ahead now, and the glowing orange of its lights bounced off Avery's cheeks. He took a shuddering breath, drawing courage from some unseen somewhere.

Winnie issued a low whistle and darted into an abandoned shop at the perimeter of City Hall's Paragon-Statue adorned plaza. We crouched over warped linoleum between shelves of molding New Delos themed knick-knacks. Naomi joined Winnie at a row of boarded windows, staring through the slats at City Hall. The wall opposite the windows boasted old graffiti.

"'New Delos is Dead'," Amanda read out loud. "Cheerful. I'm feeling great about this, guys."

Andersen and Wesley laid Fleming down next to a doorway that led into a darkened backroom. They exchanged a nervous glance, but Fleming continued to breathe ragged, rattling breaths.

"Sammy, where exactly is the Life Elixir?" Naomi asked from the window.

"Third floor in a records room. I don't really remember the way but—"

"I do," Winnie interjected

"There's people inside," Wesley warned, standing up to stretch his shoulder. "I can hear them. At least two, right at the entrance."

"I'll set a fire and draw them away." Amanda cracked her knuckles and pulled a small lantern off her belt. She handed it to Brooke, and a tiny flame popped to life inside the glass. They pressed their foreheads together for a moment, then Amanda pulled away.

"When you see the fire, wait for it to draw a crowd and then go," Amanda instructed, halfway out the door. "I won't be long."

She disappeared into the night, and Brooke held the lantern closer.

"What is that?" I asked. Brooke's smile seemed to make the fire brighter.

"A compromise," she said softly, cradling the lantern close. "After Amanda disappeared last fall, every time she has to leave, she lights this lantern just in case something happens, so I'll at least have her fire to keep."

"That's bleak," Andersen snorted.

"I think it's sweet." Naomi shot him a warning glare.

"It's better than nothing." Brooke shrugged. "More than anything, it reminds me that she's doing everything she can to come back."

"Must be nice." Wesley's tone was uncharacteristically callous and made the room feel several degrees colder. He leaned against the doorframe next to Fleming, the backroom behind him looming dark and ominous.

I'd known he was mad I'd left without warning, without a goodbye. I'd be angry, too, but this was not the time or place to bring it up.

"If you're trying to pick a fight, can it wait?" I hissed. "Let's survive first, then you can be mad about whatever it is you want to be mad about."

"That's just it, though. You were going to come here alone. After everything we've been through, you weren't even going to say goodbye."

I looked back at Naomi, hoping for back-up, but she was still at the window, looking out at City Hall.

"Wesley, stop." I lowered my voice, trying to get him to do the same. "I'm sorry, but this is the worst time—"

"Selfish." His laugh was cold and hollow. "That's what you are. You pretended you wanted to join the team to do the right thing, but now I get it. You just wanted to feed your own ego and quench your own guilt over your miserable roommate."

My mouth turned dry.

"Wes, I—"

"I lost my arm for you." He lumbered forward, and his face was unrecognizable from the one he'd worn in the sunset. "I *died* for you. And I don't think you ever once said thanks."

He stopped a foot in front of me, and I shook my head again. I couldn't think what else to do. Everything he was saying was true, but why was he being so cruel?

"I didn't mean to hurt you," I whispered.

"Yes," he growled. "You did."

His hand shot from his side to wrap around my neck, and I raised my own hands to try to pry carbon-fiber fingers off my trachea.

"Wesley, please!" Why weren't the others helping? And when had Wesley put on the prosthesis Adrestus had made for him?

His carbon-fiber fingers tightened, cutting off both air and blood. Stars burst in my vision, but then bright silver split the image. Wesley's smile stayed in place, but his eyes widened as dark blood blossomed across his chest, staining his armor.

His grip relaxed, and he fell over, dead.

"NO!" I screamed and stumbled back against a rusted shelf. A woman stood in Wesley's place, wielding a silver sword.

Wild, tawny hair was pulled back in a messy braid, and black paint and ash adorned her cheeks. Her cornflower blue dress was muddied and ripped at the hem. Twin bronze brooches glinted into the lantern light at her shoulders, and the strings of glass beads that hung between them glittered.

"Why—" I choked. I looked to the others for help, and my body turned numb. My friends and brother lay strewn across the shop floor, ripped open by ugly gashes. "What've you done?"

"It wasn't me," the girl whispered.

I drew my sword and gagged when I saw the blade dripping with fresh blood.

The silver clattered against linoleum as I dropped it, and it landed next to Wesley, whose face stared up at me empty and unseeing.

"They're all dead because of you," the girl said.

"No." I shook my head. "You stabbed him, you—"

The girl smiled and brandished her blade. It was identical to mine. She pushed loose locks of tawny hair from her face, and the eyes that stared back were my own.

Eydis.

A strangled cry ripped from my throat, and I stumbled backwards, but where I had expected my back to meet wall, I found empty space instead.

Disorienting darkness closed over my head, and I choked on air thick with acrid smoke. White light permeated the darkness, muted and shifting.

The light brightened, highlighting the heavy smoke and fog that rolled over me, and my fingers dug into the dirt and moss.

No.

I'd been here before. I knew what was hiding in the smoke of my ransacked village. I staggered upright but only made it a few feet before tripping over the first body.

Havard, my once tall, strong, and proud father, stared blankly at the smokey sky. I knew my mother Solveig would be next to him, but when I looked over, it was Alison's burnt face I saw instead.

I clapped a hand over my mouth and fought the urge to vomit. The wind picked up, blowing smoke away to reveal Vidar next to her, his button-up shirt stained with blood.

Everly and Trev Baker were next, marred with the bruises left by Mira's toxins.

And there she was, standing over them at their shoulders, dwarfed by her fur cloak. A single streak of white hair framed her little face, but the look she bore was not that of a young child, but an embittered, millennium-old woman.

"Look what you did," she squeaked. "If you hadn't buried me, maybe they would've survived."

"It's not my fault," I cried, even as my heart screamed with guilt. This couldn't be real. None of it made sense, but it felt so visceral, I knew it couldn't be a trick. "I didn't— I don't—"

"You should've just sewed your sails like I'd told you to." Havard sat up, his eyes clouded by death and his tunic bloody where Adrestus had stabbed him. "The longer you've lived, the more who've had to die."

"We could still be with our son." Mom sat up with Vidar. Her burnt skin crackled like sandpaper and flaked away as blackened dust.

"With our real child," Vidar added, and Mom nodded.

"I could've been happy and whole." Wesley's voice echoed in the fog. "But you've brought nothing but pain since you arrived in New Delos."

I shook my head and put my hands over my ears, but I couldn't block out the voices.

"I wouldn't be dying." Fleming's voice cut through the smoke, and I turned to face him. His face was pale and sweaty, his cheeks gaunt. "You're a murderer, Eydis. That's all you've ever been."

The bandages around his chest bled red, and he staggered forward and fell face down.

"No!" I rolled him onto his back, but it was too late. He was gone.

I was lost in the smoke and the fog, surrounded by my failures and all the many lives I'd ruined, and I screamed at the invisible sky, begging the universe to take me, too.

"You should've died when you were supposed to, Scourge Queen." The blue eyes of a young Adrestus glinted in the fog. "Look at the destruction your prolonged life has wrought. None of this would've happened if you hadn't insisted on being the hero."

I scrambled back on the heels of my hands, searching blindly for an escape, but no matter how far I got, the visages of those dead on my account followed while my friends admonished me from the unseen reaches of the smoke.

"Sammy."

I bumped up against someone's shins. I slowly raised my gaze to find Avery staring down at me through eyes identical to Mom's. Of all the lives I'd ruined, Avery's was the one I regretted the most.

My family had been taken from me, and I'd personally seen to his being taken from him.

"I'm sorry," I gasped before he could add his voice to the ones still taunting me from the fog.

"What for?" He cocked his head to the side.

"For everything. For getting Dad and Mom killed. For being a bad aunt and a worse sister. For the world ending."

"None of that is your fault, Sammy," he murmured, and he reached down to help me to my feet. "You don't really think that it is, do you?"

"I—yes. Of course I do."

"I know I get mad at you sometimes, but I know you could never hurt me. I love you, and even if most the memories are fake, you've always been my big sister." He looked past me, and his frown deepened. "And you didn't hurt them, either. Bad people did, but, Sammy, you are not bad people."

I blinked at him, feeling a weight lift from my chest.

"But what if I am?"

"Because I know you. Now, would you please wake up?"

"What?"

He pushed shaggy, blond hair from his eyes.

"*Wake up.*"

The world jolted, and the smoke sucked away to reveal a dark room lit by a flickering lantern. Avery looked up at me in concern, and a shuddering gasp shook my body as I twisted around, taking stock of my friends, bracing to see them dead on the ground.

Instead, they all stood still, staring into the distance. Brooke cradled her lantern, tears running down a blank face. Winnie and Naomi stood at the window, unmoving and unseeing while Andersen was frozen in a crouch next to Fleming. Wesley still leaned in his doorway, just as immobile as the others.

"Avery," I gasped and pulled him into a hug, but he pushed me away at the sound of footsteps.

Gregor pushed Wesley aside to enter from the darkened backroom, and I pulled Avery behind me as my adrenaline mounted.

"Clever," Gregor murmured. "Mr. Havardson, you must have quite the talent to break free of my nightmare. And then to break Samantha out as well? Amazing."

I drew my sword.

"What've you done to our friends?" I demanded.

"Oh, a whole myriad of things," Gregor beamed. "The hardest part was choosing what to haunt them with. Crushing guilt, overwhelming inadequacy, a sense of total helplessness. You name it, and it's in this room."

"Let them go," Avery said, injecting as much force into the words as he could.

Gregor laughed, and I hated how he sounded just like his creation Adrian Schrader.

"Good try, little man. You're strong, but you'll never be able to influence an Inculcator as strong as I am. Much like your poor mother."

Avery bristled and stepped forward, but I pushed him back again.

"Really, a fighter to the end," Gregor taunted, smoothing back his gelled hair. "It's best that she's dead. Too dangerous to be kept alive and quite frankly, a waste of talent, much like you, I'm afraid."

"Leave him alone." I leveled my sword at his neck.

"Are you going to stab me? And run the risk that I'm not me at all but another one of your idiot friends?" He looked at Fleming lying on the floor, and a silent laugh played across his lips. "Little Inculcator, if you come with me, we can put your powers to *actual* use."

"No," Avery snarled.

"If you won't listen to me, then perhaps you'll listen to your parents?"

Two grisly apparitions appeared behind him in the dark and stepped into the room. Mom and Dad, burnt and stabbed, limped forward, their joints cracking with every movement.

"Avery, close your eyes," I commanded. "They aren't real."

"No," Avery said again, more forcefully, and stepped to face Gregor. "No, I'm stronger than you."

Gregor grinned, but then Avery spoke again.

"Mom. Dad." Avery's chest swelled as he mustered up every bit of his powers as he could. "*Leave.*"

The apparitions hesitated, then dissolved into dust that disappeared before it hit the ground. Gregor's cocky smile disappeared with them, staring where his creations had stood.

"That's not possible," he growled. "You shouldn't be able to—"

"And you."

Avery stepped forward again, and Gregor recovered his look of amusement.

"Yes, little man?"

Avery lifted a single hand to point at Gregor's chest.

"*Die.*"

The first hint of a laugh passed over Gregor's face, but it was fleeting. His face drained of color, and he shook his head in confusion. A thin stream of blood issued from his nose, and he lifted a disbelieving hand to dab at it.

"No," he chuckled softly. "That's not possible."

And then he collapsed, very much dead.

53

The Best of Us

Gregor lay face down on the linoleum, and I waited for him to move. He himself had said it with his final breath. It wasn't possible. And yet—

It was hard to say which was the cause for more horror: the visions Gregor had forced on me or the callous ease with which Avery had killed him.

"I didn't know I could do that." Avery's voice was airy and weak. He swayed next to me, and I turned just in time to catch his little body as he collapsed.

"Avery!" I laid him on the floor and tapped his pale cheeks. "Avery, wake up!"

"What the hell happened?" Winnie shuddered as she woke up from her reverie. "Is that—"

"What's wrong with Avery?" Brooke crawled to my side. Her cheeks were stained with tears that glowed orange in the light of her lantern, and I wondered what horrors Gregor had forced her to witness.

"Move." Andersen pushed her aside with shaking hands and pressed two fingers under Avery's chin. "He's alive."

I pointed at Gregor's body.

"What about him?"

Andersen approached the body carefully while Wesley cowered in a corner. Naomi held his hand.

"It wasn't real," she insisted. "Wesley, you're okay."

"I can still hear screaming." His eyes met mine over Naomi's shoulder. Like Brooke, he'd been crying.

Andersen nudged Gregor with the toe of his boot before stooping to check his pulse. He shook his head and drew away.

"Dead. You still haven't told us what happened."

I looked at Avery's unconscious face, looking more peaceful than he had in months.

"Avery told him to die, and he did."

Brooke flinched away from Avery, but then regained her composure and went back to brushing the hair from his face. The others watched me with unreadable expressions.

"That's not possible," Winnie laughed. "Gregor must've finally found his limit and keeled over."

Andersen nodded along with the theory, though the looks on their faces betrayed that neither of them really believed it.

"So were we all..." Brooke let the question die on her lips, and I clenched my fists.

"It's over now," Naomi asserted, still comforting Wesley.

"I still hear screaming," Wesley said. "Naomi, can't you?"

Naomi frowned and then tilted her head to the side.

"I—yes." She pulled her hand from Wesley's and looked around at us wildly. "He's right."

"I don't hear anything," Andersen said.

"I feel it," she clarified.

"It's Remi." Winnie was back at the window, peering through the cracks in the boards. "Gregor kept her complacent with illusions and dreams. If he's dead, then Remi's mind is free until Adrestus sends Mira to get her under control."

"Then we need to move fast." Naomi crept to the main door. "As soon as Amanda has a good enough fire going, we move."

"But Avery—" I started, before looking back at Fleming. I hoped Gregor's visions hadn't affected him, too.

"I'll stay with your brother," Brooke insisted. "I'll be more help watching over him than I will be inside City Hall."

I nodded a silent thanks. It was hard to look at my friends with the ghosts of their accusations still playing in my mind, even if it had been a trick.

"There's Amanda's fire," Winnie snapped. "We need to go."

I gave Avery's pallid face one last look, brushing his hair back even though Brooke had already cleared it from his face.

"I've got him," she reassured me, but I was unable to speak over the lump in my throat. After seeing how easily he'd done what he'd done to Gregor, I couldn't fathom how much farther he might descend if I didn't come back.

Wesley and Andersen scooped Fleming into their arms. It was hard to tell since I was still avoiding looking directly at Wesley out of shame, but I got the sense he was avoiding my eye, too.

I joined Naomi at the door. Several blocks away, smoke curled into the sky, and several figures rushed from the entrance of City Hall, tripping over themselves to run towards Amanda's growing fire. Purple flames erupted from one of them.

Good. With Felix out here, that was one less Pantheon member to worry about. Amanda would welcome the challenge.

"Now!" Naomi barked, and I chased after her into the plaza. We paused at the base of Paragon's statue and peered around the edges, double checking that Amanda's fire was doing its job.

Silhouettes moved in front of the growing flames and a column of purple fire sizzled against Amanda's orange. Her flames reared and crackled in response.

"She's fighting them!" Winnie said, and I thought there might be a nervous apprehension in her tone that I'd never heard her display in regards to her sister. "She was supposed to get out of there."

"She's keeping their attention, so let's move while she's got it!" Andersen snapped, though he waited for Naomi to take the first step out from the statue.

She stopped at the bottom of the grand entrance steps and ushered us past her, glancing around to verify we hadn't been spotted.

"Watch his head," Andersen growled to Wesley as our ascent up the steps made Fleming jostle in their arms.

"I've got him," Wesley retorted, and Winnie skirted into the building first with a flourish of her cloak. I followed close behind with my sword drawn, ready to clear the way of any adversaries.

However, the grand entrance was empty and dark, and I craned my neck to look at the floors that towered overhead.

"Up there." Winnie pointed towards the third floor. "Be quiet. There will be others nearby. City Hall is more of an outpost rather than a main base, but it's well protected. Plus, Mira will be on her way now that Remi's awake. The Epsilons are probably going haywire, too."

"That's good, though, isn't it?" Andersen said as we followed Winnie up the sweeping marble staircase where I'd hobbled after Felix as an intern. "They can be on our side now."

I shook my head, remembering the last time Remi had been in proper control over Epsilons, when Hackjob had been driven to leaping from Schrader Tower's upper stories just to free himself.

"I don't think Remi is in the right mind to safely do that," I murmured.

"She's still screaming," Wesley added quietly.

Naomi stopped on the second floor.

"I can help her," she offered, "but it means I won't be able to sense if anyone is nearby."

"Do it." Wesley set his brow.

Naomi nodded and let out a heavy sigh as she redirected her powers.

"Is that it?" Andersen asked. "Does she feel better now? Should we split up? Some of us can go to help Fleming while the others save Remi?"

"As much as it pains me to stay with you all, we stick together," Winnie asserted. "We barely stand a chance as is, let alone split up."

Andersen grunted in response, his agitation clear on his face, but he didn't argue. We passed to the third floor silently, and I caught up with Winnie as she led the way down the open-air hall.

"Thanks, by the way," I whispered. "You didn't have to come with us."

She cast me an annoyed glare.

"I helped Adrestus get to where he is, even after I knew what he'd done to Amanda. And then he killed my mother. I've got a lot to make up for."

"Like getting me kidnapped?"

"No, you're annoying. I would've done that with no regrets whether or not I was working for Adrestus."

She stopped in front of the records room door, and I sheathed my sword.

We were here. We'd made it. We'd saved Fleming.

But then Winnie pushed open the door, and I grimaced.

The dull, blue light of a computer screen on standby glowed in the far corner, illuminating the edges of overturned filing cabinets. Papers littered the floor, and entire aisles of records had collapsed. I shifted through the mess, making my way to the computer. Its desk was on its side, and the computer sat sideways on a pile of folders.

"Sure." Winnie tripped over a downed fluorescent light. "Make the entire island a secret boat, but don't bolt anything down."

"It's good news," Naomi insisted. "It means no one has been here in a while, so the bottle of Elixir should still be in here. Sammy, where did you leave it?"

I shook my head, looking at the rows of upturned cabinets.

"In one of those." I pointed. Andersen grunted as he telekinetically pushed an entire row upright. The drawers clanged, shifting back into place. Winnie and Naomi violently shushed Andersen, and he threw his hands up as if to ask what else he was supposed to do.

Wesley set Fleming down as gently as he could next to the computer, propping him up against the overturned desk.

"Guys," he said, his voice wavering. "I don't know— I think—"

I tripped over my own feet in my hurry to join him at Fleming's side.

"What? What is it?"

Maybe it was the dull glow of the computer casting a ghastly pallor across Fleming's face, but he looked worse than ever. Andersen pulled at the bandages around Fleming's chest. Underneath, the cauterized skin was red and angry, and the infection was spreading under his skin like tendrils.

I ripped myself from his side and began tearing through the nearest cabinet, pulling papers out and casting them aside in a mad search for Mira's bottle.

It had to be here. It *had* to be here.

"Sammy, careful!" Naomi warned as metal reverberated with each drawer I ransacked.

"There's no time for careful!" *Why* wasn't it here? "Wesley, can't you smell it out?"

Wesley glanced around the room wistfully.

"What should I smell for?"

"Elixir tastes like metal, so probably something like that."

"Sammy," he said slowly, and his voice told me he'd already given in. "Everything in here is metal."

I looked at the filing cabinets.

"It's here. We can find it. I stashed it somewhere in a middle drawer."

I moved onto the next cabinets, grabbing armfuls of records and dropping them on the floor, becoming more desperate with each passing second.

A hand touched my shoulder, and I spun around, already on the defense, but was met with Wesley's tearful face.

"It's okay," he said. "Sammy, you tried."

"But it's here! It has to be!"

I spun back towards the cabinet and let loose a fist. The hit broke the skin across my knuckles, and I cried out in pain and desperation.

An arm wrapped around my shoulder, and I turned towards Wesley's touch, crying.

Fleming would die.

"He only has moments left. Let's sit with him. That's what he would want." Wesley murmured. I looked at Fleming through a film of tears.

Andersen, Winnie, and Naomi stood over him, solemnly accepting the inevitable.

I pulled away from Wesley, slipping on the papers I'd strewn across the floor. The computer was on. City Hall had power. I couldn't save Fleming, but maybe there was one last thing I could give him.

"What are you doing?" Naomi asked as I righted the computer and pulled the keyboard into my lap. The desktop populated with electronic files.

"What is that?" Wesley asked this time.

"Project Heracles," Winnie answered for me. "It's all the old Paragon videos."

I clicked into the trash folder, where I'd dragged every video clip that made mention of Fleming. They had been useless in pulling Roy Hendricks to Adrestus's ranks because Paul Fleming, for all his many flaws, had loved his brother.

"It's stupid." I shrugged. The first video began to play.

Paul Fleming with his cocky smile and perpetually windswept hair popped on screen. He looked around with anticipation, shuffling the papers in his hands.

"Are you ready for your fitting?" a voice asked offscreen, and Paul blushed, no older than twenty-years-old.

"Actually, I had some ideas over the weekend!" He grinned and laid his papers down on the table, showing off sketches of white and red. "I don't think I like the black. But what about this?"

"We've already made the costume—"

"Right, right, right." His head bobbed. "But I thought I was supposed to be a paragon of hope and strength? Oh, I like that. 'Paragon'. Anyway, I found these in my brother's desk."

"Your brother hasn't been recruited into—"

"Right, I know!" Paul gushed. "This is what he was envisioning for himself. He likes the colors and, I don't know, how is the city going to look up to me if my own brother doesn't?"

"You want us to change your entire costume to appeal to your brother's favorite colors?" the tailor drawled. Paul flashed an apologetic smile.

"Alex has good taste. And who do I talk to about names? Paragon is sticking with me."

The tailor's exasperated sigh cut, and I looked to Fleming as the next video started. He looked as lifeless as he had before, though his chest still rose and fell in shallow breaths. Whether or not he could hear his brother was a long shot, but it was better than nothing when there was so little I could offer him now.

"That's very nice of you, Sammy," Naomi murmured, and I turned away.

"We should still be searching," I said, but when the others didn't say anything, I knew they all thought it as fruitless as I feared.

The next video showed Paragon in a training session against an older-looking version of Adrestus, shot from a ceiling camera in the Schrader Tower training gym.

"You're quick for an old man, Dr. Cunningham," Paul panted, still wearing the same cocky smile. "You really aren't an Apex?"

Adrestus smiled back.

"Does that surprise you?"

"Not really. You should see my brother. Do you know if the recruitment team looked over his information yet? You could put in a good word for him, you know, being a non-Apex yourself!"

"I'm sure they're working on it."

"Oh, yeah, I know!" Paul nodded earnestly. "But I'd hate to debut Paragon before Alex can join—"

"Your brother is still a freshman," Adrestus chided, a hint of irritation flashing across his brow. "In time—"

"Sure, he's young," Paul pushed, "but Alex really is the best of—"

"How sweet." A voice cut through the video, and we all whipped around towards the door. "Giving Alex a send-off. Stupid, though, coming here just to play a couple of meaningless videos."

Winnie was first on her feet, taking up a stance between us and the door, and I instinctively grabbed Fleming's wrist. I would not be taken from his side.

Fire crept into the room, illuminating the doorway and spreading to the papers that covered the floor. A figure stepped through the curling wisps of smoke.

Fleming couldn't even die in peace without being interrupted by Roy Hendricks.

54

Into Ash

Winnie, as calm and deliberate as ever, pulled her dark hood up over her hair, ready in her fire-proof cloak. I knew she'd likely had a hand in the cloak's design. She'd always intended on someday fighting her father. Their first fight had been in the rain, but this time, we were trapped in a tinderbox of dusty papers.

"Step aside, Winnie," Roy warned. His black armor stood out against the red of his fire. "Adrestus may still forgive you."

"I don't want forgiveness," she growled back.

"No? Is that not what this suicide mission is? Trying to remedy some misplaced guilt?"

Winnie charged. Roy extinguished his fires and blocked her attack, spinning her over a downed file cabinet before launching towards us, fire flaring back to life.

Andersen leapt to our defense, and a metal cabinet lurched into the air to slam Roy into the far wall. A line of papers on the floor burst into flames, their light bouncing off something metallic under a far desk.

Hope burned in my veins hotter than any fire Roy could procure, and I pointed a shaking finger across the room.

"There!" I shouted. "It's there! We can still save him!"

The metal bottle must've rolled free of the file cabinets when they'd overturned and, with the help of the rolling ocean, made its way to the far corner. I could only see it now thanks to Roy's fires.

Roy tracked my pointing finger, and the desk over the bottle burst into flame.

"I've got it!" Andersen cried, and the bottle zipped into the air at the bidding of his outstretched hand. I opened my arms to catch it, but a burst of fire bloomed towards us, breaking Andersen's concentration as he threw himself over Fleming to protect him from the flames.

Wesley, Naomi, and I scattered, leaving Fleming under Andersen's care. Wesley and Naomi went at Roy from the sides, drawing his attention while I vaulted over cabinets, trying to reach the Elixir.

Wesley launched a cabinet across the room, and Roy rolled out the way. The cabinet's contents combusted, but I ignored the explosion as I dove for the bottle.

I was feet away when a creaking overhead caught my attention. Fire spread across the ceiling and support beams buckled and gave way, forcing me to dodge and avoid being crushed under their weight. The bottle disappeared under the rubble of the collapsing fourth floor, and Naomi cried out somewhere to my left.

"Naomi!" I shrieked. "Are you okay?"

Another cabinet crashed somewhere behind me, but I could no longer see the room through the smoke and rubble.

"I'm fine, keep fighting!" Naomi's voice broke with pain.

I ripped at the rubble where I'd seen the bottle disappear, pulling away piping and ceiling tiles. When I finally saw the glint of metal, it was surrounded by flame.

I forced my arm into the fire, but recoiled, crying in pain and frustration. Mom had burned to save me. Why couldn't I bring myself to burn to save Fleming?

"Sammy!" Winnie stood at the end of the aisle with her fire-proof cloak balled in her arms. She hurled it through the air, and I stumbled forward to catch it as she dove back into the fray against her father. I swathed it around my arm and shoulder and braced myself as I jammed my hand back into the fire.

Heat licked at my face, and I turned away from the flame as my cloak-protected fingers searched for the round edges of Mira's water bottle. Wesley screamed in pain somewhere out of sight, and my desperation increased.

Then, I hooked something smooth and pulled it towards me, dislodging the bottle. It rolled from the fire, and I made the mistake of trying to grab it with my unprotected hand. I dropped it, swearing through clenched teeth and wrapped the Elixir in the cloak.

"Andersen!" I screamed, trying to see through the choking smoke. The ceiling blackened and crumbled, and I dodged more falling tiles as I sprinted back towards the computer.

The computer videos continued to play, and Andersen kept his body over Fleming's. His uniform had burnt off his back, leaving ugly, painful burns where there had once been fabric, but he kept up a barrage of flying cabinets towards Roy while trying to avoid hitting Naomi, Winnie, and Wesley.

"They want Alex?" The Paul on the screen looked hopeful, but since the last video, he'd become gaunt and sickly, in the middle of his battle with cancer.

"Not the way you initially planned, but yes." Adrestus's voice offscreen was cool and calculated. Paul's smile faltered but remained in place.

"Is Fleming alive?" I demanded.

"Barely."

I pushed the bottle into Andersen's arms, and he unscrewed the cap to give it a sniff.

"Pour it in his mouth!"

Winnie grunted behind us, and Wesley was forced to abandon his fight against Roy to come to her aid, stopping a falling beam from crushing her. Wesley, trapped holding the ceiling in place, craned his head around to look at us as Roy marched forward.

"Run!" he screamed through the smoke.

But there was nowhere for us to go.

"Give it to Fleming, then take some yourself and get out of here," I commanded, standing up in front of Andersen and Fleming.

"What about you?" Andersen held the bottle back to me.

"Won't work. Mira's Immortality Cure is still in my system, so drink up."

Roy stopped a few paces away, his favorite fire-whips in hand.

"Adrestus is here, you know." He grinned. "He doesn't know yet that you're here, too, but he will soon."

A confused laugh issued behind me, and Roy screwed his face up and tilted his head to get a better look at the computer.

"You want Alex for what?" Paul's voice asked with a slight quiver.

"I know it sounds unconventional, but unfortunately, it is the only way forward."

"But he'll die!"

"And if you don't agree, you'll die!" Adrestus crooned. "You didn't think everlasting life came for free, did you?"

"I'm Paragon," Paul asserted. "I help this city. Is that not payment enough? When the city sank—"

"My dear hero, you don't really think that it was *you* that saved New Delos that day?" Adrestus laughed. "That was your beautiful fiancee and Alex."

"No, but I thought—"

"Tell me, how *exactly* did you save the city from sinking?"

"I—I guess I—"

"You don't know what you did because you did nothing. You had no clue that Alison Taylor and Alex found the control system under City Hall and stopped it themselves."

"What is this?" Roy demanded. "He's lying. Paul saved the city."

His fires weakened.

"He's not," I said. The videos had brought Roy to Adrestus's side. Did I dare hope they'd drive him away?

"All I have to do is let you kill Alex for your experiments, and you'll cure my cancer?" Paul asked, his voice desperate. "I get to continue being a hero?"

"Exactly! We've tried inviting him ourselves, but he won't bite. If you —"

"No." Paul's chair grated against tile. "He's my brother."

"And he could hold the key to creating an army of superheroes like you!"

"Like me?" Paul repeated. "I'm a liar! I just didn't know it! I'm *nothing*! Why would I give over Alex? He's the hero. New Delos needs *him*, not me. So keep your magic cure. I don't want it."

"Why?" Roy seethed, his fires growing. "Why would he do that for *him*? He could've lived!"

"Paul did that?"

I tore my eyes from Roy at the sound of Fleming's rasping voice. He leaned against the overturned desk with his head lolled to the side, but his eyes fluttered open, searching for the source of Paul's voice. Andersen sat next to him with an empty bottle.

"You're alive!" I flung myself at him, pushing Andersen out of the way to pull Fleming into a sitting position with my arms around his shoulders.

I'd done it. I saved him. He wasn't going to die, or if he did, he'd bounce right back thanks to the Life Elixir.

"I don't feel very alive," Fleming murmured. "Where are we? What happened to my shirt?"

Then he saw Roy burning behind me, and his confusion gave way to sobriety.

"Samantha," Fleming croaked, "where the *hell* are we?"

"City Hall?" I winced.

"You made him do that, didn't you?" Roy growled, pointing a flaming finger at the computer.

"Stand down, Roy," Fleming said. "I know we've rarely seen eye to eye, but this isn't you."

"Paul could've lived." Roy's hair flaked away, burning off in his rage. "But he didn't, because of you."

Fleming looked back at the computer, and his lips parted in surprise.

"I thought that was a fever dream." He swallowed. "Andersen, what did you give me? It tastes awful."

"We'll explain later," I asserted, throwing Winnie's fire-proof cloak over Fleming and standing up to put myself between him and Roy.

"Move," Roy growled. "Adrestus wants you for himself, but I can do whatever I want to *him.*"

"Dad, stop!" Winnie called. Wesley still stood over her, his arm shaking with the effort of holding the room up, and he looked at me with urgent desperation.

"Adrestus wants me for himself?" I sneered. "Andersen, get everyone out. He's not allowed to hurt me."

I launched at Roy, and he was forced to extinguish his flames. He bent backwards, out of range of my swinging fist, but came back with a sweeping kick that knocked me off my feet just as Andersen passed with Fleming.

Roy tried to lunge for them, but I grabbed him around the waist and pulled him to the ash and paper littered floor.

"Run!" I shouted, my limbs tangled with Roy's. I met Wesley's eyes. "I'll be fine!"

He waited until Winnie had scrambled clear and let the ceiling fall. He was supposed to escape with the others. I wasn't surprised when instead he charged at us.

Roy spun free of me before Wesley could reach him and deterred his attack with flames that shot up out of the floor.

"This is over!" Roy bellowed. The heat became unbearable as the fire in Roy's hands grew. He gathered the ball of flame in his arms, looking at me with hatred where I was still sprawled on the floor. I felt Wesley's arms around me, and we both turned away with nowhere left to flee.

But the heat died, leaving our backs cool.

"If you want a fair fight, *father*," Amanda drawled, "then come get it."

She stood in the doorway, and the others fled down the walkway behind her.

"If it isn't my elder disappointment," Roy snarled.

"The only disappointment here is you." She made a show of closing her fists, and all the fire in the room snuffed out. "What would Mom say if she saw you like this?"

"Your mother knew to support me!"

Wesley helped me to my feet, but the room reeled. I'd inhaled too much smoke.

"Adrestus has already won!" Roy shouted. "It isn't too late to join the winning side! Our family's legacy—"

Amanda howled with forced laughter.

"That's all Winnie and I ever were to you! Means to further your own legacy that neither of us wanted to be a part of."

"I was raising heroes!"

"You were raising *daughters!*" Amanda raised her voice, and Wesley helped me skirt into the next aisle while Roy was distracted. "But you were only interested in *weapons!*"

"Hero, daughter, weapon. Call it what you want," Roy said. "But I stand by what I said. At the end of the day, you turned out to be nothing but a disappointment."

Heat and light flared on the other side of the rubble. My lungs felt like glass was crawling its way up and out of them, and I coughed, tasting blood, but Wesley kept us moving.

He pulled us out the door behind Amanda just as fire erupted inside. We fell to the walkway tiles, and heat tore at our backs. I looked out from under Wesley's arm as Amanda was thrown from the room and fell through the air like a meteor, soaring over the railing towards the main atrium floor three stories below.

Winnie screamed from where she and the others were escaping down the same stairs we'd come up, and I pushed Wesley away to better see Amanda's trajectory. She released a burst of fire just before crashing into the marble floor. It softened her fall, but she rolled across the marble, landing sprawled on her side.

"I'll teach you respect yet!" Roy bellowed, leaping from the room and kicking off the railing to follow Amanda to the floor.

He caught himself much more gracefully, landing on his feet as fire rolled out from under him.

Winnie pushed the others out of the way, sprinting down the stairs and throwing herself over Amanda.

"Get away from her!"

Roy stood across the atrium from them, but despite the distance, he still seemed to tower over his daughters. Shrouded in flame, he marched forward.

"Come back to us," he implored, and Winnie looked up at him with loathing.

"You hurt her!"

"Like you haven't done the same!" The marble at Roy's feet cracked with heat. "You who helped enslave her! Come back to Adrestus and let *him* be the great equalizer between us! We can be a family again!"

"No!" Winnie asserted. Amanda lay beneath her, stirring feebly.

"Winnie, *please*." Roy's voice turned desperate. "If you don't, you know what he'll make me do. You know what happened to Alison Havardson."

"We made our choice, and you made yours." Winnie pulled Amanda into her arms, clutching her sister.

"But I don't *want* to do it!"

"Then don't! I don't give a crap anymore what you decide. Stop blaming all your problems on the choices of others!"

Roy took another step and shuddered.

"You don't understand. They'll *make* me do it!" His fire grew, stretching high enough to reach Wesley and me on the third floor. "They'll make me kill you both, Winifred! They're in my head, they're—"

He pushed his hands against his ears and then clawed at the back of his neck.

"He has a chip," Wesley breathed. "Oh, my god, Sammy, he's really going to kill them. They're going to make Remi make him do it."

Across the atrium on the stairs, Andersen and Naomi seemed to realize too late what was happening. They hurried down the steps, unable to reach the Hendricks family fast enough.

"Winifred!" Roy roared. He fought a lurching step forward. He threw his head towards the ceiling and spoke to some unseen someone. "I—won't. I won't kill them! Don't make me!"

Winnie grabbed Amanda under her arms and tried to pull her away. The marble continued to crack and splinter with every step Roy took.

"Then fight it!" Winnie sobbed.

"I can't!" Roy howled and lurched forward again. "Winnie, Amanda. Girls. I'm—"

He stopped, and his fire burned bright like it had the night he'd killed Mom. Winnie twisted around to hold Amanda to her chest, keeping her back to the fire than engulfed Roy. I pressed my face against Wesley, hiding from the burning light and the screams of torment that echoed through the building.

When the light faded and the screams died, Winnie still sat with Amanda, crying into her sister's shoulder, but where Roy had stood, only ash remained, scattered across the marble floor.

It was like Amanda had said at the beginning of the night.

Even Roy Hendricks could burn, and as terrible of a father as he'd been, he'd sooner see himself reduced to dust than harm his daughters.

55

Solveigsdotter

Amanda did her best to brush the ash into a pile while Winnie wordlessly took her cloak back from Fleming, using its folds to contain the dusty remnants of their father.

Wesley and I leaned against each other as we took the stairs down to the others, and Fleming was berating me before we'd even reached the second floor.

"You've done stupid things before." He lay against the heavy, wooden doors of the main entrance while Andersen inspected his wound. "But, Samantha, *this*—"

"Is the stupidest yet? You say that every time. It's starting to lose its punch." I stumbled down the last steps with Wesley.

I'd never been so grateful to be receiving a lecture. Fleming could harp all he wanted. He was *alive*. Or, at least he was in a manner of speaking. The gray pallor of death hung on his face. I wondered if that was how I'd looked every time I'd died.

"Andersen," I said, "take Fleming to Brooke and Avery—"

"You brought *Avery*?" Fleming seethed.

"I'm not leaving until we have Remi," Andersen asserted.

"Absolutely not." Fleming struggled to rise, but had expended too much energy yelling. "We're leaving. All of us. Now."

"You're technically dead." I shrugged. "You aren't the boss of us right now."

"I'm not—"

Andersen stooped and pressed his fingers against Fleming's neck.

"Nope. Dead."

Fleming's jaw dropped in horror.

"I don't like that."

"You'll be alive again in a few minutes," I promised. "That's how the Elixir works."

"And if I die again?"

"It'll keep rebooting you until you get better. Andersen will take you to Angie, and you'll be fine."

"I'm not leaving Remi," Andersen started.

"We know," Naomi sighed. "Amanda, how are you feeling?"

"Concussed," she mumbled, looking at the pile of ashes that Winnie held in the cloak.

"We'll take Dad to Brooke." Winnie folded the cloak over the ashes. "And Fleming, too, if you want."

"Not happening." Fleming glared up at me. "My students are done marching into battle without adult supervision."

I rolled my eyes and ignored the clenching in my stomach. If Roy was right and Adrestus was here, none of us were safe. Once Adrestus found out Gregor and Roy were both dead because of us, he'd reign chaos at the school. We'd only survived this long because he'd allowed it, and I couldn't see his graciousness extending any further.

If we didn't stop him now, the teams and all the delegates and families we'd saved were dead.

"You're all injured," I said. "I know where Remi is. I can—"

"We aren't leaving you," Wesley said.

"We are." Winnie steadied Amanda, and together the sisters pulled Fleming to his feet between them.

"Careful," I said when Fleming tried to protest. "It's hard to get air in your lungs when you're dead. Best to conserve it."

"Samantha, if you face him, I might never—"

"I know," I cut him off before he could finish his sentence. We both knew Adrestus would finish me easily in a fight, and my own immortality was long gone. There would be no coming back for me.

Fleming craned his head to give me one last panicked glance over Winnie's shoulder as she and Amanda carried him into the night, but then the heavy door swung closed, and he was gone.

I turned to face the dark atrium of City Hall, drawing my sword and stepping over the cracks Roy had left in the marble floor.

"You said you know where she is?" Naomi asked.

"She's underneath us," Wesley sighed. "Right where the control booth used to hang over that whirlpool."

I nodded. Andersen and Wesley had been there when we'd destroyed the old control booth. Now, Remi sat in its place as the new Heart of the City.

I led the way to a far door. If I remembered correctly, there would be a stairwell on the other side that led to the top of the massive underground dome in which Remi would be suspended.

"If Adrestus is down there, then this ends tonight." I'd spent a lot of time wondering if I had it in me to kill. When it came to Adrestus, there was no question. I would do it without hesitation. As for Mira, I wasn't sure I was ready to face my sister again.

Wesley stepped up to take the space at my side, and his green eyes glittered in the dark. He set his jaw and nodded.

"If you choose to fight, then I choose to fight with you."

"Good god," Naomi groaned. "Then let's get this over with."

I ripped the door open and reeled backwards into Naomi.

Where there had once been a barren stairwell, there was now a metal catwalk jutting out over a massive well of stone. This part of City Hall had been gutted and now looked down into the expansive dome that sat beneath the building. The dome was large enough to fit the entire school hall of New Delos Prep and still have room left over. It glowed sickly green beneath us, lit by inlet lights that spiraled all the way down to an expansive pool of ocean water that sat where the maelstrom once had. The lights extended beyond the surface of the water, illuminating several yards of dark water that faded to the black of the ocean's depths.

The light had a shifting, watery quality that bounced through a sprawling framework of metal catwalks and rickety steps of steel, like a haphazard spider's web suspended over water, leading into the eight gaping tunnels that surrounded the dome. They'd once gushed with water, controlling the rise and fall of the island with the tide, but now gentle streams poured from their mouths, dripping into the pool below.

The largest platform was suspended midway down the dome. The light from the sconces bounced off black armor, glinting up at us next to long, white hair.

Between them, Remi stood at the center of a web of wires, still in the black underclothes of her uniform. Andersen tensed next to me, and Naomi held him back.

"Careful," she warned. "It's four versus two, but they're stronger than we are."

"Yeah?" Andersen growled through gritted teeth. Steel groaned as the system of catwalks shuddered with Andersen's mounting rage. "All I see is a room full of metal."

He took a running start and leapt into the air.

"Andersen!" Naomi shouted after him, but he was already hurtling towards a platform, several floors of metal walkways below. Metal bowed and bent at his command to aid in his descent, cushioning his landing so he could continue his plummeting sprint to next level below.

Naomi, Wesley, and I thundered after him, sprinting down dizzyingly high metal steps, tracking Andersen's controlled fall. A cold, booming laugh signaled that we had Adrestus's attention.

Fine. Maybe this was better, being direct. The end would come faster, one way or another.

We reached the top of the dome just as Andersen landed at the end of the walkway that held Remi's platform. The lights that lay in the wall behind him pushed his shadow forward, reaching for Adrestus and Mira.

"Don't do anything stupid!" Naomi yelled.

"Aw, Naomi, and here I thought you hated me." Andersen gave a haughty laugh. Adrestus drew his sword, but a flick of Andersen's wrist sent it spiraling towards the water below.

"That was genuine Roman bronze, boy!" Adrestus roared, but then his armor creaked, and he rose into the air, thrashing against Andersen's telekinetic grip on his armor. For a shining, naive moment, I thought Andersen had actually done it. We'd won.

But before he could send Adrestus and his metal armor into the drink after his sword, Mira surged forward, sprinting across the catwalk to grab Andersen by his neck. He locked up, and Adrestus crashed back to the metal grate.

"A foolish attempt, but he's got more gall than the rest of you!" Adrestus called up to where we leaned over the railing to get a better look through the network of criss-crossing cables. "I'm surprised, Eydis. It's not like you to let someone else take the leading charge."

I adjusted my grip on my hilt. Mira looked up at me through loose locks of white hair with a gleeful hunger stretching her lips into a smile. Adrestus came up beside her to inspect Andersen.

"It's over, *Quintus*," I called, and Adrestus's face fell at the sound of his old name. "You can't win."

It was a weak bluff at best. We all knew Adrestus very well could, and most likely would, come out on top.

"I told you once that's the sort of insolence that gets even those closest to me killed." His eyes darted from me to Naomi. "Is that you, Miss Bradford? I'm impressed."

"What is he talking about?" Wesley hissed, and Naomi's throat bobbed as she swallowed.

"I thought, maybe if I made him feel guilt—"

"That's a new trick, isn't it?" Adrestus leaned back against the railing next to Mira, who kept her hunter's gaze trained on Andersen, her lips parted in a hungry grin. "Don't bother, child. I'm aware of the destruction I've wrought over the centuries, and I do feel bad for the pain I've caused.

That's what sets me above the rest of you. I know the sting of sacrifice, and yet I still do what needs to be done."

He turned back to Andersen, and I clanged my sword against the metal railing to get his attention.

"Don't touch him!" I warned.

"Or what?" Adrestus sang. "Eydis, how about you come have a chat and maybe Mr. Lewis makes it through the night, though I'm quite unhappy about my sword."

I pushed away from the railing and sheathed my sword in an insincere gesture of peace. I made my way to the next set of mangled metal stairs, and Naomi and Wesley's footsteps rattled the catwalk as they followed.

"Alone, Eydis," Adrestus called up. "You come down alone or Mr. Lewis takes a *very* long swim."

I looked back at Wesley and Naomi, but they frowned in defiance.

"It'll be fine," I hissed.

Wesley responded with a harrowed look that betrayed he could hear my traitorous heart beating too fast for me to believe my empty assurances. I took a heavy breath and marched down the metal steps.

I felt them track my progress through the mess of cables, wires, and walkways while Mira and Adrestus walked Andersen back towards Remi. Up close, I could see that her left sleeve had been cut to make room for the wires that stuck to her skin via electrodes.

They snaked up her shirt and disappeared into her tangle of blonde hair. Her right sleeve had been cut at the elbow, exposing her burn-scarred arm and the IV that was presumably keeping her nourished and alive, though only just, judging by the gauntness of her hollow cheeks.

I swallowed my rage, trying to keep my cool as I approached Adrestus and Mira. What they'd done to Remi was horrible, but it was just another list item for their bloodstained ledger.

"It's been a harrowing night," Adrestus said. He reached for his waist, as if to grab his sword hilt out of habit. He scowled when he came up empty. "When the Epsilons started acting out, we feared something might have happened to Gregor. It was his illusion, after all, keeping Miss Whitlock under control. You haven't seen him, have you?"

I tried to look casual, forcing an air of control. Mira watched me with weary eyes, but I knew better than to underestimate her no matter how exhausted she appeared.

She'd tried to bury me under a building after I'd saved her from her own ally's flood. Maybe Erika really was dead. Maybe the woman before was an enemy too dangerous to let live, no matter who she had been.

But even with her hand on Andersen's neck, I couldn't help but see my sister.

"Yeah, I might've seen Gregor." My mind raced against Adrestus's patience. A control panel stood in front of Remi, resting on a podium. Ripping a USB from a computer port could corrupt the files without properly closing out. Did the same apply to Remi? If I released her too quickly, would it cause more harm than good?

And how was I going to save her *and* Andersen?

"Don't play coy," Adrestus warned. He rested his hand on the controls, tapping his fingers. "Where's Gregor? What aren't you telling me?"

"Safe," I lied. "We'll give you Gregor, and you give us Andersen and Remi."

"Don't push your luck." Adrestus growled. I chanced a step forward, but Adrestus held a hand up to me. "You're lying."

I gulped.

"I killed him," I said. "He's dead."

Mira's eyes widened, and she twisted her head around to look at Adrestus, who's nostrils flared.

"How?" His question came out as a breathless, disbelieving grunt. I drew my sword, as if to show him, using the moment as an excuse to arm myself. "That's a clean blade, child."

"I cleaned it."

"She didn't kill him," Mira growled. "One of her friends did, and now she's protecting them."

Adrestus looked up towards Naomi and Wesley, scrutiny wrinkling the skin around his eye.

"Either way, Gregor is gone," Adrestus mused. "Which is very bad news for Mr. Lewis. Do it, Mira."

I lunged, but purple bruises were already spreading up Andersen's neck, fanning out from Mira's hand as she infected him with the same toxin she'd used on Everly. His eyes widened, and he choked my name as I reached out for him, but Mira pushed him over the railing before the toxin had finished its work. Andersen plummeted past cables and walkways to the water so many feet below.

"NO!" I swung my sword too haphazardly, and Mira ducked out of the way as Adrestus surged forward, tackling me into the railing.

A bolt snapped beneath me, and the railing gave way, sending me tumbling into open air with Adrestus still holding on. Wesley and Naomi screamed overhead, but the catwalk below broke my fall.

The force of our landing sent Adrestus rolling off of me, his helmet bouncing over the edge and dropping to the water as the walkway shuddered.

"Mira!" Adrestus bellowed, untangling himself from his red cloaks. "Have Miss Whitlock send the Epsilons to the school. The Apex Teams have overstayed their welcome in my capital. And then see that those two follow their friend to the bottom of the ocean!"

Metal rattled overhead as Wesley and Naomi thundered down the maze of walkways, trying to reach us, but Mira was already at Remi's side, brushing her fingers across her face.

Remi's eyes flew open, staring unseeing at the far stones of the dome. The Epsilon army Adrestus had accrued would be on their way to our friends and family at the school.

Adrestus ripped my attention away from the others as he lumbered forward, and I staggered to my feet, still gripping my silver sword.

"What a pity it has to end this way." Adrestus's voice was a manic purr. I lashed out with my sword, but he stepped to the side and grabbed my wrist, using my momentum against me to push me past him and pluck the sword from my grip.

I fell to the metal grate, sore from our fall and wheezing after inhaling so much of Roy's smoke upstairs. Metal creaked overhead and catwalks crashed, mingling with the sound of Mira's laughter as she dissolved cables, trying to get Naomi and Wesley to fall into the water.

"I'm not afraid of you." I wiped away the blood that trickled from the corner of my mouth. It tasted like Mira's poison from the other day.

"That was always your biggest mistake." He looked up to watch Naomi and Wesley scramble out of the way of a falling catwalk. "Your friends are loyal, I'll give them that. Too bad they'll be dead soon."

"Why me?" I staggered to my feet. "If I'm going to die here, I want to know what made you pick me, all those centuries ago, when I found you on that beach."

His face softened, and he ran my blade along the railing, making it sing.

"You had an incurable bitterness that made you desperate enough to bend to my whims." The catwalk shook as metal rained behind me. Adrestus didn't seem to notice, instead holding me in an unbreakable, grinning gaze. "The world has changed in so many ways over the years, but one thing stays the same. There will always be a girl so hungry for station and freedom that she'll do anything to get it. And that was you."

"Between Ignatia and me," I asked through clenched teeth, "how many girls did you manipulate?"

He grinned, and the shifting water below cast bending light back up at his face.

"So many. You weren't anything special."

"Then why are you still obsessed with me?"

"Because you derailed everything!" His careful composure dissolved, and his face contorted in sudden rage. "You were supposed to give me what I wanted! You weren't supposed to be different!"

He flew at me with the sword glinting the eerie green light of City Hall's underbelly, but in our training sessions together, I had become very good at dodging.

I ducked around him, and he growled in frustration.

"I wasn't different," I sneered. "I was lucky. Because you got sloppy when you murdered my family."

Metal creaked overhead as Mira dissolved away brackets holding more catwalks in place. Naomi and Wesley, again, barely made it to the next walkway over, and the falling metal buffeted the catwalk where Adrestus and I faced each other.

"Ignatia turned on you," I said. "I stabbed you. You couldn't even keep Winnie Hendricks by your side."

"True," Adrestus crooned, "but not every desperate, lonely girl turns coat. Some stay loyal for a very, very long time."

He pointed a single finger upwards towards Erika. A bit of metal, fallen from a railing rolled into my foot, and I scooped it up to brandish it.

"You think you're some great legendary general, but regardless of Erika, you keep getting tripped up by teenage girls," I scoffed. "All you are is a sad, old man in a costume. You are nothing."

"I'm *everything*!" His one eye widened. "You are nothing more than an idiot child I found on a beach!"

Screams echoed up above, and I craned my head to see Naomi hanging over the edge of a platform by her feet, clutching Wesley where he dangled overhead. Mira grinned and prowled towards them.

"Uh, oh," Adrestus sighed. "That doesn't look good for your friends."

Naomi strained, but didn't have the strength to pull Wesley up. Mira, however, took her time drawing nearer, and I laughed.

"She's running out of toxins," I sneered. "I know she can't be fully recovered yet."

"She's strong," Adrestus asserted. "Unlike her sister. Perhaps I should've set my sights on her to begin with."

I swung at him with my bit of metal railing, but Adrestus was playing with me now, batting away my attacks, making no effort to attack back.

"Leave Erika alone!" I screamed.

"A bit late, don't you think, Samantha?"

"Don't call me Samantha!" I swung again.

"Eydis then." He deflected the bar. I hated the sight of my sword, the sword Vidar had given me so long ago, in Adrestus's hands. "Or, what is it that precious Wes calls you? 'Sammy'?"

"You can call me *nothing*," I snarled.

"Watch out!" Naomi screamed, and Wesley slipped from her grip twenty yards overhead. He slammed into our catwalk behind Adrestus, howling in pain. A bolt popped off the anchor brackets, and the walkway shifted with a groan.

Adrestus turned his back to me to grin at his new quarry, too focused on Wesley to hear the raspy cry that called out below.

"Sam!"

I looked down into the water. My heart leaped in my chest. Andersen, against all odds, treaded water at the surface, bruised but miraculously alive. A flash of bronze streaked upwards, propelled by his powers. "Catch!"

I snagged the sword out of the air as Adrestus loomed over Wesley's feebly stirring form.

"I'm glad you aren't dead yet, Sammy," Adrestus purred, his back to me. "I would've hated killing pretty Wes without a satisfying audience. Maybe I'll do it in parts? Start with his other arm, perhaps. I so enjoyed taking the first one."

The bronze sword in my hands cut easily, slicing through red cloak into the muscle of Adrestus's back and through his ribs, the same way he'd killed my brother. I ripped the sword back, leaving a jagged gash that gushed dark blood.

I stumbled backwards, and Adrestus turned to look at me in shock as he fell to his knees.

"Don't call me Sammy." I used the tip of Adrestus's sword to push black curls from his sweat-sheened forehead. "It's Scourge Queen, Killer of Adrestus the Unkillable, or nothing at all."

"You know you can't kill me," he growled through the blood that spilled from between his lips.

"Then I'll keep you down here, away from your Elixir until you finally fade into nothing."

Wesley staggered to his feet and limped forward. He pushed Adrestus onto his stomach and knelt down with one knee on Adrestus's back.

"I've got him." Wesley pushed his hair away from his face. "Go help Remi. If the Epsilons get to campus—"

I hated leaving Wesley with Adrestus, but he was right. I sprinted to the nearest stairway, glancing up to check on Naomi as I rattled up the steps to Remi's platform. She'd pulled herself back onto her walkway and was dodging Mira's attacks.

"I wouldn't unhook her if I were you!" Adrestus growled from below as I approached Remi. The control panel was mercifully small, and I had a good feeling about the large, blue button in the upper corner. "You free her, and all of us die. Me, you, and your precious friends."

I hesitated. He was probably lying. I knew that. I was about to foil his plans, of course he'd say I was making a mistake.

"What do you mean?" I asked, my hand hovering over the blue button.

"We didn't put Miss Whitlock here because we thought she might like the view," he sang. Blood spilled from his mouth and slipped through the metal grating, dripping into the ocean pool below. "It's a safety net, ironically enough. You uninstall the Heart of the City, and this entire metal structure collapses, sinking to the bottom of the ocean and bringing us all with it.

"He's lying!" Wesley called.

"Why would I lie? Of course I put precautions in place to keep my city's heart safe from anyone wishing to remove her from her home. But go ahead, Scourge Queen. Do it. Die. I'll rise again." Adrestus choked on bloody laughter. "Can you say the same?"

"He's telling the truth. I can feel it." Metal rattled overhead, and I looked up to see Naomi looking down at me through the metal grates. She was forced to dart away as Mira descended over her.

Remi's face stared forward with a strange degree of serenity for someone with cheeks so pale and hollow. She'd been doomed from the moment Adrestus had connected her to the city. She'd live as a supercomputer, trapped in her own mind, or she'd die at the hands of her rescuers.

Naomi, Wesley, Remi, and Andersen would all die.

"Our families are at the school! They'll kill them all!" Naomi shouted, dancing away from Mira's outstretched hands.

They'd sacrificed too much to save their families for me to throw it away, so why couldn't I do it?

"Come on!" Wesley pleaded. "We knew the risks coming here. Sammy, there isn't a choice here!"

"I know," I murmured. Of course I knew. We'd save not just our friends, but the world. Thing was, I didn't like the thought of a world without Wesley and Naomi in it. Was it really any better than Adrestus's vision?

Hands grabbed at my shoulders and spun me around, and I was face to face with Andersen's bruises. Wet hair plastered his face, and his chest heaved with heavy breaths.

"You're scared," he said. "It's okay."

"I'm going to do it," I said, but part of me continued to hesitate.

"I know you will. You don't want deaths on your conscience, but it's us or everyone else." Andersen squeezed my shoulders. "We've survived worse, though I get that's easy for me to say at the moment because I'm pretty sure I just came back from the dead because you told me to take a drink from that bottle upstairs."

I clenched my fists. Maybe we'd be okay. We'd survived so much.

"When we came here to sink New Delos," I said, "you told Remi if something went wrong and we fell, if you could only save one of us, it would be her."

His eyes watered, and he nodded.

"I remember."

"Keep that promise. Get her out of here. If anyone can escape, it's you."

"Of course." His chin trembled, and his fingers tightened on my shoulders. "I'm sorry, Sam. For everything."

"Old water under the bridge." My laugh was weak and garbled by tears. "Really, it doesn't matter. I'm dead anyway."

And I turned around and slammed the blue button.

A shuddering gasp racked Remi's body, and her knees gave out. She dropped like a puppet whose strings had been cut, the wires snapping off of her. Andersen caught her and was running to the stairs with her in his arms before I could process what I'd just done.

For a moment, I thought Adrestus had been bluffing. A cautious stillness fell over the tangle of walkways, but then the metal trembled, and the first cables snapped.

"Naomi!" I screamed, trying to run across shaking metal to the stairs. "Wes!"

I fell to the metal grate, looking down at Wesley where he lay on his side, clutching his ribs. Adrestus was gone.

"It takes a lot to make me admit a mistake," a growl sounded behind me. "I should've killed *you* instead of your backwater family!"

I flipped to my back as Adrestus limped forward, twirling my sword.

"They weren't backwater!"

"You don't get to die without first hearing how they begged for mercy. Your sisters went down so easy, but Knut? He put up a fight. I think he was my favorite to kill."

"Shut up!" I screamed.

"And Erika," he grinned, "oh, how I loved corrupting her. It was so easy, too. Thank the gods she survived the Epsilon procedure."

Naomi screamed, and more metal crashed, but Adrestus in his dark armor and tattered cloaks took up my entire field of vision.

"They were better than you," I spat. "We *are* better than you!"

"They were weak! They were *worms!* And *this* is a thousand years overdue!" He swung the sword down, and I braced for its sting. It would at least be quicker than drowning.

But Adrestus froze mid-attack, stopped by the long, pale fingers that wrapped around his neck.

"You killed them?" Mira hissed in his ear.

"You didn't really believe Eydis capable of their murders? She couldn't even kill Gregor and made her friends do her dirty work!" Adrestus jeered. "She's weak, and she's always been weak."

Mira's lips parted as she took in Adrestus's words, oblivious to the walkways above us collapsing.

"You lied."

"You've heard me do that a thousand times. You didn't think you were special, did you?"

Her fingers tightened around his neck.

"You killed them. You killed *me*."

"Stand down, Mira. You can't hurt me. I took a sword to the back, and I'm still standing."

"I have the Immortality Cure," she hissed and rubbed the fingers of her free hand against her thumb. "I can kill you."

"You have no energy to heal yourself if you do." Adrestus grinned. "You'll die, too."

"Maybe I don't want to heal myself."

"Mira—"

"My name is Erika." Her voice cracked. "And you never should've come to our home."

Adrestus's eye wavered from Erika to me.

"If you—" He cut off, choking on the words.

"How does it taste?" Erika purred, getting in his face as it worked into a final snarl. The veins in the white of his eye turned black, but he continued to gasp for breath.

"Stupid village girls," he gurgled. "I'll—"

A single, drawn out gurgle rattled from his lungs, and he collapsed, falling to his knees, and then keeling forward, face down, the clang of his armor just barely perceptible as metal fell and broke around us.

After two thousand long years, Quintus Dio, Adrestus the Unkillable, was actually, properly dead.

I waited for him to move. It couldn't be over. He would have another trick up his sleeve.

But he stayed still. Erika fell next to him, her hand withered and bruised.

"Erika—" I pulled her into my lap, brushing white hair away from her face.

"Eydis," she murmured. Tears tracked her cheeks. "I'm sorry. Do you think they'll forgive me?"

She didn't have to specify who. I nodded.

"All of them. I promise."

Her fingers closed over mine, and her other hand reached for my face.

"Even Vidar?"

Her gray eyes watered with worry, and I petted her head as the metal grate beneath us shuddered.

"Especially Vidar."

"I'll tell them you say hi," she whispered. "I'm glad you got to see me again."

The veins in the whites of her eyes darkened, and her eyes fluttered closed.

"Erika?" I whispered. She didn't respond.

A mighty, metal groan swallowed my grief, giving way to a cacophony of heavy clangs, screaming, and the screeching of metal against stone as the floor dropped beneath me.

56

Sunrise

The darkness, the sensation of floating— I was sure I was dead. I was familiar enough with the feeling, and everything was quiet. Quiet, eerie, and cold.

And—wet?

My eyes fluttered open. The smallest bit of orange morning light streamed from the cracks in the distant City Hall roof, but its dusty tendrils barely reached the bottom of the basin where I lay under a tangle of metal grates and bars.

"Wesley? Sammy?" Naomi's voice croaked in the darkness. Metal splashed and shifted somewhere to my left. I sat up, half-submerged on top of a metal shelf that was bolted to the stone wall just beneath the water's surface.

"I've got you," Wesley grunted in response to Naomi. Their shadows moved in the dark, and Wesley stooped to lift a mess of metal. Naomi pulled herself out from underneath. "Careful. You might have a concussion."

Naomi felt her way to my side, splashing in the murky dark. The water was cold but refreshing after the night. Blood and ash washed away, and Wesley joined us, staring up at the distant ceiling.

The entire labyrinth of walkways had come crashing down. What hadn't sank had caught on the metal platforms hidden just below the surface around the dome's perimeter or had become lodged overhead in a weblike tangle of steel.

The door we'd come in through was impossibly far. We had no way to climb that high, let alone to the dark tunnels that encircled the massive pool.

"Andersen and Remi—" I started.

"They made it," Naomi said. "He had to pull some tricks with his powers, but they got out."

"Wait." I stood up in the water, scanning the dark, suddenly remembering.

"What is it?" Wesley asked, and Naomi sighed. I couldn't put a name to whatever emotions were gnawing at my stomach, but they seemed to be affecting Naomi as well.

Faint, orange daybreak glinted against a darker metal than the cage that surrounded us, and I exhaled at the sight of the armor, half-submerged in water. Wesley and Naomi splashed after me as I approached Adrestus's body.

The gash I'd left in his chest was still open, though he didn't bleed, indicating his heart hadn't restarted, and he lay with my silver sword still in hand. I took it from his grasp, and tucked it into my scabbard.

Adrestus's eye stared up at the faraway ceiling. I closed my own eyes to block him from my vision, but the image of a boy with curly black hair that brushed against his porcelain face in the bitter wind of a gray, pebbled beach stood out on the inside of my eyelids.

I opened my eyes. The body in front of me didn't really resemble the boy in my memories, but they'd been the same. Manipulative, callous, and destined to fall at the hands of his victims like every villain deserved but a tragic few reaped.

I knelt in the water, and Naomi and Wesley joined me on either side.

"He shouldn't come back anymore," I said. "Eri—Mira saw to that."

"But just in case," Wesley said, "should we do something? He's come back before when he wasn't supposed to."

I nodded and placed my hands against Adrestus's side. Naomi and Wesley did the same, and together we rolled him the short foot to the edge of the platform and watched him sink, weighed down by his armor, as the ocean depths claimed him.

I looked up after the dark enveloped his body, and there she was, lying nearby, her white hair floating up around her face.

"She doesn't have any armor on," Wesley said. "I'm not sure she'll sink."

"Wesley," Naomi whispered.

"What?"

Still on my knees, I sloshed to Erika's side and pulled her into my arms. Why did she look in death so much more like the Erika I remembered?

"I failed her."

She at least looked more peaceful than Adrestus had. I hoped that meant she'd already found her way back to our family.

"She tried to kill us how many times?" Wesley asked. "Pretty sure she *did* kill you once."

"She's my sister."

"Oh." Wesley dropped into the water next to me. "Sammy, I'm sorry. I didn't—"

"I didn't know for very long, either." I shrugged. "To me, Mira and Erika are still two different people. Erika died a thousand years ago, though she came back for a few moments there at the end. If we make it out of here, I don't think I can leave her behind."

I sat back in the water and leaned against a metal grate, still holding Erika. Naomi and Wesley flanked me, and we shivered together in the dark, cold wet.

"You won't have to," Wes promised, and I let my head drop onto his shoulder, the number "7" of his shoulder pad pressing against my face. "I'll carry her out myself."

"Not to be that person," Naomi sniffed, "but I don't feel anyone nearby. I'm not sure we're getting out."

The nearest exits were the massive tunnels overhead, but I wasn't foolish enough to hope we'd be able to climb the slick wall of the dome that high. The cold was already settling deep in my bones.

"But Peru," Wesley whispered.

"Shut up, we didn't invite you to go to Peru with us." Naomi laughed, but the sound was wet and feeble.

"So?" Wesley shrugged. "Sammy never invites me anywhere, and I still show up. At least this time it was going to be a vacation and not Schrader's Tower."

"You can come to Peru." I found his hand in the dark. Tears mingled with the salt water on my face. It wasn't fair. There was so much I wanted to do with them still.

Wesley's fingers tightened against mine with sudden urgency.

"Sammy." His voice trembled over the two syllables.

"Oh, god," Naomi groaned. "Here it comes."

"What?" I asked them both.

Wes took a deep, careful breath.

"I love you," Wesley admitted.

"I know." The tears in my eyes made the webs of metal overhead look evermore disorienting. "I think I love you, too."

"You both always have to make things so awkward." Naomi choked on a sob-laugh.

"We love you, too, Naomi," I insisted and put an arm around her.

"Yeah, I know, idiot," she sniffed. "I have superpowers, remember?"

I swallowed, trying to force the muscles in my throat to relax.

"I know I spent most of my life asleep," I said, squeezing both their hands, "but the last year was the best one I had in an entire millennia."

They leaned into me.

"It was our favorite, too, Sammy," Wesley murmured. "Ten stars out of ten. Would definitely break you out of a car trunk all over again."

We fell silent, listening to water splash from the tunnels and drip over metal, hoping someone might find us but taking comfort in the fact that we at least had the company of each other.

The cold was becoming too much to bear, and I shivered against Wesley while Naomi curled up against my other side. She faded off first, and I kept a finger on her slowing pulse, as if doing so might keep her with me. But the cold pulled on me, too, and my hand slipped from her neck as I leaned into Wesley.

"Sammy." His teeth chattered with sudden urgency. "Sammy, wait—"

"It's okay, Wes," I murmured, my eyes fluttering closed. "I'll be fine."

"No, I hear something."

A warmth spread along my arms, and I thought maybe I was finally losing all feeling. However, of all the deaths I'd suffered, I'd never grown warmer as I died.

Water rose off me in puffs, and I struggled to sit up, watching the steam rise off Wesley, Naomi, and me.

"You guys really thought I'd let you pull that sacrifice crap without me? You know I'd look better as a statue than any of you." A voice echoed through the cavern, and we craned our necks to look at the tunnel overhead. Glowing, white light cast long shadows that curved upwards against the rounded wall, and a bright smile flashed at us.

Sergio's arm was still in a sling, but what was left of his hair was pulled back in a neat bun. Candice stood with him and extended what looked like a miniature star that burned white in her hand. Vines snaked their way through cracks in the wall, courtesy of Boonsri, shifting collapsed metal out of the way for the staircase of ice that rose from the water.

The college team had come to rescue us.

Dazzling orange light refracted against every building, casting deep shadows where walls had collapsed and windows had shattered, but limping down the boulevard back towards campus, the city had never looked more spectacular.

Naomi was conscious again and on her feet thanks to Sergio's warming abilities, and Wesley, true to his word, carried Erika in his arms as we followed Sergio back to the school.

Helicopter blades whirred overhead, and, between the buildings, I could see frigates floating on the water. The lawns of both campuses were overrun with the freed Epsilons reuniting with their compatriots. Military uniforms from around the world ran to and fro, helping the most severely injured into helicopters and lifeboats headed to the military ships.

Sergio pointed ahead at a cluster of black-suits. At their center, a woman stood with a clean blanket over her shoulders, looking disheveled but composed. She was deep in conversation with a tall man with hair that stood up on one side after what must've been hours of running his hand through it, as Fleming always did when he was stressed.

He turned and saw us drawing closer, his face still pale and hollow, but he was *standing*.

I took a couple staggering steps forward and then broke into a run. He broke free of the crowd, limping forward to meet us.

"You're alive," I gasped.

He held his arms to stop me.

"I should be furious," he said, and seeing his brow furrow in admonishment sent flutters of relief through my chest. He was okay. He was alive.

He tried to look stern for a moment longer, but sighed in defeat.

"Are you okay?" he asked, trying to sound serious. "Is Adrestus—"

"Dead," I assured him. "Properly, very dead."

"Food for whatever is at the bottom of the ocean," Wesley added.

"Wesley!" Mrs. Isaacs pulled away from a group of gathered families to fling herself at her son while Mr. and Mrs. Bradford did the same for Naomi.

Fleming looked at me through cracked glasses, and his eyes watered.

"New Delos is officially no more," he said matter-of-factly. "Everyone is being transported back to their homes. I wasn't sure what you wanted to do."

He looked to the side, watching a group of my classmates help carry supplies to a lifeboat despite their injuries. Anthony piled blankets on Heather's lap and pushed her in her wheelchair after the others. Justin and Marcus applied fresh bandages to minor wounds sustained by our teammates. Andersen caught my eye from the bench where he and Remi shared a blanket. A military medic tended to Remi as she stared at the lawn with her hand gripping Andersen's knee, keeping him at her side.

"Everyone's okay," Fleming said. "Avery's on a medical ship. He hasn't woken up yet, but the doctors say he will. He'll be okay."

I nodded, unable to shake the lump in my throat. The world was better off without New Delos, but without the city, I wasn't sure when I'd see all my friends together like this again.

"I'm sorry." I couldn't think of what else to say. This had been their home until I showed up a year ago. Fleming frowned.

"What for?"

"I ruined your life a little bit, I think." I was trying to make a joke, but fresh tears welled in Fleming's eyes.

"No." He pulled me in and wrapped his scarred arms around me. "You made it so much better, Sammy. You had me so worried. If something had happened to you—"

I choked on a sob.

"Does this mean Avery and I can come live with you?" I dared to whisper. Fleming's arms tightened.

"You and Avery can live with me for as long as you like. It doesn't matter that New Delos is done. As long as I'm here, you have a home. You know that."

The sound of a clearing throat pulled us apart. Dr. Parker stood next to us, beaming.

"Thought you'd want to know they caught John Ratcliffe," she said. "He was trying to pass himself off as a common citizen on a lifeboat, but he's too recognizable for his own good."

Fleming nodded, and the final knot in my stomach released. It really was over, then. Dr. Parker smiled at me and clapped me on my shoulder.

"I'd kill you if you were my student, but I gotta say, you did great." She winked at Fleming as she walked towards her students. "You've raised a good kid. You should be proud."

"It wasn't me." His eyes glistened in the rising sun. "I wish I could say it was."

57

Homecoming

Two Years Later

For seven hours, I sat with my seat in the upright position, bowing my head to better watch the world pass beneath us. Wesley snored next to me, his head lolled to the side in a way that made me certain he'd wake up with a nasty crick in his neck.

Early morning sun flooded through my window, and after a dirty look from a woman across the airplane aisle, I pulled the window cover closed and instead focused on the map on the seat-back screen in front of me.

I ran a nervous hand through my hair, unused to how quickly my fingers found the ends. However, the few inches Brooke had left when she'd given me a haircut still offered plenty to twist in anxiety. An unseen force worked to loosen the knot in my stomach, and I made a mental note to thank Naomi for at least trying to put my nerves at ease.

The intercom dinged, and the captain came on to announce we would soon begin the descent into Keflavik. I'd tried my best to learn Icelandic after Fleming had gifted me the graduation trip to my old home last Christmas, aided by the Old Norse in my head, but over the static, it was hard to understand the captain.

"Did you sleep?" Wes mumbled sleepily, wincing as he straightened his neck.

"Yeah. No. Not at all."

He smiled and reached for my hand to give my fingers a gentle squeeze. We'd both come out of New Delos with too much of our own baggage, and the decision to remain friends until we were both in a better place had been a mutual agreement, but tiny moments like this made me wish things could be different.

Not that it would've mattered. He lived so far from McMillan Island that I only saw him, and most my friends, on breaks when they came to visit the rebuilt camp in the woods where I lived with Fleming, Avery, Winnie, Amanda, and Brooke. The property had belonged to Mom, after all.

"It's okay to be nervous," Wesley assured me.

"I'm not nervous."

"I'm not nervous, either." Avery's seat snapped upright on Wesley's other side. "It's our birthright!"

He grinned at me, his hair hanging in his face.

"I for one can't wait for my personal tour from my favorite local," Wesley teased. I pulled my hand away and rolled my eyes.

"Somehow I don't think I'm going to be the best tour guide."

I glanced around the plane, locating Naomi and Andersen on either side of Fleming several rows ahead of us. Amanda, Brooke, and Winnie would beat us all off the plane being up in First Class. I looked back at the grumpy lady across the aisle and slid my window cover back open.

We dropped low over the water as we approached the seaside airport, and I reached back for Wesley's hand. He took it silently and let me squeeze his fingers until the wheels of the plane bumped against the tarmac.

"It's green," Avery whispered in awe, leaning forward to get a better look out my window. "Why is it green?"

"Because it's July," I snorted.

My heart didn't stop racing. Not when we filed off the plane, not when we met the others in customs, not when the border agent looked over my passport.

I kept a vice grip on Wesley's hand as we pushed through baggage claim to Arrivals and while we waited for Fleming to check in for the rental cars.

He jiggled the keys at us, easy to find in the crowd in his white and red wind-breaker, and we followed him to the door. I hesitated, and tourists grumbled as they elbowed me out the way.

Avery rushed ahead to claim his kingdom, laughing at the wind, and Fleming grabbed the back of his jacket to keep him from running in front of a bus.

"You coming?" Naomi stopped with Wesley just beyond the doors and held a hand out to me. The knot in my stomach finally gave. I took a deep breath and stepped back into the Icelandic air for the first time in centuries.

We spent two days in Reykjavik, where Avery spent his entire souvenir budget on every kitschy, puffin-themed trinket he could find. Fleming asked me nearly every hour if it was "anything like I remembered" and I reminded him every time that I'd never been to Reykjavik when I'd been here.

But the wind felt familiar, as did the cool, summer rain that hammered the capital the two days we were there. There'd been more trees in my memories and definitely less cobbled roads, but something about the city felt like it was happy to be welcoming me back so many years later.

The ache in my heart grew on the third day when we loaded into the rental cars and headed for the southern coast.

Every weather-beaten beach looked like the one in my memories, and I sat with Vidar's black journal in my lap with the page that described our settlement carefully bookmarked.

"Anyone decide yet?" Fleming asked. I raised my eyes to meet his in the rearview mirror. The car that Avery had dubbed "The Fun Van" wound along the coastal highway ahead of us, and I suddenly wished I'd joined him with Amanda, Brooke, and Winnie instead.

"I think I'm going to go back." Naomi spoke first, and I twisted in the middle seat to look at her in shock.

"When did you decide that?" Andersen demanded from the front.

She shrugged and looked out her window absently.

"I know a lot happened on New Delos, and I know it was created to serve an evil purpose, but the people who lived there weren't bad. If the city is reopening and Dr. Parker has reformed the University team, why not go? New Delos needs me more than ever."

"That's very noble," Fleming said, eyes back on the road.

Wesley shifted next to me.

"Not going is also noble," he murmured.

"Are you not going?" I asked. His gray fingers whirred as he clenched and unclenched the robotic digits. It had taken a long time before he felt comfortable replacing Everly's old prosthesis model and was still getting used to this one.

"No, I think I am." He avoided my eye.

"I'm not," Andersen grunted in the front seat. "They could pay me, and I wouldn't go back."

"That's okay, too," Fleming assured him, his eyes back on me in the mirror. I looked down at Vidar's notebook.

New Delos University had accepted my application months ago but had set their decision deadline later than most schools due to the nature of its reopening.

And from what I'd seen on TV, New Delos *did* look different. Schrader Industries didn't exist anymore. Most of the city had been torn down for scrap metal and rebuilt.

The Paragon statue in the bay remained the same, but I'd seen the news coverage of the new statue outside City Hall with its braided hair and sword— a tribute to the girl who stood up to the monster at the Peace Summit.

Luckily, the Scourge Queen statue didn't much resemble me, otherwise I might've taken more of an issue with it. However, the day it was unveiled was the day I went to Brooke and asked her to do my hair short into a pixie cut in an attempt to look even less like the edifice.

Wesley set his robotic hand on top of my knee. I'd spoken to him more than anyone about going back, how I wanted to, but how I also didn't want to. I'd hoped this trip might give me clarity, like I might find the answer inscribed in runes under some moss.

I didn't want to decide either way. I wanted time to freeze so I could spend an eternal summer exploring Iceland with my friends.

We stayed in a small seaside inn, where Avery found yet another puffin keychain in the gift shop next door and conned Fleming into buying it for him. I raised an eyebrow at him, but he insisted he hadn't used his powers.

"No powers on family," he promised and disappeared into the room he was sharing with Andersen and Wesley.

I slunk into my room where Naomi was journaling and Winnie was scrolling through the pictures on her camera, the strap still around her neck. The smallest of smiles flitted across her face, and I looked at her in suspicion.

"What did you do?" Winnie smiling was never a good sign.

"Brooke proposed."

"What?" Naomi and I both cried, and Winnie smirked, turning the camera screen to face us. Brooke knelt on a black sand beach with a ring in hand while Amanda's expression was unreadable.

"And?" I demanded.

"At first, Amanda said no, but only because *she'd* planned a proposal at our next stop." Winnie grinned. Her hair leaned more strawberry than blonde these days. "Idiot."

"But she said yes afterwards, right?"

"Sure, but she's still proposing tomorrow." She clicked through her pictures, grinning to herself.

I settled into my bed and stared at the ceiling. It was about time Amanda and Brooke proposed, and I was glad that no matter what happened in the next few days, something happy had come out of the trip. My eyes drifted to the open suitcase on my bed, unzipped and opened so that I could see the small, purple box that sat atop of my clothes.

My stomach tightened, and I rolled over to try to sleep.

We spent the next day and a half celebrating Amanda and Brooke after Amanda's follow-up proposal under a waterfall. The other tourists clapped for them as Amanda slid her ring over Brooke's finger, and they embraced, but apprehension pushed my happiness to the side.

We'd stopped at a glacier field a few days ago, and the tour guide had talked about how much Iceland's geography had changed over the years. We could pass right by what I was looking for, and I would have no idea.

But then, back in the car, moving onto our next stop, we rounded a bend, and I clapped a hand over my mouth.

"Stop the car."

Fleming pulled over, and the so-called "Fun Van" pulled over behind us. I leaped from the backseat, pushing Wesley out of my way.

Coastal wind blew my hair back, battering the bluff that overlooked the fjord in front of me. A gravel parking lot sat ahead, and pathways wound their way over moss and grass to the black pebbles that lined the beach. In my mind's eye, I could still see the boats turned on their hulls on the far end of the cove.

The few tourists that braved the July wind and rain walked over pathways that lay where longhouses once had, before they'd been burned a thousand years ago, leaving no trace they'd ever existed.

I was home.

Fleming sent most of the others ahead. There was a waterfall a few miles inland for them to explore, and I wanted privacy for what came next. Avery had never quite forgiven Erika, and while Brooke, Amanda, and Andersen knew Mira's real identity, to them, she'd only ever been Mira.

To me, Erika was still my baby sister.

I waited in the car until the few tourists outside grew bored of the park and moved on down the road. With Erika's purple box and Dad's journal in hand, I led Fleming, Wesley, and Naomi down to the beach.

There was no doubt that this was it, and it was the perfect park for my old homestead. From the beach, it was easy to retrace my steps, even if the building landmarks were long gone. In my head, I passed my neighbors's homes. I passed their goat pens and their log piles. I passed the clearing where the men used to beat the crap out of each other for fun in the middle of the town. I passed where I used to sew sails with whale bone needles and where Gunhild used to sing for the whole settlement to hear.

And then I stopped, rereading the passage describing our home in Dad's journal. The clump of seagrass in front of me was patchy and filled with rocks. I wondered how quickly archeologists would uproot it if they knew of the Viking grave that lay underneath.

We had buried them where our home had been. Havard, Solveig, Gunhild, Knut, and Hjordis.

And Erika.

I opened her box and pulled out the bag of ashes. I still wasn't sure how Fleming had gotten it through customs. I suspected Avery and his powers may have played a role.

I stepped off the trail to kneel down in the grass and pushed aside dirt and rocks until I had a shallow hole. I emptied Erika inside, then pulled the earth back over her ashes. If she hadn't found our family in Valhalla yet, she would now.

"Do you want to say anything?" Fleming asked. I stood up and found Wesley's hand.

"I'm glad she was the one who killed him."

And I turned away. There was nothing left to say that anyone else needed to hear.

We walked back to the beach, and I looked up at the bluff. Fleming caught my eye and nodded, understanding what I was asking.

"Naomi, help me back at the car for a moment."

Naomi glanced back at Wesley and me as she followed Fleming back to the parking lot.

"Are you okay?" Wesley asked. "Is that a dumb question?"

I sighed, relishing the bitter wind on my face, and pulled him towards the bluff.

"I'm a lot better now, actually." The clarity I'd been hoping to find on this trip was finally settling over me. "I want to show you something."

The path up to the lookout was rocky, and Wesley and I helped each keep upright against the elements. The wind snatched our laughs and dragged them away on the breeze as we stumbled together up the hill, falling into each other.

Everything that had happened, it finally felt over. Erika was the final loose end, and now that I knew she could rest easy, it was like the entire world had opened up.

I looked at Wesley with his wind-tossed hair, thinking of our agreement to focus on being friends, but lately, with college approaching, I'd been forced to consider the possibility of a life with less Wesley, one where he might get tired of waiting for me to catch up.

And frankly, I was tired of waiting, too.

"Wow," he breathed, taking in the view of the fjord as we reached the top of the bluff.

"That direction, too." I pointed him in the direction of mountains, and Wesley sighed as he beheld the gleaming glaciers.

It had been so long since he'd been able to set my stomach aflutter with the uncertainty of a first crush. Instead, he felt like sitting next to a crackling fireplace, safe and cozy, in the middle of a raging snowstorm. Wesley was everything warm and secure, and when I was with him, I was home. Standing with him on the bluff overlooking my Viking home, I could feel the final cracks that still lingered between Eydis and Samantha sealing shut.

"Why didn't we come here sooner?" Wesley laughed.

"Because, it wasn't time yet." I wrapped my arm around his, standing close.

I turned him towards me, taking in his green eyes. He raised his robotic hand and made a show of grabbing his glasses.

"See that?" He held the frames between two digits. "That took me three weeks to learn to do without breaking them."

"It's *very* impressive," I said.

"As impressive as this?" He hooked the glasses on the front of his jacket before using his prosthetic hand to fish inside his pocket. When he withdrew it, a silver chain glinted between the gray fingers. My heart caught as I took the bent dog whistle in my hand.

"How—"

"Stole it, back when— you know. It was in his kitchen when I had to carry his damn propane oven up. I didn't know if you'd want it still, because maybe it would be a bad reminder after everything—"

My fingers twisted in his, pinning his arm at my side even though I knew he could move it away any time he wanted. My weight shifted forward onto my tip-toes, and I silenced his lips with mine.

His robot hand pressed against the small of my back, holding me close, and his hand escaped mine to play with the short hair that brushed at the back of my neck.

When he pulled away, he rested his forehead against mine.

"You told me back then that you would make sure I got everything and anything I wanted," I said, closing my eyes.

"I still mean that, Sammy."

"Even if everything I want is still you?"

"Especially if that." He held me tighter. "Have you decided about New Delos, then?"

I bit back a grin and opened my eyes to see Fleming and Naomi making their way up to join us. I pulled away from Wesley, blushing, looking at the long, thin, fabric-wrapped package in Naomi's arms.

"That's not—" Wesley started but cut off as I took the package and unwrapped it, revealing the silver, engraved blade that had wreaked so much pain.

"A thousand years ago," I explained, "my father made me throw this in the bay. The next day, I swam out to get it back and almost drowned."

Naomi and Wesley frowned, but Fleming nodded. I'd already explained to him what I wanted to do.

I took the sword in my hand. It had hurt so many people that I loved, but it had been loyal. It had been there every time I needed it to be.

I walked as far out onto the bluff as the wind allowed, and, to the sound of Wesley and Naomi gasping behind me, I threw my sword over the fjord.

I tracked its progress through the air, where it spun in the low sun and dropped into the water with a distant splash.

"Why?" Naomi asked.

"So you aren't going back," Wesley said blankly.

"For the first time ever, I get to decide what I do," I said. "I get to decide who I want to be and what I make of myself. I've been told I can't be a warrior, that I can't join Apex Team, that I'm nothing but a girl and a Beta. That sword made me feel like I could be more, but I *am* a girl and a Beta, and I don't need a sword to be a warrior."

I stepped back between Naomi and Wesley, retaking Wesley's hand.

"I'm going to New Delos," I announced. "I'm going to try out for the university team. I'm going to do it without my sword because I'm Eydis Solveigsdotter, and I'm Samantha Havardson, and I'm Sammy Fleming. And who needs a sword when I have all of you?"

"Well said," Fleming murmured.

And we stood there for a long while, drinking in the wind, thinking about whatever lay ahead for us, knowing that whatever happened and whatever came our way, we'd be facing it together.

The End

ACKNOWLEDGEMENTS

In the spring of 2018, I walked into Emerald City Comic Con excited to meet Scottish actor David Tennant. I'd spent months rehearsing in my head exactly what I would say, so of course when I reached his table I turned into a blubbering mess, and my husband had to talk for me. I was so mortified by the interaction that when I later lamented to my co-worker Melissa, she offered me the only course forward: make it so that next time we crossed paths, Mr. Tennant would be the one in fangirly tears.

I'd distracted Melissa from work enough times with random ramblings for her to know I was brewing a story in my head. She said this was the sign I needed to finally put that story to page and turn the tables on Mr. Tennant. She was only half-joking.

Several years later, we're standing at the end of the trilogy, and while I'm fairly certain Mr. Tennant has yet to read my story, I couldn't be more grateful for the incredible friends, authors, readers, and booksellers I've met along the way.

My writing friends, you all inspire me to continue to improve. Joseph especially helped get me to the end of EPSILON, which was inexplicably the most difficult of the three books to write. If you ever need someone to enthusiastically swear at you in all caps from the margins of your working document, hire Joseph.

My artist friends, Gigi and Maria, you bring these books and their characters to life with your character art and stunning book covers. I'm in constant awe of your talents.

My bookish friends, you make me feel at home in the wider book community. Sydney, your unwavering love for Fleming never fails to make me smile and Bethanie at the Prince Kai Fanpod podcast, I'm forever grateful to you for helping me boost my platform and for cheering me on.

And then there are those who've supported me in so many other ways. Sally and Madi, you never make me feel bad for only talking about books and you show up when I need you to.

Some of you I haven't seen in years, but I see you reading my books and supporting me quietly from the corner. I hope I've made you proud, and I hope you enjoyed your time in this silly world of superheroes.

To my readers in general, thank you. I've loved sharing my story with you all and meeting you at events. There's something surreal about introducing your imaginary friends to strangers, and I wouldn't trade it for anything.

I can't write my acknowledgements without thanking Melissa, my friend-editor who never once wavered when she prompted me down this journey, spurred on by jokes about David Tennant. You met these characters before anyone else and you never lost faith in my work, even when you saw the worst of my drafts (long live AnkleGate). Everyone deserves a Melissa, and I'm so thankful that I've found mine. These books would not exist without you.

Finally, Connor. I liked superheroes before I met you, but something about having a fat crush on a giant superhero nerd threw me even deeper into the world of capes and secret identities. You have been an exhaustless cheerleader, the biggest fan, and the most supportive husband. You encouraged me to write before anyone and it was because of you that I started concocting the ideas that would become The Apex Cycle. You've helped me accomplish so much, and I can't wait to see you do the same for Nora. I promise, now that these books are done, I'll finally go clean the garden.

CHARACTER GLOSSARY

Samantha Havardson: Everyone's favorite amnesiac with poor decision making skills. After finally regaining her memories of her life as a Viking child in medieval Iceland, she lost all her memories again. Without powers to protect herself, she's under the protection of her high school history teacher.

Alexander Fleming: History teacher, former Apex Team coach, and Samantha's stand-in guardian, this man does it all and *without* Apex abilities.

Everly Jacobi: Apex Team's doctor and resident cat lover. His powers that allow him to assess physical wellness and injuries serve him well when caring for injured team members.

Sergio Silva: A college freshman with the ability to control temperature. He uses his power to create ice-swords out of the moisture in the air. He's missing his right eye and goes between a glass prosthesis and an eyepatch depending on whether he's fighting or not.

Amanda Hendricks: College student with fiery abilities living with Sammy and Fleming in Fleming's farmhouse. Her father is the current head of Apex Team and her sister has joined the villains.

Brooke Graham: A Non-Apex college student and girlfriend to Amanda. Her aunt runs the coffee shop in town.

Joni Bradford: Younger sister of Naomi Bradford and in possession of the same empath abilities as her sister. Unfortunately, this keeps them from being able to be near each other.

Vic "Vidar" Havardson: The man who posed as Sammy's father but is actually her one surviving Viking brother, Vidar. He was killed by Adrestus while protecting Sammy and her friends.

Alison Taylor-Havardson: Vic's wife who Samantha believed to be her mother. Alison once used her powers to give Sammy fake memories of a normal life but can't recover the memories Sammy has recently lost.

Avery Havardson: Samantha's fake brother who is technically her nephew. No one knows that he is the one who wipes Samantha's memories with his powers of coercion.

Roy Hendricks: Winnie and Amanda's father and the fiery head of the high school Apex Team. He has a vendetta against Fleming and a dislike for Non-Apex.

Valerie Hendricks: Mother to Winnie and Amanda. Her powers keep her from getting burned, making her the perfect match for Roy.

Quinn: A local resident of McMillan island.

Team Members

Wesley Isaacs: An Apex with super strength, super senses, and a super cool prosthetic arm. He wears glasses to stave off the migraines that come with his super-sight.

Naomi Bradford: She's an Apex with empath abilities and feels everything those around her feel- but she can't turn it off.

Andersen Lewis: High school Apex with telekinetic control over non-organic material. He helps out in the medical bay.

Anthony Schultz: An Apex against his will. His new wind-based abilities cause him more trouble than he would like.

Remi Whitlock: Wesley's ex-girlfriend with computer-interfacing Apex powers.

Heather Hisakawa: Apex teammate and powerhouse who can control and travel through darkness. She is known for always wearing a bow in her hair.

Skyler Cripps: Apex with the ability to control the appearance of his face.

Everest Archer: A dark haired and reserved Apex teammate with the power to change his body density.

Freddie Williams: Apex teammate with the power to create and disperse fog. He has fluffy, hay-colored hair and freckles.

Olivia Chase: Apex teammate with the ability to turn herself and those she touches invisible.

Justin Pomeroy: A senior with the ability to lock those he touches in a stasis.

Marcus McDougall: A senior with the ability to see heat signatures.

Isabelle Abarca: Junior on Apex Team and Anthony's cousin. She shares in their family's wind-powers.

Desirae Sheffield: Twin to fellow junior Mike. They share a telepathic link.

Mike Sheffield: Twin to fellow junior Desirae. They share a telepathic link.

Candice Lloyd: A college sophomore who can bend and control light.

Boonsri Malee: A college junior with the ability to control plants.

Other Apex Team Faculty

Dr. Diane Parker: The head of the University Apex Team.

Trev Baker: Council Representative from Schrader Industries. Sammy believes his boss, Adrian Schrader, is working for Adrestus and that he shouldn't be trusted. In turn, Baker thinks Samantha doesn't belong on Apex Team.

Vanessa Reiner: Team Combat Specialist and Apex PE teacher. Her Apex abilities allow her to perfectly replicate hand-to-hand combat techniques.

Angie Le Roux: The team doctor for the University Apex Team. She has the ability to dull the pain of those around her.

Adrestus: Adrestus is older than the young man he appears to be. Thousands of years old, he believes the earth belongs to him and he will stop at nothing to have it.

Adrian Schrader: New Delos celebrity and business mogul, head of Schrader Industries. However, he's secretly working for Adrestus. Despite not being an Apex, Apex abilities don't seem to work on him.

Winnie "Dion" Hendricks: Samantha's former roommate who has joined Adrestus under the alias "Dion". She's a non-Apex, bitter at having always been her father's second-favorite daughter.

Mira Aimes: Adrestus's right-hand woman with the power to take control over the motor function of anyone she touches.

Gregor: One of Adrestus's followers with powers that allow him to manipulate memories and create illusions.

Lana: A winged follower of Adrestus and skilled tailor.

Felix Grimaldi: A follower of Adrestus who can create purple flames that exude cold instead of heat.

Kory: A follower of Adrestus with the ability to manipulate electric fields.

Hackjob: Another follower of Adrestus. His raw strength and durability make him a difficult opponent.

Miles: A follower of Adrestus with the power to make force fields.

John Ratcliffe: City councilman known for his Anti-Apex views. His daughter Jamie attends New Delos Prep and is dating Andersen.

Jamie Ratcliffe: A classmate of Sammy's and daughter of New Delos's new Prime Minister. She is the Head Intern at Schrader Industries.

Families and Parents

Gabriella Bradford: Naomi's mother, who she hasn't seen in years due to their empath abilities.

Mrs. Isaacs: Wesley's non-Apex mother. She isn't always sure how to handle her Apex son, but loves him all the same.

Melody Hisakawa: Heather's Apex mother. Her powers of light and dark manipulation are similar to those of her daughter.

www.ingramcontent.com/pod-product-compliance
Lightning Source LLC
Chambersburg PA
CBHW051305190726
48290CB00001B/13